HOMEWARD BOUND

Also by Elizabeth Walter:

A Season of Goodwill
In the Mist
Dead Woman
The Sin Eater
Snowfall

HOMEWARD BOUND

Elizabeth Walter

St. Martin's Press
New York

Library of Congress Cataloging-in-Publication Data

Walter, Elizabeth.
    Homeward bound / Elizabeth Walter.
      p. cm.
    ISBN 0-312-04854-8
    I. Title.
    PR6073.A4285H6   1990
    823'.914—dc20   90-36136
                                            CIP

First published in Great Britain by Headline Book Publishing PLC

First U.S. Edition: November 1990
10 9 8 7 6 5 4 3 2 1

For my fathers,
and for
RK,
mentor, laughter-sharer, friend

CONTENTS

Part I: BOMBAY – ADEN   1

Part II: ADEN – SUEZ   85

Part III: SUEZ – GIBRALTAR   167

Part IV: GIBRALTAR – ENGLAND   259

PART I

BOMBAY – ADEN

I

The SS *Karachi* sailed at dawn.

On the bridge Angus Meiklejohn watched the water widen between ship and shore, soundlessly at first, and then, as her engines came to life and her twin screws began to churn, with a throb as reassuring as the heartbeat of one who makes the journey back from death to life.

His presence on the bridge was mandatory whenever the ship left or entered port. Although he had every confidence in his officers – even the new young Third was shaping well – a ship entering or leaving port, changing her state as it were, was vulnerable; she needed the talisman presence of her captain on the bridge.

Behind him the Bombay waterfront receded: cranes, masts, funnels; the harbour offices and the godowns; the sprawl of the city rising to Malabar Hill where the rich merchants, administrators, entrepreneurs, who had made their fortune in India, were determined to enjoy it before they sailed for Home. Angus Meiklejohn did not blame them – who in this heyday of Empire would? – but neither did he envy them. There was no fortune to be made on the high seas, and when he retired in ten years' time on the non-existent pension of the Australasian Line it would be to the narrow-fronted house in the Old Town of Aberdeen where he had lived for the past fourteen years; but from its upper windows he could see the sea, and for him those cold northern waters would hold all the indigo of the Indian Ocean, the Pacific's azure, and the green, white-plumed swells of the English Channel. He asked no other wealth.

The *Karachi* was getting under way. Already they were passing Salsette Island and she was turning, turning, flirting her frilly wake behind her like a girl at her first ball. No girl, though, but a mature woman; built in 1911 by Caird and Co. at Greenock, with four years' war service behind her, and now thirteen years old. She had been his ship from the beginning; he had stood on the rudimentary bridge when she was launched, looking down on the top-hatted, frock-coated Owners and their ladies, all shivering in the raw March wind. The Chairman's wife stepped forward and swung the champagne bottle. 'I name this ship *Karachi* –' he could not hear the words, but he knew them by heart and added his own 'Amen' to the hope that God would bless her and all who sailed in her as the daft woman stepped back clutching at her hat – a big affair, not like the close-fitting, pulled-down bonnets the ladies were wearing now – while to the cheers of the workforce the *Karachi* slid faster and faster down the slipway and gave herself to the sea.

Somewhere in the crowd Ailsa had stood with Andrew. The boy had cheered himself hoarse, explaining to anyone who would listen that 'my father is the captain of that ship'. Ailsa, whose bonnet was far too sensible to fly off in even the wildest squall, had stood smiling proudly and nodding in confirmation and saying no word at all. When later he returned to Aberdeen while the *Karachi* was being fitted out and they had lain together in the deep feather bed, she had whispered, 'I ken fine ye have a mistress now, Angus, but I'm no jealous; at least your wife doesna have ribs of iron.' He had taken her in his arms – no iron anywhere in that lissom body – and vowed that for as long as she lived there would for him be only one woman, and Ailsa Cameron was her name.

One wife, one mistress, and now the mistress was slowing briefly to drop the pilot before heading for the open sea. A week from Bombay to Aden, where she would bunker; then the tedious passage of the Red Sea and Suez; a Mediterranean cruise to Marseilles; and once through the Strait of Gibraltar, the rigours of Biscay and the English Channel in winter before berthing at Tilbury in twenty-five days' time. He would have Christmas at home this year, his first since 1920, but he would be away again before Hogmanay. As well. He had no heart these days for festivities. The shipboard ones were bad enough.

On the desk in his cabin was a diary of all the social events for First Class passengers: a dance, a treasure hunt, deck tennis, a cocktail party, another dance, this time with fancy hats. The round seemed endless, the events of every voyage identical, differing only in the order in which they occurred: a cocktail party might replace a dance, a bridge tournament the tennis match, but all would make their appearance during the voyage. And all would be eagerly attended by passengers, anxious to fill the days. And nights.

They had been unaware of their captain's scrutiny last night as they came aboard, for although he would begin meeting them next day Angus Meiklejohn still liked to have some forewarning; a list of names was not enough. There were far too many passengers for him to know them as individuals; even so, as he watched them come up the gangway one or two stood out: a young army officer; two pretty girls – sisters, surely; a tall old man bowed tenderly over a dumpy wife. There was a Reverend – there was always a Reverend, differing only in denomination; wife and daughter accompanied this brand. And there was a woman with a small boy: Mrs Cynthia Vane and son Bobby. It was the child who had caught his eye. He was the only school-age child in First Class this voyage. It had been easy to look them up on the passenger list. He was surprised he remembered the name, for he would not know the woman again if he saw her, but there was no doubt she had a fine lad. Just such another as Andrew had been – that must be why he'd noticed him.

4

The sun was climbing rapidly. Already the new-swabbed decks were awash with light, the white superstructure gleaming, portholes glinting, and ten thousand diamonds decorating the sea. Of all departures, dawn was the Captain's favourite. There was something about a new day, a promise, a hope that even what had been officially declared hopeless might none the less come to pass. Then the last eight years, which had turned Ailsa's hair white and thickened her figure, would somehow be blotted out, and all be as it had been that July morning before the telegram came.

It had been a brilliant day, the North Sea sparkling and dancing, the Aberdeen granite scintillating in the light. He had never since looked at that combination of light and water without remembering it. He had been home on leave. Ailsa, bare-armed in a cotton frock, had been hanging out the washing. He had just turned in at the gate from fetching the daily paper whose headlines screamed 'Somme Offensive Gains Ground. British Troops Continue Advance' when he heard the slither of bicycle tyres against the kerb. The telegraph boy – Wattie's lad, he'd known him since he was knee-high – was dismounting, tendering him an envelope, trying not to meet his eye . . . And suddenly the sun had no warmth, the sea no splendour, and a gull screamed derisively overhead.

There were gulls screaming now, following the ship in a dipping cloud of hopefulness as breakfast began to be prepared. Their tenacity never ceased to intrigue him; a few of them would accompany the ship all the way. But whether they were the same gulls or whether they worked in – relays, embarking and disembarking like passengers at different ports of call, he neither knew nor cared. Their cries accompanied every arrival, every departure. If they were silent he would miss them, might even think it an omen if he did not curb his superstitious mind and put his trust in the Lord as the Chief was always urging, but he would not be seriously perturbed. Disaster was not presaged by omens; it came suddenly out of a sky of cloudless blue much like today's. The Chief could put that in his pipe and smoke it, as he doubtless would – that and so much else – in the half-hour they snatched together most evenings in the Captain's cabin before the social round began.

At the thought of the Chief Engineer the Captain's face relaxed a little: James Sutherland, a fellow Scot, stern disciplinarian, God-fearing true believer, considered the finest chief engineer of the Line, who had refused promotion to larger, faster vessels in order to remain with the *Karachi* and her captain; James Sutherland – his friend. Since the day he had first come aboard as wartime replacement for the original chief engineer who had been killed when the ship, serving as an armed merchant cruiser, had been struck by a torpedo (the *Karachi* still had a patchwork of steel plates on her hull), the Captain and the new Chief had been drawn to one another, had become in private Angus and Jamie, travelled north together at the end of every voyage, and had learned to count on that half-hour when each was conscious of being himself; a man, not a uniform; a name rather than a rank.

5

If they did not open their hearts to each other, it was because both had long since thrown away the key; yet the Chief was the one person aboard to whom Angus Meiklejohn had ever talked about Andrew; there were times when he had kept going on the Chief's strength.

As he turned to leave the bridge, acknowledging the salutes of his officers, aware of the mounting throb of those engines deep in the hull amidships which were the *Karachi*'s heart, he knew that Jamie, like himself, would have risen to supervise the ship's departure whether he were on duty or no. Sleep was for those off duty, for the passengers, the early birds among whom would soon be up on deck, sniffing the air, extolling the weather, taking a turn or two before breakfast to whip up an appetite; but the Captain and the Chief, the head and heart of the vessel, slept as a mother sleeps, alert to signs so small that others might have termed them non-existent, yet sure portents that somewhere, somehow, something was amiss.

And yet on that November morning, as Captain Meiklejohn went below, he felt no forewarning as he passed within feet of the unlisted passenger he did not know he had aboard.

From the porthole of her cabin Nina Martin also saw the dawn, and watched the Gateway to India close behind her as the ship drew away from Bombay. Silly, really, to think of it as the Gateway to India, despite the arch of that name erected as a landmark. She, like her sister, had been born there and had never lived anywhere else. If you were going through it in the direction she was, it was just as much the gateway to the rest of the world; or so she must think of it. 'You are not leaving home, you are going home,' Reverend Mother had said firmly before she kissed her goodbye, allowing no nonsense like homesickness. Yet the old nun's eyes had been troubled, thinking, Nina was sure, of the home she would not see again and had not seen since she came out to India, more than thirty years ago.

Nina had been roused by the long blast from the *Karachi*'s funnel as the ship cast off her mooring lines. In the bed opposite Connie stirred briefly, then settled into deeper sleep. Not for her the agonies of wakefulness that had beset her sister. As always, Connie slept like a child, stretched out in complete abandon with one hand under her cheek. How she could after the events of the last twenty-four hours since they arrived in Bombay, Nina could not imagine. It had begun with Daddy getting so disgustingly drunk. Fortunately no one knew them in Bombay, and in any case he hadn't actually been *seen* drunk, having kept to his room, so that all that was visible was the monumental hangover which might have passed for migraine among those who did not know. It was sad that this should be her last memory of him; he had not drunk like that since Mummy died, and that was nearly two years ago, God rest her. He might have waited till the ship had sailed.

'Well, my dears,' he had said last night, looking round the cabin with eyes that hated the light, 'if you're sure you want to go, this is it. It'll be too late to change your minds tomorrow. They've just requested All Visitors Ashore.'

'I shan't change my mind,' Nina assured him.

Connie said impatiently, 'Oh, Pa.'

'Very well. Give my love to your aunt and – write occasionally.' He was speaking to Connie, who squeezed his arm and said, 'You bet I will.'

Then he was bending to kiss them – sour breath and the brush of his moustache – before hurrying down the gangway and plunging into the crowd. His daughters, who had remained in their cabin, watched him from the porthole, but he did not turn and wave. So long as he did not return to the hotel and repeat last night's over-indulgence . . . Nina voiced her thoughts aloud.

'No fear,' Connie said. 'He'll catch the mail train home tomorrow and marry Mrs Moloney within a year. She's got her eye on him. She's only been waiting till we were out of the way.'

'Really, Con!'

'What's so shocking about it? He's only fifty-three. Do you want him to be lonely for ever? Then he really might take to drink.'

'Yes, but Mrs Moloney after Mummy . . .'

'You've got to take what's to hand. Besides, Mummy was pretty trying, even before she was ill.'

'How do you know?'

'I'm older than you are. And I never thought Mummy was a saint.'

'I know she was a sinner.'

'You don't know anything about it. Perhaps it's as well she's dead. Otherwise you'd only have been even more disillusioned.'

'That's a wicked thing to say.'

'I didn't mean it that way. Come on, Nini. We've got twenty-five days ahead of us in which to have a good time. There's deck tennis tomorrow morning and a get-to-know-you cocktail party tomorrow night, and I've been down to the dining saloon to check our places and we've got the ship's doctor between us. Wonder what he's going to be like.'

'You're always thinking of men.'

'That means I'm thinking lovely thoughts, dear. Wouldn't Reverend Mother be pleased! She was always on at me for being deliberately superficial and not going to the heart of things. Well, you can't go deeper than a man's heart, can you? Or do I mean lower? His stomach, liver, bowels –'

'Con, stop it! It's disgusting.'

'Sorry, little one. But I mean to enjoy myself this voyage and I want you to do the same.'

'I can't.'

' 'Course you can. It's your last chance, so take it.'

'It's different for you.'

'No, it isn't. You can still call the whole thing off tomorrow if you want

7

to. No one's going to mind. Buck up, Nini. I want to see you enjoying life.'

'I don't think I ought . . .'

'Rubbish! You're eighteen years old, with everything before you. You ought to taste the good things, at least. Otherwise you're refusing God's gifts, aren't you?'

'I never could argue with you.'

'Then don't try. Which bed do you want? I'll be unselfish and give you the choice, then we ought to unpack – everything crushes so. Oh, Nini, think of it. Three whole weeks of freedom. We're going to have the time of our lives.'

The time of their lives. Leaning her head against the porthole in the growing daylight, Nina tried to steady her thoughts. The physical and emotional upheavals of the last few days had left her drained whereas Connie seemed stimulated by them, but she was in no doubt about her chosen course. Once betrothed, you went forward to marriage. There was no backing out. The bridegroom was impatient, waiting, and she was anything but a reluctant bride. Each day of the voyage would bring her nearer. Aunt Maura and Uncle Charles would meet them at Tilbury and escort her, and then just before Advent she would begin on her new life. And live happily ever after, if God willed it. And He would. She was sure of that.

She pulled her light dressing-gown more tightly round her. The morning was still fresh and cool. It would be pleasant on deck. She could leave Connie sleeping if she dressed quietly. Their underclothes lay folded at the bottom of their beds, covered by a square of silk as the nuns had taught them. Hers was blue, Our Lady's colour, but Connie had chosen red. It lay, a great scarlet slash in the strengthening sunlight, but the underclothes it protected had escaped. Nina bent to collect them: pure crêpe de Chine was slippery, but Connie had insisted and had made Nina have some too.

'After all, it's for your trousseau,' she had said, laughing.

Nina had acquiesced.

What she could not admit, even to Connie, was the pleasure the silk gave her against her skin. The sleek feel of it, the delicate colours – peach and eau-de-Nil – the ecru lace edging. She glanced at herself in the cabin mirror, smoothing her slender flanks. The reflected image pleased her. She raised her arms and stretched.

Her figure was slim but rounded. Connie's was more boyish, more fashionable; it wasn't done to have breasts – no, bosom. She corrected the unguarded thought while enjoying the whiteness of her arms and shoulders against the ecru lace. Daddy had been generous, no doubt of it: a First Class cabin and a trunkful of new clothes. 'I shan't need all that,' she had protested, but he had answered, 'I want you to have more than you need.' 'You can always give them to me,' Connie suggested. 'It's lucky we're much the same size. No one would guess that I'm three years older. What if Mummy could see us now!'

What indeed? The soft Irish voice would ripple (Nina had allowed herself to forget that it could also be shrill): 'Would you look at them, Geoffrey.

8

Aren't they the finest girls in Nullumpur?' It wouldn't be mere maternal pride, either. 'I do declare,' said Mrs Major Barrett, who was fond of declaring, 'Connie Martin would be the prettiest thing ever if it weren't for her sister – don't you agree?' The other ladies of the garrison town sipping tea nodded before Mrs Magistrate Beer said, 'Pretty, but – flighty.' She did not quite say, 'Fast.' 'What can you expect, with no mother?' Mrs Adjutant's Widow Moloney sighed. 'I'd have thought Reverend Mother might have had more influence,' Mrs Barrett criticised. Mrs Beer, who did not mince matters, said shortly, 'Some say those nuns have already had too much.' She did not elaborate because Mrs Moloney was a Papist, but all the ladies knew what she meant. There was a general feeling that it was just as well the Martin girls were going Home to England, where poor Bridget Martin's sisters could take care of them.

England. Home. Ireland. Which ought also to be home. It would have been pleasant, Nina thought, to visit their Sheehan relatives in County Wicklow, but perhaps Connie would be able to go. It would be appropriate, because she was more like their mother: her curls were the same red-gold, and while her own moon-pale fairness fell in gentle waves which hung below her shoulders, Connie's hair was fashionably bobbed. Nina pivoted in the narrow cabin, appreciating the sheen of hair complemented by the sheen of silk, and stopped aghast at the direction her thoughts were taking. She bowed her head and crossed herself.

'What sin have you committed, spotless lamb?' Connie's voice came lazily from the bed where she had been watching her sister at the mirror.

'Don't call me that,' Nina said.

'Then what sin have you committed, O sinner? I must say I prefer sinners to spotless lambs. Sinners are so much more interesting. Don't you think Our Lady who conceived without sin must have been something of a bore?'

'Connie!'

'There, now I've shocked you. I'll say a decade of the rosary for that and you can pray for me. That'll be more effective. I'm sure my prayers aren't heard.'

'What makes you think that?'

'All sorts of things.' Connie placed her hands behind her head and stared up at the cabin ceiling. 'You know, I think I'm rather bad.'

'No.'

Her sister flicked a glance at her. 'Darling, how would you know?'

'I do. It's like Reverend Mother said – with you it's all superficial.'

'You mean I'm superficially bad.'

'Yes.'

'If only that were the whole of it.' Connie's voice was almost a groan. 'But I know one thing,' she said, sitting up and revealing apple-green silk pyjamas: 'I'm going to enjoy this voyage. I'll dance every dance, play every game, kiss every man who asks me – oh, I'll be careful, I'll keep my legs

9

crossed . . .' She caught a glimpse of Nina's averted face. 'Do stop blushing, Nini. I'm not being coarse, honest. Besides, I think you ought to know.'

'I know quite enough about that sort of thing, thank you.'

'Do you? Where did you learn? Little talks with Reverend Mother? Or is Sister Julian really a man?'

Sister Julian had a deep voice and the dark hairs on her upper lip resembled a moustache. The convent girls, Nina among them, had often speculated on her sex. But now Nina began to dress hurriedly, putting on the crêpe de Chine underwear under cover of her dressing-gown, turning her back to her sister, unaware that the mirror revealed all.

'You've got a nice bos,' Connie pronounced, causing Nina to drop garments in confusion. 'Pity bosoms aren't in. What are you going to wear? Wear the blue dress with the sailor collar. It's nice and nautical for the first day, and the colour flatters you. And in any case why are you getting up so early? First breakfast isn't till eight.'

'I thought I'd go up on deck, blow away the cobwebs. I didn't sleep very well.'

When I did sleep, I dreamed. I dreamed I wasn't going to England, wasn't about to be a bride. I was back in Nullumpur and Mummy was alive and well, just like she used to be. She was leaning over me and crying, 'Nina, I'm sorry I had to die like that. I didn't think you'd take it so hard. I thought you'd be more like Connie.' Nina hit out at the phantom and woke up. How could anyone not take it hard? Those long bouts of nightly coughing coming from the room next door, the thinness, the white face with its twin spots of colour beneath the large, over-bright eyes. 'Mummy, are you ill?' – 'Just a little cough, darling.' 'Mummy, are you going to die?' – 'No, no, I'm getting better. I walked round the compound today.' Yes, but last year you went out riding with Major Orrey, you went to the races with him. 'Isn't it a terrible thing to be a gambler?' you said when you came home. That night you had a little cough and you gambled that the little cough wouldn't get bigger. It's not gambling that's terrible, it's losing, knowing you're going to die. Yet still her mother couldn't admit it, didn't see her daughters often now. 'Don't kiss me, lovey, it's unhygienic. Save it till I'm up and about.' But she didn't get up, didn't even walk round the compound. Just lay in bed and read feverishly – every novel, every newspaper and magazine they could supply her. 'I'll be the best-read woman in Nullumpur,' she said, smiling because laughing would set her coughing. And no one contradicted her: not Daddy, not the doctor, not Major Orrey who called only when Daddy was out; only perhaps Father Farrell, who increasingly found reason to call until at last she flared, 'I'll not see that priest again, he's morbid. He brings the smell of death into the house.'

Late one night – or was it early morning? – there was commotion in the room next door. They heard her cry out, then Daddy's voice soothing,

10

soothing. Lights went on. The servants were roused, sent running. Daddy came in, ashen-faced. 'Girls, you must be very brave and say your prayers because Mummy is dying.' – 'She can't be, she's getting better, she said so,' Nina burst out. 'Not now, Nina. Connie . . .' It was Connie whose arms were round her and they clung together, hearing the doctor come, hearing the priest. When the priest came in later to see them, Connie said only, 'Did she . . .?' He shook his head. 'Pray for her, your prayers will help her.' Since then each night, each morning, Nina had repeated the prayers for the dead. Eternal rest, perpetual light for the soul of Bridget Mary Martin, née Sheehan, who died without the Last Sacrament.

'Want me to put your hair up?' Connie's voice broke in upon her.

Without answering, Nina knelt at her sister's feet. Connie's fingers were deft and gentle, twisting the gold into a coil at her nape. Twenty-five days, and then a week or two at most before their parting. 'I'll miss you, little one,' Connie said.

'I'll miss you too,' Nina answered. It was something she did not want to think about. Like saying goodbye to Daddy last night. Later it would hurt, but for now it was all Impressionist confusion. She did not want the details to stand out. Instead she concentrated on the future: she was doing what she wanted, craved, to do, loving whom she wanted to love, who most deserved it, who – this was the bewildering thing – had chosen her out of all those he might have chosen. Beside that fact all else was insignificant, even her sister's distress, for a part of her had caught the tremor in Connie's voice, had felt her fingers tremble. 'I'll pray for you,' she said.

'I'd rather you prayed for yourself,' Connie retorted. 'Oh, Nina, are you sure?'

'Quite sure,' Nina said, composed and perfect as she opened the cabin door.

The breeze came sweetly to meet her. The sun sparkled on the sea, dazzling her, filling her eyes with tears – that must have been the reason – so that for a few minutes she could not see. Which must have been why she walked to the rail to gaze at the receding shoreline and the Gateway to India without even registering the existence of the person who passed only a few feet from her, and who was to change her life.

'Bert! Bert, wake up. We're moving.'

' 'Course we're moving, you silly cow. The old tub sails at dawn, don't she? What d'you want her to do – sink here in Bombay harbour and us with her? That'd be a fine how-d'ye-do.'

Florrie Gurslake was untroubled by her husband's bad temper. Bert was always irritable first thing, especially if he'd been drinking, and he'd had a skinful last night. Still, he hardly ever knocked her about these days, and thanks to him they were returning to England a wealthy couple. First Class travel all the way.

Admittedly, she'd had to pack up quickly. When Bert moved, he moved fast. And she hadn't really understood the need to sell up their home in Sydney and catch the first available boat. The *Southern Cross* had taken them only as far as Bombay, where they'd had to idle for two weeks before the *Karachi* sailed, but now they were well and truly on their way to England for the first time since they'd left eight years before.

Theirs had been a wartime departure. At forty-five Bert had at first been too old to fight, and he wasn't like some fools who lied about their ages just to get into uniform. But he'd seen the opportunities from the start. 'Government contracts,' he'd said, winking, when she asked him why he was suddenly so flush. He was generous, though, that was one good thing about him. She'd bought all sorts of things, for the house, for herself, for him. It was too bad there were no children to spend on, but the children hadn't come. 'Nothing to keep us here,' he'd said that night when he came home to tell her they were going to Australia. 'What for?' she'd asked. 'Government contracts,' he'd said. And winked.

She'd told him then. She hadn't been sure until that morning, when Dr Jakes had confirmed it. 'Yes, my dear, we're there at last. Have to be careful, though; take things easy. Not the best age for a first child, forty-two.' She was so out of the habit of thinking about it that she hadn't even noticed the first time she'd missed, and here she was nearly three months pregnant and Bert was storming at her to get rid of it.

'I won't,' she said. 'I want it.'

'Bleeding 'ell, woman, we can 'ave another go.'

'It's the first time it's ever taken.'

'Gawd, what a time too. All that wire-pulling to get us passages and you're in the family way.'

'It's not for months yet. I can still go. It can be born in Australia.'

'If they find out there's a bun in your oven – and there's a medical – they won't allow you to go. Not with them U-boats sinking all the blinkin' shipping. You'll have to get rid of it.'

'No,' she'd said. And then he'd struck her. She told Dr Jakes when she met him that she'd turned giddy and fallen against the door. But she did not tell Bert what the doctor had said: 'You'll have to take it quietly. Rest more. We can't afford to lose another life, not with all those fine young men at the front being slaughtered. You're helping redress the balance, Mrs Gurslake – Nature's way.'

In the midst of so much destruction, what was one life more or less? To pacify Bert she'd allowed herself to visit a back room smelling of dirt and disinfectant where, with the blinds drawn, a not-unskilful operation was performed. She'd always been resistant to infection. There were no after-effects beyond a small blood clot in her leg. Phlebitis, Dr Jakes called it, though he explained it wasn't spelt as it sounded when she went to see him to tell him she'd have no need of him. 'Very sad for you and your husband,' he commented, 'but of course it was always on the cards. Women over forty don't carry a child so easily, and then there's the risk of physical or mental impairment in the infant. It may be a blessing in disguise.' When she told him they were emigrating, he seemed delighted. 'The best thing for you,' he enthused. 'New horizons, new friends, a new country. But not another baby. Not for you. Meanwhile I'll give you a prescription, and keep that leg up as much as possible. You'll be able to rest it on the voyage.'

And indeed she had, lying in her Second Class bunk moaning and vomiting from the day they left Tilbury almost as far as Marseilles. A torpedo would be welcome, she told Bert, whose sea-legs were as sturdy as the rest of him. After eight years the misery of that week was still vivid. It was the part of their return journey she dreaded most, especially since a man in their Bombay hotel who seemed to know everything about shipping told her the *Karachi* had a tendency to roll. Bert had been angry that they hadn't been able to get a cabin on the new P.& O. liner *Mooltan*, but she was fully booked. As usual when money did not buy what he wanted, he had taken it out on her.

Florrie did not mind. It was just Bert's way of showing disappointment. He had wanted the best for her. And why not? Money was for spending, and during their time in Sydney Florrie had learned to spend it with a will. Which made it all the more puzzling why, when she had come in from the bazaar in Bombay followed by a porter with her parcels, Bert had shouted at her.

'She thinks I'm made of money,' he informed the other residents in the hotel lounge, pointing. 'Mr £.s.d., that's me. But she's going to find out different, I can tell you. She'll have to economise, same as you lot. From now on, if she wants anything she asks me.'

There was a murmur of agreement at this declaration of masculine domination, and a softer undercurrent deploring when and where it was made. One or two guests, who did not need to economise, wondered what had given that common fellow Gurslake the impression that they did. Florrie, scarlet-faced and hoping it looked like heat-stroke, escaped with her parcels to their room, to be joined by Bert who, she now realised, had been drinking. He only ever drank midday when upset. But he had done so several times during those two weeks in Bombay while they waited for a sailing. 'What's up, love?' she had asked, knowing he would not answer. To her surprise, he did.

Not that she was any the wiser. It was all to do with the price of gold which had suddenly fallen but was bound to go up again, and the interest on a loan. (What loan? Bert never borrowed money.) When it did they would be sitting pretty; meanwhile they had to be careful, so no more jaunts to the bazaar.

Florrie might have asked herself why, if this was only a temporary embarrassment, Bert had taken to drink. Instead she put a plump arm round his shoulders and said, 'Want to see what I've bought?'

'Why the hell should I?'

'I mean, what I've bought for me.'

13

'If you like.' The assent was grudging, but Bert really did care what she wore. 'Reckon you look as good as any of 'em,' he would say, jerking his head towards a group of socially prominent Sydney ladies, or the obviously wealthy among the passengers on board the *Southern Cross*. He watched now with interest as she unwrapped a small thin package; after gazing blankly at its contents, he demanded to know what it was.

'It's a hair ornament.' Florrie picked up the long, intricately carved ivory hairpin in order to demonstrate.

'Looks more like a meat skewer. You could stick somebody with that.'

Florrie tested the point. 'Yes, it's sharp, but it isn't a weapon. You twist it through a bun.' And she proceeded to thrust it through the thick coil of hair which she wore piled insecurely just off-centre from the crown of her head.

Bert muttered that you could have fooled him.

'Watch out I don't use it on you!' Florrie withdrew the hairpin and prodded him.

'Hey, you randy old tart . . .'

'Not now, Bert!'

'You tell me what time's better. C'mon, off with 'em.'

'My hair . . .'

'Stick it up with that great bloomin' hatpin. Proof against anything, that is.'

And it had been. Since then Florrie had worn it daily, thrust like a dagger through her bun. The effect was certainly distinctive. Mrs Gurslake could be instantly identified. Even Captain Meiklejohn, watching them come aboard, still arguing over what Florrie called the mean tip Bert had given the taxi-wallah, had registered her existence and resolved their acquaintance should not improve.

Florrie was a large woman, highly coloured. Her hair was still so astonishingly dark that it caused other ladies to hint among themselves at walnut juice, and Florrie to stare them down from bold, black, defiant eyes. They were eyes whose sight was as keen as when she was twenty; they softened only when they came to rest on her Bert.

Herbert. Her Bert. It was the only pun Florrie was capable of, and she did not call it that. Since he had first come into the bar of the Goat and Compasses in Wapping, she had been his slave. Florrie behind the bar was a magnificent presence, Bert in front of it an insignificant one, yet there had never been any doubt about where the power lay. They had been married twenty-five years ago at St Stephen's. Christmas Eve it was, because Florrie wouldn't have to work the next day and they could have a nice lie-in in the brand-new double bed in the front bedroom of the terrace house Bert had rented, and the docks wouldn't reopen until after Boxing Day. Not that her Bert was a docker; he hadn't the build for that, Florrie thought proudly; he was as weedy as a gentleman. Just how he made his living she never did discover, but he handled a bit of this and a bit of that.

14

Handled it profitably, too. There was always money for the rent and the insurance, and he gave her the housekeeping regular. He had a drop too much some Friday nights and then he knocked her about a bit, but he didn't have other women; and Florrie, who could have laid him out with a blow if she had ever thought of such a thing, accepted these unavoidable disadvantages in what was otherwise a perfect mate.

Her one dread was of losing him. Widowhood had always lurked. An accident at the docks, pneumonia – she'd seen it happen to others. So long as it didn't happen to her . . . Not to hear his step along the pavement and his whistle (he came home regular as clockwork every night, took off his coat and cap and muffler, unlaced his boots and sat down to tea in his braces) would have condemned her to a limbo in which she went on living without a reason for life. When she attended weddings and funerals, the only time she set foot in a church, Florrie did not articulate prayers but her whole being cried out to the emptiness of the nave roof and the spaces above the aisles: Don't take him away from me, don't let me be left. There was no answer – you couldn't expect one – but he went on living and it would be their Silver Wedding this Christmas. She'd get him something really nice. A jewelled tiepin and spats – she fancied spats; they looked classy, and presumably the winters in England were still cold; though after the warmth of Sydney and the post-monsoon freshness of Bombay, it was hard to imagine unpacking the warm clothes in the trunk in the hold which wouldn't be brought up till after Suez. In any case they'd be out of fashion. She'd be able to go shopping as soon as they arrived.

'Where shall we live in England?' she asked Bert dreamily.

'Now how the 'ell would I know? Where shall we live, she says. We got to get there first, ain't we, and to start off with we'll stay in a hotel. Just till I get me affairs sorted out. Then you can go 'ouse-'unting. Live where you like so long as it's in London. I got to be near me work.'

Florrie allowed her mind to dwell on the prospect of a fine house rather than on Bert's business. Kent, now. Kent was all right. As a kid she'd been there for the hop-picking. Proper day out, it was. And country! Talk about real country! Lots of places had no streets at all, just a green and a duck-pond and one or two houses, and a church and a pub, of course. But Bert would prefer London and it was big enough, God knows – all the way from the heights of 'Appy 'Ampstead to the mansions of Park Lane, and new suburbs springing up in all directions keeping pace with the Tube. They could have one of those modern houses with electric bells that set off pink stars in an indicator in the kitchen to summon a live-in maid. And a shelf above the picture-rail in the front room to show off your collection of plates. They'd have to get new furniture but that wouldn't be a problem. Everyone said Maples was the place . . .

'You going to spend all day looking out of that porthole?' Bert demanded.

'I thought I'd go up on deck.'

15

'What, think they can't sail the ship without you? Come on back to bed.'
'No, Bert, I want air, this cabin's stuffy.'
'Switch the fan on, then, create a draught.'
'It makes such a noise.'
'My, my, we're choosy. Sorry there's nothing better than First Class.'
'I wasn't grumbling.'
'I should 'ope not. So come and take your mind off things.'
'I don't feel like it.'
'All right, ain't you?'
'Yes, of course. It's just that . . . I don't know.'

Just that it's your answer to everything and I sometimes think there might be others. But that response wouldn't satisfy Bert.

She said: 'Perhaps it's the change of life.'

'There's one thing doesn't change, I can tell you. Still, I could do with me beauty sleep. If you want to watch the dawn, you can do it on your tod, see. Eight o'clock is dawn enough for me.'

So Florrie Gurslake dressed and left her Bert sleeping, and made her way up on deck, passing as she did so several passengers and crew members, one of whose lives she was to wreck.

John Joseph Fitzgerald was one of the first on deck. As deck steward, he had every excuse for being there, although his duties did not begin until the first passengers appeared after breakfast, eager to secure a lounger chair to port or starboard, depending on their preference for sun or shade, and to be waited on attentively during a morning spent reading, writing letters, chatting, smoking, snoozing, and sipping long cool drinks, among them a concoction of pineapple juice, soda water, crushed ice and Cointreau which was known as Joe's Special and was famous throughout First Class.

But even a man as conscientious as John Joseph Fitzgerald could not claim that there was any need for him to be astir at sun-up. It was simply that he could not stand any longer the close, airless dormitory cabin in the bowels of the ship and the bed next to Preston. Preston's thoughts were mainly of female passengers: those whose favours he claimed to have enjoyed on other voyages, and those whose charms he hoped to be invited to sample on this. At intervals he farted explosively, the sound ripping off like a machine-gun in the cabin's cramped space.

'You want to get yourself a bit of crumpet, Joe,' he advised. 'Just be discreet and sod the regulations. I remember one voyage there was this old biddy . . .' And he was off again.

John Joseph had learned how not to listen, though the talent was one he would have preferred not to employ; but nothing was proof against the explosive release of gas from Preston's bowels, which in any case made itself known to nose as well as to ear. As newcomer, he had drawn the short straw among the stewards, for the hazards of being next to Preston were well known and it had so far proved impossible for the chief steward to find a solution by rooming like with like.

Nevertheless, John Joseph considered himself fortunate: he had a job; he was housed and uniformed and fed; and he was seeing something of the great wide world beyond the back streets of Dublin. He could have done a great deal worse.

The decision to leave home had not been easy. Mam had wept and Da had got fighting drunk; four of his five elder sisters and three of his four brothers-in-law had berated him; the fourth had clapped him on the shoulder and slipped him a quid; and his fifth and favourite sister Ellen knew nothing about it, immured in her convent in Connaught. The rest had pointed out to him, individually and in chorus, that he already had a job as a waiter in one of Dublin's better hotels; that no place on earth was fairer than Ireland, or at least the new Irish Free State; that things must get better after the Troubles, for indeed they could hardly get worse; and that as sole surviving son of the Fitzgeralds it was his duty to remain, to cheer the declining years of his parents, and (in so far as it was possible for such a runt) to take the place of Kieron, God rest him, who would surely never have forsaken home and country for other, wilder shores.

John Joseph did not see it quite as they did, pointing to the long tradition of emigration that had taken the Irish all over the world. America now, there was the land of opportunity, but even the cheapest passage was beyond him, whereas a one-way ticket from Kingstown – Dun Laoghaire, that is, for the old names died hard – would take him to Holyhead and thence to a waiter's job in Liverpool or London, where for sure there were always people wanting to eat.

He was nearly right. There was indeed a steady demand for waiters, whose jobs were non-unionised, but very little demand for Irish waiters, whom it was thought the customers might dislike. Far from working in good hotels, John Joseph found himself working in sleazy eating-houses and decrepit dockland pubs. But at least he learned to pull a pint and squirt a mean measure of spirits into a smeary glass. When the Labour Exchange, which he haunted despite the fact that he was in work, informed him that the Australasian Line was recruiting stewards, he was one of the first to apply. He had no hope, but to his surprise he was accepted, and at once his volatile spirits soared. They knew a good man when they saw one. Attention all ports of call east of Suez, here comes an Irishman.

He would have been less elated had he known that the reasons for his selection had more to do with his small stature (handy in a confined space), his soft voice (soothing to the seasick), and his large dark eyes (appealing to the lady passengers), than with his professional expertise or the much-folded reference in laborious copperplate from the good hotel in Dublin. And of course he was spick and span down to the toes of his polished black shoes, which let water but the day of the interview was a dry day, thank God. So, due ultimately to Mam's insistence that cleanliness was next to

17

godliness (in which conviction she differed from most of the inhabitants of Munster Street), John Joseph Fitzgerald became a deck steward aboard the SS *Karachi*, sailing between Tilbury and Bombay. To his relief after the first few nights of the crowded dormitory cabin, he found that once past the Pillars of Hercules he spent most of his time on deck in clean air, clad in a white mess jacket and dark trousers, and run almost off his feet. He had little leisure to reflect that he was serving the hated English, who ate and drank, got drunk and were seasick, very much like anybody else, as they sailed the high seas on the business of their Empire on which the sun never set.

John Joseph had not been born hating the English. They were a fact of Irish life. They made the laws and enforced them, but not all their laws were bad nor all their enforcement oppressive. They were Prods, of course, and as such unable to enter Paradise or to achieve a martyr's crown, but for that it was possible to feel sorry for them, spiritually segregated in the imposing buildings of the Church of Ireland in much the same way that they were socially segregated in their handsome houses around Merrion Square or out at Ballsbridge and Sandycove. People who lived in Munster Street had other things to worry about than the English – things like rent and food and fire. Indeed, Kate Mullen at No. 32 who worked for an English family was full of praise for them. Certainly no one could have been kinder when Michael Mullen, a sober, honest, hard-working carpenter, was knocked down and killed by a tram. They bought mourning for Kate and the children, and paid the family's rent for six months. But at the end of that time, with Kate unable to feed and clothe her family and meet the demands of the absentee landlord's agent, the Mullens and their few belongings were out on the pavement one morning and thereafter disappeared from Munster Street and from the Fitzgerald family's lives.

Except that it was from then on that Kieron began to talk about Home Rule. To John Joseph, ten years old, it was just something else for Kieron to get excited about, and heaven knows there was something different every week. If it wasn't the horses it was a wager he had with Bart Collins about which of them could beat the other when they went out for a swim; or else it was the bright eyes of Miss Louise Dunphy, or whatever girl he was walking out. But Home Rule was different; it lasted; until one day John Joseph asked him what it was.

'What it says: government from home, by us here in Dublin, not by them in London. What right have they to frame our laws? Self-government, as for every self-respecting nation. We've been asking long enough. This time they've got to give it.'

John Joseph said, 'What if they don't?'

'Why, then –' Kieron seemed uncertain – 'we have to make them.'

'Yes, but how?'

'By force. By fighting them.'

'But we don't have an army.'

'Don't you be too sure of that.'

18

John Joseph said nothing, but he watched with a small boy's observance the men who came to the house: how they seemed to have signs and passwords; how they trained athletically. In none of this did Kieron receive encouragement from his family. 'How's the Fianna, then?' his sister Ellen would ask, referring to Finn MacCool's legendary band of warriors. 'Can you leap as high as yourself and bend as low as your knee while still running?' And all the rest of them would laugh. Kieron didn't answer, but he took to spelling his name 'Ciaran', which he said was the Irish way, and he attended meetings of the Irish Republican Brotherhood at which men like Pearse and Connolly spoke. 'You should have heard him, heard Padraig Pearse,' he told his family on returning home one afternoon. 'He made a speech to tear the heart out of your body when he welcomed home O'Donovan Rossa's bones.' – 'O'Donovan Rossa – wasn't he the Fenian fellow?' his father queried. 'He was.' – 'Then I'd as lief he stayed away, bones and all.' And one of the girls – Ruth or Maggie, which one John Joseph couldn't remember – had chanted quietly but very distinctly, '*Glory O, glory O, to the bold Fenian men.*'

One night when Kieron returned late and came up to the bedroom he shared with his brother he carried a long parcel wrapped in sacking which he hid under the bed.

'What's that?' John Joseph asked.

Kieron spun round. 'You should be asleep.'

'I'm not. What is it?'

'It's a rifle,' Kieron said. 'But if you ever breathe a word to Mam or Da or any of the girls I'll cut your tongue out, so I will.'

'What are you going to do with it?' John Joseph persisted.

'Fire it when the time comes.'

'Who are you going to kill?'

'Only Englishmen, nothing for you to worry about. When you're older you'll maybe be doing the same yourself one day.'

John Joseph savoured the idea but did not find it appealing. 'What have the English done?'

Kieron sat down on the end of the bed. 'If boys are taught nothing of the history of their own country, that's one thing they've done,' he said. 'What do you know of the Boyne? Of Athlone and Aughrim and the siege of Limerick? Do you know how many Irishmen died at Drogheda, burnt alive in a church, some of them, by the Devil's own saint, Oliver Cromwell? Have you heard of Robert Emmett, hanged and then beheaded, and Wolfe Tone, who cut his throat rather than face a traitor's death? Rebels they call them, but I say they were martyrs for the cause of Ireland, and so was Lord Edward Fitzgerald whose name we bear. Oh, I'm not claiming kinship, but there's no denying 'tis one of the proudest names of Ireland and I'd be ashamed for the Irish Republican Brotherhood to march without me when the day comes for us to march.'

The day had come, John Joseph reflected later that morning as he set about his duties. Kieron had marched – and died. Since when his hatred of the English had flared like naphtha; even so, there was only one he would have liked to kill. And that was an unknown, unnamed khaki figure whom he had watched raising a rifle in the heart of Dublin, sighting it and firing in one smooth motion, like a sportsman at a shoot. Each night when he knelt to pray in his cabin, which he did much to Preston's openly expressed disgust, he added a private petition that God would see fit to allow his path to cross that of the unknown English officer, and then grant him as much advantage over his enemy as he had granted that enemy over Kieron Fitzgerald, patriot.

Meanwhile he lived and worked among the English, and in the main he liked them well enough. And they liked him: his cheerful, easy manner had soon made him a favourite with the *Karachi*'s passengers outward bound. So much so that John Joseph found himself positively looking forward to the new faces on the homeward voyage. And then, amid all the happy bustle of that first morning, he encountered the Haldinghams.

The coast of India was fading to a blur behind them as the passengers established themselves on deck. They had come aboard the night before and now, having unpacked and breakfasted, they were preparing to enjoy their first lazy morning and begin making one another's acquaintance. John Joseph moved among them, attending to their needs.

He paused before an elderly couple.

'Madam? Sir?'

The little white-haired lady looked up from the magazine she was reading, but made no attempt to speak.

'What can I get you now?' John Joseph asked, thinking she had not realised he was taking orders.

To his astonishment he saw dawning horror in her eyes.

'Sir –' he tried the old gentleman – 'will you take coffee, fruit juice, mineral water? Something stronger? Would the lady be fancying one of my specials? It would be a pleasure to mix it for her.'

For answer the old lady turned away from him. The tall old gentleman put out an arm as if to shield her, but managed to say, 'Nothing, thank you,' before he too turned his head away.

Baffled, John Joseph retreated. Perhaps they did not drink between meals; perhaps the old lady was deaf, or on a diet – but in that case surely they could have said? In any case, these theories were refuted within the next half-hour when the old gentleman summoned Preston and placed an order for drinks.

John Joseph's cautious enquiries about the couple only deepened the mystery. Mr and Mrs Ivo Haldingham had lived in India for more than fifty years, even choosing to remain there when Mr Haldingham retired from the Forestry service. For some reason they had now decided to sell up and return to England, leaving behind them an empty bungalow and desolate servants, and presumably facing genteel impoverishment in

Cheltenham or somewhere such. Nowhere in their humdrum existence did there seem any reason for their dislike of him. It was as well the rest of the passengers weren't like that, John Joseph told himself.

On the whole he found the English kind if patronising, tolerant if uncaring, slow to act in anger but retaliatory when they did. It was obverse and reverse, no one without the other; no altering them and no accommodating them. No altering or accommodating him either; he would not attack but nor would he defend. Which was why he lingered when the luncheon gong sounded and the deck had emptied: he had a self-imposed mission, which was to help all those who sought to beat the English system, whether of government, justice, worship or snobbery.

So, after glancing round to make sure there was no one watching, he ran lightly up to the boat deck and moved swiftly along to the third boat from the stern on the port side. Its black tarpaulin cover looked undisturbed, but he knew better. From his trouser pocket he produced a packet of sandwiches; from beneath his jacket a bottle of lemonade. Reaching up, he thrust them beneath the boat's cover and felt them taken from him by a delicate, slender hand.

II

Two days out from Bombay, and Edmund Bladon's morning surgery was busy. Nothing serious, thank God, and not the least qualm of seasickness anywhere on an ocean calm as a lake, but a succession of minor ailments. Insomnia – 'It's the throbbing of those engines, Doctor'; headaches; hangovers; period pains; sunburn incurred through rash exposure; bruises sustained by falling down the last few steps of a companionway – he would not suggest while drunk. The First Class passengers included a diabetic and several with high blood-pressure, all on standard medication, which he dispensed. They also included Mrs Cynthia Vane and son Bobby, who stood before him now.

Bobby was an intelligent-looking, dark-eyed child, a-quiver with energy. His eyes darted round the surgery; his feet were never still. He was naturally pale, but it was not a sickly pallor. On the contrary, he seemed vibrantly alive.

'What's the trouble?' Edmund asked.

'He keeps being sick, Doctor.' Cynthia Vane's voice was low, pleasant despite an edge of anxiety. 'After every meal, it seems.'

'Sounds as if our chef's cooking doesn't agree with you,' Edmund said to Bobby. 'How long has this been going on?'

'Oh, only since we sailed, Doctor. He was never sick before.'

'Well, if you can survive what some Indian cooks put before you, there can't be much wrong with your stomach,' Edmund said. No other passenger had reported sickness; it couldn't be the food.

'Do you have any pain? A stomach ache, for instance?' he asked Bobby.

'He's never complained of anything like that.'

'How long after meals does this happen? Three hours? Four hours?'

'Much quicker, Doctor. Sometimes he's sick almost as soon as we get back to our cabin.'

Something nervous, then.

'It must spoil your appetite,' Edmund suggested.

'That's the funny thing, Doctor; he eats well enough. He just can't keep it down, can you, darling?'

Bobby Vane shook his head.

Edmund glanced at his watch: ten-thirty.

'Have you been sick since breakfast?' he asked.

'No, today is one of our better days,' Mrs Vane answered, 'but we can't go on like this.'

23

'Well, let's have a look at you. Show me your tongue.'

Edmund examined a rosy organ and at the same time took stock of Cynthia Vane. The resemblance between mother and son was unmistakable: they had the same dark eyes, pale skin, and cloudy dark hair, their likeness accentuated by the mother's fashionable shingle which revealed in both a thin, vulnerable nape of the neck. She was about his own age, early thirties, Edmund guessed, as he took out a thermometer and stuck it under Bobby's tongue.

'Is he your only child?' he asked.

She looked meltingly at her son. 'I'm afraid so,' she murmured. 'His father was killed in the war.'

'I'm sorry.'

One more of the tragedies. But at least she was comfortably off: good clothes, First Class travel, no financial worries . . .

He said, 'Oughtn't Bobby to be in school?'

'He's going after Christmas. To his father's old school.'

'You'll miss him.'

Mrs Vane inclined her head. 'We've been staying with my brother. He's in the Army, stationed at Quetta. Do you know it?'

'I know nothing of India except the waterfront of Bombay.'

'It was our first visit. My brother suggested it. He thought it might do us good.'

Thought you might find a husband among the garrison or the civil servants, Edmund suspected. He removed the thermometer, noting it read normal, and asked Bobby, 'Are you looking forward to going to school?'

'Of course he is,' Mrs Vane answered.

This time Edmund ignored her and repeated his question to Bobby.

The boy shot him a venomous look, turned and buried his face against his mother. 'Mummy, I feel sick,' he said.

'Oh, sweetheart, not again!'

'I'm going to *be* sick.'

Edmund pointed. 'You'll find a washroom in there.'

Bobby disappeared, and a moment later came the sound of violent retching.

Cynthia Vane twisted her hands. 'Poor darling, he does suffer.'

'So, I think, do you.'

'He's all I've got. His father never saw him. He was killed on the Somme a month before Bobby was born.'

Making Bobby eight . . .

'Had you been married long?'

'Two years. We were childhood sweethearts. Our families lived near, in Lincolnshire. We were married in June 1914, just a week before that Austrian archduke was assassinated. It never seemed possible there'd be a war.'

No, Edmund thought, it didn't. The assassination had rated a small

24

paragraph in *The Times*. The Balkans were a well-known trouble spot, and the death of the Austrian Emperor's nephew and heir was not significant – there was, after all, another one waiting and one whom it was said Franz Josef much preferred. At the time, to Edmund as to most Englishmen, Cowes Week had seemed more important, and the end of the Season's balls, at one of which he had asked Rosemary to marry him. Rosemary . . . He tried not to think of her.

'Robert's two brothers were also killed,' Cynthia Vane was saying, 'and the shock finished off his parents, so Bobby's the last of the line. That makes him doubly precious.'

'You mean he's heir to an estate.'

'Hardly. It was sold – there was no one to run it. But at least he bears the name. That's why I'm so frightened – oh, Doctor, am I going to lose him?'

'Heavens, no,' Edmund said. 'There's nothing wrong with him.'

She looked at him reproachfully as further distressing sounds reached them, and he explained, 'I'm afraid he's having you on.'

'What do you mean?'

'He's making himself ill to frighten you.'

'But why should he do that?'

'I don't know. Perhaps you've done something to upset him and he's trying to punish you. Perhaps he doesn't want to go away to school. Whatever it is, he wants you to think he's ill so that you'll give way to him.'

She turned on him. 'How can you be so heartless? He *is* ill. I shall report you to the Captain. I shall demand we take on another doctor at Aden, otherwise I shall sue the Line –'

'Mrs Vane, if you will sit down and be calm while I talk to Bobby, perhaps I can convince you I'm right. You owe it to your son as much as anyone. After all, if he's speaking the truth and I'm wrong, you'd never forgive yourself, would you? Now please sit down over there and let Bobby give his own answers when I talk to him. He'll be out any moment – he can't keep this up indefinitely, you know . . . Ah, I can hear him coming. Don't answer for him, please!'

The child who emerged from the washroom was not noticeably paler, but his head drooped, his feet dragged, and he made great play of wiping his mouth with his handkerchief.

'Do you feel better?' Edmund asked.

A nod.

'I'm so glad. Now, I'm going to give you a dose of physic –'

Bobby backed away from him in alarm.

'– and you'll be as right as rain. I'm sorry it's not very pleasant, but you'll find it'll do you good.'

'I don't want any physic. I don't need it.'

'Surely I'm the best judge of that. You're not a doctor, are you?'

'I tell you I don't need it.'

'Not when you've been sick several times a day for the past forty-eight hours? You'll be lucky if one dose cures you.'

'I won't take it.'

'Doctor's orders.'

'You can't make me.'

'No, but the alternative is to put you in the ship's hospital where I can keep an eye on you, make sure you get only the plainest food, go to bed early –'

'Mummy . . .'

'Doctor, this is cruelty.'

'I think not, Mrs Vane. Besides, you promised to keep quiet, remember. Now, Bobby, open wide.'

The child stood with head lowered and lips clamped into a thin line.

'Some people deliberately make themselves sick,' Edmund continued, holding spoon and bottle poised. The mixture was one of his placebos. He had no qualms about administering it. 'It's unkind,' he went on, 'because it upsets people who love them, but of course you wouldn't do a thing like that. Which is why I'm going to give you this medicine. You want to get better, don't you?'

A nod.

'Well then, what are we waiting for? Open up.'

Bobby turned his head to one side, looking neither at Edmund nor his mother.

'Unless you'd care to tell me what you do.' Edmund made the suggestion matter-of-factly, and continued, 'Some people drink salt and water, or mustard and water, but I don't think you do that. Others tickle the back of the throat with a feather – have you got a feather?'

The child almost shook his head.

'So I suppose you stick two fingers down your throat,' Edmund went on. 'It works pretty well, doesn't it? But now that we know what you do, perhaps you could stop doing it. It's not very clever and, as I told you, it's unkind. And it won't make a scrap of difference to your going away to school,' he added, 'so there isn't even any point. Now I suggest you and your mother go and have elevenses – you must be hungry – and I don't want to see you here again.'

Bobby shot him a look of hatred.

Cynthia Vane stood up. 'Thank you, Doctor.' She did not sound grateful. 'Bobby dear, come along.'

Edmund watched them go. They walked side by side, not touching. The backs of their necks were very white. He hoped they were going to forgive him; it would be awkward at the dinner table, if not. He sat between the two Miss Martins, but Cynthia Vane was only a little farther down and the talk and laughter could easily involve her, as it had done last night.

Last night. He allowed himself to dwell on it with pleasure. It was a long time since he had enjoyed himself so much and he had not expected to as a

26

ship's surgeon: the bitterness of becoming one was still too keen. Were all his hard work and his prizes reduced to this? The most brilliant student of his year at Guy's a ship's surgeon? He still could not credit it. Yet door after door had closed in his face at one interview after another as one of the smiling, self-congratulatory faces on the other side of the table asked the dread question which for them was mere formality: 'What about your war service, Doctor?' As he answered, he had become accustomed to seeing their faces assume mask-like expressions, like the skinning over of a wound. 'I see. Thank you.' A hurried confabulation. 'Thank you, we'll be in touch.' And a few days later a letter regretting that the post was filled, or deploring politely that his qualifications were not what they were seeking. What were they seeking, then? The second rate? It was bad enough that he had come late to medicine, was newly qualified at thirty-two as compared to men of twenty-four or -five, the bloom of inexperience still on them and too young to have fought in the trenches or indeed anywhere else. That these were the men hand-picked for junior registrars, for junior partnerships in comfortable general practices, was more than he could bear. The consciousness of worth ill-rewarded ate into him like acid until Curtis had taken him on one side – Curtis the senior gynae man who had eyed him with favour ever since that night when he had been on duty as houseman and a patient had haemorrhaged. Not that there was anything to show. 'She can't sleep, Doctor,' the brisk night sister said, 'but I've told her the baby's fine and she'll see him in the morning, so there's nothing for her to worry about. If you could just give her something . . .' She looked at him expectantly.

Edmund glanced at the woman moving her head from side to side upon the pillow. A high forceps delivery, prolonged and painful, but she'd come through it heroically. Now she was pale and sweating, gazing up at him from sunken eyes as she murmured apologies for being a nuisance. And suddenly he knew that this was not just restlessness.

Afterwards Curtis had congratulated him. 'Diagnosis by instinct, you said. I'd rather call it diagnosis by inference and observation carried to the nth degree. Either way you saved a life, and that's worth doing. That's what a doctor's for.'

Thereafter Curtis had extended his favour wherever possible, though it hadn't succeeded in landing him a job, until at last he'd taken Edmund aside and asked bluntly, 'What is it? Your war record?'

'Yes.'

'Tck, tck.' The consultant had a way of sucking his teeth while considering; many a patient knew the sound. 'These things have a way of blowing over. Why don't you go abroad for a bit?'

'I can't afford to. The training took all my savings. Besides, I want to work in my own country.'

'Tck, tck. I understand. Ever thought of becoming a ship's surgeon for a year or two?'

'You mean on a cargo boat?'

27

'No, no, on a passenger liner. I've a friend in the Australasian Line . . . A couple of years with them and this war service thing will get forgotten. What do you think of the idea?'

'It's very good of you, sir . . .'

Even though it was the last thing he wanted, it was still good of Curtis to try. And his intervention proved effective. Within six weeks Edmund found himself a ship's surgeon with the Australasian Line, appointed to the SS *Karachi* under Captain Angus Meiklejohn.

'At least,' he wrote to Aunt Anne, 'I'll be sailing the high seas and seeing a bit of the world.' And she'd written back, warm and funny and affectionate as ever, warning him that what he'd mainly see was sea. At the end of his first outward voyage he'd written to tell her she was mistaken: what he saw was the gleaming surgery and ship's hospital and bodies, young and old, male and female, in sickness and in seasickness, in decrepitude and in health. Dear Aunt Anne! She kept him abreast of all that went on in their Gloucestershire village: how she'd been down and found his father very frail; who was married and who buried; how the new Memorial Hall had been opened; how she'd heard that Rosemary . . .

He switched off. It was better not to think of Rosemary, except that last night he had done so because Connie Martin, with her bright curls, her neat little teeth, her lilting way of talking, had reminded him of her time and time again. He had to force himself to remember that Connie was a stranger, so easy did he find it to respond. On his other side was Nina, the quiet sister, with full lips and downcast eyes and soft young breasts that not even current fashion could flatten as they rose and fell with laughter and indrawn breath. The middle-aged woman on her left, who had astonishingly dyed hair and an even more astonishing hairpin which could put someone's eye out at a dance, smiled down on her benignly; opposite Nina a young army officer with a scarred face made play; but she remained remote, serenely smiling, sensual, like some Renaissance painting of the Virgin which made one doubt the spirituality of the Holy Ghost. He gathered she was going home to England to be married, and thought to himself: Lucky chap.

But Connie, the elder, wasn't about to be married. She talked gaily of getting a job. To begin with, the two girls would stay with an aunt and uncle near Reading, after which, as Connie said, Who knows? Who indeed? Certainly not Edmund Bladon. Marriage was not feasible for him until he acquired a shore base and a more settled existence, and that would not be for a few years yet. He might well be forty before he could ask any woman to marry him, and with the rekindling of desire bitterness rose in him like bile.

After Rosemary he had vowed there would be no other heartbreak. After the war he had immersed himself in work. It had been a stroke of luck getting into Guy's, though he suspected Aunt Anne had pulled strings with her Red Cross contacts. If she had, he had more than justified her efforts in the world of students, but not in the world of men. The consciousness of having much-needed skills to give which were not wanted because of the stigma associated with his name not only embittered him, it had made him reclusive, skilled at parrying the questions he knew must come. But not yet; not on this voyage; the passengers were only just getting acquainted; they had had no time to form that network of shipboard friendships which might or might not last, the mutual antagonisms and alliances of convenience which lay like a web over First Class. It was amusing to speculate on what would develop. It was already obvious that the hairpin woman longed to 'adopt' the two girls; that he and the young army officer had little to say to each other; that Cynthia Vane was prospecting for a man. He was less sure about the Reverend and his wife and their insipid daughter: had they cast an assessing matrimonial eye on Julian Strode, the young third officer who had joined the *Karachi* on this voyage just as he had, though that seemed their only link? Strode was small but well built and classically handsome, too young to have fought in the war, to bear those scars, concealed or otherwise, which marked the bodies and minds of those who had. He was correct in carrying out his duties, in his manner; he had attracted so far only good reports; so why don't I like him? Edmund wondered. Am I to go through life being jealous of all handsome, unscarred younger men?

But then, how am I going to go through life? The last ten years have seen so many changes. In 1914 I was twenty-two, home from studying in Leipzig to become a singer and my first recitals for the autumn already booked. In 1924 I am a newly qualified doctor, knowing I want to be a gynae man like Curtis but unable to find the opening in hospitals or general practice which would give me the experience I need. Instead, I am a ship's surgeon with only one pregnant passenger aboard and she nowhere near term, so that, barring accidents, she will not need my help. And all that lies between my two selves, between the younger son of a comfortably off family in Gloucestershire who could afford to indulge a musical talent that was not perhaps so very great, and the restless, friendless, impoverished ship's surgeon, is signified by the years 1914–18.

The war was said to have eroded class distinctions, to have reversed in many instances the roles of master and man, to have touched with tragedy homes throughout the kingdom from highest to lowest, to have advanced the cause of equality; yet here in this hierarchical world of an ocean liner, where did Edmund Bladon fit in? A specialist, as narrow in his skills as chief engineer or steward, one of the ship's company. For all the good he had done so far he might as well not have existed. Common sense could have dealt with the minor medical problems that had presented; they had not required specialist skill. Even the surgery he had held for the crew that morning had produced nothing of significance: an upset stomach; the Purser's usual headache due to eyestrain – he'd already told him to get his glasses changed; a Lascar stoker with a burnt hand, nothing serious but the

29

engineering officer on watch had been right to send him – the Chief was a stickler for such things.

'How d'you do that?' Edmund had asked.

The man eyed him sullenly, saying nothing.

'How did you do it?' Edmund asked again.

The native crew were all supposed to understand English, it was one of the Line's requirements, but below decks he sometimes had his doubts. These were now dispelled by the man's uttering the one word, 'Furnace.'

'What happened?'

The man mimed a fall.

It wouldn't be the first time such an injury had occurred. It was something the Australasian Line's chief medical officer had mentioned in the course of their interview. 'Usually happens only in rough weather,' he had elaborated. 'Despite all precautions, a man can get thrown against the furnace doors, which is like putting him on the hotplate of a stove and frying him. There've been one or two fatalities.' Edmund shuddered; it had happened also in wartime, when shells or torpedoes struck. Some of the unlucky survivors were still being treated at Guy's . . . But this was flat calm, and peacetime.

'What made you fall?' he asked.

This time the man shook his head, his dark face tight with anger. Without warning, with his good hand he gave Edmund a shove.

'Do you mean you were pushed?' Edmund said when he had recovered.

'Pushed. Yes.'

Presumably he should report this, though doubtless the Chief already knew. He was rumoured to know everything that happened in the engine-room, including what happened while he slept. Still, it was as well to cover himself. If the man made trouble later . . .

He finished dressing the hand and dismissed the stoker, who departed without thanks. Then he picked up the internal telephone and rang the engine-room, asking to be connected to the Chief.

'Sutherrland.' The Scottish accent was very noticeable.

'Bladon, ship's surgeon, here. I've just treated one of your stokers for a burnt hand, nothing serious, but I thought you should know he alleges he was pushed against the furnace door.'

'Does he now? That's maybe because I've just docked his pay for insubordination and he's trying to get his own back.'

'I just thought you should know.'

'I'm obliged to you, Doctor. I'll deal with the man, never fear.'

Fear for whom? Edmund had wondered, replacing the handset. For the man? For himself? For the Chief? He would have dismissed the incident at once had he had more to occupy him, but now, as he took off his white coat and prepared to close the morning's surgery, it lingered in his mind. What was it like for the native crew on these ocean liners, Australasian or P.& O., with their white officers and crews composed of every race along the

30

waterfronts of Calcutta, Madras, Bombay? The structure was parallel to that of the British Army of India, white officers of native regiments backed up by native NCOs on whom the officers depended, the whole maintained by discipline, tradition, and more or less precarious goodwill. Except that these days there were rumblings: thousands of Indian troops had perished in the war, a war in which they had no conceivable interest. Was it surprising if questions were being asked? If the newly formed Indian Congress Party was beginning to talk of Independence, as the Irish Republicans did? Well, for the past two years the Irish had at least had their Free State. Would India have Independence some day?

His thoughts were interrupted by a knock on the surgery door. Edmund glanced at the clock: eleven. Surgery was technically over. Nevertheless . . . 'Come in,' he called, reaching once more for his white coat.

To his surprise, Archie Johnson came in, smiling hesitantly. Captain Archibald Johnson, MC. Tall, well set up, handsome despite the scar, in the way that any young male animal is handsome: proud, confident of masculinity. The scar ran diagonally from above the left eyebrow almost to the top of the ear. In places it formed a deep indentation. Edmund judged him lucky to be alive. There had been times, listening to Archie Johnson's conversation, when he had wondered if this was not due to thickness of the skull, which appeared to be solid within the frontal cranial cavity. Or was that jealousy?

Connie Martin, at any rate, had seemed to find his banalities amusing. The banter flowed to and fro, encouraged by the hairpin woman – what *was* her name? Gosford? Gursley? – while the Reverend's limp daughter listened wide-eyed. Nina Martin also listened, with her remote, sensual smile, lips parted as if awaiting kisses, head filled with thoughts of them, no doubt. It was astonishing how often a convent education (he had learned that both girls were convent bred) seemed to enhance the flesh by emphasising the spirit; it was something he had noticed before. But in Connie physical animation complemented quick wit and high spirits. She it was who led the way. Yes, of course they would join Captain Johnson in deck tennis. They were looking forward to the first ship's dance. Did he know how to tango? He must teach them. How marvellous that he had his gramophone. Did Dr Bladon know how to tango? Oh well, there were lots of other dances, weren't there; of course he knew some of those.

Edmund had not danced since he had danced with Rosemary, her small, pointed face turned up to his.

'When are you going to join up, darling? Most people have already gone.'

'Are you so anxious to lose me?' he asked lightly.

'Of course not, though I'm resigned to you doing your duty. And you'll look splendid in uniform.'

He had worn uniform all right, and looked anything but splendid. Come to that, he was wearing uniform now, carrying out his duties as laid down by the Line's official regulations. His eyes assessed Archie Johnson.

'What can I do for you?'

Johnson certainly didn't look ill. Bursting with health as a beanpod bursts with beans. Not even hung over, though there had been some heavy drinking going on last night, him and that ugly little husband of the hairpin woman's. Had they anything in common except a taste for Scotch?

'I wanted to have a little chat, Doc,' Johnson said, ingratiating. 'You're not going off duty or anything like that?'

When surgery hours were ten to eleven, what did he expect to find at eleven o'clock?

'No, no,' Edmund said, surreptitiously rebuttoning his white coat and indicating the patient's chair opposite his desk. 'I must say, you're the healthiest-looking patient I've had in here this morning.'

Johnson cleared his throat. 'I take it we're alone?'

'The nurse has gone off duty. I was about to follow.'

'Yes, well, sorry and all that. I won't keep you long. Fact is, I've been waiting till I could be sure you were on your own . . .'

'What's the trouble?'

'I don't really know. These below-the-belt jobs . . .'

'Which organ is affected?'

'*The* organ – know what I mean?'

Of course I know. What do you take me for? But we'll stick to the form, if you please.

'Any difficulty passing water?'

'Oh no, nothing like that.'

'Any swelling?'

'No.' A hesitation. 'Not of the organ itself.'

'Of what, then?'

'It's more a swelling on it.'

'Right, better let me have a look.'

And I hope for your sake I'm wrong in my suspicions, he thought as Johnson struggled with his braces. Then: 'How long have you been suffering with this?'

'Only the last few days, Doc.' As if that minimised it.

'And when did you last have intercourse?' Don't frown with the effort to remember. It must have been recently.

Archie Johnson was silent.

'Have you had intercourse since we sailed?'

'Good Lord, no! There hasn't been a chance. I mean . . .'

Thank God at least for that.

'It was in Bombay. I was stuck there waiting for a sailing. Some fellows and I went out . . .'

'All right, I can guess. As a result, you've got a primary syphilitic lesion. Half the whores of the East are riddled with it.'

'Christ!' Johnson muttered, fumbling for his trousers. 'You mean I've got the clap?'

32

'Yes.'

Johnson sat down heavily. He was noticeably paler.

'Is there anything you can do?'

'I can give you an injection and some mercury ointment. That should stop it developing.'

'You can't cure it?'

'No, for that you need specialist treatment. But it can be cured, no doubt of that.' And if it teaches you not to go whoring, it may be a lesson well learned.

'Christ!' Johnson said again. He seemed unable to believe it.

Edmund relented slightly. 'How old are you?'

'Twenty-six.'

'I take it you've never had anything like this before?'

A violent shudder.

'Well, don't worry. You'll survive. Bathe it as often as you can and apply the ointment – that'll help to soothe the burning – and get yourself to a specialist clinic as soon as ever we dock. I'll give you an address.'

Johnson continued to sit, stupefied.

'The ointment will be ready for you this afternoon as soon as the dispensary opens,' Edmund said, dismissing him.

The young man turned glazed blue eyes upon him.

'She was so beautiful,' he said. 'You couldn't tell. You'd never have guessed she was infected.'

'It's safer to assume they all are.'

'Damned wogs!'

Why not damned Englishmen? Who knew where infection began?

Johnson stood up. 'I take it this remains confidential?'

'Of course. It has to go down in my log, but no one sees that except the Captain, and port health officials if need be.'

'The Captain?'

'Only if he so requests.'

He would, of course. There was no aspect of the *Karachi* that Captain Meiklejohn did not oversee. But Edmund saw no need to say so. There were other, more urgent things to be said . . .

'One last thing.'

Johnson paused.

'No intercourse. A celibate existence.'

'That tops the lot,' Johnson said, not quite banging the surgery door behind him.

So long as he obeys, Edmund thought. But what if he doesn't? He could infect others, particularly the innocent. The Martin girls. Connie. No, she'd never give in to him. Or would she? That last time with Rosemary he'd realised how easy it would be, as she alternately coaxed and taunted, herself the unacknowledged reward. He had only to do as she was asking, to do as others did, to heed the recruiting posters – 'Your country needs

33

you' – and she was willing to be his. Without benefit of registrar or clergy. A soldier's unblest bride. Already her body was pliant, yielding, the sparkle of desire in her eyes. He knew that his own eyes shone in return, his limbs were quivering with constraint. He had only to put aside his own pig-headed principles, which might quite possibly be wrong, and all would be as he had dreamed it might be between them. Yet still a voice within him cried 'No!' If she could not, would not, understand, what union was there except of bodies? At the very brink, he had drawn back.

He watched the sparkle die, leaving her face pinched.

'So you're afraid to go,' she'd sneered.

'I hope not.'

'Some hope!'

'Dearest,' he'd pleaded for the last time, 'couldn't you try to understand?'

'I understand very well. You don't love me enough to defend me. What sort of a man are you?'

'Just because we disagree . . .'

'It's more than disagreement, Edmund.'

He was silent, knowing it to be true.

'I think it's best if we don't meet again.' She avoided looking at him. 'Let me give you back your ring.'

'No! I don't want it. Keep it.'

'Do you think I have no pride?'

'I meant as a keepsake, a memento . . .'

'I want no memento of a coward.'

She'd flung it then, with deadly accuracy. He felt the sting of it against his cheek and put his hand up in an involuntary gesture as it fell with a tinkle to the floor.

Even as she turned, her small figure stiff with dignity, he'd had to restrain himself from running after her, from casting himself down at her feet, despite the fact that she would only glory in his abasement and he be shamed by it. Instead he'd stood, watching her go, his mind an echo chamber in which her words resounded ceaselessly.

'I want no memento of a coward.'

And echoing still through all his days and nights, those ultimate syllables: Coward, coward, coward.

'*Requiem æternam dona ea, Domine, et lux perpetua luceat ea. Requiescat in pace.*'

Nina rose from her knees.

Prayer was so difficult. 'Think of it as a conversation with God,' Reverend Mother had advised. 'You don't get distracted when talking to your friends, do you?' But conversation with friends was ever varied, not the same thing repeated by rote. No wonder one needed a rosary to keep count of all those Our Fathers and Hail Marys. Even so, one was constantly startled into realising that the lips were moving, beads sliding

34

through the fingers, while the mind was otherwhere than on the Mysteries. Yet this was the spiritual discipline to which she had pledged herself.

Hot with shame, Nina sank down again in the cabin and bowed her head over her folded hands. This was no way to pray for the soul of Bridget Martin now in Purgatory who had died unreconciled.

'Have mercy on her soul, O Lord, and on all Christian souls . . .'

But what about the non-Christians who knew not the Lord Jesus? Were they to suffer for what they could not help? Ought one to join a missionary Order? It was not only prayer that was difficult. The whole of the religious life was a challenge. Why else should anyone take it up? Certainly not as an easy way out, as people sometimes dismissed it. It was not easy to be called by God, chosen as one of his handmaidens, for ever set apart.

She had felt the shock waves today at the lunch table when Connie told them she was going to enter as a nun. It was all Mrs Gurslake's fault, really; her questions had been impossible to evade. She had been probing ever since they sailed, but so far Nina had managed to parry – or Connie had parried for her. This time there was no escape. Was it true there was somebody? That she was going to England to join him? Who was the lucky man? The woman had passed from the arch to the importunate; it was no longer possible to put her off. The half-truth that she was engaged had seemed such an easy solution to her desire to take no part in shipboard social life, even though Connie said this was foolish: she ought to enjoy it while she could. It was like the silk underwear: she needed to know what she was missing before she gave it up. But you couldn't barter your mother's soul for silk underwear and dances. Ever since that dreadful night when Mummy had died and she had clung sobbing to Connie, hearing her sister ask the priest, 'Were you in time?' and hearing Father Farrell's voice in answer: 'Pray for her, your prayers will help her,' she had known what she must do. If she gave herself to God in a contemplative Order like Aunt Eileen's, surely he would have mercy on Mummy's soul.

There had been tremendous opposition. Daddy had had a fit and gone storming off to see Reverend Mother, but of course Daddy wasn't a Catholic. Reverend Mother's refusal to see her desire to enter as anything other than adolescent fantasy had been more daunting. The nun had tried to talk her out of it, arguing that she should wait a while, see something of the world before deciding, because she was really too young at eighteen.

'You were eighteen when you entered,' Nina said, for Reverend Mother's history was well known, although it sometimes seemed impossible to her pupils that that austere, handsome face had ever been young.

'How do you know I don't regret it?' Reverend Mother had said in her soft voice. 'Not my vocation, of course – that is God's blessing – but having seen so little of life.'

Nina's determination had naturally thrived on opposition, and in the end Connie had talked their father round. 'If it's really what she wants to do – and she's never wavered – have we the right to stand in her way?'

'But this nonsense about your mother –'

'Daddy darling, you and I know why Mummy refused to receive the Last Rites, but Nini's an innocent. Isn't it perhaps appropriate that her innocence should be offered for Mummy's guilt?'

'Don't use that word!'

'I'm sorry . . . What else am I to say?'

'Say I failed her. It takes two to wreck a marriage.'

'Only one of you went astray.'

'You're a good girl, Connie. Thank God you don't fancy you've got a vocation. All right, I'll tell Reverend Mother she may write – see if Eileen will have her. But you'll have to take her home to England, get her safely settled in.'

So a letter had gone off to Mother Imelda of the Child Jesus, née Eileen Sheehan, in her Yorkshire convent to ask if she would be willing to receive her niece Nina as a postulant, and in due course a letter had come back giving cautious agreement. There was also a formal note for Nina, telling her she looked forward to welcoming her at the beginning of Advent and signed 'Your loving sister in Christ'; and there was a list of the clothes she would need: two black serge dresses, ankle-length; six pairs of black lisle stockings; three pairs of black directoire drawers; two woollen vests and two cotton; plain lace-up black walking shoes.

'We'll go shopping in England,' Connie said. 'Aunt Maura will help us. It's like going to school, isn't it?'

Only there would be no half-terms and holidays, no visits from parents and friends. She would no longer be Nina Martin, but Sister whatever name the community gave her. There would be no letters, no newspapers, no wireless; she would be dead to the world and the world be dead to her. The first did not matter; it was what she asked in her role of postulant; but the second – ah, that was harder: to accept that great events would happen and she not know of them. She would not know if Connie married or her father remarried, though if one of them sickened and died Mother Imelda would be informed and the community's prayers be asked for. She would add them to those for her mother that she offered every day.

'*Requiem æternam dona ea, Domine* . . .'

Poor Mummy. No more dancing and going to the races with Major Orrey, no more early-morning rides; no more dressing for dinner, pirouetting in front of the mirror in the bedroom she shared with Daddy; no more coughing her life away. 'The gay Mrs Martin', they had called her; men said it admiringly; but Mrs Magistrate Beer and Mrs Major Barrett said it in tones of disapproval, as if a civil servant's wife should be as staid as they. 'Your father's position requires it,' they had said firmly ever since Mummy had died, whenever she and Connie had jibbed at some boring ceremonial of the kind Mummy had hated and on occasion refused to attend. Daddy had never insisted; he had just dressed with especial care and fended off enquiries: 'I'm afraid my wife is unwell . . . no, nothing serious

... the heat (or the rainy season) ... a chill (or a fever) ... a little over-fatigued.' And everyone made sympathetic noises and hoped she would soon be better and raised their eyebrows as they turned away.

Of course it was illness that had changed her. Before that she had gone regularly to Mass in Father Farrell's simple church, so different from the imposing edifice of the Anglicans on Nullumpur's main road. But Nina could hardly bear to think of the last time her mother had come out of church, feet foremost, before being hurried away to burial. As for her state since, that was something she dared not dwell on. She sometimes woke screaming in the night, because if that wasted body was now a mass of putrefaction, how much worse must be the state of her soul ...

'*Requiem æternam dona ea, Domine* . . .'

At that moment Connie came bursting in.

'Sorry! I thought you'd have finished.'

'I have. It's perfectly all right.'

'Good. Come on up on deck. It's cooler now and Captain Johnson's brought his gramophone and he and Mrs Vane have been teaching me and Imogen Stiles a new two-step. It's the most tremendous fun.'

'Who's Imogen Stiles?'

'That clergyman's daughter who never says a word. She's got as far as telling us her name, so she could be said to be blossoming. Luckily the Third Officer's off duty and he's been dancing with her.'

'I oughtn't to . . .'

'Of course you ought to. See a bit of life before you give it up.'

'But now everyone knows . . .'

'It doesn't matter. You haven't yet sprouted wings.'

Nina said nothing, remembering the silence that had swelled along the lunch table when in answer to Mrs Gurslake's insistent questions Connie had announced, 'My sister isn't going to marry in your sense. She's going to enter as a nun.' An elderly gentleman at the far end who was telling an anecdote to a crony was suddenly overwhelmed to hear himself saying in the hush, 'And then the damned horse farted . . .' He had had a diplomatic coughing fit and Connie had laughed, dispelling the embarrassment, setting everyone chattering again.

Dr Bladon had turned to Nina. 'That's a very big decision to have taken.'

She waited for him to ask if she was quite sure – people usually did – but he said nothing. She glanced up at him and said, 'Yes.'

He looked so kind that she wanted to say more but couldn't think how to put it, so she laid her spoon down on her plate (they had reached the sweet course and it was mango sorbet) and said: 'I'm very happy – just as happy as if I was really getting married.'

He smiled at her. 'Then I'm happy for you,' he said.

After that he turned back to Connie. He liked Connie – you could tell. There was an intentness about the way he looked at her, even when she

37

was talking to other people, that was unmistakable. But then everyone liked Connie. The little Irish deck steward was already devoted to her. Even Captain Meiklejohn who was so polite but never seemed to smile had almost smiled at Connie during the captain's cocktail party. Archie Johnson liked her a lot. And Mrs Gurslake's puny husband, whom everyone except Mrs Gurslake seemed to detest, bared his rodent teeth at Connie in what must be assumed to be a grin.

Giving up the world was easy compared to giving up her sister, even though a community of sisters would take her place. Sister . . . Sister . . . The sibilants whispered in Nina's brain. Could sisters of the spirit ever take the place of a sister of the blood?

She said impulsively to Connie, 'I do love you.'

'And I you. What's brought on this outburst of affection?'

'I hate the thought of losing you.'

'Not half as much as I hate it.'

'But you're not choosing to and I am. I feel so guilty. That makes it all the worse.'

'The passive suffers less than the active?'

'Oh, don't be clever, Con.'

'I didn't come down to be clever. I came to fetch you up on deck. That Irish steward is making us iced tea – it's delicious.'

Nina allowed herself to be led away.

On deck the group of young people had swelled and an impromptu dance was in progress. Dr Bladon had put himself in charge of the gramophone, winding the handle vigorously so that the tempo did not slacken and the needle start to scratch. 'You left me like a broken-hearted doll,' moaned the machine, as a pale young man with freckles came up and asked Nina to dance.

She loved to dance. In that she was 'the gay Mrs Martin's' daughter, light as thistledown. Now and again she caught glimpses of Connie dancing with Captain Johnson and recognised in her the same sense of release. But from the look on Dr Bladon's face you might have thought she was wantoning stark naked. How romantic if he and Archie Johnson fought a duel over Connie – except that duels weren't fought any more, and in any case Dr Bladon might not win (she discovered she wanted him to) and that would be difficult.

She did not really like Captain Johnson. It was nothing to do with the scar, which was disfiguring but somehow not unattractive; it was something about his manner, his attitude. He was politeness itself, rising by automatic reflex the instant a woman approached, holding doors and chairs, offering his arm to older ladies, Mrs Gurslake in particular, yet eyeing all of them as if they were only bodies, as if it did not matter what they thought and said, because their heads, though pretty, were clapped-on afterthoughts which need not be considered seriously.

It was the same with the dining-saloon waiters, the stewards. He saw

38

them as functionaries and addressed them as such. At this moment he was summoning the little Irish steward, ordering drinks for the ladies – 'the gels', he called them – as if he ruled the universe. Their father had insisted on courtesy to inferiors, which of course meant Indians. 'They may not be white, but by Jove the best of them are as good as,' he maintained, and he had daily dealings with them. 'They're not to be spoken to like dogs.' Captain Johnson would probably be more civil to a dog, Nina reflected. He referred to their steward as 'a Mick', 'a Paddy', or in moments of unusual tolerance, 'that Irish leprechaun', and he did all this in the steward's hearing as though the man were deaf. All Nina could do was to thank John Joseph with her sweetest smile, which did not go unacknowledged. She was glad to note that Connie did the same.

The little man was so deft, so unobtrusive, it was easy to overlook his services; an order appeared, a pen was proffered for signature of the chitty, and then the space he had occupied was empty; you never saw him go. She had asked his name and he had said, 'Joe, miss,' but Connie had done better than that. 'His name's John Joseph Fitzgerald and he comes from Dublin,' she told Nina. 'He's the youngest of seven children and one of his sisters is a nun. This is his first voyage. He joined the ship at the same time as Dr Bladon and Third Officer Strode, but they're the only ones who are new among the officers and deck crew; the rest have been with the *Karachi* for years. He says she has the reputation of being a happy ship, thanks to Captain Meiklejohn, who is always stern, but just. He's stern because he lost his only son in the war and has never been seen to smile since – isn't it tragic? For all that, lots of people choose to sail in the *Karachi*. The same names recur in her passenger lists year after year.'

'Will you sail in her when you return?' Nina asked in a small voice.

'I might. I haven't thought about it. Let's get you settled first. In any case, Daddy's not expecting me back for a twelvemonth. A lot of things may have changed by then.'

He's not expecting me ever, Nina thought in one of the surges of sorrow that occasionally rushed over her. I shall never see him again. No wonder he got drunk that last night in Bombay – I should have been more understanding. I must write and tell him so. Mail would be dispatched at Aden, where they were due in three days' time. So it was with thoughts of beginning a letter that evening that she made her way to the boat deck. Connie was dressing for dinner – like their mother, she made a thing of dressing – but Nina was practising simplicity, unaware of the impact it made, coupled with her freshness, her naturalness, her air of perfect certainty.

The boat deck at this hour was deserted because it had no bar, and everyone wanted a cocktail or a peg before dinner. It suited Nina perfectly; she did not drink and she wanted solitude. She settled herself in a deck-chair and had written 'Daddy darling' when she heard a sound overhead. Something had moved in one of the lifeboats. Something quite big – an animal. It couldn't be the ship's cat – the Chief Engineer was devoted to her and rarely let her out of his sight – but could one have become trapped there while the ship was docked at Bombay? Or could it be some other, more noxious creature? Alarmed, she gathered up her writing materials and moved away. She must tell someone – but who? One of the deck officers? She could see nobody about. The Captain? She had seen the signs saying 'Bridge', but they also said 'No Admittance'; one surely could not disturb the unsmiling Captain Meiklejohn because of an animal trapped in a lifeboat. She was about to go in search of assistance when John Joseph Fitzgerald appeared at the top of a companionway. She turned to him with relief.

'Oh, Joe!'

'Miss?' He was still wearing his white mess jacket and dark trousers.

'I thought you went off duty hours ago,' she said. 'While we were dancing to the gramophone.'

'I did, miss.' His watchful stance emphasised that he was not on duty now.

He was carrying a packet of sandwiches and a bottle of something. Was he planning to eat his supper up on deck? Where did the crew eat? It was one more thing she did not know about a liner. Were members of the crew when off duty even supposed to visit the boat deck?

'Joe, I think there's something alive in that lifeboat.' She pointed to the third from the stern, trying to remember whether that side was port or starboard. It was always Connie who knew these things.

John Joseph shook his head. 'I don't think so, miss.'

'But I distinctly heard something move.'

'Just the boat swinging in the davits, miss.'

He was obviously not prepared to go and see.

'It didn't sound like that,' Nina persisted.

'You get some very odd noises in a ship. Don't you be letting it worry you, miss. Take it from me, there's nothing there.'

She looked at him, wanting to believe yet doubting. He stood waiting for her to go.

'If you're sure . . .' She did not want to intrude on his off-duty.

'Quite sure, miss. Would you stop being anxious, now. I'll not let him come after you.'

'Him?'

'Him or whoever's in the boat,' he said, smiling to show her it was a joke.

'I . . . Thank you.' She bowed her head, and a sweep of hair fell forward, revealing her soft white neck.

'Good night now.'

'Good night.'

She went below, feeling his eyes upon her, conscious of a sense of dread. There had been something in the lifeboat, she was certain, but had it been

40

something alive? If it had been dead and rolled, it would have produced a sound very similar. She was depressed by the ubiquity of the dead. Even here, in this world floating between two continents, death could strike a fellow passenger down and Dr Bladon be powerless to do anything about it. And with no priest – she did not count Mr Stiles – they would die unreconciled, just as Mummy had done. But the Church catered for that; it was not like refusing Extreme Unction. It was when people preferred their sin and chose to die in it rather than confess it and renounce it that things began to look black. When only prayers could help, prayer became a Christian's duty, especially the intercession of a nun.

Requiem æternam . . . This time the prayers went far beyond her mother as she prayed for all the dead; that they might know eternal rest and light perpetual; that they might rest in peace.

'It's not right, Bert. It's a wicked shame.'

Florrie Gurslake was up in arms. Ever since Connie Martin's calm announcement of her sister's intention at lunch the day before, her mind had been in a whirl. She could not have said why it mattered to her that Nina should turn her back on life before she had even tasted it (for so Florrie interpreted her resolve), but she felt deeply that it was a mistake and that it was for her to prevent it, though how she was to do so she did not know.

Asceticism was not a word in Florrie's vocabulary and its practice was foreign to her life. She had had to deny herself many things, but the denials were not from choice. To give up, as Nina was proposing to do, the things for which woman was created, seemed to Florrie both perverse and wrong. She knew nothing of the Church of Rome, but she had an inbred Protestant dislike of it; it was something nasty and foreign – you could tell that by the name; whereas the Church of England, though of no concern to anyone's daily existence other than a vicar's, was at least the national church and as much to be respected as any other national institution – the Royal Family, say, or Derby Day.

So Florrie was up in arms at the waste of a young life at the behest, as she saw it, of a foreign body. It was as bad as Englishmen being slaughtered by Germans in the war. And when Florrie was up in arms her voice rose, her bosom rose and fell like a heaving billow, and since there was no room to do anything else in the small airless space of their cabin, she subsided like a beached hulk on the bed.

Bert Gurslake sighed. Normally Florrie getting worked up did not worry him; he seldom troubled to ascertain the cause of her distress; but the present outburst on someone else's behalf, coming at a time when his own affairs were in such disorder that any railing at Fortune should surely be for him, struck him as an act of wifely sabotage. In this he was unfair: since he had not told Florrie the extent of his financial predicament she could hardly be blamed for dismissing it. Bert, however, was a man of instinct, not of reason.

'It's none of our business,' he snapped.

'It's everyone's business, a young girl like that going into a convent.'

'What you going to do, then? Kidnap her?'

'If someone could talk to her . . . She can't realise what she's doing. D'you think that parson could help?'

'Wrong sort, ain't he?'

Florrie overlooked this irrelevance. 'Do you suppose she knows what it's really like in a convent? The nuns whip each other, and they cut off all your hair.' Her hand went to her own pile, which was ready to tumble in sympathy with her general agitation. 'They sleep in hair shirts in their coffins and they never have enough to eat because they have to depend on what they're given and if no one gives them anything they starve.'

In the course of reading innumerable magazines and works of romantic fiction Florrie had come across an approximation of all these statements and had blended them into one. Result: Mother Imelda in Yorkshire and Reverend Mother in Nullumpur would have been equally surprised on behalf of their respective Orders, could they have listened to her account. But there was only Bert to listen, and he was not interested.

'It's none of our business,' he repeated.

'But, Bert, she's only eighteen. And so pretty.'

'Silly bint. What do her parents say?'

'Her mother's dead. There's just her father and her sister.'

'That sister's a bit of all right. She's already got the quack and Captain Johnson panting after her. Want to bet which of 'em'll have had her by the time we get to Tilbury?'

'Don't talk like that!'

'Wouldn't mind having a go myself if I hadn't got you along, old lady.'

Florrie smiled. She knew how to take such remarks. And indeed, Bert had no real desire for other women. Girls like Connie Martin were all right to titillate; it took Florrie to satisfy. But in the midday heat, with the fan stirring the air in the cabin like syrup, even desire petered out, leaving him a prey to anxieties that seemed to draw strength from his lassitude. Oh for the wharves of the Thames, their warehouses, the east wind sneaking round corners, the cafés with their hot peas and thick black char – for Bert never drank during working hours; he said it fuddled the brain and he needed his razor-sharp. Instead he relied on others drinking, on the moment when a hand would be slapped down on the counter and another bargain sealed. In such situations a man could trade to his own advantage, especially if in the first place the goods had been dishonestly 'won'.

It had been much the same in Sydney: he pushed his luck, but not too far. He should have left it at that, not listened to siren voices promising instant fortune in exchange for a large lump sum. Gold. He ought to have known better, but the word had a seduction all its own. A new strike near Bendigo. A glossy prospectus. The chance to get in on the ground floor. He hadn't recognised his own line in sweet talk when it was played back to him, though the difference was that he always had the goods in hand. There was nothing speculative about Bert's dealings. It was just a matter of the difference between buying and selling price.

When he went along to the office named on the prospectus he hadn't been able to credit that it was no longer there, even though the doorman was roughly sympathetic: 'You ain't the first to come asking after 'em and I don't suppose you'll be the last. They ain't here, mate. They never was, except for a week or two at the first, just so long as it took them to skin you and a few more silly buggers. Reckon no one's ever going to hear of 'em again.'

Bert reckoned so too when he thought about it; reckoned he too would need to disappear before those to whom he owed money came looking for him with a good deal more success than he as creditor had had. He had sold up quickly and booked passages for himself and Florrie aboard the *Southern Cross*. Like any injured animal, Bert's instinct was to head for home. It would take time for the Consolidated Finance Company to find him there – even if they pursued their debt-collecting that far. Meanwhile he must raise money for himself and Florrie to live on, and that could only mean a loan. Surely among all these well-heeled First Class passengers there must be someone he could gull. A thousand pounds would do it, though two might be better, but it was important not to pitch the sum too high. And he'd pay it back, of course he would, once he'd had a chance to begin trading. Money made money. You only needed some to start.

It was important, too, to look as though you did not need it, as though you were merely putting a good thing someone's way. It had been a mistake to burst out at Florrie for extravagant spending, as he had done in the hotel in Bombay. So on board the *Karachi* Bert jingled the coins in his pocket, spent with a lavish hand, tried to tip the Mick steward whose respectfulness was balm to one more used to the cold shoulder, and assessed his fellow passengers for wealth. Mrs Vane, a well-heeled widow if ever he saw one; Captain Johnson, bound to have a private income as well as army pay; the ship's doctor, nothing to suggest money except that he was obviously class and in Bert's mind the two still went together; the Reverend, unlikely but with the Church you never knew; several business and civil service types with whom he had not yet managed to scrape acquaintance but whom he had earmarked as possibilities, including old man Haldingham, the retired Forestry officer, who had such an inexplicable dislike of the Mick. He had three weeks to raise the capital that would enable him to make a fresh start in those same streets of London's dockland where he had begun twenty-five years ago. Florrie might have to wait a bit for her Silver Wedding junket, but a year more or less made no odds. She'd understand – she'd have to – and by the time they were in the Bay of Biscay and the Channel she'd be in no state to care about anything, if the voyage out was anything by which to judge.

Meanwhile she was fretting about some stupid kid going into a convent.

43

Well, of course it was a mistake; stood to reason if the girl was normal; but how would they know if she was not? In Bert's eyes the sister would be a greater loss; Nina was too palely pretty, though of course she was still only half alive. One good fuck and she might look very different, discover it was more fun on your back than on your knees . . .

He came to to hear Florrie saying, ' . . . and they take all your money, too.'

'Who do?' Mention of money was guaranteed to rouse Bert's interest.

'Convents.' Florrie had been culling her mind for other information gleaned on religious Orders. 'You have to give them your dowry when you go in.'

'Thought you said nuns lived on charity.'

'They do, but they take your money just the same.'

'Mug's game, innit? Why do women do it?'

'They say they enter for the love of God.'

So the Martin girl had money which she was about to make over to a convent. Suppose instead she made it over – temporarily, of course – to him . . .

'She's too young for a convent,' Bert said with sudden conviction.

'That's just what I've been saying all along.'

'You'll have to talk to her.'

'Me? No, Bert, I couldn't.'

'You're old enough to be her ma, ain't you?'

'Yes, but I'm not religious.'

'Just tell her what she's missing.'

'I couldn't.'

'You just get matey and start chatting, sometime when that sister's not around. Push her off with the quack or Captain Johnson. Then you get Nina on her own.'

'What do I say?'

'Look, love, I wouldn't know what women say to each other. But put her off the idea of the convent, see.'

A girl with a dowry. She'd be glad to double it, and he, Bert, would see she got it back. A temporary loan, that was all he needed. If Florrie tackled the girl and he had another chat with Captain Johnson, similar to the one he'd had a night or two ago when he'd touched on the opportunities for a young man with capital to increase it, things should be looking up by the time they docked at Tilbury. Hope, volatile as always, flared in Bert. He'd made one fortune, he could make another. There was nothing to it once you got started, so long as human nature didn't change. He reached for the sweat-filmed body of his wife supine beside him.

'Come on, old girl, you get a load of this.'

Captain Meiklejohn watched the Chief Engineer fill and tamp a pipe with a finger so blackened that not all the soap and nailbrushes in the world would get it clean. The pipe was the Chief's great luxury; he never drank,

44

regarded cards as one of the Devil's inventions and women as another, though it had not stopped him from taking one to wife some twenty years ago and fathering three sons and a daughter upon her. It was perhaps as well, the Captain reflected, for the Chief was a handsome man, and though he rarely mixed with the passengers, when he did many a lady had fluttered a fan or an eyelash at him, or turned quickly to let him catch a whiff of expensive scent. To no avail. In the engine-room the Chief was said to be a man of iron; he was a man of iron out of it as well. James Sutherland did his duty with the thunderous precision of his engines and acknowledged God as the same ultimate source of power for both.

Since leaving Bombay Captain Meiklejohn's social duties had excluded their evening half-hour together. It was always the same at the beginning of a voyage: the Captain had to be seen, not only because First Class passengers expected to meet him, but to demonstrate that he was there, master under God of this vessel and for the next twenty-five days of their lives. Now, with only two more nights to go before they reached Aden, the ship had settled into a routine which, barring storms and accidents, should last as far as Gibraltar, when the weather would change for the worse.

Despite all his voyages, this transition from summer to winter, or winter to summer on the outward run, never ceased to fascinate the Captain. It was like a time machine, the seasons telescoped so swiftly that a month became a day. Here in the Indian Ocean it was high summer, hot but not yet swelteringly so; that was reserved for the slow passage through the Red Sea and Suez, when everyone's temper frayed. The Mediterranean would see a return to summer, though storms were not unknown; and then, once they left the coast of Africa behind them and turned northwards, skies and seas became colder, greyer, with fog sometimes lying in wait in the Channel.

The ship reflected these climatic changes, the white ducks of the deck officers giving place to navy, the women's summer dresses to winter coats and furs. The ship's surgeon treated sunburn at the commencement of the homeward voyage and seasickness at its conclusion. The menu changed from mango sorbet to Christmas pudding and brandy sauce. Each outward voyage was an escape from winter, each homeward one a return, for even when they docked in June or August, it was still winter in his heart. That had had its cruel onset on the day the telegram came. Eight years of hope fading to a despair ever darkening. Eight years of quiet hell.

The Chief's voice came, deep and quiet. 'Ye'd a letter from Ailsa at Bombay.'

It was statement, not question. There was always a letter and always its news was the same.

'Aye.' Angus Meiklejohn knew that more was expected, even though the more was already known. 'There's no change.'

The Chief nodded. 'And Ailsa?'

'She says she's managing all right.' Managing a child in a man's body. 'The boy's not difficult.'

'I'm aware of that. The Lord tempers the wind, Angus.'

Angus Meiklejohn restrained himself. From no one but Jamie would he have accepted such a statement, nor did he accept it now; but to argue would be to create a needless tension without affecting James Sutherland's belief. It was no good asking where the Lord had been in July 1916. Jamie's answer would be, 'The Lord knows.'

Of all those aboard the SS *Karachi*, only to Jamie had Angus admitted the truth: that Second Lieutenant Andrew Meiklejohn, reported missing believed killed in action, had been found very much alive. When they had dug him out of a shellhole from beneath a tangle of mutilated bodies, his wounds had been miraculously superficial: it was his mind that was wounded and missing; missing and now believed dead. 'Shock,' they said at first, 'he'll get over it;' changing to, 'Shellshock, but no physical cause . . . time the healer . . . keep hoping;' changing to, 'We know so little about the mind . . .' So Andrew – bonnie Andy still, handsome as a god – trotted at his mother's heels, did simple tasks and errands, responded to his name and not much else. In vain Angus had talked to him of former interests, taken him to places he used to love. The blankness behind the large, once-bright eyes remained blankness; a shutter had come down between eye and brain. Only between ear and brain was there still communication: sounds excited him, sometimes piteously. The skirl of a pipe band; thunder; a shout; running footsteps; a child crying – these could cause distress. But never joy. The smooth, blank-surfaced features did not light up from within. The horrors had gone so deep that they had poisoned the very well-springs of happiness. *We know so little about the mind . . .*

'Ye're not giving up hope?' the Chief asked gently.

'No.' It was a lie. Hope had been abandoned long since. There was only endurance now. And even endurance must give out some day. What happened when he and Ailsa died, leaving Andy alone in a world at worst hostile, at best indifferent? Sometimes, watching his son eat with a man's appetite and childlike enthusiasm, Angus had caught himself thinking: If only he weren't so fit; if only he could die, God forgive me, and that tormented spirit be at rest. Did Ailsa feel the same? He had not asked her. She it was who had given Andrew life one cold January morning in the cramped front bedroom of their first home, a terrace house that was just above being a slum in Glasgow, before the midwife could arrive. The woman from next door, who had come in to help in time-honoured fashion, had laughed as she held the red, slippery body in her hands: 'Was ever a wean in such a hurry? Dinna ye ken this world's no worth coming into? Ye maun watch him, Mrs Meiklejohn, that he doesna seek to slip out of it as cannily as he came in.' But Andrew had lived and thriven. Each birthday was a milestone of happiness. Not only was he handsome, he was intelligent; at the academy they began to say brilliant. There was talk of the university. Different masters vied for the honour of presenting this outstanding candidate in their disciplines, but Andrew made up his own mind.

It was to be medicine or nothing. He was to begin his course in the autumn of 1916.

At first when war broke out all the fear was for Angus, as the *Karachi* became an armed merchant cruiser painted battleship grey and with guns mounted on her decks. A lad of sixteen seemed safe enough with his studies; it was his father who was at risk, and never more so than when that torpedo struck but did not sink her. Angus still shuddered at the memory. The *Karachi* had been on escort duty in the Channel on a clear-sunned, cold March day, the sea a mass of small lace-edged billows like frills on a petticoat. Angus, on the bridge, had been about to go below when the lookout's cry alerted him. Far away, a straight white line was travelling towards them. The engine-room telegraph shuddered as Angus drove it full ahead, as the helmsman spun the wheel, as the ship responded slowly, how slowly, her wake beginning to describe a great arc. And all the time the deadly white line came speeding towards them and its point of inter-section with that arc. There was a great staggering blow, as though a mighty hand had struck them, followed by a muffled explosion below the water-line. In those few minutes, in the hours that followed, Angus Meiklejohn aged ten years, the relief when he realised they were not sinking counter-balanced by fear of another attack. Meanwhile from the wrecked engine-room the dead and injured were brought out. Destroyers raced up and down, the choppy sea fountained with depth charges, the rest of the convoy drew steadily farther ahead, until at last the destroyers signalled that they too were leaving: 'Safe home and best of luck.'

Throughout the long dark night that followed, with every nerve at breaking-point, Angus strove to guide the slow, wallowing hulk that had been the proud *Karachi* towards the safety of the nearest port. Sometimes he thought of Andrew and Ailsa, but they were unreal figures far away; it was his ship who claimed all his love, all his skill and attention, who responded to him, so he fancied, as he willed her to go on. 'I ken fine ye have a mistress, Angus . . .' Ailsa's words had been said in jest, but in that keen March night they became reality as Angus Meiklejohn brought his wounded mistress home.

She had repaid him. After the telegram – and Angus divided life into before and after the telegram, as the Western world divided it into before and after Christ – she had welcomed him back with her dear familiarity in which there was relief from pain, because Andrew and Ailsa did not belong here but existed only in some bleaker, other world. In war and later in peace she had been his refuge. He knew that he would die for her, not just because it might become his duty as her captain but because he would choose it that way. Except that there was always Andy, and there too duty lay.

As the war had dragged on and Andrew's eighteenth birthday had drawn nearer, the hope of a medical career began to fade. True, Edinburgh had accepted him, but only after active service, when Kitchener's finger stopped pointing: 'Your country needs *you*.' Instead of a white coat

Andrew donned a second lieutenant's uniform, which became him very well. Many a girl had looked after him wistfully – he was bonnie Andy still. His letters were short and cheerful, like his leave. Angus had been at sea, but Ailsa assured him that the boy had left smiling, waving till she was no more than a speck on the platform as the train curved out of Aberdeen. They knew he was in France. He wrote of base concerts, of a certain *estaminet*, of books he had read, of his atrocious French, of the miracles of nature that survived amid a ruined landscape, of everything except the war. There was talk of a big push – but the whole war had been a series of big pushes, each advancing over a few bloodstained miles until a big push from the other side turned it into a strategic withdrawal, leaving only a fresh quota of shellholes and corpses to decorate No Man's Land.

In Aberdeen you could not hear the guns across the Channel. In Southern England you could. So they knew the big push of 1 July 1916 was something special, while further north it was the same old newspaper headlines yet again. But the casualty lists were longer. The grey wartime paper of *The Times* carried page after page of names close-printed: name, rank and number, the soldier's sole identity. More and more women appeared in black – the mantlemakers were kept busy; more and more men wore black ties and armbands; more and more eyes were red. And through it all the summer blossomed as children shouted from the beach, gulls screamed, the girls wore pretty dresses; while from the War Office to post offices and homes all over the country the dreaded telegrams went out.

With every one the nation's patriotic fervour wore a little thinner. In 1914 men had rushed to join up before the show was over, to teach the Hun a lesson, to save little Belgium; by 1916 conscription had to be introduced. Some businesses limped on with only boys and a few old men called out of retirement – and women, whose working presence became more and more a matter of course. Angus came home on leave to find Ailsa had taken a job in a local lawyer's office – 'It's something to do while the two of you are away. I canna sit at home and knit socks, Angus, I must be busy. It's better I have a job to do.' Well, she had a job now, looking after her son of twenty-six summers whose mind had obliterated twenty of them, yet who in moments of repose still looked the handsome, gifted lad she had seen off at Aberdeen station, who had waved and waved as the train crossed the bridge over the Dee and began its long journey southwards and she was no more than a speck.

'Ye've a fine woman in Ailsa.' The Chief's voice came again.

'Aye.'

'The Lord knew what he was doing when he sent her to ye, Angus.'

'Aye.' If that was what the Lord had done; if he had decreed that a young third officer, just such another as Julian Strode, should come home on the sparse leave the Australasian Line granted its employees to find that a new family had moved in next door. Moreover, they had a daughter with the neatest waist and ankles, the brightest eyes that Angus had ever seen.

Those eyes had rested on him as the minister pronounced them man and wife two years later. They rested on him now from the sepia photograph on the desk beside him, and an equally bright-eyed eight-year-old stood at her knee.

Only that morning Angus had found himself looking into another pair of eight-year-old eyes sparkling with intelligence and mischief: the eyes of Master Bobby Vane. Their encounter had taken place on the bridge, when he had turned to see a small figure standing at the top of the companionway, looking about him with a mixture of bravado, curiosity and hope.

'I do not recall inviting you on to my bridge, sir.' Angus was at his most magisterial.

'You didn't.' A deliberately engaging smile. 'I thought you'd be glad to see me.'

'And why should I be that?'

'Don't you like small boys?'

That was a poser. 'On my ship I have no reason to be aware of them,' Angus replied.

'*Your* ship! Are you the captain?'

'I am.'

The quick eyes took him in. 'How long have you been a captain?'

'Thirteen years.'

Since that cold spring day on the Clyde when the *Karachi* slid down the slipway, with Ailsa and Andrew somewhere in the crowd . . .

'My father was a captain, but not like you. Like Captain Johnson.'

Angus noted the past tense.

'A captain in the army is somewhat different.'

'My father was killed on the Somme. That was a battle in the Great War,' Bobby explained for the benefit of the ignorant.

'I know. Do you remember your father?'

' 'Course not. It was before I was born. I was born on 17 August 1916.'

'Making you eight years and three months old.'

'Yes.'

'And at your age a captain's son can read, I take it?'

'Yes.'

'So what does this notice say?'

With pretended hesitancy Bobby mumbled, 'No admittance.'

'Do you know what "no admittance" means?'

'It means you mustn't spit.' The bright eyes were defiant.

'It means you mustn't come up here.'

'Why not?'

'Because I'm the captain and I say so. And I don't like ignorant young gentlemen on my bridge.'

'I'm not ignorant.'

'Not to know what "no admittance" means is ignorant.'

'If I weren't ignorant, would you let me stay?'

'No, because you're also disobedient and a liar. You knew what that notice meant and you disobeyed.'

'Don't you ever invite people on to your bridge?'

'Sometimes.'

'Will you invite me if I'm good?'

'I am going to invite you to leave under escort. Mr Strode,' Angus called to the Third Officer, 'will you return Master Bobby Vane to his mother with my compliments and request her to keep him in leading strings from now on.'

The look he got from the young gentleman left him in no doubt of his unpopularity. Bobby was obviously unaccustomed to the failure of his charm. But Julian Strode's hand was on his shoulder and he allowed himself to be led away, while Angus amused himself by wondering in what form his message would be delivered. He suspected young Strode of being a diplomat.

Not that life could be easy for women like Cynthia Vane, whom he had identified early on the voyage as one more casualty of the war. Brought up to fulfil the role of wife and mother and now left high and dry, with adequate income but inadequate human resources, she was one of many whom life was passing by. Not only her husband had been killed but her potential husbands; she was too old for the boys who in the past eight years had become men, while for the survivors, those who were whole and free, there was determined competition – sometimes for those who were not free. The Court might frown, the Churches fulminate against moral laxity, but in worlds removed from both divorces flourished, together with cocktails and co-respondents, skirts above the knee and lewd dances – only yesterday Angus had observed a party of young people on deck practising the latest American imports to the strains of a gramophone; the party had included Cynthia Vane and those two pretty sisters, and also Julian Strode; Angus had been shocked to have to number them in the category of men without morals and women who had no shame. He had read of such conduct in London, seen something of it on shipboard, but could detect no trace of it in Aberdeen, where he and Ailsa lived by the rules laid down by their elders, which were accepted as the rules laid down by God for man. If Angus had doubts, he smothered them; God's ways were not man's ways. But if God's hand was in what had happened to Andy and all those like him, could that God be just and good? And if not, why follow his ways . . .? The Chief would have an answer because the Chief always did. He was convincing in his magnificent assurance . . . but what if the Chief were wrong?

No such thought could ever have occurred to Chief Engineer James Sutherland. The rules of human conduct were laid down in the Old Testament, modified only slightly by the New, and expounded by ministers of the kirk, the Lord's servants, according to the letter of the law. He followed those rules with a fervour only a little less than that with which he saw to it that they were administered, and ensured that the way of the transgressor was hard. The Chief was notorious throughout the Line for his strict discipline, though it was conceded he was also just. He enquired zealously into any misconduct, and some felt that to be the focus of his enquiries was already punishment enough. When the Chief sank to his knees to pray, which he did each night in his cabin, it was to petition the Lord that he would turn men's hearts from wrongdoing, aided by suitable deterrents at his own unworthy hand. He asked no mercy and gave none; the Lord was a just God, and the keen bright blade of justice did not falter or turn aside. As for the heathen – that is to say, most of the engine-room's crew – they might not have received the Gospel, but the rules applied to them no less. If as a result there was a great gulf fixed between Chief and crew, that was as the Good Book would have it, and so it would be maintained by James Sutherland.

He had before now suffered engineer officers under him who had advocated understanding the crew, spoken a few words of their language, even dabbled in their heathen religions, which God and the Chief forbid. These officers had never lasted; as soon as their term was up they had sought other berths, with the result that the Chief had by now gathered round him a staff as dedicated as himself. If their motives were sometimes less exalted, the Chief was unaware of it; they were only sinful men, after all, and if one of them gave way to temper, as had happened that morning with a sullen and stupid stoker, both officer and man must be disciplined, but there was no question of who was to blame.

As he related the incident to his captain, who as captain had a right to know and as friend had the right of advice – not that James Sutherland would have asked for it but he was not above listening to what might be offered – he was aware of something troubled in Angus's gaze, and the expected confirmation, 'You did right, Jamie, as always,' was lacking in wholeheartedness.

'What's troubling ye?' he asked the Captain.

'A nothing, Jamie. The man was pushed, you say?'

'Hardly pushed, but a hand was raised against him. After extreme provocation, I may say.'

'Was he a trouble-maker?'

'They're all trouble-makers.'

'Granted, but nothing in particular?'

'An idle beggar. Always skiving. It was his carelessness, I'm certain, that caused the fire last night.'

'What fire?'

'Och, a wee conflagration –' the Chief allowed himself to smile. ' 'Twas nothing, Angus: a few glowing coals in a bunker. A good hosing quickly put it out.'

Both men knew that fire in a bunker could be serious: it could go on smouldering for days, and the constant hosing necessary to contain it often damaged valuable cargo, to the distress of the Owners of the Line.

51

Angus said only, 'You were lucky.'

'Aye, thanks to the same officer I'm now disciplining for having raised his hand against black scum. If he had not been alert and vigilant, the fire might well have got a hold. Like me, he's convinced it was due to one man's carelessness and we think we know the man. I canna altogether blame my officer for what happened when the fellow provoked him next day.'

'But the man was not fomenting trouble among the crew?' Angus insisted.

'He set an example of dumb insolence. In the army a man can be flogged for that.'

'And in the Australasian Line he can be pushed against the fire-doors.'

'Ye're exaggerating, Angus. The man lost his balance, that's all.'

'He was injured.'

'A burnt hand, nothing serious. I sent him to the doc at once. It'll all be there in the medical records. He'll be back at work within days.'

'Nevertheless, I wish it hadn't happened, Jamie.'

'So do I, man, so do I. An infraction of discipline's always to be regretted, but we've had many such, as ye well know.'

'I do, and many more serious than what seems to have been no more than a flare of temper, though the officer concerned is maybe lacking in control. But I want no trouble with the native crew on my ship, and there's no doubt agitation's in the air. Oh, not on board –' as the Chief made to protest – 'but on the waterfront at Bombay there were men out trying to stir up the crews, get them to form unions, demand higher wages, better conditions, withdraw their labour if need be –'

'A pack of Socialists!'

'Maybe, but the movement's spreading, Jamie. A few more years and we'll be giving them what they want.'

'Over my dead body.'

Angus smiled. 'Perhaps more than a few years, then, but India's not what it was. There's a new breed of barrack-room lawyer, and they maintain that Indians have rights. We may have put that fellow Gandhi in jail, but it hasn't stopped them. The talk's of Independence now.'

The Chief snorted.

'I agree with you, but you can't stand against the tide, you must go with it. Anyway, you'll be able to discuss it if you wish with the new passenger we're taking on at Aden.'

'Aden's a bunkering station, not a port of call.'

'I know that, but I've instructions telegraphed from Head Office. His Majesty's Government requests that the *Karachi*, as the next liner due at Aden, send a boat while she bunkers to pick up a certain Stafford Briscoe who needs to leave the Protectorate at speed.'

'What's he been doing?'

'Nothing sinister. He's one of their politicos. But he's finished whatever mission took him out there and they're giving him the chance to get home quick. I've no doubt he'll talk for hours on the situation in the Middle East and in India –'

'I have no doubt he will.'

'– so you might learn something.'

'If it's how to rid myself of careless black scum who can't observe simple safety precautions, I'll be grateful. You realise, Angus, that if it hadna been for the officer you castigate as hot-tempered, yon fellow might have endangered the ship.'

'I'm aware of it. Now tell me what's worrying you about your "wee conflagration", Jamie. You put it out easily enough.'

The Chief's handsome head came up, his shoulders settled, as he prepared to face his conscience and his God.

'It was a fire in a peculiar place, Angus. Spontaneous combustion, maybe, but I dinna see how it can have happened, and I confess it troubles me.'

'What are the other possibilities if it wasn't spontaneous?'

'There's only one: gross carelessness. But the carelessness was so gross that I'm wondering if gross carefulness wouldna be a better description. Ye talk of agitators stirring the crews up, and disaffection. Well, that fire, Angus – it could just have been deliberate.'

III

Captain Archibald Johnson, MC, leaned on the rail of the deck of the *Karachi* and thought how ill-used he was. In late afternoon the port side was in shadow, but around him the sea was alive with light, winking with a thousand helios if he could only read the signals. It was so calm that the liquor in his glass was unmoving. It was his third double already, and it was not yet six o'clock. He knew he was drinking too much, but what the hell. A fellow had to have some relaxation, something to blot out thought.

It was easier said than done. He could chat up the girls – the ship seemed suddenly full of desirable damsels – but what was the good of that? A celibate existence, the doc had said. Why whet an appetite he could not satisfy? Even thinking of it caused him to acknowledge his need and the burning discomfort in his groin which both provoked and forbade it. God, what a fool he'd been! It wasn't ignorance – young officers were warned from the start. 'No matter how seductive they seem, they're nothing but rotten whores – and I mean rotten,' the MO had lectured. 'If you must, well, there are places we inspect – I've a list of addresses – but it's impossible to guarantee. If you think I'm exaggerating and you decide to risk it, let me pour cold water on the idea. In fact, cold baths are safer, gentlemen. More hygienic, too.' The MO smiled to show it was a joke and went on lecturing about native women. Did he ever lecture about the white? There was that sergeant's wife on Victory Road – half the regiment had been with her; it was whispered the Colonel had as well; was she inspected? Did her complaisant husband care for nothing but his share of the takings – well over eighty per cent, it was said?

Of course, Archie told himself, he would never have ventured into Bombay's red light district if he'd been going home on leave in the usual fashion. For one thing, he'd have timed his arrival by the mail train to coincide more nearly with when the *Karachi* sailed. It was the speed of his departure which had thrown him. In a sense he was still in shock. 'I've reserved you a compartment on the train leaving at midnight,' the Colonel had concluded. 'Better get your bags packed tonight.' And then, because he was a humane man and liked young Johnson – a damned good officer in the making, it was a rotten shame – he'd added: 'You're young. Best thing you can do is to put this episode behind you. Go home and start again.'

It was good advice but it made nothing easier. Archie heard himself say, 'Thank you, sir.' There was a firm handshake and the Colonel remained standing as he turned, sleepwalking, towards the door. Still sleepwalking, he made his way back to his quarters, thankful that there was no one about. His brother officers had tactfully absented themselves. Only his bearer was there.

It seemed to Archie there was a glint of curiosity in the man's eyes, but he said only, 'The Captain sahib would like a bath?'

'No, thank you.'

'I have put out the Captain sahib's mess tunic.'

'I shan't be messing tonight.'

'But, sir, it is Captain Lane's birthday –'

'I know, Abbas, I know.'

Lane and the rest of them would have to get on without him, not just tonight but all the nights to come. Resignation. He'd had to resign his commission. He was technically a civilian now, though he'd still wear uniform, drive to the station in army transport, return salutes as he boarded the train. But the world that had enfolded him since he first set foot in India was his no longer. The Colonel had been brief and to the point: 'I want your resignation, Johnson. It's the quickest way of hushing this matter up.'

'But, sir, I –'

'I understand what happened, Johnson. I consider you were provoked. All the same, a British officer doesn't order his men to open fire on unarmed civilians – and of course they say they were unarmed, which is true enough in most cases, though I'm not saying you imagined seeing guns. But there are fifty of them and half a dozen of you, and their lawyers plead lawful assembly, in the course of which they claim you murdered a man. We've heard your story and, speaking personally, I believe it, but it's a political matter now. The Resident feels strongly that the Nawab and the native populace have got to be appeased. The claim for compensation by the dead man's family can drag on in the civil courts, but we've got to defuse a potentially dangerous situation, and that means action now. The Resident believes, as I do, that your resignation will go a long way towards settling the matter, and I may as well tell you His Highness the Nawab has indicated he won't accept anything less. I'm sorry, but after Amritsar we can't be too careful. We don't want another Jallianwala Bagh.'

But the two episodes had been quite different, Archie wanted to protest. General Dyer in a situation of unrest five years ago had marched his men into an open space surrounded by high walls where thousands of Indians were peacefully camping and simply opened fire, withdrawing his men afterwards in perfect order with their rifles at the slope; whereas he with six men had been returning from a routine inspection patrol when they had been surrounded by a hostile crowd, and though with hindsight he conceded that a short cut through the native quarter might have been ill advised, he could not, even with hindsight, accept that it was a serious mistake. The Colonel could have told him that a more politically aware officer would not have made it, after an incident involving a sacred cow and an army vehicle, but he recognised that Johnson was not politically aware. He was a magnificent fighting animal, that was the trouble, and when he was cornered he'd opened fire. Admittedly he'd had the sense to do so over the heads of the crowd, but a bullet ricocheting from a building had killed an unarmed man. In the circumstances Johnson and his party had been lucky to escape unscathed. There was no doubt some of the men in that crowd had had rifles and had fired at them as they withdrew; the bullet marks on surrounding buildings were clear testimony (and the Colonel, the Resident, his advisers, and lawyers for the dead man's family had all inspected the spot), but the fact remained that a British officer had given the order to fire on civilians and propitiation had to be made. The propitiation took the form of a letter from Archie Johnson resigning his commission. His army career was at an end.

So Archie was homeward bound for England, travelling First Class, a last taste of the high life. For in England unemployment was rampant among ex-officers, of whom there still seemed too many, despite the horrifying number who had been killed. Trained in nothing but fighting, for he had been called up straight from school and on demob had been offered a regular commission, largely because of his MC, Archie had neither skills nor private means to fall back on. The future had been bleak enough before that night out in Bombay.

He looked down and saw that his glass was empty, although he had no recollection of downing the drink. That damned barman was never there when wanted. It only went to show you could never trust a Mick. All charm and blarney on the surface and out with the knife as soon as your back was turned. That was what had happened in 1916. He could still remember the thrill of anger that had run through his training camp in Easter Week, when news of the Dublin Rising broke. It wasn't that anyone took the Rising seriously, even though in the event it was to cost more than 120 lives of soldiers, men of the Royal Irish Constabulary and the Dublin Metropolitan Police; everyone in England knew it could be stamped out in a matter of days, as indeed it had been; it was the fact that it had occurred that hurt. There were Irishmen, Irish regiments, fighting in the trenches with the British Army; no one questioned but that in a tight corner English and Irish would fight side by side. Why, the brother of one of the leaders of the Rising had lost two sons in France and a third a prisoner of war. Yet here was a handful of crazed idealists proclaiming Irish independence from the main Dublin Post Office and taking up positions with guns, while crowds gathered on the other side of Sackville Street in the April sunshine and asked one another what on earth was going on.

They might well ask. The authorities in Dublin Castle were asking themselves the same thing. The wires buzzed between London and Dublin, but the outcome was never in doubt. A week or two later the leaders were shot as rebels and traitors, and Archie, like the rest of his countrymen, felt that justice had been seen to be done. After all, if the Germans could execute a dedicated nurse like Edith Cavell who had never harmed anyone, merely aided prisoners to escape, what were the English to do with those who had not only taken life but had assisted the enemy, and had even been caught running in German guns? Since then, of course, the Irish had revealed their true colours, fighting among themselves like Kilkenny cats and ending up calling themselves the Irish Free State with the rebel de Valera as President, except for the Protestant North. England was well rid of Ireland. It was a pity the whole damned island couldn't sink beneath the sea instead of remaining a source of disaffection at the back door. It was even more of a pity that blasted barman couldn't be on hand to serve a drink when needed. Just because the deck was empty while everyone dressed for dinner didn't mean he could desert his post.

Archie was in no way mollified to see the little steward bob up from behind the bar where he had been busy checking stocks in readiness for the cocktail hour. There was a note of unusual arrogance in his shouted 'Hey!'

John Joseph Fitzgerald crossed on catlike feet to stand beside him. 'Sir?'

'Same again,' Archie said, indicating the empty glass before him. His speech was slightly slurred.

'Very good, sir.'

The steward retreated. He had been hoping the Englishman would go below and leave the deck empty long enough for him to nip up to the boat deck and visit the third lifeboat from the stern on the port side. He had not been there since he had slipped up on deck in the small hours, making the need to escape Preston's offensive presence his excuse if he were challenged by any crew member, though there had not been any such need. Instead he had handed in the parcel of broken dinner rolls, of fruit pinched from desecrated dessert dishes, of odds and ends of cheese, and felt it seized by a hand which a moment later grasped his in gratitude. It was water he had not been able to bring. At the thought of the stowaway hidden all day beneath the stifling tarpaulin lifeboat cover, John Joseph Fitzgerald licked lips parched in sympathy. Without water the stowaway would die, or be forced to give himself up while the ship was still nearer to Bombay than England, thus ensuring his return to Indian soil. It was essential he should hold out till after Aden; otherwise all the endurance would be vain. It was essential for John Joseph to supply the bottle of water and the small soda waters he had secreted (a good steward could always lose a few of those) to the eager hands which were dependent on him, with which he was so curiously allied.

It was chance that he had encountered the stowaway. That first night, while still in Bombay harbour, he had crept up on deck for air and literally bumped into a slim figure coming swiftly round a corner. John Joseph had begun apologising to this nocturnally ambulant passenger when he realised he was no such thing. Implored to secrecy, he had hesitated. Dismayed by wretchedness, he had been lost. At stake was his job, but also his humanity.

58

It was his humanity which had won – that and a fellow feeling with some-one out to beat the Imperial system aboard an Imperial ship. It was the old story: he had nothing against the English as individuals, with one excep-tion, that is, but the brother of Kieron Fitzgerald owed them no loyalty. His loyalties were to the rebel, the renegade.

As he brought Captain Johnson his drink and waited while he signed the chitty, John Joseph looked down at the Englishman, handsome but for the scar down his face (and even that was dashing rather than disfiguring) and wondered what he would do about the stowaway if he knew. What would any of them do? Mrs Cynthia Vane would report it, if only to draw favourable attention to herself. Bobby for the same reason – he was not her son for nothing, and in any case he was too young to understand. Nina Martin would not so much report as reveal in innocence, but her sister was different: John Joseph recognised in her the same streak of devilry that he knew existed in himself. It was just as well she wasn't the one to take the veil: a convent's discipline would break her. His sister Ellen now, how had she ever been able to subject her strong will to the vow of obedience – Ellen, who was the fieriest of them all?

It had been Ellen who had found the gun under Kieron's mattress when in a burst of sisterly affection she had come in to change his bed. She had shouted at him at first – 'If the police ever come here searching, it's destroyed we are for sure' – but she had ended by weeping and embracing him. 'Ah, Kieron, aren't you the brave boy and the hope of Ireland, you and Bart Collins and the rest. But don't go thinking the English are only waiting for you to point a popgun at them to evacuate Dublin Castle.' And then she had wept again.

After the Rising there had been no more brightness in her. She spent long hours on her knees praying for the souls of Kieron, and of Bart Collins with whom she'd been walking out, and of all the other brave boys who had died – were still dying – as Ireland's lifeblood drained away. No one had been surprised when she informed them she was going to enter a convent in Connaught – 'Anything nearer home and I'd be tempted to run away,' she said with a touch of the old Ellen. The whole family had assembled at the station to see her off, and as the train pulled out John Joseph, dismayed by his weeping elders (for would Ellen want her last memory of them to be tears?), had raced down the platform keeping pace with the carriage window until almost the very end. 'Goodbye, Ellen. Don't forget how to smile or we shan't recognise you in Paradise – that's if we ever get that far.' And as her face lit up for a moment in the old way, he had looked fixedly at the railway lines stretching before him, for it was now his turn to weep.

Ellen would have kept silent about the stowaway, and so would Connie Martin; he was convinced of that. But Captain Johnson would frogmarch the stowaway before the Captain and demand he be clapped in irons. John Joseph was not sure if irons existed on a passenger liner, but there was no

59

doubt some punishment equally severe, and while Captain Meiklejohn as master of the vessel could overrule a mere army captain, John Joseph was by no means certain that he would. Captain Meiklejohn was a terrifying figure glimpsed only from afar, except when he mixed socially with the First Class passengers, smiling with a smile that never reached his eyes. Only once or twice when the eyes dwelt on Bobby Vane or his mother did John Joseph detect a softening, as Ellen's face would soften at mention of Bart or Kieron before composing itself back into rigidity. The Captain liked the child, for all that he was spoilt and wilful; it was an unexpectedly humanising trait.

But if Captain Meiklejohn liked Bobby Vane and his mother, Captain Johnson liked Connie Martin. He made no secret of it, though so far as the steward could judge she did not return his liking; she was polite and friendly, but that was all. Whereas Dr Bladon, who sat next to her at meals and talked easily, drew an altogether different response. Ah, sure she liked the kindly doctor – everyone except the doctor himself could see that. John Joseph also liked Dr Bladon, who went out of his way to smile and speak, even stopping sometimes for a chat as one new crew member to another in his quiet, beautiful voice. It was almost possible to forget that in Ireland he would have belonged to the Protestant Ascendancy; there was no difference in his manner to an Irish steward and a First Class passenger; he seemed to rate both equally. Would he rate a stowaway as an equal? John Joseph suspected that he would. He had already resolved that if things became desperate it was Dr Bladon's help he would seek.

He would certainly not seek Mr Gurslake's. He did not trust him, though he could not have said why. Bert Gurslake never quite met your eye; or if he did he would look away again, as though afraid you might read him too well. Whether he really had something to hide John Joseph had no means of knowing, but whatever it was he was certain Mrs Gurslake was unaware of it. She chattered incessantly about herself, her Bert, her fellow passengers; there was nothing she was not prepared to ask and comment on. 'That poor young thing,' she had said with a jerk of her head in the direction of Nina Martin when the steward brought her a pink gin. 'She's going to be a nun – isn't it a shame? I think it's dreadful. Fancy wasting herself like that.'

John Joseph did not think it dreadful. To give a son or daughter to God was common in Irish families. He himself had felt no call to the priesthood, much to his mother's disappointment, and Kieron quite evidently had not, but it had not seemed to any of them a cause for mourning when Ellen announced that she was off to the convent in Connaught. True, they would no longer see or hear her; there would be no letters, received or sent; but everyone knew she would be praying for them and that the prayers of a nun were specially blest. He smiled at Mrs Gurslake, who did not understand these matters, and received a glare in reply.

'I suppose you're a Papist,' she challenged.

60

John Joseph inclined his head.

'My Bert says the Pope's responsible for half the trouble in this world, and the Archbishop of Canterbury for the rest.'

John Joseph did not doubt the Archbishop's responsibility, but the Holy Father was not to be criticised. Of course Kieron had criticised him, but Kieron was a Catholic, for all that he refused to go to Mass. Only on that last Easter Sunday had he dumbfounded them all by accompanying them and taking communion with the rest. 'Feeling all right, are you, Kieron?' Ellen had twitted. Kieron had growled, 'Shut up!' – 'The prince of courtesy, our Kieron,' Ellen proclaimed. ' 'Twould put the saints to shame to have you with them. For their sakes I dare say you'll be among us a while yet.' She had been wrong. Did she remember it in her convent? Did she acknowledge it when she knelt to pray?

John Joseph smiled a second time at Mrs Gurslake, as if the reference to the Pope and the Archbishop was a joke. 'You'll be having the Devil on the dole at this rate.'

Florrie Gurslake slapped his hand. 'Naughty boy! My Bert says you Irish are the ones for back answers. As punishment, you can get me another pink gin.'

If only all punishments were as easy, John Joseph reflected, trying not to watch Mrs Gurslake's efforts to conceal her plump legs behind a bamboo table, since her skirt barely covered her knees. Had she no modesty? His own mother wore dresses down to her ankles. Did her Bert not care that she made herself ridiculous? Did he perhaps not care for her?

It looked very much like it, for Florrie had spent several evenings alone while her Bert devoted himself to Captain Johnson, whose company he seemed to seek. So it was with heart sinking on behalf of the stowaway that John Joseph saw him now, already dressed for dinner, making his way towards the Captain at the very moment when, having finished his fourth drink, the young man at last stood up to go.

'Not leaving me to drink on my own, are you?' Bert greeted him.

'Why not? I've been drinking on my own.'

'Not good for you.' Bert snapped his fingers at John Joseph. 'Steward, the same again for my friend here, and you'd better make it mine as well.'

'Very good, sir.'

Or very bad. At least for Captain Johnson, who was on the edge of truculence. Another double would take him over it. John Joseph wished the ladies would appear. Their presence acted as a restraint, and the Chief Steward had warned him that Captain Meiklejohn took exception to raised voices aboard his ship. As he served the drinks, he longed to be out of earshot, fearing trouble, but all he could do was busy himself behind the bar polishing glasses already polished, and will other passengers to arrive.

'Enjoying the voyage?' Bert asked.

'Very pleasant.'

'Your good health. Bottoms up!' Bert raised his glass.

61

Archie Johnson lifted his more slowly. What was the little runt getting at? What did he know about a fellow passenger's health? If that blasted doctor had talked . . .

Archie did not pause to consider that this was unlikely. He said curtly, 'Up yours!' And drank.

'There's some nice bits of skirt around,' Bert confided. 'Makes me wish I was a young fellow. Like you.'

Another dig? Archie let it pass.

'Yes, I'd like to have it all before me,' Bert continued. 'Just starting out, so to speak. Bloody hard work, but there's nothing like the satisfaction of making your own way in the world.'

Of being forced to resign your commission. Of making your way homewards with your tail between your legs . . .

' 'Course I didn't have your advantages. I envy young officers like you. Decorated for gallantry, with a field marshal's baton in your knapsack, I shouldn't wonder, and retirement on a comfortable pension at the end of it. The Army's a fine career.'

So long as you don't confuse peacetime with wartime. So long as the skins you pierce aren't brown . . .

'Only snag is, I reckon you've not much chance to accumulate the ready.'

Too right.

'Apart from what you start with, I mean.'

And what was that, Archie Johnson thought sourly, when you came from a middle-class home? What money there was would go to his two sisters. A boy was expected to fend for himself.

'I know how hard I found it. How much I'd have appreciated a helping hand.'

Archie pricked up his ears. Was this the offer of a job coming? Had he underestimated this detestable little man?

'All you need is some capital to start with. Money makes money, see?'

First lesson in economics.

'I say all you need, but of course it isn't. You need some good advice as well. That was what I never had, but I learnt the hard way, even though it's others as gets the benefit.'

First lesson in philanthropy.

'Now I don't suppose you've done much in the way of investing –'

Archie Johnson shook his head.

'– but if you was interested, there are things I could put you in the way of.'

'What things?'

'Well, of course, on board this ship I can't exactly say. The opportunities for investment are what you might call limited, but once we're back in London town – well, to them in the know there's always bargains. I'd be glad to help a pal.'

'How much?'

'Couple of thou should do it nicely.' Bert hoped Archie couldn't hear his relief.

'Forget it.'

'I could probably get you a snip for a thou. 'Course you'd have my IOU,' Bert continued when Archie remained unresponsive. 'If you like, you can wait till we disembark –' he could hold out that long if he was careful – 'but a lot depends on being quick off the mark. Say we dock at Tilbury on November 25th as per schedule, you don't want to wait till December 1st. When my old mates know I'm back on me native shore they'll be round me like flies round offal –' The comparison struck him as inapt. 'I mean, first come, first served,' he concluded.

'First come, first fleeced, you mean.'

'What you getting at?'

'I mean, Mr Gurslake, that German shrapnel may have sliced my face open, but it's left my brains intact.' (And it'll be a year or two yet before syphilis, even if untreated, has any effect on them.) 'In short, I don't fancy your proposition.'

'All right, all right, it ain't done you no harm.'

'And I don't care for your company either. In future, you can bloody well leave me alone.'

'I don't think I like your tone, *Captain* Johnson. I thought you was an officer and a gentleman.'

No longer an officer . . .

'As a gentleman, I don't appreciate your efforts to touch me for a loan.'

'No harm in it.'

'Not to me. I haven't got the money. But how do I know you won't go trying it on someone else?'

'They can say no, can't they, same as you did. In any case, you got no right to tell me what to do.'

'In this instance might is right, Mr Gurslake.'

'Here, you let go of me coat.'

'I've a good mind to chuck you overboard.'

'Help! Murder!'

John Joseph surfaced from behind the bar. Before he could decide what to do, he heard swift, firm footsteps. Third Officer Julian Strode appeared, immaculate and clean-cut as ever.

'Everything all right, Steward?'

'I think so, sir. The gentlemen are a little excited.'

Strode moved towards them nonchalantly.

'A warm evening, gentlemen.'

The two men drew apart.

'Easy to get overheated.'

Strode's nod was more towards the empty glasses than towards the westering sun.

Archie Johnson wiped his brow. He was swaying slightly. 'Time I went below to change.'

'Have a drink, Mr Strode,' Bert offered.

'No, thank you, I'm on duty.' Strode made it sound like a rebuke.

Bleeding little prig. Just such another as *Captain* Johnson. Officer class. Bert would have liked to spit. Instead, he cleared his throat noisily.

'You young fellows have to work too hard. I was saying to Florrie, you don't get no chance to enjoy the voyage.'

'We have our hours off duty. And even duty has its compensations. Like the fancy hat dance tomorrow night.'

'You going to that, are you? Florrie's on at me to go.'

'Then I shall hope to have the pleasure of dancing with Mrs Gurslake.'

He knew how to please, young Strode.

'She'll be tickled pink.'

She would too. Florrie still loved to dance, though Bert refused these days to take the floor with her: it was too embarrassing. In her younger, slimmer days it had not mattered that she was a head taller, but now when he couldn't see round . . . You needed a ruddy periscope to steer her. Not like it used to be. Now the Martin girls or that clergyman's pale daughter, or better still Mrs Cynthia Vane – you could dance with them without looking daft. Find out a bit about 'em too. There was no shortage of cash aboard the old *Karachi*. It was just a matter of whose pockets it was in.

'I hope you won't mind my mentioning it,' young Strode murmured, 'but that very striking hair ornament of Mrs Gurslake's reminds me: does she keep her jewels in the Purser's safe?'

'Jewels? Florrie ain't got no jewels.'

Too late Bert cursed himself for revealing the fact.

'That's all right, then. I became concerned when Mrs Vane inadvertently mentioned that she keeps hers in her cabin. There is a notice in every cabin advising passengers to lodge valuables in the Purser's safe, but it's surprising how often it's disregarded, usually by those with most to lose.'

Bert struggled to recall details of Cynthia Vane's costume. Something glittering . . .

'Got some nice sparklers, hasn't she?'

'Very nice. Of course one doesn't like to think of such a thing as dishonesty aboard the *Karachi* . . .'

'But better safe than sorry, as you say.'

Strode laughed. 'That wouldn't make a bad cabin notice. You're quite a wit, Mr Gurslake.'

'Does no harm.' Bert smiled uneasily. What exactly had he said?

'I hope you and your wife are enjoying the voyage?'

'Oh yes. So calm even Florrie hasn't felt queasy.'

'Is Mrs Gurslake a bad sailor?'

'I should say so! On the voyage out I thought she wasn't going to make it even to Gib. That was 1916, of course. Poor old Florrie. At least she wasn't worried about subs. Said she reckoned a torpedo would be a mercy.'

'We'll do our best to give her a smoother passage home. She shouldn't need to worry for the next two weeks at least. At this time of year things should stay calm as far as Gibraltar. After that . . .' The Third Officer allowed himself a shrug.

Bert saw there was still liquor in his glass and raised it. 'I'll drink to a good trip home.'

The Third Officer, having done his duty, turned on his well-shod heel.

'Better than that, I'll give you the old seaman's toast, Mr Gurslake. Calm seas and a prosperous voyage.'

He did not know with what fervour Bert Gurslake drank to both.

'May I have the pleasure of this dance?'

Edmund Bladon bowed over Nina Martin's hand.

She looked up at him through a fringe of lashes beneath a peasant's head-scarf and murmured she would be delighted. He led her on to the floor.

The *Karachi*'s ballroom had been made as festive as festoons of coloured lights and paper streamers could make it. Huge Chinese lanterns hung like exotic moons. The band plaged ragtime, musical comedy hits and Edwardian waltzes from a dais at one end. At the other a bar, served by several stewards, John Joseph among them, dispensed a wide variety of fashionable cocktails more or less expertly mixed, as well as straight drinks and fruit juice. Around the edges of the room a few small tables and smaller chairs were ranged, though most of those who were not dancing preferred to sit out on deck and enjoy the tropic night, warm and caressing, through which the *Karachi* steamed like a moving isle of light.

It was the first ball of the homeward voyage – fancy dress from the neck up. Captain Meiklejohn himself would attend (no fancy dress for him!) moving from group to group and chatting, gazing benignly on the animation, and smiling, though never with a smile that reached his eyes.

'I'm so glad you decided to take part this evening,' Edmund said to Nina as the band struck up a waltz.

'Connie said I should.'

'Not too much against your will, I hope?'

'No-o.' She sounded uncertain. 'I used to love to dance.'

Edmund noted the past tense. She wasn't yet twenty. It was no business of his, but: 'Are you sure you're doing the right thing in entering?' he asked.

She did not resent his question. Instead, she raised lambent eyes to his. 'More than anything this world has to offer, I want to give myself to God. I'm sure it's difficult to understand if you're not a Catholic; perhaps even if you are . . .'

She paused enquiringly, but Edmund did not respond.

'. . . but even when I was a little girl the religious life drew me. I used to play at being a nun.'

'Then I hope you will be very happy.'

'Thank you. I hope so too. It's in the family, you see. My aunt is the Mother Superior of the convent where I am to enter, and her aunt was a religious of the same Order. It would be wonderful if some day . . .'

'If someday what?'

'I was going to say, if Connie's daughter were to join me.'

'Connie doesn't have a daughter yet!'

'No, but I'm sure she'll marry and have children. Otherwise it would be such a waste.'

Edmund glanced across to where Connie with a mantilla on her red curls was dancing with Archie Johnson who was trying to look like a sheikh. It could only be good manners that had led her to accept Johnson, he told himself, who had beaten him by a head. They had asked her to dance simultaneously, but her eyes had been on Johnson first. She had apologised, laughing.

'Ah, Dr Bladon, I can't bear to disappoint myself by saying no to you. Do make it up to me later on. Otherwise I'll spend the whole evening wondering what I'm missing.'

'It shall be my pleasure to help you find out,' Edmund said.

Meanwhile it is my pleasure to dance with your sister, who used to love to dance and has not forgotten how to give herself to the music. I hope she finds it as easy to give herself to God. I hope she knows what she's doing. Why am I so ill at ease? Surely it's not just Protestant prejudice, my conviction that hers is a useless sacrifice. If she were joining a nursing or a teaching Order I'd feel happier; I've seen them do wonderful work; but to spend her life in prayer and penance and fasting – what does she hope to achieve? I cannot help seeing it as adolescent infatuation, only with God, not some star of the cinema screen. Why, she's probably never even seen a moving picture. What does she know of what she's giving up?

'You'll miss your sister,' he remarked as they cornered.

'Dreadfully. I don't know how I'm going to bear it, except that I know I'll be given strength. We've never been apart, and since Mummy died we've been closer than ever.'

'Did your mother die long ago?'

'Two years. She had consumption. But she was so bright and gay you wouldn't ever have known until she had to stay in bed, and even then she read voraciously. I didn't know it was possible to read so much.'

'Some consumptives have a feverish energy.'

'Mummy certainly had. I couldn't believe she was going to die. And yet, you know, her death was a blessing. It's what decided me to dedicate myself to God.'

So there had been hesitation . . .

'How was that?' Edmund asked as the music finished. His eyes sought Connie, but she and Johnson were nowhere in sight.

'Mummy's death was very sudden,' Nina explained, 'and she died unreconciled. The priest couldn't get there in time, so she never confessed and received the Last Sacrament, and she will have to spend a long time in Purgatory because of that. I can help her and the other souls by praying for them. People in the world have so little time to pray.'

So little reason, Edmund thought, when prayers go unanswered. Where was Connie?

'That must be a comforting thought,' he offered, 'though I don't personally believe that prayers can help the dead. A man is judged by what he does in this life.'

'Oh, I believe that too. But in this life you'd help a friend by praying for him, wouldn't you? Why should that change because he changes state?'

What a delightful way she had of putting it. She hadn't seen what death could do. How could she have witnessed its crueller manifestations, living her sheltered life in a garrison town? She had not walked the wards of a London hospital and seen the dead come in: road casualties; men mangled in industrial accidents; despairing suicides; children too weak from under-nourishment to battle against disease; the young and vital transformed into incurables by medicine's helplessness. She prayed for their souls; he fought for their bodies.

'I wish I had your faith,' Edmund said.

Once upon a time he had, not identical, but a belief in the general goodness of creation and of all created things. But that was before he had seen the created turn against one another, degrade, dehumanise, in order to destroy. The people he had lived and studied with in Leipzig had become 'the Boche', 'the Hun'. Yet they were no different, no worse, than they had been, no more worthy of being put to death. He had tried to explain this to Rosemary, but his fiancée did not understand.

'I know you've lived there, darling, and of course there are decent Germans, but do you want them lording it over here?'

'Of course not,' Edmund said, impatient. 'I'm just not prepared to kill them, that's all.'

'You're so sweet.' Rosemary laid her cheek against his. 'It's why I love you so much. Don't you think you ought to decide soon which regiment you'll enlist in? You'll look wonderful in uniform.'

The commonest uniform was that of thought, Edmund reflected, and it did not flatter its wearers. The same views were held on factory floor and on the bench of bishops, among chiefs of staff and in the village pub. But the girl in his arms tonight who danced with such grace and lightness had been a child then, playing with dolls and teddy-bears, playing at being a nun . . .

'The most difficult thing was to get Daddy to agree to my entering,' Nina was saying. 'He's a Protestant, and he doesn't believe in people going into convents. I dare say you feel the same.'

'I do when they are young and vulnerable and inexperienced,' Edmund said, looking down at her.

'But that's just what I'm offering to God – my innocence. Except that no one's ever truly innocent. I'm not giving up the world; I'm giving up my chance to know it. Isn't that a greater sacrifice?'

'Perhaps.' Edmund changed the subject. 'Mrs Vane seems to be enjoying herself.'

'Cynthia?' Nina broke off. 'Oh, I'm sorry. She asked us to call her that.'

'Why not?'

'We've known her such a short time.'

'Shipboard life accelerates friendship.'

Nina looked at him again from beneath her lashes. 'I feel as if I'd known *you* all my life.'

'That's good.' He sought once more for Connie but could not see her, only the sleek dark head of Cynthia Vane as she was escorted back to her table by Third Officer Julian Strode. Young Strode was well and truly smitten, Edmund noted with amusement, watching his hand rest lightly on her elbow just below the gold slave bangle she always wore. This strictly brought up young man, only son of a widowed mother, was for the first time off the leash. Small wonder that he had fallen for the sophisticated Cynthia. Edmund hoped his puppy-dog adoration would not go too far, for he had a suspicion Mrs Vane would not hesitate to dismiss him sharply if he became an embarrassment. Meanwhile, embarrassment of a different sort awaited her, for he could see Bert Gurslake hovering hopefully, intent on asking her for the next dance.

Edmund and Nina arrived back in time to hear Cynthia say, 'Thank you, Mr Strode. I haven't had such a vigorous partner for ages.'

'My pleasure, Mrs Vane.'

'May I have the pleasure –' Bert began.

'Ah, Nina,' Cynthia said, avoiding him with practised ease, 'how good to see you enjoying yourself, dear. Does Dr Bladon dance well?'

She half turned towards him.

'He dances beautifully, Cynthia.'

'I look forward to finding out.'

'May I have the pleasure –'

'And what have you done with your sister? She seems to have disappeared.'

'She was dancing with Captain Johnson.'

Edmund needed no reminder of this as he fought down his unease. He was aware of Cynthia expectant beside him, but he had glimpsed Florrie Gurslake sitting statuesque and despondent in mauve chiffon, and a sudden pity swept over him. She had made no attempt at 'fancy dress from the neck upwards', as the invitations had stipulated, but with her astonishing hair colour and that bun with a dagger thrust through it, she already looked like a parody of a geisha girl.

'Mr Gurslake, I must give myself the pleasure of dancing with your wife,' he excused himself. After all, he owed Cynthia Vane and her spoilt son nothing. One dance with Bert Gurslake wouldn't hurt . . .

'What?' Bert seemed surprised. 'Oh, Florrie. Yes, she'll appreciate that. She likes to dance.'

'You beat me to it, Doctor,' Julian Strode said, in case Bert remembered his earlier promise to partner Florrie. 'Miss Nina, may I?'

Bert managed it at last. 'Mrs Vane, may I have the pleasure of this dance?'

It was a ladies' excuse-me, so Edmund had no doubt she would abandon Bert as soon as courtesy permitted. Sooner, perhaps. He had no high opinion of Cynthia Vane. Indeed, on the whole, he thought, he preferred Florrie; at least her heart was kind.

Her face lit up when he asked her to dance and she took the floor with a certain shy dignity, though, as he soon discovered, there was no need for shyness: Florrie danced exceedingly well. He was a good dancer himself, but it was years since he had had such a partner. Until this voyage it was years since he had danced, not since he and Rosemary . . . He snapped off the thought and concentrated on the large lady in his arms whose feather-light feet darted where he led with grace and precision, and somehow dominated and controlled the bulk above.

'You're a wonderful dancer, Mrs Gurslake.'

'Thank you, Doc. You're not so bad yourself. Too good to be pushing an old woman like me round the floor – not but what it isn't appreciated – when there's all them pretty girls.'

'Ah, but they can't all dance like you can.'

'I dare say you're right, at that. Real sticks they are, some of 'em. Have you tried Miss Imogen Stiles?'

Edmund glanced to where the Reverend's thin pale daughter was driving her thin pale legs like pistons in advance of her partner's feet. The ship's officer concerned wore his most dutiful expression and cast his eyes heavenward as he passed.

'No,' he said, answering Florrie, 'I haven't yet had the – er – experience.'

'Then watch it, Doc. She's got her eye on you. This is a ladies' excuse-me, you know.'

'I do know, but I'm sure you've misinterpreted the young lady's interest.'

'You'd see it right enough if you had eyes for anyone but Connie Martin.'

'Miss Martin's a very attractive girl.'

'You can say that again. Shame, isn't it, about her sister? Going into a convent, I mean.'

'Not if it's what she wants to do.'

'How can she know at her age? If you ask me, she's the sexy one of the two. Connie's all spirit and brightness, but Nina, she's got it in her flesh.'

'Perhaps that makes her sacrifice the greater.'

'Or the dafter. Depends on how you look at it. I didn't believe it when Connie first told us, I thought she was having us on. My Bert says I ought to have a little talk with Nina, tell her what she's missing, but I don't know. What do you think?'

'I'd leave well alone.'

'Perhaps you're right. But I feel for them two girls as if they was my daughters. They got no mother, you know.'

'Do you have children, Mrs Gurslake?'

'We was going to have one but I lost it. We ain't never tried again.'

'I'm sorry.'

'I expect it was all for the best. I was forty-two and we was coming out to Australia. He'd have been quite a little nipper by now.'

'Like Mrs Vane's son.'

'About that age, but with my Bert for a father he'd not have been allowed to run wild. What Master Bobby needs is a clip round the earhole, and that takes a man's hand, believe me.'

'There may be several masculine hands aching to give it.'

'Proper young limb, he is. She ought to remarry – the boy needs a father.'

'Let us hope she will.'

'Too many widows like her, that's the trouble, not to mention all the young girls coming up. You married, Doc?'

'No.'

'A broken heart, then. There must be a reason, a fine young chap like you.'

Her eyes were on him, assessing. A partial truth was better than a lie.

'I was engaged, but my fiancée broke it off.'

'Silly girl. Another fellow?'

'She has married since, yes.'

'And now Miss Connie's caught your eye and you can feel the old heartstrings flutter.'

'As I said, Miss Martin's an attractive girl.'

'And there she is, just coming in that door with Captain Johnson. My, it looks as if they've had a tiff.'

Connie did indeed look ruffled. Archie Johnson was stiffly correct, escorting her round the edge of the floor but making no move to lead her on to it.

'Looks as if she could do with rescuing, don't she? Off you go, Doc. I'm getting puffed.'

Edmund looked down at her flushed face. 'If you'd rather sit down, just say so, but I've no intention of breaking off our dance.'

'There ain't much left of it in any case, they're into the last reprise. Well, if you won't be sensible, I will.'

She broke away from him and waddled across the floor, all grace gone from her in an instant. Edmund followed reluctantly. He had no desire to intrude on Connie and Archie Johnson like the jealous swain he felt himself to be. He would have preferred to withdraw, to plunge over the side if necessary, in order not to show he cared. But Florrie Gurslake left him no option. She plumped herself down at the table beside Connie and Archie and announced, 'Sorry, ducks, but I simply got to sit down. The Doc here's been pushing me round as if I weighed no more than you do, and I didn't when I was your age. But Anna Domino catches up with you; even my Bert ain't as spry as he was. Where is Bert? He was dancing with that Mrs Vane but it's a ladies' excuse-me, so Lord knows who he's dancing with now.'

'Mrs Vane is dancing with the Captain,' Archie Johnson reported.

'How's that for flying high?' Florrie fanned herself and patted the chair beside her. 'C'mon, Doc, you sit down.'

Edmund perched himself just as the dance ended. Out of the corner of his eye he saw Imogen Stiles edging towards them. He turned his back on her.

'Mrs Gurslake is a magnificent dancer,' he informed the pair opposite.

Connie clapped her hands. 'I should have guessed it. So is Captain Johnson. They must give a demonstration. Nini –' as her sister came to join them, young Strode having vanished, presumably still in pursuit of Cynthia Vane, 'did you hear that? Don't you think Mrs Gurslake and Captain Johnson should show us how the next dance should be danced?'

'I'm afraid you'll have to wait a little, Miss Martin,' Archie answered, vowing to avoid the situation at all costs. 'This is the interval.'

'Already? It just shows how much I've been enjoying myself.' She did not look at Archie as she spoke.

'May I get you all a drink?' he offered. 'Mrs Gurslake, what will you have?'

'Oh, a pink gin for me, dear.'

'Miss Martin?'

'I'd love a Manhattan.'

'Miss Nina?'

'Nothing for me, please.'

'Not even an orange juice?'

'Oh well . . .'

'An orange juice, Bladon?' The tone was insulting.

'Let me look after myself and Mr Gurslake while you serve the ladies,' Edmund suggested as Bert came sidling up. He saw with relief that Imogen Stiles had joined another table. 'Mr Gurslake, what will you drink?'

'I'll have a scotch. I never refuse a good offer, as the chorus girl said to the – Ouch!' Florrie's dig in the ribs was obviously painful. She looked meaningfully in Nina's direction, and Bert subsided into Edmund's empty chair.

As he joined Archie Johnson in the crowd round the bar Edmund was conscious of a figure – he was sure it was Captain Meiklejohn – disappearing through the ballroom doorway in company with Cynthia Vane.

*   *   *

71

Cynthia Vane was not enjoying the dance, although her sleek little head looked very fetching beneath a saucy sailor hat. She did not lack for partners, but they were all too old/too young; too short/too fat; could not dance/converse; were engaged/married. Not one of them was a second Robert Vane, and that was the trouble: Cynthia was not prepared to settle for less.

Time had not healed her; on the contrary, it had deepened her bitterness that her husband should have been snatched from her just when she needed him most. Not only could she not remember a time when Robert, five years older, was not on hand to soothe, comfort, minister to his childhood playmate grown imperceptibly into his great love, but he had left her to bring the child he had given her into a fatherless life. If the child had been a girl she would have felt less helpless, but she was convinced a son needed a father's hand. That visit to Dr Bladon's surgery a few days earlier had shaken her. What did he mean by saying the boy was punishing her, having her on? She was aware that Bobby sometimes fantasised – she would not call it lying – but surely that was due to a combination of imagination and high spirits? He never fantasised to her. Yet now, if Dr Bladon was to be believed, he had deliberately deceived her. The question was whether the doctor was to be believed.

On the whole she thought not; there was something too uncomfortable about his cool gaze. She was not used to men who looked at her as though she were a specimen they were examining under a microscope, having no connection with flesh and sex and blood. She preferred the ardour she could read in Third Officer Strode's eyes, but of course he was too young, more like an elder brother to Bobby and not at all what she wanted for herself. The trouble was that so far as she could see the *Karachi* on this voyage carried no attractive and eligible males in First Class.

It had been the same in Quetta, though her brother and sister-in-law had ended by telling her she was too hard to please. 'Stop crying for the moon,' they said. 'You'll never find another Robert, but you could still make a satisfactory match.' But what was a satisfactory match? Her gratification or a father for Bobby? Whatever it was, it was not dancing in the arms of Bert Gurslake, whose breath smelled and whose moustache had more than once tickled her cheek. So far as was possible, she turned her head aside, but was obliged to look at him from time to time to hear what he was saying. She caught the words ' . . . always enjoy a hop.'

'Does Mrs Gurslake also enjoy dancing?' she asked him.

'Cor, yes, just look at her. She's giving the doc a real treat.'

'Do you like Dr Bladon?' Cynthia enquired, anxious to know if other passengers felt as she did. Though he had not slighted them, nor implied that they were unsatisfactory parents . . .

'He's all right,' Bert said. 'They say he's a very good doctor and the ship's lucky to have him. But I tell you one thing about him: he's a man with something to hide.'

'What makes you think that?'

72

'Ever tried asking him anything about hisself? He shuts up like a clam. All we know about him is that he ain't married and is recently qualified. What's he been doing in between?'

'War service, I suppose, and then studying.'

'He won't never talk about the war, just turns the subject. But he don't half like the Boche.'

'Really.'

'Yes, he speaks their lingo. Captain Johnson reckons he must have lived there.'

'Continental travel is quite usual.' Among a certain class, at least.

'What if he was a German in disguise?'

'Is that Captain Johnson's idea?'

'Nah.' Bert was offended. 'I haven't discussed it with him. But you start to ask yourself why the doc's so cagey when the rest of us is like an open book.'

In his own case he was conscious of having glued some pages together so that only the uppermost could be read, but instinct told him Dr Bladon's past did not include peculation. Nothing as straightforward as that.

'Dr Bladon is unmistakably English,' Cynthia said with decision. 'And a gentleman.' You couldn't expect Bert Gurslake to recognise it, but others of the doctor's class could and did.

'It seems queer he ain't never married,' Bert suggested, emphasising slightly the word 'queer'.

'I don't think so.' Cynthia was getting bored with the conversation and her partner. Could she now tap another lady on the shoulder, say 'Excuse me,' and dance off with the partner of her choice?

Of her choice. That was the trouble. There was no one she wanted to choose. Oh, Robert, Robert, come back to me. How could you leave me so alone?

'Women may not find Dr Bladon overwhelmingly attractive,' she suggested.

'Yes, but with all the spare wheels about –' Too late Bert remembered he was partnering one of them, and broke off in confusion.

'We're not all ready to take the first man on offer,' Cynthia said sweetly.

'For some ladies I'm sure there's no need.' Bert's gallantry was creaking into gear. 'Take yourself, now. You've no need of a breadwinner. Why should you marry again?'

To give my son a father. To assuage my own aching needs. These were answers Cynthia might have given, but all she said was, 'Why, indeed?'

' 'Course, when it comes to investment a man can be helpful,' Bert continued. 'Not many ladies understand investment.'

'We have advisers,' Cynthia said, amused.

'Ah, but you know the old saying: If you want a thing done well, do it yourself. Take that bracelet and those rings you're wearing –'

'I assure you, Mr Gurslake, they're insured.'

So she wouldn't even feel the draught . . . Bert licked lips suddenly dry.

'I wasn't going to suggest you might lose them. Just reinvest their value, say.'

'I'm afraid their value is sentimental. I wouldn't part with them for worlds.'

'Quite right too.' Damn sentimentality. 'But I dare say you got a few more.'

Cynthia didn't answer.

'I was only going to say,' Bert ploughed on, 'that if you was ever interested in making a bit – all straightforward and above-board – I might be able to help.'

'Thank you so much, Mr Gurslake.'

Bert was not clear what she was thanking him for, for she suddenly left him gyrating aimlessly and darted across to the ballroom door. A tall, gold-braided figure looked down at her, but Bert was not near enough to hear her say, 'Captain Meiklejohn, this is a ladies' excuse-me, but since you don't have a partner for me to excuse, may I be very forward and ask for the pleasure of this dance?'

'I should be honoured, Mrs Vane.'

Mrs Cynthia Vane and son Bobby. As Angus Meiklejohn said her name aloud he was surprised to note that it had registered. There were as yet not many First Class passengers he could name. And curiously enough, the name that most intrigued him belonged to a passenger who had not yet come aboard: Stafford Briscoe, of His Majesty's Foreign Service, whom they were due to pick up at Aden the next day.

Angus Meiklejohn had never heard of Stafford Briscoe until he received his telegraphed instructions, but he realised he must be an unusual man: one of the Foreign Service's trouble-shooters, perhaps even a secret agent; certainly a person of consequence for whom special arrangements could be made. One of the few unoccupied First Class cabins would have to be prepared for him and the places at one of the long dining tables adjusted to make room. Stafford Briscoe would be sitting near Cynthia Vane; perhaps a shipboard romance would develop between them; the Captain had seen plenty such, one or two even ending in formal engagements celebrated in champagne. He was always invited to these parties, but the appearances he put in were brief. There would never be an engagement party for Andrew Meiklejohn. What would happen to him when he and Ailsa were no more?

He suspected there might never be any such party for Cynthia Vane either. Son Bobby stood in the way. A man attracted to Cynthia might well balk at the encumbrance of a spoilt child. Nevertheless, the boy was a good conversation-starter, so he remarked, 'I met your son the other day.'

'Did you, Captain?'

Her astonishment was obvious. Had young Strode shielded her from the truth when returning the boy?

'He paid me a visit on my bridge,' he elaborated.

74

'But I thought passengers weren't allowed . . . ohh, I *am* so sorry! I'll – I'll –' Threats failed her. 'I hope you gave him a thorough telling-off.'

'I am not expecting a return visit. Unless by invitation.'

'Do you invite people on to your bridge?'

'Occasionally. Why, would you like to come?'

'I shouldn't understand anything about the instruments,' she said candidly, 'but it would be a privilege to be asked.'

He liked her honesty. Perhaps later in the voyage he would ask her. Together with her son, of course.

'We'll see. It must be quite a job keeping a bright child amused on a long voyage.'

'It is, believe you me.'

Her statement sounded heartfelt.

'He's a handsome laddie.'

'Thank you.'

'One can see he takes after you.'

'Thank you again. He's my son in looks but he's got his father's brains, thank heaven.'

'His father would have been proud of him.'

'I'd like to think so, but it's so difficult bringing up a boy alone.'

'You've no brothers-in-law, brothers?'

'Only one surviving. We've been staying with him in Quetta, but he's too far away to be much help. Besides –' she hesitated – 'he thinks Bobby's spoilt and says he needs a good thrashing. Do you think boys ought to be thrashed?'

Her eyes were on him – beautiful eyes, he noticed.

'It's not the only means of discipline.'

'Indeed not. I can't believe that brutalising a child teaches him anything but brutality.'

'It's not a view which many schoolmasters share.'

'I know. I dread sending Bobby to his father's old school. I'm so afraid he'll hate it.'

'Yet it did not do his father any harm.'

'Nothing could have harmed Robert. He was the gentlest, sweetest man –' Her voice broke. 'I'm sorry. After eight years you'd think I'd know how to be a widow, but some things you never learn.'

Like being father to a child in a man's body. After eight years you still had not learnt that.

Cynthia Vane recovered herself.

'And have you children, Captain?' she asked in a social voice.

'I have a son.'

'An only child like Bobby? No wonder you understand how I feel.'

Angus was not sure he did understand, but he was glad she thought so.

'How old is your son?'

'Twenty-six.'

'Is he a sailor like his father?'

'No, Mrs Vane, he is not.'

'What does he do?'

'At present he's at home with his mother.'

'That must be nice for her.'

'I doubt it,' Angus heard himself saying. 'Andrew's an invalid.'

For the second time in his life he had admitted it, the first time being to the Chief. Jamie Sutherland had said nothing for a few moments, merely drawn deep on his pipe before asking, 'Has he always been so, Angus?' Angus Meiklejohn had bowed his head and wept.

He did not weep now, although Cynthia Vane was asking, 'Has he been an invalid all his life?'

'Only since the war.'

'You mean he was wounded? How tragic. But at least you have something left.'

A beautiful shell. Shell of the shell-shocked. *We know so little about the mind* . . .

'Aye, we have him at home safe and sound. His mother tends him.'

'It's better than having him dead.'

'Is it, Mrs Vane? You've not seen him.'

'Is he – disfigured?'

'No, he's a bonnie lad.'

Bonnie Andy, setting off, penny in hand, to buy his sweeties. Bonnie Andy, twenty-six years old.

Slim fingers tapped his arm. 'Would it help to talk about it?'

How could talking help? Yet why had he told this woman if he did not want the sound of sympathy expressed in her soft, pleasant voice?

'You're very kind.'

'No, you make me feel ashamed of myself. Of course there are people worse off than I, or even Robert. Death is the last thing that can happen, but it isn't always the worst.'

She had slipped from his arms and was drawing him after her towards the edge of the floor. The dance was ending, the dancers dispersing into chattering, laughing groups.

'Where shall we go?' Cynthia paused. 'I know! The writing-room. This is the interval, so we have that much time, at least.'

She made it sound like an assignation, and so in a sense it was, though the assignation sooner or later to unburden himself to a woman had been made when the burden was laid upon him; only time and place and partner had been withheld. And the time was now, the partner Cynthia, the place the writing-room, an elegant wood-panelled haven of shaded lights and quiet, set in the heart of the ship.

Predictably, it was deserted. Cynthia led the way, the fringed silk tunic she wore swaying with every movement of her boyish hips and slim, silk-stockinged legs. She chose a corner table, sat down and crossed her legs, displaying them from knee to ankle. Angus looked, and looked away.

'May I smoke?'

'Please do.'

A woman smoking! The sight was rare in Aberdeen, and would in any case have met with granite-faced disapproval. He tried to keep his expression neutral as she fitted the cigarette into a long black holder and prepared to strike a match.

'Allow me.' He took the match and leaned towards her. Its brief flare showed up hollows in her cheeks and deepened her eye-sockets, in which it was reflected as two tiny points of light. Then the cigarette glowed into life and she leaned back, regarding him from under brows that were artificially arched. He blew out the match and pinched it for good measure before dropping it in the ashtray.

'You're a careful man, Captain.'

'It's second nature aboard ship, Mrs Vane. Besides –' He had been going to say that in his view the writing-room's panelling was a fire risk, but she was a passenger. He changed it to: 'I come from a careful home.'

He did not say a poor one, because that was not strictly true. There was enough to go round – if they were careful; but it made for deliberation rather than spontaneity. Perhaps that was why he now found himself silent before her. Suddenly there was nothing to say.

She blew a smoke-ring which wavered ceilingwards.

'The hardest thing about having a son,' she said, 'is the knowledge that he's never truly yours, except in the womb. A husband, yes; but a son, never. You must expect to lose him, to hand him on to someone else.'

He had heard Ailsa say something similar in the prayers she used to offer up each night, the white-nightgowned body, as slim then as Cynthia's, kneeling at the foot of the bed, asking a blessing on him, on her, on Andy, for whom her prayer was, 'Lord, let me love him but not too much.' Lord, let me love him . . . What power on earth could stop her when he was bone of her bone, flesh of her flesh? But of his father he was heart, soul, spirit, so that Angus's prayer had been, 'Lord, let me love him with all the power of love within me;' knowing that for him it could never be too much. He started to say that for a father it was different, but Cynthia cut him short.

'Why is it different? Is a father's love less than a mother's? How do you measure love?'

Angus was embarrassed by the turn the conversation was taking. He had not meant to discuss philosophical abstractions with Cynthia Vane. They were not things he discussed with anyone, even Ailsa. No, least of all with Ailsa; she had no time for them. 'When you can tell me why this had to happen to Andy, I'll maybe listen to you,' she said. 'Meanwhile I'd as soon you took him down to the beach and kept him happy, and gave me a chance to get on.' For the house in the Old Town of Aberdeen still sparkled from top to bottom, despite the time Ailsa spent with their son. Or perhaps because of it. The house responded to her efforts, whereas with Andy every letter brought the news: No change.

So how did you measure love? By hours of devotion? By self-denial of material needs? By endurance of imperfections in the beloved? By a steadfast act of will which ensured the continuance of loving even when love itself was no more? Angus did not answer his own questions. Instead he said to Cynthia Vane:

'You were asking about Andy. During the Battle of the Somme he was buried alive in a shellhole full of dead and dying. As a result, he has regressed to childhood and his mental age is lower than your son's.'

Cynthia Vane said nothing. When he looked at her, her eyes were full of tears.

She laid a hand on his. 'Forgive me for asking. I see now what you mean about better dead. At least with Robert I have my memories. And of course I have his son.'

'I envy you.'

If only there had been another child, a late one. Ailsa had not been too old. But from the day the telegram came she had turned from him. It was as though all her vital forces were concentrated on her son; first her refusal to believe in his death – wholly justified; then her refusal to accept defeat. She was convinced he would recover, despite the absence of any hopeful sign. When Angus tried gently to discourage her from hoping she quoted the doctors: *We know so little about the mind . . .*

He stood up.

'I must leave you,' he said to Cynthia. 'I have to socialise. Besides, I mustn't monopolise your time on this gala evening.'

'No, I've appreciated your confidence.'

He wanted to say, Please keep it as a confidence, but that would be to insult her.

She seemed to read his thoughts.

'I shall naturally say nothing of this to anyone. I hope we may talk again.'

Angus inclined his head and left her. He did not know whether he hoped for or feared another encounter with the disturbing Mrs Vane.

Edmund Bladon did not find Connie Martin disturbing, at least not consciously; he found her delightful, and would have been tempted to believe that she had sought him out except that that seemed too much to hope for; it was easier to think that fate had been kind.

When she had returned to the ballroom looking flushed and angry, with Johnson following hangdog at her heels, she had made straight for her sister. Edmund had noticed before the instinctive alliance between them if trouble threatened either; it was almost as though they were twins. Because he had been with Nina, Connie had accepted him as an assistant ally and a bulwark between her and her erstwhile partner, who had not lingered once his round of drinks had been served. During the interval while the band refreshed themselves conversation had been general, with Bert and Florrie Gurslake, Julian Strode and several people at neighbouring tables all joining in. When at last the band regrouped on the dais and the bandleader stepped forward to announce the next number, young Strode had immediately addressed himself again to Nina, but she had begged to be excused.

'I've danced enough, I mustn't allow myself to get into the way of it.'

As always, any reference to her intending profession silenced argument. Strode bowed and stood aside, murmuring something about God's gain and man's loss which caused Nina's face to flame.

'Your sister takes things very seriously,' Edmund observed to Connie.

'Too seriously. It wouldn't hurt her to relax. The Church doesn't demand this excessive piety. Reverend Mother back in Nullumpur thought Nina was too young to enter; that it would be better if she had more experience of life.'

'Yet she tells me she's always wanted to be a nun.'

'She's always played at it, but does she really know what it means to give up everything for love of God?' (Do you? Edmund wondered.) 'If only Mummy hadn't died as she did.'

'You think her death affected your sister?'

'I know it, but there's nothing I can do.' She closed the subject with her most winning smile. 'You're very good at getting people to talk but I notice you don't say much.'

'A doctor's training. Let the patient talk.'

'Is that how you see us – as patients?'

'We're all inmates of a sick world.'

'How cheerful.'

'I'm sorry. I'm afraid I'm not very good at being light-hearted, but I'm light of foot, so I'm told. Shall we dance?'

'Whoever told you you were light of foot was right,' Connie said later as they progressed round the dance-floor. 'Who was it?'

'A girl I used to dance with.'

'Tell me something I can't guess. What was her name?'

'Rosemary.'

'For remembrance, evidently.'

'It wasn't why she was named.'

'Goodness, you're guarded. Don't you ever let up?'

And open my heart to you, as I should like to? No, my dear, I've kept it locked for too long. A man like me lives by not living. I am sailing away from life, limiting myself to the miniature world of a passenger liner. It would take more than you to draw me back.

'This is your first voyage, isn't it?' Connie queried.

Edmund admitted it. There was safety in admitting a known fact.

'What would you choose to be if you weren't a ship's surgeon?'

'I'd specialise,' he said cautiously. Why were her questions so awkward? 'Gynaecology, perhaps.'

79

'Why don't you?'

'There are difficulties. It takes money, for one thing. And I need the right opening.'

'Can't your family help?'

'My aunt did what she could. It's thanks to her I took a medical training.'

'Aren't your parents alive?'

'My mother is dead.'

'What about your father?'

Was there no stopping her?

'My father and I are estranged.'

That was putting it mildly. The old man hadn't actually said, 'Never darken my doors again,' but he'd certainly meant it. What was it he had said – 'a disgrace to our family name . . . an insult to your brother's memory . . .' He'd pitched it pretty strong. And Mother, who'd lost one son and was now about to lose another, had wept quietly in a corner and never said a word. It was left to Aunt Anne to speak out – 'the disgrace may be in your eyes, Jeffrey, but it is not in mine, I'm thankful to say. Edmund has a home with me whenever he needs one. God forgive me if my prejudices ever grow so strong that I turn my own flesh and blood away.'

He had needed Aunt Anne often in the years that followed, and his father's sister had not failed. Miss Bladon was respected throughout the county, but she chose now to make her home in town. The leafy avenue in St John's Wood, the small house built as a rich man's love-nest but now a spinster's property, had welcomed him whenever he needed a refuge. As soon as the door was closed behind him by Bertram, who had been his aunt's maid ever since Edmund could remember, the world outside was shut out. Books, music, Aunt Anne's amateur but gifted watercolours, the work she did for the Red Cross, the letters she wrote on behalf of the wounded she visited in hospital, all blended in a fine disarray, while from the basement rose a delicious smell of cooking, for even during the worst wartime shortages Bertram could prepare a tempting meal.

Aunt Anne would issue from the drawing-room to greet him. By consent they said as little as possible on what they called his 'leaves'. Instead she would eye his gaunt face, feel the thinness through his clothing, and draw her own conclusions. Once or twice, when he woke in a nightmare, he found her in his room and apologised, realising he must have disturbed her – a fact she shrugged away. If she was out when the time came for him to return, he would scribble her a note; 'See you next time. Thanks for everything. Love, Edmund.' If she was at home, she never broke down. Only long afterwards did he learn from Bertram that each time he went back his aunt took to her bed. It was through Anne he learned of the death of his mother, and thought: Now the old man really is alone. 'Shall I write?' he asked next time he was at the house in St John's Wood, but she merely shook her head. He had asked the same question at intervals ever since, most recently just before the *Karachi* sailed, but the answer was always the same, and he had come to accept that by his father's express wish they would never see each other again.

Connie raised her face to his. 'Do you mind about the estrangement?'

'Yes,' Edmund said, wondering at himself for admitting it to this stranger. 'He's old and ill. He won't live long. I'd have liked to see him once more.'

I was always his favourite, as Roger was Mother's. I'd hoped he'd understand. Not approve – that would have been asking too much, but at least not conclude I was a coward, as the rest of the county did. Even people I'd known all my life. Even Rosemary. No wonder I never want to revisit my old home, though I'd have gone back to see my father if he'd wished it.

'Where does your father live?'

'In Gloucestershire.'

'Where's that?'

Of course: Connie had never set foot in her own country.

'In the middle of England, to the west.'

'Is it near Berkshire?'

'It's not impossibly far.'

'Berkshire's where our aunt lives. We're going to stay with her. But she comes from Ireland, like Mummy, and Aunt Eileen in the convent. Do you know Ireland at all?'

'Only as a troubled country.'

'Joe the deck steward calls it troubled too. His accent reminds me of Mummy's.'

'Are you like your mother?' *My turn to ask questions now.*

'Too much so, I'm afraid.'

'Don't say that. Your sister makes her sound delightful.'

'So she was, but it didn't stop her dying in sin.'

Edmund was too startled to answer. Instead, he said, 'Would you like to sit out this dance?' They had to raise their voices to be heard above the howl of the band's saxophone. Confidences here were out of place.

He led Connie out on deck. The sea was black and the night sky blacker. Along the horizon a paler rim divided sea and sky. Other couples were leaning over the rail or grouped in deckchairs. One pair were entangled in a passionate embrace. Edmund led the way to a point beyond the deck awning and towards the bows of the ship.

Connie accompanied him without speaking, perhaps regretting her extraordinary remark. Looking about him, Edmund pondered how to reintroduce the subject but she forestalled him.

'I oughtn't to have said what I did.'

'Then let's forget it.'

'No, because I want to talk. Nini's too innocent, and there's no one else I can turn to. You're used to listening – you said so. Do you mind if I talk to you?'

'If you think it will help.'

'I don't know what I think any longer. Tell me: do you believe in sin?'

'I believe there's evil in the world, so I suppose I must do, but don't ask me to define sin.'

'Adultery.'

'It's against the Seventh Commandment, but mightn't what you call sinfulness depend on circumstance?'

'You mean it takes two to wreck a marriage. That's what Daddy said.'

'If we're talking about your mother, I couldn't offer an opinion.'

'I'm not asking you to. I just want you to know about us and why Nina's as she is.'

'Very well. Talk if it will make you feel happier, though this sounds like matter for a priest.'

'No!' Connie said, startling Edmund for the second time. 'Mummy wouldn't have the priest because he tried to make her give up Denis Orrey and she preferred Denis to saving her immortal soul.'

'Can you be so sure the two were mutually exclusive?'

'They must be. You see, Mummy chose not to confess and receive the Last Sacrament rather than give up her lover and so renounce her sin.'

'And your sister was distressed by this?'

'Oh no, no, no! You don't understand. Nina knows nothing about it. She thinks Father Farrell arrived too late because the end was very sudden. It was the middle of the night when he had to be sent for, but Mummy wouldn't see him. She turned her head away.'

Was it obstinacy or a great love, Edmund wondered, that had made her do it? Aloud he said: 'So your sister's decision to enter is founded on a lie?'

'My sister is entering to pray for the souls in Purgatory, our mother's among them.'

Edmund realised he had gone too far. 'Then what is it that's troubling you?' he asked, doctor to patient.

'Do you think conduct like Mummy's might be hereditary?'

'My dear girl! You're not even married. How can you commit adultery?'

'I wouldn't, I'm sure I wouldn't. Only – men can't keep their hands to themselves.'

Remembering her flushed and angry face as she rejoined the group with Archie Johnson, Edmund felt his own hand clench.

'I'm sorry if you've just had an unpleasant experience.'

Connie shrugged. 'It wasn't the first time. But it's always me, it's something about me.'

'You're an attractive girl.'

'That's what Denis Orrey said when he tried it while Mummy lay dying. For his sake she'd imperilled herself for ever, and all he could think of was seducing me.'

'Men aren't all like that.'

'I know it. I just seem to attract the ones who are.'

'Like Archie Johnson.'

She did not deny it. 'He was vile. Because I wouldn't let him put his hands where he wanted, he called me names and said I was a tease.'

Edmund's knuckles were white. 'Does it matter what a man like that calls you?'

'I hadn't thought of it like that.'

Her smile when it came was brilliant. Edmund's hand relaxed. He leaned down and kissed her lightly. She did not draw away.

Her lips were cool and fresh, not covered in gluey lipstick. Rosemary's lips had been the same. And scornful. He could still see them spitting out rejection as she broke off their engagement, could hear her contemptuous *Coward, coward, coward.*

'If you have any more trouble with Johnson, tell me,' Edmund said, keeping control of his voice.

'You're a dear.' Connie looked along the deck, empty now except for the entwined couple. 'Do you think we ought to go back?'

'If you would like to.'

'I'd rather go on talking, but I promised Mr Strode a dance. And I suppose I'll have to have one with Mr Gurslake, if only for politeness' sake.'

'I can see you have a full programme.'

Another of her brilliant smiles.

'With everything in life before me, how could I not?' Connie said.

It was over an hour later when she made her way back to the cabin she shared with Nina to make sure her sister had gone to bed and was not engaged in those excessive devotions on which Reverend Mother had poured such scorn. 'A regular life,' she had said. 'Discipline, including discipline in prayer, Constance. This is what Nina needs if she is not to find life as a postulant too irksome. You can help her in this.' The old nun's eyes were wise as she continued: 'You know very well what I mean. Nina has always been dependent on you as big sister. She needs a guiding hand. We must pray that God will allow her to find it in her life as a religious, but it won't come of itself. Discipline can become an aridity of spirit and prayer an emotional wallowing. This is something Nina has not yet realised and I fear she will find the learning hard. All her life she will need the help you give her, which means the help of your prayers.'

She hadn't done much praying this evening, Connie reflected, though she'd certainly eased her spirit. It was astonishing what talking to Edmund Bladon had done. She no longer felt alone. She no longer minded about Archie Johnson and his bitter taunting. She had danced every dance with partners whose names she had already forgotten and felt her heart grow light. She was 'the gay Mrs Martin's' daughter, but independent of her. Free.

She wanted to laugh and skip and shout, but she remembered to open the cabin door quietly, hoping to find Nina in darkness and in her bed, or at worst on her knees before the little statue of Our Lady. To her astonishment, the main light was on and Nina was lying face downwards, fully clothed, across her bed.

'What's the matter?' Connie demanded.

Nina did not move. Her long hair was in disorder about her shoulders. Her dress was rucked up – no, torn – revealing petticoat, stocking top, suspenders.

'What is it? Are you ill?' Connie said again.

She forced herself to put a hand on Nina's shoulder, fearing for one dreadful instant that she was dead. To her relief, the shoulder twitched, but twitched away from her, as though her hand were red hot.

'Nini, it's me, Connie.'

She made to gather her sister in her arms, but Nina rolled away from her and sat up, back to the wall, glaring at her from eyes like burnt holes in the blanket whiteness that was scarcely recognisable as her face. Her arms were crossed over her breasts. It was as though a corpse had reared upright in some form of zombied life.

Connie reached out, but Nina drew her knees up, making herself as small as possible on the bed. Her voice, when it came, was a croak, a whisper.

'Go away.'

'Darling, what is it? Tell Connie.'

The old childhood command got through. The black holes focused for an instant.

'I've been raped,' Nina said.

PART II

ADEN - SUEZ

I

Stafford Briscoe came aboard smartly.

He and his luggage – experience had taught him to travel light – had been down on the waterfront ready and waiting when the boat from the *Karachi* arrived. From the window of his hotel he had watched her glide into harbour that morning, though sea views could hardly be described as one of the hotel's attractions, for the sea here was as unappealing as the land. Dust and aridity, a few stunted palms and a great bloodied lump of rock – that was the Aden Protectorate to those who protected it. It had its strategic advantages at one end of the Red Sea, just as Suez had at the other, but Suez was not impossibly far from the fleshpots of Egypt. Aden was a red dot on the map all by itself.

It had always been an unpopular posting. Stafford Briscoe could quite see why. The heat alone was enough to sap a European, the absence of greenness an affliction to the English eye. Dining last night with the Resident, who had not troubled to conceal his envy that in the morning his guest would sail for home, Briscoe had agreed politely that Aden was one of the less attractive corners of the British Empire, though it was not a view he shared. Aden itself might be drab, but behind it was Arabia – Araby, Arabia Deserta, the Moslems' Mecca, mysterious, still largely unexplored. He had seen more of it than most Europeans, had spent the last few months travelling by camel very much as he might have done a thousand years ago, visiting one Arab ruler after another, bearing gifts and greetings from His Majesty King George V. He agreed with the Resident that his mission was important. 'We've got to keep 'em sweet,' the Resident said, 'because if they ever turn they could throw us out of the place tomorrow. Government is still by consent of the governed, no matter what the colour of their skins.'

Stafford Briscoe did not care about the colour of their skins. In the case of the Arabs, he liked it; he liked their dark, sliding eyes. He did not trust them, but they did not trust him either. Paradoxically, this created a climate of trust. The rules of Arab hospitality ensured that he was unlikely to be slaughtered, and every ruler saw him as a potential ally whose name at least could be invoked in his ceaseless quarrels with other rulers, even if British troops could not. Briscoe listened and responded in his fluent Arabic, implying plenty but never saying too much. While not disagreeing with the Resident's view that it would be all too easy to pitch the British

87

out of Aden, he thought this unlikely so long as the Arab princes continued to quarrel among themselves. It was useful that so many of them were related: it lent an extra dimension to bitterness. Even in his native Gloucestershire he had seen families riven. There was more than one way of interpreting the phrase 'bad blood'.

Briscoe was human enough to deplore such situations and cynical enough to exploit them. He was a subtle and wily negotiator, who had wiped the stars from his eyes together with the first tears he had shed as a man. He was fifty-nine years old, within measuring distance of retirement, and even closer to honours, for in the briefcase which he carried with him at all times reposed the letter that had been waiting for him at Aden, in which one of His Majesty's private secretaries enquired if Mr Briscoe would be prepared to accept the honour of a knighthood in the New Year's Honours List. Briscoe had already drafted his letter of acceptance which would be posted at Marseilles, the overland route being quicker than carrying it by sea mail all the way. He was gratified by the recognition of his services, but he did not pretend to be surprised: he had seen knighthoods given for far less. War profiteers, political supporters, how many now had handles to their names! It was difficult not to conclude that honours once conferred for services to King and Country were now sold in the market-place. Still, Jean would be pleased. His sister and only living relative held a special place in Stafford Briscoe's heart. There had been letters from her, too, waiting at Aden, full of local news and gossip. He had read them, but neither had yet sunk in.

He was glad to get letters – Jean knew that – but she also knew that no letters now quickened his heart. The last one to do so, written on a page torn from a notebook and enclosed in a wartime Forces envelope, lay faded, folded and decaying in the wallet he carried next to that same heart. There would never be another Maurice. Such beings were made once and then the mould was broken. Friends, lovers, need not expect to find their like again. But once that was accepted and a dark, slender figure no longer aroused a surge of hope, it was possible to lead an existence (he would not call it living) rich in interest and material prosperity, and to which now honours were to be joined. No matter that the heart was as dry as the sands of the Empty Quarter. Only doctors considered it a vital organ. Those who had survived the war knew that it could be amputated as effectively as an arm or leg. Not being obvious, the maiming evoked no sympathy. And that too was as its victims would have it. Sympathy was emotion, after all.

Nevertheless, as he greeted the boat's crew and made conversation during the short trip out to the *Karachi*, Stafford Briscoe was animated enough, and he climbed the rope-ladder awaiting him with an agility that would have done credit to a man half his age. He was aware that his unscheduled arrival was putting the Australasian Line to some trouble, and he was grateful both to the Line and to those in Whitehall who had arranged it, and gratified that he should rate their trouble and time. Even so, he did not expect to be greeted by the Captain, for so he assessed the gold braid on the cap, and on no other ship would this have happened, for Captain Meiklejohn was unique. Briscoe, of course, did not know this, though he sensed the officer escorting him was not surprised. Indeed, the officer would have been surprised only if the Old Man had not been on hand to greet his new passenger, for it was well known that there was no detail relating to the *Karachi* that the Captain did not make his concern.

Already that morning he had listened to the Chief's demand to put ashore at Aden the troublesome stoker whom he alleged was responsible for the fire in the bunker – listened, and refused. The terms of service for native crewmen with the Australasian Line stipulated that they could be laid off only in Bombay or London, where welfare organisations existed to ensure that they did not starve. In London some sort of berth would be found which would at least return the man to his own country. In Aden there were no such facilities. To put him ashore here was little better than leaving him a castaway on a desert island. Besides, it was against Company rules.

Angus reminded the Chief of this, not without a certain wry amusement, for it was normally the Chief who was a stickler for rules.

'Right, sir. It shall be as you say.' The Chief's voice over the engine-room telephone was at its most formal, most Scottish. 'I'll have him kept under close surveillance for the rest of the voyage and we'll give him his discharge in London.'

'Thank you, Mr Sutherland.'

'But don't say I didna warn ye if there's trouble – and trouble there will surely be. Ye ken what they say about one rotten apple in a barrel.'

'I'm aware of the saying, aye. But I rely on you to contain the trouble, Mr Sutherland, and protect the rest of the apples. I trust I make myself clear.'

'Aye, aye, sir.'

The Chief managed to make the sound of replacing the handset a comment in itself. Angus smiled. The 'trouble' was no doubt real – Jamie was not sufficiently imaginative to invent it; it was equally likely to be exaggerated. In the eyes of the Chief native crew were human robots; they were not expected to think or feel. Any indication that they did so was a form of insubordination because it disturbed the Chief's view of them. Within the engine-room of the *Karachi* Angus accepted that view; elsewhere he was unsure, not so much because he attributed higher faculties to Lascar seamen but because he was aware that there were other Indians. The wealthy among them played cricket, like Ranji; wrote poetry in English, like Tagore; or took the Prince of Wales on tiger-shooting expeditions; they could hardly be classed as robots even though their skins weren't white. Moreover, they travelled First Class on vessels like the *Karachi*. The ship automatically provided special diets for those who ate no meat, or only certain kinds of meat. With many of them the Captain had made

89

conversation, finding little difference in the views expressed regarding the lower orders, whether the speaker's skin was brown or white. He had heard sentiments uttered in singsong accents which made the Chief's seem liberal. He suspected, though, that he would hear no such openly stated opinions from Stafford Briscoe, and if he did he would be wary of believing them. He had learned to distrust diplomats.

Nevertheless, his voice was cordial as he welcomed the man aboard. Influence, the curse and blessing of the British way of life, was not to be despised, and he was certain Briscoe had influence. Or at least his masters had. The Owners of the Line were not given to telegraphing instructions which might delay the sailing of a vessel, and even if the time were to be made up it meant full steam ahead and more coal for the Chief's greedy engines. Which meant a reduced profit on the voyage. Already there were empty First Class cabins – unusual, but not unknown – but one of those would now be occupied by Stafford Briscoe, who was welcome because of it. Captain Meiklejohn had scarcely finished shaking hands with the new arrival before he was suggesting that he would no doubt like to see his cabin. A steward would show him the way.

The steward on duty happened to be John Joseph Fitzgerald, busy as usual with his meticulous preparations, though it was as yet too early for passengers to be up on deck. The Captain noted his trim turn-out with approval. It was no bad thing that the man of influence should be impressed.

'If you'll kindly come this way, sir . . .' John Joseph had already seized Stafford Briscoe's suitcase, a heavy leather affair plastered with labels from hotels and shipping lines in every corner of the Middle and Far Eastern worlds, when there was the sound of running footsteps, followed by a shout and heavier feet pounding along the starboard side of the ship. The group turned as one man, but Captain Meiklejohn was first through the nearest gap, the rest crowding behind him, eager to hear and see.

John Joseph saw a slight, fleeing brown figure whom he recognised instantly, pursued by an officer. He could not tell more because at that moment the officer launched himself at the fugitive in a flying rugger tackle that brought both of them down on deck.

Three things happened: the officer rose to his feet lithely and delivered a vicious kick; the brown figure cried out in pain and something long and bright and glinting slithered along the deck; and a furious voice cried 'No!' as another figure, that of Edmund Bladon, pinioned the officer from behind at the precise moment that his right foot drew back to deliver a second kick at the unprotected man before him.

'Mr Strode, what is all this?'

The Captain's voice cut in smoothly like a knife through butter. Julian Strode shook himself free, glared at Bladon, saluted, and reported, 'Stowaway, sir.'

'How do you know?'

90

Strode's glance took in the sweat-stained, stubbled figure in dirty shirt and trousers who lay retching and gasping on the deck.

'I observed him climbing into a lifeboat, sir, the third from the stern on the port side. I shouted at him but he took to his heels. I pursued him down to the bridge deck and caught up with him, as you see.'

'Indeed, Mr Strode. You showed commendable quickness. Perhaps less commendable force.'

Strode's face was red, though no one could be sure whether it was due to exertion or embarrassment.

'Sir, the man was armed.' He pointed to the jewelled dagger which had come to rest almost at the Captain's feet. 'Stolen, most likely,' he added.

The figure on the deck gave a convulsive heave and reached out a slender hand towards the dagger. Strode kicked the weapon aside.

'A dangerous little cuss, sir, if you'll pardon the expression. Do you want him arrested and put ashore?'

'Sir, the man needs medical attention.'

Edmund Bladon spoke for the first time. Dressed in sandals, shirt and trousers, the shirt none too securely tucked in, he did not cut quite the figure as ship's surgeon that Captain Meiklejohn could have wished. He was off duty, of course, but that did not seem to have prevented him from obstructing an officer in the carrying out of his. If only Strode's youth and hotheadedness had not led him to go too far. He should have brought the man down and left him there; he had no excuse for that kick.

'Get up!' Captain Meiklejohn commanded the stowaway.

The man got shakily to his knees. The deckboards had abraded the skin of his right cheekbone and a smear of blood stained his face.

'Holy Mother of God!'

John Joseph could not repress the exclamation, for he had not seen the stowaway in daylight before. Despite the stubble and the bloodstains, the face looking up at them was beautiful: dark, liquid eyes, a short straight nose, broad forehead, lips chiselled over flashing teeth. If the girls could get a sight of that they wouldn't be swooning over Rudolph Valentino, John Joseph thought, looking at him.

With an effort, the stowaway stood upright. He staggered, and Bladon put out a hand, but he brushed it aside and they saw a man of medium height, narrow-shouldered and narrower-hipped, but lithe as a cat, his every movement graceful. Beside him, the athletic young Strode looked an oaf.

'What is your name?'

There was no answer to the Captain's question.

'What are you doing on my ship?'

Again, no answer.

The Captain held out his hand for the dagger which Strode was caressing. 'Is this weapon yours?'

John Joseph thought he saw the beginning of a nod, but the stowaway checked it.

Stafford Briscoe stepped in, repeating the Captain's questions in excellent Hindustani.

The dark eyes swivelled towards him, but there was no other sign.

'Can't or won't answer,' the Captain commented.

'Won't, I think,' Briscoe said.

'Perhaps. Well, Mr Bladon, do you wish to treat this patient? If so, I'll have him sent down to the surgery under guard.'

'I'd like to make sure there's no serious damage, sir.' Bladon gave Strode a look. He knew now why he had been unable to take to the young Third Officer. There was something of the school bully in him: all the arrogant assumption of superiority on racial or religious grounds which he himself had resisted so strongly and for which he had paid so high a price.

'Shall I arrange for a boat to put him ashore, sir?' Strode interposed swiftly. 'After the doctor has attended to him, of course.'

Captain Meiklejohn hesitated. His instinct was to say yes. Something about this stowaway spelt trouble. He was anxious to be rid of him. But the *Karachi*'s departure from Aden had already been delayed. The tide was now ebbing strongly: he could not risk losing that tide. If he did, he might well lose his place in the queue for Suez and the slow, dispiriting crawl through the Canal. That could mean docking a day late at Tilbury, especially if there was bad weather in Biscay and the Channel. Neither passengers nor owners would be pleased.

'No,' he said. 'He'll have to work his passage.'

It seemed to John Joseph that the stowaway relaxed.

The Captain's mind, however, was on where this could best be done. Not where the Chief could get at him, that would be asking for trouble. Nowhere where he might encounter passengers, who, when not the victims and when the thief was handsome, were apt to romanticise stealing, which was how the Captain regarded the young man's act. Certainly nowhere where, in the course of domestic duties, he might have access to their cabins in case he was indeed a thief; the Captain was well aware that not all valuables were deposited as requested in the security of the Purser's safe.

'When the surgeon has looked at him,' he said, 'have him taken to the Second Class galley and see that some menial task is found.' The native cooks and their assistants, very different from the white, tall-hatted chefs, could be relied on to give him the worst jobs and to keep an eye on him. They would also ensure that he slept on the worst pallet in the communal dormitory. The handsome lad who had tried to cheat the Australasian Line of the fare from Bombay to London would not enjoy the voyage. Not that he could have enjoyed it so far; it must have been stifling under the heavy tarpaulin cover of the lifeboat into which young Strode had seen him climb. How had he managed for food? And, more important, drink? Had someone kept him supplied? Did he have allies on board? Was he some sort of agitator? All these thoughts went through the Captain's mind. But not a muscle of his face moved as he watched Strode lead the stowaway away, escorted now by two deckhands who marched one on each side of him. Throughout, the unscheduled passenger had said no word, though the Captain was inclined to agree with Stafford Briscoe that it was a case of won't, not can't.

He turned now to his other new arrival, who was standing quietly to one side.

'I'm afraid you're having a dramatic introduction to the *Karachi*, Mr Briscoe. I assure you, the event you've just witnessed is unusual. I've never had such a thing happen aboard my ship before.'

'All the more reason for me to be impressed by your smooth handling of it, Captain.'

Angus Meiklejohn's distrust of diplomats flared. All right if the remark could be taken at face value, but had there been a sneering undertone? To conceal his unease, he continued with the same smoothness with which Briscoe had just credited him: 'One of the disadvantages of such incidents is that they destroy the social graces. I have made no introductions as yet. The officer in charge of the boat crew will already have introduced himself –' Briscoe nodded – 'and Mr Strode, the Third, to whose alertness we owe the capture of this felon, is at the moment otherwise engaged.' He avoided looking at Edmund Bladon, to whom the remark had really been addressed, but went on, still turning to Briscoe: 'But perhaps I may introduce the ship's surgeon before his concern for humanity obliges him to go below. Mr Bladon, who joined us on the outward voyage – Mr Briscoe.'

He stepped back to allow the two men to shake hands.

Neither moved. Both of them stood tense, waiting. At last Bladon held out his hand. 'An unexpected meeting – Stafford.'

Briscoe looked at him – and looked away.

'We have met many times in rural Gloucestershire,' he told the Captain, 'but it is some eight or ten years ago. I'm afraid I don't care to shake the hand of an ex-jailbird, a conscientious objector who refused to fight for his country.' (Like his betters; like Maurice.) 'If that's what you carry as ship's surgeon, I can only hope it's not my misfortune to fall ill.'

Angus dared not look at Edmund Bladon as he said, 'I hope so too, Mr Briscoe. Sick passengers are something any captain deplores, though I flatter myself the medical attention aboard the *Karachi* is as of high a standard as everything else.'

He did not know whether he was defending his ship or Edmund Bladon; he had an uncomfortable feeling it was both, though he could not but despise a man who left boys like Andy to face the horrors of the Western Front while he skulked behind prison bars. Except that ugly rumours had begun to trickle out about the treatment of conscientious objectors, for whom there was still no amnesty. Deprived of the vote by a government which had been unable to break them by other methods, they had no part in the land fit for heroes to live in which was allegedly being built. Yet 'No more war' was now everybody's slogan; in peacetime there was a plethora of pacifists. It was not so much Bladon's views which were wrong as the time chosen for expressing them.

Angus switched off. At least Bladon was a good doctor, with qualifications second to none. And he was no weed: there had been nothing unscientific in the way he pinioned young Strode, who should have known better than to use unnecessary force, let alone be vindictive, when making a shipboard arrest. As captain, he was going to have to speak to both of them. He did not relish the thought as he nodded in dismissal to the doctor and turned to Stafford Briscoe once again.

'If you're still prepared to sail with us, Mr Briscoe, I'll have you taken to your cabin.'

Briscoe bowed slightly. The Captain beckoned to the Irish steward who had been standing silently by and instructed him where to take the new First Class passenger. As the steward picked up his bag Briscoe spoke.

'Captain, a word in your ear if you'll not think me impertinent. That stowaway – watch him.'

'Trouble?'

'Not in the way you're thinking. The man's not political.'

Beneath the sweat and dirt and blood Briscoe had detected a caste mark. A high-caste mark. The jewelled dagger, forgotten in the Captain's hands, might well turn out to be the man's own property.

He said carefully: 'I think he's a potential embarrassment. You might like to bear that in mind in your treatment of him, for unless I'm much mistaken, he's something very different from what he seems.'

At four o'clock in the afternoon of the following day, with Aden well behind them, Edmund Bladon knocked at the Captain's door. It was unbearably hot. The ship had begun the slow passage up the Red Sea which at Suez would reduce to a crawl, and no breeze of passage freshened the still air. Most passengers lay flat in cabins loud with the whirr of fans whose disturbance created no coolness. Ice in drinks melted before they could be downed, and the jugs of iced water in every cabin were reduced to tepid insipidness. For those passengers who consulted him about their discomfort Edmund could do nothing beyond reminding them to take plenty of salt, to rest during the worst of the midday heat, and to eat lightly – this last unnecessary because no one had appetite.

He had none himself, bowed with the news he carried, as he sat, saying little, through lunch. There were many absentees, but Bobby Vane was present, fretful and capricious and still avoiding Edmund's eye; his mother, over-indulgent as ever, dabbed discreetly at the beads of perspiration on her face; Bert Gurslake informed everyone (as if they did not know it!) that Florrie was feeling the heat; and farther down the long table, Stafford Briscoe in a lightweight tropical suit was correct and neat and eating sensibly, every inch His Majesty's representative.

It had been rotten luck running into Briscoe. For Edmund it brought back all too much of the past; the comfortable house in Gloucestershire, his parents, his brother Roger, music spilling out on to the terrace on summer evenings – his own voice and, at the piano, Rosemary. The Briscoes had often enough been guests on that terrace. Jean Briscoe was Aunt Anne's best friend, the two organising spinsters of the parish who between them had everything under control. When in 1916 Anne abandoned Gloucestershire for St John's Wood, she abandoned Jean as well. There was something about a quarrel, though she had never been specific and Edmund, fearing he was the cause, had never asked. There were too many things of which he was the cause, witting or unwitting: the slow decay of the estate which his father, paralysed by a stroke, could no longer manage but from which by the old man's wish he was debarred. Anne did what she could; there was a manager; but how different it had seemed ten years ago, with Roger all set to inherit and Edmund's own career in music opening up. If Roger had lived . . . but if he had, might it not have been to figure as a name in the casualty lists which appeared under the heading 'On Active Service' day after day in *The Times*? The brothers had seldom agreed but it hadn't mattered: Edmund had been Roger's best friend, as Roger had been Edmund's until his death from a wasting disease. Thereafter their father's hopes had been concentrated on Edmund, whose refusal to take part in the war had been seen as a double betrayal resented with double bitterness.

Edmund ran a finger round his collar, clean half an hour ago but already beginning to go limp and sticky as sweat soaked into the starch. But Captain Meiklejohn expected his officers to be correctly dressed at all times. He had intimated as much yesterday when suggesting to Edmund that even though he was off duty when the stowaway had been arrested, his appearance had left much to be desired. Particularly since he had chosen to obstruct an officer in the performance of his duty, which was that of arresting an armed man.

'With respect, sir, Mr Strode did not know he was armed. We none of us did until the man fell and the dagger clattered from his clothing. He made no attempt to use it on Mr Strode.'

'He'd not drawn it so far, I grant you, but we cannot be sure what he'd have done. You've no wish to be treating knife wounds, have you, Mr Bladon? Especially not fatal ones?'

'No, sir.'

'Then perhaps you'll be good enough, should we have another such incident –' the Captain allowed himself what passed with him for a smile – 'to allow the officer concerned to proceed with the execution of his duty, which will not in future include delivering a kick.'

'Yes, sir.'

'So as long as we understand each other on that point, Mr Bladon, I believe there is no more to say. Incidentally, I assume you found nothing much amiss with our unscheduled passenger when you examined him?'

'No, sir. The man is basically well nourished, about eighteen or twenty years of age, and though he's suffering from the effects of his recent deprivation and some bruising, there's nothing wrong with him.'

'Did he answer your questions?'

'No, sir. He refused to say a word, but I have the impression he understands English. He was quick to obey my commands.'

'Mr Briscoe also maintains he understands English. And by the way, I was unaware that you and he were socially acquainted. The Line's chief medical officer is sparing on personal details – it's your medical qualifications he thinks I ought to know.'

The chief medical officer had had reason to be sparing in his own case, Edmund reflected, though he liked the Captain for this form of apology. It would have been easy for him to say nothing. It made all the worse the tidings he was bringing now.

When he had asked this morning for an appointment, the Captain had shown no curiosity. He had merely asked if four o'clock that afternoon would be time enough, and put down the telephone. Now he sat behind his desk and looked at Edmund.

'You wanted to see me, Mr Bladon. Does that mean one of the passengers is ill?'

'Yes, sir. Miss Nina Martin, eighteen years old and travelling First Class with her sister.'

'Something infectious?'

Every Captain's dread . . .

'No, sir. I hope not. She alleges she's been raped.'

If Captain Meiklejohn was shocked, he did not show it.

'Alleges.' He seized on the word. 'That implies you doubt her.'

'Not necessarily, sir, but there's no proof.'

'Hm. And isn't this the young lady who's all set to become a nun?'

The Captain's voice was loud with unvoiced suspicion.

'Yes, sir.'

'Have you examined her?'

'I have, sir, but the alleged incident took place two days ago, on the night of the fancy hat dance.'

'Yet you're only reporting it now?'

'It was never reported to me, sir. She did not appear for meals yesterday and her sister claimed it was due to the heat. When she was still unwell this morning, I insisted on seeing her.'

Edmund did not enjoy the recollection of his visit to the Martin girls' cabin. Connie had stood at the door insisting that there was nothing wrong with her sister except the heat, which was affecting other passengers, though it was kind of the doctor to call.

'Then if there's nothing wrong, you won't mind my examining her. It'll only take a minute,' Edmund said. Then, as Connie still blocked the doorway: 'Come, my dear, it's only common sense. To say nothing of

96

Company regulations. What do you think we carry a doctor for? We want you and other passengers to enjoy the voyage. You can't do that if you're ill.'

'She's not ill.'

'Don't you think I might be the best judge? You don't look too good yourself.'

She didn't. In the last two days something had happened to Connie's sparkle. She was like a jewel dulled. She had appeared punctually at mealtimes, fended off enquiries about Nina, and played with the food on her plate; but she said little, escaped to her cabin at the first opportunity, and never appeared on deck. Edmund missed her, and had asked himself repeatedly if he were responsible for this change. Had something he had said or done on the night of the dance distressed her? Was she avoiding him?

She was certainly avoiding his eyes as she stood in the cabin doorway. Beyond, he glimpsed Nina lying on her bed, her face to the wall, her long hair in disorder, the rumpled sheet pulled tightly round her a testimony to restlessness.

The fan whirred uselessly as Edmund pushed past Connie and said in his most professional voice, 'Good morning. I'm sorry the heat's too much for you. I came to see if I could help.'

He sat on the end of the bed. Nina shrank away from him. If she could, she would have pressed herself into the wall.

'Nina, what is it? I thought we were friends.'

He laid a hand on her shoulder.

'Don't touch her!' Connie cried.

'Has Nina lost her voice? Is that the trouble?'

'Go away! Please go away!' The wail from the sheeted form answered that question.

'Nina, look at me,' Edmund commanded. 'You know who I am. You feel as if you'd known me for ever, or so you said the other night.'

The sheeted form shuddered. 'That was before . . . before . . .'

'Before she was raped,' Connie said.

'Good God!'

Edmund jerked the sheet from the girl before him and saw an almost unrecognisable face. The smooth, voluptuous cheeks were puffy; the reddened eyes were watery and shrunken in dark pools which Edmund at first took to be bruises but realised later were no such thing.

'What happened?' he asked Connie.

'I don't know. I came back to our cabin about midnight on the night of the dance and found her like – like this. She'd come down earlier – you remember her going – and I thought she'd be asleep . . . She won't talk to me, won't tell me what happened . . .' Connie's voice broke.

'Did it happen in here, Nina?'

'Next door . . . the cabin next door . . .'

Now occupied by Stafford Briscoe, but empty on the night of the dance.

'Do you know the man?'

A shudder. 'He had something over his face. A mask. I thought it was fancy dress. He came at me from behind, from the shadows . . .'

'Did you scream or struggle?'

'I was afraid to. He had a knife.'

Into Edmund's mind came the vision of a jewelled dagger, long and glinting, clattering along the deck.

'What was it like, this knife?'

'Long and sharp.' Another shudder. 'Oh, please don't make me go on.'

'You must,' Edmund said. 'He might attack others. Would you want this to happen to someone else? Imogen Stiles, say; or Cynthia; or Connie.' He realised he did not doubt what Nina said.

There was a long silence.

'Did he speak to you at all?' Edmund prompted.

A shake of the ravaged head.

'Was he a big man? Tall or short?'

'I don't know. I couldn't believe it was happening.'

She was still in shock, he judged.

'Why didn't you send for me at once?' he asked Connie.

'She wouldn't let me, wouldn't let me leave her. She swore she'd kill herself.'

'You could have asked your stewardess to fetch me.'

'I was too upset. I didn't think of it.'

It was all too likely, he supposed, framing his next question.

'What immediate steps did you take?'

'She had a bath. Several baths. We used up a whole bottle of disinfectant.'

A useless precaution, but all trace of evidence would be gone.

'I'll have to examine you,' he said gently to Nina. 'Your sister will stay with you.'

Nina's passivity frightened him more than her earlier protests, but he was as quick and thorough as he knew how.

'May I know the result of your examination, Mr Bladon?' Captain Meiklejohn was asking now.

'Inconclusive, sir, I'm afraid. Miss Nina is not technically a virgin, but that proves nothing in itself. There was some slight swelling and bruising, but of course all trace of semen had been washed away, and since the alleged rape occurred thirty-six hours before I saw her, I could not swear on oath that it took place.'

'But you think it did?'

'I believe her, yes, sir.'

Even as he spoke Edmund thought of Bobby Vane and the self-induced sickness brought on by the prospect of school. Nina Martin had wanted to enter a convent, but now that its portals gaped who knew what revulsion

98

might have overwhelmed her and made her seek a means of invalidation? What better than a rape?

'Hm.' Captain Meiklejohn considered. Whatever the doctor believed, he himself was sceptical. 'Is Miss Nina an attractive girl?'

'Any such evaluation can only be subjective, but I would say so, sir. Yes.'

'Think she led some man on and then alleged she wasn't willing?'

'Not deliberately, sir, but . . .'

Into Edmund's mind came a picture of Nina's innocently voluptuous body, unexploited, unexplored. She might without realising it have aroused some man to a pitch of dangerous desire. Her very refusal to become involved in the give and take of social converse represented a challenge. Had someone taken advantage of the masked ball to follow her, waylay her? Where did truth end?

'. . . but I have to allow it is not impossible,' Edmund concluded.

'Then for the time being, Mr Bladon, I must ask you to say nothing about this. I am sure we can rely on the discretion of the two young ladies –' though the Captain was sure of no such thing, for if it was a bid for attention the victim would want it to be known; yet at stake was the safety and comfort of his passengers, the honour of his ship and of the Line. 'Let us not conclude without more definite evidence,' he said firmly, 'that we have a rapist on board. A stowaway and a rapist on the same voyage, that would surely be too much of a good thing.'

Or were they the same . . .?

He refused to contemplate the possibility, and the ship's surgeon took his leave.

Florrie Gurslake tapped at the door of the Martin girls' cabin and entered without waiting for a 'Come in'.

She had not wanted to come, but Bert had insisted. 'Go on, old girl, it's as good a chance as you'll ever get to spell things out to little Nina. That sister of hers has got to leave her sometime. I'll keep watch and let you know the minute Connie's up on deck.

'It don't seem hardly fair, Bert. Not when the kid isn't well.'

'She's only feeling the heat, same as you are. She makes more fuss about it, that's all.'

'Dr Bladon's been with her.'

' 'Course he has. He's sweet on her sister. And maybe little Nina's sweet on him. Maybe she's jealous of her sister. What better way to get the doc's attention than by saying she feels ill.'

'You mean she's just pretending?'

'I mean she's not just suffering from the heat. There's something more to this "sudden indisposition".' Bert brought the phrase out triumphantly.

Florrie was inclined to believe him, if only because Connie's behaviour was so odd. Her small face looked older, tighter, under its cluster of red-gold curls. Poor Captain Johnson had spent the whole of lunchtime attempting to draw her out. She just said yes and no, and that nice young doctor abetted her. The pair of them had been almost rude. And Captain Johnson such a fine young man, with his good looks enhanced by that scar. And his decoration – he must be quite a hero. Most girls would jump at him. As Miss Imogen Stiles was not far off doing. She gazed at him adoringly. And the Reverend Septimus and Mrs Stiles were ever on hand to push her forward whenever Miss Connie was up to her cold-shoulder tricks.

It wasn't only his daughter that the Reverend Septimus was pushing, either. He was pushing himself as well. It would be Armistice Day before they reached Suez. He wanted to hold a ceremony on deck. For a variety of reasons, heat being only one of them, his fellow passengers were unenthusiastic. 'But two minutes. For the Fallen,' urged the Reverend Septimus. It was difficult to refuse, even though everyone knew that something like half an hour would have elapsed by the time they had all assembled and sung a patriotic hymn, followed by a short prayer and an address, which was the object of the exercise (no one was in any doubt about that) and the dance band's trumpeter had played the Last Post to introduce the two minutes' silence and a wavering Reveillé to mark its end. And half an hour at eleven o'clock in the morning while the ship crept like a barge through the Canal would be a purgatory of flat brown banks and flat brown water which not even a breeze of passage would dispel.

'What do you usually do on board?' Cynthia Vane asked the First Officer. She had no wish to participate; she would prefer to spend the two minutes in her cabin, alone with Robert's photograph. The First Officer explained that as a rule the flag was lowered, with the Captain and his officers at attention on the deck, and everyone, passengers and crew, stood for the two minutes' silence before returning to their everyday tasks. Only the ship's great engines continued to drive forward, untended for two minutes by Chief and engine-room crew, though in the Canal where speed was minimal they might very well stop too.

'I should have thought that was sufficient,' Cynthia said pointedly.

It would have taken a sharper point to pierce the Reverend's hide. He hastened to explain that without the presence of a cleric it was as much as could be expected of the Captain. Cynthia, filled with memories of other Armistice Days, including that one when for the first time in four years the guns had fallen silent while in homes all over the country the full realisation of loss and peace sank in, could only murmur that she thought the act of remembrance was essentially private.

'So it is, dear lady,' the Reverend Septimus assured her. 'So it very rightly is. The many private acts come together in an act of public remembrance. Every hero lies buried in the Unknown Warrior's tomb in Westminster Abbey, and the Cenotaph in Whitehall stands for every unmarked grave.'

The Reverend Septimus was a small man with a fine voice, which he cultivated, tutored by Mrs Stiles, who had early realised that her husband needed to make the most of his slender assets if preferment was to come his way. People assumed that his name, Septimus, indicated a seventh child, whereas in fact he had been named for a rich relation who had then left his fortune elsewhere. It was the first of many disappointments that had starred the clergyman's life, his decision to enter the mission field being the biggest. He had seen himself administering from headquarters in London, or Calcutta at the very least. Instead, he had been moved from one remote station to another, accompanied by his ever more grimly disappointed wife. Imogen had been educated at a school for missionaries' daughters in New Delhi, but that had been a disappointment too; not even the city's elevation to administrative capital status in 1911 could conceal the fact that Calcutta was still the business and social capital of the Raj. Now, at his wife's insistence, they were taking Imogen home to launch her on the marriage market, and it was on his wife's money that they were travelling First Class. In her view the money was well spent, not only for the comfort but for the contacts: you never knew who you might meet. People like Captain Johnson and Third Officer Strode, or even Dr Bladon, all unmarried, made up for the vulgarity of those like the Gurslakes, or the presence of a native stowaway on the ship.

The discovery and capture of the stowaway had been a major talking point. Julian Strode found himself elevated to the status of hero, a situation to which he was not at all averse. The tale lost nothing in the telling; indeed, it gained accretions every time, and those like Stafford Briscoe who had witnessed the episode had some difficulty in recognising the variant versions, which included a knife attack on the Captain and the need for three strong sailors to hold the mad native down.

But all the passengers were agreed on one thing: the stowaway's colour made everything about the episode worse. A white stowaway might have been romantic; a black one was a dangerous liberty. It was only right that he should have been consigned to the kitchens; 'a slave to the galley', as someone said. The *Karachi*, like the Empire, ran on unskilled native labour, and by means of this placement the balance was restored.

Stafford Briscoe observed all this with the same wry detachment which he had donned as armour through life. Since Maurice died at Loos he had forced himself to see the world as a comedy of manners lest it topple into tragedy. Comedy evoked amusement, intellectual appreciation, but it did not tear the heart. A man could almost believe such an organ no longer existed were it not for the occasional remembrance such as he had felt at sight of the stowaway on the deck before him and banished to the back of his mind. He no longer felt desire, although he had occasionally accepted one of the boys offered him as acts of hospitality in Arabia, and hated himself for sullying Maurice's memory with a purely carnal act; yet he was achingly aware of incompleteness. The figurehead who was shortly to become Sir Stafford Briscoe was only half a man.

101

Would Bladon remember Maurice? The boy had visited him only occasionally in Gloucestershire. Prudence required that their life together should be in anonymous London, or on the Continent. The boy's delight in Paris had been infectious, causing Briscoe himself to view the well-known city with new eyes, and later there had been walking tours in the Alps and one splendid, heady summer in a villa near Fiesole. Everything implicit in being a man of means and culture had flowered for Briscoe in the two years before the war, and had ended in August 1914 with pulling strings to get Maurice a commission in a good regiment, which had all too soon embarked for France. There had been letters, accounts of leave in Paris, still the capital of the arts; then a silence which had driven Briscoe almost to the verge of breakdown before the listing 'Missing, Believed Killed'. That was the end. All trace of Maurice had vanished. His commanding officer wrote to the boy's 'uncle', since that was how Briscoe had been styled as next of kin, that Maurice had last been seen leading his men into action and that the loss of such a gallant officer would be keenly felt. Briscoe threw the letter into the fire burning that chill autumn morning in the study in Gloucestershire and set about reconstructing his life. He was fifty-one, but he offered his services to the War Office, and found himself engaged on secret work, which had led naturally into diplomatic assignments when peace came back again. He had heard at a distance of the death of Roger Bladon, of the disgrace of Edmund's refusal to join up, the breaking off of his engagement and the deeper disgrace of his appearance before a conscientious objectors' tribunal and subsequent imprisonment. He had heard, too, from his sister of her quarrel with Anne Bladon when Anne had taken Edmund's part, and had grieved as for any loss of love, whatever its nature, but had felt nothing in what used to be his heart.

On his rare visits to Gloucestershire he had avoided the Bladons. He had heard that Anne had pulled strings in London and in part financed Edmund's medical training, but he had never thought to meet him here. The shock of seeing him on the deck of the *Karachi* and hearing Captain Meiklejohn introduce him had shaken his usual calm and led him to react with a vehemence he believed he had forgotten. While not disowning it, he regretted it. His few ill-chosen words had lost nothing in their inevitable repeating, with the result that many passengers had turned away from Bladon, which had never been Briscoe's intent. The Reverend Septimus Stiles almost had his womenfolk draw in their skimpy skirts in passing; Mrs Vane and Captain Johnson, war widow and war hero, avoided speaking to him; but the redhead with the Irish lilt in her voice continued to make conversation, though on Bladon's other side at mealtimes there was now an empty place: the redhead's sister, struck down by the heat, 'or so she *says*,' Mrs Gurslake informed him under cover of another of her Bert's pointed comments on those who had not done their bit.

'And what did *you* do in the war, Mr Gurslake?' Stafford Briscoe asked smoothly.

Bert looked affronted. 'Me? On government contract work I was.'

'Indeed. Did you make much profit?'

'What's that got to do with you?'

'Nothing, I'm thankful to say. Some men gave their lives, their time, their talents, and others received back an hundredfold.'

Bert suspected he was being got at. He'd distrusted Briscoe from the start, acting superior when no one knew a thing about him. What had he been up to in Arabia that he wouldn't talk about?

'There's something I can't take to about him,' he confided to Florrie.

'He's quite a gent,' Florrie said.

'So what? So are half the fools who run the bleedin' country, and look what a mess they got it in.'

'What you want? Trade union government?'

'Nah. What we want's a strong man, someone we can all get behind and show the wogs and socialists and commies we ain't going to be pushed around. Take that wog what stowed away: d'you think such a thing would have happened in the old days?' (He meant before the war.) 'We gone soft, that's what it is, talking about giving them a say in the way they're governed. Might as well hand it to 'em on a plate.'

'They managed before we got there.'

'They was just savages then.'

Florrie held her peace. She had no interest in wogs or savages, only in supplying her Bert's wants, and if he thought that by deflecting Nina's desire to become a religious he could lay hold of her dowry for a while, Florrie was ready to do what she could to help him, no matter what Dr Bladon had advised. Of course now that they knew Dr Bladon was a conchie (and Bert said they ought to have guessed it from the start) who had spent much of the war imprisoned by his own side, Bert maintained that his medical opinions were as tarnished as his war record, but Florrie was not sure she agreed. She liked Edmund Bladon; she would gladly have consulted him about the indigestion that had troubled her lately, but if her Bert thought otherwise she was not going to go against his wishes. Not after twenty-five years.

For the same reason she was prepared to call on Nina Martin when Connie was out of the way, though only she knew the hesitation behind her assured-sounding knock on the Martins' cabin door, or that her hasty entrance was due more to nervousness than to discourtesy.

The girl lying on the bed jerked convulsively as the door opened, and sat up, knees to chin and arms clasped round her knees, squeezing herself into as small a space as she could manage, her back pressed against the wall. At sight of Florrie she relaxed to the extent that her eyes became less staring, but her body remained taut.

'Hello, dear, how are we? Feeling a bit better, I hope?'

Florrie advanced into the cabin, which seemed to her unusually airless.

'This heat's quite something, ain't it? It had me knocked out flat. My Bert was quite worried, I had to pull myself together for his sake.'

103

Receiving no response, Florrie advanced further and lowered herself on to Connie's bed, dabbing at her face already wet with perspiration which was causing her make-up to run. Her dress shields too were soaked – so much for underarm protection! – and her clothes clung stickily. The dagger-like hair ornament impaling her topknot had slipped and was askew.

Nina made a great effort. 'Thank you for calling, Mrs Gurslake, but all I want is to be left alone.'

'All you think you want, dearie,' Florrie corrected, 'but sometimes we have to make an effort for others, like I did for my Bert. Your sister now, she'd be so much happier if you was up on deck.'

'Connie understands.'

'I'm sure she does. We all do. But you can't stay moping in this cabin. It's like the Black Hole of Calcutta in here.'

'The fan's on.'

'It'd take more than a fan to cool this lot.'

'Please, Mrs Gurslake, I don't want to see anybody. I want to be alone.'

'Time enough for that when you're in your convent, dearie. No need to practise in advance.'

A shudder went through Nina which Florrie misinterpreted. She reached out to pat the girl.

'If you've had a change of mind or heart about it, it's nothing to be ashamed of. We all of us make mistakes. Look at marriage: how much better if some couples had thought twice before they tied the knot. So if it's the convent that's worrying you, dear, don't let it. It's only natural for a girl to want a boy. And a boy to want a girl. It's what Nature intended. Believe me, Auntie Florrie knows.'

'Don't talk like that!'

'I don't suppose you and your sister was brought up ignorant. You know what's what, I dare say, but with your poor mother gone to her rest it may be that an older lady . . . I mean, you don't know it all, do you? Of course every girl's got to be careful, though even if she ain't there's a way . . . I should know, though I was a married woman, but my Bert didn't want no family. Reckoned kids was a nuisance, and when I look at Mrs Vane and that spoilt brat of a Bobby I must say I agree. But your own kid's always different, as I hope you'll find out some day. Tell me, dear – because you know you can tell anything to Auntie Florrie – have you ever, well, really kissed a boy?'

It wasn't what Florrie had been going to say, but something about Nina's rigidity was getting through to her. The little talk wasn't going as she had planned.

'I thought perhaps you hadn't,' she went on when Nina failed to answer. 'An older woman can always tell. There's something about a girl who hasn't . . . Well, dear, you know what I'm getting at.'

'Mrs Gurslake –'

'Auntie Florrie, dear.'

'Mrs Gurslake, I don't want you here. Please go away.'

'I can take a hint, as well as another.' Florrie shifted her bulk on Connie's bed. Her Bert would be disappointed, but there was nothing more she could do. She made one last effort as she stood upright. The action sent a trickle of perspiration down her back.

'There's nothing so romantic as being on board ship,' she assured Nina. 'Why, you can see it going on all around you, what with the Doc and Archie Johnson making sheep's eyes at your sister, and the Captain himself getting a bit sweet on Mrs Vane. Oh, I've watched him –' as Nina's body jerked again – 'and it's like I say: a woman of experience can soon tell. There's something in the way he looks at her, though his face don't move a muscle. I bet he'd like to get between her legs . . . So you see, dear, Bert and me, we don't want you to miss what Nature intended just because you've got this fancy you want to be a nun. And you're made for love if ever a girl was. My Bert says so, and believe me he should know.'

'Get out!'

The sheeted form that rose up violently before her could have been the Angel of Death as Nina advanced on her.

'Get out, get out, get out!'

The little fists rained blows on Florrie's shoulders as the older woman turned, shielding her face which, streaked with mascara and smeared with lipstick, resembled a carnival mask.

'You filthy, evil monster! You devil in human flesh! Get out before I kill you. Oh God, what am I going to do?'

Nina's voice had risen to a scream. Feet were running down the corridor. A frightened stewardess. Then Connie. Dr Bladon. 'Nini! Nini, what is it?' as Connie took her sister in her arms and turned an anguished face on Florrie. 'You wicked, cruel woman! Can't you see what you've done?'

'I ain't done nothing,' Florrie said with dignity, though she found she was addressing the wall as the other three busied themselves with the sobbing writhing bundle that was Nina. 'We was just having a little talk, that's all.'

II

'What is the matter with Nina Martin?'

It was Cynthia Vane who spoke, but the question was on everybody's lips. Even among those First Class passengers who did not know Nina, rumour was beginning to run riot, and strangers stopped Connie as she scurried between her cabin, the dining saloon and the hospital to ask how her sister was. To all of them, as to those she knew better, Connie made the same reply: 'She's resting. She'll be all right in a day or so.' Dr Bladon said the same; but which was voice and which was echo no one liked to ask. The Reverend Septimus Stiles, who had appointed himself guardian of public health by extension of what he deemed to be the clergyman's role as guardian of public morals, did go so far as to ask Dr Bladon if Miss Nina was suffering from an infectious disease, and received the reply: 'Not noticeably. In any case, there are strict regulations governing any such outbreak on board ship and you may rest assured that they are being followed to the letter.' Which left the reverend gentleman as ignorant as he was before.

Florrie Gurslake was markedly reticent in her questions; her comments were something else. 'She's gone mad, that's what,' she informed anyone who would listen. 'Stands to reason she was unbalanced, going into a convent like that, and it's all been too much for her. She's had to be put under restraint. Shrieking and screaming, she was, something terrible – I saw her.' – 'When was this? Where were you?' someone asked her. Florrie did not elaborate.

She had been more shaken than she cared to admit by the results of her 'little talk'. She had been prepared for hostility or incomprehension, but not for what she got. To be called a devil, a filthy woman, because for her Bert's sake – not to mention Nina's – she had ventured to play a mother's part, left her breathless with indignation, a sentiment not soothed by Bert's unfeeling 'You must've done it wrong.' Done what wrong? Florrie asked herself, for she considered she had been the soul of tact; yet Nina's small clenched fists raining blows upon her, her contorted face and those dreadful, rending screams, derided her, made her wonder if she was indeed to blame. She would have liked to ask Dr Bladon, but she could not forget his face as he turned to her, hovering helpless on the fringes of activity: 'You stupid woman,' he had said. 'Go away.' So she had not consulted him about the indigestion that had assailed her once again and refused to be assuaged by bicarbonate of soda, her Bert's sovereign remedy. Time enough for that when things were back to normal – if there was such a thing as normality aboard this blasted ship, what with its native stowaway and now her Bert muttering something incomprehensible about Captain Johnson having threatened him. Which did not make for an easy atmosphere in the dining saloon. Only the newcomer, Mr Briscoe, seemed unaware of it.

In this, as in much else, Stafford Briscoe was deceptive. He was a trained observer, after all, and although he did not know the reasons for the network of sympathies and antipathies that lay like a cobweb gathering the dust of confrontations, he was aware of them. There was Bladon, another trained observer, dignified in isolation, saying little because few people spoke to him, but watching all the time. There was Captain Johnson, who also polarised opinion; Connie Martin, Herbert Gurslake and Bladon obviously detested him, while the Stiles family considered him the pattern of young manhood, and Mrs Gurslake hovered somewhere in between. There was Cynthia Vane, who kept herself discreetly distant, especially from the puppydog antics of young Strode. There was her son, a detestable little brat except that even at eight he had the dark slenderness that would make him just such another as Maurice some day. And over all, present even in absence, was Captain Meiklejohn with whom he, Briscoe, was invited to have a drink that night.

The invitation had been delivered by a steward. 'Captain Meiklejohn presents his compliments and would be glad if Mr Briscoe would join him and the Chief Engineer for a drink in his cabin at six p.m. this evening.' Briscoe had treated it as the royal command it was. He could not know how honoured he was to be invited to share the Captain's precious half-hour with the Chief. The two men had discussed inviting him to join them (for naturally Angus had told Jamie of what had befallen Nina Martin) because he was, as Angus said, despite his dislike of diplomats, the one male passenger who could be totally exonerated of any suspicion of the rape.

'Aye. If the lassie speaks truth.'

The Chief's voice was loud with doubt. He distrusted Papists; he distrusted women; he doubly distrusted Papist women who wanted to become nuns. It would be an exaggeration to say that he was uncharitable enough to feel Nina deserved what had happened to her, but he felt she was in some way to blame. And if, as he suspected, the rape existed only in her fevered imagination, she was solely and entirely at fault. He listened without interrupting while Angus gave Stafford Briscoe an account of the situation, but could not repress a snort.

'Mr Sutherland is sceptical,' Briscoe noted.

'To some extent I am myself.' It was a delicate balancing act to keep a foot in both camps, but Angus managed it. 'It would not be the most difficult thing in the world for the girl to invent such a story – for what reason we can only guess; but if it's true, then every woman on board is at risk and I can't afford to take chances.'

'And every man is a suspect,' Briscoe said.

'Not every man,' the Chief objected. 'I can vouch for the engine-room crew on duty. I was with them myself at the time. We'd had trouble with a gasket – och, 'twas nothing – but I'd looked in on them to make sure all was well.'

Angus suppressed a smile. It was so like Jamie. The least hint of trouble with his beloved engines and he was there, like an anxious parent. Stafford Briscoe, however, was unmoved by this devotion to duty.

'Surely it would be difficult in any case,' he murmured, 'for a man in oil-stained overalls and black with coal dust to make his way unchallenged from the engine-room to First Class. It is difficult enough to pass to First Class from Second, let alone from the bowels of the ship.'

He was stating the obvious and they knew it. For similar reasons most of the rest of the crew could be ruled out.

'Moreover, rape is seldom premeditated,' Briscoe continued. 'It arises from chance and circumstance. The likeliest suspects are those in First Class, whether passengers, crew or officers, who were present in some capacity at the dance.'

'You mean someone who knew the girl?'

'Perhaps. At least by reputation. To some sick minds there is a morbid fascination about a nun. The dedicated virgin, attractive because forbidden. Or she could have been the victim by pure chance.'

'In which case every female is in danger, as I said to begin with.'

'Yes,' Briscoe said. 'What steps are you proposing to take?'

'None, beyond keeping our eyes and ears open and seeing to it that Miss Nina is never alone. We cannot be sure a crime has been committed. I see no point in alarming passengers needlessly.'

'Very wise, Captain. And for what should we be looking or listening?'

Angus Meiklejohn spread his hands. 'Any undue interest in Miss Nina. Any man on the night of the dance seen near her cabin when he had no business to be there. Any boasting . . . The thought's distasteful but men do it.'

'Any more revelations on her part.' The Chief had not abandoned his suspicions of Nina, but a more attractive explanation had occurred. 'Check up on the whereabouts of yon blackamoor,' he suggested. 'That stowaway who had a knife.'

'For a man his colour and in his condition to get from the boat deck to Miss Martin's cabin is almost as incredible as for a man from the engine-room.' His own quick defence surprised Briscoe.

Angus corrected him on one point.

'The alleged rape did not take place in the girl's cabin, Mr Briscoe. I'm afraid it took place in yours, which at the time was empty.'

'Wouldn't an empty cabin have been kept locked?'

'It should have been, but the cabin staff are occasionally forgetful.'

'Then if the attacker knew the door was open, doesn't that point to a member of the crew? Her own cabin was locked, I take it?'

'A key can be very quickly produced at knife-point. He need not have gone next door.'

'Except that in her own cabin there was always the risk of being disturbed by her sister, and if he'd tried the handle of my cabin by accident and found it open, it would have seemed the ideal place. You searched my cabin?'

'You were already in it before the incident was reported to me. Did you notice any disorder yourself?'

'Your excellent stewardesses had been busy. There was nothing.'

'There's no proof anywhere.'

The Chief and his theory were not to be parted, Briscoe noted, and indeed it had credibility. A novel had been published that very summer, *A Pas̲ge to India*, in which a young woman had falsely alleged sexual molestation against what the Chief would call a blackamoor. The Chief would not know of the novel and nor would Nina Martin – indeed, he had had no chance yet to read the book himself – but it was quite possible Nina Martin had invented the whole episode. It would be so much easier if she had.

He rose. 'Thank you for confiding in me, Captain, but it seems there is little any of us can do beyond, as you say, keeping our eyes and ears open. Let us hope the girl will soon recover from whatever happened, and that will be an end of it.'

Nevertheless, it was a poser, Briscoe reflected, and the girl in no fit state for further interrogation. She was now said to be suffering from a nervous breakdown, precipitated but not caused by the unwise questioning of a fellow passenger. No name had been mentioned, but after less than twenty-four hours in First Class Briscoe suspected that Mrs Gurslake was the passenger concerned.

He was far too used to parrying questions to have any difficulty with hers, which encompassed his past life, present activities and future prospects, all posed more or less in public and at a volume which suggested that his answers were expected to be the same. He had amused himself by lowering his voice deliberately as he made his noncommittal replies. He suspected that she had not always heard these clearly, and looked forward to learning what garbled nonsense emerged. He felt sure of hearing in due course because the woman was a born gossip: no item of information was of value until opportunity arose to pass it on. He had encountered such women both in village life and in London society; in neither had he any use for them.

Mrs Vane was another matter. She was a lady and as such deserved respect. The rootlessness and insecurity he detected in her were typical these days of too many of her class. Deprived of husbands, actual or potential, they had a choice between frivolity and good works. Those who chose the former adorned the pages of the *Tatler* and the *Illustrated London News*; those who opted for the latter might receive in middle age an OBE.

This portrait of Cynthia had been painted largely by Bobby, who had attached himself to the newcomer despite discouragement. The two Miss Martins, the only people on board who ever played with him, apart from his mother, had mysteriously disappeared, Miss Nina completely, Miss Connie as good as, though she still took her meals in the dining saloon, hurrying away afterwards as if she had an appointment.

'Where's Miss Nina?' Bobby asked his mother.

'She's ill.'

'What's the matter with her?'

There was no reply. Instead his mother began to talk brightly about a forthcoming bridge tournament, in which Bobby knew she had no interest. So there was something odd about Miss Nina's illness. He set his wits to work.

'Is she going to have a baby?' he demanded, recalling the mystery surrounding the temporary disappearance of other ladies he had known.

Cynthia laid down her pen – she was writing to her brother.

'Heavens, no! What makes you think that?'

Had the child heard something she hadn't? What a scandal in a girl who had been going to be a nun!

'I just thought it,' Bobby said, pretending to lose interest, which he had learned was a sure way of getting his mother to say more.

'It's not a very nice thing to think, dear. Only married ladies have babies.' In the consciousness of eight-year-olds, that is.

'I shall ask Dr Bladon,' Bobby announced. 'He goes to see her every day.'

'Just since she's been poorly. Today and yesterday.'

'And the day before that. During the fancy hat dance.'

'What do you know about the dance? You were tucked up and sleeping.'

Bobby's eyes sparkled knowingly.

With sudden misgiving, Cynthia demanded, 'Weren't you?'

'I had to get up,' Bobby explained, 'so I opened the cabin door to peep out and there was Dr Bladon.'

'Where, dear?'

'Skulking in the corridor outside.'

Bobby was very proud of this new addition to his vocabulary – 'skulking'. He had been longing for a chance to use it, and this one was too good to miss.

'What was he doing?'

'Nothing. But I don't think he wanted to be seen.'

'How do you know?'

'When he heard someone coming he dodged into an empty cabin. The one where Mr Briscoe is now.'

How odd, Cynthia mused. It sounded as if he had an assignation with one of the sisters, though she could have sworn it was Connie rather than Nina who had taken his eye. Perhaps one or other had arranged to meet

111

him. Still waters. Quiet, nunlike waters . . . The poor girls didn't have much taste. Though perhaps it was unfair to judge, since they hadn't then known he was a conchie, one of those creatures who had skulked at home – how apt was Bobby's innocently chosen expression! – while men like Robert fought and bled and died.

'I should say nothing about seeing Dr Bladon,' she cautioned Bobby. Not that she cared about a man who had implied in his professional capacity that all was not well between her and her son, but she could not quite dismiss the thought that Bobby was capable of lying, and the thought flickered like a picture on the cinema screen. With an effort, she willed herself not to think of it. The doctor's presence near the Martin girls' cabin had no significance, she wasn't jealous, she didn't care which one he fucked. And then, aghast at the language of her thoughts (no lady even *knew* such an expression!) she clapped her hand to her mouth as though about to vomit.

'Do you feel sick?' Bobby asked.

Yes. Sick of my life. Sick of myself, of my future. Sick of other men existing when Robert had to die. Sick of the random fate that plucks happiness like a flower and offers it, and next moment snatches it away.

'Shall I fetch Dr Bladon?' Bobby persisted.

She shook her head. 'I'll be all right by and by.'

In the sweet by and by. In the hereafter. In Nirvana. What was it the ballad said? *'I only know Nirvana, When safe in your loving arms.'* Someone had sung it recently at a garrison concert in Quetta, a strong, unmodulated baritone belting out the words at the rows of blob-like faces. A wartime base concert must have been like that. Robert had written of one in his last letter:

> Pretty awful as art, but the men enjoy a singsong, though if I have to hear 'Roses of Picardy' once again I think I shall go mad. But it's only right they should have a little pleasure, for everyone seems convinced (as usual) that there's something in the wind. Take care of yourself, my dear love, and of our baby. I'll see you both when I come home.

That was written in June 1916, 'somewhere in France' – she learned later it was near Abbeville. And Robert had never come home.

'I think I'll lie down,' she told Bobby. (Lie everlastingly alone.) 'Can you amuse yourself without annoying the Captain? Promise me you won't go near the bridge.'

Captain Meiklejohn had also suffered; like her, he still suffered every day thinking of the shattered young life at home, the bright promise darkened. Only in his grief had she briefly forgotten her own. Next time she must find some words of comfort, something beyond compassionate silence . . .

'Mummy –' Bobby's voice broke in upon her, ' do you think the Captain will ever invite me on to his bridge like he said?'

112

'I don't know, dear.' (He had invited her, hadn't he?) 'We'll have to wait and see.'

And find some way of reminding him. Of enjoying his company – for she had enjoyed it. It was secure and restful, without that flicker of hope too quickly fading to disappointment that eligible men aroused. He was not quite a father figure, but in his presence she had felt a certain peace. And he had understood her feelings about Bobby, as perhaps she had his – a little – for his son. She would see him again; she must see him. And with this thought, although she lay down alone, as always, in the heat of that Red Sea afternoon, Cynthia slept.

Bobby, dismissed, wandered in search of company along the shaded decks. There were very few passengers about, and those were all men who lay supine in the long verandah loungers with a newspaper over their heads. The view of the coast was uninspiring; the sweat dripped into his eyes; the glare of the sun on the water was painful; even school might be preferable to this.

'Would you like a lemonade, now? I have one ready.'

There was an encouraging clink of ice, and Bobby looked round to see the Irish steward smiling invitingly and holding a tall frosted glass with two straws in it.

'Yes, please.'

With some difficulty Bobby scrambled on to a high bar stool and swung his legs to and fro. His trousers were sticking to him, but as he clasped the cold glass and rested his forehead against it, he knew a moment's relief from the heat.

'Not all at once, mind, or you'll chill your stomach.'

Didn't grown-up people ever stop cautioning you? Bobby drew on the straws to show he wasn't going to take any notice, but not for long because he didn't want to be ill.

John Joseph watched with amusement, remembering how he had done the same, though in his case the cautions had come from Kieron and were often accompanied by an elder-brotherly clip. 'Wash your hands.' 'Watch where you're stepping.' 'Touch your cap, now – Mrs O'Halloran's a lady, so she is.' Or his mother: 'Joe, the Father will take another cup of tea, won't you, Father? And a drop of something in it for the cold.' Or Ellen: 'Will you look at him – tie under his ear and not even a clean handkerchief for church, the little heathen.' Ah, if only they could all see him now.

John Joseph was happy as a steward aboard the *Karachi*, except for the puzzle of the Haldinghams' hostility. Why would this dignified old couple not speak to him or accept service at his hands? Apart from this he was proud of the ship; he was beginning to be proud of the Australasian Line even though it was British. After all, its captains included Angus Meiklejohn, who had not only not put the stowaway ashore but had intervened to stop Mr Strode from kicking him, though Dr Bladon's intervention had been more effective still. And was it not Dr Bladon who had taken food and water to the stowaway when he, John Joseph, had been unexpectedly pressed into service for the dance.

He had been overwhelmed with dismay when the Chief Steward, without any warning, had drafted him to help at the bar. No matter that he was technically off-duty. Another steward had reported sick, they were short-handed, John Joseph would have to take his place. At once, please. John Joseph knew better than to argue with the Chief Steward, but the stowaway would be hungry; thirsty too. The provisions he had saved made a bulge under his neat mess jacket as he sought out Edmund Bladon in his cabin, on his way to take his place behind the bar.

'What is it?' The doctor was shaving for the evening, though in his case it was unnecessary.

'Sir, would you be kind enough to save a human life?'

'Since my Hippocratic Oath obliges me to do so. Whose life am I required to save?'

'Sir, I don't know. He's a stowaway.'

The doctor dropped his bantering tone. 'Do you mean to say you know of a stowaway and haven't reported it? That's a serious offence, you know.'

'Sir, I know it, but . . .'

'But your soft heart overcame you,' Edmund finished. 'Where is he, and how did you learn of his existence?'

John Joseph told him.

'I ought to report him. And you.'

'It'll cost me my job, sir.'

'It'll cost me mine if we're discovered. But we can't let the poor devil die of thirst.'

John Joseph relaxed. It was going to be all right. 'Everyone will be at the dance, sir,' he offered. 'I was going myself, only I've got to serve at the bar. I've some sandwiches here, sir –' he produced the packet, 'and I can slip you a bottle of water right away. You've only to slide them under the tarpaulin – he'll be expecting them. And it would save his life, sir.'

'Very well, yes, for tonight I'll stand in for you, and tomorrow we must decide what to do.'

'You're very good, sir.'

And very foolish, Edmund reflected, as later, after dancing with Connie, he made some excuse and slipped away. It took him only a moment to fetch the food and drink from his cabin, but then began a nightmare progress through the ship. He had not the effrontery to march straight up to the boat deck, though he suspected he would have gone unremarked if he had. Instead he crept from corner to corner, an excuse ever ready on his lips. Once or twice he heard footsteps, real or fancied, and pressed himself against the wall. Tomorrow, he promised himself, he must find some way of reporting the matter without involving the steward, who had acted like a fool; though not more so than he himself was acting in throwing his career away. He could expect no mercy from Angus

114

Meiklejohn if it became known that he had abetted a breach of discipline, and in any case, on the high seas stowing away was a crime. It had come as almost a relief when, emerging on deck early next morning, he had witnessed the discovery of the stowaway and Julian Strode's pursuit.

Had it not been for Stafford Briscoe's early-morning arrival, the man might have remained hidden for several more days, though whether even a body accustomed to hot climates could have survived under that sweltering tarpaulin Edmund had his doubts. Instead, the stowaway, taking air in the dawn coolness, had been surprised by Julian Strode, who was officer of the watch and officious with it. Edmund struggled unsuccessfully to be fair. Any officer or crewman might have seen the man, have given chase and overpowered him; but Strode had delivered that kick. And if he, Edmund, had not also been taking the air early, obsessed by his own thoughts, he had no doubt the young officer would have delivered another. The first could have been attributed to over-zealousness; the second looked like cruelty.

The early morning was the time when the past came back to torment Edmund. It brought with it memories of the jangle of keys, the hoarse shouts of the warders, the crash of cell doors, the ritual of slopping out; the stench of prison; the foot skilfully hooked round his ankle to send him sprawling with his slop bucket, for a conchie was fair game for all. Within the prison hierarchy he was lower than murderers and robbers with violence; only men convicted of sex crimes against children ranked lower than he. The warders turned a blind eye; worse, they found their own ways of demonstrating contempt in a world of killers for one who refused to kill. Mouldy bread (and wartime bread went mouldy quickly), stew that was little more than greasy water; the last serving – these were the conchie's share. And even then the warder ladling out the skilly, in which one or two pieces of meat accidentally remained, was apt to miss the bowl held out to receive it and pour it over feet and floor.

From twelve stone Edmund dropped to ten, then nine. His cheeks were hollow, his eyes sunk deep into his skull. His shaved head added to the spectral appearance which caused Aunt Anne to clasp him tighter each 'leave' and Bertram to descend to her kitchen, muttering, there to concoct delicacies which he often could not eat. The 'leaves' became ever more farcical. At the end of each sentence 'for refusing to obey military orders' – three months or six months, as the case might be – he was released a free man, but it was only an illusion of freedom. Barely had he returned to St John's Wood, for which Aunt Anne gamely sent the fare whether from Wakefield or Wandsworth prisons, Gloucester or Wormwood Scrubs, than a fresh set of call-up papers would reach him, requiring him to report at such-and-such a depot on such-and-such a day; and when that day passed it was a matter of a week at most, often less, before two uniformed police constables arrived to re-arrest him and he was bundled into a Black Maria and whisked away.

115

It seemed sometimes to Edmund that this interval of waiting was the ultimate refinement of torture. Around him was a civilised way of life from which at any moment – in the midst of a meal, while reading a book, or bathing – he might be torn away. Some policemen were more humane than others and allowed him to scrawl Aunt Anne a note if she were out, but some took pleasure in making his humiliation as complete as possible. He was only a conchie, after all. And he was being given a chance to do the decent thing, wasn't he, and go and fight like everyone else. They'd put the age-limit for conscription up to fifty-five after the Somme's losses. Men old enough to be his father were fighting. Why couldn't he?

Edmund had given up trying to explain his position. The principle of non-violence was no longer understood. Besides, the men who fought were at least as reluctant as he was, the lust to kill having been one of the war's first casualties. The one thing all were agreed on was that war must never happen again. But when it did, Edmund supposed that they would still go like sheep to the slaughter, the tribunals' questions to conscientious objectors reducing once again to the imbecilities of, 'Would you stand by and let a German violate your sister?' Would you stand by and let a German violate a German girl?

Each time the day came when he was required to report at a depot, Edmund struggled with himself. It would be so easy to give in, and for misery and discomfort there was not much to choose between the alternatives of life in the trenches and life in prison. Many conchies ended by surrendering to the State's dictates, the justification for this so-called Cat and Mouse Act. Others, broken in health or spirit, died or went mad; one or two hanged themselves.

One man hanged himself in the cell opposite to Edmund's. 'It's what you ought to do,' a kindly warder suggested, leaving the door open to allow the purple-faced corpse to remain in Edmund's view. Edmund could think only of the despair on the other side of the corridor, and the slow tightening of the ligature made from the man's own clothes. Had he regretted it as his body fought for life despite him, soiling him in a final ignominious act?

What kept Edmund from suicide that last summer, as his weight went down to eight stone and the lack of ventilation added to the bad food left him drained of normal human responses, was a kind of obstinacy; to give in to their system was to acknowledge that in any contest between the individual and the State, the State was destined to win. And though against the State not every rebel cause was worthy, yet the very act of rebellion seemed the worthiest cause of all. So his sympathies, like John Joseph's, were with the stowaway. Was he any more of a criminal than Edmund himself, or those Irishmen who had led the abortive Easter Week Rising and been hurriedly executed ten days afterwards in the courtyard of Kilmainham Gaol?

Like everyone else in England, Edmund had been stunned by news of the Rising. What could it hope to achieve? The forces which had defeated Home Rule for a generation lay as much in Ireland as in England. Had Irishmen at last decided to unite in favour of an independent country, as Pearse's proclamation from the steps of the General Post Office in Dublin called on them to do? '*The Irish Republic is entitled to, and hereby claims, the allegiance of every Irishman and Irishwoman.*' But had they really found overnight oblivion of the differences fostered by an alien government which divided a minority from the rest? It was all very well to '*place the cause of the Irish Republic under the proctection of the Most High God*' and invoke His blessing on their arms, but that same Most High God would surely demonstrate once again that He was on the side of the big battalions, of the British gunboat *Helga* on the Liffey and a rain of incendiary shells.

Fine words butter no parsnips. The old saw came relentlessly back as the fine words died away in a hail of bullets and life in Dublin went on outwardly as before. True, Sackville Street and its surroundings were a shambles, with their burnt-out, crumbled buildings, their heaps of rubble, their notices that this or that edifice was unsafe, but most Dubliners were intent on reassuring themselves by re-establishing normality as soon as possible. The Rising had not happened; the new Republic was stillborn. Small parties of the curious, mostly schoolboys, made visits to the Four Courts and Mount Street Bridge, scenes of the major British reverses, but most avoided them. Some of the poor who had looted in Sackville Street before the shocked eyes of Pearse's Irish Republican Army (what price the prayer in their Proclamation that no one would dishonour the cause?) were enjoying their spoils, watched with resentment by neighbours less bold or higher principled. And in some houses the blinds were drawn: those where missing sons, husbands, brothers had been identified in one or other of the hospitals' mortuaries – unless they had already suffered hasty interment: 217 dead of gunshot wounds were buried in Glasnevin cemetery alone.

Nevertheless, as the aftermath of the Rising wore on there were more and more private funerals, including that of Kieron Fitzgerald. John Joseph would never forget the strange familiarity of the church on that late April evening, the candles flaring and guttering in the dark, the clicking of rosary beads, the uncertain shadows, the murmur of prayers broken by a sob. In that box before the altar lay Kieron, who so short a time before had knelt here at his side, had taken on his tongue the Body of Christ and received it into his own body, which now lay, washed and shrouded and anointed, before making its last journey to the worms. The funeral Mass would be tomorrow. 'Lift up your hearts.' – 'We lift them to the Lord.' But you could not lift a heart weighed down by sorrow. A sideways glance at his sister Ellen showed tears trickling through her fingers as round as her rosary beads.

And imprinted for ever on his retinas, like a transparent filter for all future scenes, was the figure of Kieron as he emerged from the blazing

117

ruin that had been the General Post Office and stood for the last time in the open air.

Kieron had left home early on Easter Monday, although it was a Bank Holiday when a clerk in the Royal Bank of Ireland could have afforded to roll over and address himself to sleep. But Kieron had been up as if for early Mass, except that even Mass was later on a Bank Holiday. He had dressed with especial care (had some other young lady replaced Miss Louise Dunphy?) and stood before the spotted mirror in the bedroom he shared with John Joseph adjusting a slouch hat and a sash.

'What's that?' John Joseph asked.

Kieron turned and struck an attitude. He had his good suit on and a clean shirt.

'You are looking at an officer of the Irish Republican Brotherhood at a moment in history,' he declared.

'Another parade, is it?'

One or other of the nationalist movements was always having a parade, especially the Irish Volunteers who were even allowed by the British to drill with rifles, and James Connolly's Irish Citizen Army wasn't far behind. The Brotherhood was the smallest of the movements, and in the eyes of many, including those of John Joseph's father, the least effective of the three. The older Fitzgerald maintained that it was typical of Kieron to get himself involved with that outfit, with its Gaelic culture and Celtic twilight and led by the headmaster of St Enda's College at Rathfarnham, which he called the College of St Enda everything.

'More than a parade.' Kieron's eyes sparkled. 'Come down to the GPO about eleven and you shall see what you shall see.'

'Terry Mulligan and I are going fishing.'

'Not today you're not. Today's the day when Ireland becomes a free country. You'd not want to miss seeing that.'

Something in Kieron's voice made John Joseph decide to put off the fishing, for all that Terry Mulligan would gripe. But in fact it proved surprisingly easy to persuade Terry to accompany him, and eleven o'clock saw the two boys idling on the opposite side of the street to the Post Office, pretending to take an interest in shop windows which would not normally have rated a second glance.

The General Post Office was open on this Bank Holiday, and there was much coming and going. An unusual number of young men seemed to have business there, several of them in Irish Volunteers uniform, which consisted of a slouch hat and sash like the Brotherhood's, but worn over khaki. Indeed, there was a lot of khaki about. Down the street a detachment of Volunteers came marching as if they were on parade, though there was no parade-ground uniformity about their weapons: German Holtz and Mauser rifles, British Army issue, sporting guns, revolvers – anything. Suddenly they wheeled and charged into the Post Office. John Joseph and Terry, like those about them, stared disbelievingly.

118

People were coming out of the Post Office; they had a frightened, flustered air. Men with rifles were escorting them. Passers-by stopped to look. Those evicted from the Post Office were explaining, pointing. The crowd soon swelled, and the two boys, all agog now, joined its outskirts just as a man emerged on to the portico, unfolded a paper, and began to read aloud. But no one realised the historic nature of his words as Padraig Pearse, headmaster of St Enda's and Commandant General of what was now the Irish Republican Army, read aloud the Proclamation of Irish Independence to listeners who regarded him as some sort of Bank Holiday freak.

'Irishmen and Irishwomen: in the name of God and of the dead genera- tions from which she receives her old tradition of nationhood, Ireland, through us, summons her children to her flag and strikes for her freedom . . .'

The Proclamation was a long one, and many did not linger till the end. Besides, posters of it were being plastered on every available surface: you could read it if you wished. And a volley of rifle fire from within the Post Office, shattering its windows, reminded everyone that the pubs were open- ing and there was dinner to be got. By one o'clock the trams had stopped running as barricades in the streets went up, and by the time it became clear that those occupying the Post Office represented something called the Pro- visional Government of Ireland (and what would Dublin Castle say to that?) the crowds who had taken refuge in the pubs had shifted their attention from the portico of the Post Office to its roof.

There, the Provisional Government of Ireland were mounting a machine-gun, would you believe it, and someone was struggling to hoist a flag. Suddenly, against a blue, cloud-scudded sky the new banner broke and unfurled. Green, with a device upon it . . . Stars . . . the Plough and the Stars. There were a few cheers almost indistinguishable from jeers and the crowds began to disperse. Whatever would the lads think of next? It was great to be young and full of spirits. It was a typical Bank Holiday lark.

For the rest of that Monday the holiday atmosphere continued, the crowds gathering to watch for a while, then melting away, and the young men – and young women too, now – coming and going, very correct and serious and saluting smartly, as they brought in provisions at bayonet point, and messages through the GPO's guarded doors. Less than a mile away, at the far end of O'Connell Bridge, loomed the bulk of Dublin Castle, the Union Jack streaming from higher vantage above the Plough and the Stars, but the authorities made no move. Nothing happened. It would have been boring if one or two shops hadn't been ransacked, among them Lemon's confectionery store in Lower Sackville Street and Noblett's toffee-house . . . When John Joseph and Terry returned home at tea-time, they had no appetite.

'Doesn't anything ever happen on this ship?'

A small voice recalled John Joseph to the present. A small boy looked up at him.

119

'Do you not call it exciting that Mr Strode caught a stowaway the other morning?'

'No, because I didn't see it. I haven't seen the stowaway either. It was before anyone was up.' (Bobby obviously considered this unfair; someone was going to have to tell Julian Strode not to catch stowaways before breakfast.) 'And Mummy says the stowaway was black.'

He was of no interest, therefore. Not to the British. John Joseph tried again.

'When you go away to school there won't be many young gentlemen who'll have seen as much of the world as you have.'

'I haven't seen all that much. Quetta was dull, and the voyage is even duller, and my Uncle Edward was awfully strict.'

'What would you like to happen?'

Bobby considered. 'There was an earthquake in Quetta but it was ages ago, and ships don't sink any more since the *Titanic*, and there isn't a war on. Life's uninteresting, isn't it?'

But it's life, John Joseph longed to say to him. You're not lying in a coffin before the altar with a British bullet in your heart, or falling riddled with them in the bloodsoaked courtyard at Kilmainham where the leaders of the Rising died. You belong with the firing squad, will grow up to suppress rebellion, never asking yourself if it's justified nor what its far-reaching effects might be: a civil war in Ireland, Ellen in her convent in Connaught . . .

If it was possible to hate a child John Joseph hated Bobby in that moment, but all he said was: 'Will you have another lemonade?'

'No, thank you.' Bobby slipped from the high stool. 'I'll go and see if anyone would like to play deck tennis.'

John Joseph thought he had scant chance of finding anyone willing in this heat. If Miss Connie were around, or Miss Nina, it might be different . . . He switched off. He did not want to think of them. It was too painful, with the whole of First Class speculating about Miss Nina's mysterious illness, Miss Connie's obvious distress, Dr Bladon's attentiveness, Mrs Gurslake's horror stories which were becoming more lavishly embellished with every hour that passed. Nina Martin had gone mad; developed leprosy and become unsightly; been found to be pregnant and maintained it was by the Holy Ghost; the Captain had telegraphed to the Home Office, the Vatican, the Institute for Communicable Diseases; the doctor was lying to prevent panic; Connie Martin ought to be in quarantine. All these and other theories were aired freely around the bar and the stewards could not help but hear them; they in turn repeated them among the crew. It went without saying that Preston's versions were the lewdest, the least repeatable. John Joseph alone of those in a position to indulge in speculation on the fate of Nina Martin did not do so.

He did not need to.

He knew.

* * *

His Highness Prince Ravi Rabindranath Banai, only son of the Nawab of Maggapore, had developed an aversion to the potato. It came from peeling it. Never in all his nineteen years had he been so insulted. Peeling potatoes was women's work, or possibly that of some low-caste cookboy in the Palace kitchens. It was not work for a ruler's son. Yet here he was, in the Second Class galley of this liner in which he had stowed away because she was bound for England and he could not think of any other place to go, and he was peeling potatoes as if his life depended on it. Which in a sense it did.

Potatoes had figured largely in the diet of his English public school; they had appeared regularly on the tables of the English homes he had visited in the holidays; they were a staple on the menus of even the best restaurants; but until he found himself in the Second Class galley aboard the *Karachi* he had never realised the English ate them in the quantities they did. Chipped or boiled, fried or roasted, sautéed, mashed, puréed, the variations were endless but they all required the potato to be peeled. Ravi had never before seen a paring knife, let alone used one. His efforts aroused ridicule among the other cooks. Maintaining impassivity when he longed to lash out at them was a strain, but he was determined not to establish communication with anyone aboard this ship. Neither English nor Hindustani must evoke response in him, although he was bilingual in both. He kept his head down, and after two days was even acquiring a certain facility with the paring knife. Or at least the potatoes were larger and the pile of peel smaller and the head cook didn't shout at him so much.

Another two weeks and they would be in England. He was not sure what would become of him when they docked. Would he be allowed to land without papers? Would they put him in an English gaol? Of course there were people who could vouch for him – his headmaster, his friend Waterman, people in the India Office – but only if he revealed who he was. And if he did, then once his father knew he was in England he would insist on his immediate return. His effort to escape would have been futile, and he dared not think what punishment awaited him.

He had never got on with his father, who was sixty-five years old and had ruled Maggapore since he was younger than Ravi, with the help of the British Resident. The Resident changed – Ravi himself could remember four. It was said that the Nawab ran rings round them, but all Ravi could see was their alien presence: the adviser and the foreign army in their midst. Ever since he came home from school to cool his heels and face an arranged marriage, he and his father had been on a collision course. Predictably, the row which had decided the prince to run away to escape his father's domination had been sparked by an Englishman.

This unknown officer, leading a small patrol on a short cut through the city's poorest quarter, had been surrounded by a hostile crowd. Understandably, since an army vehicle had recently collided with and killed a sacred cow and the people were angry. The officer had panicked and ordered his patrol to open fire, and while Ravi accepted that it had not been their intention to slaughter Indians and that they had fired above the heads of the crowd, a bullet had ricocheted and killed a man. Burning with indignation, Ravi sought out his father.

'Father, this officer is a madman.'

'Before he has been accused, tried or sentenced? Really, my son, what kind of justice is that?'

'A man has been killed and his family left destitute.'

'Your first statement I do not dispute. But who killed him? Was it not fate that he stood in the path of a ricocheting bullet?'

'And who fired the bullet?'

'We do not know. When six men fire into the air, which the English say is what happened, who can say which bullet came from which gun? It is the old firing-squad principle of collective responsibility. Am I to insist on the punishment of six men?'

'The men were only obeying orders. It is their officer who should be punished.'

'A fine young officer who was decorated for gallantry in the Great War and whom his colonel highly esteems? Will that bring back life to the dead man?'

'You know very well it won't.'

'So you wish for an act of revenge?'

'A deterrent.'

'My son, you have much to learn. The Resident and I have discussed it and we have agreed this captain must go, not just from Maggapore but from the Indian Army. His career is at an end. Do you not think that is sufficient punishment for a man only seven years older than you?'

'And the poor man who was shot – what about his family?'

'The lawyers are already feasting like vultures on the case, though I believe Mr Patel, who is of course a Congress-wallah, has offered his services free of charge. In due course the Resident and I will ensure that the British pay generous compensation. Which means that even after the lawyers have had their pickings, the dead man's family may have cause to bless this day.'

It was true, and Ravi knew it. Once again matters had been arranged, as they always were, by his father and the Resident. Or the Resident and his father – he was never quite sure which. The present Resident was the Nawab's favourite, but he had cooperated with them all, though Ravi was sure 'cooperation' was only a gloss for taking orders. Things would be different in his day!

'Could you have arranged matters better?' his father was asking. 'The officer has been punished, the dead man's family indemnified, and the British are in our debt. This last is perhaps the most important. Generosity is the offspring of guilt. They are not used to thinking themselves inferior to natives; when they do, it is the natives who benefit.'

'According to you and your tame Mr Edwards, with whom everything can be fixed.'

'The Resident and I understand each other. Besides, unlike his predecessors, he is an excellent chess-player. If he were recalled, I should miss our games very much.'

The Nawab sighed, wondering if his son would ever learn the art, or perhaps the craft, of government. Born late in his life to a favourite young wife who had died in giving him birth, the boy was at once the joy and despair of his old age. It was at Vernon Edwards's suggestion that he had sent him to an English public school, dreading the long separation but allowing himself to be convinced. And what happened? The boy who came back speaking like an Englishman wanted nothing but to throw the English out, unable to see that his own survival as a ruler depended on the continuance of the Raj. Did he really suppose that those like the Congresswallahs who clamoured for Indian independence would endure any power except their own? Especially not the power of the Princes which was old before they were born. The followers of this Gandhi they called the Mahatma were not aristocrats; they would see no virtue in the enlightened rule of the Princes. His great-grandson, perhaps even his grandson, might never sit upon a throne.

But first he had to ensure a grandson's existence. A bride for Ravi was imperative. The Resident concurred, though for different reasons, muttering something about it being better to marry than to burn. The Nawab did not see them as alternatives, but then the English were peculiar about sex. Worshipping a god not born of fleshly delight who had seemingly died a virgin, they could not be expected to understand the pleasures depicted on Indian temple carvings, though they always took a good look at them before turning decorously away. So long as they had not infected Ravi with their strange attitudes; though the Nawab feared the worst, for when marriage to a neighbouring rajah's daughter was suggested, the boy refused to hear of it.

'I shall choose my own bride.'

'Very well, my son. We will send to all the parents of eligible daughters and ask for photographs from which you may make your selection – if the parents are willing and if the dowry can be agreed.'

The Nawab was sure the parents would be willing. The dowry was something else, for the princely coffers emptied faster than they filled, and while he had assured his personal fortune like a wise ruler, money was still necessary for the running of the state. Drought, bad harvests, famine, all these things took their toll. Ravi, with his 'enlightened' ideas of wells and irrigation, would have to learn that a land without money was always destined to be dry. As for his 'enlightened' ideas about marriage, it was time for him to get rid of those. Love – pleasure, rather – had its place and there were plenty of young girls willing to give pleasure, but a man married for heirs and the dowry with which to support them. In a bride broad hips and rich jewels counted for more than perfection of face or form.

Unfortunately Ravi saw differently. 'She's fat,' he had exclaimed on being shown a picture of the rajah's daughter whom the Nawab had pre-selected, though he did not of course know this. 'And stupid,' he added, looking at the plump, pouting features.

'That is very desirable in a bride,' the Nawab said gently. 'She will not question your decisions.' (Though alas, I doubt if it is intelligence that makes you question mine.)

'I don't like her.'

'But you do not like any of the others.'

'Then I shan't marry them.'

The Nawab sighed. 'You are young. Mr Edwards agrees we can afford to wait a little.'

'It's my marriage. Edwards has nothing to do with it.'

'Of course not. A Resident acts only in an advisory capacity – but it makes sense to listen to his advice.'

'On political matters, maybe. And let's not beat about the bush, Father: you mean he calls the tune.'

'The marriage of a ruling prince *is* a political matter. For the rest, you will have to learn that it does not matter who calls the tune providing that the melody is pleasing. You must not confuse the trappings of power with power.'

You must not, but you did, and in India it was more difficult than in England, for in India the trappings of power were to the fore. Uniforms, retinues, costly gifts and jewels, the Raj and the princes matched each other step for step. Yet behind the scenes it was officials in the Indian Civil Service who made the decisions, and below them it was the ordinary Indian who did or increasingly did not carry them out. Was this non-cooperation the answer to the Army's guns and the Civil Service's chittys? One man like Gandhi with a doctrine of non-violence had caused the British more trouble than many a full-scale insurrection in the past. If he, Ravi, refused to go through with this marriage, what would happen? And immediately in answer to his question came the one word: imprisonment.

Not bread and water in a gaol with common prisoners, but a loss of freedom equal to theirs. His father could withdraw his allowance, make it impossible for him to leave his princely quarters, have him watched by guards and spied on by informers until his spirit broke. His father would doubtless 'agree' with the Resident that something must be done to tame his unruly son, and the Resident, taking care not to advise on a non-political issue, would quietly marshal the Raj in support. Ravi had been prepared all along to believe he could hold out against an unwanted marriage, but now the hushing up of the murder of one of his father's subjects was something else. He could secure justice neither for himself nor for the victim. There was nothing for it but to run away.

The problem was where to run to, for anywhere in India he could be rapidly found and brought back. England, then; the only other country he knew and where he had at least one friend. Barry Waterman and he had been friends all the way up the school and he had stayed with Barry's family in the holidays. They had even exchanged a few stilted letters since his departure from England, where Barry now worked in his father's bank. Ravi did not pause to consider whether the circumstances of his return might make him unwelcome, nor what he would do in England with no allowance and no job. The Watermans had always been kind to him; he assumed they would still be so, and in particular Dorothy, Barry's younger sister, whose slight, blonde beauty had made a deep impression upon him.

Yet even after the decision to escape was taken, Ravi still found it hard to carry it out. For one thing he had no ready money, since a prince had no need of it. Everything he wanted was ordered from the Palace and paid for by his father's comptroller of accounts, but a request for train and steamship tickets would be checked with the Nawab and a stop put on it at once. Anxiously Ravi counted his token pocket money; there was not nearly enough. At best it would purchase a third-class ticket to Bombay, but with nothing over for board and lodging, and in any case he was locally too well known. If he bought a rail ticket for cash in his own person, it would be all over Maggapore by the time he returned to the Palace. In despair he turned to the one person he could trust, his old ayah, who grudgingly agreed that her husband would procure the ticket which would enable her beloved princeling to sample the delights of Bombay. It was the best reason Ravi could think of, for it was accepted that a young man needed to sow a few wild oats before marriage, and Ayah knew all about the impending bride. It was understood that his father must know nothing of the excursion, even though – if it were for the reason given – he would not necessarily disapprove. Ayah even cooperated to the extent of lending him some clothes belonging to her son, which did not fit but by that very fact contributed to Ravi's need for disguise.

So at midnight the Prince boarded the night mail for Bombay, with a good deal less ostentation than had attended the departure of the disgraced army captain some ten days before. He travelled in closer proximity to his subjects than he had ever experienced hitherto. In the fashion of the poor, they shared their meagre provisions with the young man who had been so improvident as to embark without sustenance on a twelve-hour journey, for although it was by no means the first time that Ravi had travelled between Maggapore and Bombay, it was the first time he had done so without servants to minister to his comfort and fetch his meals from the first-class dining car.

Once arrived in Bombay, he made his way to the offices of the steamship companies and learnt that the next liner homeward bound was the *Karachi*, due to sail the following dawn. All day he haunted the waterfront and watched the passengers going aboard, forcing himself not to walk up

125

the gangway by right, as was his instinct, and be turned humiliatingly away. No more inept stowaway had ever boarded a liner, but his very inexperience helped and beginner's luck aided him to come aboard with the baggage, with everyone assuming he was employed by someone else. By now it was dark, and although cargo was still being loaded, on the passenger decks lights were dimmed. Gliding between shadows, halting at every corner, Ravi climbed one companionway after another until he found himself on the boat deck. He had to struggle with the tarpaulin lifeboat cover, looking over his shoulder all the while, but long before dawn he was bedded down with much discomfort, his few possessions close at hand.

The possessions consisted of a few rupees' change from his rail ticket; a bottle of water and some fruit; two chapattis, already hardening but capable of assuaging hunger; a clean shirt; and the jewelled dagger given him for his fifteenth birthday and which had belonged to his grandfather. At best he might last twenty-four hours before being overcome by thirst, but he hoped by night to steal as far as a cloakroom and have a chance to wash and drink. He was helped by his recollection of previous voyages, for though he had never sailed on the *Karachi*, he had sailed on a sister ship, and since the design of the Australasian Line's vessels was very similar, he was not totally disoriented. Even so, things would have gone ill with him had he not encountered a sympathetic steward on his first nocturnal prowl.

Ravi knew nothing about the steward except that he was short and slight, but in the days of dependence that followed he fantasised about this saviour. He was a revolutionary who planned to sink the *Karachi* and all aboard her (Ravi forgot briefly that he was also a revolutionary in his way); he too had been a stowaway and was now working his passage home in reparation; he was the rightful heir of a duke or marquis, snatched from the cradle at birth and brought up in poverty, from which he was about to be rescued by the recognition of a locket or birthmark which had previously been kept hidden; best of all, he was an illegitimate son of the Nawab (who was reputed to have many such), a long-lost half-brother who could become a friend and return with him to the Palace as a kind of junior Resident. Someone his own age would be welcome in the sumptuous world of his elders where young courtiers were conspicuously absent, the Nawab preferring to enjoy power unchallenged by the views of the younger generation, much to the Resident's dismay.

Had Ravi but realised it, the despised Mr Edwards was eager to be his friend, seeing in the young prince with his English education and liberal ideas a happier future for Maggapore, which, like so many of his country-men serving in India, he had come to love as his own. In vain he had pleaded with the Nawab to give the boy more scope, something to do, responsibility, an introduction to the duties of a ruler. He had watched with unease the young man's sympathy with the new Congress Party and the whiff of independence in the air, for, like the Nawab, he believed that

India's future lay with her princes rather than her people, if only the princes could be trained to lead aright. He had sympathised with Ravi over the arranged marriage, because although it was desirable in itself (if only because, if the boy took after his old goat of a father, a legal outlet for his urges must be found), the bride had been chosen with no thought of personal suitability; she might be rich, but she was, as Ravi said, fat and stupid. It was asking for trouble to expect the handsome heir, who the Resident suspected was still a virgin, to accept as his consort a maiden whose virtues seemed likely to consist solely in wealth and fecundity. Arranged marriages need not ignore the tastes and temperaments of the partners; often these were a parent's first concern. Had the Nawab forgotten that his only son was the child of his only love-match? There was a certain justice in such things.

So the Resident was not altogether surprised to receive an urgent summons to the Palace and be told that Prince Ravi had run away. Once he had satisfied himself that this was true and had intervened to stop the old ayah being beaten as the likeliest accomplice, it became necessary to consider where the Prince might have gone. The Nawab had already sent messages to neighbouring rulers, but the Resident was for casting a wider net.

'He will make for England, Your Highness, I am convinced of it. I would advise a watch on the ports.'

'My son has no love for the English, Mr Edwards.'

'I suggest, sir, that that is only partly true. He has no love for us in India, but he has been brought up among us at home. He has friends there – Barry Waterman, for instance.'

'He does not have the money for the fare.'

'Nevertheless, sir, we should check with the steamship companies. He will use an assumed name, so they should be asked to check any single passage booked by a young Indian gentleman to England on liners sailing in – what? The past four days?'

The Nawab looked unhappy as he confirmed this. He knew what the Resident thought: that a closer relationship between father and son would have prevented the boy from having such a head start. In which direction had he gone? From Central India it was possible to reach Madras, Calcutta or Bombay. If England was Ravi's destination, the western seaport was the most likely. He gave instructions to telegraph first to Bombay.

But when after two days the replies from all the ports and steamship companies were negative and the old ayah still refused to talk (there were ways of making her, but the Resident was a considerable obstacle), the Nawab's fear exceeded his anger. He did not need to be told where danger lurked. Even penniless, disguised, Ravi was still a high-caste Brahmin, a young man accustomed to command and one who might have hidden wealth upon him. For more than a hundred years the practice of thuggee had been outlawed, but in 1924 his country had robbers still. At the thought of his son beaten unconscious, garotted, throat cut, left on the roadside for birds of prey to pick, the Nawab's guts twisted in a spasm of belated love and terror. He sent for the Resident again.

'My friend –' Such a form of address was not used every day and the Resident prepared himself for a difficult interview. 'My friend, my only son is missing. I appeal to you for your help.'

'What more can I do, Your Highness?' Vernon Edwards surveyed the fat old man whose yellowed eyes were dulled, his cheeks sunken, and thought: He's only half hamming it up this time.

'My friend, would you go to New Delhi, see the Viceroy, implore him to ask the King-Emperor for aid, for the help of detectives such as we read of in your novels, perhaps for the assistance of Scotland Yard.'

The Resident refrained from saying what he thought of these suggestions. Instead, he made a suggestion of his own.

'Why don't you let me talk to the ayah? I might get something out of her.'

The Nawab shrugged. 'The woman is ignorant. And obstinate. She should be beaten. It is the only way we shall get her to talk.'

'Possibly, sir, but whatever she tells us or does not tell us, I must ask for an assurance that you will order no such thing.'

It was one of the Nawab's strengths that he knew when to give way gracefully. 'Very well. It shall be as you say.'

Within the hour the Resident was able to report that the future ruler of Maggapore had left a week ago, disguised and with a few rupees in his pocket, by the night mail to Bombay.

'I was right, he's making for England,' the Resident said a trifle smugly. 'He intended to stow away. He may not have managed it, but as a first move I suggest we arrange to contact all shipping already homeward bound for England from Bombay.'

It had never occurred to Ravi that his father would go to such lengths. Once out of India, he had believed himself beyond the Nawab's jurisdiction and he had to some extent relaxed. True, he had to hold out till past Aden if he was to be sure of reaching England, but even as he fell to the deck and felt the Third Officer's foot drive into him, he knew a moment of relief that he had escaped the worst. As he peeled potatoes in the Second Class galley, he comforted himself with the thought that each day brought him nearer to Barry, to the Watermans' Lutyens-designed home in leafy Surrey, to Dorothy Waterman.

Dorothy had been sixteen on his last visit, two years younger than her brother, and she had not yet 'come out', a procedure which she referred to with a mixture of disdain and excitement and which involved, he gathered, being presented at Court. As this event took place in the company of several hundred other debutantes, all dressed more or less alike, Ravi could see little remarkable about it; he took for granted a court. But the Watermans considered it something special and he had no wish to prick this particular balloon, 'though when you come to my court,' he told Dorothy, 'you will make your curtsey to me all on your own.'

'Oh, Ravi, shall I really? Can we come and visit you?'

'Why not?' A visit by Barry had already been mooted. Why shouldn't his sister accompany him?

'You shall have the most beautiful rooms in the women's quarters,' he promised, 'with peacocks on the terrace outside, and the scent of frangipani, and perfumed water in the fountains.'

Dorothy clapped her hands. 'I can never quite believe you're a prince, Ravi . . . When you come here with Barry you're just like one of us.'

And so he was, included in all the family's parties and outings, treated kindly by all their friends. Mrs Waterman regarded him as a motherless boy and spoilt him a little; Mr Waterman was affable. Indeed, the banker listened indulgently to the young prince's ideas for modernisation in the state of Maggapore, and never failed to remind him that such schemes cost a great deal of money but that Waterman's Bank might be ready with a loan. As for Dorothy, she adored Prince Ravi and followed him about like a dog, so that it was with some surprise that he realised on that last visit that she had emerged into womanhood.

It was April, and the two of them were in the roomy attic that ran the full length of the house. Below them was a sea of blossom and young green leaves and swelling buds. Next week the boys would return to school for their last term.

'It seems so empty after you two have gone away,' Dorothy said, looking up from sorting through a pile of magazines for jumble, the ostensible reason for their being there.

'I'll miss you,' Ravi said. It was not politeness: he was suddenly aware it was true. He would see her once more when he stayed with the Watermans in the summer, and after that who knew when they would meet again.

'We have such fun, don't we?' Dorothy went on wistfully. 'There's so much to talk about. More than there is with Barry, because you and I always like the same things.'

'I wish you could see Maggapore, you'd love it, especially the Palace.'

'The terrace with the peacocks where the perfumed fountains play.'

'How well you remember.'

'It's as if I'd been there. Tell me about it again. You said there was hibiscus and bougainvillæa and – what was that tree with the lovely scent?'

'Frangipani,' he said, and told her, conjuring up every detail in his mind and seeing it as a background for this English maiden whose pale beauty glowed like the moon.

'It must be wonderful to see it basking in the sun.'

'By moonlight is better, for then the scents come into their own.'

'*All the perfumes of Arabia . . .*'

He did not recognise the quotation.

'No, India.' He added softly, '*Jai Hind.*'

'What does that mean?'

'Hail, India. No – India for ever. It's somewhere between the two.'

'You love India, don't you?'

'Yes. I want you to love it too.'

'I shall. I shall, dear Ravi, because it's your country.' She did not add, 'And I love you,' but she flung her arms round him, almost overbalancing him. 'India will always mean Ravi for me.'

'And for me, Dorothy is England.' His arms tightened as he spoke and his lips touched her hair, shining clean with its faint good soap smell and the fainter good scent of her scalp.

She was unaware of the caress and broke free, laughing. 'We must go, we've been up here for ages.'

Flushed with happiness, she ran down the two flights of stairs, Ravi carrying the magazines behind her. Mrs Waterman met them in the hall.

'Where on earth have you been all afternoon, dear?'

'Sorting the magazines for jumble, like you said.'

'Oh, of course. I did not realise Ravi was with you. You look flushed, dear, do you feel all right?'

'Perfectly, Mummy. Ravi was a great help. Mummy, may I go with Barry to India one day?'

'Perhaps when you're grown up. We'll have to see, dear, won't we? Yes, Ravi, put the magazines down there.'

As he set the pile of magazines down in the lobby, Ravi had the impression Mrs Waterman was not pleased, but it was so fleeting he thought it was imagination.

He never saw Dorothy alone again. Her mother, or Barry, or her father always happened to enter whatever room they might be in, and for all that the garden was a big one, its secluded corners seemed to have disappeared. But otherwise things went on as usual, and on the night before the boys returned to school they drank a toast. 'To Anglo-Indian friendship,' Mr Waterman, said, rising. 'And to India herself. *Jai Hind.*'

The words sounded strange on his lips, but Ravi was touched and delighted. His heart warmed to the Watermans. When he came in the summer on his last visit, he would come bearing princely gifts. For Mrs Waterman a gold bangle; for her husband and Barry diamond tiepins; but what for Dorothy? A sari as blue as her eyes, a silver filigree of moonlight to lay on her shining hair, the sandals of dawn to bring her feet skimming towards him, the rings of eternity for her hands – all the wealth of his father's coffers held nothing worthy. Besides, the English were peculiar about gifts. Far from appreciating the munificence poured out upon them, they talked about ostentation and bad taste. He was sure Mrs Waterman would consider a Swan fountain pen more suitable for Dorothy. Could it be a gold-plated one?

He need not have worried. There was not to be another visit. Towards the end of the summer term Mrs Waterman wrote. Instead of Cornwall where Ravi had so often joined them, her husband had taken a villa in Biarritz. They would be away until the end of August, and unfortunately it was necessary to leave at once. In September Dorothy was departing for a finishing school in Switzerland and Barry would be starting at the bank. They were all so sorry not to see him one last time, but alas, it was impossible. Dorothy was desolate, as indeed they all were. They sent their fondest love.

Disappointed, Ravi had sailed for India and the princely state of Maggapore, where the presence of Mr Edwards reminded him of a different England and Dorothy Waterman's image began to fade. He had not thought of her for months until his impulsive decision to return to England, and her sudden appearance before him on deck. Not that Dorothy Waterman was aboard the *Karachi*, but someone very like her was. One evening, when the ship was only a few days out from Bombay and the boat deck was deserted, a girl had come up there alone. He had been on the lookout for the steward who befriended him when he saw her, and had watched, lifting the tarpaulin slightly, as she chose a chair and settled herself to write. He could see the blue notepaper on her knees as the fountain pen – was it a Swan? – began to traverse it. She wore a blue dress with a sailor collar and her hair was long and blonde. She wasn't Dorothy, but she reminded him of her in a fuller, more rounded way. Her breasts were heavier, her arms less sticklike, no dress could disguise the swell of her haunches as she moved. But she had the same shining fall of hair which parted as her head bowed, to reveal the white nape of her neck. Dorothy had been the new moon and here was the full one. Dorothy had been a bud, but here was womanhood coming into bloom.

His foot slipped. Grabbing at the nearest support, he scrabbled to retain his balance, desperate not to give his presence away. No good. She had heard him. She raised her head, an animal alerted. Gathering up her writing materials, she stood, uncertain what to do. Would she scream? No. She would go for help, then. She would bring someone to examine the boat. He was wondering where to find another hiding-place, and quickly, when he heard her say, 'Oh, Joe.' To his relief, he saw his benefactor steward caught with sandwiches and water bottle in hand, heard him reassure her that nothing was lurking in the third lifeboat on the port side, and watched him stand stolid and unmoving until she went reluctantly away.

He had not seen her again, and peeling potatoes in the Second Class galley, he doubted if he ever would, but whether for her or for the remembered Dorothy, he was startled at the knife-thrust of desire he had felt. It was almost as though the jewelled dagger hidden so cunningly in his clothing had pierced his vitals without drawing blood, leaving him shuddering with shame and self-knowledge as he took the food and water from the little steward's hands.

A voice cut into his reverie. 'You there! You with no name!'

Ravi looked up. What was wrong now with the potatoes? Hadn't he peeled enough?

But the head cook was not interested in potatoes. His eyes gleamed with curiosity as he said, 'You've done nothing but ruin good spuds since you got here, but what did you do before? I know you stowed away – we all know it – but you must have done something worse than that. Here's two sailors and an officer sent to bring you before the Captain. What crime have you committed? Murder? Rape?'

Requiem æternam dona ea, Domine . . . requiem æternam . . . requiem . . . requiem . . . But there is no rest, neither in heaven, nor earth, and certainly not in Hell . . . Father Farrell says Hell is a place without God, without hope therefore; if you are in Hell you are there for ever and there shall be weeping and wailing and gnashing of teeth. Hell is a place of torment where the damned go. If you are in Hell you are damned. If you are damned it is because you have sinned mortally in this life and not repented. But we all sin, we are born sinners, only Our Blessed Lady was conceived and born without sin. Connie says she must have been a bore, but that's just Connie. Our Lady prays for us, prays for Connie. *Sancta Maria, Mater Dei, ora pro nobis peccatoribus nunc et in hora mortis nostræ* . . .

I wish I were dead, but I know that's wicked. We have to live as long as God ordains, and in the state He has ordained for us – even mad, blind, paralysed, unclean. Unclean. I can still smell the disinfectant, I scrubbed myself until I was sore, and all the time there was a greater soreness that no salve or disinfectant could reach. I am unclean. I am not a virgin. I can never be a bride of Christ.

They don't believe me, don't believe it happened. Connie does, I think she does, but Dr Bladon has twice asked me if it happened just as I described. Do they think I could invent such things? Do they think I tore my dress and rent my hair and said a man had forced me to do the unspeakable? Yes, of course they do, it would make it so easy for them, and by now I hardly know what I believe. *I believe in God the Father Almighty* who has ordained that I shall be befouled, whose will I must accept, *be it unto me according to Thy word*, who has ordained I shall not be believed. But did it happen? Last night when he laid in wait for me again, when his hands came from behind and I felt his breath on my neck and the knife was glinting, glinting, when I lashed out at him and screamed, I woke to find Connie bending over me looking frightened. She said it was a nightmare, the stewardess said it was a nightmare, they gave me something bitter to drink. And I slept, I plunged into blackness, but it was a blackness where there was no rest. *Requiem aeternam dona mihi, Domine* . . . But I must not wish for death.

Who was he and why did he choose me for violation? Because I was there? Because he was there? Did we simply coincide or had he been stalking me? Then it must be someone I know! Dr Bladon suggested as

132

much, but I never saw the man, only felt him. I never even heard his voice. A knife-point is an eloquent persuader. Thank God it was in the cabin next door. I couldn't have borne it if it had been our own cabin, though it's been pointed out to me that if it had there'd have been evidence which Connie would have noticed, whereas if it was somewhere else – that's to say if I imagined it, if it took place only in my mind . . . Oh God, is my mind such a sink of depravity that I could have imagined *that*? I ought to have swabbed my mind with disinfectant as carefully as I swabbed my body, but if I had I still shouldn't feel clean. That awful woman who forced her way in here with her indecent suggestions . . . Auntie Florrie indeed! A girl wants a boy. Had I had second thoughts about the convent? Her black eyes popped with curiosity. I suppose by now she knows what happened, what they allege I allege happened . . . How she'll savour it, feasting on the details like a fly on excrement. I can never face any of them again, they'll all be looking when they think I'm not, whispering, 'That's the girl who claims she was raped.'

Connie says I've got to face them, I can't go on lying here. There's a big service for Armistice Day and if I make that my first reappearance in public no one can question me. But I bet Mrs Gurslake could, and if that little clergyman says anything about 'the fallen' she'll look right across at me. A fallen woman. I might be pregnant. Oh Holy Mother, please not that. They say God doesn't ask you to bear more than you're capable of, but in that case why do so many people break down? If I'm pregnant I shall go mad. But would they even believe I was pregnant? Isn't there something called a false pregnancy? They might say that was what was wrong with me, that I wanted a child so much that I'd developed the symptoms. As if anyone would want a rape child! Ah, but the rape never occurred. Just look at her, my dear, she couldn't bring herself to enter the convent so this is how she saved her face.

It isn't that I don't want to enter, I *can't* enter. Not now, not after I've been defiled. I must stay for ever on this side of the parlour grille, one of the unenclosed because I'm shop-soiled and you can't give God damaged goods. A priest must be a whole man, a nun a virgin. At the convent in Nullumpur Sister Julian of the deep voice and the moustache taught us what happened to women who lied and took the veil when they had no right to. According to her, such women went straight to Hell and in the pictures she showed us they were being tortured by demons with misshapen bodies and weird faces who were doing the strangest things. Someone asked her to explain one bit of the picture and she went red and snapped the book shut. She said it was symbolic (though it didn't look it) and we were much too young to understand Hieronymus Bosch. I've always remembered the name Bosch though I've never seen any more of his paintings. He had a very clear idea of Hell. Those women were being forced, there were demons holding their legs open and other demons forcing open their mouths. I tried to open my mouth to scream, but his hand was across it, I tried to bite him but my jaws just wouldn't move. He was panting like an animal, I could hear him grunting as he drove himself into me. And I could do nothing. His will was stronger than my flesh, *be it unto me according to Thy word*, Blessed Mary pray for me.

What do I write to Aunt Eileen? Do I just say I've changed my mind or do I tell her the truth? But would she believe it or would she too say I'd fantasised? Dr Bladon doesn't actually say he disbelieves me but he told Con there was no evidence and he couldn't say positively I wasn't lying, though I think he believes me in his heart. He's so kind, I wanted him to marry Connie, I was going to pray for them every day after I'd prayed for Mummy and all the souls in Purgatory, oh God what's to become of me? If I can't be a nun I am nothing. My whole life has been directed towards that end and is now violently deflected because a man got between my legs, which is where that horrible Mrs Gurslake says the Captain would you believe it wants to get with Cynthia Vane only Cynthia would never let him unless he raped her as that other man did me.

It could be any man on the ship including the Captain, including Dr Bladon, Archie Johnson, all the rest, even the crew, Mr Strode, the little steward whose sister is a nun in Connaught . . . Only the new passenger who came aboard at Aden is not suspect, I wonder what he's like, if I go to the Armistice Day service I shall see him and all of them and they will look at me, and somewhere among them is one who knows me as Adam knew Eve his wife, in whom the act of love is an act of hatred. Dr Bladon says not necessarily hatred for me but hatred for all women because he fears us and so all women must fear him. Suppose he strikes again. It could be any of us but somehow I know it will be me, his hands will reach out from behind me, closing my mouth, poising the knife at my throat, I shall never dare to be alone for an instant and in every crowd he will be there, he and I of all the ship's company joined by that terrible bond.

Requiem aeternam dona ei, Domine – O Lord, grant him eternal rest where he can no longer prowl like Satan seeking whom he may devour, grant us peace, O God, grant me oblivion, the dark of death, as now, the blackness closing round me down-sinking, sinking into the depths, the depths of Hell . . .

NO! Not that, never, never, never, Hell is for ever and the demons come as in that dreadful picture of Sister Julian's. *He* comes, his hands are on me, I can feel his breath, hear him pant, O God hear me, give me the strength to fight, he is holding me, saying my name, it is me he seeks and no other, I am the scapegoat and the sacrifice, let me kick him, claw him, bite him, oh but he has the strength of ten and mine is failing, I cannot move, he is talking to me, soothing, soothing, *I will not open my eyes*, worst of all he has enlisted Connie, my sister is holding me down so that he can have his will of me *according to Thy word* but I will fight you I will never stop fighting you shall find no pleasure in me and as for you my treacherous sister I can think of no fate cruel enough for you. Take your hands off, stop saying Nini, my name is defiled in your mouth the touch of all flesh is defilement I reject you I spew you forth no No NO!

'Nina,' Connie said, 'it's me, Connie. Look at me. Open your eyes.'

With an effort Nina did so. The bedside light was on, the electric light that answered to the touch of a switch and was so magical after the oil lamps and candles of Nullumpur. A servant at the bungalow did nothing but trim and refill lamps, the outdoor lanterns as well as the lamps for the house, lanterns like the one the chowkidar carried when he patrolled the compound after dark. At intervals they would hear his call, long-drawn-out and mournful, and the distant cries of other watchmen answering. It was the chowkidar who had been sent running for the doctor the night that Mummy died. Then, too, Connie had been there, holding her tight as she sobbed her heart out for Mummy, just as she held her tight now while she wept with equal abandon for herself.

'It's better to have nightmares, Nina, and get it out of your system than to keep it all bottled up.'

That was Dr Bladon's voice. What was he doing here? What time was it? She did not realise she had put her thoughts into words until he answered, 'Nearly half past eleven, but I hadn't yet gone to bed.'

'How did you get here?'

The presence of any man was suspect.

'Your sister sent the stewardess for me.'

No need to add that the stewardess had said Miss Nina was raving like a madwoman and ought to be put under restraint. He looked down at her: the nerve-storm was exhausted, leaving her spent and wide-eyed.

'Tell us about your dream,' he commanded. 'Why did you cry out NO?'

'Because he was going to . . . to . . .'

'Force you again? Who was he?'

'I told you, I never saw him, I don't know.'

Edmund sighed to himself. She knew something that would identify the rapist, he was certain, but it was locked away in her mind together with the horrors she could neither deny nor assimilate and which burst forth in nightmares when she slept. He knew about nightmares: it was some time since he had wakened drenched in sweat and teeth chattering because there were two policemen at the door and he was about to be dragged back for a further round of insults and degradation which he feared this time he might not be able to endure, but even the recollection of the recollection could set him trembling like a leaf. From being an act of conscience, his refusal to fight had become a pitting of himself against the State, a duel between an individual and a system in which the system seemed bound to win, except that if it did it was not one individual who would be blotted out but *all* individuals, as they were already being blotted out in Flanders mud. He had had a belief in conscience to sustain him, but Nina did not have even that. His torments could be called self-inflicted; she was victim *par excellence*.

135

He said gently, 'Will you tell me if you ever remember anything about this man who forced you, any little detail that might help us to identify him before he strikes again.'

'Do you think he's going to?'

Edmund cursed himself. He should never have implied that the attack might be repeated – Nina had enough to bear without that. Except that if she was ever to emerge from this cocoon of terror in which she had wrapped herself, she would have to admit the possibility.

'I don't know,' he said. 'I hope it was just a moment of madness of which he is deeply ashamed, the result perhaps of drinking too much.' (By the time the dance ended there had been plenty of over-loud laughter and lurching footsteps.)

'He wasn't drunk,' Nina said.

'How do you know?'

Connie intervened. 'Daddy got drunk the night before we sailed, and once before in Nullumpur. And Major Orrey, that friend of Mummy's, he sometimes smelt of drink.'

She was telling him Nina was no stranger to it. Above her head he nodded to Connie to show he understood.

'All right, I can't make that excuse for him. Not that I want to make excuses. I'm ashamed of my own sex, Nina. Will you let me apologise?'

'You're the last person who should –' Connie began, and broke off in confusion. What proof had they that Edmund was not the man? It seemed unlikely, but all the men so far encountered seemed unlikely. Was Edmund more so than the rest? After their dance together she had lost sight of him, had danced with several other men. Where had he been meanwhile? In the comings and goings of a dance involving all the First Class passengers, whose movements could be accounted for?

Above Nina's head her eyes met his for an instant. Again he nodded to show he understood. She felt the beginnings of a blush, but faced him despite it. What if his kindness were remorse, his apparent acceptance of Nina's story a kind of double bluff?

Edmund, knowing her thoughts as clearly as if she had spoken them aloud, turned back to Nina with a little shrug. It was like those job interviews: all geniality until the question, 'What about your war service, Doctor?' Unless or until he could prove past doubt who had attacked Connie's sister, there could be no forwarding of their relationship.

It surprised him that he thought of it that way. A few dances, some conversation at meals, he must have had the same with whoever he sat next to on the voyage outward, yet he could scarcely recall her name. Whereas Constance Mary Martin (when had he learnt her second name was Mary?) was engraved on the substance of his heart, where the name Rosemary was being effaced by time and distance; even a heart turned to stone crumbles, or transmutes again into living flesh. It was what Aunt Anne had hoped for: 'There'll be someone for you, Edmund dear. You must forgive Rosemary –

she's young and shallow and thoughtless. It would take sterner stuff to stand out against this war hysteria.' But Edmund did not believe he would ever forgive her. It was one thing to toss him back his ring and scald him with her taunt of coward; the episode on the church path was something else again.

It had come after morning service in the village church where they were to have been married – Edmund saw no reason why he should not continue to worship God, although some members of the congregation had made it plain that they thought God should feel as insulted by his presence as they did. The vicar, too old to become a chaplain to the Forces, felt free to proclaim how much he would have liked to be, and showed singular success in transposing the more jingoistic pronouncements of politicians into the mouth of God, to be plucked thence the following Sunday at Matins for the congregation's benefit. In vain Edmund reminded himself that God was all-encompassing and that every shade of opinion could be found in Him; it did not minimise the hurt when at Easter, at which he had always sung the solo in whatever musical programme was arranged, he the trained singer was passed over in favour of a draper's assistant with a powerful, unmodulated bray. Nevertheless, he continued to worship at St Michael's, 'the warrior saint', as the vicar was fond of reminding them all; and if on occasion he glimpsed Rosemary across the aisle, demurely virginal as one of the saints in the bad Victorian stained glass above her, he had learnt to pretend he had not noticed that she would seek every opportunity for publicly ignoring him.

So he was surprised, on emerging into the sunlight one summer morning, to see her waiting on the path where the congregation lingered to chat, exchange gossip and news, and – with increasing frequency – to condole with the bereaved. On this occasion the blacksmith and his wife were making their first public appearance after the loss in Flanders of their only son. People were shaking hands, clapping the blacksmith on his bowed shoulders, speaking kindly to the crushed little woman at his side. But Rosemary was standing alone, eyes fixed on the church porch, waiting for someone – could it be for him? Despite himself, Edmund felt hope flare as she started towards him, came to a halt in front of him. He had never believed that this estrangement could continue; sooner or later tolerance and good sense must prevail. He took a step towards her, hands outstretched. She turned her head away.

But her fingers were busy in her handbag, she drew something forth, reached out and thrust it into his lapel. He looked down, and she turned on her heel in the instant that he recognised the white goose quill. Someone tittered. People were turning, whispering. 'Good for Miss Rosemary,' a voice said, as Edmund, face aflame, pulled out the quill and let it flutter obliquely earthwards as he strode down the path which suddenly cleared before him. The blacksmith spat as he passed.

He had gone to church the next two Sundays because he had to face them, but he had ceased to pray. The god of this stone temple dedicated to a warrior was not his god, and thereafter he stayed away – only to find that the god of battles had taken up his abode in many institutions and spoke through many mouths. One of those which seemed created especially to receive him belonged to the Reverend Septimus Stiles.

Edmund and the clergyman had taken an instant dislike to each other, which civility held in check but could not hope to conceal.

'You don't fancy him much, do you, Doc?' Florrie Gurslake asked in her outspoken way.

'We hold opposing views, I suspect,' Edmund murmured.

'I don't care about his views, but he's a nasty piece of work. Have you noticed how he keeps eyeing the girls?'

Edmund had noticed but did not wish to discuss the subject with Florrie, whose reputation for tactlessness grew apace. The Reverend Septimus watched young women with something akin to hunger in his eyes, but there was no reason to think there was anything sinister about it; many middle-aged men did the same. So why am I uneasy, Edmund wondered, his thoughts coming back to Nina Martin lying before him on her bed. Surely I do not suspect Mr Stiles of violating a girl even younger than his daughter, and one intending to become a nun? He didn't do it, of course he didn't, I am a victim of my own prejudice. All the same, I shall make it my business to find out where he was during the last hour of the dance. I do not remember him dancing. No doubt we shall find he was in his cabin composing the sermon with which we are to be honoured on Armistice Day. But if that is the case, who is to prove that he was really there? Whose word can be trusted on this accursèd ship?

The Reverend Septimus had got his way and there was to be a service on deck for First Class passengers. Naturally all would attend; it would be impossible not to. And I, Edmund thought, must be there in a triple capacity: as ship's surgeon and a member of the ship's company; as medical man in case anyone collapses from heat or emotion; and as mourner in my own right for all those who went to the war and did not come home again. Already there were whispers that his presence would be unwelcome. Captain Johnson called it 'an insult to the dead', making Edmund regret that professional ethics made it impossible for him to call Johnson an insult to the living. Bert Gurslake opined that there wasn't no room in the world of the 'twenties for someone who hadn't done his bit. Julian Strode, too young to express a survivor's opinion, made a point of withdrawing from any circle which Edmund happened to join; and Imogen Stiles, who was also too young but saw no reason why she should not express her father's opinions, made a bid for attention, Archie Johnson's especially, by announcing that she did not want to stand beside a coward. On the whole, Edmund reflected, he was a considerable embarrassment in First Class, equalled only by the presence among them of Prince Ravi of Maggapore,

138

the stowaway translated overnight from the Second Class galley to the best available accommodation in First Class. Of course the colour of the Prince's skin was lightened several shades by his title, but he remained uncompromisingly dark, though his wealth and birth and education, when discovered, had mysteriously changed wrongdoer into wronged.

The first intimation of his identity came in a telegram from the Owners sent at the request of the India Office (Mr Edwards had been busy behind the scenes), requesting all captains to check passenger lists for a young Indian gentleman, description followed, who might be travelling incognito aboard one of their ships. If found, he was to be given every possible assistance and discreetly prevented from leaving the ship. The Purser had reported that the *Karachi* harboured no one who fitted the bill.

'How about yon blackamoor stowaway?' the Chief asked.

He was alone with Angus Meiklejohn in the Captain's cabin during their half-hour at the end of the day.

With sinking heart Angus re-read the description: nineteen years old, height five foot seven, slim build, clean-shaven, caste mark on forehead, speaks perfect English as well as Hindustani and local dialect. Stafford Briscoe had warned him that the silent stowaway spelt trouble. It looked as though he might be right.

Angus summoned a steward. 'My compliments to Mr Briscoe, and would he be good enough to join me and Mr Sutherland in here.' If the diplomat had scented imposture, he could help in its unmasking.

Stafford Briscoe listened with trained impassivity to the story, then said: 'We shall have to interview the young man. I suggest we allow him to think that all is discovered and note his reactions.'

Captain Meiklejohn bowed his assent.

So it was Briscoe who rose to his feet when the stowaway was brought in by two sailors who stood holding him on either side. At a nod from him, the Captain signalled to the two men and the escorting officer to let go of the boy and withdraw.

'Ah, Your Highness,' Briscoe said in English, watching the boy's face as he spoke, 'you choose an unconventional mode of travel. I trust you are enjoying life below decks.'

To Ravi it was as though the Resident were after him in person, for though there was no outward resemblance between Vernon Edwards and the speaker, the tone, the approach were the same.

He closed his lips and looked at a distant corner of the cabin. When the escort had come to fetch him from the Second Class galley he had expected to be accused of some crime. There were wild rumours that a First Class passenger, a woman, had been attacked and left for dead. If true, he might have to speak to attest his innocence. The last thing he had expected was to be greeted as himself. He listened without appearing to as the tall man in front of him went on:

'I ought perhaps to introduce myself: Stafford Briscoe, of His Majesty's

Foreign Service. Captain Meiklejohn you already know. And this is Mr Sutherland, Chief Engineer of the *Karachi*. Will Your Highness not sit down?'

Will Your Highness do this . . . that . . . take orders. The Resident spoke in the same way. But at least these men commanded the ship, whereas in Maggapore it should be the Nawab who commanded. As it would be the Nawab some day.

Involuntarily Ravi sat, but sprang up immediately, hating himself for inbred subservience. The other men had relaxed, he noted. Stafford Briscoe drew up another chair.

'Please, Your Highness. English hospitality will be offended if an Indian prince refuses to sit. Your father is a good friend to the King-Emperor. For his sake his son is an honoured guest on this vessel, as well as for his own.'

Afterwards Briscoe could never decide what caused him to add the last words, but at least the young man sat down and made no attempt to deny his identity. The Nawab would be relieved. Grateful, too. Briscoe was already concocting the telegram in which he would announce that the missing prince was safe and well. Meanwhile lavishness was indicated. He was confident it would be lavishly repaid.

'I hope Your Highness will forgive the misunderstandings that have so far dogged your presence aboard the *Karachi*,' he continued, smooth as silk, avoiding all mention of the circumstances that presumably lay behind this desperate attempt to return to England. 'Fortunately there is now a First Class cabin at your disposal –' he glanced at the Captain and received a nod of confirmation, 'and with your permission we will have you shown to it at once.'

'I have no money.'

They were the first words Ravi had spoken. His voice was unexpectedly deep, the accent the equal of Briscoe's own.

'Among friends such matters need not be discussed, Your Highness. I have no doubt a loan can be arranged with the Purser to cover immediate needs.'

'And no clothes.' Ravi indicated the overalls which the head cook had grudgingly provided. 'I can't travel First Class in these.'

'Of course not, but I am sure we can borrow something suitable to fit you from among the officers' off-duty clothing, and in a few days' time we can go shopping in Port Said.'

That is to say, you can't, because of the risk of your absconding, but someone can go on your behalf. Meanwhile young Strode's about your height though a bit heavier. Too bad he's the officer who actually arrested you, but with luck you needn't know that. Briscoe tasted his future celebrity. What a story all this would make. He pictured himself telling it to Jean, to men in clubrooms. One of Sir Stafford Briscoe's anecdotes.

He held out a hand. 'I am sure there are no hard feelings on your side for

140

the way we have treated you. Please be assured that there are none on ours.'
He wasn't too sure about the Chief but he would sort that out later, and he
had taken care this time not to wait for the Captain's confirmatory nod.

Angus Meiklejohn rose in a gesture of dismissal. Already a steward was
hovering at the door. 'I can only say what I say to all passengers, Prince.
May you have a pleasant voyage.'

He judged that it was time to stop using the formal 'Your Highness' to a
boy of Andy's age – at least Andy as he had last known him, before the
telegram came.

The Chief also shook hands, though his good wishes were conspicuously absent. All three men stood as Ravi was ushered out. Then, as the
door closed behind him, the Chief's scorn and anger burst forth.

'Yon laddie's defying his father, defrauding the Line, and you're
condoning it. D'ye call such behaviour right?'

'Politic, Mr Sutherland, politic,' Stafford Briscoe murmured.

'Politic! Have ye no regard for the Ten Commandments? The Lord
says, "Honour thy father and thy mother." He also says, "Thou shalt not
steal." That's two for a start yon prince of yours has broken.'

'Perhaps he does not subscribe to them.'

'A heathen!' James Sutherland glared at Stafford Briscoe as though he
were responsible for this deplorable state of affairs. 'Then a good English
education's been wasted on him. Did ye note his hands, as delicate as a
girl's?'

Stafford Briscoe had indeed noted them. Many Arabs had hands like
that: all bones and veins and sinews, darker than Maurice's but otherwise
much the same. He glanced with distaste at the Chief's hands, meaty and
powerful, with a sprinkling of black hairs on their backs which were
echoed by the sprouting black hairs in his nostrils.

'Ideals of beauty vary from race to race, and sometimes within a race,' he
said mildly. 'Ideals of conduct are the same.'

'There's no tampering with the Word of the Lord, and no calling black
white, either.'

'Can we not compromise on infinite shades of grey?'

'Ye canna compromise with evil, Mr Briscoe.'

'That implies that we know what evil is.'

'Would ye no agree that it was an evil act to rape a young lady?'

'Certainly, though we have yet to learn how it came about.'

'What difference does that make?'

'There may be extenuating circumstances; if, say, the lady's behaviour
was misunderstood.'

'We're not talking about fast women, Mr Briscoe. This lassie was going
to be a nun.'

'And is therefore inexperienced in the ways of men and women. Innocence can be its own danger as well as its own protection, Mr Sutherland.'

'So in your book the innocent are blameworthy?'

141

'Sometimes. As I say, it depends on circumstance.'

'And the guilty are to be excused?'

'Sometimes. Again, depending on circumstance.'

'Then where are your moral values?'

'Where are yours, Mr Sutherland, but in your head? Mine are in the same place, but our heads happen to be different. Who's to say which of us is right?'

'I believe ye'd even seek to find excuse for a disaffected stoker who tried to set fire to the ship.'

'Like everyone aboard, I have a vested interest in ensuring that such a man, if guilty, is punished, but I'd still want to know how he came to be disaffected.'

'You've no proof, Chief,' Angus Meiklejohn said in warning.

'True, sir, I did not see him strike a match. But I consider that a man who has been rightly rebuked for insubordination –'

'By yourself, Mr Sutherland?'

'By one of my officers – and is then found loitering round the bunkers when off duty –'

'You did not tell me that.'

'Did I not, sir? You'll pardon the omission. The man had too much time for idling when yon doctor took him off work.'

'Why did he do that?'

'He burnt his hand, sir – I told you.'

'So you did.' When the rebuking officer pushed him and he fell against a fire door. Angus began to understand why the Chief thought the fire in the bunker had been deliberate, and did not like what he understood. He guided the conversation into safer channels.

'Mr Briscoe will be thinking we have a fire-raiser on board. As he already knows we have a rapist, he must be wishing some other ship had called at Aden first. Quite apart from the excitement of the stowaway, though that at least has a happy ending. Do you think we shall be able to persuade Prince Ravi to forgive us, Mr Briscoe?'

'I hope so, Captain, in time.'

'It may be tricky ensuring he doesn't make a dash for it when passengers go ashore at Port Said and Marseilles.'

'The Nawab will be grateful for your vigilance, Captain. No doubt in a typically Oriental way.'

Angus Meiklejohn allowed himself to savour the prospect of a little extra money. He did not consider himself ill-paid, but there was nothing for luxuries by the time his careful nature had apportioned his salary to cover various needs. Most important was some financial provision for Andy; he and Ailsa had long ago agreed on this. Each month the sum which in happier times had provided holidays, a trinket for Ailsa, a treat for Andy, some long-desired item for the home, went into a savings account in the name of Andrew Meiklejohn. He would have that much at least against the day when, uncomprehending, he attended the second of two funerals and strangers came to take him from his home.

Meanwhile another man's son was his problem. He said to Briscoe, 'Why d'you think His Highness is running away?'

Briscoe shrugged. 'Some peccadillo, no doubt. The Nawab is said to be a stern father. Or perhaps he can't bear life at court.'

The Palace at Maggapore was known to be vast; some parts of it were beautiful, but it lacked the amenities of the West. And when you reached its heart an old man with an ivory chess set beside him sat moving pieces, playing against himself. To a boy fresh from English public school the tinkle of fountains must be as maddening as the peacock's sunset cries, and the endless plains of brown dust visible from every window as dispiriting as idleness. How did you reconcile two conflicting cultures? Instead of straddling them, the boy was being torn apart. He had witnessed a similar struggle in Maurice, torn between their life together and the last clinging remnants of home. In the end home had lost. When he joined up Maurice had described himself as an orphan. Stafford Briscoe (uncle) was officially listed as being next of kin.

'If we knew what he'd done,' the Chief said, his voice heavy with foreboding, 'I'm thinking we might be one stage nearer knowing who Miss Martin's attacker was.'

'In Maggapore, Mr Sutherland, such an act would not be regarded with the same disapproval that it naturally excites in us. There would have been no need for flight, though much might have depended on the wealth and caste of the victim.'

'We are all equal in the sight of God.'

'But we are talking about the sight of man, in which we are decidedly unequal, not to mention the sight of man's gods.'

Captain Meiklejohn hastened to the rescue. 'The Ten Commandments might be only nine somewhere else –'

'Not if the Lord has given them.'

'– and they might not carry equal weight.'

Stafford Briscoe's presence imposed formality. 'Which ones, sir, were ye thinking might be dispensed with?'

'Perhaps the prohibition against graven images.'

'The Papists would agree with you.'

'For the rest, it's more a matter of degree.'

'Are there degrees of killing? A man's either dead or alive.'

'Might not the circumstances of the victim determine the seriousness of the offence?' Stafford Briscoe suggested. 'To steal sixpence from the poor might be considered worse in the Hereafter than stealing a thousand pounds from the rich. And to destroy a happy marriage is surely worse than a mere technical infringement of the Seventh Commandment.'

The Chief raised his eyebrows. 'A mere technical infringement. Now what's that?'

'If the marriage has broken down, exists in name only, is another relationship so very wrong?'

This intervention from the Captain was unexpected. The Chief turned to him, caught off guard.

'I never thought to hear ye defending adultery, Angus. What would Ailsa say?'

She need not know . . . Angus drove the thought from him, astounded that it had surfaced at all. Both men had briefly forgotten the presence of Stafford Briscoe, who listened mesmerised.

'I'm not saying adultery isn't wrong, Jamie, just that there may sometimes be excuse.'

'There are excuses for disobeying man's laws, but the courts do not recognise them. They still treat those who do as lawbreakers and punish them as such.'

'Since when has punishment been a deterrent? No lawbreaker expects to be found out. Whereas those who break the Lord's Commandments do so in the light of His all-seeing eye. Does that take courage or not?'

'You must not confuse courage with human weakness, Angus. We are all sinful men. The Devil tempts us with specious excuses, but I'd not thought to hear them from your lips.'

They were talking, Angus realised, as if he had broken all Ten Commandments. He said in a lighter tone: 'Who's to say I wasn't testing you by playing Devil's Advocate?'

The Chief looked mollified. 'You were aye one for a disputation. Mr Briscoe will be reassured to know that ye're still master under God of this vessel and not master under something worse.'

Stafford Briscoe was not reassured. He did not believe in the Devil. He did not believe in God. The world turned, the sun rose and set, men died and were buried and did not rise again; or they rose and were not buried, disintegrating into shards of bone and flesh while the earth rocked with shell blasts and Heaven looked on unconcerned. It had nothing to do with the words mouthed on formal occasions, world without end amen, when the bowed heads raised with an air of relief as though oppressed by this instance of folly in the presence of nullity. The forthcoming Armistice Day service would be a prime example: the trappings of Church and State united in an act of remembrance which at the next behest of political necessity they would perforce forget. No more war. It was a good slogan. The League of Nations was, no doubt of it, a fine thing – especially for Geneva and Swiss prosperity. All insisted they were brothers, despite the fate of Adam's sons. History taught, and those who made history learned nothing. God and the Devil had as much to do with it as a ceremonial sword with modern weaponry: they were outmoded figures of speech which he had never expected to hear bandied about in this cabin by Captain Meiklejohn and his Chief Engineer.

'I'm always glad to be in good hands,' he said easily. 'I've enjoyed your discussion, gentlemen. As for Prince Ravi, I'll endeavour to keep an eye on him. We'll see what diplomacy can do.'

He had seen diplomacy achieve a good deal, had even been instrumental in enabling it to do so. With this handsome, haughty princeling it would be a challenge to try. An amusement for the voyage, for brief acquaintance did not dispose him to rate his fellow passengers highly. Edmund Bladon was the one man in First Class who interested him, and that chiefly for his past. When last encountered Bladon had been a young singer home from two years in Leipzig, and because of his refusal to join up when war broke out, as everyone around him was doing, suspected of German sympathies. Because of him, his sister Jean had quarrelled with her best friend, Anne Bladon, and the breach remained unhealed. With the old baronet Sir Jeffrey semi-paralysed after a stroke and the elder son Roger dead and buried, this ship's surgeon stood to inherit title and estate. Title, at least; that was inalienable; but the estate was running down. There was no money in farm land, it was an encumbrance, everyone said so. If Sir Jeffrey's second son was not cut out of his will, as rumour had it, his inheritance might well be debts. And he would not be welcome in the county, where war wounds still went deep and memories were long. How and why had Edmund Bladon become a doctor? What did he think the future held for him?

Edmund Bladon could not have answered. For him the future was a blank. He could see no further than the next voyage of the *Karachi* . . . and the next voyage . . . and the next. Like the Flying Dutchman, he was condemned to sail the Seven Seas, or those of them which lay between Bombay and Tilbury, until the curse of the past was lifted, until his father died; until such time as he had something to offer and could ask Constance Mary Martin if she would be his wife.

Some relationships progress like bushfires. The spark travels along the ground, doing little damage, leaving barely a hint of its presence, until the flames erupt faster and farther ahead than anyone could have guessed. So it was with Edmund's feelings for Connie Martin. No sooner had he recognised that she was important to him than she became important in a very special way that carried with it its own torment: he could not speak for her, but other men with better prospects could. She could not spend the rest of the voyage at Nina's bedside, for Nina could not spend the rest of the voyage in bed. Somehow they had to live again despite the flicker of fear aroused by every masculine presence, including of course his own. Only by catching the man responsible could that fear be laid to rest. And how, in a ship where crew and passengers numbered hundreds, did you set about identifying one man? Even after eliminating women and those with watertight alibis, there were still a great many left. Colour of skin would not help, for in the dark and masked Nina had not seen him. She had not heard his voice. Only the urgent pricking of the knife at her throat told of sadism, murderous intent.

Nevertheless, he said again to the girl lying on the bed before him, 'Are

145

you sure there's nothing you remember that might identify this man?'

Nina raised her head from Connie's shoulder long enough to shake it. She doesn't want to remember, Edmund thought.

'No scent?' he persisted. 'Cologne, for instance, or tobacco?'

The headshake was more of a shudder this time.

'Leave her alone,' Connie pleaded.

'I'm going to,' Edmund said, 'but I want you both up on deck tomorrow, that's doctor's orders.'

'For the Armistice Day service?'

'Not specifically. You needn't go if you don't want to.'

Connie said, 'I think we should.'

She said it as much to Nina as to Edmund. If they knew of the service, Mrs Magistrate Beer and Mrs Major Barrett would surely expect them to be there. To plead indisposition was to be like Mummy. To be like Mummy was to let Daddy down. It was also to die in adultery, but Nini did not know that, must not know it, for now that she could no longer spend her life in intercession for the souls in Purgatory, she would grieve immeasurably if she learned that the soul of Bridget Mary Martin stood more in need of prayers than she had thought.

She said more firmly, 'We'll go, won't we, Nina?'

A quiver. 'People will stare . . .'

'They don't know what's happened,' Edmund assured her, wishing he could be certain it was true.

'He'll be there.'

They did not need to ask who 'he' was.

Edmund said, 'He'll be everywhere,' and realised too late the significance of his statement, for this unguessable 'he' would be a part of all Nina's future relationships unless he could be identified and laid to rest. That is, if he existed . . .

Edmund tried one last time. 'Nina, are you sure it happened just as you described it, the man seizing you from behind?'

'Yes.'

'And he was wearing a scarf tied over his face, you never saw him?'

'No.'

'What about when he forced you into the empty cabin?'

'It was dark. He put out the light.'

She had thought of everything. If not true, it was well invented.

'And there's nothing more you can tell me about him?'

Nina looked at him with clear blue eyes grown suddenly opaque as though their very depth were sullied. For an instant she seemed about to speak and Edmund's hopes rose. Then she turned back to Connie, burrowing her face against her sister's shoulder like a blind kitten, but not before uttering a mewling little cry of 'No.'

146

III

November 11 dawned hot and humid like every other day the Red Sea knew. Waking after a night that felt sleepless even if it was not, passengers could see through their portholes that the light already had a hazy quality as though filtered through fine spray, and the effort of turning the head to inspect it sent sweat slithering over skin already glistening, to fall on a damp and rumpled bed. Some slept naked, but they were a minority; most preferred to make concessions to decency 'in case the ship sank', as Florrie Gurslake proclaimed with ghoulish relish, although the Red Sea's oily calm soothed her nerves better than the rolling white-flecked greenness of waters nearer home.

Archie Johnson wore his pyjama trousers. Nakedness was a luxury he could no longer afford. The chancre remained visible, had even, he fancied, increased in size, though the quack Bladon assured him it was not so. 'All I can do is prevent it spreading,' he told Archie. 'I can't make it go away. For that, you'll have to wait until we're home and you can get specialised treatment at a clinic.' Archie shuddered. Quite apart from his dread of the treatment and the even greater dread that the treatment might not work, he would have to stay in London to be certain of anonymity and the cheapest hotel was more than he could now afford. This homecoming was very different from what he had imagined when he heard the magic words 'Home Leave'.

He had supposed he might stay in London to do a show or two, go to tea-dances, take in a night club, always accompanied by a girl, preferably a different girl each time unless the incredible happened and one of them turned out to be *the* girl. After a few days he would return home to his indulgent parents, to admiring glances from his sisters – and their friends. He was well aware that everyone went out of their way to spoil young Empire defenders, from offering them temporary membership of the golf club to the riding stable's best hacks. Retired officers in the vicinity made a point of inviting one for a 'peg', while their mems, less given to alcohol and anecdote, assessed one with shrewd if faded eyes. And it was the mems' verdict which mattered. If favourable, more doors were opened and jealously guarded daughters paraded for inspection at the tennis club, boating parties, perhaps a private dance. A young officer could easily find himself engaged before he knew it and reduced thereafter to a three-year courtship by post, unless the bride grew impatient of waiting for his next home leave and married someone else, or came out from England for a ceremony in the garrison church at Maggapore. Archie had attended one of these, had formed part of the guard of honour as the young couple left the church, bowing beneath the arch of swords, she with buck teeth and he already balding (it was the heat that played havoc with a man's hairline, everyone said so), while confetti showered them and voices shrill or hearty assured them that this was the happiest day of their lives.

But for Archie – never. He no longer held the King's Commission. He was no longer part of an ordered, stable world in which promotion came slowly but surely and one knew precisely who addressed whom as 'sir'. He could no longer count on the ministrations of bearers, native servants, who emerged from and receded into shadow much as they entered or left his consciousness. Abbas would already be drawing a bath for another officer, polishing someone else's boots. And in those shadows to which he had receded he would be sniggering over Captain Johnson's fate as the tale of his departure was unfolded, doubtless with accretions of ignominy. What the bearers did not know the lawyers would fabricate, exaggerating their own cleverness until it would sound to those who did not know better as if they had run an officer of the British Army of India out of town.

Archie closed his eyes against the humiliation. For him, life outside the Army did not exist. Just as he was wondering what to do when demobilised in 1919, the offer of a regular commission had come through. 'We need young fellows like you,' the interviewing major told him when he presented himself before the Selection Board. 'Chaps who've had a bit of experience and know what this war game's all about.' The major had lost a leg, so was entitled to call it a game, though it was not the term Archie would have used. He had fought his war in deadly earnest, intent on killing to survive. To a schoolboy steeped in tales of Hun atrocities (for which supporting evidence tended to be contradictory or vague), the slaughter of Attila's hordes had become a crusade that not even the filth, cold and squalor of trench warfare could diminish when set against the exaltation of consciously killing a foe.

Only twice had Archie known that supreme personal satisfaction. The first time was when he took aim at a head which kept bobbing above the parapet of a supposedly empty German support trench a couple of hundred yards away. The sector was quiet; in the summer silence they could hear the young German whistling a jaunty, catchy tune with a refrain so often repeated that it imprinted itself on the ear. The young man was either supremely confident or supremely careless. They almost expected him to wave as he paused at intervals to peer in the direction of his enemies – if he bothered to consider them as such. He must have been alone or leading a small detachment; no CO would have allowed him to be so rash. After a few minutes Archie assessed the periodicity of his appearances and rested a borrowed rifle on the parapet. 'Be you going to shoot him, sir?' someone asked in the thick accents of the West Country. Archie

148

answered, 'I'm going to try,' feeling himself concentrated into a pair of eyes and a tensing trigger-finger which moved without act of will.

The head jetted scarlet; the helmet fell backwards revealing a flash of fair hair; the whistling stopped. In the silence the echoes of the shot extended to what felt like infinity. 'Reckon you got him, sir,' said the same West Country voice, at once respectful and reproachful. 'Any one of you could have done the same,' Archie said, aware suddenly that none of them had tried to, that there was something accusatory in their awe. Weeks later, when one of them who could carry a tune began whistling the same jaunty air that had floated over No Man's Land that summer morning, Archie had shouted at him to shut up.

The second time he had killed was in retrospect more satisfactory, though at the time all he had felt was fear. He had been leading a wiring party back to base through a shattered village when they had turned a corner and run slap into a German patrol. Their only hope lay in quick reaction. The less surprised party won the day. Archie had run forward firing before he registered what he was doing, uncertain even whether he had been hit. A German fell as if pole-axed. Another twisted into a twitching heap. Behind Archie his own men fired in fright and fury. The Germans took to their heels, demoralised by the death of their officers. The British continued firing as they ran, and Archie felt again that surge of exaltation at seeing a man go down.

This time there was neither awe nor accusation. His men crowded round him full of praise, even one nursing a shattered arm, the sole exception being a khaki carcase lying in the angle of a building, their one fatal casualty. In recommending Archie for the MC his commanding officer had been lyrical: 'Put to flight a superior force . . . courage in the face of the enemy . . . an inspiration to his men.' So why had it ended in disgrace and humiliation when he had acted similarly in Maggapore? Similarly, not identically, for he had had no intention of killing – this was peacetime, after all – but faced with superior hostile numbers and responsibility for the men he was leading, he had once again opened fire. Would they have had him turn tail, have British soldiers run from a jeering native mob, perhaps even be massacred? The Colonel had avoided answering such questions. It seemed they did not arise.

So now, because he had acted like a soldier, he would don a soldier's uniform for the last time. He laid it out with all the loving care of a bearer and contemplated it on his bed: shorts and knee-high khaki socks, brown shoes polished to a mirror finish; short-sleeved shirt with a captain's pips on the regimental shoulder flash; his medal ribbon over the left breast pocket – that at least they could not take away; Sam Browne belt and pistol holster; flat khaki cap and cane; everything that went to make up the hot-weather uniform of an officer of one of the Indian Army's crack regiments; all that was lacking was the officer himself.

Of course no one on the *Karachi* knew he no longer had the right to wear

149

it, except perhaps that little pipsqueak of an Indian prince. Of all the places in the Indian sub-continent he might have come from, it had to be Maggapore. Not that they'd ever met. An infantry captain didn't go calling on the Nawab in that vast rose-coloured edifice set on the only hill for miles around. And it was unlikely that the princeling, who until recently had been at school in England, would know anything about an episode in the town's poorest quarter which had left one of his father's subjects dead, still less know the name of the English officer responsible. There had been no glint of recognition in his eyes when Captain Johnson had been introduced to him in the dining saloon, though Captain Johnson had taken care to say nothing about being stationed in Maggapore. No, the ship's stowaway knew nothing, and could therefore say nothing to undeceive. To Mrs Vane, Stafford Briscoe, old man Haldingham; Miss Stiles and her parents, he was still Captain Johnson MC, going home on leave, gallant and dashing and with the world his oyster; a thoroughly enviable young man.

The contrast between appearance and reality couldn't have been greater, but there was no one to share it with except the doctor who turned out to be a conchie. He might have guessed there was something wrong there. Would the news make any difference to Connie Martin's crush on him? There was a Snow Maiden if you like! All very fine and friendly until a chap did what ought to have been expected and then a look guaranteed to freeze your balls. Though if they had indeed become ice balls, might that not ease the burning throb that reminded him that he was as hollow as his uniform? The outward show of a man, nothing better. In any case Miss Connie had made herself scarce since his ill-fated pass on the night of the dance, and her holy virgin sister had made herself scarcer still. 'Locked up, she is, or ought to be,' Mrs Gurslake had reported. 'She's gone stark raving mad if you ask me.' No one had, but Florrie was ignorant of the dictum that a lady waited to be asked. Besides, she had been so shocked by Nina's outburst that she had had to unburden herself, and since the girl's sudden and mysterious indisposition was the subject of speculation throughout First Class, Archie's had been among the attentive ears when she gave a suitably crafted account of Nina's condition without vouchsafing how she knew of it.

Had the girl really gone off her rocker, Archie wondered, as a result of what had happened to her, for while no one knew what precisely, everyone was aware that something had. Not that screaming at old Ma Gurslake to get out was any indication; the sanest passenger might have done the same if subjected to a tête-à-tête with that upholstered bosom, those beady black eyes, and that ridiculous topknot skewered by a dagger. Still, the pious little sister whom Connie guarded so jealously might well have had a screw loose all along and no one any the wiser. Suppose that story about the convent was an invention and the girl was going into a nursing home. There were places that specialised in nervous disorders, or whatever the phrase was when someone went off her head. There were also clinics that specialised in other unmentionable diseases, such as that which afflicted him. Wasn't madness one of the delights they threatened if treatment was ignored? Could little Nina . . . Archie checked his imagination. He already had enough on his mind.

But when after breakfast he returned to his cabin to don his uniform for the service and shower afresh, for already his clothes clung damply, he was startled to find Edmund Bladon waiting for him. Archie paused, enquiring and unwelcoming.

'May I come in?' Bladon asked.

'I suppose so.' The corridor was no place for a showdown, if that was what it was going to be.

Bladon followed him in and closed the door behind them.

'What is it?' Archie asked, tapping a foot to show he had no time to waste.

'This is confidential . . .' Bladon began.

Archie waited, deliberately not helping.

'I want you to give me your word as an officer and a gentleman,' Bladon said, 'that you've not had sexual intercourse with any woman aboard this ship.'

Archie was suddenly guarded. 'You asked me that when I consulted you.'

'Yes, but since then.'

'I'm not prepared to answer. I've still got some rags of dignity and privacy. It's not your business anyway.'

'Of course it's my business. You could spread infection.'

'You mean there's an epidemic of the clap?'

'Your word, please.'

'I can't give it.' Not the word of an officer.

'Why not?'

Archie was silent.

'I'll ask you again. Have you had intercourse since we sailed?'

'What if I have?'

'I want the name of the woman.'

'No gentleman's going to give you that.'

'For God's sake, Johnson, this is serious. She's in danger.'

'I haven't admitted she exists.'

The quack was certainly worked up about it. It was diverting to lead him on.

'What about the night of the fancy hat dance – did you have intercourse then?'

Archie began to put two and two together. 'Has someone been saying I did?'

'No-o . . .'

'But little Miss Nina was too drunk to know who tupped her, is that it?'

'Miss Nina Martin was not drunk.'

151

'And not a virgin either by the end of the evening, I'll bet. My, my, these would-be nuns do fall hard.'

It was guesswork, but the pieces fell into place with such precision that Archie was convinced he was right. Besides, Bladon's face was a giveaway. Archie had seen that look before. It meant: for two pins I'd knock you down.

Edmund forced himself to breathe deeply. He would not give way to anger, he would not! He had feared all along it might be a mistake to tackle Johnson direct, and now the anxiety and distress that had led him to do so had caused things to misfire. If Johnson were guilty he was not going to admit it. Could he instead shock him into admitting innocence?

'Nina was raped,' he said. Surely Johnson would deny it and he could assess his truthfulness.

Instead Johnson whistled. 'What price the nunnery now!'

'What price her health and sanity.'

'Yes, Ma Gurslake said she was teetering on the edge.'

'Mrs Gurslake is an interfering fool.'

'Carried *nem. con.*, as they say.'

He had admitted nothing, damn him. Edmund tried again.

'Now that you're aware of the situation, can't you see it's vital I should know?'

'What makes you think I'm the only man aboard the *Karachi* to have a communicable disease?'

He had a point, Edmund admitted. His was the only known case of syphilis, but it was at least possible that other cases existed among passengers and crew.

He said stiffly, 'I'm sorry you're not prepared to help.'

'I'm not prepared to incriminate myself on a rape charge. She's not pregnant, is she?'

'It's far too soon to say.'

'You could try blaming the Holy Ghost, if need be.'

The suggestion was in character.

'Johnson, you'll keep quiet about all this, won't you?' Edmund insisted.

'It won't do much good,' Archie said. 'Everyone's already speculating on what's happened to Nina Martin.'

'Suppose it were *your* sister, how would you feel?'

'Oh, very well.' Archie glanced towards the bed where his uniform lay waiting. Would Bladon never go?

Edmund followed his glance and withdrew, defeated.

'I'll see you up on deck.'

'You don't mean to say *you're* going?'

'Why not? I too have dead to remember.' And a host of other things . . .

Archie shrugged eloquently and turned towards the bed, thus presenting his back to Edmund. Edmund went out and closed the door.

In the corridor he found that he was shaking. Was there no end to the humiliations he must endure? He existed in a kind of limbo, unwanted despite his qualifications, deprived even of the right to vote. What would happen when his father died? He had no wish to return to Gloucestershire where memories were painful for him and others. Unless he had Connie at his side? She had not changed towards him since learning he was a conscientious objector, though she must know what it implied. She even sought his company – or was that because of Nina? He was in no position to offer marriage, but suppose that altered. Suppose his father died soon. 'Very frail,' was how Aunt Anne had described him in the letter awaiting Edmund at Aden. It could happen any time. He could surely salvage enough from the estate to buy a practice. Would Edmund and Constance Bladon be more acceptable than Edmund Bladon alone? Edmund and Connie Bladon – he allowed himself to dwell on the words. They had a rightness to his ear. Her body would feel right against his. He understood suddenly that they would be one flesh, their separate entities dissolving so that she was part of him as he of her, and the world outside could growl and sneer and threaten and they would remain untouched so long as they two were one.

It was a dream which he forced himself to relinquish; though later, watching the Martin girls come on deck, almost hidden under their deep-crowned, wide-brimmed hats yet to him instantly distinctive, it resurfaced in his consciousness. What did this Remembrance Day service signify to young women who had been children in another country when the Armistice was signed? They could know nothing of the awed hush when the guns fell silent, when men clasped hands, wept openly, sank to their knees in prayer, and later raised their heads uncaring above the parapets of trenches or took the first tentative steps into No Man's Land. They trod carefully because unnameable horrors, some of them lethal, lay hidden in the November mud, but they also trod boldly because under the ravaged fields lay farmland, reclaimable, eroding the very name of No Man's Land. And at home people came forth into the streets, at first cautiously, to shake hands, dance and sing, erupting into a wild euphoria of hugs and cheers and kisses, drowned briefly when church bells began to ring. Even in prison the atmosphere had penetrated. The warders went round giving out the news, grinning because for them too and their charges the end of the war must bring relief.

One of them drew back the shutter of Edmund's peephole. 'Well, two-six-nine, peace has broken out. No thanks to you, and if I had my way they'd shoot every one of you cowardly skulkers, but at least when they let you go this time we shan't be having you back.' He spat, made expert by long practice. In the narrow cell there was no place to hide. After the first few times Edmund had learned to stand with face averted, but a slimy trail of tobacco-stained saliva still slithered down his arm. He glanced round. Already the walls of his cell seemed to have expanded. There was a whiff of freedom in the foul air. Like the crowds outside whose commotion reached him faintly, like men everywhere, in hospitals, base camps, trenches, he knew an amazed awareness. He had come through. He had survived.

Angus Meiklejohn had felt the same sense of wonder, but for his ship, not for himself. Painted battleship grey, the new steel plates in her hull as hideous as scars on a body, HMS *Karachi* had also survived. Two of her sister ships had gone to the bottom, one of them with all hands, but she would sail the seas of peace, her passengers voluntary again, and once decked out in the colours of the Australasian Line and refitted, she would have nothing but her secret scars to tell of wartime travail. She would be as good as new, and to her captain she would be even better, for not only were the links that bound them stronger than her new steel plating, but James Sutherland was now her Chief Engineer, and with this fellow Scot Angus felt an affinity such as he had never previously known. Looking back from the plateau of firm friendship, he could scarcely recall a time when Jamie had not been there. On that first Armistice Day the Chief had knelt down in his cabin and offered thanks to what he called the living God. Angus, equally thankful, had remained standing, uncertain whether God was dead or living. Was He perhaps another casualty of those four holocaust years?

But by Armistice Day 1924 most of those travelling First Class on the *Karachi* seemed convinced that God was living. Angus surveyed them as he took his place on deck. The Reverend Septimus Stiles had shown an unexpected talent for the theatrical, and passengers and crew were drawn up in a hollow square. In its centre was a flagpole from which the Union Jack drooped in the still heat. A trumpeter – now where had he found him? – was positioned to one side and a sailor stood ready to lower the flag at the appropriate moment. A small dais made from trestles laid across what appeared to be three tea chests had been draped in something black, an appropriate setting for the wreath which Angus was to lay upon it and which young Strode clutched ready to present.

Instinctively, Angus's eyes sought Cynthia Vane's. There she stood on the very edge of the crowd. She was wearing a simple black dress, and between the blackness of the dress and the darkness of her straw hat and the hair beneath it, Angus could barely discern the white triangle of her face. Bobby stood beside her, turning round, shifting from one sandalled foot to the other, until Angus longed to reprimand him and say, 'Don't.' He was not a bad child, there were moments when he was endearing, but he was growing up undisciplined. Not like Andy Meiklejohn, though of course it was hard for his mother with no man to turn to and her own grief still as raw as on the day it was born. The pity Angus felt for her blinded him to the fact that he was making excuses for her in an uncharacteristic way. He had never been tolerant of weakness, of his own least of all. It was something he had in common with James Sutherland, a stern clarity of thought and judgement that could never permit an issue to be blurred by considerations of intent or extenuating circumstances, or even of character.

The task that lay to hand could not be shirked or delegated. If that task was bringing up a son, then no indulgence – which was really self-indulgence – must be allowed to warp or distort the upright lines between which a man walked in the sight of – what? his God? But if God were no longer living, had never lived, did not begin to exist, what use then the self-denial? Cynthia Vane was surely right to spoil the only relic of the man she had loved to distraction. What was love but the desire to give? His own love longed to give her strength and in return draw on her sweetness, in the act of procreation above all. She was born to be the mother of a son. Not Bobby, but *his* son. His son most of all.

'*God so loved the world that He gave his only begotten Son, that whosoever believeth in Him should not perish but have everlasting life.*'

The mellow orotundities of the Reverend Septimus Stiles who, unnoticed, had ascended the dais, floated forth and hung in the still air, seeming to fill the hollow square like a miasma.

In the pause following the Reverend Septimus exhorted, 'Let us pray.'

Angus was glad to bow his head and save his eyes from straying in the direction of Cynthia. He could think of nothing but the awfulness of the admission which his own heart, racing ahead, had just made. He was old enough to be her father, he was a married man, the father of a twenty-six-year-old son. Yet the more he reminded himself of these considerations, the less they mattered. Marriage today was no longer indissoluble. For everyone – married, single, divorced, widowed – there loomed the promise of a new start.

'Grant, O Lord, that in this act of remembrance . . .'

Yes, he must remember Ailsa and Andrew. But he'd support them, he'd keep in touch. Would the boy even notice if he ceased to visit – for that was what he had become: a visitor. Someone home from sea who after the first week was eager to be back on his bridge, on the deck of his mistress, fast in the embrace of his true and only love.

It was a joke he made every voyage, usually in answer to some question at the dinner table about his marital state. 'Yes, sir, I have a wife – and also a mistress.' Then in the shocked hush that followed: 'My mistress weighs some 10,000 tons.' It never failed to get a laugh. Passengers were heard to murmur that Captain Meiklejohn had a sense of humour after all. The Captain, if he heard them, smiled at this interpretation. For him, the statement was no more than the truth.

He had sometimes wondered what personification of womanhood the SS *Karachi* might represent. Beautiful, certainly, with her slender lines and raked funnels; gallant, unquestionably; but also ageing, ailing and demanding, which made her all the dearer in his eyes. She needed him – needed him to steer her through narrow channels; to decide how much speed she should make; to cosset her when the ocean heaved beneath her, for as the man in the Bombay hotel had warned Florrie Gurslake, she did indeed have a tendency to roll. In emergency he was her saviour, not only when

155

the torpedo struck, but once in a storm when her cargo shifted and she developed a list to port. Yet when he retired and a new captain took over, the fickle jade would do as much for him if treated kindly, more perhaps if he were younger and primed with all the latest techniques of seamanship. There was talk of aeroplanes replacing ships; already men had flown the Atlantic, and the newly formed Imperial Airways dreamed of linking distant parts of the Empire to London in a series of short hops; but no one seriously believed that the days of the passenger liner were numbered, Angus Meiklejohn least of all. For as long as men felt the need to know what lay over the next horizon, there would be ships upon the sea; and for as long as he sailed it would be in command of the *Karachi*, which he suddenly saw personified as a small, slim, straight-backed woman with shingled hair and lustrous, expressive eyes.

He could not have said when for him Cynthia Vane became identified with the *Karachi*, but he knew that the love he bore the woman was clamant for satisfaction in the flesh; knew too that he must deny himself that satisfaction; she would never bear his son. How could she? He was nothing to her. His thoughts were tantamount to rape. And they already had one rape victim aboard, for almost opposite him in the front row with her sister's arm about her stood Nina Martin, eyes downcast, still the very picture of a nun.

She looks so holy, Cynthia thought crossly. Does she have to make it so obvious? If I were going to be a nun I shouldn't want anyone to know. I should dance and flirt and drink and go to wild parties so that no one even suspected what was in my heart. They say it's always the most unlikely people who become nuns. Thank God I never wanted anything but to marry Robert in the village church that was half-way between my home and his. It was a glorious June day – that summer of 1914 was glorious – and the men were working in the hayfields as we passed, my father and I, in an open carriage. They stood up, leaning on their scythes, and saluted. Daddy raised his top hat and bowed. Everyone knew us; they were our people who had worked all their lives on our estate or Robert's father's. There was a grand supper laid on for them that night in the largest barn. Robert and I went across there from the reception and they cheered us till the rafters rang. 'Miss Cynthy – Master Robert, God bless 'em. Come on, lads, let's give them a cheer.' They loved Robert. He had been trained from boyhood to take over the estate, and already he was respected. What's left of it now he and his two brothers are gone?

'We do not grudge those who went gallantly to defend their country . . .' The Reverend Septimus had begun his address.

His wife stood with downcast eyes and ears alert for every nuance. There might not be any bishops in the congregation, but someone might have a living in his gift. What more suitable than that a labourer in India's vineyard – she checked herself; metaphors, like clichés, were apt to run away with her. (Her husband's had a tendency to do the same.) But surely

156

some of those listening would be sufficiently impressed by his melodious utterance to remember it and mention his name. 'Heard a jolly good address last Remembrance Day aboard the old *Karachi* –' she could almost hear the conversation in her mind. 'Fellow by the name of Stiles. Wasted in the mission field, I fancy. We could do with a few of his sort over here.' And before one knew it, there would be the offer of a living, a country vicarage perhaps, and the prospect of Imogen married to someone like that nice Captain Johnson and settled near to ageing parents in England's green and pleasant land . . .

'. . . in the immortal words of the Bard,' the Reverend Septimus was saying, 'this earth, this realm, this England" is something more than a blessed plot or a geographical expression, or even an island off the coast of France . . .' (Was that too much? Was he verging on humour? He drew breath and with barely a glance at his notes went on.) 'It is a land that has bred heroes since Caractacus withstood the Roman legions; since Harold's housecarls fell round him one October eve; since a young king led his troops into battle on the hallowed field of Agincourt with the immortal cry of "God for Harry, England and St George!" '

One or two faces were looking blank (history was not taught as it should be), and he sped on with a haste that left Good Queen Bess breathless at Tilbury, down to Waterloo ('a David against the Goliath of tyranny'), and so to the present day.

Bert Gurslake, bored and uncomprehending, wondered how much longer the dog-collared little bleeder was going to go on. The last time he had had contact with the cloth had been at his wedding, and that was near a quarter of a century ago. The old Queen was alive then, it wasn't even the twentieth century, and there hadn't been no Great War, as they now called it. He'd never dreamed there'd be the opportunities it had offered for making money and that he, Bert Gurslake, would be rich. Nor had he supposed he'd end up on the other side of the world getting even richer, only to lose it all at one go. Twenty-five years later he was back where he started, older and wiser maybe, but without the sharpness, the agility of mind and body that had enabled him to keep one jump ahead of everyone else, including on occasion the law. He ought never to have been talked into borrowing money to buy shares in that goldmine, but he'd be all right so long as he could lay hands on a couple of thousand of the ready by the time this old tub docked. Or a week later at the outside. It'd take them that long to catch up with him; he'd always got off to a flying start. His eyes shifted over his fellow passengers; loaded, some of 'em. There was no shortage of money aboard. The difficulty lay in getting a suitable amount of the necessary transferred from their pockets to his. Cynthia Vane – forget it. And Florrie'd cocked it up somehow with the Martin girl; he should have known better than to ask her to try it, but who would have guessed the kid would go off her head and upset Florrie like that? Florrie hadn't been the same since, complaining of indigestion and then eating enough for two. If she thought he was wasting time on sympathy she'd another think coming. All the same, it was a pity they'd put a bun in her oven when they did. A kid would have given her something else to think about, but who'd ever have believed that after seventeen years of marriage she'd be in the family way, and just when they were leaving the country for their own and the country's good. There'd been nothing for it but a visit to old Mother Sisley, who called herself a herbalist, and it had gone like clockwork, not like some you heard of. A touch of white leg, but you got that anyway very often, and the voyage out had soon put paid to that. Gawd, what a fuss the old girl had made coming through the Bay of Biscay. Would she be as bad coming back? The doc might give her something. He wasn't bad even if he was a conchie. Daft, mind, because if he hadn't wanted to fight he could have found a way round their blooming Conscription Act if he'd been smart enough. Still, he might have inherited money – his sort never made it – and it wouldn't do no harm to sound him out. At least he wouldn't react like Mr *Captain* Johnson. Murderous little bastard. Who the hell did he think he was? And who did he think Bert was? Threatening him as if he was a bleeding native. Let him have a go at Prince Ravishing whatsisname if he was in search of someone to bash.

'. . . These men, schoolboys, some of them, fathers of families, sons and brothers, made the supreme sacrifice . . .'

The Reverend Septimus, glancing round his audience, encountered Ravi's dark features and decided to extemporise.

'. . . From far corners of the Empire, regardless of creed or colour, they came with haste and dedication to defend the Motherland . . .'

That should do it. Follow the golden rule and include everybody. This was, after all, a vote of thanks. They were coming up to the hymn. Was it a mistake not to have chosen 'Land of Hope and Glory'? At least they would all have known the tune. Too late now. Besides, the dance band had been practising, though they hadn't quite eliminated a tendency to syncopate.

'. . . In remembrance of that sacrifice, let us pray that we too may be ready when the call comes to give our lives that those coming after us may live . . .'

They had indeed been schoolboys, some of them, Ravi remembered. In the autumn of 1918 he had just graduated from preparatory to public school. Prominent in the new school's assembly hall was the Roll of Honour, two boards on which the latest additions shone in the brightest gilt. But no one talked about the supreme sacrifice. Instead, the headmaster paused one day before commencing morning prayers and Ravi felt a premonitory shiver run through the rows of boys behind him at sight of the head's grave face. Who was it this time? Their speculation was soon ended. 'I regret to inform you,' the head said, sounding bleak, 'that W.J. Chalmers, Harris House, 1913–18, has been killed in action on the Western Front.' And then, in the same breath: 'Let us pray.' The clatter of several hundred boys falling to their knees subsided. Harris House,

1913–18. So. W.J. Chalmers must have left in the summer term. This was October and he, Ravi, was in Harris House. Which meant that all around him were people who had worked, played and laughed with the unknown W.J. Chalmers who was now for ever set apart. '*O God, who art the author of peace and lover of concord* . . .' The headmaster's voice had no tone. Outside, autumn leaves showered past the window. Ravi noticed that the Roll of Honour already filled one board, but had only two names on the second, where W.J. Chalmers would shortly make a third.

Prayers ended, the boys shuffled out subdued. The masters too were grim-faced, all of them elderly, frail or crippled. One, who taught classics, was blowing his nose as if he had a cold. All day a hush lay over the classrooms. That night in the washroom Ravi heard a snuffling sound and realised the boy next to him was crying. 'What's the matter?' he asked. 'Nothing.' The boy scrubbed at his face with a towel which was not improved by the process. 'I was Chalmers's fag last year. He gave me a cricket ball when he left. He was jolly decent. And now –' the voice quavered into a higher register – 'now he's bloody well dead.'

Three weeks later the whole school had been summoned unexpectedly to assembly and the headmaster, his voice quivering, informed them that at eleven o'clock that morning an armistice had been signed. Ravi, looking at the Roll of Honour on which W.J. Chalmers's name had not yet been inscribed, felt that there was something menacing about that brown wooden board with so much space upon it. It had an empty, waiting air.

The rest of the day was a holiday, aimless because unexpected. The younger boys gathered in the common room. Ravi, only half accepted because in addition to being new he was a foreigner, stood at the window watching the day shut down. They had been told that 11 November 1918 would be a date in history only a little less memorable than 1066, except that that had been a defeat and this was Victory. He wondered why he did not feel victorious.

'Look at His Highness celebrating,' someone said.

They had not yet assimilated his title, which of course was never used. It did not rank with the English titles, of which there were several in the school, but it marked him out among the commoners as clearly as did his brown skin.

Several boys, eager for distraction, sniggered.

'It wasn't his war,' someone else observed. 'Why should he celebrate?'

'Let's make him!'

'Let's bump him!'

They surrounded him in a trice. Two of the biggest seized his ankles and shoulders. He twisted and wriggled, uncertain what indignities were about to be perpetrated, but they only laughed and let him drop. The floor was hard, and before he could gather himself together they were bumping him up and down to the accompaniment of raucous laughter, neither he nor they could have said at what.

159

'Leave him alone,' a quiet voice commanded.

The answer was a further series of bumps.

'You've got it all wrong,' the quiet voice continued. 'He's got as much right to celebrate as we have.'

The speaker, a tall, fair boy, had managed to insinuate himself into the centre of the crowd, where he stood, hands in pockets.

'Don't be a spoilsport,' someone said.

'That isn't sport.' The voice was scornful. 'I'd call it ignorance.'

'And what do you know, Mr Clever Dick?'

'I know the Indian princes gave millions to the government for the war.'

The fair boy was a banker's son and his words carried weight. The crowd began to thin around Ravi. Besides, there were other, better things to do.

Yet still the two boys who had hold of his ankles and shoulders gripped him. Ravi wriggled a leg free and kicked out. There was a howl of pain as his foot connected with a kneecap.

'You little bastard, you've crippled me!'

The boy let go his other ankle in order to hop about rubbing his own knee, but the boy holding his shoulders shook him roughly and struck him a dizzying blow on the side of the head.

'That'll teach you, you brown-skinned little bugger!'

'And that'll teach *you*,' the fair boy said, and stood looking down at his victim as if unconscious of the speed and power of the blow delivered by a fist that a moment earlier had been in his pocket. 'If I were the son of a war profiteer, as you are,' he went on, 'I'd leave Indian princes alone. They did more to help this country than your old man did. Try to remember it.'

He turned away. The other boys stood aside to make way for him. It was as though he were the prince. Ravi, the page, dusty and bruised and breathless, hurried after him.

'I say – thanks.'

The fair boy looked down at him. They were the same age, but Ravi barely reached his shoulder.

'That's all right. Here – want some toffee?'

His trouser pocket yielded a piece adorned with hairs and fluff. Ravi accepted it like manna.

'My sister makes it,' the boy said.

Ravi was enchanted at being admitted to this family intimacy. He plucked up courage to ask, 'What's your name?'

The boy seemed surprised that anyone should not know it.

'Barry Waterman.'

The two of them had been friends from that day.

John Joseph Fitzgerald also remembered, as the Reverend Septimus exhorted them to 'sing that fine hymn which expresses what every right-thinking man, woman and even child –' here he looked directly at Bobby

160

Vane – 'must feel.' He had had copies of the words run off on the Purser's duplicating machine, to the annoyance of the Purser. They were smudged but legible, and as the band struck up rousingly but at too slow a tempo (they had been warned about sounding cheerful) here and there voices joined in, hesitant, becoming stronger, until by the end of the second line they were almost in unison.

John Joseph listened to the English congratulating themselves. They were good at it – they had had plenty of practice and very little justification for thinking they were God's chosen people destined to rule by a kind of divine right over as much of the earth as they could lay their hands on. Beginning with Ireland, their first conquest, even before they had subdued Wales. His own name bore witness to the arrival of those Anglo-Norman invaders, for already the English were of mixed blood. What other nation paraded the fact as if it were an honour? 'I'd a Spanish grandmother;' 'My great-grandfather was Irish;' 'My mother's people were Huguenot refugees.' He had heard many such claims, all made in the same lordly tones, as though the blood of alien races was purified by being mixed with English blood. They were rather less vocal about some other admixtures, such as the hero Field Marshal Lord Roberts being the grandson of an Indian princess, even though a title was, as always, a mitigating factor. Would that stowaway be travelling First Class if he hadn't turned out to be the son of a nawab? He looked very different now from the frightened, sweating, starving youngster who had dined off scraps from the rich man's table purveyed to him by Steward Fitzgerald on the strict Q T.

But His Highness Prince Ravi was grateful. He went out of his way to stop and chat. 'Probably fancies your bum, lad,' Steward Preston suggested, to John Joseph's acute dismay, but when no indecent overtures followed he began to relax again. Except for his anxiety about Nina Martin. He knew what had happened to her. 'Says she was raped at knife-point,' her stewardess confided to a crony, because naturally she had to tell someone. The crony too had felt a need to talk. Before long most of the staff knew what had happened, though they kept it to themselves. Preston's comments were so crude that John Joseph had actually blushed, which called forth further indecencies. The worst was that he might be the rapist, for every man aboard was under suspicion except Mr Briscoe who had not then joined the ship. Everyone else, even Dr Bladon, was suspect. His Highness Prince Ravi most of all.

Raped at knife-point. The phrase lingered. John Joseph knew that Ravi carried a knife. He had known it long before it fell clattering to the deck as Mr Strode brought the stowaway down in a flying tackle. He had seen it during that first encounter by night on the deserted boat deck, when it had glinted at the stowaway's waist. 'Don't be frightened,' the stowaway had said. 'This dagger was my mother's father's. I could not bear to part with it. See the workmanship – but it is ceremonial only.' It was none the less very sharp, and a terrified girl would be in no condition to assess the nature

161

of a weapon she could not even see. He glanced at her now, pale and quiet beside her sister. If her story was true, she could never now be a nun. Her soft, full fairness was appealing. It might be even more so to a man with a dark skin and hot blood. Who knew what effect privation might have had on Ravi? John Joseph recalled hearing from the Christian Brothers that the sexual appetites of heathens were unrestrained. It was one more reason for sending priests to the missions. The speaker's eyes travelled hopefully over the young faces before him, which remained unresponsive to a degree. 'It's a mug's game being a priest,' Kieron had warned his young brother. 'Forget about giving yourself to God. Capons, that's all the priests are, living off the fat of the land and never the sweetness of a girl's legs opened to them. They're half-men at the best.' Perhaps. But Kieron was now a non-man. He was one of the holy souls sweating it out in Purgatory for sins which might well include mocking at priests. And it was an English bullet that had put him there, so why should his brother now join the English in their annual ritual of self-praise? John Joseph clamped his lips against the words of the hymn on the paper before him. In any case, he did not know the tune.

'*What heroes thou hast bred, O England my country.*' Edmund knew the tune all too well. It was a good tune, though difficult to sing – that ugly interval before the 'O' which too often became a glissando, particularly when played at this pace. Like everything else about today's ghastly service, it was an inappropriate choice. He could not bring himself to sing the words and kept his lips closed. Besides, he had every reason to know his voice stood out. 'What heroes thou hast bred...' Edmund glanced at Archie Johnson, though his was not the only medal ribbon in evidence that day. 'A little less of a solo, Number two-six-nine,' the prison chaplain would say on Sunday mornings. 'Give the harmonium a chance.' The rest of the prisoners would snigger dutifully. They knew the chaplain thought himself a wit. '*What heroes thou hast bred*' – and cowards too, and those who, as in every nation, were somewhere in between. 'I see the mighty dead pass in line.' Only the dead were not mighty; they were powerless, pathetic, heaped up in trenches or, as they themselves had put it, 'hanging on the old barbed wire'. And to what end? *They died that we might live*, proclaimed the village war memorial on which his father every year until incapacitated by his stroke stepped forward to lay a wreath on Armistice Day, standing doubly straight and saluting (though he was never a soldier) to wipe out the disgrace of having a son who would not fight. If he had tried to understand me I might forgive him, Edmund reflected; if he had only accepted that I had a point of view. I was his favourite son, yet he wouldn't even listen when I tried to talk to him. And Mother never intervened. After Roger died she cared for nothing. Only Aunt Anne thought I might deserve to be heard. And to this day I don't know (and have never asked) if she defended me as a beloved nephew or because she believes as I believe. Which is that man is a fighting animal, he has fought down all the centuries – and every war gives rise to more. But man is more than an animal with reflex urges; for him there is something between fight and flight. He can comprehend abstractions, moral forces, he has knowledge of good and evil, right and wrong. Yet he knows no way to settle differences but by the wholesale slaughter of other men, whereas I seek to find another way. I will not kill, in the belief that others like me must exist in every country. My death at the hands of foes does not demand retaliation, it is too small a thing. The differences between us are always less than the resemblances. My friends in Leipzig, those who survived the war, are my friends still . . .

'*Making thee what thou art . . .*' warbled Mr Stiles's congregation. The Germans spoke of the Fatherland. The English opted for the softer, all-embracing Motherland of Empire, drawing her children in. Yet looking at the faces around him, Edmund wondered whether parental affection obtained in either case. Men fought for whatever cause the propagandists skilfully presented to them; they fought because they feared – or were made to fear. How could he promise this Mother, as Mr Stiles's congregation were promising, that he would stand '*ready to hear her call, ready whate'er befall, ready to give her all*' when she was as great a destroyer in her way as the goddess Kali in the Hindu pantheon, an entity who aroused both love and dread? He glanced at Prince Ravi who was also standing silent: what did he make of this ceremony? And young Strode, ramrod straight as at a passing-out parade, stepping forward now to hand Captain Meiklejohn the wreath which he in turn would prop against the dais – what meaning had this ceremony for him? Or Nina and Connie, side by side; Bobby Vane clutching his mother's hand; all of them cushioned by youth against the horrors their elders lived with and were preparing to hand on to them.

The Last Post sounded, a little flat on the top notes, the trumpeter slightly off-key. Slowly the flag came down the flagpole to lie in folds on the deck. The two minutes' silence began with most people staring at their feet or else straight ahead of them, their faces masklike except where a muscle twitched or an eye let fall a tear.

Stafford Briscoe's face was certainly masklike, though there were those who said it was expressionless at the best of times. They had not noticed the eyes which, withdrawn and hooded, concentrated in themselves all the vitality and animation of the face. Behind them lay a subtle, scheming brain that was even now brooding on ways of negating Prince Ravi's first unfortunate impression of the *Karachi*, and perhaps winning for the British Empire a new friend. Briscoe did not make the mistake of thinking Ravi stupid, as some First Class passengers had done, nor dismiss him as an uneducated native when his scholastic background was at least as good as theirs. But he was aware of the boy's simmering resentment at having been set to work in the galley, all the greater for having brought the humiliation on himself. He had yet to learn why Ravi had fled from home in the

first place, and where he hoped to go. He must win the boy's confidence –
God, but he was beautiful! – find out his plans, and perhaps procure for
him some discreet India Office aid. At a time when the bonds of Empire were
slackening (and paradoxically more and more subjects chafed against
them), the happiness of a future native ruler acquired a new significance.

Meanwhile there was the two minutes' silence to be got through, and he
found it difficult to maintain self-control when all around him the dams of
emotion were overflowing and in danger of being swept away. But nothing
could be as bad as that first anniversary in Piccadilly, when traffic and
pedestrians stopped as if caught in some gigantic game of Grandmother's
Footsteps and for two minutes there was no sound anywhere save a horse's
nervous stamp. In the road beside Briscoe a bus had halted; the driver sat
with tears streaming down his face. Women in black and men with black
armbands wept openly, while in Whitehall the King laid a wreath on the
temporary plaster cenotaph soon to be replaced by a more permanent one
in Portland stone. There was still argument about whether the word
should have a Greek or an English pronunciation, some classicists, Briscoe
among them, opting for kaynotaph, but in the end he had adopted the
popular rendering of what too few of those who passed it with bared heads
remembered was a deliberately empty tomb. An empty tomb for such as
Maurice who had no resting-place, or an empty tomb signifying resurrection, despite the careful absence of a cross or any religious symbol?
Stafford Briscoe was not sure.

He was sure of nothing beyond the immediate present; the heat, the
sweat, the silence on this crowded deck. And somewhere in that crowd
there was a rapist, and each man seemed more unlikely than the next.
Short of a miracle – and he did not believe in miracles – how could the
man be identified? Already the voyage was half over. He had twelve days
in which to prove a case, less if the man chose to leave the ship at Marseilles, as would be prudent, and make the rest of the journey more swiftly
overland. He looked at Nina Martin. No help was forthcoming there.
Bladon had forbidden him to question her further, saying she was in too
precarious a mental state. In fact Bladon was being thoroughly obstructive
– or over-protective, which came to the same thing. Nevertheless, he felt a
reluctant respect for the man. His views were naïve, misguided, but the
courage with which he maintained them was worthy of a better cause. If
friendship were still possible between them after his first outburst, Briscoe
admitted, he would welcome Edmund Bladon as a friend.

To Nina Martin Edmund was already a friend. He was the one man
whose presence did not frighten her, for somewhere among these
decorous, bare-headed gentlemen was the one who had forced her on to the
bed in that empty cabin, splayed her legs, clamped his hand over her
mouth and thrust himself into her with a mechanical ferocity more
humiliating than the act itself. Now, whenever she tried to pray, she felt
again the violent movement that drove coherent thought away, leaving a

164

dark, empty coldness that not even Red Sea heat could dispel. She swayed, and felt Connie's arm about her. Would the two minutes' silence never end? A lifetime's thoughts flashed through her head in seconds, their speed darkening the sun. The airlessness of that empty cabin. Reverend Mother's quiet voice. Her own mother dressed for a party, Major Orrey in attendance. Daddy drinking the night Mummy died. There had been no smell of drink in that airless cabin. She had told Dr Bladon that. But then, the mask had covered nose and mouth . . . She shook her head to clear the blackness, and emerged again into light.

It was a peculiar light, far brighter than sunlight. Surely the two minutes were two hours? The band of her hat pressed like an iron crown upon her temples; she could feel her face filmed with sweat. She knew she was conscious because she could see Mrs Gurslake opposite, still with that dagger thrust into her astonishingly black, black hair. A shadow eclipsed Auntie Florrie – no, she could never call her that – but she could see the wreath of poppies glowing bloodily where Captain Meiklejohn had just placed it against the dais. The deck had tilted. Things were no longer vertical and horizontal. Was the ship going down? Why did no one move? Where's Connie? I want Connie. I cannot bear this brilliance across which drift patches of darkness edged with light, great floating blobs of blackness trimmed with radiance, emerald and gold and rose and blue and white, shifting in patterns, forming tunnels down which I am inexorably drawn . . . She jerked upright, aware that Connie's arm had tightened about her. The dark receded and she saw each detail sharp and clear.

Captain Meiklejohn raised his head to indicate the two minutes' silence was ended.

The trumpeter lifted the trumpet to his lips.

The sailor in charge of the flag began to hoist it.

The first notes of Reveillé rang out.

The trumpeter was in tune this time. Heads lifted. Shoulders squared. There was an almost sensible lightening of hearts. And a puff of wind, a hot wind from nowhere, caught the Union Jack as it crawled up the flagpole and sent it billowing forth. For an instant it hung there, floating proud and free in the updraught.

The Reverend Septimus intoned, 'Let us pray.'

And as he pronounced the benediction, the flag subsided limply against the flagpole and Nina Martin fainted dead away.

PART III

SUEZ – GIBRALTAR

I

Bobby Vane was bored. It was all very well for grown-up people, whose ideas of amusement were peculiar anyway, to exclaim over the blueness of the Mediterranean, the freshness of the air now that they had left Port Said behind them, and the taste of summer they hoped to enjoy between here and Marseilles; but there was no point in summer if you did not play on deck, and you did not play on deck because there was no one to play with, the grown-ups being too immersed in their own concerns.

On the evening of Armistice Day the Captain had called a meeting of the First Class passengers. Bobby did not know what had been said, but since then his mother had been very insistent on locking their cabin door at all times, and she and the other ladies tended to go about in groups escorted by several gentlemen. Only married people strolled in couples. Horrible Dr Bladon no longer walked arm in arm with Miss Connie, if only because Miss Connie could not be found. 'She's looking after her sister,' his mother said when Bobby asked her. 'Poor Nina's not at all well.' And she looked at him strangely. What had prompted the child to ask some days ago if Nina was pregnant, as all the ladies were now convinced she was?

'I fainted just like that with my first,' a Mrs Barrie-Jenkins informed anyone who would listen; she had a clear, carrying voice. 'It could be the heat,' another lady demurred. 'It was even hotter than this on my first outward voyage – in fact it was a record. Several of us fainted, and I assure you we were not *enceinte*.' This last was said with a glance at Bobby, who as usual was on the fringes of the group. 'Talk about apron-strings,' the ladies said when Cynthia was not present. 'They can't have cut the cord.' 'He should be in school,' Mrs Stiles said firmly. 'All other boys are, at his age.'

This was true, and explained why there was no one to play with. Bobby was the only school-age child in First Class. For company he depended on his mother, and such of the passengers as took pity on him, the Martin girls most of all, though Edmund Bladon had several times made vain offers and was being made aware that an eight-year-old can hate. Bobby was sustained in this attitude towards the doctor by his mother, who also disliked him and for similar reasons. Administering the unpalatable truth was even less endearing than administering an unpalatable dose of physic, as Edmund Bladon was beginning to find out. But there was no trace of apology in his manner. Thick-skinned, Cynthia told herself. He must be,

169

to have stood among us at that Armistice Day service knowing he'd been afraid to risk his life. Whereas men like Robert . . . As always when she thought of her husband, the wellsprings of grief gushed afresh. If Robert were here she would not need to lock her door against the rapist who was apparently prowling the ship.

Captain Meiklejohn's announcement to the First Class passengers had been made only after much heart-searching and discussion with the Chief. Mr Sutherland was still of the opinion that Nina had invented the whole story. Captain Meiklejohn was growing less certain by the hour.

'She'd have had to be mad to do it, Jamie, and the surgeon swears she is as sane as you or I.'

'That isna what I hear, but rumours are maybe distorted by the time they reach the engine-room.'

'What have you heard?'

'That one of the ladies visited her and found her raving.'

'She became hysterical, it's true, but only because of that lady's visit.'

'And how do you know that?'

'The surgeon informed me of the incident.'

'I wouldna place too much reliance on what *he* says. Is he no walking out with the sister?'

'The engine-room is exceedingly well informed.'

'Aye, well, we are not deaf nor blind, Angus. We can see the direction in which a man's eyes turn, and when it's a married man we pray he may be recalled to righteousness.'

'Why are you looking at me?'

'Are ye not looking a little too often in the direction of Mistress Cynthia Vane?'

It was something only a close friend could say, but even so, Angus was angry. 'I must ask you to withdraw that remark.'

'Verra gladly, if you can assure me I am mistaken.'

'Mrs Vane is no more to me than any other passenger.'

'Then that shall be the end o' that.'

Or the beginning. Had he ever before lied to Jamie? And by admitting to a lie thereby acknowledging the underlying truth. When he lay lonely in his bed it was Cynthia who lay beside him. When he stood on his bridge he saw not the instruments but her face. He conversed politely with other ladies and compared their every feature with hers. He watched Bobby Vane running about the decks and saw in his mind's eye another child, a compound of Andy and Bobby, who did not exist yet was more real to him than if he did. And when he discussed with Jamie whether the passengers should be told what had happened to Nina Martin, it was of Cynthia that he thought. She must not be put at risk. She must be safeguarded. She had a right to know.

'The passengers have a right to be told,' he said aloud. 'If there was another such incident and I had not warned them, I should be blamed, and rightly so.'

170

'Ye're spreading alarm on the word of a disturbed young woman. Ye canna trust a Papist, Angus. Ye know that.'

'I cannot see that rape is affected by the victim's religion.'

'Yon doctor isna certain it was rape.'

'He cannot swear to it in court, but he assures me privately that he believes her.'

'Ye're the captain, Angus. Ye must do as ye think best.'

The ultimate responsibility. Master under God of this vessel. And what if God were not there? If the paths of righteousness did not exist except as each man charted them for himself on the sea of destiny? He was more than master of this vessel; he was master under God of his fate.

He said, 'I shall tell the First Class passengers this evening.'

Jamie Sutherland bowed his head.

In fact his announcement was very bland, which did not prevent the spread of alarm among the ladies. 'To think it might be any one of them!' exclaimed one lady. 'Not my husband,' defended another. 'My dear, how can you *know*? On the night of the dance we were all dancing with other partners. No one can vouch for any man for very long. And I believe rape is quite quick.' The lady lowered her voice, anxious not to appear to know too much about it. 'I mean, there are no . . . preliminaries to be gone through.' – 'That poor girl,' someone else said. 'What a thing to happen to you when you're going to be a nun.' – 'Of course she can't enter now,' a new voice informed them. 'That Order's one of the strictest. I wonder what will become of her?' – 'Teaching, perhaps,' suggested a doubtful lady. 'I believe some convents have lay teachers.' – 'Or nursing,' someone else put forward.

'Why shouldn't she marry?' Cynthia said.

There was a silence. 'Not very suitable, surely,' a voice murmured.

Cynthia again: 'Why not?'

The group broke up. It was all right for Mrs Vane, a war widow; she was eligible enough. But a girl who had been seduced – raped, rather: well, a slice off a cut cake and all that.

For the first time Cynthia felt herself in conflict with conventional attitudes. Nina Martin was a victim, for heaven's sake. No one could accuse her of setting out to captivate, except that her very refusal to do so might be seen as a challenge by some. Whereas Connie . . . Connie was a good-time girl in the making. These demure convent-bred schoolgirls often were. Once cast them loose and loose was the word for it. No one could have felt surprise if Connie had been the victim. She'd been asking for it all along.

Cynthia did not acknowledge the jealousy she felt of Connie, ten years younger and as yet untouched by life, free of grief, free of emotional commitment to the past, of the child who occupied and demanded to occupy her every moment; this girl who already made it evident that she would have a wide choice in becoming a wife. All the men responded to

Connie, even those like Captain Meiklejohn who seldom smiled. It was particularly vexing that the Captain of all men should not see through this shallow little hussy who played the field. He certainly couldn't have seen her with young Johnson the night of the fancy hat dance. Talk about leading a man on! And then obviously a refusal at the last minute. Cynthia had not been too busy dismissing the callow advances of young Strode to notice, like others, the pair's obviously antagonistic return to the dance-floor; she had thought it none of her business, but now, with the sister a victim of rape, who knew whether Connie or someone like her had aroused some man to the utmost limits of desire and then left him furious and frustrated, the restraints of civilisation cast aside? She must mention the possibility to Captain Meiklejohn next time she saw him alone. Because there would be a next time; she would engineer one; it would do him good to talk to her again.

But it was on Edmund Bladon that Cynthia first tried out her theory, only to find that Connie had got there first.

'Miss Martin mentioned her anxieties to me on that score,' Edmund informed her, 'but I was able to reassure her, I hope.'

A memory of Connie's eyes, huge and pleading, came back to him.

'Edmund, was it my fault?'

In the last few days they had slipped easily into using first names. They were closer than they had ever been.

'Why should it be your fault?' he asked her.

'People are suggesting I led Captain Johnson on.'

'What people?'

'Mrs Gurslake. Oh – and others.' She could not bring herself to mention Cynthia Vane, though it was Cynthia's suggestion that had disturbed her. She had the measure of Florrie Gurslake now and, curiously, did not dislike her. She could not be called harmless, but at least she never intended to do harm. Whereas Cynthia . . . About Cynthia, Connie was less certain. 'We could all see you two had had a row, and of course when a man is angry . . .' – 'But it was me he was angry with, not Nina.' – 'Yes, but Nina is your sister. Besides, you weren't alone in your cabin and she was.' – 'You mean he took it out on someone innocent?' – 'I don't know, my dear. It's a possibility.' That possibility beat like a caged bird in Connie's head. She could not bring herself to give it the freedom of expression, except to Edmund, who was professionally qualified.

'You can forget Mrs Gurslake,' he said with unusual vehemence, resolving to have a word with her when he could.

Connie had already dismissed her, but persisted none the less with what troubled her. 'Could it have been anything to do with me?'

'That's assuming Captain Johnson is the attacker.' Which please God was not the case. Edmund felt his nerve failing at the thought of explaining to Connie and her sister the implications if he was . . .

'Could it have been Prince Ravi?' she suggested, feeling round for another suspect. 'We all know he had a knife.'

'Nina never saw the knife,' Edmund said gently, 'and any man could have taken one from the dining saloon. No, I'm afraid you must both learn to live with the knowledge that it could have been any one of us. Even me.'

'Oh no!'

'Why not? I was present in First Class that evening, and contrary to what some passengers believe because of my war record, I am still very much a man.'

'I know.'

What do you know? Edmund wondered. Do you know how much I care for you? Do you know that if I were in a position to ask you to marry me, I should do so? That is, if my father died and I came into money, because there would certainly be something, even though the estate is so run down. We need not live in Gloucestershire as neighbours to the Briscoes. I could buy a country practice somewhere else. Or even get a hospital job, if it's true that wartime prejudices are fading. I'm sure Curtis would help me if he could.

But all this was in the future. Pipe dreams. Pie in the sky. For the present there was only Connie standing with bowed head before him. He allowed his hand to caress her hair.

If she was aware of it, she gave no indication. Instead she said, 'Mr Briscoe is making enquiries about the attack on Nina. The Captain asked him to.'

'As the one man in First Class above suspicion he's in a good position to do so.'

'Has he talked to you?'

'Not yet.'

He'll have to, of course, and he'll hate doing it. Almost as much as I shall hate talking to him. There are too many bonds between us that are broken. He knows my home, my father. He knew Roger and my mother. He knew Rosemary.

'Do you think he'll find out who did it?'

'It's possible.'

'I'm not sure I want to know.'

'Perhaps you needn't, but we must do what we can to make sure there are no more such attacks, on the ship or off it. It may be a matter for the police.'

'No! Nina could never stand it.'

'She may not have much choice. The victim in such cases is victim of far more than the physical outrage.'

'Edmund, promise me you won't let it come to that.'

'My dear, I can't.'

She did not notice the endearment. 'If it became a police matter, I think Nina'd kill herself.'

And the Church had no place for suicides. They could not even be buried in consecrated ground. For that sin there was no absolution, for you did not just break God's laws; you thwarted His purpose in creating you. Small wonder that the State also called it a crime.

Edmund said, 'People are stronger than you think.'

'And weaker.'

'Yes.'

He had seen instances of both, whether precipitated by the Cat and Mouse Act or by life in the trenches. And it was not the expected ones who cracked; the weaklings often lasted when the seemingly strong gave way. What would Connie do if her sister committed suicide? If her sister were pregnant, which was what worried Edmund most?

The thought did not so much worry Florrie Gurslake as excite her.

'That poor young thing,' she said to Bert. 'Don't suppose she'd know what to do any more than I did, and she don't have no opportunities to find out.'

'You're not going to tell her, are you?' Bert asked in some alarm. He was not certain what had occurred between his wife and Nina, but he was determined it should not happen again. The doc even indicated to him that Florrie ought to leave both girls alone.

'Not good enough for them, you mean?' Bert had demanded.

'I mean nothing of the sort, Mr Gurslake, but Miss Nina is understandably in an overwrought state and your wife appears to exacerbate it. I'm asking your help as a matter of tact.'

Bert was not sure of the meaning of 'exacerbate', but the drift was clear enough.

'I'll have a word with Florrie,' he promised. 'Little Nina's got a bun in her oven, has she, and it's making her nervous, like?'

'I'm afraid I cannot discuss her condition.'

' 'Course you can't,' Bert said. Quite the toff, this doctor. It took class to carry off a remark like that. And class meant brass in Bert's estimation. He leaned beside Edmund on the ship's rail. 'How long are you going to go on doing this job, then?'

'Why do you ask?' Edmund countered.

' 'Cos you're too good for it, that's why. Anyone with half an eye can see that. Now if you was in Harley Street . . .'

'You're an expert on ships' surgeons, are you, Mr Gurslake?'

'Nah, I don't need to be. There's a brass plate somewhere with your name on it, but like all these things, it takes cash to get started, don't it, and that's what you young men don't have.'

Edmund's silence was acknowledgement. Emboldened, Bert went on, 'Florrie thinks the world of you, and it takes some doing, I can tell you, to make her speak well of a quack. She don't think too highly of 'em – not since we lost a little 'un – did she tell you?'

'Yes,' Edmund admitted, though she hadn't put it quite like that.

'Shouldn't be surprised if she don't consult you about this indigestion she's been having.'

174

'I am at Mrs Gurslake's service any time.'

There was no denying the doc knew how to put things. Bert swallowed and said, 'If it's a matter of cash, then Florrie and me, we might be able to help.'

What was coming? The offer of a loan? Edmund braced himself to refuse. In the world today you could no longer tell who was rich. There were plenty of rough-diamond millionaires, war profiteers, armaments manufacturers. The little man beside him could be any or all of these, though war profiteer seemed most likely. What was it Aunt Anne had said? 'For every hundred men who died, there's one who did well out of their deaths.' Not that their profiteering was illegal; a desperate government had been forced to buy where and at what price it could. The result was that in the post-war world the profiteers lived luxuriously. Where too many had lost all, they were ostensibly rich, and were becoming even richer as they bought up failed family businesses or sold jerry-built housing on cheaply bought agricultural land. Inevitably, these profiteers were older men who had not had to go and fight and resentment of them ran deep. It was all too probable that Bert Gurslake, so unexpectedly rich, belonged among them, in which case his help was unthinkable. Tainted money, Aunt Anne had called it, her nose wrinkling as if the stench of corruption were real.

'It's kind of you to suggest it, Mr Gurslake,' Edmund answered, 'but I am adequately provided for.'

It was a fine phrase and Bert appreciated it. It had the smell of cash.

'A bit of sensible investment's what you need,' he assured Edmund. 'Let me handle it for you. Say a couple of thou to start.'

Edmund, who had been expecting the offer of a loan, was left gasping. 'I assure you, I've nothing like that.'

'No matter. Make it a thousand and I'll double your money in six months.'

This was rash, but Bert was getting reckless. The voyage was almost half done and he was no nearer to solving his problems which would begin the moment he disembarked. Florrie's twenty-fifth wedding anniversary was going to be very different from what she hoped. What would she do? She hadn't had to shift for herself since they were married, and before that – well, it was no secret that there'd often been a gentleman friend to help out. If he'd had any sense, Bert thought, he'd have bought her a bit of jewellery; that at least she could keep. But she'd never cared for it, claimed it didn't suit her, and so far as the ladylike stuff was concerned she was right. Not for Florrie the discreet string of pearls, the delicate floral brooch in which the stones were real. She liked her adornments massive and showy; the costume jewellery counter was for her, or the Indian bazaar – Lord, did you ever see anything like that bloody great meat skewer? Suited her, though; she knew what was what; and though ivory wasn't valuable, it was strong, no snapping like the artificial stuff they were making nowadays. She'd be wearing it for their Golden Wedding – that's if they got that far.

Couple of old dodderers they'd be by then; he would, at least. They said prison shortened a man's life and you could still get sentenced for debt. But a thousand would see him in the clear, though of course two would be better. He glanced shrewdly at Edmund and said:

'Take my advice and get in on the ground floor with Miss Connie. You won't never get no chance like this again. Once she's ashore, a girl like that, there'll be others falling over themselves to pop the question and she'll get more choosy, see. Take a chance. Invest your money and your feelings. I'll look after the cash and the feelings you can look after yourself.'

'I can't afford to risk either, Mr Gurslake.'

'Go on. Nothing venture, nothing have. Besides, it ain't risky. Double your money, see.'

'I don't have a thousand to invest.'

Bert considered this. The doc had the hallmark of gentility, but he wouldn't be the first gent Bert had met on the way down, keeping body and soul together in decreasingly acceptable ways. Sydney had had its share of them. Failures desperate to make a fresh start, which all too often ended in further failure, the degradation of waterfront bars, bums with posh Pommy accents, the occasional suicide. Not that he could see Dr Bladon in such a situation, but the medical profession had its failures too – those struck off the register, for instance, and earning their living in various doubtful ways. It had been a choice between one of them and old Mother Sisley when Florrie had her spot of bother – Bert always thought of it like that. And now little Nina . . . No convent for her, if even half her story was true. The doc might do himself a bit of good with both sisters if he played his cards aright . . .

'The first thou's the most difficult,' he encouraged. 'But keep your eyes skinned and it's astonishing what a medical gent can pick up on the side.'

'If I had it I couldn't risk it in speculation. That's strictly for the idle rich – of which I am not one.'

Bert accepted defeat.

'Course you ain't. You don't get no chance to be idle aboard this blinking ship.'

Indeed you didn't, Edmund admitted. His surgery was often full, though the ailments were either minor or mildly chronic, many of them caused by excess. Compared to the poverty he had seen in London, the *Karachi*'s passengers and crew were well off. They did not suffer from deficiency diseases, and though there was overcrowding in the native crew's quarters, it was less than they were used to at home. Even the stoker with the burnt hand was not ill-nourished, although he had hinted as much on a subsequent visit when, the hand healing perfectly, Edmund had passed him fit for work.

'Hand hurts,' the man protested.

'Work will distract you,' Edmund said. He was not sure how much English the man understood, but he noted with amusement that he was now attempting to speak it, whereas on his first visit he had pretended no knowledge at all.

To make clear his dismissal, Edmund rose and opened the surgery door.

The man raised a fist – it was the burnt one. 'Doctor sahib unfair to Gopal. White man –' he salaamed. 'Brown man –' he spat, expertly missing the toe of Edmund's shoe.

There had been too many spittings in the past which Edmund had been powerless to object to.

'Clean up that mess,' he ordered, tight-lipped.

In the background he was aware of the surgery nurse reaching for the telephone, but he signalled to her to leave it alone.

'Wipe up that mess,' he repeated. 'Nurse will give you a cloth.'

Gopal regarded him with insolent eyes, and for a moment Edmund thought he was about to refuse to obey and wondered what he should do next. Then the man stooped – the movement was graceful – and with the smallest of bows offered Edmund the now befouled cloth.

Edmund choked back his anger. 'Put it in the bin over there.'

The man walked – or rather, swaggered – to the waste-bin, deposited the cloth and wiped his palms ostentatiously against his shirt. Edmund had read somewhere that the native crews who served aboard ships like the *Karachi* were men without caste; any they might once have had having been destroyed by contact with forbidden substances, or with Europeans, which was worse. He had a flash of understanding of the man's resentment, before discipline reasserted itself.

'I shall have to report this,' he told him.

The man's face had returned to impassivity.

'I am sorry,' Edmund added.

For an instant the eyes flickered with something very like contempt. Then the slender figure in the white dhoti which proclaimed he was off duty marched through the door which the nurse was holding open, as though he were the master and the white people his servants. Edmund entered the incident in his log and reached for the telephone.

'Sutherland.' The Chief's voice was brusque; he disliked telephone calls unless they were from the bridge.

'Bladon here. I've discharged your stoker. He can return to work right away.'

'I'll ensure he does. Thank you, Doctor. You'll forgive me if I say it's not before time.'

'There's always the risk of infection.'

'These people arena subject to infection, Doctor. I've seen verra few cases in all my years at sea. What they are subject to is a disinclination to work, even to the extent of inflicting a little discomfort on themselves if need be.'

'Are you saying that burn was self-inflicted?'

'I wasna there, Doctor. How should I know what happened? But I have

177

seen it happen before. When ye've been at sea as long as I have, ye'll appreciate things arena always what they seem.'

Not for worlds would the Chief reveal to the doctor that Gopal did indeed have just cause for complaint. Within his own domain the Chief reigned supreme, subject only to the Captain. A parvenu ship's surgeon was no fit recipient of his confidence.

It was at that moment that Edmund decided to say nothing about the spitting episode. He did not want to cause further trouble for Gopal. And in the same instant the Chief enquired, 'Was the heathen grateful for your ministrations, Doctor?'

'I'm sure he was,' Edmund said.

'Did he no thank you?'

'No.'

'He will do so tomorrow. He will report to the surgery.'

'There's no need –'

'There is need. I will have courtesy in my department, Doctor, and I'll thank ye for your help in obtaining it. Is there anything else I should know?'

'No,' Edmund said without hesitation.

'Good day to ye, Doctor.' The Chief put down the phone.

To his surprise, Edmund found he was shaking. It was the second time he had breached the regulations of the Australasian Line. First there had been the stowaway. Well, only the Irish steward knew of that and he had good reason to keep silence. But this failure to report a breach of discipline to a man's superior officer might be more difficult to hide. It was down in black and white in his log-book, which the Captain might decide to check at any time, and it had been witnessed by the nurse, who would no doubt relate it to the stewardesses among whom she spent her off-duty hours. Having entered it in the log, he would find it difficult to claim he had 'forgotten' to tell the Chief, or if he had, why he had not repaired the omission. Captain Meiklejohn would be justified in taking a stern line. Would it warrant dismissal? Edmund wondered. Was his first voyage to be his last? Though less rigid than the Chief, the Captain was none the less a strict disciplinarian, and Edmund was aware of the awe he inspired when he made his unsmiling rounds. Even the passengers sensed his reserve when he attended social functions, at which he seldom stayed long. Did they, like him, speculate on what lay behind that impartial courtesy that was so effective a screen?

But what lay behind any of them? His own past had been brutally revealed; Nina's ruined life was public knowledge; he had glimpsed the void at the heart of Cynthia Vane's, and knew Archie Johnson's guilty secret. But what of the Reverend Septimus Stiles and the amateur theatricals of his Armistice Day service; what of his pained wife and painful daughter? What of Florrie Gurslake and her Bert? Did she realise how desperate he was for money? Or was she as obtuse as she had been with Nina Martin?

178

What brought the aged Haldinghams home at last to England after more than fifty years abroad? And what of Julian Strode and John Joseph Fitzgerald, his fellow novices on this voyage? Their faces were young and innocent; perhaps they had nothing to hide. He must not assume every face was a mask, even when the mask had become fused with the features, as in Stafford Briscoe's case.

No muscle had twitched when they had come so unexpectedly face to face in that first dawn after leaving Aden. If he had not claimed acquaintance, would Briscoe have admitted as much? To take the unexpected in his stride was part of his training. 'Engaged in various diplomatic missions,' Aunt Anne had said on one of the rare occasions when she had mentioned the Briscoes. 'Something high-powered, I believe, and confidential. I can see him doing it, can't you?' I can indeed see him doing it, dear Aunt Anne, quietly quizzing and assessing every male in quest of whoever aboard the *Karachi* might have committed rape. By the time we dock at Tilbury, Captain Meiklejohn will have a report. Will there be an arrest, or will the matter be hushed up in time-honoured British fashion – to protect Nina, to protect the man if sufficient excuses can be made for him, to protect the man's wife? For of course the man may well be married. There is no need to confine enquiries to single men. The Reverend Septimus Stiles is not the only husband to have a lascivious eye; that is, if Florrie Gurslake is to be trusted, and in such a matter I think she probably can. The whole atmosphere of life on board ship is morally relaxing; small wonder if romance flourishes transiently in such an air.

It was heady stuff, as heady as the alcohol that flowed freely. Had someone somewhere found it all too much? Among some of the men who frequented that bar night after night had there been a dare, a wager? Bet you can't make it with the one girl who's off limits. Had the attempt gone suddenly, horribly wrong? He did not doubt that Nina had been forced, but was it really by a masked attacker who had held a knife to her throat? Might she not only know his identity but have played some part in her own downfall? In which case, was she not at risk? The man would find it desirable to ensure her silence . . . Horrified, Edmund pulled himself up short. It was bad enough to have a rapist among them. Was he postulating a murderer as well?

It was with relief that he locked the surgery door behind him and made his way up on deck. Blue sea and sky and a gentle breeze were better than clinical whiteness and the odour of antiseptic. He turned a corner and came face to face with Captain Meiklejohn and Bobby Vane.

Bobby was bursting with pride that the Captain had stopped to speak to him and suggested a stroll along the deck. More than anyone aboard, he revered the Captain, who had so much gold braid on his uniform. Only Prince Ravi had equal glamour in his eyes, partly because he was a prince and partly because he had stowed away like a hero in the *Boy's Own Paper* until discovered and caught by Mr Strode. Of course he was not a prince

179

like the Prince of Wales; he was foreign royalty, and Indian royalty at that. His mother had explained it all, but said it was still correct to address him as Your Highness, and Bobby enjoyed doing just that. He received a flashing smile in return and a 'Good morning, Bobby' – for the Prince had asked him his name. Not many boys at school would be able to say they had had a stowaway prince in a cabin near them, nor that they had walked the deck of the *Karachi* at her Captain's side. His mother also liked Captain Meiklejohn. 'He's a good man,' she had said. 'You could trust yourself to a man like that.' Of course you could, Bobby thought, with officers and crew scurrying to do his bidding, and passengers striving to be noticed in the hope of one of the much-sought-after invitations to join the Captain for drinks. They all deplored the fact that he was not more sociable, and having heard this so often, Bobby had been surprised to be addressed by name. Unlike Prince Ravi, the Captain had never asked it, but he seemed to know it just the same. And now here he was strolling importantly beside him, and everyone smiling as they passed. Tall man and handsome laddie: they made a good pair, people thought.

Angus Meiklejohn also thought they made a good pair. The boy was unmistakably Cynthia's son. Would another son inherit her dark, slender beauty, along with something of his own ruggedness? Another son . . . He curbed his erring thoughts with images of Ailsa and Andy, but the flesh-and-blood boy continued to walk at his side, head bowed and hands clasped behind him in admiring imitation. If Cynthia was on deck would she see them? Correction: would they see her? If they did, would she come across to them or should he deliver the boy to her? Either way they would engage in conversation – though it was not her conversation he craved. He forced his steps to keep an even measure lest a glimpse of her should cause them to betray by altered tempo the heightened beating of his heart. His eyes were fixed on the deckboards for fear that they might too obviously cease their searching if once they rested on her. He was playing with fire and he knew it. In his way he was as culpable as whoever had started that 'wee conflagration' in the bunker that the Chief maintained was deliberate. Arson and rape: an assault on the ship and an assault on the person, and both of them in one voyage. Truly, as captain he had more to think about than the glow in a pair of dark eyes.

He was almost grateful to Edmund Bladon for hurrying round a corner, stopping short and apologising, breaking the flow of his thought which had begun, like certain rivers, in dozens of small streams that converged to flow on inexorable and strong. Cynthia . . . Cynthia . . .

A river ran down to the ocean and was lost in the immensity of the sea. If he could only be lost so in Cynthia. If she could bear him a son . . . In vain he strove to remember his denial to Jamie Sutherland that she was more to him than anyone else aboard, when she was the very soul of his ship, the embodiment of his longing . . . What had the doctor just said?

'Glad to see you taking the air, sir. A relief after the Red Sea, isn't it?'

180

'Yes.' His tongue felt for words. 'Much fresher.'

'Everyone's feeling the benefit.'

'Yes.' Another struggle as he wrenched his mind. 'Less than a week now to Marseilles.'

'How about you, Bobby?' Edmund asked. 'Enjoying it?'

'Yes – thank you.' The 'thank you' could barely be heard.

Angus became aware that his small companion had gone rigid and was eyeing the doctor's shoes with dislike.

'Do you know Mr Bladon?' he enquired.

'Yes.' Bobby did not raise his eyes and seemed determined not to.

'One of my patients,' Edmund explained. 'But you're all right now, aren't you, Bobby?'

The boy nodded. Angus noticed that he had tightened his lips.

Something of his hostility communicated itself to Edmund, who looked at him in puzzlement.

'You're just going off duty, I take it, Mr Bladon?'

'Yes, sir.'

'Then I wish you a very good day.'

As Edmund hurried off, the Captain turned to the boy beside him. 'Why don't you like the doctor, son?'

It gave him pleasure to use the word to Cynthia's boy, even though this was no son of his.

Bobby debated with himself. To tell the truth was dangerous because he was aware it did not show him in a good light, and he wanted very much to appear in one to the Captain. He played for time.

'Because I don't,' he said.

'That's no answer. Did he give you a dose of physic?'

This was uncomfortably near the truth. 'He does funny things.'

'What sort of things?'

Bobby cast about for examples, but these were in short supply. 'He hides in Mr Briscoe's cabin,' he said desperately. 'Before it was Mr Briscoe's, I mean.'

'You mean when it was empty?'

'Yes.'

'Well, there's no doubt a good explanation . . .' Angus Meiklejohn was beginning, when he fell silent, remembering that Cynthia and Bobby's cabin was near the Martin girls'. Stafford Briscoe was between them, but when they had left Bombay that cabin had been vacant, and by the time they reached Aden it had been the scene of a rape. And Bladon's cabin was on another deck, on the other side of the ship . . .

'What exactly did you see him do?' he demanded.

'He heard someone coming, so he went into the empty cabin. Then he kept peering out to see if the coast was clear.'

Or if the right person was coming . . .

'How do you know all this?'

181

'It was one night when I was watching.'

'You ought to have been in bed and asleep.'

'Oh, I was in bed. Mummy came and tucked me up before she went back to the dancing, but I could hear the band and it made it hard to sleep, so I got up and opened the door a wee bit in case there was anything to see.'

'And was there?'

'Only Dr Bladon. So I shut the door and went back to bed.'

'Do you remember when this was?'

After all, there had been music and dancing most nights, but Bobby's next words confirmed all his fears.

'Of course I remember,' the boy said scornfully, as if there could be any doubt. 'It was the night of the fancy hat dance.'

II

'Do you think he did it?' the Chief asked.

'No,' Angus Meiklejohn said automatically, 'but he's done something he shouldn't have, I'm sure.'

Why else should Bladon have refused to give an explanation when he and Stafford Briscoe had questioned him. 'I'm sorry, sir, I've nothing to say,' he had answered. 'Don't be a fool, man,' Briscoe had said. 'We've a witness that you hid in the empty cabin next to Miss Martin's around the time that this alleged rape took place. Now you may be as innocent as the babe unborn, but you can see for yourself it looks bad. You can talk to us in confidence, but some explanation is due.' 'I'm sorry . . .' Threats, arguments had been of no avail. Briscoe remembered hearing that Edmund had behaved similarly before the conscientious objectors' tribunal when, having stated his objection, he had refused to elaborate. Then, as now, it had not helped his case.

The Chief had not been present at the interview, but in the first cool of the evening, with the glare on the water dimmed and the soft air through the open porthole mitigating the smoke from his pipe, he was hearing an account of it and was aware that Angus was worried; the frown lines between the eyes were a sure indication of that. Yet if this new anxiety took his mind off Mistress Vane, might it not be the Lord's own mysterious way of recalling him to righteousness? True, Angus had denied that the woman meant anything to him, but the Chief was uneasy none the less. There was some subtle change in Angus which he sensed but could not pinpoint; a softening in the hard outlines of judgement which, if not checked, could cause them to disintegrate.

But the change was in Angus the man. Angus the captain remained as upright and inflexible as ever, calmly ordering the running of his ship. If he thought Edmund Bladon not guilty of rape it was not due to weakness or partiality, but to a lifetime's knowledge of men. The Chief accepted that. What he could not accept was that Angus had a lifetime's knowledge of women, any more than he had himself. Women were the very devil. If the personification of God was masculine, surely the arch enemy should be female? Who had decided that their eternal opposition was between male and male?

'He's protecting someone,' Angus said suddenly. 'He knows something we ought to know. If he was in that area, however innocently, he may have

183

heard or seen something vital. I'll have to question him again.'

'Maybe he was there by appointment. He was friendly with the Martin girls. Who's to say he did not have an assignation with Miss Nina and things somehow got out of hand?'

The Chief could not know how closely his reconstruction parallelled Edmund's, but the Captain tossed it aside.

'If you had said Miss Connie, maybe . . .'

There was talk that he was sweet on her. Certainly, if it had not been for this tragedy, Angus would have expected to see her at the heart of a shipboard romance. On every voyage there was one girl who stood out as the focus of masculine interest, but he himself was immune to Connie's charms. He could admire and appreciate, but her immaturity did not draw him like the womanhood of Cynthia Vane. And it was Cynthia's son who had set this latest enquiry in motion, with his revelation of what he had seen.

His first thought had been that Bobby was lying, seeking to incriminate the doctor whom he so obviously disliked, but Edmund's own refusal to admit or deny his presence in the area strongly suggested guilt. Yet not for a moment did Angus believe the ship's surgeon was a rapist. Some other episode lay buried here.

Of the two aboard who could have told him what it was, only John Joseph Fitzgerald stood to lose, for Ravi, now something of a fêted hero, no longer had anything to hide. Except that in the stinking darkness of the lifeboat, he did not know whose merciful hand had brought him food and water, but assumed it was the steward's each time.

John Joseph was only too thankful that Ravi had been discovered and he himself relieved of his role of providing the necessities of life. Purveyor to His Highness Prince Ravi of Maggapore. It sounded good, until you remembered that what he purveyed was all too literally the crumbs from the rich man's table. The bread of sorrow and the water of affliction. No, the bread of sustenance and the water of life. And all the time he had worried that he might somehow be prevented from performing this act of mercy, that the unknown man in the lifeboat might starve, might sicken and die. Then the death would be on his conscience as much as the life was. Whatever happened to the stowaway was his affair. It still was, even though the stowaway had been translated and now occupied a cabin in First Class, where that unmentionable act had taken place. There were those who whispered that Ravi had committed it – John Joseph heard them from behind the bar, where he was deemed to be deaf and blind, so that anything could be said or done in his presence and he none the wiser. Nor was he until after the event, when things sometimes had a habit of clicking into place. Like Captain Johnson saying, 'The trouble with India's teeming millions, princes and paupers, is that they're all in a perpetual state of rut.' Or Mr Gurslake: 'I wouldn't trust any of 'em an inch. They don't really like us. It's the same as the Micks.' He did not

184

trouble to lower his voice. 'Look at 'em now they got their independence, fighting like the Kilkenny cats. Why –' the thought seemed to strike him forcibly – 'they was a lot better off with us.' – 'If we ever pull out of India,' Captain Johnson drawled (his speech was slurring), 'there'll be a bloodbath.' He found the prospect interesting rather than disturbing; he was not speaking of human beings, after all. The enemy was – The Enemy. That was one advantage of wartime. You knew who your enemies were. You killed them not from personal malice but because it was your duty and because they might otherwise kill you first. Whereas in peacetime it was different; you must not kill them even when they were armed. Would the Colonel have preferred to see him dead? A funeral with full military honours? Like doctors, the Army had a long tradition of burying its mistakes.

Bert, who was anxious to get away before the half-cut young officer remembered their last encounter, decided that a common enemy was his best hope. 'Murdering bastards,' he observed to no one in particular.

'Yeah,' Archie affirmed with alcoholic wisdom. 'That just about sums it up.'

He watched Bert slide from his bar stool and stroll with feigned nonchalance from the room. Had he touched anyone yet for the thousand he was after? At least he wouldn't try it again with him. The thought made him feel good. He must have put the fear of God into the little runt. Which was as it should be. People like Bert, despite their colour, belonged in Archie's view to Kipling's 'lesser breeds without the law', and the law was that White is Right. It was unwritten, unspoken, though some of the Pinkos occasionally murmured against it and everyone knew of cases where it hadn't worked, his own among them. Nevertheless, the law was the basis of Imperial rule and it extended by gradations unspecified but perfectly clear to those charged with administering it to other subject races like the Irish, where colour was not the deciding factor, and into England itself. There was a distinction between Bert Gurslake and the Mick behind the counter, but it was not as great as either of them supposed.

He pushed his glass forward. 'I'll have another.'

The barman moved with alacrity but conveyed his disapproval none the less.

'You think I've had too many, don't you?' Archie demanded.

John Joseph attempted to turn away wrath. 'I'm sure you're the best judge of that, sir.'

'Too right I am. Do you know what I'm going to do when I get home?'

'No, sir.'

'I'm going shooting.' Archie laughed at the look on the other's face. 'Oh, I don't mean running amok. I mean real shooting – pheasant, partridge, rabbit even – in God's clean English air.'

There was not much rough shooting in suburbia, but Archie had temporarily forgotten that. He was overcome with longing for the kiss of frost on his cheek and the sparkle of a winter's morning, something cold and clear and pure. The last time he had enjoyed such sport, he and three brother officers had treated themselves to a few days' shooting in Norfolk. Archie had had the biggest bag. He had a natural eye and a smooth, easy swing which had won him the instant approval of the beaters: no fumbling, bloodstained massacring here. It had been another moment of triumph. Like killing Germans.

He slid from his bar stool. 'Ever been shooting?'

'No, sir.'

'Ah, boyo, you don't know what you've missed.'

Boyo. It wasn't the first time John Joseph had heard the word on English lips in bantering good humour. Would Captain Johnson say 'Begorrah!' next? He schooled himself to smile politely and remember that they were talking about the slaughter of animals, not men. Except that there was no distinction. An autumn day in the Wicklow hills when he and Terry had lain in the bracken and watched a group of sportsmen move diagonally across a hill in front of them, had been horribly parallelled by an April day in Dublin when the quarry, flushed from one blazing building to the next, had fallen before a rifle raised with the same easy swing and precision, the same casual insouciance.

Had the English ever taken Easter Week seriously? They had certainly been slow to react. For the rest of Easter Monday, after the rebels had seized the General Post Office, the English seemed to lie low. The Royal Irish Constabulary prudently allowed things to take their course, and the people of Dublin, having had their dinners, took to the streets to watch, though there was not much to see except a constant coming and going of messengers and volunteers to the Post Office, and the carrying in of bedding commandeered from the Hotel Metropole next door. Other points in Dublin had also been taken: St Stephen's Green, Jacobs' biscuit factory, Boland's flour mill, the Four Courts. It became the thing to do the rounds, strolling in the chequered April sunlight from one rebel stronghold to the next.

There was an absence of news, which fuelled speculation. Had the rest of Ireland risen in arms? It seemed not. The story of bungling and misunderstanding emerged only later, by which time it had ensured that Dublin's Easter Week Rising had gone off at half cock from the start. But on the Monday afternoon, while the spectators laughed and joked and speculated, and a local licensee sent in a case of stout to the gallant defenders (or attackers?) of the General Post Office, the atmosphere was one of holiday. As indeed it was: Bank Holiday Monday, and the show better than any circus or fair, especially when a cornet-player appeared on the roof of the Post Office at dusk and began to play 'Who Fears to Speak of '98?' and 'A Nation Once Again'.

The first ugly incident came as dusk was falling, when there was a crash of broken glass and the windows of a liquor store were seen to have been

186

shattered – no one could say by whom. A number of looters emerged with what they could carry in arms or bellies. The middle-class elements of the crowd began to retreat. After all, they had to go to work tomorrow, and it was chilly now the sun had gone. The looters, drunk with success, whether literally or metaphorically, went on the rampage and attacked other shops in Sackville Street. It was all very well for Pearse's proclamation to pray that no one who served the new Republic's cause would disfigure it by cowardice, inhumanity or rapine: Pearse was an idealist. So the first shots fired by his own men were an attempt to discourage looters; symbolically, perhaps, they failed; and John Joseph, not daring to tell his mother of his own and Terry's small part in the looting of the sweetshops, went home to his tea (cold meat and beetroot, and the remains of yesterday's Swiss roll) with nothing definite to report.

But despite severed railway lines, the English reinforcements were streaming into Dublin. By next day the first were in position, and rumours of casualties began to come in. Near the Four Courts it was said a troop of Lancers had been decimated and put to flight (subsequently reduced to four men killed and several horses out of control). The Dublin Veterans Corps was reported to have been annihilated in an ambush – but only five men were found to have died. Everywhere there was rumour and counter-rumour. The trams still weren't running and you had to walk to work. If you were going, that is, now that the British machine-guns were in action and things were hotting up. Besides, streets were barricaded and cordoned off, and that made things difficult, especially after Tuesday evening when martial law was declared. You needed a pass to show to the soldiers even to get to your own home, though there were still plenty of ways through for those who knew the area as well as John Joseph and Terry did. The boys had set off on Wednesday, their pockets full of bread and cheese and chocolate, prepared to make a day of it. 'I don't like you going,' Mam had said. 'You mind and be careful.' Ellen had laughed and said, 'They won't shoot little boys.' She did not say who 'they' were and Mam didn't ask her. No one knew who was the enemy.

'Begorrah,' said Captain Johnson, swaying slightly and resting a hand on the bar, 'there's nothing like a day's shooting for making a man feel a man.'

John Joseph forced the smile that was expected and wished Third Officer Strode would come to the rescue once again. He had admired the way in which the young officer had dealt with Johnson's quarrel with Mr Gurslake; he had shown the confidence and authority of a much older man. But he knew that this afternoon Strode was off duty. Perhaps Dr Bladon might come, or the tall gentleman who had joined the ship at Aden and never came into the bar. Because of this someone said he was a Moslem, but he didn't look dark enough for that. What everyone seemed to know without being sure how was that he had been appointed by Captain Meiklejohn to investigate the rape. And the whisper was that he need look

187

no further than a certain medical gentleman whose past was already a disgrace.

John Joseph knew it couldn't have been Dr Bladon. Hadn't the doctor been up on the boat deck provisioning Prince Ravi at the time Miss Nina Martin went below? Or had he? John Joseph could not remember clearly. He had been too busy serving at the bar and trying to ignore Preston's vulgarer asides, made as they dived below the counter for replenishments but perhaps audible to the customers none the less. John Joseph expended his widest smiles upon them to mitigate any possible offence, and appeared to have been successful in that no complaints had been made.

He now bestowed a similar smile on Archie Johnson.

'You're an outdoors man, are you, sir?'

'You could say that.'

'Do you hunt at all?' the steward asked eagerly.

Now there was a sight if you like. Glossy horses and glossier riders, the sheen of the beast's coat matched by the rider's top hat. Snowy white stocks; the glow of a hunting pink coat; the scent of leather and horse sweat; and a running river of hounds. Only once had he seen it, smelt it, but he had never forgotten. It was a memory from another day spent playing truant in those same Wicklow hills . . .

'No, I don't hunt,' Archie said. Too bloody expensive, and no certainty of a kill. None of the excitement of swing, sight, aim, fire, and a plunging whirl of feathers. 'I'd sooner be out with the guns.'

He mimed the actions in a single arc aiming at John Joseph.

'Bang-bang,' he said, 'you're dead.'

'NO!'

The little Irishman's shout was loud in the empty bar, but attracted no attention. Archie, momentarily sobered, asked, 'What's up?'

'Nothing, sir. I was startled.' Nothing you can understand and nothing I can tell you. I have fought to forget what I saw.

Thursday, 27 April 1916. He had gone once again with Terry to the area round Sackville Street where two boys who knew the district could still find a point of vantage, though now that the English artillery was in position the place looked like a battlefield. There were soldiers with machine-guns at street corners and others with rifles on the rooftops. The air was thick with dust and smoke from the crumbling, burning buildings; it almost obscured the sun that would otherwise have sparkled on the broken glass carpeting the pavements that crunched like ice when men ran. And run they did: carrying messages, seeking escape, striving to drag a wounded comrade into the shelter of a doorway, sometimes pausing long enough to fire back – a useless gesture, for by now the British troops were well protected; it was only in occasional ambushes that they fell. The whole of Dublin was agog with the exploit of Eamon de Valera, who had led British reinforcements into a trap at Mount Street Bridge, where many of them had been killed in a five-hour battle – but that was twenty-four hours before, and since then the gunboat *Helga* on the Liffey had added her bombardment of Liberty Hall to the destruction of Dublin's heart. As the boys watched there was another *cr-rr-ump*, and the wall of a building swayed outwards before disintegrating into rubble and smoke.

It was then that a figure emerged from a doorway and zigzagged towards the GPO, a lithe, hatless, dark-haired figure, one of the runners who kept the lifelines free. 'Can you leap as high as yourself and bend as low as your knee while still running?' Again John Joseph heard his sister Ellen's scornful voice. And now Kieron, big brother Kieron, ran like one of those heroes of old making his way through a spatter of bullets, seeming to bear a charmed life. John Joseph did not know he was holding his breath; his whole being had fused with Kieron's, when from the corner of his eye he caught a movement by one of the rooftop soldiers silhouetted against the sky. Swing, sight, aim, fire – the action was as graceful as a dancer's, the expertise as great, the foolhardiness in thus exposing himself as great as Kieron's own. Almost before the crack sounded, Kieron spun round and fell. John Joseph heard him gasping and did not realise it was himself he heard.

'He got him,' Terry said. 'The bastard got him.' He began noisily to cry, but John Joseph stood like a statue, while Kieron twitched and lay still. The boy never doubted that it was death he had witnessed. What was he going to tell Mam?

But: 'It's nothing, sir,' he assured Archie Johnson. 'Nothing you need be troubling yourself about at all.'

Requiem æternam dona ei, Domine, et lux perpetua luceat ei. Requiescat in pace . . . pace . . . pace. May Kieron rest in peace.

'*Requiem æternam dona ea, Domine* . . . Grant her eternal rest. My lips move but my mind is otherwhere, as it often is these days despite the familiar words of prayer. Perpetual light seems such a strange blessing. I want nothing now but the dark, a warm dark burrow into which I can crawl for ever and never see the light of day. 'You want a grave,' Connie said, half laughing half frightened, when I told her. I did not bother to contradict. To go up on deck is torture, to run the gauntlet of those lustful, prying eyes, all wondering (as I do myself): Am I pregnant? All longing to overwhelm me with their slick, sick sympathy. Edmund explained that it was necessary for the Captain to tell the First Class passengers what had happened because other women might be at risk, but I do not accept that. It was me the man came for. I know it. What I do not understand is why.

Reverend Mother would say that I ought to pray for him. I have tried, but no words come. Forgive us our trespasses as we forgive them . . . I am not Christian enough to forgive. Perhaps I was not Christian enough to be a nun. Is that what God is trying to tell me? If so, His ways are indeed mysterious.

Daddy will have to know what's happened, but Con says she'll take care

189

of that, which is good of her because it won't be easy, but she says I've got to tell Aunt Eileen myself. Only I mustn't think of her as Aunt Eileen. She's Mother Imelda now. I asked Daddy once what she was like, this younger sister of Mummy's who was everyone's darling, and he said she was beautiful. There's a photograph of her in the family album, but it was taken a long time ago. She's wearing a ball gown, there are flowers in her hair, you can almost hear music in the background, I never saw anyone look less like a nun. When I wanted to enter, Daddy said it was history repeating itself. No one could believe it when Aunt Eileen announced she intended to take the veil. She'd already been spoken for twice but she'd said no and my grandparents wouldn't force her. They said someone better was sure to come along. And so He did, but it wasn't what they were expecting. Their darling became the bride of Jesus Christ. Daddy said my grandfather wept at her clothing, she looked so lovely in white. He died soon afterwards, but by then Daddy and Mummy were in India and Connie was on the way. And all those years, since before I was born, Aunt Eileen has stayed in the convent where she is Reverend Mother now.

Dear Reverend Mother, I am afraid I shall not be joining you at Advent because I have been raped and cannot now enter as a nun, please pray for me, your affectionate niece, Nina. Is that what I'm going to write? What will she say when she opens it? Am I going to have to add: as a result I am expecting a child? Please God not that, but my breasts felt heavy this morning and I read somewhere that this could be a sign. I was due last week, but Edmund says the lateness is nothing to worry about, it could be shock, we shall have to wait and see. Connie says she's always wanted to be an aunt, but I wanted to be an aunt to Connie's children and perhaps some day welcome her daughter into the convent with me. And now – never. All because some man forced me into that cabin and flung himself on top of me and – No, I won't think of it. They've put Mr Briscoe in that cabin, Edmund brought him to see me, the Captain's asked him to investigate the incident, as they call it, and he asked the same questions all over again. He was cold and distant, he didn't believe me, I'm certain, he looked at me as if I were something distasteful but Edmund says I mustn't mind because he's seldom at ease with young women; when he is, he can be good company. It seems Edmund knows him, they live near each other in Gloucestershire, his sister and Edmund's aunt were great friends but because Edmund wouldn't fight in the war they quarrelled – as if it was anything to do with them.

Some people thought Edmund shouldn't have attended the Armistice Day service. Captain Johnson said it was an insult to the dead, but I don't see why, Edmund lost people he knew and so did everybody else, no wonder they call it the Great War. In other wars there were no conscientious objectors because civilians didn't have to go and fight, but now decisions by professional armies are no longer accepted. Edmund says the next step will be the refusal by the diehards to accept that any war ever ends. He thinks that in war as in peace we are witnessing the breakdown of all the rules we thought we lived by. I said if that was so I didn't want to go on living, but he just laughed and patted my hand. He wouldn't have done that if Connie had said it. I think he is in love with her.

Is she with him? I know she likes him, she sparkles when he is around, like Mummy when she came in with Major Orrey from the races – why do I remember that day? I suppose because it was the beginning of her illness, though there must have been other times when she sparkled – at balls and parties and the races, she was 'the gay Mrs Martin', after all – but she didn't sparkle much on Daddy's arm at official functions; instead, she looked almost plain. Mrs Magistrate Beer said she wore unbecoming hats on purpose, though no hats could have been more unbecoming than Mrs Beer's. Mrs Major Barrett said she had a want of public spirit and personal charm could not make up for it, she said it with a little snap of her teeth like a spring lock shutting; she was always very nice to Daddy, I recall. When Major Orrey's regiment was moved from Nullumpur she said what a pity it couldn't have happened six months sooner, but I think Mummy would have been even more wretched if it had. He was the only visitor she would see; for him she would stop reading her eternal magazines and books, but as she got worse he didn't come so often; he said his visits wearied her. After that I used to tell her if I saw him and she always said I had a pair of eyes in my head, but once when I told her I had seen him out riding with a Miss Mason who had come on a visit to her brother she burst into tears and beat her pillow and had such a fit of coughing that Daddy had to be sent for. After that Daddy said it might be better if I didn't mention Major Orrey since it seemed to upset Mummy so. I never spoke of him again, but I asked Connie why it upset Mummy and she said I didn't understand.

She said the same when I asked her if she was in love with Edmund. 'You don't understand,' she said. 'No one does. It's so lonely.' And then she turned aside and shook her head. For a moment she reminded me of Mummy, but she didn't raise her fists and start to cough. Instead she slipped her arm through mine and drew me out of the cabin and suggested we take a walk on deck.

On the deck we met Captain Meiklejohn. He always looks so sad, but he smiled as people do at Connie, and wished us a very good day. He said he hoped we were enjoying the fine weather, it should last as far as Marseilles and tonight we should see the coast of North Africa on the port side and Sicily to starboard the next day. I cannot believe this voyage is more than half over and that in ten days' time we shall dock at Tilbury, where Aunt Maura and Uncle Charles will meet us. What is to become of me? Connie talks about finding me a job, perhaps with a milliner or a modiste, I'm good with my hands and she thinks my appearance and manner would help me, because thanks to Reverend Mother's strictness and despite what Mrs Magistrate Beer and Mrs Major Barrett used to hint about Mummy, we've turned out ladies after all. Perhaps we should add grateful thanks to St

Jude, the patron saint of lost causes. Should I pray to him for my lost vocation? No, not even St Jude can restore what that man took from me. I won't think of it, yet all the time I keep coming back to it. Why did he do it, why? Edmund says I should think of him as sick, but I keep thinking have I spoken to him, shaken hands with him, danced with him? Until I know that I want only my dark, narrow burrow. The touch of any man makes me shrink.

I want a grave, Connie said, but the grave is cold and lonely. The grave is where Mummy is now, imprisoned, fighting to get out, the gay Mrs Martin in the company of worms and slugs and snails, unreconciled with the Church, the gates of Paradise closed against her, rotting in the stench of sin, my stomach heaves at the thought of it, *requiem æternam dona ea* . . . Oh God, am I going to be sick? Not this time, it will pass – like the faintness. All things pass. O God, if it be Thy will, let this cup pass from me, let me not be pregnant, *requiem æternam dona mihi, Domine* . . . Grant me eternal rest.

Nina was unaware how often her lips moved automatically as she put up her petitions. Reverend Mother had encouraged physical participation in prayer. 'At least it will keep you awake,' she had said with that half-smile that lurked in her eyes and in the corners of her lips and reminded pupils and their parents that under her habit was a woman who knew more of the world than might be thought. But other passengers, watching Nina's pale lips move in the greater paleness of her face which had once had the pallor of the moon but now had more the clay colour of earth, shook their heads in knowing commiseration and tried not to meet Connie's eye.

Ravi was one who did not share in this communal complicity. The girl had lost her virginity – so? Why else had she been given it in the first place? Virginity was made to be lost. Admittedly it was not something which should be taken by force – not in English society, at least, where, just as in his native India, it reduced a girl's value as a bride. But in India girls were kept in purdah; in England no such precautions seemed to exist. The restraints were moral only. Small wonder if they sometimes broke down. In any case, Miss Nina Martin was not destined for the marriage market. Her initial story about an engagement had been false, as several passengers had explained to him; she was going to be a priestess, one of the nuns who in India touched untouchables and did good works with the aid of disinfectant and prayer. When Miss Connie disabused him of the notion that Nina's role would have been like that and he understood that she would have spent the rest of her life immured within a harem of holy women whose sole task was to pray for those without, Ravi could see no reason why she should be debarred from this unnatural existence merely because the natural had overtaken her.

Of course, if it had been Dorothy Waterman it would have been different. In connection with her it was impossible to think of the natural as

192

anything but repellent. The exchange of smut in senior boys' stories, the boasts of prowess, had nothing to do with anyone so pure. They had nothing to do with him either. The very thought of what was expected of him in marriage – oiled, scented, coupled with a fat and greedy bride in a travesty of those temple carvings from which the Resident liked to be seen averting his eyes – caused Ravi to sicken physically. Anything rather than that! Even the sweltering, stinking misery of his stowaway existence, the humiliation of work in the galley, was preferable to the enforced copulation of alien bodies conjoined. To his surprise, Mr Briscoe had seemed to understand what he was saying when they had gone ashore together at Port Said.

The reason for the excursion had been Ravi's wardrobe. He could not spend the rest of the voyage in Third Officer Strode's spare clothes. When they docked Ravi had acquiesced eagerly in Captain Meiklejohn's suggestion that he should go shopping in the bazaar. Those crowded lanes of shops with their innumerable dark doorways offered infinite possibilities of escape. He was only mildly disconcerted when informed that Mr Briscoe was to accompany him; they could scarcely be manacled together; it would be easy to give him the slip.

After the first half-hour Ravi revised this opinion. The Englishman might have grey hair, but he moved as lithely as Ravi himself and seemed in addition to be something of a mind-reader; whichever way the boy turned, he was there. Moreover, he spoke fluent Arabic; the stall-holders' salaams were low; their fawning became respectful; the English voice, unraised, would be obeyed. If Ravi tried to escape, he would find his way blocked by apologetic figures, bales of merchandise, the contents of a stall inexplicably spilled, for all of which the Englishman would offer compensation and remain persistently at Ravi's side. In a different way it was like arguing with the Resident. Whatever you did, there was no hope that you could win. The young Prince's frustration mounted as each purchase was haggled over and dispatched to the ship.

As length he turned. 'Mr Briscoe, why do you accompany me when I prefer to be alone?'

'Not a good idea in this place, dear boy. So easy to take a wrong turning and get lost.'

The voice was bland, the explanation blander, but Ravi was not ready to concede defeat.

'You also are a stranger here.'

'Not so, dear boy. I have been here many times.'

Stafford Briscoe spoke the truth. He was well acquainted with the souks of the Middle East and that of Port Said in particular as he journeyed to and fro. His offer to accompany Prince Ravi on his shopping expedition had been gratefully received by Captain Meiklejohn, who had been wondering how he was to keep his prisoner under tactful restraint. Should Ravi escape, it was difficult to say whether the displeasure of the Nawab or of

193

the Owners of the Line would be greater, but both would make themselves felt. The presence of Stafford Briscoe on board took on an air of Providential organisation: the Lord looking after His own. He was conscious of it as he said, 'I should be grateful to you, sir, if you would keep an eye on him, not just when he goes ashore at Port Said but throughout the voyage.'

Stafford Briscoe was amused by Ravi. The boy had courage of a sort, and his transparency reminded him of Maurice in the early days of their relationship when Maurice too seemed anxious to escape. Had he wanted to? Stafford Briscoe had never been certain. Or had he been playing hard to get? The distinction might have been too nice for some, but for him it had been important that in the end Maurice had come to him of his own free will. There must be no hint of force or even persuasion. One stood still and let the object of desire approach, hesitant at first but ultimately beseeching, begging to be desired in return. Only then was it possible to embark on a relationship, or – if impossible – to spurn.

He had no feelings about Ravi beyond the pleasure he found in contemplating so much physical perfection in the person of one young man. And of course the added thrust of memory when some gesture, some turn of the head, reminded him of Maurice. But this was not Maurice. Maurice in the end had been pliant, adoring, but Maurice had not been a prince. This time, Briscoe recognised with a frisson of interest, he might be the one to be spurned. At the Nawab's court there would be no shortage of attendants eager to gratify the ruler's every whim. And Prince Ravi was the future Nawab. What more natural than that some of the courtiers should already fawn on him?

It was this possibility that had troubled the Resident and had led him to acquiesce in the idea of early marriage, thereby achieving at least a dynastic succession to ensure stability. After that, well, there were already Indian princes disporting themselves when and where they pleased, defiling their caste with European women and sometimes with European men. The first risk had been taken with the decision to send Ravi to school in England. From then on there was always the possibility of the wrong kind of influence or the wrong kind of reaction, though young Waterman seemed all right. The Resident had made discreet enquiries about the banking family and been reassured by what he learned. Although the boys were friends, he half suspected that it was the sister who was the real attraction, but that problem would solve itself in time. Distance, and their respective engagements (for Dorothy's first Season was a success and a suitable matrimonial alliance could not be long delayed), would put an end in a final and painless way to any boyish tenderness that might have existed. The Prince's disappearance and the news that he was now half way to England had upset the Resident considerably. Had the boyish tenderness been stronger than he had allowed for? How would the Watermans react?

Such considerations had not troubled Ravi. Once get to England and an English telephone and he would phone Barry or his father in the City,

194

and—for the moment—his troubles would be at an end. The Rolls with Mr Waterman's chauffeur would whisk him to the Lutyens-designed home in Surrey, where Mrs Waterman would be waiting, warm and welcoming as always, and also Dorothy . . . Beyond that he did not go. There would presumably be an English Christmas such as he had spent with them in other years, trying not to marvel at the customs so rigidly observed by people who found Indian customs quaint or foolish, and then they would all see in the New Year. Toasts would be drunk – would Mr Waterman again raise his glass and say *Jai Hind*? In which case he, Ravi, would respond with, 'God save the King', Mrs Waterman would embrace him, and Dorothy – what would Dorothy do?

She would not embrace him, of that he was certain. Their physical contact was limited to shaking hands, except for that magical moment in the attic among the dusty piles of magazines. Shaking hands was the accepted limit of physical contact between the sexes, and even that could represent defilement for a strict Hindu. But he had now shaken hands with a number of ladies aboard the *Karachi* on being introduced to them: the two Misses Martin; Mrs Haldingham, her thin fingers brittle with age, and Mrs Vane, her thin fingers heavy with rings; Mrs Stiles and her daughter, whose hands were like damp dough; and then there was that ridiculous Mrs Gurslake who had embarrassed everyone by curtseying because he was a prince. Aware of the ill-suppressed smiles around him, Ravi drew himself up stiffly:

'There is no need, madam.'

A little puffing. 'Oh, Your Highness is too kind. Still, if you say so . . . It's my knees, when you get to my age . . .'

Afterwards she had seemed to think this social gaffe conferred on them a special intimacy. She would come seeking him to ply him with questions about his voyage out. Had it been very rough in the Channel and the Bay of Biscay? He had experienced it more recently than she. She spoke as if the ocean might have changed its habits, as indeed she hoped it had, and was not reassured when Ravi recalled that he and most other passengers had spent a very unpleasant few days.

'Mr Gurslake don't understand how much I dread it,' she confided. 'He thinks I exaggerate. Trouble is, he ain't got no imagination and I'm full of it.'

She patted her bosom. Ravi had not supposed its amplitude to be composed of imagination and said as much to Stafford Briscoe as they were wandering through the bazaar at Port Said, their major purchases completed and their time briefly their own.

'Apprehension, perhaps,' Stafford Briscoe suggested, 'though of course imagination can take many forms.'

'*And as imagination bodies forth* . . .' Ravi quoted. (They had done *A Midsummer Night's Dream* at school in his third year.)

'Precisely.' Stafford Briscoe expressed no surprise that he should quote

Shakespeare and went up in Ravi's estimation as a result. When not fawning on him like Mrs Gurslake, or Mrs Stiles less obviously, the English were inclined to patronise. Even Mr Haldingham, whose years in India should have taught him better, had enquired, 'Educated in England, were you?' and raised an eyebrow on learning the name of the school. Only Stafford Briscoe took such background for granted, as though they were not men of different race but simply men, one older and one younger, and capable of being friends in spite of it.

In fact Stafford Briscoe's thoughts were much occupied with imagination. Had Nina Martin imagined that attack? Edmund Bladon was convinced she hadn't – yet Bladon was now number one suspect, seen by Master Bobby Vane in the vicinity of Nina's cabin at about the appropriate time and refusing to give any explanation when the Captain questioned him. Stafford Briscoe did not believe him guilty, but it was a complicating factor none the less, if only because it helped to shield the guilty – assuming a guilty party did exist.

He found himself almost hoping the girl was pregnant. At least that would remove any doubt. He was not going to believe in a second virgin birth – he was not sure he believed in the first one. If she was pregnant there had been an attacker all right. Could it have been the boy beside him, whose revulsion he so well understood but who might have felt obliged to prove himself? Or had revulsion followed from the act? At the time, since no one had known of Ravi's presence aboard, he had had remarkable freedom to come and go, provided only he did so under cover of darkness and did not let himself be seen. But why should he have singled out Nina Martin, whose cabin was several decks below the boat deck where Ravi had hidden himself? Coincidence, then –

His thoughts were interrupted by Ravi observing, 'Miss Nina Martin has imagination.'

'What do you mean?' Briscoe asked, thinking that the boy too was about to express the view that the attack had no reality.

'When she sits down to write a letter, her expression is far away. She is thinking herself into the presence of the person she writes to. Good letters are written like that.'

'How do you know how Miss Nina writes letters?'

'I watched her one evening when she climbed up to the boat deck. She was almost directly beneath the boat where I was hiding. I could have dropped on her like a leopard on its prey.'

But you didn't. At least, not then. You watched her, Briscoe thought. You followed her. Later you sought her out. Was it your jewelled dagger whose edge she felt against her throat? He was already deep in the political complications which Ravi's assumed guilt would entail when he heard him say, 'She looks a little like Miss Dorothy Waterman, the sister of a friend of mine.'

Was this the explanation? A transfer of boyish passion, a confused identity . . .

196

'But so much fuss I do not understand,' Ravi went on. 'Miss Martin is not betrothed. She does not even intend to marry. Therefore she is not devalued in the market-place.'

'In England women aren't viewed quite like that,' Briscoe began, and broke off, wondering. Wasn't that precisely how they were viewed? The other women aboard pitied and despised Nina. The men regarded her as fair game. Not that she was at risk from them, but she had lost that aura of untouchability. Where one had been, others could follow. Even by God she was outcast, the convent's doors closed against her. Would she voluntarily have brought such a fate upon herself? But when she invented her story, she would not know the consequences; she was an innocent. And innocents were a danger – to others as much as to themselves. They had no place in a sophisticated world where everyone understood the rules even while breaking them. Innocence was something best lost.

So was he condoning what had happened to Nina Martin? No, but neither was he altogether condemning it. He was saying with Ravi, 'So much fuss I do not understand.' The thought jarred him briefly, but it was only a matter of rearranging his mental furniture to accommodate a new idea – something in which he had had plenty of practice – and all would function as smoothly as before. He glanced at the young Prince walking slim and brown beside him, noting with pleasure the delicate flaring of the nostrils, the perfect curve of the lips, and decided that it would be a challenge worth while to stand still and let the boy come towards him. After all, innocence was something best lost . . .

Lightly he placed an arm round Ravi's shoulders, turning him from contemplating the merchandise on a stall.

'Dear boy, it grows late, and time and tide wait for no man, not even in a sea like the Mediterranean where tides do not exist. Captain Meiklejohn will not be pleased if we delay his sailing. Shall we return to the ship?'

III

'And this is our position today, Mrs Vane.'

The hand that came over her shoulder at the chart table was strong and sinewy. The veins were supple beneath the skin, the pointing finger ended in a short, neat-cut nail. The wrist with a few light hairs upon it disappeared into an inch of glistening white cuff and above that was so much gold braid it was dazzling. It was a firm, capable hand, without softness. Very much a masculine hand.

Robert's hands had also been firm and capable, but surprisingly delicate in their touch as they probed the secret areas of her body, rousing her to a frenzy of desire. That had pleased him. He had set his fingers to work harder, commanding her to respond even beyond the response that had surprised her already. It seemed that ecstasy was limitless.

'You see we are at latitude thirty-five degrees and ten minutes north, and longitude nineteen degrees and ten minutes east. I'll not trouble you with the seconds.'

Captain Meiklejohn's voice was resonant. Not deep like Robert's, but reassuring in its unhurried articulation. It would not turn shrill in anger, nor bark contradictory orders in an emergency. It was solid, dependable, like his body positioned behind her, not touching her, but guarding her, reserving her to himself.

'It is all most interesting, Captain.'

Cynthia hoped this was not too much of a lie. The chart was a mystery, the instruments bewildering, the explanations floated somewhere above her head. Yet it was certainly interesting to see this man in his own domain, master of himself and of this vessel, and unselfconsciously in command. Robert in discussion with his estate manager had been similar. He knew what had to be done and what he wanted to do. A series of decisions slipped into a pattern as the future of a great estate was laid out.

The finger moved across the chart. 'By tomorrow noon we should be at this point.'

The future course of a vessel indicated with the same assurance. Robert would have liked the Captain, she was sure. Did she? Yes, for all that he was such a sad man. It was good to see him smile as he had smiled when they had met on deck that morning, crinkling the corners of his eyes. 'You're abroad early, Mrs Vane.' She assented. How explain to him that she could not sleep, not with Bobby restless in the bed opposite and

199

clamouring to go up on deck. He was bored, she knew. There was no one for him to play with and his own inner resources were small. Her suggestions for activities were met with 'I don't want to,' but a sulky silence was the only answer when she asked him what he did want. 'He wants a father, little brothers and sisters,' her brother in Quetta had said. 'Why don't you marry again? Robert wouldn't have wanted you to spend the rest of your life as his widow, and it's certainly bad for his son.' Yes, but remarriage wasn't easy. There was a shortage of eligible men and no shortage of competition for them. What chance had a widow with a child? The men who had survived the war wanted someone young and giddy. The Connie Martins of this world had suitors at their feet. They could tango, foxtrot, one-step, sip cocktails and flaunt their cigarettes, show their silk-stockinged legs, their bobs and shingles, their vivid, grease-stained lips. Bold earrings swung against their cheeks, their laughter tinkled, a swizzle stick within an empty glass. No one plucked at their short skirts crying, 'Mummy, what shall I do now? I've no one to play with.' Captain Meiklejohn's suggestion of a visit to the bridge had been heaven-sent. It would occupy the next half-hour at least.

The bridge was not what Cynthia had expected. So much glass and such a view. A hundred and eighty degrees of sea and sky as you looked for'ard, blue merging into blue. A dark rim of sea and a pale ring of sky blended, deepening to the zenith overhead, sparkling at her feet in a flurry of wavelets cascading either side of the bow. The stem of the ship cleaved the water like an axehead, the thrust of the great engines visible rather than felt, the steady advance marked only by the thinnest line of white as the *Karachi* surged forward. Powerful. Unstoppable.

'We're making sixteen knots,' the Captain told her. 'With a flat calm like this we should make Marseilles dead on time.'

And no using precious extra coal, which should delight the Owners. So long as Biscay and the Channel were as good . . .

'At the moment Mrs Gurslake doesn't have a thing to worry about,' Cynthia said for the sake of something to say.

'What's troubling her?' Captain Meiklejohn was concerned for all his passengers, even those he did not know.

'She's afraid it'll turn rough. She's a poor sailor and had a horrendous voyage coming out.'

'With the *Karachi*?'

'I don't think so. It was seven or eight years ago.'

'Then it wasn't the *Karachi*. We weren't ferrying passengers in wartime. Convoy escort duty was our line.'

'That sounds dangerous.'

'Aye, we've a few scars to show for it, but nothing that hasn't healed with time.'

Those new plates in the hull would always be with them, the Chief fretted that they were not as strong, but there were other scars than those to mark the war years, scars like those on Andrew Meiklejohn's mind. We know what to do with damaged hull plates, but: *We know so little about the mind* . . .

Cynthia changed the subject. 'Is it always very rough in the Bay?'

'No, I've known it as calm as a millpond. But of course at this time of year . . .'

With winter approaching, it was too much to expect the calm voyage all captains hoped for. Already the northern clime was reaching out towards them. He touched the rough serge of his uniform: no white ducks after Port Said. It was custom only, for in the Mediterranean it was still summer, though without the tropical heat of the Red Sea. But Port Said had always been the key to India, the gateway between East and West. There had been the usual ceremony as the ship left port when those who were returning home for good cast their sun helmets overboard because they would not be needing them again. Mr Haldingham had sent his spinning far out like a discus; for all his years, he still had a good aim. Mrs Haldingham had dropped hers overboard gently, as if reluctant to let it go. It was old and worn, survivor of many seasons. He had wondered, not for the first time, what had decided these two old people to sell up and sail for home. But you couldn't ask, and there was a cloak of privacy about them that fell in impenetrable folds. The captain of a ship saw many dramas, but never more than one act of the play.

Once he had enjoyed telling Ailsa about the dramas. She had listened avidly. What would he have said about Cynthia Vane? 'A young war widow, attractive, with a spoilt but handsome son.' And Ailsa: 'Isn't that just like a man to say she's attractive and think he can leave it at that! Is she dark or fair, tall or short?' – 'Dark and about your height. The boy's a bit like Andy – Andy as he used to be.' Silence. He would have said the unsayable. They never mentioned Andy in the past. Ailsa's letters were full of Andy in the present: Andy has been restive . . . has been playing with a celluloid doll . . . has been frightened by a thunderstorm. Angus hoped the lad had been indoors when it thundered. Uncomfortably vivid in his mind was the first occasion when the lightning flashed and the thunder rumbled, and the devastating effect it had had.

They had been in the garden as the storm was approaching, black clouds gathered over a leaden sea. It was a Sunday, and Andy in his best clothes had accompanied them to church, where he had fidgeted throughout the sermon, to Ailsa's embarrassment. Suddenly the storm, which had been muttering, decided to declare itself. A jagged streak ripped open the heavens simultaneous with an ear-splitting crack. With an animal cry of fear, Andy flung himself to the ground, clawing at the bare garden earth in frantic terror, seeking to bury himself. Before the long, rumbling echoes had swelled and diminished, Angus had sunk to his knees beside his son, seeking to relax the rigid fingers, to calm the staring eyes and babbling lips. There was earth in Andy's hair, his clothes were muddied, foam trickled from the corner of his mouth. Another flash, another rumble, and again he clawed at the earth. As the first drops fell they had dragged him indoors, Ailsa white and trembling, where for the rest of the afternoon he had cowered under the stairs moaning and whimpering, until the storm had passed and the sun was out again. Since then they had kept him indoors at the first hint of thunder, fearful that a second exposure might provoke a crisis worse than the first, and one which might lead to his incarceration in some mental hospital, a fate which Ailsa refused to contemplate.

'You were asked not to touch that, sir.'

Angus was jerked back by the voice of the officer of the watch, young Strode, immaculate as ever and even handsomer in his dark uniform, addressing Master Bobby Vane. In the few moments since his mother's interest had been distracted he had wandered to the far side of the bridge and now stood, head hanging and meddling hands behind him, before the Third Officer, whose small size was no disadvantage when dealing with juvenile crime.

'Trouble, Mr Strode?'

'No harm done, sir.'

Angus looked the delinquent up and down. 'When you invaded my bridge uninvited,' he recalled, 'I had to ask Mr Strode to escort you back to your mother. This time your mother is here. Since you cannot behave even in her presence, I suggest you be denied it. Mrs Vane, have I your permission to have this young man returned to your cabin and kept there under the stewardess's eye?'

His tone brooked no denial. Cynthia nodded.

'Mr Strode!'

'Sir, I will see to it. Under escort, sir?'

Angus hoped his eyes did not twinkle. 'That might be a good idea.' He watched with amusement as two sailors were summoned and Bobby Vane marched away. Then he became aware that Cynthia was weeping softly.

'My dear, there is no need to cry.'

'Yes, there is. He is such a handful and I can't control him. I apologise, Captain, for my son.'

I apologise for my son. Ailsa had made excuses when Andy had fidgeted in church and the minister had been gracious. Now it was Angus's turn.

'He's maybe a touch high-spirited,' he suggested.

A watery smile. 'That's a kind way of putting it.'

'He'll grow out of it – or into it. He'll learn to control himself.'

'Do you really think so, Captain?'

No, Angus thought, I don't. Not unless someone takes him in hand, acquires some influence over him, but I can't tell his mother that.

'Did you not say he was going away to school?' he countered.

'His name's down – if I can bear to let him go.'

'You must. You want what's best for him, don't you?'

Her lips trembled again. 'It's just that he's all I've got.'

'Of the past maybe. Not of the future.'

202

'What do you know about that?'

'You're an attractive woman, Mrs Vane. Some gentleman will be lucky.'

'If I could only believe that was true.'

They were still standing by the chart table, though both had turned when Julian Strode called out. It was the weariness in her voice which distressed Angus. Then, like a child, she laid her head against his chest. And as if she were a child (but she was all woman) his arm came round her. They were alone with the sea, the helmsman gazing straight ahead of him, young Strode busy correcting the instruments tampered with by Bobby Vane.

I apologise for my son, she had said. But your son is your existence, your justification for being on this earth. And you have other sons in you. You have my son. My son's mother is in my arms.

Gently Angus released her. 'This is not the time or place.'

She shook her head as if to clear the wonderment. Did he mean some other place, some other time?

He did. He was speaking quickly, urgently. A part of her mind made notes. My cabin. Tonight. After dinner. Once the boy is in bed and asleep. She heard herself repeating the details. She had never made an assignation before. It was something people did in novels. She had not known it would be like this. The part of her that agreed to meet the Captain – Angus – was a part of herself she did not know but which was stronger than her everyday self, maturer, more confident. Doing what she had to do.

'I think I should leave now,' she murmured.

There was no restraining arm. Correct as ever, Angus Meiklejohn escorted her to the companionway. 'I trust you have enjoyed yourself,' he said for the benefit of listeners.

'Oh yes. It was most instructive. And exciting.' She raised her face to his. Despite the presence of young Strode and the helmsman, it was only the knowledge that there would be other times and other places that kept him from giving her a kiss.

For the rest of the day it was as though he was watching a moving picture, the filmed life of the captain of a ship. Once he had taken Ailsa to the pictures and she had sat entranced before the grainy screen on which figures with cavernous black mouths and lashes laden with mascara acted jerkily the story of their lives. Now, as he received the day's reports, moved about the ship, took his place at the luncheon table, he almost expected piano accompaniment; but the only music came from a tinny gramophone and a record endlessly repeated: 'Let's Do It.' It was the hit song of the day.

Tonight she would come to his cabin. He surveyed it in the quiet of the afternoon. It was as immaculate as always, but what would it tell her about him? The books: never read – he had no time for reading. The Bible: yes, he found time for the Good Book. The stack of wireless messages. The photograph of Ailsa with Andy – he looked at that long and hard before laying it face down so that they should not witness his betrayal. Then, deliberately, he repositioned it so that he could see it from the bed. If a man decided to break the Seventh Commandment, he should at least be reminded of the fact.

Jamie Sutherland noticed that the photograph had changed position when he came as usual at half-past six. Since Port Said their evening communion had been suspended because of various cocktail parties that had taken place. Angus could not refuse all invitations – the Captain had to socialise – but he would much have preferred his own or the Chief's company. Better still, Cynthia's . . .

'Ye've done some rearranging,' the Chief observed. 'Ye're maybe expecting company after dinner.' Angus said nothing. 'Well, at least ye serve a decent whisky.'

He swirled the liquor in his glass appreciatively; the Chief's views on cocktails were well known. 'When I want them to tip the fruit salad into my glass, I'll ask them,' he said grimly. Whisky sours rendered him all but profane.

'I'm not entertaining,' Angus managed. Cynthia was surely more than that . . .

'Ye're getting like a woman, fussing with the curtains. Sit down, man, and enjoy your drink.'

Angus moved away from the porthole. He had not realised he was adjusting the curtain's folds.

'What's the matter wi' ye?' Jamie demanded. 'There's something on your mind.'

'No, blank as a schoolboy's slate.' Or Andy's. 'We're making very good time.'

'Aye. Marseilles the day after tomorrow. Have you caught your imaginary rapist yet?'

'No.'

'Nor will do. I tell you, Angus, the man does not exist. And even if he does, you can soon say goodbye to catching him. He'll leave the ship at Marseilles and go overland.'

It was more than likely. A number of passengers were due to disembark and one or two always made last-minute decisions, especially if the weather report was not good. Perhaps the Gurslakes would go. It would resolve Mrs Gurslake's worries about the last leg of the voyage. A three-hour Channel crossing was very different from five rough days at sea. Ought he to suggest it? The possibility might not have occurred to them. It cost more, but Bert Gurslake had obviously made his pile in Australia. Since the war there was no certainty about whom you might encounter in First Class. The old barriers were breaking down.

'I almost wish the man would leave the ship,' Angus said, answering Jamie. 'At least we need not fear another attack.'

'Ye needn't fear that in any case. Yon nun lassie's a wee bit fey. I saw her myself, wandering along the boat deck, her lips moving and no sound

204

coming out. She didna see me. I was looking for Minna and I took care to keep out of her way.'

Like a figure on the silent screen. A moving picture. An image unable to speak. She no longer raved. The surgeon said she was withdrawn and he was worried. How much deeper could withdrawal go?

'She'll be jumping overboard next in a bid for attention,' the Chief prophesied. 'Naturally when there's someone around to jump after her and maybe lose his life as well.'

'She'll not kill herself,' Angus said. 'Her religion's against it.'

'So are all religions, but that doesna stop the many who disregard the Lord's commandments.' The Seventh Commandment most of all. 'We're all sinners, Angus.'

'Aye . . . For that reason we should be charitable towards one another,' Angus suggested, thereby confirming Jamie's fears that he was growing soft.

'Provided charity does not prejudice discipline.'

Angus said heavily, 'What do you mean?'

From the moment the Chief had come in he had known that it was Jamie rather than he who sought to unburden, and something in him did not want to know what. Silently he rebuked himself for indifference to a friend's troubles, for failing, however briefly, as captain of his ship.

'It's yon conchie doctor,' the Chief said.

Angus's heart sank.

'Ye'll have to get rid of him.'

'What's he done?'

'Failed to report a breach of discipline to a man's superior officer.'

'What is it, and how do you know?'

'That stoker with the burnt hand was insubordinate. Yet he said no word to me. I grant you he dealt well with the matter, but it should have been logged and reported none the less.'

'When did it happen?'

'Two days ago, when the man went to him to be discharged.'

The Chief gave a succinct account of the episode. Angus listened with mounting dismay. As usual, the Chief was right; the matter should have been reported. Bladon was undermining discipline on the ship.

'It may have slipped his mind,' he suggested. 'He's not yet used to our ways.'

'If he logged it he's no excuse for forgetting.'

'You've not told me yet how you know.'

The Chief permitted himself a bleak smile. 'His nurse is associating with one of my officers.'

Angus savoured the choice of words. Was he 'associating' with Cynthia?

'It's hearsay,' he said.

'Not if it's in his log.'

'And if it isn't?' (But he would have to inspect it.)

'There's no smoke without a fire. The girl would hardly invent such a tale

205

and it fits all too well with what we know of yon idle stoker. Gopal has been trouble from the start.'

Gopal. So the troublemaker had a name. Might even have a grievance, as the men along the Bombay waterfront thought they had. It would be like Bladon to be sympathetic to the underdog, but on board ship there had to be discipline.

'I want an investigation, Angus.'

'You shall have one.'

'I'm thinking Mr Bladon's first voyage could verra well be his last.'

Angus was already thinking that, for the surgeon was still steadfastly refusing to account for his movements on the night of the fancy hat dance. Like Stafford Briscoe, Angus believed him innocent of rape, but without a satisfactory explanation the disquiet among the First Class passengers was gaining ground. It had been put into words by the Reverend Septimus Stiles, their self-appointed spokesman. 'You see, Captain, we're not accusing Dr Bladon of anything, but we all know Bobby Vane saw him there. The child's evidence is quite specific on that point. Some explanation is surely due. Even if some other peccadillo is involved –' and the Reverend made a supreme effort to appear charitable – 'we are men of the world, after all; but to refuse any kind of explanation looks very like an admission of guilt.' Angus did not agree, but a captain on board ship was both judge and jury, and could only find according to the evidence.

The trouble was, he liked Edmund Bladon. There was something about him that compelled respect. And there was no doubt he was an excellent doctor; even his detractors granted that. As for the past, well, Angus did not agree with his position, but the man had the right to make a stand for what he believed. And if all he had gathered about the treatment of conscientious objectors was accurate, he had paid a heavy price. Angus could guess now at the reasons that had led him to become a ship's surgeon; the doors closed against him, the opportunities denied. If at the end of his first voyage he faced dismissal, it might be just but it would certainly be hard. Nevertheless, the path of duty lay clear before him, and this time there would be no turning aside as he had turned from the path that led to Ailsa and Andy.

He told the Chief, 'I shall support you. You know that.'

'Aye. Ye're a good man, Angus.'

What would Jamie say if he knew? What would any of them say if they knew the truth about their captain? He had wondered at intervals throughout the day and he was still wondering after dinner, when, counting the hours and minutes until he could expect Cynthia in his cabin, he passed a group in the lounge.

'Come and join us, Captain, if you've a moment.'

It was Stafford Briscoe who spoke from the depths of a large armchair, one elegant leg crossed over the other, the light glinting on a patent leather shoe. Ravi was in attendance beside him. At least, Angus reflected, there was no

206

problem there. Since Port Said the boy appeared devoted to him and seldom left his side. Far from wishing to abscond, Prince Ravi wished only to be of service. Stafford Briscoe had merely to express a wish and His Highness sprang to grant it, often discovering in the process wishes Briscoe did not know he had. Even his pose now mirrored Briscoe's, but in a more upright chair the effect of controlled abandon gave place to eagerness, as though at any moment Prince Ravi might leap to his feet to procure whatever Briscoe sahib wanted, from cigarettes to dancing girls, from the jewels of his father's treasure to half his princely state.

How had this come about? Angus wondered; but not even Stafford Briscoe could have enlightened him. He did not desire Ravi; he desired him to seek to be desired, to be as Maurice had been, suppliant. And after that, who knows? From the depths of his chair he summoned Captain Meiklejohn to join the group and began introducing them.

'Prince Ravi you already know...' He smiled slightly. 'Ivo Haldingham, retired Forestry officer, returning I suspect to lay his bones with others of his kind in Cheltenham rather than Ind ... Captain Johnson, on home leave ... Mr Gurslake, a box-wallah, except that he hails from Sydney where they call them businessmen ... Mr Stiles, whose concern is our spiritual health, our physical being in Dr Bladon's hands...'

Angus bowed and smiled around the circle, regardless of whether they had met before. The absence of ladies did not surprise him; after dinner they would be titivating, indulging in gossip of their own. Cynthia would not yet have joined them; she would be putting Bobby to bed. Was she, like him, counting hours, minutes, seconds? 'I'll not trouble you with the seconds,' he had said when showing her the ship's position – was it only that morning? Now every second smote like a labouring heart.

'Captain Johnson has put forward a most interesting thesis,' Stafford Briscoe continued with relish, well knowing that Johnson, who was sweating slightly, had not intended to put forward any such thing. 'He thinks that our Indian Empire, which to us seems at the zenith of its glory, is beginning to slip from our grasp.'

'I didn't exactly say that...'

Indeed he hadn't. How could he, when it was so patently untrue? For this was the year of the great Empire Exhibition at Wembley which had been opened in April by the King. A whole new London suburb had sprung up around it; it even had its own new station on the Underground. Half England had flocked to see its Imperial splendours, the Indian Pavilion above all.

'You may not have put it into words, my dear fellow,' Stafford Briscoe said, smiling, 'but if you military men can't keep the peace...'

'With all the agitation that's going on now for home rule, let alone the hostility between Hindu and Moslem,' Archie said hotly, 'I'd like to meet the man who could.'

'Then permit me to introduce him to you, Captain,' the old Forestry

207

officer intervened. 'My district comprehended both religions, but I assure you the Pax Britannica prevailed.'

Archie was unimpressed. In rural areas it was different; there, trouble if it came amounted to no more than local ill-feeling; it was in the towns that things got out of hand. He said as much.

'Surely the principle remains,' Ivo Haldingham said. Beneath his tufted eyebrows his eyes were bright and keen. He had seen all too many young men like Archie: they either learnt, or went home on extended leave. Occasionally they got themselves killed, which was awkward, though the matter could usually be hushed up, the civil and military powers cooperating to maintain an unbroken façade. It was when they killed someone else, whether Hindu or Moslem or any one of India's myriad other sects, that British India was in danger because the Pax Britannica was breached.

'I'm not sure what principle you mean, sir, but when you've got a riot on your hands . . .'

'Need it come to a riot, Captain?'

'With respect, sir, these people aren't civilised. Even if you speak their lingo, you can't reason with them.'

'I have often noticed that the word "reason" in this context means getting others to adopt your point of view. Have you thought that there may be something to be said for adopting theirs occasionally? Things look quite different if you do.'

Archie had clearly never considered such a possibility. 'Isn't it a waste of time, sir, when they've got to do what you tell 'em in the end?'

'There speaks the military mind.'

'You can't reason with a crowd of strikers at home,' Edmund Bladon broke in with a glance at Ravi, whose face was expressionless, 'but if you can understand their point of view you're half-way to a solution. The great British virtue is compromise.'

'But India's uncivilised: compromise would be regarded as weakness. They don't see things our way.'

'A remarkable definition of civilisation, Captain.'

Stafford Briscoe judged it time to intervene. 'Suppose we hear from a different kind of captain. Tell us, sir, how you deal with breaches of discipline aboard your ship. I believe you no longer hang men from the yardarm.'

'We have not done so for some time now. I suppose the ultimate sanction is economic. A man's employment is at stake.'

Angus tried not to look at Edmund Bladon. Did he realise the gravity of his offence in not reporting Gopal?

Briscoe spoke again. 'I'm sure we're all glad you have such a powerful weapon at your disposal, sir, to keep officers and men in line.'

'Yes, we carry no guns in peacetime, though we follow basic naval discipline.'

'That makes you a specialised case, Captain, since the rest of the world does not.'

208

'All professions have their disciplines, Doctor,' Mr Stiles said meaningfully. 'You can be struck off and I can be unfrocked.' He had no intention of letting the conchie get away with snide undermining of the world as it existed; the man was probably a socialist. 'When God created order out of chaos,' he expanded, 'he intended that order to be maintained.'

'Immutably and indefinitely?'

'It is not for man to tamper with God's laws.'

'What about disease? Are you saying we shouldn't check it?'

'We should not go too far.'

'And who decides how far is far?'

Mr Stiles selected a rebuke. 'These are not matters to be taken lightly, Doctor.'

'I was never more serious in my life. Is it not, like so much else, a matter for the individual conscience?'

'Like the decision whether to go and fight.'

'Yes, Stafford.' Edmund heard the name come out quite naturally, but then they had argued so often in the past, on the terrace, round the fire of a winter's evening, before the world turned upside down. And now that it had, the same issues were re-emerging. At the centre of a whirlpool all was still.

'If we'd all decided not to go and fight we'd have had the Jerries here, mate.'

'Unless they'd felt the same, Mr Gurslake.'

'Not much hope of that. The only good German's a dead German.'

Archie Johnson said, 'Amen to that.'

'No doubt their view of us is similar.'

'Here, who began the bleedin' war?'

'That is for the historians to tell us.'

'It don't need no historians to tell the truth. The Huns invaded little Belgium, didn't they, and I s'pose we was just to go on standing by. But if a man draws a gun you got to shoot him. Otherwise he'll shoot you first.'

Which was precisely what had happened, Archie remembered, when he and his men had entered that narrow street in Maggapore, only to find it led into a small square where a demonstration was in progress. The meeting had been orderly and peaceful – it was one of many such – until his little detachment had marched unsuspectingly into it and everyone had taken fright. The memory of Amritsar was too recent and nerves were still on edge. British troops, armed, and a gathering of peaceful natives still spelt Jallianwala Bagh. Suddenly there were rifles, excited, angry shouting. Someone fired a shot. His men looked expectantly to him. Retreat was unthinkable – and dangerous. Reluctantly, Archie gave the order to open fire. They fired above the heads of the crowd, and it was with a sense of unreality that he saw a man stagger and fall. The crowd wavered. For a moment it was touch and go whether they would attack the British, but the little detachment stood firm. A long, wailing cry went up from where the man had fallen. Two or three others began to drag him away.

209

And suddenly they were all running and the British were alone in the square. One of the men looked at Archie. 'That was nasty, sir.' Archie wiped the sweat from his forehead. 'You mean it will be nasty,' he said.

In the event it had been worse than he imagined. The midnight mail from Maggapore, the long hot journey, the boredom and bitterness at the hotel in Bombay, and then the brief, sweet, scented solace in that house in the red light district and its legacy of shame and fear. He stirred uneasily, conscious of his groin throbbing. What did these men know of shame and fear?

He became aware that the little Irish steward was standing beside him. Stafford Briscoe had ordered a round of drinks.

'Thank you, I'll have a peg. A chota peg,' he added, anxious not to give the impression that he was used to knocking it back. He noticed that Bert Gurslake had no such inhibitions. Briscoe too ordered himself a burra peg, but the Captain and old Haldingham had settled for something more modest, and of course it was fruit juice for His bloody little Highness who sat metaphorically at Briscoe's feet, like a white man's servant in the first trading days of the East India Company when India was still a private fief.

From behind his lowered lashes Ravi surveyed Archie Johnson and disliked what he saw. Captain Meiklejohn and Mr Haldingham were worthy of respect, if only because in his eyes they were old men and old age was an honourable estate. Besides, the Captain had been kind to him even before he knew his identity, though not as kind as Dr Bladon had been. Bert Gurslake he dismissed with contempt. A box-wallah indeed! Briscoe sahib had been charitable in his introduction. The man was no better than a clerk issuing chits and thinking himself superior to the babus who did the same, often more efficiently. But Briscoe sahib was a wise and charitable being who understood many things, including the fact that he, Ravi, was not to be manipulated into marriage because of some dynastic concept of duty, but was as free in this respect as an Englishman. And Englishmen did not always marry. The Resident hadn't, for which Ravi considered some woman should be thankful, and neither had Briscoe sahib. Mr Haldingham had, of course, but he and his wife were so mummified they were scarcely man and woman. It was strange she was not with him; they were hardly ever apart. In that respect they reminded him of the Watermans, for Mr Waterman also seemed to enjoy the company of his wife. Or was it that since in England there were no women's quarters, the Englishwoman's quarters were inevitably at her husband's side. Which might explain why Englishmen were slow to marry . . .

The drinks came and Briscoe sahib signed the chit with the same insouciance that Ravi associated with Barry Waterman. 'Money's only paper,' the banker's son explained loftily, 'or any other agreed medium of exchange.' To Ravi, accustomed to his father's treasury where gold bars lay cheek by jowl with precious stones, the concept was still bewildering. He too could now sign for drinks, for the money reimbursed to Briscoe sahib for the clothes bought in Port Said, for the cash which would be made available to him when they docked at Tilbury. His father would honour the chits – provided he returned with the *Karachi*'s next sailing. All this had been explained to him by Captain Meiklejohn and Briscoe sahib who seemed to think it not unreasonable. And when he returned? Would his father and the Resident produce the same arguments, the same blandishments, worse still, perhaps, the same bride? Or would Briscoe sahib succeed in making them recognise that it was too soon for him to wed?

For Stafford Briscoe had offered to intercede. He would write to the Resident, who was known to have influence with the Nawab, and put Prince Ravi's case. It would amuse him to play a part in this small drama of Empire. It would be something to do in rural Gloucestershire, where after the nine days' wonder of knighthood, time might hang heavy on his hands. Until the next mission: for there would be another, he was certain. He wasn't being put out to grass. An embassy? His Excellency Sir Stafford Briscoe. It had an appropriate ring.

Meanwhile the need for diplomacy near at hand was apparent. He said easily, 'Mr Gurslake is quick on the draw. It sounds as if he's been wasted as a box-wallah. The Wild West should have been his scene.'

'Cowboys and Indians?' Bert brightened. 'We used to play that when I was a kid. We had to draw lots to see who was going to be cowboys, 'cause the Indians always lost.'

'These were American Indians,' Stafford Briscoe said in an aside to Ravi, who whispered, 'I know, I have played it too.'

'An excellent example of historical falsification,' Edmund Bladon suggested, 'for in fact the Indians didn't always lose. They were every bit as brave and fearless as the white man, but they were no match for the invaders' guns.'

'And of course they wasn't white,' Bert interjected.

'That too,' Edmund said.

'It is amazing how often throughout history the false gods yield to the true.' The Reverend Mr Stiles noted this fact with satisfaction. Archie Johnson was thankful to find the Padre on his side.

'And how often the missionaries were followed by the soldiers.'

'Meaning what, Doctor?'

'That the victory was to the guns.'

'I cannot accept that.'

'Regrettably, Padre, it's true. But that is not to despise the work of the missions.' Ivo Haldingham was also a diplomat. 'It is merely to say that in this world the best things can be perverted – by time, if by nothing else.'

'I'm afraid I don't follow.'

'Take British rule in India, for example, with which this discussion began. I yield to no one in my admiration for the British achievement, but isn't it possible that a change in the Indian people may make our presence less desirable than it was?'

Mr Stiles pursed his lips. 'If that's your thinking after a lifetime in the country, then our grasp is indeed slipping.'

Archie broke in. 'Sir, isn't that just where the rot begins? A soft line with agitators – seeing their point of view – makes the work of the police and the Army that much more difficult, and we are there for your protection, after all.'

'I need no reminding of the role of police and army, young man. When two of my colleagues were slaughtered by extremists the forces of law and order could not protect them, but they saw to it later that a number of men, some innocent, were hanged.'

'Are you saying we should stand by and let such murders happen?'

'I am saying we should enquire into their cause. We are less welcome in India than we were – if we were ever welcome, except as individuals here and there.'

Bert Gurslake could not believe his ears. 'You mean we should get out of India?'

'I forecast we shall have to some day,' Stafford Briscoe said, assuming the mantle of prophet. 'Can a handful of white men hold a country that size against the will of its inhabitants?'

'What's the Army got to say to that?'

'Of course we can hold India – if the politicians will let us,' Archie retorted.

'The politicians, as you call them, may be all that stands between the Army and a bloodbath,' Ivo Haldingham said quietly. 'You see, I am old enough to remember the Mutiny. Oh, I don't mean I was there, I was a boy at school when it happened, but I heard my elders talk. Of course it was months before the news reached England and the worst was over before we knew it had begun, but I remember hearing of the horrors of Cawnpore and the Round Tower at Jhansi, and always the worst horror was that those we trusted had turned on us. Now perhaps the British presence is all that prevents another bloodbath: that between Moslem and Hindu.'

'But they're only natives.'

Really this little runt Gurslake was impossible. Even in the uniform of evening dress it was impossible to mistake him for anything other than what he was. Stafford Briscoe turned to Captain Meiklejohn before Ravi could have a chance to intervene.

'You run a happy ship, Captain, with a largely native crew. What's your formula?'

Angus, who had heard nothing since Bert Gurslake's reference to cowboys and Indians, came to with a start. In his mind's eye was a picture of a long-legged, laughing boy uttering wild war whoops. Andy had loved to be an Indian; for while it was usually the cowboys who were the victors, the Indians had all the fun – bows and arrows, feathered headdresses and tomahawks, pow-wows, wigwams, not to mention scalps. To be asked suddenly about other Indians and how he dealt with them was like jerking him back from one world to another, but he answered readily enough.

'I have always found that firmness and justice work wonders.'

'Backed by naval discipline.'

'You must not make too much of it, Mr Bladon. To say it's there is not to say it's used.'

'I am glad to hear it, Captain.'

Was this why the young fool had jeopardised his career by not reporting Gopal's insubordination – some notion that the underdog was victimised? Angus wished very much that discipline, naval or otherwise, would permit him to shake Edmund Bladon as he had shaken the child Andy on occasion in a frenzy of love and despair. For Andy could be obstinate, like his mother, and when embattled there was no reasoning with him. Later, of course, when things had calmed down, Angus would return to the issue and explain his point of view, and Andy, who at other times was a ready listener, could usually be persuaded to it. Perhaps it would be possible to do the same with Edmund Bladon. At least it would be worth a try.

In the meantime Mr Stiles, like Bert Gurslake and Archie Johnson, was struggling to assimilate what he had heard.

'You surely can't mean,' the Reverend protested to Stafford Briscoe, 'that we should withdraw from India and hand it over to the natives.'

'Who are natives of India, after all.'

'But India is part of the British Empire.'

'*All empire is no more than power in trust*. No, that's not me: the poet Dryden said it some two hundred and fifty years ago. Before we had an Empire. We don't realise what parvenus we are.'

'Sir, as a servant of His Majesty and, I assume, a member of the Church of England, it ill becomes you to speak so slightingly of one of the great civilising forces of the world.'

'It hasn't had much effect on the Indians, has it, Padre?'

Before anyone could answer Archie Johnson's crassness, Ravi was on his feet.

'We are not savages!'

'Of course not, dear boy, Captain Johnson didn't mean that. Sit down and don't behave like one.'

Stafford Briscoe laid a hand on Ravi's arm, but the Prince shook it off. He had heard more than enough.

'You are right to forecast the end of your Empire,' he told Briscoe, but courteously; this was Briscoe sahib, after all. 'And yes –' he turned to Archie with less courtesy – 'you have already lost your grip on India and some day we will throw you out.'

'Some day is a long day.'

'Perhaps, but already shadows fall. Your sun will set and darkness overwhelm your Empire that you boast the sun never sets on. And you will deserve all you get.'

Ivo Haldingham stirred in protest.

'I am sorry, sir. I am sure you have had a long and honourable career and done much good among our peoples, but there are others of whom the same cannot be said. Our civilisation was old before your Empire existed – it is a parvenu, as Mr Briscoe points out. Yet for every British member of Calcutta's Asiatic Society who is steeped in our culture and whose learning has contributed to it, there are hundreds of you who think we have no culture. You think we exist to be your servants, and when we protest you think we are targets for your guns.'

Stafford Briscoe reflected that an English liberal education had its disadvantages when the recipient was a hereditary foreign ruler, but he decided to follow Ivo Haldingham's advice and see the other point of view.

He clapped Ravi on the shoulder. 'Well said, dear boy. I couldn't have put it better myself.'

Startled and gratified, Ravi turned, but not before Archie Johnson had retorted, 'Your peaceful protests, as you call them, are designed to stir up civil disorder. Of course they must be quashed.'

'Civil disobedience is somewhat different from military insurrection,' Edmund Bladon pointed out.

'*You* can hardly be expected to know anything about it,' Archie said scornfully, 'but these peaceful demonstrators are capable of opening fire on British troops.'

'And British troops on peaceful demonstrators – as happened at Amritsar, you may recall.'

'I'm sick to death of hearing about Amritsar. We've been pussyfooting ever since.'

'Not everyone, Captain. Only a few weeks ago in my father's capital of Maggapore British troops fired on a peaceful demonstration and an innocent man was killed.'

This distortion of fact took Archie's breath away.

'We only fired to break it up. And after they'd drawn guns.' Too late he realised he had betrayed himself.

'Ah,' Ravi said softly. 'You were there.'

'Yes, I was. Which is more than you were.'

Ravi took a leap in the dark. 'You were the officer in charge of the detachment. You gave the order to fire.'

'Over their heads. The bullet ricocheted.'

'My father had you cashiered.'

'I was not cashiered. I resigned my commission.'

'And we ran you out of Maggapore.'

Archie's face had flushed a dull red. His hands were clenching. 'You didn't run me anywhere. *You* ran. What crime had you committed that you had to run away from your own country? Some girl, was it, whom you raped and abandoned? Did you think you could do the same thing here, creeping out of your hidey-hole with that jewelled knife and prowling the ship in the darkness until you found a defenceless girl alone –'

'There's no evidence for any of this, Johnson,' Captain Meiklejohn said in warning.

214

'No, sir, he's too fly for that.'

'Sir, he accuses me because he may himself be guilty. "Come on, girlie, give a chap a break." Isn't that what you said to Miss Martin when you had her alone on the boat deck? Except that you weren't alone. Stowed away in a lifeboat, I could hear you, I could see you. She tried to push you away. And then she slapped your face and ran, and you ran after her. I wonder, *Mister* Johnson, what you did next?'

Archie writhed at the civilian appellation.

'Well, Johnson, what did you do?' Stafford Briscoe spoke calmly, despite the speed of his heartbeats. Imperceptibly, the circle of men closed in.

'I escorted Miss Martin back to the dance-floor. I'm not an animal.'

'You mean it is Miss Constance Martin of whom you have been speaking?' Edmund Bladon's hands were clenching now.

'Yes, of course.'

'And you did not, in frustration, assault her sister?'

'Where would be the fun in that?'

He had not answered the question, Edmund noted, and ached to knock him down. He could imagine him half drunk and leering over Connie, though he dared not allow himself to imagine more than that.

But Johnson had sounded so aggrieved that Stafford Briscoe almost decided he must be innocent. He looked at Captain Meiklejohn. 'I think, sir, there is nothing to be gained by pursuing this discussion. I suggest we break it up.'

'Good idea.' The Captain had been trying to glance not too obviously at his watch when the accusations started. Now he made his escape. 'You will excuse me, gentlemen. There are matters to which I must attend.'

In particular, Cynthia . . .

As Archie Johnson was escorted away by Mr Stiles and Bert Gurslake, who was more nervous of him than ever now he knew him to be quick on the draw, Stafford Briscoe was reminded of seconds in a duel. Which left him and Edmund to second Ravi, who seemed to have come off the better of the two. But if he had scored a personal victory, the racial wounds must go deep. He had been confronted with a cross-section of English opinion on India and the Indians, and he could hardly like what he had heard. He turned to him now and held out his hands, all charm and expansiveness.

'Dear boy, what can I do but apologise for my countrymen, or some of them. Don't take it too much to heart. Men like Mr Stiles, Bert Gurslake, and Captain – no, *Mister* – Johnson have little to do with framing England's laws or with administering her vast overseas territories.' (That sounded better than Empire.) 'Don't take them too seriously.'

'Mr Gurslake can exploit the people commercially, Mr Stiles can interfere with their beliefs, and Mr Johnson can kill them,' Ravi said flatly. 'I am sorry, Mr Briscoe sir, I cannot feel reassured.'

How like Maurice he was when Maurice was being prickly and difficult. The trick then had been to take no notice; above all, not to let him think you cared. Maurice had had no hesitation in abandoning an unproductive attitude. He had the realism of a child.

'You're right, of course,' Stafford Briscoe said. 'It is deeply disturbing to discover certain aspects of any society. Your own demonstrators in Maggapore must have taught you that.'

The hit went home. Ravi's gaze faltered. 'I am not saying we are perfect . . .'

'No nation on earth is that.'

'But you British perhaps approximate?'

Was there the beginning of a twinkle in the dark eyes looking into his own?

'You are gracious enough to see it from our point of view.'

'I have been brought up among you.'

'So an English education may take some credit?'

For the Watermans' friendship. For Dorothy. Ravi inclined his head.

'Then you will join me in another drink. With the doctor.'

Edmund excused himself.

'Then we two alone will continue the discussion.'

'Forgive me, sir, I am tired. Some other evening.'

'Some other evening of your choice.'

That put the ball in Ravi's court. He would have to suggest it, would have to seek him out. A first lesson in asking – and the request would be granted. Soon he would ask for more. Which might or might not be granted. Stafford Briscoe watched him walk away. Slim hips, narrow back and shoulders. A sinuous, catlike grace. A smooth, almost hairless body. Those delicate, fine-boned hands. No nation on earth was perfect, but physically individuals were.

'You're a dangerous man, Mr Briscoe.'

The slow, quiet voice took him unawares. From the corner to which he had withdrawn Ivo Haldingham was regarding him with those keen, all-seeing eyes.

Briscoe shrugged. 'You exaggerate my power.'

'I suspect I underestimate it. You are a manipulator of men.'

'Someone has to pull the strings.'

'And some have to be puppets.'

'Don't take me too seriously.'

'I don't.' Haldingham rose stiffly. 'But then, you have no strings on me. You are an accomplished puppet-master, Briscoe, but beware lest you do it too well. What happens if you in turn are manipulated?'

Briscoe considered the possibility. 'I don't know. It's never happened.'

The old man regarded him an instant before moving towards the door.

'That I can believe, but may I recommend you consider it? It is not so much other men you need beware of as circumstance. Circumstance – or fate – pulls all our strings, some more than others. What will you do when you feel the unfamiliar jerk, I wonder? Well, time alone will tell.'

IV

In the early-morning light coming through the porthole the splash of scarlet silk dripped to the floor. At the foot of the bed, where it should have covered her underwear, it was the first thing Connie's eyes registered, its fall a witness to another restless night. Then her ears heard the silence and her body recognized that the ship was no longer in motion. They were in port, their first port in Europe. Outside was the waterfront of Marseilles.

She glanced at Nina, who lay supine in the heavy, drugged sleep induced by the tablets Edmund had given her. She lay with her mouth half open, her features flaccid, all semblance of beauty gone. The square of blue silk at her feet had scarcely shifted; her underwear remained in a neat pile. She would not wake for hours yet. Connie slipped from bed and went to the porthole to look down at the dock far below.

Cargo was being unloaded, and the luggage of those passengers who were leaving the ship. The passengers themselves stood in disconsolate groups, waiting. Blue-bloused porters hurried hither and thither. There were shouts in an unfamiliar language. And everyone was white.

Until then Connie had not realised how much she took brown bodies for granted. They were around her all the time. At home the retinue of household servants belonged to a different race. The idea of a white person performing menial duties was disturbing. Those porters were all wrong. They should be brown and thin, clad only in dhotis and turbans, like the ones left behind in Bombay. Nothing could have brought home to her more clearly that East had finally given way to West.

Of course the staff on the *Karachi* were British – she mustn't say English, not with Captain Meiklejohn being a Scot and her favourite steward Irish – but the *Karachi* was a world apart. Or rather it was a world between worlds, touching both East and West. The vast substratum of native crewmen, of whom for the most part First Class passengers were unaware, performed the necessary menial tasks, and above them was a thinner layer of white or near-white passengers whose small animosities and factions might or might not be due to race. She could understand, though she did not share, some people's animosity towards Edmund, but why should the Haldinghams refuse to have anything to do with John Joseph, who was all Irish courtesy and charm? She knew it worried him, for the steward had asked her privately if she knew what he had done. 'I never set eyes on them, miss, until I asked them if they'd care for a drink on

217

that first evening,' he confided. 'The old lady seemed to shrink away, but the old gentleman now, though he put his arm around her as if to protect her from me, did at least manage to say "No, thanks." But they'll place an order with any other steward. I let Preston look after them, but...' He shook his head. He did not think highly of Preston, a view which Connie and most of the other First Class passengers shared.

The *Karachi* was not due to leave Marseilles until eleven o'clock in the morning, so those passengers who wished could go ashore for a couple of hours. Few did. The time was not sufficient to allow of exploration, and the thought of coffee and croissants in one of the café-bars around the port was less attractive than the good breakfast served in the ship's dining saloon. But Connie was one of the few. From the moment she had learned that there would be an opportunity to set foot on dry land in the forenoon she had been determined to take advantage of that chance, though she did not hunger for what the café-bars could offer. It was a different sustenance she craved.

She had not heard Mass since Father Farrell had said it in the little wooden church at Nullumpur, when Nina had knelt beside her and the Father's hands had rested briefly in blessing on their bowed, mantilla'd heads. The blessing had really been meant for Nina, who was about to embark on the religious life, but she had not felt totally excluded: some part of it was for her. Of course if Father Farrell really knew her, that is to say if she had confessed her sins as she should, he would have held up his hands in horror rather than blessing, but he did not know her: no one did. Except God who, according to one of the good Father's sermons, could see into every corner of your soul, all the stained and shabby places, all the crevices where dirt and fluff might collect. He made your soul sound like an aged soutane, such as he himself often wore, and his exhortations to amendment were more like an advertisement for some spiritual dry-cleaner's than pointers to a regenerate life. 'Father Farrell preaches such beautiful sermons,' Nini said afterwards, and Connie had not liked to disabuse her. She would have no more opportunities to evaluate them.

But there was no priest aboard the *Karachi*, for the unpleasant Mr Stiles did not count, and after all that had happened since the Gateway to India had fallen away behind them, Connie ached to lose herself in the blessed familiarity of the Mass. She had said nothing about her resolve to Nina, partly because she believed it more important for her to sleep, and partly because, since the Occurrence (which was how Connie thought of it), they had not mentioned religion, let alone the religious life. What must Nini feel, Connie wondered; what accommodation would be asked of her as she struggled to come to terms with a new life? A new life. If Nini were pregnant, what were they going to do? Suppose Aunt Maura and Uncle Charles did not believe her story? There were times when Connie hardly believed it herself.

Each time that happened – as now – she reproached herself for doubting her sister. Nini had enough to bear. Pausing only to leave a note so that her sister should not worry, Connie escaped up on deck into the sparkling, salt-laden, many-odoured air.

'Going ashore, Miss Martin?'

It was Third Officer Strode's voice.

'Yes.'

'Alone?'

'Yes. Any reason why I shouldn't?'

Young Strode's teeth showed in a neat smile. 'Only that it seems such a waste. Sorry I can't offer to escort you, but I have to take the forenoon watch. Don't get lost. I'm told there's a warren of little streets behind the harbour, and you'll need to be back by ten.'

'I'll be careful,' Connie promised, relieved she was to be spared his company. She did not like Julian Strode. Then she reproached herself. He was courteous, helpful, pleasant in manner. It was just that she found him a bore. If only Edmund could have accompanied her! But she knew he had a surgery and could not leave the ship. Besides, his presence would have been too distracting if he knelt beside her at Mass. 'Remember what is meant by communion,' Reverend Mother had said. 'The opportunity to commune with Our Lord as you take His body into you and open your heart to Him.' Connie had a fleeting vision of the grubby soutane Father Farrell thought of as the soul, but Reverend Mother's voice went on: 'Try to hear Mass daily, not just on Sundays. It offers food for your journey through life, and when the time comes for you to make your heavenly journey, you will be well prepared to receive viaticum.'

I am not prepared, Connie thought. I am not even prepared for this morning. *Introibo ad altarem Dei* – I will go in unto the altar of God. But a thousand new sensations assailed her: the unfamiliar cobbles beneath her feet; the strange language spoken all about her; the salty tang of the air. She passed a market, where gleaming fish and piles of many-coloured vegetables beckoned to her from the stalls, and women with baskets on their arms haggled with stallholders, apparent hostility overlying the reality of comradeship. A man pushed his way through the bead curtain in the doorway of a café-bar, paused to light a cigarette, and shouted something after her; she inferred from his tone that it was a compliment. Several heads turned to look at the slim girl with the red-gold colouring who was so obviously a foreigner.

A foreigner. *Un étranger*. Connie remembered the words from school French, taught painfully by Sister Ursula who had never set foot in France. *I was a stranger and ye took me in*. Our Lord Himself had been a stranger, and was so still to many hearts, not just to those in countries unvisited by the missions, but even to those within the Church. Like her own, locked and barred against him. But He would take care of her unworthiness. When the priest uttered the absolution none would rise more thankfully than Constance Mary Martin. Except that absolution

219

implied the desire to amend and cast out sin and, like her mother, she would still carry the burden of hers within her because the sin was sweet.

The streets had already narrowed into the rabbit-warren Julian Strode had mentioned. Glancing back, she could no longer see the port although it was only a few minutes since she had left it. Water dripped from washing already hung overhead. High up, where the early sun entered top-floor windows, a caged bird burst into song. The street opened suddenly into a little square, irregularly sided, and there before her was a church. A woman with a topknot that made her think of Florrie Gurslake's and the broad, bony haunches of a mare pushed her way in despite two well-filled market baskets. A moment later Connie followed her.

She almost stumbled in the darkness against a padded inner door, which swung to noiselessly behind her, disturbing nothing but the air. Before her were columns, the altar still in darkness save for the sanctuary lamp; the sound of chanting from a side chapel; a bank of candles. She sank to her knees in a pew. A priest was reciting the Litany of the Virgin; it was November – the month of the dead. The woman with the market baskets had gone to join the group before the Lady altar, but Connie stayed where she was. She had last attended Mass on All Souls' Day and prayed for the repose of her mother's soul. It was two years since she had died – did they measure time in Purgatory? Who kept the records and totted up those Days of Indulgence which prayers were supposed to buy? What remission would Nini's vows purchase? And now that she could not take vows, was the remission to be snatched back, like a prize falsely awarded? Would her mother know?

She heard again the hoarse whisper – 'No, I won't see him' – when Father Farrell called. 'I'm sorry, Father, she refuses . . .' It had been her task to explain. The priest had looked at her sorrowfully and made the sign of the Cross. 'I shall pray for her.' – 'Thank you, Father.' *But that isn't what she wants.* It was three weeks since Denis Orrey had visited. Connie was well aware why: he was escorting a young woman fresh out from England who was handsome, healthy – and free. Innocent Nini had almost let the cat out of the bag and provoked an outburst which Connie, striving to calm her mother, had been unable to forget: that repeated pitiful whisper, 'Is Denis coming soon?' After that Daddy had told Nini not to mention Major Orrey because it upset Mummy so. He was right: the man would be better forgotten, but Connie knew that she at least would never forget.

One afternoon she had gone to see him. Women were not allowed in the military cantonment, except of course in married quarters, but he often spent off-duty hours at the Club. It was where he had first met Mummy, which made it an inauspicious rendezvous. The Martins, like all Europeans in Nullumpur, belonged to the Club, though they seldom went there since Bridget Martin had been ill. One or two acquaintances greeted Connie with pleased surprise, but she dodged their efforts to detain her and refused invitations to a drink. So long as Denis was not with that Miss Mason . . . But no, he was alone, sprawled in a wickerwork chair on the verandah with the *Times of India* over his face. An empty glass was on the table beside him; she watched the paper's gentle rise and fall; he was asleep. She went and stood beside him and said, 'Denis, I have to talk to you.'

He woke with a jerk. 'Good God, Connie, do you have to steal up on a chap like that?'

'Yes,' she said, 'since there's no other way of seeing you.'

He sighed resignedly. 'Sit down – though of course I'm flattered.' He leaned over and patted her knee. She was obliged to sit close to him so that they should not be overheard, but her flesh flinched at his touch.

He noticed it. 'Not shy, are we? I thought we knew each other too well for that.'

'I don't think so,' she said politely. 'I thought it was my mother you knew well.'

He adjusted his tone. 'Poor Bridget. How is she?'

'Worse,' Connie said.

'So I heard. You've no idea how much her illness distresses me.'

'No,' said Bridget's daughter, 'I really have no idea.'

There was a silence. Connie broke it.

'Will you come and see her?'

'Of course. You don't think I've given her up?'

'It's nearly a month since you came.'

'Time goes so fast. I must get better organised.'

'Will you come back with me now?'

'Sorry, my dear. Other commitments.'

'When will you come?' Connie asked.

'As soon as I can – if she's up to receiving visitors.'

'You're not a visitor,' Connie said. And then: 'She's been asking for you.'

She felt colour flood her face. To reveal her mother's desperation to this man who lay back so coolly indifferent was betrayal. She hated herself, and hated Denis Orrey even more.

He was smiling. 'Kind of you to say so, my dear. I must admit I've felt like part of the family, but it's good to know you feel the same.'

'She's dying, Denis.'

'I grieve for you.'

'But you won't come back with me.'

'Look, Con, you know it'll only upset her. I realised that last time. You don't want a crisis, do you?'

'I want her to have a little happiness.'

'You're a good girl, but believe me, I can't give it to her. If you were older you'd understand. Why not give yourself a rest from home nursing? Come riding with me this afternoon.'

'I thought you had other commitments.'

'For you I'm prepared to break them.'

'For me, but not for her.'

'Haven't you just told me she's dying?'

Connie turned to hide her tears and felt his arm slide round her shoulders. It might look like a brotherly embrace but he was fingering her breast, his breath warm on her neck.

'If anyone could persuade me, you could,' he murmured. 'You're the prettiest little bawd in Nullumpur.'

She forgot people were watching and slapped him. Heads turned, but she did not care.

His eyes went on lazily smiling. 'Come on, girlie, give a chap a break.'

They were the same words Captain Johnson had used on the boat deck on the night of the fancy hat dance. Then too she had slapped him. Then too she had perhaps acted as a bawd. An unwitting one, of course, but if she hadn't said no . . . She checked herself. Edmund said there was no evidence to suggest Nini's attacker was Archie Johnson. Stafford Briscoe had come up with none. The field was still wide open. It could be any man aboard.

In the side chapel the priest was exhausting the Litany of the Virgin, hurling her attributes at the small congregation of women, who in turn volleyed back each response. It sounded like a game. 'Prayers of repetition have their uses,' Reverend Mother had said. 'It requires an act of will to concentrate on them, which itself is a good thing, but if you cannot make one, at least make the responses. They empty the mind of other thoughts.'

'*Rosa mystica* . . .'

'. . . *ora pro nobis.*'

'*Turris eburnea* . . .'

'. . . *ora pro nobis.*'

Pray for us. Pray for me.

Connie bowed her head. There was activity now at the high altar where a server lit candles. Behind her the padded door swung several times, admitting a waft of air with each new entrant. Some half-dozen congregants had joined her now. An old priest shuffled in and genuflected stiffly. *In nomine Patris, Filii et Spiritu Sancto* . . . The morning Mass had begun.

Connie struggled to follow the Frenchified Latin, to concentrate on the mystery unfolding before her that would transform bread and wine to flesh and blood, but her mind darted like a shoal of minnows, each fish a separate thought. Edmund (that thought recurred) . . . what is going to happen to us when the *Karachi* reaches port? Do we go our separate ways or . . . Have I the right to leave Nini? What do we do if she's pregnant? Will Aunt Maura and Uncle Charles help? . . . I can't imagine Nini with a baby. And yet I can, she's made for motherhood. So can it ever have been right for her to be a nun? If Mummy hadn't died as she did, would she have thought of it? Would she if she had really understood? . . . Edmund says people have to make their own adjustments, which means I have to make mine. That's easy. More than anything in this world I want to be with

Edmund. I want to be his wife. I want to be at his side when he is reviled for following his conscience. I want to bear his sons. And I ought not to want all this . . . *mea culpa, mea maxima culpa*, oh yes, pray for me to the Lord Our God and all the angels and saints, but angels and saints can't save me, for it would be wrong for me to marry Edmund and yet everything in me says I will. That is, if he asks me. Dear God, please let him ask me. Mrs Edmund Bladon. The words are sweet on my tongue. For the sake of a worthless man my mother defied her Church and her upbringing, but Edmund isn't worthless, he is the finest man I know. Surely it cannot be wrong to give him happiness when he has endured so much? It's ridiculous to think he could have assaulted Nina, and all on the word of a little boy who fantasises, as even his mother admits. So why won't Edmund clear his name? Mr Briscoe is convinced he's protecting someone. But he wouldn't shield a rapist – or would he? Might it depend on who it was?

Have we reached the Gospel already? I haven't heard a word. Reverend Mother says that not to concentrate during Mass is to insult God in His own house, like going out to dinner and then ignoring your host. I'm sorry, God, it's just that . . . Reverend Mother gave me such a searching look when we went to say goodbye, as if she could see into my mind. I don't want my mind read by anyone, I don't want to read it myself, I'll turn the page and . . . Edmund. All things come back to him. Will he ask me to marry him? He has already told me he has no money, no prospects, but surely he won't hold back because of that? To deny love fulfilment because of material considerations is to mock the power of love – only isn't that what I'm doing? Denying another love for the sake of material considerations, the most material of them being love itself?

Someone coughed behind her. During the recital of the Creed she allowed her eyes to roam. This dim, dark church whose columns had stood for centuries was so different from the shack-like church in Nullumpur. The stones breathed incense, the air was heavy with the smell of candle-wax, the floor was worn by countless generations of feet. There were flowers in pots massed untidily before the Lady altar, deserted now that her worshippers had gone. Instead, all the drama was concentrated on the high altar, where the old priest intoned '*Let us pray,*' and proceeded to pray in an inaudible mumble, though his little congregation duly responded when he paused.

Requiem æternam dona eis, Domine . . . He had reached the prayers for the dead in this funereal month of November when the year's obsequies were observed. And then, in Nature's sleep of death and darkness, came a birth, a pinpoint of light, growing ever stronger and brighter to become the risen sun, the Risen Christ. '*Let light perpetual shine upon them*' – Connie's prayers were heartfelt now – upon Mummy, who loved man more than God, and upon her daughter, who is well on the way to doing the same.

Before her lay all the rich experience of womanhood: love and marriage; childbirth and motherhood; the black habit of a widow – Oh no! Oh, never that! Let Edmund live on after me, let him marry a second time, so long as I do not have to live without him. Widow's weeds are not for me.

Aunt Eileen, in the photograph which so fascinated Nina, had put off her ball gown for the postulant's clumsy dress and waited now, black-habited as any widow, to receive a bride of Christ. Only there wasn't going to be a bride. Nina could not enter. What would become of her?

Before they left Nullumpur Daddy had insisted on having them photographed by the little Indian photographer everyone used. The two portraits hung side by side in his bedroom, above the one of Mummy on his desk. 'So that I can say hello to you occasionally,' he said, half joking. Connie felt tears prick her eyes. She had forecast to Nina that he would marry the widowed Mrs Moloney but she wished she could be sure of it. Her father was too much of a loner ever to be happy in a bachelors' chummery, the civilian equivalent of the mess. In the past two years she had wakened sometimes in the small hours to see his light still on, or had watched him pacing round the darkened compound, distinguishable only by the glow of his pipe. He missed her mother, she knew. He reproached himself, she suspected. What remarks would he address to those portraits in the empty years to come?

He had been so opposed to Nini's entering. 'Waste of a young life,' he had said. 'Look at Eileen. Prettiest girl you ever saw, apart from your mother, and walled up for twenty-five years in a convent. What's the point of it?' As usual, it had fallen to Connie to try to explain, for Nina just wept and whimpered, but her father had not accepted what she said. 'A life of prayer because the rest of us don't pray enough!' he exploded. 'You might as well spend the rest of your life in a bath because the rest of us don't wash.' They had both laughed. It was one of the joys of being with him that they laughed at the same things. With Edmund too she was at ease. She had only to catch his eye in company and a smile of complicity would pass between them. Later, when alone, they would compare notes and enjoy the joke. It would be wonderful to share such things with him in future, to know that at the end of every day its content of good and ill would be assessed and then forgotten in the delicious preliminaries of love and sleep.

A small thrill of pleasure ran through her, to be succeeded by shame. She was in church. On the altar the passion and death of Our Lord were being re-enacted, and all she could think of was lust. She forced herself to use the ugly word, though with Edmund there was no such thing. And then she checked: if you denied the prior claim of one who loved you, if you cheated a husband, say, did you not compound the offence by claiming that love was the name of your lust? Was that how Mummy had justified her relationship with Denis Orrey? That relationship had led to death. The death of the soul . . . No! Connie jerked to her feet as the priest enjoined them to lift up their hearts. Despite the ten-thousand-ton weight that pressed upon hers, she could not, would not believe that. When she knelt with Edmund to receive the sacrament of marriage, their two hearts would be as one as surely as the priest now lifted up the chalice. *This is my body . . . my blood . . .* This is the symbolic act that makes of Christians one family, blood brothers in the Lord . . . *Do this in remembrance of me.* Yes, Lord. As if it were possible to forget.

I remember the first time I saw Edmund and wondered what the red bars meant on the epaulettes of his white ducks. Later, when I knew they meant surgeon, I asked if they were bars of blood. He laughed – up to then he'd been so solemn – and suddenly his face was transformed. He looked ten years younger and I realised he was handsome – and that I was in love with him. We were one day out from Bombay. That was all the time it took for my life to be refashioned, all the time it took for me to fall. From grace? In love? I no longer know. *Lord, I am not worthy . . .* No, I am not worthy of him, but say the word and my soul at least shall be healed.

A few women from the congregation shuffled forward as the priest turned to offer them the Host. Connie found herself among them, though she had not consciously commanded her body to move. The woman in front of her, old, bent, black-habited, smelt as musty as stale air or books mildewed in the rainy season; between toothless gums she mumbled the body of Christ. And now it was her turn: before her the priest's green vestments, his hand upraised, the white circle of the Host – she closed her eyes in the old childish game of 'Shut your eyes and open your mouth and see what God will send you', and felt upon her tongue the bland body that promised eternal life.

'*Corpus Christi.*'

'Amen.'

His body in me. Edmund's body . . .

Appalled, she almost choked. How could her thoughts have taken such a direction at this most solemn moment! The Host was already mushy in her mouth. She sank to her knees – her neighbour in the pew noted with approval her air of devotion – and buried her face in her hands. Dear God, forgive me that I confuse the earthly with the heavenly, but when the heavenly comes to earth we call it love and for a fleeting instant the veil between heaven and earth is drawn aside. The spirit made flesh, the flesh made spirit. The Bridegroom united with his Bride.

The concluding words of the Mass passed over her unheeded. When others left she remained kneeling in her place. A sacristan snuffing the altar candles looked at her curiously; she did not even know he was there. The dark-shadowed church invested her like a habit; she knelt in the midst of its folds woven of holiness, dedication, mystery, and felt herself grow small, smaller, smallest, a pinpoint, a speck of light, one soul in a sea of souls, an ocean upon the face of whose waters there moved the spirit of God.

Time, when at last she raised her head, had no meaning, though perhaps ten minutes had gone by. She thrust open the padded door and emerged into the little square which in the past hour had shaken off the last of its torpor and was vibrant, bustling with life. The smell of fresh bread from a baker's reminded her she was fasting and breakfast waited back aboard the ship. At the port gulls screamed, masts bobbed, light danced on the water, the sky grew steadily more blue. A boy, whistling, broke off to gaze at her in frank admiration and she gave him a dazzling smile. She picked her way over ropes, around bollards, to where the *Karachi* lay, smoke drifting from her funnels as she rose serene above the antlike activity below.

Aboard her was Edmund. And Nina. The one joy, the other care. And aboard her too was the unknown man who had assaulted Nina and whom Stafford Briscoe had pledged himself to find. She could see Briscoe now, leaning on the rail and looking down at her, the light breeze lifting his thin hair. It was the first time any element had dared disturb that immaculate appearance. She waved, and his hand lifted in salute. Always there was that air of royal acknowledgement: His Majesty's representative, before whom even men as tall as Mr Haldingham seemed diminished, and men like Mr Stiles, Archie Johnson, or that dreadful little man Bert Gurslake, were suddenly of no account.

As she watched another figure joined Stafford Briscoe. Edmund. She said the name aloud, causing a porter to turn in surprise, but since there was no accounting for the ways of foreigners he shrugged and turned back again. She could not see Edmund's features beneath the uniform cap, but she knew his gaze was on her, and that there was a highway between them as sturdy as the gangway up which she walked. She had only to go on walking, to go right up to him and be enfolded in his arms, for all troubles, even Nina's, to be erased in that embrace. But of course she did no such thing. Reverend Mother – Mummy too, for that matter – said that in all circumstances a lady waited to be asked. So presumably Mummy had waited for Denis Orrey to ask her, only he had asked her – what? Whatever it was, it had involved betrayal, but with Edmund there could be no such thing, except . . .

Connie put the thought from her. First he had to propose. Surely God would not be so cruel as to make supreme happiness the supreme temptation? My cup runneth over; when I go to drink from it, will it be dashed from my lips? Lord, let this cup pass from me – the cup of temptation, that is – for if it does not, I know I have not the strength of my own volition to say no and turn it aside.

I love Edmund. More than anything in this world I want to give myself to him. I want to be his wife.

If I am not that, I am nothing.

Dear God, forgive me if I do wrong, but if he asks me I shall accept him. Because in this world you give me only one life.

*   *   *

226

Captain Meiklejohn looked up from the surgeon's log before him. There it was in black and white: '*November 18. Gopal, stoker, suffering from burn to hand. Discharged.*' And underneath: '*Patient insolent. Reported for breach of discipline.*' No such report had been made.

Angus sighed. False entry; condoning insubordination; failure to report the man – the list of Edmund Bladon's misdeeds would have been formidable even without the suspicion of rape. Had it not been Jamie who had complained, he would have been tempted to ignore the accusation and leave the surgeon's log unread, but not only had he promised: he had a duty. No captain could ignore that.

Ailsa. The thought of his wife was unwelcome, for there too he had a duty, though in ignoring it he had acted not as captain but as man. And Cynthia as woman. Her response had been unexpected, but the more exciting for that. He recalled their roiling and tossing – who would believe it now? Even young Strode, in whose eye he fancied he detected a knowingness ever since that morning on the bridge, might have been surprised by the violence of their passion. What had the young Third Officer overheard? Most likely he had heard nothing and it was imagination on Angus's guilty part. He had never been accused of being imaginative, but all men were born sinful, he no less than the rest. Without Jamie's watchwords, Watch and Pray, there was no control over a man's baser nature. For the last few nights he had neither watched nor prayed.

Ailsa still prayed. How often had he looked down at that white-nightgowned figure kneeling beside the bed, her hair which by day she wore braided round her head swinging forward in a schoolgirl's pigtail, her hands folded, the picture of mature innocence. He had been faithful to her. Till death do us part – death, not distance. But distance had nothing to do with it. So why had he succumbed to Cynthia? No, that was an unfair interpretation, implying artfulness on Cynthia's part. Instead, he had deliberately sought out Bobby Vane's mother that she might present him with just such another son.

From his first cry in the Glasgow tenement that cold January morning Andy had been an extension of his father's life, a loving parallel which would continue on into the future long after his own course had stopped. Without that gage of immortality his existence was pointless. Who would choose to leave nothing behind? Jamie had three sons and a daughter, he could afford fidelity. Afford too to pass judgement on others, knowing he himself had not transgressed. He would be shocked into incomprehension at discovering his friend and captain had abandoned the straight and narrow path laid down in the Old Testament's Ten Commandments. No, Jamie must never know.

Which meant he must be given no cause in any other quarter to suspect a slackening of discipline aboard. His charge against Edmund Bladon would have to be investigated. Angus reached out and pressed a bell.

'Ask the surgeon to come and see me in my cabin,' he instructed the

227

answering steward. Better get it over with at once. It would mean dismissal, and Bladon could not afford another black mark against him, but that was his lookout.

All the same, it was a pity, Angus thought when the young doctor stood before him. The few days in the Mediterranean had given him a light tan. His eyes were bright; he was less gaunt; there was a confidence about him. He was undeniably an attractive man.

'I've been inspecting your log,' Angus said without preamble. 'There's an entry here I do not understand. On November 18th, last Tuesday, you've recorded that you discharged a stoker, that he was insolent, and you reported him. The Chief Engineer tells me he has no record of any such incident. Who did you report the matter to?'

'I'm afraid, sir, I didn't report it.'

'Are you telling me you forgot?'

Such carelessness was inexcusable, but there might be some way it could be overlooked.

'No, sir, I decided not to report it.'

'*You* decided?' Damned out of his own mouth. 'Since when has discipline aboard this ship been at your discretion, Mr Bladon?'

'Sir, it was not a matter of discipline but of justice.'

'And what qualifies you to be a judge of that?'

'Humanity, sir. We all think we can recognise justice.'

'And what if we are wrong?'

Edmund was silent.

'It is to avoid leaving such decisions to individual fallibilities,' Angus said evenly, 'that the rules of discipline are framed. It is for a man's superior officer to decide if an infringement has occurred and what is the appropriate punishment. *Your* duty is clearly laid down. You are to report any such matters to the senior officer concerned. That means, since this man is a stoker, you should have reported him to the Chief Engineer.'

'That is why I did not report him.'

'Kindly explain what you mean.'

'I had reason to think there was prejudice against the stoker and injustice had already been done.'

Angus waited.

'The man alleged his injury occurred because an officer pushed him against a fire door.'

'Did you inform Mr Sutherland of that?'

'I did, sir. He appeared to dismiss the allegation.'

'He may have had good cause. Are you aware he had already had occasion to discipline this stoker?'

'Yes, sir.'

'Who may have borne a grudge.'

'Sir, it was six of one and half a dozen of the other. Mr Sutherland would

228

not give him the benefit of the doubt. He implied the injury could have been self-inflicted.'

'How do you know he wasn't right?'

'Because the man had a brown skin and was being damned because of it. I've seen injustice, and I know that once a man is tagged as a member of a group rather than as an individual justice flies out of the window. Justice is always for an individual in the end.'

Edmund stopped, aware he had gone too far. Discipline aboard the *Karachi* was impressive. He had come to respect Angus Meiklejohn, but that was more than he could say for James Sutherland, who embodied everything he most disliked. Sutherland stood for all those warders who had allowed the bullying of conchies to take place and even joined in on occasion because these prisoners of conscience were fair game. It satisfied their sadistic instincts to make the conchies stand at the end of the line when the daily ration of skilly was doled out. It was amusing to trip a man up so that the precious bowlful went flying and there was nothing, not even the bread, which someone's heel would have 'accidentally' trodden into the ground. Best of all was to withhold the longed-for letters which were the prisoners' only contact with home. Anne wrote once a month and Edmund knew it; other men's families did the same; and every month some prisoner would be singled out for special treatment when his mail allegedly failed to arrive. Every man nursed the secret fear of all prisoners that his woman would desert him; the conchies were no different from the rest; and there was always a warder on hand to be gloatingly sympathetic. 'Given you up, has she? Can't say I blame her. Any woman worth her salt wants a *man.*' Edmund had seen men reduced to tears by such insinuations. Then, two or three days later, the letter would be handed over with a smile. 'Afraid this got left in the bottom of the bag. So sorry.' And as the hand stretched for it, it would be jerked away, the frail wartime paper tearing. 'Oh dear, isn't that a pity – you've got two letters now. Can't have that, it's against regulations. Have the other one another day.'

Those men who never received letters because their families had cast them off could be made to suffer even greater torment as the warder delivering post stopped outside the cell door. 'Letter for you at last, Number so-and-so. Family must be getting soft. Now where is it? I know I saw it. Too bad, must have left it behind.' The hope that dawned in the eyes of even the most hopeless was noted with satisfaction as the warder moved on. With care, the fiction could be maintained for several rounds, each time a fresh excuse forthcoming, until one of the more humane among the warders told the truth.

But James Sutherland was not a prison warder. Moreover, he was Captain Meiklejohn's best friend, and the Captain was now regarding Edmund thoughtfully.

'Are you saying Mr Sutherland is unjust?'

229

'I think, sir, that his prejudice blinds him in this case.'

It was possible, Angus knew. The Chief's stern code and sterner justice were a byword among the crew. 'Only way to keep black devils in their places,' he would say heartily, 'and most of my devils are black' – referring to the oil and grease and coal dust which effectively masked every engine-room crewman's face. His engineering officers were devoted to him because he was a first-class engineer, but the Lascars who stoked the boilers and greased the engines regarded him differently. Moreover, when it came to running his own domain the Chief was as prickly as a sea-urchin. Angus knew well that it was difficult even for him to intervene. Besides, quite apart from his technical qualifications, there was no more conscientious, loyal and hard-working officer aboard the *Karachi*. And, most importantly, they were friends. Without the support and understanding on which he drew most nights in that precious half-hour in his cabin, every voyage would be that much more of a strain. He owed more to Jamie than to any man aboard. Both discipline and friendship demanded that he support him, even though he might be in the wrong.

'What reason have you for thinking Mr Sutherland's prejudiced?' he asked Edmund. 'Apart from your own prejudice, that is.'

'I've told you, sir: his attitude to Gopal on several occasions as conveyed to me over the telephone.'

There was a silence. Then Angus said, 'You're already under a cloud, Mr Bladon, in that you're suspected of rape. I'm not saying you're guilty, but you're unable – or more likely unwilling for some reason – to prove your innocence. Now I find you're in breach of discipline and accusing a senior officer of prejudice and injustice. Would it not be better all round if you resigned at the end of this voyage?'

Edmund heard the suggestion unflinching. He had not flinched before the tribunal's sentence when his conscientious objection was dismissed. Other, lesser men had been directed to non-combatant duties, but something harsher was reserved for him because he was not just betraying his country by refusing to fight for it; he was betraying his class. He was 'poor old Jeffrey's boy', and a ripple of antipathy ran through the tribunal as they sentenced him to six months. Beside him he heard Anne gasp. She had insisted on attending the hearing, and his heart was torn with gratitude and pain. Impulsively she clasped his hand. 'Oh, Edmund, it's too cruel. It's only because of who your father is.'

Now, with only the slightest inclination of his head, he heard another sentence. 'I shall do as you suggest, sir. I'll write the letter tonight.'

And with it would go all thought of asking Connie to marry him. A member of the unemployed did not propose to a well-brought-up young lady. His prospects had been unenticing before, but at least he had a job, he could support her modestly if she was prepared for the long separations of the voyage. He had watched her come aboard the ship that morning from whatever brief excursion she had made in Marseilles and had thought

230

there was an even greater radiance than usual about her as she waved to him leaning on the rail. Beside him, Stafford Briscoe had assessed her. 'Damned pretty girl,' he said. 'Spirited, too. Your mother would have liked her. She'd go down well in Gloucestershire.'

Edmund threw up his hands. 'Do I make myself so obvious?'

'What harm is there in that? Your feelings are permitted and I envy you. I'd give half my life for the freedom you possess.'

Edmund said, 'I own I find Miss Martin attractive, but you know the position I'm in. I can't ask a girl like that to marry me – her family would never consent.'

Stafford Briscoe watched the light dancing on the water. 'I understand she's of age.'

And Ravi wasn't. He must be careful. This was not some Arab prostitute. He wasn't even Maurice, whose family had been remarkably understanding once they'd grasped that for Maurice he represented cash. No, the boy must come to him not only because he wanted to taste power in his coming, but because he must not be seen to seek him out.

'Are you suggesting an elopement?' Edmund asked, smiling.

'Hardly. But relatives aren't an insuperable obstacle.'

'I'm afraid poor Nina is.'

'Oh, the mysterious rapist's victim. You know, Edmund, I wonder in all seriousness if he really exists. You realise that at present you're chief suspect?'

'I realise I was seen in the area, but I saw and heard nothing.'

'What were you up to?'

A work of mercy. Feeding the hungry was that. If John Joseph had not taken Ravi food and above all water, the youth would have died in that lifeboat. Edmund had merely aided and abetted what the Captain would call a breach of discipline, but for that the steward could be dismissed, and now he found himself in the same position out of loyalty to an Irishman and an Indian.

'You're a fool,' Briscoe said, parallelling Edmund's own thoughts. 'You never learn, do you? The world still has to revolve around you because you think you're too important to accommodate, as the rest of us have to do. If you don't want to tell the truth, then lie, but for heaven's sake say something to dispel the rumours that are going round.'

'I can't tell a lie.'

'Bravo, George Washington!'

'I'm sorry, Stafford, I know you're trying to help –'

'But you'd rather be damned by your own efforts than saved by any of mine.'

'No, I –'

Briscoe turned and left him. When he looked over the rail again, Connie too had gone.

And now she would go out of his life for ever as soon as the *Karachi* docked. There'd be other men . . . At the thought of her in someone else's arms Edmund felt like running amok in the Captain's cabin, but the Captain's voice broke in.

'Thank you, Mr Bladon, you may go.' And then: 'Allow me to say I'm sorry. I did not think when you joined us that our acquaintance was to be so brief.'

The unexpectedness of it was almost too much for Edmund, who could only manage, 'Thank you, sir.'

Angus Meiklejohn watched him go and cursed silently the code of conduct that forbade the surgeon to save himself. Never had he been more aware of the undercurrents among crew and passengers that slapped to and fro like water in the bilge. For so many of them the voyage was a turning-point: the Haldinghams, leaving at their age their beloved India to return to a land where they would no longer feel at home; the Gurslakes, also returning home, but apprehensive of what awaited them – Mrs Gurslake reportedly feared the voyage itself, but what did her husband dread? Since Marseilles he had seemed increasingly uneasy, one might almost say running scared. And for Nina Martin the voyage had certainly been a turning-point, a reversal of fortune, no less – as it had been for Prince Ravi, from stowaway to princely personage with a question-mark over his future when they docked.

And Cynthia – was the voyage a turning-point for Cynthia? Angus lingered lovingly on the name. Cynthia – the moon, and as swiftly changing, from poised, controlled young widow to elemental woman in his arms. He was not expecting it – but had he known what he was expecting? Not Ailsa's gentle response, but certainly not that abandon of restraint which in turn had broken through his own barriers. This was not love – it was more like hatred, the marks of her nails were in his back – and yet what else was love but two bodies violently conjoined, the quest of hands, lips, seeking to fulfil the imperative that there should be one body, total fusion, in a sharp cry of agony. For it was agony, that death of the spirit subsumed into ecstasy. A little death, a great lassitude, which he feared as much as she to disturb.

When at last she slipped away from him, his body had remained curled, seeking to maintain the impress of her body as proof that she was more substantial than a dream. He had not dared to hope she would return, but the next night and the next she had been with him. She was as much in love as he.

Disjointedly she had talked. Her love for Robert. Their fairytale wedding. The happiness of both families. The war. Their letters. The changes in him when he came home on leave which she was quick to notice and he as anxious to conceal. The secret knowledge of the child she carried. His certainty that it would be a son. And then the telegram that July morning: 'Regret to inform you Captain Robert Vane killed in action.' After which she said no more and he could only hold her, thinking of another telegram among the thousands spawned by the Somme.

On another night she added further details. The whole village had shared her grief. She had been overwhelmed with kindness, but it was unreal, distant. Only the child mattered now. He had been born one bright August morning in the double bed where he had been conceived. For the first time she shared it with a living creature other than her husband, a male, another Robert, for it was unthinkable he should not take his father's name. And then, when she had believed herself beyond fate's reach, successive blows had fallen. Her two brothers-in-law killed within a year. Her father-in-law old and broken. The decision to sell the estate. 'I can never go back there,' she had whispered, 'I feel like a traitor. It isn't even farmland now. They've built houses all along the road that used to be a farm lane, they've felled timber and left good land lying fallow, rented for grazing while they decide what next to build.'

It was a foreign world to Angus, though he was aware of her distress. Small tragedies: good land lying fallow . . . *we know so little about the mind* . . . But she had one thing out of it: she had Bobby. 'He needs a father,' she said when he reminded her. 'A father like you.' – 'And my son needs a mother to give him being.' The words were out before he could stop them and he cursed his clumsiness. He had thought she would turn away, perhaps leave. Instead she lay looking up at him, her eyes dark peat-bog pools. 'Why not?' Her voice was so husky it rasped, and again they fought each other's separate bodies in their driving need to be one.

'*Those whom God hath joined together let no man put asunder.*' He had heard the minister pronounce the words with Ailsa beside him, both of them a little troubled by the deep solemnity of it all. It had seemed then so easy to be faithful. They would grow old together, one of them would die, but there could be no other woman than Ailsa Cameron; he had convinced himself of that. And he still loved her and the son she had borne him. They would not suffer – he would see to that. But Cynthia and her sons, present and future, were all-important. For eight years he had lived with what he believed to be a broken heart, only to give the lie to the old song, for he knew a second spring more glorious than the first because there was a hint of autumn in it, just as in their love there had been a hint of death.

And only Cynthia would understand. Andy was beyond understanding. Ailsa would look at him, her blue eyes big with hurt, tears drowning the last of their harebell colour which had faded with the years. And Jamie? Jamie would denounce him. He could almost hear the Chief's ringing tones. 'Ye'd not neglect your duty as a captain, Angus, and your duty as a husband is as plain. "*Thou shalt not commit adultery*" – the Lord has laid it down as one of His Ten Commandments, and He casts into outer darkness those who will not walk in His ways. Beware, among the weeping and wailing, that ye do not repent too late. Ask His help now, man, while the temptation is yet to be resisted, and I'll pray with ye and for ye that ye may be given strength.'

Jamie's God moved as inexorably as his engines, or perhaps his engines were subject to divine laws of cause and effect which had in them justice but no mercy, for Jamie and his God were made in each other's mould, and Angus wondered sometimes which had come first. He had wondered in the case of Gopal, the stoker, when he informed the Chief of the entry in Edmund Bladon's log.

'Ah!' There was satisfaction in the Chief's tone. 'If it's official, I'll proceed against the black devil.'

'Go gently,' Angus said.

'I'll pretend I didna hear ye, Angus, undermining discipline on your own ship.'

'There's more than one way of maintaining discipline.'

'Aye, there's yours and mine. But this stoker falls within my jurisdiction and I'll see justice done.'

Angus kept silent.

'I can do no other – even if I so wished. The least softness with that rabble and ye'd have insurrection.'

'You're only delaying it.'

'I beg your pardon?'

'Oh, I'm not talking of your engine-room, Jamie, but how long can we go on holding down a quarter of the globe by consent of the governed? For that's what it amounts to. And the more cause we give them for dissatisfaction, the sooner that consent will be withdrawn. Young men like Archie Johnson hasten the day of reckoning. If I may say so, so do you.'

The Chief shook his head. 'Ye've been listening to yon conchie doctor, Angus. It's terrible the rot he spreads. I'm thankful to hear ye've requested his resignation. Let him take his pernicious ideas elsewhere. I'll be glad when this voyage is over. There's too much aboard that I don't like, what with stowaways and that would-be nun alleging there's a rapist, and a doctor who's too scared to fight. I tell you, Angus, for all your running down of young Johnson, I'd rather be with him in a tight corner any day. And then there's your Mr Briscoe. I canna take to him.'

'I didn't know you'd met.'

'Aye, he's one of those pretends to take an interest in the engines. Wanted to see the engine-room, him and some others, but he doesna know a screw from a crankshaft. And he had that Indian laddie in tow. Do ye no think, Angus, that there's something a wee bit unhealthy in the way the boy follows him around?'

'I asked Briscoe to keep an eye on him in case he made a break for it while we were in port.'

'Did ye now? Then he should be able to relax his vigilance. We don't dock again till Tilbury. Another six nights and we'll have dry land beneath us, and you and I'll be travelling north.'

Another six nights. Six more nights of Cynthia. Six more nights in which to conceive a son. And then what? If he travelled north with Jamie, as they had done at the end of every voyage in the past, it would be to tell

Ailsa that he was leaving her and starting out again. But it was not Ailsa's reaction which troubled him: it was Jamie's. Would Jamie sail with him again, or would he hasten to accept one of those transfers to a newer, faster ship which Head Office was always urging upon him and which he had as consistently refused? He could not imagine the *Karachi* without Jamie, yet he knew it might come to that. Cynthia and her sons would then be everything. But would Cynthia marry him?

Cynthia was wondering the same thing during days which had steadily reduced themselves to intervals between the nights. Like some nocturnal animal emerging diurnally from its burrow, she felt naked in the sharp Mediterranean light. The warmer clothing which had become desirable on deck seemed suddenly transparent, leaving her inmost being exposed. Surely everyone must know she was the Captain's mistress? Yet when she made her nightly way to his cabin she met no one, or if she did it was the ship's cat, or else a member of the crew accustomed to the vagaries of passengers who came on deck at the oddest times in search of a breath of air – and sometimes other passengers' cabins. With the freshening breeze the ship's motion was more apparent; the decks were emptier now; but Cynthia was not only a good sailor, she scented with every inspiration the approach of the green fields of home.

Home. Home with Angus. Home was Angus. Not since Robert died had she felt so deeply at peace and at the same time so stimulated that every nerve-ending was laid bare and a thousand sights, sounds, scents never before noticed came crowding in on her: the smoothness of the deck rail, as hard and firm as Angus's body; the bells which rang throughout the ship, each seeming to signal a step in their relationship; the sight of Bobby, child of her womb and Robert, and pledge of other possibilities. But when she bore Bobby she was surrounded by loving relatives and servants, whereas a new pregnancy would have to be faced alone. For even if Angus obtained a divorce and she married him, he would be away at sea. He would never be happy without a deck beneath him. There could be no returning to her world of landed gentry, which had shaped her as surely as geology had shaped the land.

Would they be happy? Would Bobby be happy?

'You like the Captain, don't you?' she said.

'Rather!' The answer was emphatic.

'I'm glad. I think he likes you too.'

'Does he really?'

'Yes, of course he does.'

'I bet he wouldn't if he –'

Bobby broke off. Not even to his mother could he make the admission that he had told the Captain something that was not true. The Captain would not approve; and since his approval mattered, he must never learn the truth. Only six more nights before the voyage was over. Surely he could keep silent that long?

235

'If he what, darling?' his mother asked tenderly. She was always tender towards him these days.

'If he knew I didn't like spinach,' Bobby improvised.

Cynthia's laugh came silvery and true. 'He wouldn't hold that against you. Besides, you'll get to like it. When you go away to school.'

School, always school. Bobby looked mutinous.

'What Angus – Captain Meiklejohn – wouldn't understand,' his mother went on swiftly, 'is cheating, stealing, anything dishonest.'

'You mean like telling lies?'

'Yes.'

That settled it. No confession was possible. 'Would he want me to go away to school?'

'Yes, because it's the best thing for you. That's why I want it too.'

Cynthia spoke sincerely, realising it was true. She no longer clung to Bobby. If only she could let that detestable ship's doctor know!

'I love you.'

The childish voice broke in upon her. She looked down.

'You know I love you too.'

'Do you love Captain Meiklejohn?'

'I like him,' she said carefully.

'So do I. I wish he was my daddy.'

'Perhaps – perhaps he might be some day.'

'I'd like that. Wouldn't you?'

Yes, Cynthia thought, the three of us and then another added – I'd like that more than anything in the world.

Aloud she said, 'We don't always get what we want, but we'll have to see about this, won't we?'

Bobby nodded, and said with all the faith and experience of childhood, 'You can make things happen if you want them to.'

V

Bert Gurslake was on the track of the money he needed. At the thought his pinched nostrils flared slightly, as though he were literally on the scent. The necessary cash, and more where that came from – his troubles might soon be at an end. Of course there were problems; the whole thing might blow up in his face. But not if he was careful – and by God he would be careful! You didn't get a chance like this twice.

And it was all due to that Mick steward, though the lad didn't realise what he'd done. Stood to reason: no Mick was ever deliberately helpful, not to an Englishman. They said they wanted independence; they could have it where Bert was concerned. No point in keeping that lot in the British family of nations; they were outside the pale. Bert did not realise the appropriateness of the expression and would not have cared if he had, but he knew Ireland spelled trouble for England and would continue to do so even if you spelled it Eire. Not that spelling had ever been Bert's strong point and he found writing a nuisance, but he could read all right; and it was because he could read, because of a letter, that for the first time since he and Florrie left Sydney he could lie down and sleep at nights.

Those last few days in Sydney had been a nightmare, far worse than Florrie knew. When he returned from his visit to the gold mine's vanished office, he had lost everything he possessed except the cash in his pockets and the contents of his house. But he had managed to keep the extent of the disaster from Florrie, so much so that she had protested at going home. She had grown to like it in Sydney. Besides, there was the voyage to be endured. 'I can't face that rolling and lurching,' she objected. 'Just thinking of it makes me heave.' 'Come on, old girl,' he had encouraged. 'Thought you fancied a mansion in Park Lane. Might as well see about getting one. There ain't nothing more for us here.'

That wasn't strictly true, but the things awaiting him he hadn't cared to contemplate. A prison sentence was the least of his fears; most men, after all, survived prison, but he wouldn't survive what he was threatened with. That loan had been a mistake and he ought to have known it, but the thought of gold had blotted out all else; not just dust, the prospectus had assured him, but nuggets the size of hen's eggs. A few of these were on display, closely guarded, at the mine's office: dull, ugly, glinting, but gold. The men at the desk had been very ready to take Bert's money – he was the last in a line of six – but when they were alone they had deplored politely that for his sake it wasn't more. Such a pity, when this was the chance of a lifetime. Did he know that loans were available on very favourable terms? Oh, not from them, but there was a loan office next door with whom they had an arrangement. The loans were in cash; he couldn't really lose. Bert hesitated. He had made his fortune buying and selling, but he had never borrowed in his life. On the other hand, he had never before invested in anything as precious as gold and in all probability he would never have the chance to again. It could do no harm to see what was on offer, and the loan office was only next door. He didn't have to accept, but it was folly not to listen – and at the end of it he could always say no.

Half an hour later he had said yes, had signed some papers, and returned to invest his cash. The men behind the desk congratulated him on his shrewdness and again assured him he couldn't lose. And that was the last time he had seen them before they vanished into thin air – but they had his address and soon demands began to arrive for the loan's repayment, to be swiftly followed by threats. Bert hadn't taken them too seriously; you couldn't get blood out of a stone, and he had an idea the loan company wasn't above suspicion; they'd be reluctant to go to court. Then, one dull, chill evening, two men caught up with him and walked one on either side; big men, well dressed but rough-spoken, and terrifyingly polite.

'Evening, Mr Gurslake,' said the one on his right.

'Good evening,' Bert responded.

'Glad we've met up with you,' the man went on. 'You was out when we called, but your missus said you'd be home shortly. Me and Red's been on the watch.'

There was no need to wonder how Red had got his nickname. A flame of hair rose above the face of a pug, broken-nosed, gap-toothed. His fists too were raw and red, like steaks. He kept them flexed in readiness, and the mincing steps he took to accommodate Bert's short ones were those he must have used in the ring.

'We're from the Consolidated Finance Company,' the big man said, crowding Bert a little. 'Our principals asked us to call to collect the first instalment of your repayment. It seems to have got overlooked.'

'I ain't got it,' Bert blurted. 'You'll have to give me time to pay.'

'You've had all the time we're going to give you,' the big man said patiently. 'If I was you, I'd pay up now.'

'I can't.'

'Hear that, Red? This gentleman can't pay what he owes.'

Red smote one steak upon the other and spat expectantly.

'Seeing as that's the case, we turn off here, Mr Gurslake.' The big man laid a hand on Bert's shoulder and almost swung him off his feet. They entered an alleyway which Bert had seen a hundred times without noticing it. People were passing the end of it, going about their legitimate business, but suddenly he was alone. Except for the two men who had manoeuvred him against a wall and now stood watchful, like two cats waiting for a mouse to run.

238

'The Consolidated Finance Company don't like bad debts, Mr Gurslake,' said the big man. 'I'm sure you appreciate that. The terms was set out in the document you signed when they assisted you with your investments –'

'It was all a bloody con!'

'The Consolidated Finance Company does not enquire into the purposes for which a loan is required.'

'Because they bleedin' well knew it was for that fucking gold mine. They was hand in glove with them.'

'The Consolidated Finance Company has sent you several reminders about repayment,' the big man went on as if he had not heard. 'Our principals regret they ain't prepared to wait no longer than a week for your first instalment, including interest of course. You'll find the sum written here –' he held out a paper – 'and to help you remember they asked me to give you this.'

The blow was vicious, and Bert doubled up retching and gasping, until a kick to the knee brought him down and he lay there, unable to move, with the men's feet inches from his eyes. The feet seemed enormous. There were metal toecaps to their boots.

'Sorry about that, Mr Gurslake,' the big man said (Red had never spoken). 'It's the first and let's hope it'll be the last, 'cos we get nastier as we go on.' (Red sniggered.) 'But if you're sensible you won't see us no more. Only don't think we're not there just because you can't see us. We'll be keeping an eye on you.'

Red's feet executed a stepdance. Bert braced himself for the blow, but instead the feet receded. Did he fancy reluctance on Red's part?

Then they stopped. 'Don't think you can hide from us neither,' the big man cautioned. 'Whatever you'd do, we'd know. Why, if you was to go back to England there'd be a reception committee to greet you, and they wouldn't be none too pleased. Be sensible and pay up, Mr Gurslake. It hurts less that way in the end.'

The boot thudded into his ribs like a sledgehammer. He could not think for pain. But before he blacked out he had the distinct impression that it had not belonged to Red.

Later, when he limped home to Florrie with some story about a fall (she was concerned about his clothes, but he managed to conceal the damage to his person), he lay awake sweating with fear. He believed their threats now (with every breath he drew, his bruised ribs convinced him they meant business), but he did not believe they could pursue him across the world. In England he would be safe, penniless but safe. Next morning he broke it to Florrie that they were selling up and going home.

The fact that there was no immediate passage available, which had first angered, then frightened him, began to seem providential by the time they left Sydney behind. If the Consolidated Finance Company chose to check on sailings and passenger lists, they would find he was aboard the *Southern*

Cross outward bound for Bombay and calling at Madras and Colombo, at any of which ports he might have disembarked. In Bombay he had hardly left the hotel, but once aboard the *Karachi* he had begun very slightly to relax. He had been in tight corners before and got out of them. Somehow he would get out of this, and step ashore with a thousand pounds in his pocket, ready to start afresh. They couldn't know where he was; he'd given them the slip good and proper, and there'd be no reception committee waiting for him at the other end. So when shortly after leaving Marseilles a wireless message was brought to his cabin, he had opened it with interest rather than dread.

'*The Consolidated Finance Company looks forward to welcoming you to England.*'

Innocuous words of welcome to a businessman, but to him a threat that turned his bowels to water. They had caught up with him. Sooner or later, one dark night he would hear those overtaking footsteps and two men, the same only different, would fall into step beside him and the nightmare would begin all over again. He *had* to have money, but several more attempts at touching fellow passengers for a loan had come to nothing, and he was becoming desperate.

Ivo Haldingham had simply said, 'My dear fellow, I have no money, and if I had I shouldn't lend it to *you*,' and said it rather loudly, making neighbouring heads turn. Other passengers had been as brusque, though some had produced rambling excuses which Bert had tired of long before they ran their course. He was convinced his best hope lay among the ladies, but he was mindful of Archie Johnson's threat. Would he really have thrown him over the side? Probably not, but the Mick steward had done nothing to prevent it. All the more amazing that he should have signalled the way to relief.

Bert had been paying a surreptitious visit to Cynthia Vane's cabin, well knowing that because Bobby was in and out of it, it was often left unlocked. Daft when you came to think of it, considering the jewellery she had. Though of course the best was always with her: those sparklers on her hand – must've been her engagement ring – they were worth a bit. Her pearls too were constantly round her neck, a double string that hung almost to her waist, but she occasionally wore other pieces, and everything she had was good. Nevertheless, Bert found it hard to accept that he was reduced to stealing; he had always had his code, and though he had never defined it, he knew it didn't include theft. He thought of himself as a law-abiding citizen, maybe a bit smarter than some, but not a person who could be arraigned on charges of dishonesty. Fraud, now – that was something else: an accidental mistiming, leading to a temporary shortage of funds; three months either way and the deficit would have been covered; it was the kind of accident that could happen to anyone in business and in Bert's eyes no stigma was attached. But to take property belonging to another – that was stealing. Six weeks ago he would never have thought of it.

Small wonder, then, that he was nervous when, about eleven o'clock in the morning, as the coast of Spain slid by to starboard, he made his way

240

below. It was the quietest time of day. Passengers congregated in the lounges, or took the air on deck. He had checked that Mrs Vane and Bobby were both enjoying a game of shuffleboard. The stewardesses would have finished the daily cleaning of cabins. The stewards on duty were serving coffee, chocolate or beef tea. There was another hour before the watch changed, and an hour and a half till luncheon. This was as good a chance as he would have.

Even so, his heart was beating wildly as he stood outside the row of polished mahogany doors, identical save for their brass numbers, and tried the handle of Cynthia Vane's. It moved: the door opened. Sweating with relief, Bert closed it and leaned against the corridor wall to get his breath back. No point in going in like this. His legs were so weak he would have subsided on the bed instead of going quickly to work trying drawers, feeling in the pockets of clothes hanging in the wardrobe, thrusting under piles of underwear. Most of all he dreaded a locked jewellery box, too bulky to be easily hidden on his person, too difficult to open on the spot. Oh, let the baubles be lying loose – on a tray, in a drawer, beneath her pillow, so that he could act swiftly and be away.

He pulled on the gloves he had brought with him – no sense in taking risks – and was about to wipe the door handle when a triangle of white caught his eye. Someone had half pushed a letter beneath the door of a cabin further down the corridor. Who to? Bert's curiosity overcame him. He winkled out the envelope.

Afterwards he was to thank his lucky stars he had done so, for it was as he was kneeling on the carpeted floor that he realised someone was behind him, and looked up to see John Joseph Fitzgerald, dapper as usual, smiling down at him.

'Can I help you, sir?'

'No, thanks,' Bert improvised, showing the addressee's name. 'I was just posting a letter to His Highness Prince Ravi.' How patly the words came out. Would the steward notice his gloves, and wonder? He added, 'I was about to go up on deck.'

John Joseph nodded and passed on. He was in a hurry and was using the First Class corridor as a short cut. There was nothing odd in passengers delivering notes to one another – they did it all the time: invitations to drinks, challenges to deck games, suggestions for concert turns. Not that there'd be a better turn than they'd had last night, when Dr Bladon had sung. The trained voice had stood out and the applause had been heartfelt, for all that the lady accompanist had confided that she was uneasy at the thought of playing for a man who might be guilty of rape. And that was a cod, if you like. You'd only got to look at Dr Bladon to know the idea was ridiculous, as ridiculous as – John Joseph sought for the unlikeliest thing he could think of – and came up with a permanent peace in Ireland in the wake of the Irish Free State.

To begin with, it wasn't free in the eyes of the Republicans; it still owed allegiance to the Crown – the same crown that had once graced the brow of William of Orange, the victor of Aughrim and the Boyne. And not even all of Ireland was free: there were still the Six Counties in the North, insisting in their hard Ulster accents, more Scottish than Irish, that they could not, would not, belong to a country ruled from Catholic Dublin. Was it for this travesty of a united free Ireland that men like Pearse and Connolly had died?

Not that anyone had thought they'd die. They'd surrendered honourably like soldiers after the General Post Office had become a pyre and the leaders had evacuated it, carrying the wounded Connolly on a litter and taking anguished counsel throughout Friday night. But by the Saturday following Easter Monday it was apparent that the Rising was over; everywhere the British, aided now by reinforcements, had the upper hand. The Four Courts were still holding out, and so were other scattered Republican positions, but it could only mean further loss of life. At four p.m. on Saturday Pearse signed the document of unconditional surrender '*in order to prevent the further slaughter of Dublin citizens, and in the hope of saving the lives of our followers*'. This document was not read aloud from the steps of the gutted General Post Office; those steps were obliterated under smoking rubble and dust. Instead it was taken round from post to post by a young nurse, a member of Cumann na mBan, the Irish Women's Organisation, while Pearse and the other leaders of the Rising were on their way to gaol. And the Fitzgerald family, broken and weeping, began the long round of the morgues and hospital mortuaries where the Rising's unburied dead lay.

John Joseph was not with them; he spent the day queuing with his sisters at one of the free food depots that had been opened, since provisions of all kinds were running short. He was quiet, answering only when spoken to, still seeing in his mind's eye the swift-running figure stop and spin round, frozen in surprise that death should have found him, before collapsing to the ground. 'He got him! The bastard got him!' He heard again Terry's unsteady voice, and then he was running, running through the back lanes that led to Munster Street, back to the arms of Mam.

She was washing at the kitchen sink when he burst in, his face dirt- and tear-streaked. 'They shot him, Mam, Kieron's dead!' She turned in slow motion, made the sign of the Cross, and then she was gripping him, shaking him. 'What's that you're saying – lies, is it? What d'you mean, frightening me, saying that Kieron's dead?' – 'It's true, Mam. I saw it.' His da had come into the kitchen – he was home because it was impossible to get to work. 'Easy, now. It wasn't Kieron. You'd not have been near enough to tell.' – 'It was! It was! I saw him.' Ellen was with them now. 'I'll get some of the boys to make enquiries,' she said breathlessly, 'though the dear God knows what they can do. If the ambulances can't get through to reach them, they're burying them where they fell.'

They found Kieron in the Mater Misericordiae, having tried the Jervis

Street, St Vincent's and City hospitals in vain. In all of them it was the same story: the long rows of sheeted bodies lay close-packed, side by side. Although the faces were covered, the sheets sometimes reached only to the knee, and it was possible to distinguish a woman's shoes, the hem of a priest's cassock, among the endless variety of boots. At intervals someone in the file of distraught relatives would give a cry of recognition followed by an outburst of weeping, and arrangements would be made for the body to be brought home for a private funeral as soon as a coffin could be obtained.

Throughout the following week, while Dublin strove to return to normal and the first executions took place in the courtyard of Kilmainham Gaol, the undertakers were kept busy as the Fitzgeralds and hundreds like them gathered to bury their dead. Other families mourned men deported to England and imprisonment far from home; and on 4 May George V, King of Ireland, sent thanks to his gallant troops, the Royal Irish Constabulary and the Dublin Metropolitan Police, now that what he called 'the recent lamentable outbreak in Ireland' had finally been quelled.

To John Joseph, the most obvious change brought about by the Rising was that he no longer shared a bedroom, though Mam refused to have Kieron's bed removed. The rifle that had been hidden under the mattress was never seen again, nor was the slouch hat, but the stained sash and suit were preserved, and each Easter Monday thereafter they were lovingly laid out on the bed. And each Easter Monday John Joseph spent a restless night on the sofa in the front room for fear lest Kieron should come back to flesh them out. And each Easter Monday too Ellen spent long hours at her devotions, though the churches were empty that day and their congregations, their Easter duties over, were out making holiday. When she informed them that she was going to enter a convent, it was something John Joseph felt they should have seen coming, though he added his dissuading voice. But Ellen was obdurate, and since the other sisters had all married, the house in Munster Street soon contained just him and his parents – and Kieron's ghost. And then it was his turn to leave, for by now all Ireland was the battleground for a war waged by those Republicans who, having tasted independence, would not accept the Dominion status granted to the new Irish Free State, and those Irishmen who were prepared to do so, aided willy-nilly by marauding British Auxiliaries and Black and Tans.

One by one the great houses of the English Ascendancy, each one a treasury of Ireland's past, were reduced by the Irish themselves to smoking ruins: the castles of Antrim, Lohort, Dunboy and Mitchelstown; Bessborough House, Portumna and Mount Shannon; Renvyle and Summerhill. The English mercenaries, men who had found their trade in fighting and for whom there was no place in Civvy Street – men, John Joseph suspected, like Archie Johnson – neither gave nor were given quarter; the bitterness on both sides ran too deep. Small wonder that young men decided

243

to leave Ireland, and if America was too far, the next best place was England, where the easygoing indifference of the population made it hard to remember that these were the countrymen of those same Auxies and Black and Tans.

Occasionally there was prejudice, and there was always good-natured contempt for a Mick, but John Joseph had never encountered anything like the stone-faced, sustained hatred that the Haldinghams showed him, which puzzled as much as it hurt. For these people had nothing to do with Ireland. They had lived in India for more than fifty years. At the time of the Rising they had been retired in their bungalow in the hills, in a world where they were loved and respected and where they intended to end their days. He had ascertained that they had no sons who might have fallen to an Irish bullet as Kieron had to an Englishman's. Yet every attempt he had made to serve them, or even to be polite, had been chillingly repulsed, so that he now left them to one of the other stewards, though he did not cease to fret.

'They are prejudiced,' Ravi told him during one of the conversations they managed from time to time, for His Highness did not forget that he owed his life to the steward, even though that fact must not be betrayed. Many British people were prejudiced, he explained, especially the uneducated – 'people like Mr Gurslake,' he added with a smile. 'He does not like my brown skin but his wife adores my title. It puts him in a spot, wouldn't you say?'

'The Haldinghams are a cut above Mr Gurslake.'

Ravi had to concede that this was true. Ivo Haldingham was like another Resident, older and pleasanter, but with that same arrogance that melted suddenly into understanding and took you unawares. Men like him had given India and her people good service. If they had now decided that it was time for them to go, Ravi could only regret that they had not chosen to end their days in their adopted country where so many of their compatriots slept.

'There's no cut-off point for prejudice,' he told John Joseph, thinking of school where he had first discovered that fact. You knew, almost as if you smelt it, who disliked the colour of your skin. It existed equally among boys and masters, though the masters tried harder not to let it show. Sometimes they were even over-generous to compensate. Ravi suspected that he had not always deserved the high marks he was given in certain subjects. Or was his title to blame? It was one of the joys of his friendship with Barry Waterman that in it neither race nor place played a part.

In less than two weeks he would see Barry again – and Dorothy. Would Mrs Waterman invite him to spend Christmas with them, as he had done once or twice in the past? He had revelled in all the English traditions, from mince pies to stockings at the foot of the bed. They took these domestic-religious rites so seriously: everything must be the same as in other years; even a variance in the size of the turkey was noted, or in the number of Christmas cards sent and received. Fortunately it was possible to laugh at them and even to tease them: their English sense of humour allowed it, and besides, how could a foreigner and a heathen be expected to understand? Only with a few of them – Dorothy, for instance, or Briscoe sahib – was there no element of patronage.

Each day Ravi looked forward to seeing Briscoe sahib, to being singled out for a chat while walking on the deck, even to a game of deck tennis – anything that would enable him to enjoy the company of his god. He had no hesitation in according Briscoe sahib this status: it had nothing to do with race, though everything to do with the fact that he was treated as an equal in a situation where he had not expected it. His opinion was sought on a variety of subjects, from how he would rule the state of Maggapore to the English Test cricket team and how he viewed India's chances; the imprisonment of Mahatma Gandhi; the poetry of Rabindranath Tagore. On these and on every other subject Briscoe sahib seemed remarkably well informed. Ravi could hardly believe he had never set foot in India. His god merely smiled and said the world was growing small.

'Wireless telegraphy, the telephone, fast trains and steamers, the development of the motor car, perhaps even of the aeroplane in the future – they all make distance shrink. It will take us just over three weeks to get from Bombay to London, and the *Karachi* is by no means the fastest ship, whereas before the Suez Canal was opened it would have taken more than twice as long, and in the days of sail, well, a three months' voyage was not unusual, sometimes longer than that. Today we can cut short your father's anxiety about the fate of his only son –' Ravi intercepted a shrewd look. 'You must surely be glad of that.'

'I won't go back,' Ravi said in warning.

'You'll have to go back some day. Maggapore is yours to rule.'

'I shall be an unmarried ruler. I won't bed that repulsive girl.'

'I'm sure the Resident and your father will understand,' Briscoe said, choosing the order carefully. 'They'll find you a more pleasing bride.' He would write to the Resident, suggest someone slim and supple and boyish – like Ravi himself, in fact.

'I should like to marry an English lady.'

'Have you anyone in particular in mind?'

Ravi was silent. Not even to Briscoe sahib could he mention Dorothy Waterman.

'It might not be a good idea,' Briscoe sahib continued. 'Your people would resent her and she would be unhappy.'

The answer was an English mistress, perhaps. That should get it out of his system – if it was really a woman he wanted.

He laid a hand on Ravi's shoulder. 'You don't have to decide anything yet.'

'The Resident thinks I should marry and my father agrees with him.'

'Nevertheless, they'll consider your feelings.'

245

He would have to spell them out – having first made sure they were what he suspected. No, Briscoe corrected himself, what he hoped. Maurice too had been uncertain of his own nature until it had been revealed to him. Of course a relationship with Ravi would not last; there were too many forces pulling against it; and when it ended he would be the one to be hurt. But at least let it exist: one brief, glorious taste of youth before going into the shades of age and loneliness and the respect accorded the good colonial servant: Sir Stafford Briscoe, retired in Gloucestershire, late agent of His Majesty.

He could imagine all too well the boredom of that existence, though perhaps with Bladon for neighbour it might not be too bad. Old Sir Jeffrey couldn't last much longer, from what Jean told him, and there was only Edmund to inherit the estate. The title too. How many of the First Class passengers realised that the ship's surgeon would be a baronet some day? Would it make any difference to the attitude of the idiotic Cynthia Vane, for example, who complained that Edmund had told her (quite truthfully, in Stafford Briscoe's opinion) that she was spoiling her son?

Ravi too was a spoilt son, but the very thought of the boy offered anticipatory pleasure. He was coming on nicely, bursting with ideas which no one had ever asked him to express, and hanging on every word of his mentor, Briscoe sahib. Briscoe allowed himself a half-smile at the thought of the name. It was deliciously feudal, like so much else about the Indian Empire, and an anachronism as such. Men like Bladon were right in saying it could not continue, but the time for its demise was not yet. *Swaraj* – home rule, which had such depressing connotations in Ireland – would some day come to pass. And when it did, where would the future Nawab of Maggapore stand? Would he be a friend to the British or to the Indian Congress Party? To the British, if Stafford Briscoe had any influence – and he well knew that he had. In seeking to forge links with the boy he could comfort himself that he was also forging links of Empire, and of whatever lay beyond.

Because Ravi was intelligent. Much more so than Maurice, though with so much beauty Maurice had not needed brains. Still, it would be fun to travel once more with a young companion eager to see the fashionable places of Europe now that the lights had gone on again: Nice, and the burgeoning French Riviera; Paris, Le Touquet and Deauville; Capri and its Blue Grotto; the newly discovered wonders of the Nile. They would be fuel to fling upon the pyre of memories by which an old man warmed his bones – perhaps in the company of his friend Sir Edmund Bladon. And Lady Bladon also, if Edmund married that girl.

Of course she was a Roman Catholic and old prejudices died hard, but there were very few that held out against personal charm and Connie Martin had that in abundance. The sister was a liability, but no doubt a husband could be found in due course and she would settle down well enough. Meanwhile there was Ravi to think of; Ravi to plan for – and to lure. He need not hurry to take up residence with Jean in the country. Stafford Briscoe would shortly have a new title conferred by His Majesty, and a new life devised by himself.

A new life. That was what Bert Gurslake had been seeking when John Joseph had surprised him on his knees outside Ravi's cabin door, and it was only after the steward had turned the corner of the corridor that Bert realised he still held Ravi's letter in his hands. His Highness Prince Ravi. The name was written in black ink, in a bold hand based on copperplate and using a relief nib. The envelope was the usual ship's stationery which all the First Class passengers used, and just sufficiently opaque to conceal its contents, despite the flowing boldness of the hand. Bert turned it over, but there was nothing to indicate the sender. He thrust it under the door again and stood up.

The steward's unexpected arrival had shaken his nerve, there was no other explanation. Beyond Cynthia Vane's unlocked door was the jewellery which, once in his hands and disposed of in London, would see him out of the clutches of the Consolidated Finance Company and with a bit in hand to start afresh. Florrie might have to wait a bit for her Park Lane mansion, but he'd be able to put a roof over her head. He'd been down but never out and there wasn't going to be no first time. Only he couldn't bring himself to walk into Mrs Vane's cabin today. There was a jinx on it: if he persisted, someone else would come along, or she would, and he'd be caught with the jewellery on him and not even an excuse on his lips. So – not today, thank you. There was still a little time in hand, though he'd look fine if she took to her cabin with seasickness, as Florrie kept threatening to do.

Very little upset Bert's stomach, but the thought of the Consolidated Finance Company did. It was the impersonal brutality of the men who had fallen into step beside him that frightened him. No deal, no appeal was possible, and Bert lived by a combination of these. Trading: that was the secret of making money. You had to have something another party'd want, and the more they wanted it the more you could put your price up. It wasn't just buying cheap and selling dear, it was buying ahead of the market, being smarter than the next man. That was how he'd got his start: gauging wartime shortages and being in a position to supply them – where was the harm in that? Profiteer, they'd called him, but he'd only filled a need. They didn't have to pay his price if they didn't want to, and if he got it wrong he'd be left with stock on his hands. That was the risk he took and it was part of what they paid for. You didn't get nothing without risk. But you didn't risk your hide, and if he'd known the Consolidated Finance Company was interested in his he'd never have borrowed a penny. He never would again.

Except just this once, this loan to pay off the last one and give him initial capital once more. He glanced down the corridor – maybe His little brown Highness would help. He was the only son of the Nawab of

247

Maggapore, who must be rolling in it like all these Indian princes, with gold coming out of his arse, some of it in the direction of his beloved son doubtless, who if prevailed upon to lend would never miss it. Should he go and try him now? No, the Prince was not in his cabin, the letter had not been taken in. The small white triangle still protruded, and the more Bert looked at it with that bold superscription upon it the more it seemed to him to cry out to become a square. It was the work of a moment to kneel down and work it back as he had done when disturbed by the Mick steward. If disturbed again, the same excuse would serve: 'I was just posting a letter to His Highness Prince Ravi.' They could make what they liked of that – and he could make what he liked of the letter, depending on its contents, of course.

Bert saw nothing wrong in reading someone else's letter. Letters were meant to be read. He'd have read it if it had been open and lying on a table; the fact that it was sealed meant only that he'd come upon it at an earlier point in time, before the rightful recipient had opened it. Well, he was the recipient now. He tore open the envelope and let his eyes travel over the few bold black lines on cream paper before breathing a sigh of relief. He was in a trading position again. He held in his hands the secret of making money. He had something another party'd want.

Archie Johnson leaned on the rail with Imogen Stiles beside him. His arm rested lightly and publicly across her shoulders. This was permissible because they had become engaged.

Archie had not intended to propose. He had attended the ship's concert with the Stileses and had afterwards found himself alone with Imogen. The mood was romantic; the quack had sung three heart-throbs, and there had been demands for an encore in which Imogen had vociferously joined. 'Doesn't he sing beautifully!' she said, and indeed he did; Archie had to admit it. Trite ballads and musical comedy hits insensitively accompanied could not disguise the beauty of the voice. Hands had slid into hands to the strains of 'Love, could I only tell thee' or the highspots of *Rose Marie*. Ivo Haldingham, sitting just in front of Archie, had closed his hand over his wife's and looked down at her with such an expression of tenderness that Archie's first reaction – 'Fancy! at their age!' – had died away still-born. Perhaps there was something in this marriage business; he'd have to try it some day. 'Better to marry than to burn,' they quoted. Well, he burned often these days. That ointment the quack had given him was as useless as he had known it would be, coming from that source, but it was only five more days before they docked; and then the indignity of a clinic – but at least the quack had assured him he could be cured. 'We're lucky to have caught it at an early stage,' he told Archie on his last visit to the surgery for an injection. 'Just don't go infecting anyone else, there's a good lad.'

So Archie burned with two shames, one secret, the other open, for thanks to that little pipsqueak of a wog princeling everyone now knew that his army career was at an end and the inglorious circumstances of its termination. Drummed out of Maggapore. Forced to resign to propitiate a native ruler. Sacrificed to a wog. It was enough to sicken the most pro-Indian officer, and Archie was never that. After the concert he found himself pouring it out to Imogen as they sat in a sheltered corner of the boat deck on one of the last evenings when it would be possible to do so, for already the nights were turning chill. Imogen had listened, pale eyes and pale face glowing, and said in her soft little voice that it was harsh and unjust and no one would believe it, and the Colonel was a horrid old man. Her words were more soothing to his spirit than Bladon's ointment to his flesh. When she shivered it had seemed natural to put his arm around her, but he had been shocked by the vehemence of her response. Nice girls, missionaries' daughters, were not expected to demand, to turn in his arms, their bodies pressing against him, their tongues seeking the way to his mouth. Imogen had none of the languorous grace of the beauty in Bombay who had infected him, but there was no mistaking her desire. He felt himself rise to meet her and wondered if she was aware of it. Licit passion night after night would have its advantages . . . It was in this confused state that he spoke and her rapturous acceptance had left no room for manoeuvre: she would tell her parents that very night.

The Reverend and Mrs Stiles had been less than enthusiastic when Archie asked formally for her hand. Their daughter might be marrying a hero, but he was a hero who was unemployed. They were not familiar with the jobless situation in England, where ex-officers tramped the streets selling brushes to bored housewives, or struggled to produce enough from a smallholding to give their families enough to eat, but even in India rumours had reached them. The state to which Imogen was accustomed might not be very grand, but they were concerned she should not sink below it. It was all so different from what they had hoped and planned.

Imogen swept all objections aside and answered for Archie in a foreshadowing of things to come. Of course he would get a job. The police, perhaps – oh, she didn't mean as a bobby, but what about the Palestine Police? They were recruiting men with Archie's qualifications. What a pity Ireland had quietened down and the Auxiliaries and the Black and Tans had been disbanded; he would have done well in either of those. Or what about Australia? Mr Gurslake might have useful contacts – he was a businessman. The world was their oyster; once opened, there was sure to be a pearl inside it for a man like Archie. Imogen's confidence was infectious, and since she was twenty-one and had just inherited a small trust from her grandfather, the Reverend Septimus reluctantly said yes. He bestowed a somewhat theatrical blessing upon the young couple, and the engagement was announced.

Everyone agreed it was the most exciting thing to happen aboard the *Karachi* since the Martin girl had been attacked. Imogen and Archie were the centre of attention, and the unaccustomed situation brought a becoming flush to Imogen's cheeks. She seemed suddenly to have grown two inches taller, and her voice had acquired a new firmness as it escaped from her small, pursy mouth, a firmness which had even extended to the jut of her weak little chin. Miss Imogen Stiles might be insignificant, but Mrs Archibald Johnson would not be. The insecure girl was receding as the matron-in-waiting emerged.

It was Imogen who acknowledged the felicitations, perhaps because those to Archie were more perfunctory. He was aware that Imogen was considered lucky and he himself was not. Imogen had none of the qualities in a fiancée which aroused other men's envy, whereas the man who won the hand of Connie Martin could be sure of congratulations of a different sort. Edmund Bladon, who seemed the likeliest candidate, had said something kind to Imogen, but his eyes when he looked at Archie were cold, and the young man was not altogether surprised when the doctor knocked at the door of his cabin and thrust unceremoniously in.

'You're not going through with this, are you, Johnson?' he demanded.

'I'm not jilting Imogen, if that's what you mean.'

'You should have thought of that sooner. It would be a crime for you to touch her.'

'I haven't anticipated the wedding – yet.'

'How long do you intend to wait?'

'Imogen wants us to be married quickly, as soon as I can find a job.'

That might take some time, Edmund reflected; on the other hand, it might not.

He said aloud, 'You ought to wait at least a year.'

'Not on, old chap. Imogen's hot-blooded.'

'You can't do it, Johnson. Do you realise what it can do to your child or children, let alone to Imogen?'

'I'll go to a clinic.'

'That's not enough. You must make sure you can't infect her. Will you give me your word on that?'

'What'll you do if I don't?'

'You know there's nothing I can do. I shall respect my oath as regards a patient's confidentiality, but if you've a spark of decency in you, you'll not touch that girl until you're cured.' And I hope to God you haven't infected any other women, Edmund added to himself. He was thinking of Nina Martin as he closed the door.

Nina was pale these days, and quiet. She moved with a listless air. The calmness of her face had given way to blankness, the translucence of her skin to pastiness. Edmund almost fancied her figure had thickened, although he knew it could not do so yet – that is, if she were pregnant, which please God she was not. She had returned to her place at the long dining table and everyone was very kind, trying to draw her into the conversation, to win some response, however slight, that would indicate she

250

was not totally cut off from human society. Nina did her best to respond. She had always been a dutiful daughter. 'My good girl,' Mummy had said, implying that Connie was a bad one, though Nina did not think that was fair. Con wasn't bad but she questioned, not just by asking aloud but by testing every pronouncement, every rule imposed at home or at school. The nuns ran out of punishments; one or two ran out of patience. 'If Reverend Mother had to endure Constance in class she wouldn't have such a soft spot for her,' Sister Anne, who taught needlework, declared. She held up a piece of gappy hemstitching. 'The child doesn't even try. She just says she can't imagine hemstitching anything once she's left the convent, so what's the point of it?' – 'A similar pragmatism may explain why her essays are good,' observed Sister Hilda, who taught English, 'except that they're never neat and some of her ideas are – well, outlandish. The trouble with Constance is, she thinks.' The good Sisters shook their heads over this unnecessary activity which Reverend Mother failed to castigate. 'Surely,' she said in that voice which could still a roomful of agitation, 'we should be glad that we are sending out into the world a young woman who is not afraid to challenge the things that are wrong with it, as opposed to young ladies with nice manners who are proficient in needlework and French.'

To Nina the convent had never seemed more desirable than now when its doors were closed to her. Deflowered. She savoured the word – she had heard Edmund use it – and it conjured up pictures of Our Lady's Annunciation, when there was always a pot of lilies beside her or a stem of them in the Angel Gabriel's hand. The lily was a symbol of purity, Reverend Mother had said, to show that, all evidence to the contrary notwithstanding, Our Lady was as pure afterwards as before. Mary Immaculate. Mary unspotted. Without the least taint of ravishment. Whereas those who yielded to a man, however willingly, even a bride on her wedding night, were for ever sullied, for how could an earthly spouse compare with the bridegroom Christ? And what of those like her who had not yielded but had been sullied none the less? It was as though the lust they had sated clung to their skin, resistant even to carbolic; they were innocent yet steeped in guilt. And no longer whole. They could not offer Our Lord their deflowered bodies because these were imperfect, incomplete, and nothing but the whole and perfect would do for His service. A broken heart He would accept, but a broken body – no. 'It's wrong,' Connie had protested on hearing of a priest who could no longer continue in the priesthood because he had lost a leg. Reverend Mother had looked severe. 'It is to be hoped your perception of right and wrong applies as clearly in your own life, Constance. It is not for you to criticise the Church.' Connie muttered, 'Then who is it for?' but Reverend Mother chose not to hear her and went on: 'When we give ourselves to God He asks us to hold nothing back. He wants from us the same perfect sacrifice that He made: ourselves whole and entire.' – 'What about Sister Ursula's squint?' – 'She has two

251

eyes; there is nothing missing.' – 'Supposing she'd had her appendix out?' – 'The vermiform appendix is not a member of the human body. We can function very well without it. Whereas poor Father Holmes not only lacks a member but he would find it very hard to do God's work on one leg.' – 'He wouldn't be able to genuflect,' Connie said. Someone giggled. After a moment the whole class, including Reverend Mother, joined in.

Then it had been an academic matter, but now it was Nina's own life, her own body, that God saw fit to reject. And man also? She hoped not, but men prized virginity. Why else make such a fuss about it? 'To ensure the heirs of their bodies,' Connie said. 'At least they know the first child's theirs.' – 'And all the others?' – 'Yes, of course.' What a simpleton Nina was. If Mummy had had a child by Denis Orrey, Daddy would have had to acknowledge it as his unless there was to be a scandal which could have wrecked his career. It wouldn't have been the first time such a thing had happened in Nullumpur. There were rumours about the Colonel's wife's last baby, only she and Nini weren't supposed to understand. But if Nini were pregnant there was no cover-up, except a hastily arranged marriage in order to give the child a name. Suppose Edmund offered – could she bear to see him marry her sister? Connie suddenly discovered how close hatred is to love. And what about Imogen Stiles's engagement? Could pregnancy be the reason for that? If so, it would account for the reserve she felt in Edmund when they gathered to congratulate.

She was becoming used to this awareness of him, as though the physical boundaries between them were weakening, turning into the thinnest of membranes through which thoughts passed to and fro. She did not need to touch him to be aware of him; it was enough that he came into a room; even if her back were turned she could sense his presence before ever she heard his voice. And it seemed sometimes as though that awareness extended to all those she had come to know aboard the *Karachi*: Captain Meiklejohn with his sad eyes – but surely they had brightened recently? Mr Gurslake, so desperate for money – but why was he so desperate? His wife, dreading the Bay of Biscay and the English Channel as though seasickness were a fatal disease. Cynthia Vane, more self-confident and less engrossed in Bobby; the child himself, with something on his mind. Archie Johnson, now immersed, thank heaven, in Imogen, and Imogen – no need to be sorry for her! The First Officer whom she liked and the Third Officer whom she didn't, without being able to say why. And the Haldinghams—no, she did not know the Haldinghams, no one did; they were the enigma of the voyage. All she knew, all anyone knew, was that they had spent their lives in India expecting to die there, and were now unexpectedly coming home. No mention of family or finance, the usual reasons for such a decision, though less so at their advanced age. They had parried or turned aside every question – and there had been enough of those. Indeed, it was felt to be in some way unsporting to play everything so close to the chest. The only chink in their impenetrable armour was their dislike of the Irish

252

steward, which was not personal but seemed rather to be a dislike of all things Irish. Was it chance that during the ship's concert, when a woman with a loud, cracked voice had sung 'I'll take you home again, Kathleen', Mrs Haldingham had made an excuse to go out? Perhaps she was musical, Connie speculated – in which case how she must have delighted in Edmund's voice. He had lifted the whole concert into another dimension, despite the banality of the songs. His eyes had kept coming back to her as if to a magnet. 'Love, could I only tell thee' – but he would, he would, please God, and she would hear him – 'How dear thou art to me.' It needed no saying, yet more than anything in the world she wanted to hear him say it, and more than anything in the world her body clamoured to respond.

It was a clamour Cynthia Vane would have understood, though her own clamour was stilled these days – nights, rather – in a comforting, cradle-like lull. It was not her passion in Angus Meiklejohn's bed that surprised her – she knew herself to be a passionate woman – but she had never expected to rediscover it with the grizzled Captain. Even now she did not know what had made her agree to creep through the sleeping ship to his cabin whose door was left unlocked. As with Robert when on leave, the knowledge that their time was limited acted as a spur to her desire, but it was the calm aftermath of passion that confounded her when she lay cradled in his arms, feeling the rise and fall of his big body like the sea beneath her; or the weight of his head on her breast where it seemed each heartbeat shook it and he was a stubble-faced child who might at any moment open greedy lips to fasten on her nipple, from which he drew inexplicable sustenance. She had known nothing like this with Robert. With him, the dawn always came too soon, whereas with Angus she lay lapped in tranquillity, accepting the natural order of day after night.

She met no one on her nocturnal journeys. Bobby, she knew, would not wake; he slept soundly, never rousing as she entered or left their cabin. The rare stewardess or crewman she encountered had learned to be discreet. Only once had one of them shown curiosity: a tall, dark, handsome man whom she had met near Angus's door. He had stopped dead, and for a moment she had wondered if he had seen from what door she emerged. But he resumed his steady tread and when she risked a glance back she saw only broad shoulders and a slight movement of the head from side to side, as if he was in search of something. Or was it that he moved with the ship's roll, now more apparent as they left the Mediterranean behind? A reminder of how few nights she had still to spend with Angus. What would happen after the *Karachi* docked?

Cynthia found she could not see beyond the end of the voyage. It was like running into fog. Fog in the Channel – she heard the officers talk of it as a hazard at this time of year, when the ship nosed forward through a grey blanket of silence rent by foghorns and passengers congregated in the stuffy, smoke-filled lounges and fretted at the delay. She hoped there would be no fog, for if there was Angus would have to be on the bridge instead of in his cabin; there would be a double frustration to be endured. His duty as a Captain must separate them, despite this involuntary extension of the voyage.

Cynthia's fellow passengers would have been amazed at the powerful meld of emotions within her. To them she appeared aloof: the well-heeled young widow with a spoilt child and insufficient to occupy her. Mrs Stiles thought she should take up charitable work. 'Perhaps she doesn't like it,' Connie said. The missionary's wife looked at her in astonishment. 'It is not a question of like. Every position, even that of superfluous woman, has its duties. She should think of those less fortunate than herself.' As the mother of a daughter who was not going to be superfluous, she felt she could allow herself such remarks. After all, humble employment and good works were all the future held for Connie Martin's poor sister. There was a girl to be pitied, if you like! No good marriage for her, such as Imogen was making. Suppose it had been Imogen the rapist found! Really, no woman was safe and Captain Meiklejohn didn't appear to be doing much about it, although it was obvious where the guilt lay. The child Bobby Vane was hardly likely to have invented his story about seeing the doctor lurking nearby on the night in question. It was only the Captain's reluctance to accuse a member of the ship's company that prevented an arrest being made.

She said as much to the Reverend Septimus, who did not disagree. Besides, he had reasons of his own for disliking the doctor, as he hastened to disclose.

'He actually sought me out the day after Imogen announced her engagement,' he reported, 'to ask me if I was sure she was doing the right thing. Didn't say anything against Archie, of course – nothing he could say – but implied he wasn't what he seemed, "He's a man who wasn't afraid to fight for his country," I told him. "You don't get the MC for skulking at home. MC stands for Military Cross, not miserable cowardice." I thought that was rather good.'

'Yes, dear,' his wife said absently, her mind already distracted by the sight of Florrie Gurslake hurrying along the deck in pursuit of the Third Officer, no doubt to ask yet again if the glass was falling, the weather worsening, if they were in for what she persisted in calling 'a blow'. The whole First Class knew of her dread of seasickness, but any sympathy they felt had long since gone. Edmund, Connie and Julian Strode were the only people prepared to put up with her. Even Bert she tried hard to avoid. Especially since last night, when he had struck her because she bemoaned the *Karachi*'s tendency to roll.

'Shut up, you stupid cow. We was lucky to get on her. There wasn't no other ship leaving Bombay.'

'I'm sorry,' she said humbly, sitting down on the end of the bed. Distress had released her indigestion, which flowed outwards in a wave of pain. She rocked back and forth, pressing her lips together to prevent a gasp escaping.

'Feeling bad, are you?' Bert asked. His voice was gentler now as his conscience tweaked him. He shouldn't have treated her like that, but she had such a knack of picking the wrong moment, just when a bloke needed time to think how best to use the extraordinary stroke of luck that had come his way and should put an end to his troubles with the Consolidated Finance Company.

'Could I have a glass of water?' Florrie asked.

He poured one. Her hand trembled as she took it, and some of the water spilled.

'Here, steady on.' He put an awkward arm around her. She was getting herself all worked up. Christ, they wouldn't pass the Rock until tomorrow morning, and even after that the sea might still be calm. She should have his problems, then she'd know what it was to worry. 'Come on, old girl,' he encouraged. 'It may not be so bad.'

Florrie sipped and nodded. The pain was easing, though she felt herself come out in a cold sweat. They all said things like, 'It may not be so bad,' but she knew with every fibre of her being that it was going to be much, much worse. Nevertheless, she was grateful for his attempt at kindness and lay back on the bed, only to sit up with a sharp cry as the ivory hair ornament dug into her scalp.

'Beats me what you want to wear that thing for,' Bert said as she removed it, 'making yourself look daft. You don't see none of the other old ducks with 'em, do you? Why don't you chuck it over the side?'

'Because I like it.'

'Well, takes all sorts, I suppose.' Bert's ill-humour had evaporated, to be replaced by his more everyday concerns. He pushed her back on the bed, but she resisted.

'Not tonight, Bert. I've still got that pain.'

'Come on. Make you forget it.'

'Please, Bert.'

'Call yourself a wife!'

She had been so good a wife throughout their marriage that he was unused to not having his own way. On another occasion he might have insisted, but he had other things to think about now, such as the change in his fortunes. Should he tell Florrie? No, it would involve him in too many explanations and what she didn't know wouldn't hurt her. He undressed and ostentatiously put the light out, before turning his back on her and muttering goodnight. He was scarcely aware of her sitting rigid in the darkness as his present and future plans slid into sleep.

The pain persisted for a little, but Florrie did not lie long awake, and though her sleep was unrefreshing, next morning saw her determinedly on deck. She intended to see the Rock of Gibraltar, which she had been in no condition to appreciate on the outward voyage, and she lingered long after the other passengers including Bert had heeded the lunch gong. Besides, she did not really want food. She had drunk two cups of tea and toyed with breakfast, and her indigestion had not returned. Still, it would do no harm

255

to miss one of the *Karachi*'s lavish menus and instead contemplate the Rock.

It towered high above her with its distinctive shape, symbol of immutability, unchanged since its first British conquerors had come this way. They said there were monkeys on the top of it. From the port you could hire a carriage and drive up to the peak, from which there was a spectacular view of the harbour all a-bob with tiny ships. Best of all, they said, was when the Fleet was in and the warships were all lit up, but today the Mediterranean Fleet was elsewhere on manoeuvres and the Rock was in civilian dress.

It gave Florrie a sense of reassurance to know that the Rock of Gibraltar really existed and was not just an expression to indicate that some things were unchanging in an ever-changing world. Her own world was changing so fast it made her dizzy – all too literally. She sat down harder than she intended on a convenient seat. The waves rose and fell before her, deep green with a ruffle of spray. She closed her eyes against the heaving, and the breeze, still gentle but freshening, came and carried her breath away.

'Are you all right, Mrs Gurslake?'

Florrie drew air into her lungs: Nina Martin, her pale face anxious. 'Yes, thank you, dear,' she managed to say. God, what did she want to come poking around now for? If she went all hysterical again, Florrie knew who'd get the blame. She forced herself to sit upright and stare straight ahead of her.

'You don't look very well.'

Nina was frightened. Mrs Gurslake's colour was terrible, a kind of ashen grey. If only she had gone in to lunch with the others, she would not have found her here. Instead, she had chosen to avoid the lunchtime banter and stumbled on something far worse. Should she go for Edmund? But she did not like to leave Mrs Gurslake, who looked as if she was going to faint.

She put out a hand and touched her. The woman's hands were cold, but there was still some strength and feeling in them, for one of them closed over hers.

'Don't leave me.'

Nina swallowed. 'No, of course not.'

She couldn't go now. If only someone would come! She eased herself down beside Mrs Gurslake (she could never bring herself to call this dreadful woman Auntie Florrie) and put an arm around her. Close to, you could see her hair was dyed, so that was one question about her answered – but did the answers matter now?

'Wouldn't you like me to go and find your husband?' she suggested.

The dyed head moved from side to side as Florrie clung more tightly to Bert's hand grown suddenly smooth and young as she remembered it; it was only recently that his hands had gone so stiff and dry. Not that she'd had much chance to notice. Bert had never been one for holding hands. It wasn't often that he put an arm about her either, but he had in their cabin last night. He loved her, she knew he did, he just couldn't show it; some men were made like that. He was taking her back to England and they were starting all over again. Somewhere in the suburbs, with a maid and one of them shelves for posh plates round the dining-room – she could see it, even though the plates swam before her eyes. Bert was beside her, holding her, she could feel his hand even through the pain. Only it wasn't a pain, more like a tightening, as though her ribs were riveted and her lungs could no longer expand. Why didn't Bert say something, help her? With her last strength she clung to his hand.

Footsteps.

'Is something wrong?'

Nina, sagging under her burden, looked up into the eyes of Julian Strode.

'Is something wrong?' he repeated.

'Get Dr Bladon – quick!'

Footsteps running. Receding. A tattoo on the deckboards – Florrie heard them. A thunder of heartbeats. A sledgehammer somewhere in her chest.

There was not breath enough to speak, but: 'I love you . . .' Florrie whispered. She struggled. '. . . Bert,' she said.

And died.

PART IV

GIBRALTAR – ENGLAND

I

'*We therefore commit her body to the deep* . . .'

Captain Meiklejohn looked up from the *Book of Common Prayer* to scan the ocean, grey and heaving all around him, unwelcoming in the chill dawn. The woman who dreaded the sea was to be buried beneath its waters, sunk in her lead-weighted coffin fathoms deep.

Since Julian Strode had come hurrying into the dining saloon yesterday lunchtime and the ship's surgeon, with muttered apologies, had risen and followed him out, it had been only a short time (though it had seemed a long one) before the Third Officer was back, standing at his elbow, murmuring, 'Dr Bladon would be grateful if you would join him, sir, port quarter of A deck.' It was his turn now to mutter apologies and follow the young officer out, well knowing that only an emergency could have required this summons and half prepared for what he heard. 'One of the First Class passengers, sir, a Mrs Gurslake—she's had a heart attack.'—'Fatal?'—'The surgeon thinks so, sir. He asked if you would come.'

The woman lying on the deck had the flaccid untidiness of death. It was not the first time Angus had seen it and noticed how the dead instinctively abandoned the little decorums of life. Who now cared that Mrs Gurslake's skirt was rucked up waistwards, showing puffy knees and blue directoire drawers? He had a sudden recollection of her struggling to smooth that same skirt downwards, despite the fact that it was too short. Edmund Bladon looked up on hearing his approaching footfalls, and briefly shook his head.

'There's nothing I can do. She's gone, sir.'

Angus looked down at the empty, wide-eyed face. 'Better get her moved at once, before lunch is over. What is the cause of death?'

'I'd say a coronary occlusion, sir, it's almost a classic case. She had a history of phlebitis, was overweight and easily became breathless, took little exercise . . .'

How easy it was to slip into the past tense, yet less than an hour ago Florrie Gurslake had had a future, albeit one filled with fears.

'Miss Nina Martin was with her when she died, sir.'

Angus noticed the girl for the first time. She was so pale these days she could hardly be paler, but her eyes were wide with shock.

'This can't have been pleasant for you,' he said gently. 'I think we should ask your sister to come and then perhaps you would like to go to your cabin.'

He looked at Julian Strode as he spoke, and for the third time the young

261

officer sped off in the direction of the dining saloon, where by now speculation must be running high. As soon as the deck was cleared he was going
to have to break it to the husband. He didn't look forward to that.

When he did, Bert Gurslake was unbelieving.

'Florrie? But there wasn't nothing wrong with her. A bit of indigestion
maybe, but people don't die of indigestion . . .'

'I'm afraid it was something more than that.'

'You mean if she'd gone to the quack he might have saved her? Christ,
and I wouldn't let her go, told her she was a silly old cow imagining things
. . .' Bert's voice cracked, but he went on: 'She was dead scared of being
seasick 'cause she'd felt so rotten on the trip out. I thought she was
working herself up. I never dreamed it could be serious.'

'Mr Bladon tells me there's nothing he could have done. You shouldn't
distress yourself. The end was mercifully quick, a matter of minutes.'

'And who knows what she thought about in that time?'

When the gentlemen from the Consolidated Finance Company had
escorted him down that alley, Bert's thoughts had ranged far and wide.
Escape and its chances and consequences. The possibility of playing for
time. Pleading – an idea hastily abandoned. Going down fighting. Naked
animal fear. And as an undercurrent: Florrie. What would become of her?
Would the bully-boys try to recover the money from his widow? Could she
face the voyage home on her own? There wouldn't be no Silver Wedding.
At least there was enough stashed away for her fare . . . If Florrie's
thoughts in her last moments had in any way resembled his, her brain must
have ticked over like a watch gone mad, despite her faltering heartbeats.
Time played funny tricks with you when you were in that state. How could
that gold-braided bastard say it was mercifully quick?

The gold-braided bastard was still speaking. 'I assume you will wish
your wife to be buried in England, since we're only four days from port?'

'Where else?' Bert dragged his mind back to the present.

'There's always burial at sea. In tropical waters it is essential, but here
. . .' The Captain shrugged. 'You have family, friends, who will no doubt
wish to attend. The comfort of their presence will easily outweigh the
cost.'

'You mean it's cheaper at sea?'

'Well, yes . . .'

'We ain't got no family.' And no friends neither. 'Won't make no
difference to Florrie,' Bert said aloud to the startled Captain. 'She can't get
seasick now. But I don't want that missionary bloke praying over her. Him
and his wife, they treated us like dirt.'

'A burial at sea is usually performed by the Captain.'

'Florrie'd appreciate that.'

'And at dawn, to spare the feelings of the other passengers.'

'It don't make no odds to me. Nor to Florrie,' Bert added quickly.

However hard he tried to make himself believe it, he could not accept that a part of his life had gone. Later in their cabin he surveyed, uncomprehending, Florrie's belongings, her make-up, the silver-backed hairbrush of which she had been so proud. Her nightdress was folded under the pillow where the stewardess had left it; it would remain there for the rest of the voyage. Her side of the bed would stay cold and empty, the nights unpunctuated by her snores. He was alone. There was no one in the wide world to care whether he lived or died. If Bert had been familiar with self-pity he would have wept, but the tears came later when Florrie's clothes were returned to him in a discreet bundle by a sympathetic stewardess. Choking, he thrust them away on the top shelf of the wardrobe. There was a clatter as something fell out – the ivory hair ornament she'd bought in the Bombay bazaar. How he'd gone on about it, and the poor cow was only spending, same as she always had. He'd encouraged her, for God's sake: no point in having money if you didn't spend; how else would anyone know you'd got it, and Florrie didn't know they was broke, hadn't never heard of the Consolidated Finance Company, wouldn't have understood if she had. No, she'd just wanted to look good. For him, Bert Gurslake, to whom she'd been married for almost twenty-five years. And now that he was about to recoup their fortunes, she'd gone and died on him. Hadn't even felt ill; gave no warning. And because it was bloody well cheaper, she'd have to be buried at sea.

Shivering on deck at dawn the next morning, Bert still couldn't believe it was true. That oblong box covered with a purple pall did not contain Florrie. She was waiting for him somewhere else. When he got back to their cabin she'd be wanting to know what he thought he was doing, going up on deck in his best suit before any of the other passengers were astir, and all because of a funeral. Hadn't he seen enough of those? Nasty depressing things. Thank goodness they were usually gentlemen only. Women had enough to do with getting the tea ready back home. Cold ham and salad, that was the usual; sometimes a nice pork pie; and cheese and pickled onions and fruit cake, with plenty of good strong tea to wash it down. Later the men might go up the road to the pub for a half-pint; anything more would imply a lack of respect; and the women would have a drop of port at home, or brandy in cases of severe affliction, and there would be red eyes, damp handkerchiefs, and of course ubiquitous black.

Nasty depressing things they might be, but there was something comforting about a funeral like that. Bert would gladly have exchanged it for these cold and windswept prayers attended by himself, the Captain, the Third Officer, the doctor, a handful of First Class passengers, and two seamen waiting to tip Florrie over the side. The Captain's voice came intermittently, blown away by the wind: '*We brought nothing into this world and it is certain we can carry nothing out of it . . .*' Except, in Florrie's case, her wedding ring. An apologetic Dr Bladon had sought Bert out the previous evening to say he had been unable to remove it from her hand. 'Let her take it with her,' Bert said. He had been tempted to hand

263

over the ivory hair ornament and request that it go too; for him it had no happy associations, but he didn't want to be misunderstood. 'Couldn't get rid of his poor wife's things fast enough' – he could hear them saying it. Sooner than give them that satisfaction, he would keep every last pin.

'*Man that is born of woman . . .*' The Captain's voice came again, something about how little time they had in this world. 'Man that is born of woman . . .' Pity she couldn't have had that kid. She'd wanted it and he'd known she wanted it, but other considerations came first, such as leaving England before anyone discovered there was good reason for insisting on his presence to answer certain questions about goods supplied. 'Helping the war effort,' they called it when you supplied what they wanted; 'profiteering' when they got the bill. As if the law of supply and demand ought to be suspended for the duration as part of the Emergency Powers.

'*The soul of our dear sister, Florence Annie Gurslake . . .*' It didn't sound like Florrie. Once she'd had brothers and sisters, but it was each for himself, she'd said. 'Mum couldn't keep us and Dad wouldn't, not once we was old enough to earn. Never mind how we earned. No questions asked, no answers given, so long as the cash came in. When it didn't, he beat us. I saw the older kids leave home, and as soon as I thought I had a steady wage coming I went off and took a room. Then the firm laid me off and for a bit things was sticky until I got a job in a pub. Washing floors and cleaning glasses, but I had my eye on the bar. Once when the regular barmaid was sick the landlord let me take over. I knew I could do it, and I did. Bit of banter and glad eye and backchat with the customers, and the landlord never took the other girl back. She laid in wait for me one night and tried to claw me, but I was stronger. Then her steady threatened to carve me up. That was when I realised a girl needed gentlemen friends and I wasn't never without one, until you happened along.'

Happened along was what it had been, Bert remembered. The Goat and Compasses wasn't his usual pub. Chance had brought him to the area and a sudden heavy shower had sent him in. He was aware of a brief pause in the talk at the bar as the regulars looked round, suspicious; then, their suspicions allayed by whatever instinctive assessment obtained on such occasions, they turned back to the matter in hand. But that pause had been enough to show him Florrie, bright-eyed, high-coloured, dark-haired (no question of hair dye then), her full breasts straining against the black satin of her blouse, the swell of her hips tantalisingly visible as she swung round to the till, its bell pinging and its drawer crashing shut with a rhythm that dominated the conversation as surely as Florrie's presence dominated the room.

Bert had edged his way forward. 'Half of bitter, miss, please.'

Two halves could be drawn out longer than a pint, gave him two chances of addressing the goddess of the Goat. Already he had satisfied himself that no plain gold wedding band lurked among the rings on her fingers. As she slapped down his beer (but without spilling a drop, he noted), her glance travelled over him.

'Half a pint for a half-pint-sized gent,' she called loudly.

Someone sniggered and several heads turned to stare.

Bert was undismayed. He was used to jokes about his stature, and there was nothing personal in this. She had registered him as mechanically as her cash register rang up the totals, but she would register him differently in future, he vowed. Like all his vows, though he did not call them that, he fulfilled it. On the night before they were to be wed there was a whip-round in the bar and Florrie found herself richer by two weeks' wages. Bert preened himself at her popularity, for from now on she would be his. These brawny stevedores and dockers could cast their lecherous eyes elsewhere. She hadn't settled for one of them, had she? It was their unlucky day when Herbert Gurslake had, as Florrie'd put it, 'happened along'.

The phrase, with its undertone of chance and fortune, did not always signify good. It rang heavily in the head of Angus Meiklejohn in the intervals of his concentration on the Order for the Burial of the Dead. 'I just happened along, Angus – ye ken, I was looking for Minna.' He heard again Jamie Sutherland's words last night, and in the intervals of commending the soul of Florence Annie Gurslake to her Maker, he cursed ships' cats who wandered and Chief Engineers who sought them and the time at which both chose to do these things.

He had known there was something wrong from the minute Jamie came through the doorway for their usual half-hour's chat. Angus had been particularly looking forward to it: a death on board had a disturbing effect, quite apart from the fact that he would be obliged to read the burial service at dawn next morning. Surely the husband could have waited four more days and had Mrs Gurslake decently buried in England? Angus resented this new task imposed. He had never before had to consign someone to the ocean. When the wartime torpedo struck they had been relatively close to land and the bodies removed from the engine-room had been sewn up in canvas by some of the crew while Angus, on the bridge, fought with every ounce of Scots tenacity to coax the *Karachi* into port. He had no time even to feel grief for the men lost and their families: he was wholly concentrated on the messages coming in to the bridge: starboard pumps working, three port pumps out of action; one engine gone, the other sluggish; answering slowly to the helm; down by the bow on the port quarter; wallowing, wallowing . . . The bad news came in, and all the time his mind worked like a well-oiled engine, selecting and discarding options, monitoring, rejecting, repeating the process until it seemed there was nothing left untried and the *Karachi*, ever lower in the water, must slide under within sight of home. Then, as darkness fell and emergency lighting cast a green-ish glow over the bridge instruments and their pessimistic dials, some change in the ship's movement alerted her captain more surely than any gauge. His ship was responding; she had heard her master and was struggling to obey. The messages now were more hopeful; Angus willed her on. He could not have said what instinct told him that his ship was alive once more, but he knew suddenly that he and she were destined for many more journeys on their lawful occasions upon the high seas.

A similar instinct had warned him of trouble the moment the Chief Engineer came in. As he poured the three fingers of Scotch which was the Chief's one daily indulgence in his otherwise teetotal life at sea he was alert for any phrase or nuance which might tell him what was to come. But the Chief merely sat down more heavily than usual and sipped his drink in silence. When he spoke it was only what Angus expected.

'I hear ye'd a passenger die.'

'Aye, a Mrs Florence Gurslake.'

'I didna ken the lady. Was she old?'

'Fifty.'

'It's young to go,' said the Chief, who was forty-eight. 'Was she travelling alone?'

'No, with her husband.'

'A terrible shock for the poor man. In the midst of life we are in death – there's nothing truer. We do well always, Angus, to look to our last end. It behoves us all to walk in the way of the Lord and to keep his Commandments. Would ye no agree?'

'Aye.' Except for the Seventh. There were special circumstances there which made it less of a sin to break it than the others; perhaps not a sin at all.

'We cannot know when a tie is to be severed.' The Chief took a sip from his drink. 'Which brings me to something I must tell ye, Angus. I'll not be sailing with ye again.'

'What!'

Angus could not believe what he was hearing. His mind refused to take it in. He went on staring at Jamie. The Chief began to explain.

'The Owners have been at me to transfer to a more modern vessel. They've offered financial inducement as well. The time has come when I canna go on shutting my eyes to the future. I've decided to accept a transfer to the *Hyderabad*.'

Angus heard the news with sinking heart. The *Hyderabad* was the new flagship of the Line, the Owners' darling, her maiden voyage just completed. For Jamie to become her Chief Engineer was a dazzling prospect – but why had they offered it now? He should have been with her on that maiden voyage, one of the ship's company from the start. He voiced his thoughts. The Chief looked uneasy.

'Aye, well, they wanted me to, ye ken, but I said I'd rather serve under Captain Meiklejohn on the *Karachi*. Then there was a letter at Marseilles offering me the job again.'

'And this time you're going to say yes, as you should have done the first time. Congratulations,' Angus said. 'It's a fine chance and you've made the right decision.'

From a great distance he saw himself hold out his hand and Jamie refuse to take it, heard himself ask, 'What's wrong?'

''Tis for me to ask you that, Angus.'

Angus Meiklejohn said, 'I don't understand.'

'I think ye do. When respect goes, it takes everything else with it.'

'Respect for whom or what?'

'Respect for a fine man and a captain I was proud to serve under.'

'What have I done to forfeit that respect?'

'When a man canna control his lust and falls foul of the Seventh Commandment at the expense of a wife and a sick bairn, I judge him to be less of a man and therefore less of a captain.'

'Do you also judge him less of a friend?'

'A man must respect his friends.'

'Even in things that are none of his business?'

'Ye canna parcel out a man like that, saying this is good and that bad and something else could be better. We must stand or fall by what we are. And – ye force me to say it, Angus – you are an adulterer.'

'How do you know? Have you been spying on me?'

'Och, man, never that. But I'm no blind, and if I were I could still feel which way the wind is blowing. Ye canna take your eyes off Mistress Vane.'

Was it so obvious? Angus reviewed the position. They had been so careful where they met. No one could have seen Cynthia enter or leave his cabin; he had always made sure of that. So what made Jamie call him an adulterer? He was surely jumping to conclusions, in which case he must be faced down.

'Mrs Vane is an attractive woman,' Angus said carefully, 'and not the first we've had aboard. I admit I'm man enough to be aware of her, but you've no right to infer more than that.'

'Not when I've the evidence of my own eyes before me? I have seen the woman leave in the small hours, and I know whose cabin she came from.'

'So you've been spying after all.'

'No, Angus, I just happened along. I was looking for Minna, she'd gone missing – the poor creature's after a tom. I came round and there was Mistress Vane coming out of that door beside you. I couldna help seeing her.'

Angus debated. The evidence was conclusive and he knew Jamie Sutherland too well to believe that a plea for sympathy would be heeded. Not for himself, at least . . .

'Mrs Vane is a widow. For eight years now she has been celibate.' (As he had himself . . .) 'She is young, healthy, vital. Is it any wonder if, like Minna, she goes in search of a mate?'

'Would you degrade her to the level of a brute beast, without control of

267

her animal urges? The good Lord gave us free will, as well as the power to distinguish good from evil. It is at our peril that we ignore these gifts.'

'But the Lord is merciful.'

'To them that fear Him.'

Angus saw that it was useless to go on. It did not matter whether the Chief was better able to resist temptation, or whether he did not know what temptation was. He understood neither the struggle nor the surrender. For him, they did not exist.

But the human dimension was not lost on Jamie Sutherland. 'What will ye do?' he asked. 'Ye canna leave Ailsa and Andy.'

'I'll see they don't suffer,' Angus said, 'but to be truthful, Jamie, I don't know what will happen at the end of this voyage. I don't know what Cynthia expects. I don't know how I can do my duty by both women and their sons, but I'll have to find a solution.' He hesitated. 'Pray for me.'

'I'll pray that ye may be recalled to the path of righteousness, and that we'll go north together at the end of this voyage as we've so often done before.'

'Let us at least part friends.'

Again Angus offered his hand and again Jamie refused it, saying unsteadily as he turned away: 'Ye're a fine man, Angus, and that makes it all the harder to see ye in thrall to a woman like Mistress Vane.'

As though Cynthia were to blame for his fall from grace. Yet the urge to defend her died on Angus's lips. If that was how the Chief interpreted their relationship he would not change his mind. The alternative to blaming Cynthia was blaming Angus, and Angus knew that was more than his friend could bear. The years of friendship could not be sloughed off like a snake's skin, for no new skin grew beneath. Instead, both men were left naked and shivering in a world grown old and cold.

'Ye'll continue to receive my daily reports,' the Chief said, his voice returning to normal, 'but I'll no be bringing them in person.'

'Very good. Anything today?'

'Only a wee bit of trouble with yon stoker – Gopal, as he calls himself.'

'What's he done?'

'He was reported to me for spreading disaffection. Urging the crew to form a union.'

'They're all at it. It's coming sooner or later. Remember the waterfront at Bombay.'

'It's no coming in any engine-room I'm Chief of. It is part of the Lord's plan who shall serve. Masters and men, he made us in His wisdom. It is not for us to unmake what He creates.'

Angus forbore to point out that Gopal answered to a different deity, to a whole pantheon, in fact, for that would only remind Jamie that the man was a heathen.

'What did you do?' he asked.

After all, the man already knew he would be given his papers in London;

he must have reckoned he had nothing to lose by urging fellow stokers and greasers to unionise.

'Relieved him of his responsibilities, such as they are, and confined him to quarters.' Confidence rang in the Chief's voice. 'In four days' time we'll be in port. It'll no hurt him to meditate on his sins till then.'

Physically it wouldn't, but to give a man time to brood on injustice – or on justice – was a bad thing. Alone in the native crew's cramped, dark quarters, troubles magnified as the day wore on. Yet to allow this man with a grievance free access to his fellows was to court trouble of a different sort.

'Has his hand healed?'

'Aye. Yon doctor laddie did a good job.' There was grudging admiration in the Chief's voice. 'The man has no case against us, if that's what ye're fearing. It's his word against an officer's.'

A situation to delight a *babu* lawyer, who could skilfully blacken the Line's name and still more the name of the *Karachi* and her Captain, even though she would have a different Chief Engineer. Guiltily Angus recognised that there might be advantages to a change in the engine-room. A new Chief might have more liberal attitudes to the Commandments of God and man. There would not be friendship, any more than there was friendship between him and the deck officers, but there might well be more accord, for he recognised now how deep were the divisions between himself and Jamie Sutherland which friendship alone had enabled them to bridge. But for the moment, looking at the Chief's tall figure framed in the doorway, all Angus could feel was loss. Cynthia Vane for Jamie Sutherland? The equation was absurd. Then there flooded through him all the sweetness of last night's remembered ecstasy, and the anticipation of the pleasure that was to come between now and his reading of the Order for the Burial of the Dead at Sea . . .

'*We therefore commit her body to the deep . . .*'

Not Cynthia's, but Florence Annie Gurslake's, a woman he had hardly known, whom he had last seen as a crumpled heap of flesh sprawled on the deck, whereas he had last seen Cynthia curled luxuriously in his bed. She was half asleep, lips parted, her breast rising and falling like the gentle swell of the sea, which now lapped the *Karachi*'s stern, grey and choppy, hungry to receive its prey.

At the words of committal the pall was withdrawn from the coffin. A gleam of watery sun caught the wood as the plank was upended, making it shine as though polished as it slid forward and began to tilt. Faster it moved, so fast that the instant when it vanished was impossible to identify. One moment the mortal remains of Florrie Gurslake were among them; the next there was only a void. Those nearest the rail glimpsed the dark object plummeting downwards, then the deep received it silently.

'. . . *in sure and certain hope of the resurrection . . .*'

Edmund Bladon had laid a hand on Gurslake's arm, as though he had compulsively started forward when the coffin began to tilt. It was the same at the graveside: that last surge of longing for a physical union once more, that ultimate attempt to rouse a sleeper who had never yet failed to respond. If he leaned over Cynthia, Angus thought, her eyes would open, her lips curve into a smile; her hands reach out to draw him to her; but if he leaned over Ailsa, her eyes would open wide and startled, her lips frame the question 'Andy?', her hands thrust her upright in bed. Only afterwards, when reassurance had taken hold, would she lie down beside him and roll over to present her back.

'. . . *when the sea shall give up its dead.*'

The Martin girls had crossed themselves. Too bad Nina Martin had been present when Mrs Gurslake died. The girl had had enough to contend with on this voyage, but presumably her presence at the death had dictated her presence at the committal, although he would not have blamed her if she had stayed away. The sister's influence, perhaps. Now there was a strong character, as well as an attractive girl. Whoever won her would be lucky. Pity it couldn't be Edmund Bladon, but without a job, how could the man propose? Yet it would have been so easy for him to clear his name, even though it had proved impossible to shake Bobby Vane's story that he had seen the doctor hiding near the Martins' door. If only Bladon had denied it, it would have been easy to suggest to Cynthia and everyone else that the child was fantasising, seeking childish revenge on someone he so evidently disliked. But Bladon refused to clear himself, and whatever the reason, that and his sympathy with underdogs like Gopal were going to cost him Connie Martin. Angus felt a pang of regret.

Because of Cynthia, Angus was attuned to relations between the sexes as never before. He was aware of the current that ran between Bladon and Connie Martin, and also of that between Archie Johnson and Imogen Stiles. Only there was something wrong there – not with Imogen, she was triumphant, already a matriarch-to-be – but with Archie, who was less assertive and had an almost furtive air. He clung close to Imogen, was uneasy in her absence, as though he feared to be alone and open to the questions of others, particularly of other men. Of course the revelation of his disgrace must be humiliating, particularly at Prince Ravi's hands, but Angus was well aware that despite it, to some passengers, young Johnson represented 'the right stuff'. 'So brave,' Cynthia had said. 'It can't have been easy to win a decoration when acts of bravery were going on all the time.' She was certain Robert had earned one many times over, only no witness had lived to report. The Big Push that Robert had insisted was coming had seen men mown down like corn in the wake of a barrage that had been heard over much of southern England and would surely have pulverised the Germans – except that it had fallen short.

Robert's father, returning from a brief trip to London, reported the capital agog as news came in from Dover almost to Portsmouth of the hammering being given to the Hun. 'They'll never stand up to it,' was the verdict. 'We'll be at the German frontier by the time this war's two years old.' And Cynthia, feeling the child stir within her, had looked forward to welcoming Robert home. She had done her share of paying calls of condolence when a villager failed to return, but because the Big House had been spared she had assumed it would continue to be so, her love and the duties of his inheritance ensuring that Robert would come back. She was still too numb with shock to register the subsequent deaths of Robert's younger brothers in 1917 and 1918 respectively. If it were not for Bobby, she would have envied her mother-in-law, who quietly yielded to a cold turned to pneumonia even before the Spanish flu epidemic arrived. Yet there was something unreal about her burial in the village churchyard when Robert and his brothers lay 'somewhere in France'. Which was perhaps why she had agreed to her father-in-law's suggestion that they should visit the war cemetery.

There were other figures in black aboard the boat train from Victoria, but Cynthia was not aware of them. She was aware only of the tall, stooped old man beside her whose hands had begun to tremble, though his hair, white now and thinning, was kept like his moustache immaculately trimmed. But there were occasional food stains on his clothes, spilt by those same shaking fingers; his clothes no longer fitted as they should; they said in the village he was failing. Cynthia was suddenly aware of it.

In the small hotel where they stayed the staff overflowed with kindness. Cynthia mustered long-disused French to thank, request information, explain. A taxi was forthcoming to take them to the cemetery – God's acres, Cynthia thought, looking at the vast expanse of green strewn evenly with crosses; no single acre here. Armed with instructions, they moved up and down the straight paths while other dark figures did the same, and found easily enough the graves of Second Lieutenant Philip Vane and Lieutenant Anthony, but Robert's grave eluded them. The *gardien* of the cemetery insisted there were only two graves of that name; he consulted a typewritten list and even showed it to them, from which it appeared he was right. Her father-in-law's trembling had now spread to his whole body; his hands were clenched on hat and walking-stick. All around them the land lay green and peaceful. It was the same landscape that Robert's eyes had last rested on in that first week of July 1916. But where was Robert? To Cynthia it no longer mattered; the essence of him was not here, but in the green, rolling acres of the estate he would never administer. She turned to her father-in-law: 'Let's go home.'

The words died on her lips at the sight of his shaking shoulders, the tears trickling down his cheeks, forcing her to lay a hand on his arm and say 'We'll find him,' before turning back to the *gardien*.

And after all it proved to be an administrative error and the *gardien* himself, with many apologies, led them to the white cross like all the other white crosses which marked the last resting-place of Captain Robert Vane, and the taxi-driver took them back to the hotel in silence and refused to accept a fare . . .

271

On the boat returning to England across a Channel wonderfully calm, such as thousands of men must have crossed with joy or dread, depending on direction, the old man said suddenly, 'You'll have to sell the estate.' Cynthia answered with the first thing that came into her head: 'But Bobby will run it.' – 'It won't be there for him to run.' Her father-in-law leaned on the rail beside her and she could feel the tremors of his body communicated to her own. He went on to explain that there were debts, and the cost of a good manager to run it was more than the estate could bear. 'I can't go on till the boy's old enough to take over,' he said needlessly, 'but although agricultural land is depressed, there'll be enough to keep you both in reasonable comfort if you sell as soon as I'm gone.' – 'You'll live for years yet,' Cynthia protested. 'No, my dear, I'm done. When a man has three sons he has a right to expect continuity. Now there's nothing left of them, and nothing left to hand on. I don't want to discuss this when we get home –' his voice took on the trembling of his body, 'I shan't say anything in the village, you understand, but I've made my Will – Stephens the lawyer has it. The boy gets everything, apart from an allowance for you. Stephens will handle the sale – his firm's dealt with us for generations; he'll see you're not sold short. And if you take my advice you'll leave Lincolnshire; go right away and forget it. You might even remarry some day.' His smile was so sad that Cynthia felt tears starting; she could only shake her head. 'It's early days yet,' her father-in-law said softly, 'but I want you to know it would please me if you did.'

What would her late father-in-law have said to Captain Angus Meiklejohn, Cynthia wondered, a married man old enough to be her father, with a grown-up but permanently disabled son? He would not approve of the situation, but she thought he might approve of the man. They both moved within a moral framework, their every action governed by a code. Duty, responsibility, these were their watchwords, whether to an estate or to a ship. And for her Angus was prepared to throw all this overboard, dead weight like Mrs Gurslake's coffin when she had been buried at sea. Her death had sent a frisson through Cynthia and the rest of the First Class passengers, as proximity to death often does, but this had been rapidly replaced by outrage at the choice of funeral. Of course it was no more than was to be expected from a fellow like Gurslake, but even people like that usually did the decent thing when it came to the last offices for a loved one. Perhaps Florrie had not been loved? Which made it all the worse, for the poor woman had been besotted by 'her Bert' and he now went out of his way to demonstrate how little she mattered. It was a scandal and a shame.

Only – who knew the ways in which grief was manifested? Cynthia had never seen her father-in-law weep for his dead sons and lost acres until he stood beside their graves in a war cemetery in what had hitherto been the unnamed 'somewhere in France'. She doubted if Angus had ever opened his heart to anyone about Andrew as he had to her on the night of the fancy hat dance. It would have been easy to think him unfeeling until he chose to reveal himself. Even now, when she looked at him as he moved among the passengers, she could not believe that that face, strong, seamed, bronzed, craggy-featured, could relax into tenderness. Did it with Ailsa? With Andy? Or was it only for her – and for Bobby, of course, for she had seen his expression when he looked in her son's direction, though Bobby was unaware of it.

How would Bobby react if she married Angus? Her first duty was to Robert's son, and if he had taken against the Captain as he had against Dr Bladon, she would never have considered it. Instead, he admired the Captain, talked already of going to sea himself some day, in the magnanimous, all-things-are-possible manner of childhood which brooks no obstacle or delay. If she married Angus and he gave up being a captain, would they be happy living somewhere within sight of the sea and devoting themselves to each other and to bringing up their son? For there would be a son, Cynthia promised. She longed to bear Angus's child and to hear again those first miauling cries which were all that had linked her to sanity when Bobby was first put into her arms. 'You have a little boy, Mrs Vane' – the nurse's voice was gentle; it was not the first time since August 1914 that she had delivered a posthumous child. And Cynthia, weak and spent, had had room only for two thoughts: A son to inherit; and: Robert will never see this child. With Angus there was no question of inheritance, but at least he would be able to take his son in his arms, and in watching him grow forget the tall, handsome man who feared thunder and loved sweeties and followed his mother like a dog.

'I mean you and your son no harm, Ailsa Meiklejohn,' Cynthia murmured, 'I shall take nothing from you that you still have. It is my money that will keep our home going, and you will continue to receive whatever Angus earns. Perhaps in time you may even come to share our love for the boy who will restore to both of us all that the past eight years have drained away, for by the time this voyage is over I may already be pregnant with Angus's second son.'

Deaths come in threes. Edmund Bladon thought of the old saying when news of the second death reached him, even though he had been half expecting it.

The Captain sent for him and handed him a cablegram. 'Bad news, Mr Bladon, I'm afraid.'

Edmund took the form, knowing what he would read there.

'Father died peacefully this morning. Funeral arranged for a week today.'

It had been handed in yesterday. The signature was 'Anne'. He guessed she had been present at the end because it would have been like her to let nothing stand in her way when the doctor who had attended Roger, his mother, his father, at last got in touch with her. 'If Jeffrey asks for me, I'll

273

come,' she had told him, 'and if he doesn't ask I still want to be there. My brother has been a fool but there's no reason why he should pay for his folly on his deathbed. A man ought not to die alone.' So she would have closed his eyes, which had never lost their piercing brightness although his brain no longer registered the messages they conveyed, and she would have folded his hands which once smote with irritation on the table when someone – wife, sons, servants – failed to be prompt in executing his commands. As a boy, Edmund had feared his father, but there had always been Roger to intervene: Roger the firstborn, the beloved, Sir Roger as he would be some day . . . And now it would be Sir Edmund. Odd how strange the title sounded when he had known for so long it would be his. Would he use it? Sir Edmund Bladon, Bt, general practitioner: it didn't have quite the right ring. But there would be enough money now to buy a practice; enough money now to take a wife. A woman might enjoy being Lady Bladon. His wife might. Connie might . . .

'Please accept my sympathy,' Captain Meiklejohn was saying.

'Thank you, sir.' Edmund allowed himself to smile. 'My father has been an invalid for years. His death is a release for himself and for others, and for me it could not have come at a better time. I should in any case have had to resign my position as ship's surgeon in order to attend to his affairs. Now that the matter is already in hand, I hope you'll allow me to get away quickly as soon as we reach port.'

Angus Meiklejohn nodded. There would be no problem. He had already informed the Owners that a new ship's surgeon would be required, and they would be aware that a new Chief Engineer would also be needed.

'I'll see that everything's made easy for you,' he promised. 'As you say, we should perhaps see it as Providence.'

Jamie would insist on seeing the Lord's hand in the turn events were taking, but he did not have Jamie's faith that those who obeyed the Lord's Commandments need not fear and that the Lord's Commandments offered no problems of interpretation – he would miss Jamie, that was all. Yet despite their friendship, Angus recognised, he knew little about him: a man from Dundee, with a fine brain and an understanding of engines in his hands that had ensured him the highest qualifications; an upbringing within the Kirk, from which he had never strayed; an iron disciplinarian, with himself first of all – cast-iron rather, for Jamie's principles would break before they would bend. They would not even bend to encompass his best friend's transgressions; Angus could expect no more mercy than the stoker Gopal, except that it might grieve Jamie more to cast him into outer darkness. Only Minna, the ship's cat, was exempt. For her there was a soft place in the Chief's cabin and a softer place in his heart; she could lie purring on his knee and feel the caress of his fingers; her frequent litters and occasional thieving were overlooked. True, the Chief drowned her kittens, but the ship could not be overrun with cats, and he did it himself, making sure the blind, helpless creatures did not suffer, and went out of his way to comfort the mother cat. Minna adored him; she would let no one else fondle her; from any other approach she sprang away. Angus had often marvelled at the gentleness there must be in those strong fingers: Jamie's wife might be more fortunate than he supposed. As for the three fine sons and the little daughter, who was a late addition to the brood, they had a father they could admire and look up to. If Andy were capable of admiration, would he be able to say the same?

But if Bonnie Andy were Dr Andrew Meiklejohn, his father would never have incurred Jamie's wrath. How much was due to his longing for a son like Bobby and how much to his love for Cynthia Vane – Mistress Vane, as the Chief contemptuously called her, stressing both her title and her role? 'When I grow up I'm going to go to sea,' Bobby informed him. 'I'm going to be a captain like you.' The admiration in the child's face was apparent, and Angus found it sweet. 'It's a fine life if the sea's your calling,' he answered, glancing at the ocean as he spoke, 'but it needs discipline, hard work. Do you think you have it in you?' Bobby nodded. 'Well, we'll see. But you'll need a good education. No more telling lies to your mother to get out of going away to school. You'll have to leave her and get used to living with other laddies. How does that appeal to you?'

Bobby swallowed. 'I expect I can do it if I have to. Did you go away to school?'

'I was not so lucky. My parents could not afford it. I began my service before the mast.'

As a deck boy, the lowest of all crew members, knowing nothing about the sea except that its salt lodged in his blood and no other life was possible. Even through that first grim winter he had known that. Cold, frightened, bewildered, obeying orders he often did not understand, warmed by rough kindliness, chilled by bullying, seasick so frequently he had forgotten what it was to keep food down – no voyage had ever been as terrible as that first one. But then, never again had he been fourteen years old, wiry, undersized, not much bigger than the spoilt child before him who glowed with advantages. What was Bobby Vane ever likely to know of the struggle to study in a bunk too narrow for books to be propped open; or those rare occasions when space could be cleared at the mess table and the books slid as wildly as the plates? Sometimes on deck in his free moments he had looked up and seen the horizon melt all round into the sky, and known that it was all worth while because the firmament above and the waters under the earth met in one vast cradle in which God rocked the world. But such visionary excesses were all too likely to be disrupted by a sudden shouted command, for free time for the most junior member of the crew on a small ship was never absolute.

Things had improved after the first two years when he became first a seaman and then an able seaman and the prospect of taking his Second-Class Certificate loomed, but too often the best times to study were when the rest of the crew went ashore. Of all those early ports of call he had seen less than anyone, for he had neither time nor money to spend, and the roisterers, returning aboard, would tumble him from his bunk for the hell of it and regale him with stories of what he'd missed. He did not mind. His sights were set on a Captain's Ticket, but he had not realised it would be such a long, hard haul, never certain at the end of every voyage whether he would be taken on again. In that respect he had been lucky; even so, there had been a period of unemployment compensated only by the chance to study ashore. And then, just as he began walking out with Ailsa, came the crucial decision whether to change Lines. He would rise more quickly in the small one, but the prizes were more glittering in the premier Australasian Line.

He had changed Lines and never regretted it. The blue and gold house flag fluttered from her masthead now as the *Karachi*, rolling a little, ploughed northwards and her captain confronted a small boy, who was even now asking, 'What do you mean – before the mast?'

Angus explained and Bobby listened. Then: 'I can do what you did,' he said.

'Good for you if you can,' Angus answered, suspecting that for Bobby his mother would demand that the Royal Navy beckon: Dartmouth, the wardroom, the White Ensign of social acceptability. Still, Bobby was her son; their own son might be different . . . Sternly Angus checked his thoughts. What could he offer Cynthia but the shame of joining him in adultery? And the shame would rub off on Bobby and on their bastard. Social acceptability? A joke. Yet to part after the next few nights, to deny each other, would be self-mutilation at its worst. He knew a sudden fierce jealousy of men like Bladon who were free to offer their hearts. And an even fiercer anger, which shocked him, against those like Jamie who felt free to judge and condemn.

It was with no great sense of freedom that Edmund sought out Connie Martin after dinner that night. All day his heart had been saying, 'I have something to offer, I can ask her,' and all day his head had replied, 'What makes you think she will accept you? She has known you less than three weeks.' Connie's every glance and gesture now seemed subject to misinterpretation; her every tone rang false. Nina still retired immediately after dinner, despite entreaties from her fellow passengers to stay, so it was not difficult to get Connie alone. As she returned from making her sister comfortable, he lay in wait for her on the pretext of asking how Nina was.

'I'm not sure,' Connie answered, her face troubled. 'She won't talk and I don't know what she's thinking, though I've always known before. When she first said she wanted to be a nun I knew exactly what lay behind it, and now that she can't I think she feels she's failed Mummy in some way.'

'Perhaps you'll be able to talk her out of it.'

'I couldn't talk her out of wanting to enter. It was only when I couldn't that I realised she had to go through with it, however misguidedly, and I persuaded Daddy to agree.'

'Have you told your father what has happened?'

'I thought I'd wait until we reached England. I have so much to tell him.' She added with seeming inconsequence, 'Nina's period's late.'

'She's not necessarily pregnant,' Edmund said, heavy-hearted. 'There could be other explanations. Shock . . .'

'She's always been as regular as clockwork.'

'All the more reason why shock should throw things out.'

'Perhaps. But I'm certain she's pregnant. Oh, Edmund, what are we going to do?'

Edmund forced himself to refrain from saying, 'Marry me,' and suggested a turn on deck.

'But it's cold!'

'Put your coat on. You'll have to start getting used to England, you know.'

Connie disappeared back into her cabin, to re-emerge in an unflattering, unfashionable coat. The native tailor in Nullumpur had done his best with good material and last year's fashion magazines, but his efforts fell lamentably short. From the too-large collar Connie's face looked out, oddly pointed, as Edmund conducted her up on deck. How Anne would enjoy shopping with this girl, he reflected. At last she would have someone worthy of her taste, for his aunt made no secret of the fact that her own dumpy figure defeated her when it came to elegance. And Anne would like this girl for other reasons, just as Stafford Briscoe had done. For a moment Edmund allowed himself to dream of life as a country squire, with Briscoe for neighbour, such as he had once dreamed of with Rosemary . . .

The chill wind sweeping down the English Channel brought him back to reality. Beside him, he felt Connie shiver, and offered her his arm. He would have liked to put it round her, but he feared to scare her away. They paced the sheltered side of the deck. The few passengers doing the same smiled indulgently as they passed them. Another engagement on the way?

Edmund and Connie paced for a while in silence, he accommodating his step to hers. It was easier than he had expected: a slight shortening of his stride equalled two of her quick paces; they were never out of step. It seemed a good omen: side by side down the aisle, down the years . . . His thoughts were interrupted by Connie's voice, oddly strained.

'Edmund, may I ask you something?'

'Of course.'

'Do you believe in God?'

It was not what he had been expecting.

'Why do you ask?' he temporised.

'I just want to know.'

'I don't mean what you and Nina mean by God,' he said, thinking of the days now ten years distant when he had accompanied his parents to the village church, never dreaming that he might do otherwise. He would have said no more, but Connie's face was expectant.

'What do *you* mean by God?' she asked.

There was no escaping her. There never would be. She would force him relentlessly to assess and re-assess his every action.

He said cautiously, feeling his way through doubt and difficulty, 'I find it difficult to explain. Perhaps I mean immanence. *I see His blood upon the rose,*' he quoted, '*And in the stars the glory of His eyes. His body gleams amid eternal snows. His tears fall from the skies.*'

'Who wrote that?'

'An Irishman named Plunkett who was executed after the Easter Week Rising.'

'A Catholic?'

'I presume so.'

'Is there any more?'

They had paused and were leaning on the rail, looking out over the dark waste of waters which gleamed like coal where the ship's lights caught them.

'*All pathways by His feet are worn,*' Edmund continued. '*His strong heart stirs the ever-beating sea. His Crown of Thorns is twined with every thorn. His Cross is every tree.*'

'*His Cross is every tree,*' Connie repeated. 'I believe that too. It means you can't get away from God even if you want to.'

'You sound as if you want to get away.'

'Sometimes.' She changed the subject. 'Do you know the Irish steward's brother was killed in the Easter Week Rising?'

'No, I didn't. Is that why – No, it couldn't be.'

'What were you going to say?'

'I was wondering if that was why the Haldinghams can't bear him. But they were safe in India, and in any case they had no son to lose.'

'It worries him that they should be so hostile.'

'You must have been talking to him a lot.'

'I suppose it's because I'm half Irish. Mummy was Irish, you know. That's why Nina and I are Catholics, but Daddy says he'll always be a Prod.'

'So you're used to a mixed marriage?'

'*That* was no problem. The problem was Major Orrey.'

'I think perhaps you and Nina take that rather hard. Your mother wasn't the first woman to find a man other than her husband attractive, and she certainly won't be the last.'

'Yes, but adultery. And then to choose to die in sin.'

'Perhaps she had greater faith in God's mercy than you have.'

'I never thought of it like that. Oh, Edmund, you open my eyes to so many things. How I wish we could talk and talk and talk.'

'Why shouldn't we?'

'Because we dock the day after tomorrow and you have duties to perform.'

'But after we land. May I call on you? I should like to see you again.'

'It would be pointless.'

'You mean your aunt and uncle would disapprove? But you're of age, Connie. Now if it were Nina –'

'I only wish it were.'

'What do you mean? Connie, you must know I love you. Will you marry me?'

She allowed herself to sink against him, and this time he made sure she was in his arms, holding her like a pinioned bird whose flutterings serve to emphasise captivity.

'I couldn't speak before because I had nothing to offer you,' he went on, 'but I heard this morning that my father has just died. No – 'as she began to condole – 'he had been an invalid for a long time, and we had never got on well. He felt I'd dishonoured him by not enlisting; we hadn't spoken for years. But it doesn't alter the fact that as his only son I inherit, and I can give up going to sea. We shouldn't be rich, but I could afford to buy a practice, set up my plate and become a GP. Somewhere, I think, in the country. England is so beautiful – I can't believe you've never set eyes on it.'

He tailed off, aware of her lack of response. After a moment's hesitation he tried again.

'I know I'm not a Catholic, but that needn't matter. You can bring our children up in your faith. And you said yourself it was no problem in your parents' marriage. In a sense all marriages are mixed in that they represent the union of two very different people. And we could give Nina a home until she finds her feet. It would be better for her than staying with your aunt and uncle, and she needs you at present more than she ever did.'

Again he tailed off, aware now that she was crying.

'What is it? Have I said something to distress you?'

She shook her head, and it was as though her whole body shook.

'I've been too sudden,' he said, remorseful. 'I love you so much I thought you must surely know, but I see now that I've been presuming. All the same, now that you know I love you, do you think you could learn to love me in return?'

The violence of her embrace almost overbalanced him.

'Oh, Edmund dear, it isn't that! I love you so much already. More than anyone, more than anything in the whole world, except God.'

His heart sang. What more could a man ask?

She rushed on, unheeding. 'But I can't marry you.'

'Of course you can,' he said, preparing to dismiss some scruple, 'once you've got used to the idea.'

'No. I oughtn't to have let you ask me. Please forgive me, Edmund dear.'

'Forgive you for my loving you? You might as well ask me to forgive myself for breathing.'

'Don't say such things. You only make me feel worse.'

279

This scruple was not so easily dismissed. 'Why can't you marry me?' he probed gently. 'You're not secretly married, are you?'

'Of course not.' She managed a little laugh.

'Well then, is there someone else?' Someone perhaps in India, a child-hood sweetheart to whom she regarded herself pledged? He was certain it was no one on board, but he ought to have been less arrogant in supposing her heart-whole. She nodded, and his fears were confirmed.

'Who is it? Some boy back home?'

She looked up at him. 'That would be easy.'

'A married man?'

'No, Edmund. God.'

At first he did not understand her. How could God get in the way? *'I see His blood upon the rose . . .'* There was surely no conflict between the natural world and their love for each other, which enhanced it.

Then she said, 'I've made up my mind. I'm going to be a nun.'

'No!' His cry was one of total rejection. For an instant he was his father's son, bellowing with frustration. Then he forced himself to be calm.

'You're talking nonsense. Just because Nina can't go through with it, there's no need for you to take her place.'

'She was taking mine. Oh, she didn't know it. It's only since Mummy's death that she's truly thought she wanted to be a nun, but I've known for years that God was calling me, only I just didn't want to hear the call. Then, when Nini wanted to enter, I thought He wouldn't want us both; Nini could go and join Aunt Eileen and I could enjoy myself. It was wonderful, Edmund, while it lasted. Almost I could forget God's call, or at least hear it differently and pretend it was to marry you. I prayed it was. I want to so much, Edmund, but then when Nini couldn't enter I knew I had been wrong and this was God's way of telling me.'

'A strange interpretation of rape.'

'Please don't laugh. You can't imagine what it costs me to have to say no to you.'

'Then don't.'

'No, I must. I can hear the call so clearly, it drowns out everything else.'

'You're imagining things. You're still upset by what's happened to Nina.'

'Yes, of course I'm upset. Particularly at the thought of leaving her. As you say, she needs me more than ever now.'

'Yet you'd desert her?'

'There will be other people to help Nina. And desert is a cruel word.'

'You're right. I wanted to hurt you.'

'Only because I've hurt you. Dearest Edmund, you're the last person in the world I would have wounded. You already have enough to bear.'

But not like this, he thought. When things were bad, there was always the hope they would get better. Now, it was as though he had seen a vision of the Promised Land and then a shutter had come down, the grille of a convent, barring him from entering. He looked down at the bright face, now serious, and tried to imagine the red-gold curls shorn and covered with a veil.

'I won't let you do this,' he said. 'Your father won't let you. He wasn't willing for Nina to enter, and you're his favourite, I know.'

'But as you reminded me, I'm of age. And you needn't tell me about Daddy's feelings. I don't know how I'm going to write to him.'

'The two men you say you love, and you're prepared to hurt both of us.'

'What's the alternative? I can't marry you and turn my back on what God has planned for me.'

'I love you, Connie, I need you. Isn't that another sort of call? I won't say from God, though you could argue it that way, but at least a call of the flesh. Can you deny it? Shut yourself off from love for ever?'

He was pressing her against him as he spoke, feeling her body tremble as she sought to evade his lips. With a jerk she wrenched herself away and leaned panting on the rail beside him. They were like two adversaries.

Introibo ad altarem Dei . . . Connie forced herself to say the words under her breath for their calming influence; to remember the church in Marseilles with its padded door . . . the worn stones . . . the unending cycle of praise and prayer and praise. It was the same at home in the convent chapel: the children crowded at one end, but beyond the screen the community gathered. When had she first known her place was beyond that screen? She could not remember, and the thought was frightening. She had tried so hard to run away, telling herself it wasn't time, praying God it wasn't, that he would call her in some other way. Now the call of the flesh was urgent. She wanted nothing so much as to abandon herself to Edmund's arms, to be his wife, to bear his children, as she had begged God to let her do. Instead, her desires were a last temptation, the ultimate barrier to be overcome.

'I shan't be shutting myself off from love,' she assured Edmund, 'except in a physical sense.' (How could the denial be made to sound so easy? She forced herself to go on.) 'I shall have the love of God and of the community; of my father and Nina. I hope I shall have yours, at least in the form of your prayers.'

'I haven't prayed since the prison gates closed behind me.'

'Perhaps you might begin again, for my sake.'

'No,' he said harshly. 'This is false. You've been filled with some romantic nonsense which you ought to have outgrown with your teens. Oh, I'm not blaming you, you've led an isolated existence, you've never been out in the world – all the arguments we've been putting to Nina when we ought to have been putting them to you. But at least give yourself a chance to know what you're renouncing. Wait six months and let me see if I can make you change your mind.' Encouraged by her hesitation, he grew bolder. 'Let me show you England – Ireland too, if you want. Let me introduce you to my Aunt Anne – I know you'll love her; almost as much as she'll love you. Let me show you where we might live. A doctor's wife has a place in society, especially a titled doctor's wife. I've never mentioned it, but my father was a baronet, so you'd be Lady Bladon. You have only to say the word.'

Only say the word and my soul shall be healed . . . Regrettably, the word was still no. She had resisted the flesh, and now the world, but it seemed no cause for congratulation when she saw the misery in Edmund's eyes.

'It would be fun to have a title,' she heard herself murmur, 'but I'll have one anyway. I shall be Sister whatever the community call me. That will suit me better, I think.'

'Very well,' he said, 'I must accept your decision. Only – are you sure it's right? How do you know what God wants? Isn't it a kind of presumption for any of us to assume we know His plan?'

The flesh, the world . . . Now the Devil.

'In my case, it's a matter of faith. I can't know God's calling me, but I believe it and I must act on that belief. If I knew, it would be easier; but knowledge isn't faith. I must forsake the rational, which up to now I've tried to live by, and trust to the irrational.'

'What if it lets you down?'

'How can it? To let someone down is a rational concept, and reason has no place in faith. Which is why faith cannot fail me. I can only fail in faith.'

'You think you've got all the answers, don't you?'

'No, Edmund. I believe I have.'

'You're playing with words.'

'Because I find them inadequate. How can they not be? The poets, prophets, seers, have all fallen silent before the mystery of God.'

'Damn God!'

A soft hand covered his mouth. 'Don't, dearest. Besides, how can you curse God when He is all around you – His blood upon the rose, His Crown of Thorns in every tree?'

'Trust a woman to use my words against me.'

'Edmund, don't be angry with me. Please!'

'Don't be angry with me,' he mimicked. 'When I see you acting the fool. Wrecking your life, not to mention mine, your father's, Nina's, for the sake of a misguided fancy you persist in calling God. Why shouldn't I damn him? It relieves my feelings, and there's nothing there to damn. I'm being sacrificed to something non-existent, and by the time you discover it, it'll be too late.' He turned. 'I'd better leave you. I'm sorry if my words hurt, but the truth can be very painful. As a doctor, I know that.'

She laid a hand on his arm, but he shook it off. 'No, leave it. In a few more hours we shall be in port. It will be better if we don't meet again. I'll keep out of your way. Please try to keep out of mine.'

She gave a stricken little cry and darted away from him. He heard the clatter of her high heels on the deck. Then she was gone, and only the glinting sea kept him company, surging with the black anger in his heart.

She was wrong. He knew she was wrong. She loved him – she had admitted it. And now she was trying to deny it, like any other tricksy little bitch. Once Rosemary had said she loved him; he had believed her, and where had that led? To taunts and a ring thrown back at him. Involuntarily he raised a hand to his face. This time there was no blood because the wound went deeper, into the inmost recesses of his heart. It was a mortal wound, from which he would never recover. He would never love again.

The chill wind made him shiver. At least, he supposed it was the wind, for in the last hour the breeze had freshened and there were occasional white caps to the waves. The Bay of Biscay had been calm – so much for the fears of Florrie Gurslake, who now lay beneath its waves – but as they approached the English Channel he could feel the beginnings of the *Karachi*'s famous roll. There would be work for him by morning, consoling the seasick; work for him every morning, doling out palliatives for all humanity's ills. Not cures – that was too much to hope for, but it was occupation of a sort; something to fill the empty days ahead of him; he refused to contemplate the empty nights. It would be sufficient if he could get through this one, whose dark hours stretched dauntingly ahead. It was not yet midnight, but the ship seemed unusually quiet, just the wind, the sea, the throb of her engines – these were what filled the night. Her decks were empty, and even the lounge as he passed through it was untenanted save for a small group playing cards and Bert Gurslake, sitting alone with an empty glass in front of him, looking at nothingness.

As he passed the door to the writing-room, closed and doubtless empty too at this hour, some instinct made Edmund pause. It was an uneasy sensation that something was deeply wrong, like the moment when in a seemingly healthy body he first sensed what would bring about its end. It was too unscientific to be called diagnosis, yet it was a knowledge science would confirm. There was a faint scent too in his nostrils, a change in the air against his cheek; his ears imagined sounds too faint to be audible, yet refusing to go away. In such situations there was only one course to follow: his instinct must be put to the test. He grasped the handle of the writing-room door and made to enter, only to be beaten back by a sudden gust of flame.

The room was ablaze. In that one glimpse he could see the panelling crackling, curling. The heat seared him. It was impossible to close the door. He heard his voice cry out, feet pounding along the deck, the horrified face of a crewman, who ran to the nearest alarm. Seconds later bells jangled, whistles sounded, men materialised from nowhere as they ran to take up their stations against the dread enemy.

Fire! Fire! shrilled the alarm bells. Fire! Fire at sea!

II

The tap at the door was so gentle that it came again before Briscoe recognised it for what it was. When he did, he strode to the door of his cabin and wrenched it open.

'Am I disturbing you?' Ravi asked.

The answer was yes. Not just in the sense of an unexpected visit, but because the boy had disturbed him all along. From the moment the young stowaway had been flung to the deck before him, he had been aware of emotions that, like Maurice, were missing believed killed. He had neither welcomed nor rejected them. A passive acceptance of fate – what the Arabs called the will of Allah – was now his philosophy. Captain Meiklejohn's request to take the boy under his wing, the lowering of Ravi's own barriers, had come about without volition on his part. It had been the same with Maurice: a chance second meeting, and everything had proceeded from there.

Years later Maurice had confessed that there had been nothing accidental about that second meeting. What thought-waves, what chemical reaction, had been involved? The decision to take no action was itself a form of action. Was there such a thing as innocence? Briscoe had side-stepped that issue – he was a skilled side-stepper and his career since the war had emphasised that skill. Where Ravi was concerned, he was satisfied he had no cause to blame himself. His Highness acted of his own free will.

In that lay the gratification: all moves must be made by the other side. But the making of those moves was confirmation of his own power, and not until Maurice had been suppliant before him had Briscoe allowed himself to act. It would be the same with Ravi, but because time was shorter on the voyage, he had been more precipitate. Once or twice he had laid an arm about the boy's shoulders, just as an uncle or a father might have done; just as Barry Waterman had no doubt done many times in friendship, though without eliciting the same response. Yet what had that response amounted to? An indefinable frisson of the flesh, a shrug, a rejection that was an invitation. It was nothing. It was everything.

Nevertheless, he would have to be careful. This was no working-class boy ready to be prised from his family in exchange for a more sophisticated way of life. Ravi had been born to luxury, to wealth and inherited power. Of course the power of the Indian princes was no longer absolute, but they were not without influence, as Archie Johnson could testify. Briscoe still

285

savoured the moment of confrontation between Johnson and the Nawab's son. On the whole, he felt Ravi had emerged with dignity and courage, whereas Johnson had been shown to be a thug. It amused him to apply to the gallant captain the Indian word for a robber with violence. There were few situations in his experience to which violence was the answer, and he regarded it as a last resort. Even the war could perhaps have been averted by skilful diplomacy, but the military mind was essentially simplistic: I'll hit him before he hits me. Several times in the past few years it had taken all Briscoe's abilities to keep the army in check when local commanders were convinced that a few bullets were all that was needed to quell incipient unrest. To Briscoe this was an admission of failure: all things were negotiable, including loyalty, for which he had bargained, flattered, pleaded, that loyalty being always to the British Crown. Small wonder that His Britannic Majesty had seen fit to reward his services. It would be pleasant to be a KBE – a knight of that same newly created Order of the British Empire for which he had toiled unceasingly.

He was surprised by his own pleasure, having thought himself above such things, but now he recognised how satisfactory it was that Sir Edmund Bladon, Bt, should have as neighbour Sir Stafford Briscoe, KBE. One title inherited, one earned. Earned! He allowed himself a moment's contemplation of how pleased Jean, his sister, would be. He had written to her from Marseilles, since the overland route would be quicker. He had at first intended taking it himself, but the mystery of Nina Martin's attacker counted as unfinished business, and that was something he abhorred. Besides, there was Ravi, though he was not yet ready to admit the extent to which the young man's beauty appealed to him, preferring to think of him as one more future ruler whose allegiance needed winning, and his own actions as disinterested.

Beyond subjection, he had not worked out what he wanted from Ravi. Another Maurice-like relationship, with Ravi spending part of each year in England staying in his friend Sir Stafford Briscoe's London flat or at his country home? And was it to be a relationship between apparent equals in which his own years and eminence counterbalanced the Prince's inherited privilege and wealth, or one more befitting teacher and pupil, in which the pupil sat at the master's feet? Whatever it was, there must be no open scandal, not at least before the New Year's Honours list and the subsequent investiture – say another three months at most. During that period he must be circumspect with Ravi. Any intercession with the India Office, any word in the Resident's ear that might delay the boy's return to his father, must be seen to be solely on the young Prince's behalf.

At the same time he must bind Ravi to him, so that he too would accept the need for discretion and perhaps even enjoy the clandestine relationship. And relationship there would surely be. Yesterday he had invited the boy to his cabin to continue a discussion begun in the lounge that afternoon, and though he had not come and had offered neither excuse nor apology, Briscoe sensed anew his growing power. The tap at the door and the gentle voice asking, 'Am I disturbing you?' was confirmation of his own ascendancy, even though twenty-four hours late.

Nevertheless, he gave no hint of his exultation. 'What do you want?' he asked

'To see you, Mr Briscoe sir. May I come in?'

Stafford Briscoe held the door open. He had a moment of feeling like a flunkey as His Highness Prince Ravi stepped in, elegant as a cat and as unhurried. He was wearing the white silk trousers and the green coat embroidered in gold that he had insisted on buying in Port Said. 'You can buy anything in Port Said,' Briscoe remembered telling him, and it was very nearly true. After the essential re-stocking of shirts, trousers, under-wear and blazer, while Briscoe had been pointing out the advisability of adding a topcoat to the list, Ravi had darted away, leaving him no option but to follow, and made his way to a stall selling vividly patterned saris. Briscoe had not been pleased.

'These are for women,' he said.

'Yes, but I must have one ceremonial dress, to wear in the evenings for dinner.'

'A dinner jacket would be more suitable. Besides, you won't find any-thing at this stall.'

'The stallholder knows where I will.'

There had followed an exchange in Hindustani which Briscoe gave up following. The upshot was that they had visited another stall, where Ravi, like an excited child, had tried on outfit after outfit, asking each time, 'Do you think this one will do?' Purple, scarlet, turquoise, yellow, the green he had finally selected – Ravi had looked resplendent in them all. Briscoe's ill-humour had vanished in the face of such magnificence. Even here, in the confines of a First Class cabin, he had a regal air, despite being boyishly awkward. The costume enhanced both qualities.

'My dear boy, to what do I owe this honour, even belated?' Briscoe hooked forward a chair for his guest and perched himself on the end of the bed.

Ravi ignored the chair and stood very straight before him. 'I wish to discuss my future with you, sir.'

This was promising. 'Very well. What of your future?'

'Sir, I cannot go back to Maggapore.'

'No one has asked you to.'

'Yes, I am returning on the next ship that sails. My father has made that plain. Besides, I have no money, except what Captain Meiklejohn has lent me.'

'Let that be the least of your worries. Now tell me truthfully: why do you want to get away from Maggapore?'

'I cannot marry this fat, oily girl my father has selected.'

'Then you must tell him so.'

287

Of all the turns the conversation might have taken, Briscoe had not expected this.

'I do not wish ever to marry.'

'Never's a long time. In a year or two you will feel differently.'

'No!'

The boy's vehemence was astounding – and gratifying. Encouraged, Briscoe tried again.

'When you fall in love it will all seem different.'

'Rulers do not marry for love.'

'I did not mention marriage . . .' Briscoe paused delicately. 'There are . . . relationships . . . outside it.'

'I do not want a whore.'

'There are other . . . ladies . . . who might not be unwilling.'

Ravi looked away, picturing the erotic carvings of certain temples in which bodies were entwined like foliage in a stony thicket of sex. They stirred him, but not to thoughts of the women about his father's palace: he saw instead Dorothy Waterman. It was impossible, of course. His letters to Barry, stilted by time and distance, could say no more than, 'Please give my best wishes to your mother and sister,' but he could allow himself to dream. And since meeting Briscoe sahib, he could allow himself to dream of counsel. Briscoe sahib would know what to do.

It had taken all his courage to come to the older man's cabin, but it was difficult to find him alone. It was as though he was on the one hand ensnaring him with discourse, arguments, asides, requests for his opinion – always with an audience – and at the same time fending him off. It would have been pleasant to continue some of these conversations in private, but the longed-for invitation never came.

'I think,' he said carefully, 'that I do not understand ladies.'

'My dear boy, what man does?'

'I am sure that you, sir, understand them.'

'Perhaps. If I wanted to . . .'

'Yet you have not married.'

Briscoe was silent.

'So there is a precedent. If I do not marry, I shall be following in your footsteps.'

'I am under no dynastic obligation to wed.'

'If my country changes and men like Mr Gandhi have their way, I too shall be spared that obligation, for there will be no more ruling dynasties.'

'Do you not like women's company?'

'I like one – some – very much, but . . .'

'But you also like men's.'

'Men's company? Yes, of course.'

Ravi spoke much more positively: he felt himself on firmer ground. Apart from female servánts, his world in India was entirely male. In Maggapore women did not count; a man visited them for one purpose only;

288

he did not linger in their company. As for the ladies in First Class aboard the *Karachi*, he had avoided them, amused and flattered by the interest engendered by his looks and his title, but convinced that there was only one Englishwoman for him. With the men, it was a different matter; for the first time, he felt himself on equal terms. Even the venerable Mr Haldingham had become no more than a frail old gentleman to whom was due the respect inspired in youth by age.

'Many men prefer the company of their own sex,' Briscoe sahib was saying. 'I confess I do myself. Women – well, where should we be without them? – but for true companionship give me a man any day.'

Ravi nodded in agreement. What he felt for Dorothy Waterman was far too rarefied for daily use; it would be like, in Dorothy's family, using the best china at every meal.

'I have been fortunate in men's friendship,' he conceded. 'At school there was my friend Barry Waterman and his father, and now you, sir.'

'There's no need to keep calling me sir.'

'Oh, Mr Briscoe sir, it would seem discourteous not to do so, to one so much older and more honoured.'

It was not the response Briscoe had hoped for. Nevertheless, he said easily, 'It is one of the advantages of male friendship that age does not matter. A man who consorts with women much older or younger than himself is open to ridicule, or at least misrepresentation. Among men that need not apply. I have enjoyed your company on this voyage. I hope we may see something of each other after we disembark.'

Ravi could not believe his ears. Briscoe sahib, the admired, the mighty, was actually suggesting seeing *him*. And just at this point when it seemed likely that the fruits of all his endeavours to escape were going to be snatched away!

'I should like that, sir, but I shall be sent back to India like a – like a parcel.'

'We may be able to arrange a delay.'

'We' may be able to! Ravi listened in gratitude and astonishment as Briscoe sahib went on: 'I do not know the Resident personally, but I have connections who do. I am sure he will be willing to intercede for you with your father once he understands the facts of the case.' Or rather, provided he does not understand them, and at this distance they should not be hard to conceal. 'Of course, he – and your father – would need to be satisfied about your residence in England –'

'I shall stay with the Watermans.'

The Watermans. Always the Watermans. There was a tinge of impatience in Briscoe's tone as he said, 'A long visit might not be convenient for them. I was going to offer you the hospitality of my home.'

'But, Mr Briscoe sir, you hardly know me!'

Someone should teach the boy not to open delighted eyes like that, otherwise it would be only a matter of time before some old queen coralled him. Briscoe did not include himself. For the time being, all that mattered was that the boy should accept him as protector. *In loco parentis*, as it were.

'Sir, what is it? You are smiling.'

'May not a man smile at pleasant thoughts? I should enjoy your company, Ravi. There is so much of England that you have not seen. We might travel a little – I am sure the Resident would be glad for you to extend your knowledge of our country. And Europe you do not know at all. You should at least see the capital cities –'

'And I will show you India,' Ravi promised, carried away by the prospect. 'Not just Maggapore, but the neighbouring states where my father knows the rulers. You shall see places not normally open to an Englishman. Even the Resident has not seen some of those I will show you. The best suite in the palace at Maggapore shall be reserved for you. My father has spared no expense. The water in the fountains is perfumed. There are even –' he blushed a little – 'girls.'

'Not so fast,' Briscoe said, laughing. 'We have yet to obtain your father's consent. And since he will no doubt have cabled his instructions ahead of the *Karachi*'s arrival, that may be difficult.'

But it was a challenge. Already his mind was racing, planning each and every move in a game with a delicious prize.

'What if my father insists?' Ravi said tentatively.

Briscoe made up his mind. 'I shall escort you home.' That ought to do it. The newly knighted Sir Stafford Briscoe taking personal charge of an Indian nawab's son. Difficult to judge whether the India Office or the Nawab would be the more impressed. He might find himself in the palace at Maggapore sooner than expected, with its perfumed fountains and its girls. And its young prince, who now said wonderingly:

'You would do that – for me?'

'Yes, of course.' It was time to return the conversation to a less emotional level, but Ravi had other ideas. A tear glistened on his cheek, sweetly salt, could one but taste it . . . Before Briscoe could banish the thought, the boy was kneeling at his feet.

'Mr Briscoe sir, you are the best, the kindest –'

'Get up, Ravi.' Briscoe was kindly, but curt.

'You do not know how relieved I am, how grateful –'

'I told you to get up.'

Briscoe bent to put a hand under the boy's shoulder at the same time that Ravi half rose. Off balance, the older man swayed, reached for support and, finding none, clutched Ravi, just as Ravi, also off balance, clasped him. For a long second they stayed locked together in an unwanted, clumsy embrace, and during that time Briscoe watched, disbelieving, his cabin door swing open and a balding head peer in.

'I did knock,' said Bert Gurslake in explanation. It might or might not have been true, for neither of them had been in any state to have heard him as they battled to remain vertical.

Ravi turned, panting a little from his exertions, a fact not lost on Bert, who said, 'Good evening, Your Highness –' for once he managed the aspirate – 'sorry to break up your little tête-à-tête but I wanted a word with Mr Briscoe.'

'Well?' Briscoe was in command again now. 'What is it?'

'Begging your pardon, sir, but it might be better if we was alone.'

'I cannot imagine what you can have to say to me. I am not aware of any confidential business between us.'

'Not between *us*, no.' Bert managed a knowing wink.

'Good heavens, man, it's as clear as day –' Briscoe was angry. 'I lost my balance and His Highness saved me. I could have had a very nasty fall.'

'Still could, sir, in a manner of speaking.' The wink had become a leer. 'People have such nasty minds. If it became known you and His Highness was so friendly, they might misunderstand.'

'They would not misunderstand that this was an attempt at blackmail.'

Bert looked pained. 'Now who said anything about that?'

Briscoe cursed. It was a measure of his dismay that he had so far forgotten himself as to anticipate what the man was after. Ravi meanwhile was looking from one to the other with an air of bewilderment.

'You'd better leave us, Ravi,' Briscoe suggested.

For answer, the young Prince settled himself firmly on the cabin's one upright chair. If Briscoe sahib was coming under attack and needed a defender, he had one.

'I shall be a witness,' he announced.

Briscoe sighed. This was going to be awkward.

'Very well, stay if you must. But remember this is a matter between me and Mr Gurslake. I don't want you butting in.'

Ravi prepared to become a tower of silence, if that was what Briscoe sahib wished. He would have preferred to be an Indian ruler in his palace and order Mr Gurslake to be taken away, but he recognised that they were aboard an English vessel in English waters and this matter must be played the English way.

The English way. That of course was the trouble. Mr Gurslake was a man whom no one liked. 'Too mean to give his poor wife a proper funeral,' was what they said about him, and Ravi was sufficiently anglicised to recognise the condemnation for what it was: Not One of Us. Mr Gurslake was a social outcast – and now the outcast was calling on Briscoe sahib, who, being an English gentleman, did not instantly show him the door, but stood waiting, impassive, rising slightly on the balls of his feet like a boxer awaiting a blow.

'You had better be brief,' Briscoe sahib said to Mr Gurslake.

'Right, sir.' Mr Gurslake raised his hand; for an instant Ravi thought he was going to touch his forelock, but he fumbled in his breast pocket instead. 'I came to return a piece of your property.' He produced an envelope.

Briscoe leaned forward and saw the superscription.

'What the – Where did you get this?'

'It came into my possession.'

'You mean you stole it.'

'That's an unfounded allegation, sir.'

'It is, and I withdraw it.' Briscoe sahib resumed his boxer's stance. 'The letter is of no value to me or to anyone else, but I am grateful to you for returning it.'

Bert nodded in satisfaction. 'Thought you'd be pleased to get it back.'

'I am.' Briscoe held out his hand. 'If you will be so good . . .'

Bert said, half to himself, 'Glad to, sir. In a minute. Wouldn't do to let a letter like this get around. People have such nasty minds, like I was saying. Seem to want to assume the worst.'

He was enjoying himself watching the impassive face opposite, behind which he guessed emotions were a-swirl. It wasn't often he'd had a nob on the run. Only once before had it happened, and that was during the war, when he had discovered that only two-thirds of a war supplies contract was being delivered, although it was paid for in full. The man concerned had been more than ready to keep things quiet – he was Lord Something-or-other now. And then the bastard had shopped him, Bert, for a similar kind of transaction, only on an infinitesimal scale. The injustice of it still rankled: forced to quit his country by someone ten times guiltier than he. It was one more thing to hold against this race of aliens who spoke as if they had a hot potato in their mouths, were polite but laughing at you behind their politeness, and weren't no better nor anybody else. This Mr Briscoe, for instance: even the Captain kowtowed a bit to him, and all the time he was trying to bugger the nancy-boy princeling. Looked as if he might be succeeding, too. Lost his balance, had he? 'His Highness saved me from a very nasty fall' – Bert mimicked the words to himself. 'Course they'd deny it, but the contents of that envelope was something they couldn't explain away.

'A letter like this,' Bert went on, tapping the envelope, 'could do you and His Highness here a lot of harm.'

'Leave the boy out of it.'

'I only wish I could, sir, but it's addressed to him.'

Ravi half rose. 'You wrote to me?' he said wonderingly, his face suffused with joy.

Briscoe dismissed it as 'no more than a note suggesting we should continue one of our discussions'. The boy should know better than to let his feelings show like that. At another time such frankness might have been welcome, but at present it was an embarrassment and so was Ravi. He said again, 'Dear boy, I think you ought to go.'

His use of the affectionate form of address was deliberate; he was going to show Bert Gurslake that Stafford Briscoe had nothing to hide. Nevertheless, what the devil had he said in that hastily penned note which the little runt had obviously got hold of and which Ravi as obviously had never received? He knew a moment's pleasure because it explained why the

292

invitation had not been accepted: the boy was not avoiding him, as he had feared. All the same, at the moment his absence was more desirable than his presence. He made a move to open the cabin door.

'Wouldn't it be better if His Highness here stayed,' Bert suggested, 'seeing as this concerns him too?'

If one of 'em wouldn't pay up, the other might do. They had enough between them not to notice a few hundred quid. Sure enough, the nancy-boy now addressed him.

'What did Mr Briscoe say?'

Bert unfolded a piece of ship's notepaper from the envelope with its boldly written address. He had to hold it at arm's length to read it, but he did so confidently enough.

' "Dear Ravi, I greatly enjoyed our conversation this afternoon in which you expressed yourself so frankly. I am glad you were able to be so open about what you felt. Perhaps you will give me the pleasure of continuing it sometime in my cabin, where we are unlikely to be disturbed. If so, may I suggest this evening –" '

At that point the paper was plucked from his hand, and he found himself looking up at Stafford Briscoe, whose mouth was folded in on itself in a grim line. The cabin doorway gaped before him. There was a hand on his collar. A voice in his ear said, 'Out!'

Bert squinted up at his captor.

' 'Course *I* know that letter don't mean nothing more than it says, sir, but other people mightn't.'

'When do you think they're going to have the chance to see it?'

'When I show it to them, o' course. That's only a copy you're holding. If you thought I'd brought the original with me, you must be as daft as you're queer.'

It was true it was only a copy. Glancing at it, Briscoe saw Bert Gurslake's scrawl instead of his own elegant copperplate. Never under-estimate an adversary. He had broken one of his own rules. It could prove a costly mistake.

He did some rapid calculations. A sum of money against his knighthood and reputation, and his sister's peace of mind. The letter was at worst ambiguous; not even the gutter press would dare to publish it, but circulated in the right quarters it could effectively damage his career. There were always those jealous enough to use it, to pass on its contents by word of mouth, and His Majesty was known to have strict views on what he was pleased to call purity: he would not knowingly knight a tainted man. As for the burgeoning relationship with Ravi, that would have to be forgone – unless it were possible to negotiate, distasteful though that might seem . . .

'What did you hope to get by showing me this letter?' he asked, still holding Bert in front of him.

'A thousand quid,' Bert muttered.

'I'd need the original for that.'

' 'Course you would.' Bert's teeth stopped chattering. The poker-faced bastard was going to do a deal. All that high-mindedness and indignation didn't count for nothing when they saw you meant business and that business was a thousand quid. How Florrie'd laugh when he told her. He remembered suddenly that Florrie wasn't there.

'I'd need cash,' he added.

'That might be difficult. I can't immediately dispose of such a sum.'

'I couldn't let it go against a cheque, sir.' None knew better than Bert Gurslake how easily a cheque could be stopped.

'Then it will have to be a transaction after we're in port.'

Bert tightened the screw a little. 'I'm sure a gent like you could raise cash if he tried.'

'Where? I doubt if even the Purser has such a sum available, especially at the end of a voyage.'

'Too bad.' Old poker-face was sweating . . .

'Perhaps a sum on account . . .'

'In full, sir, please.'

'What's the alternative?'

Bert had not stopped to think any more than he had of the difficulties of raising cash aboard a liner, but he hoped it didn't show.

'I'll take to it the newspapers,' he said glibly.

'They won't publish it. And they won't pay a thousand pounds.'

But they would see it as the start of a campaign of innuendo. 'Mr Stafford Briscoe and his young friend, Prince Ravi of Maggapore, attending a first night . . . relaxing on the Riviera . . . returning home after their tour . . . Mr Briscoe and His Highness first met aboard the SS *Karachi*, when the Prince dramatically stowed away.' Or: 'His Highness Prince Ravi of Maggapore, who is staying with his friend Mr Stafford Briscoe at Mr Briscoe's Gloucestershire home.' It would never be Sir Stafford Briscoe. His years of service to the Crown would go for naught. Of course he'd have a word where it mattered, call in past favours: he was not without influence. But he realised too late that he had no friends because since Maurice he had avoided friendship. There was no one who would spring to his defence.

But there was. Ravi rose from his chair in a single fluid movement and fumbled at his cummerbund. A slim brown hand held out something that flashed and glinted even in the cabin's dim light.

'I suggest you take this, Mr Gurslake. It is worth much more than a thousand pounds.'

In his hand lay the jewelled dagger that Briscoe had last seen beside him on the deck.

'The Captain returned it to me,' Ravi said in explanation. 'He said my costume needed it.'

'It does. You mustn't part with it.'

'I'm only offering it as a pledge. Until you can raise the money.'

Bert licked his lips. 'It's a fair offer, sir.'

The dagger's hilt glistened with diamonds. A single emerald glowed like grass-green fire. Rubies like blood drops dripped towards the point. It was worth a fortune, quite apart from its historic worth.

Flushed with gratification at the success of his gesture, Ravi turned to Briscoe sahib. 'He cannot hurt you now.'

'Then he had better leave us.'

This time when the door was opened, Bert did not linger to hear old poker-face say, 'Out!' It had worked. In his hands was more money than he had ever hoped for. He'd be daft to hold it as a pledge for a thousand quid. In the right quarter it would be worth more than that, even at the price paid by fences. He could pay off the Consolidated Finance Company's agents and still have something to spare. Under his coat Bert clutched the dagger to him, and tried not to swagger as he walked.

In the cabin Briscoe faced Ravi.

'Why the hell did you do that?'

'He was threatening you. Because of me.' (Why was Briscoe sahib angry?)

'He was threatening me. Not you.'

'But, Mr Briscoe sir, you have befriended me. I wish only to repay.'

'And you choose to do so with a valuable item which is easily identifiable. Gurslake need only show that dagger for it to amount to an admission of guilt. Why else would you have given it to him?'

'I wanted to help you.'

'I told you when you insisted on staying that I didn't want you butting in.'

The bitterness that welled in Stafford Briscoe was the greater because he knew his defeat to be undeserved. He had trusted in his sharp wits, in his skill in negotiation which had brought him through more ticklish situations than this, and it had all been brought to naught by Ravi's inexperience and folly. Maurice would never have done such a thing.

'Should I ever require your help in the future,' Briscoe said, making it sound unlikely, 'I am capable of requesting it. Until then, I should be grateful if you would refrain from interfering in my business. As in this case, your intervention can only make things worse.'

Ravi's eyes filled with tears. Briscoe sahib was angry and he had sought only to be of use. He had given his most precious possession, and his action was resented. So much so that he was convinced Briscoe sahib would never now intercede over his return home, his marriage, his reunion with Dorothy Waterman; would never now sit in the court of the fountains in the palace at Maggapore. The friendship which had meant so much was being withdrawn, English fashion, in an atmosphere of increasing chill.

'I shall respect your wishes, Mr Briscoe sir,' Ravi said with what dignity he could manage, reminding himself that he was an Indian prince.

'Then why the hell couldn't you have done so this time?'

Dignity fled before the truth.

'Because I love you,' Ravi said, catching his breath in wonderment at the discovery.

Briscoe too caught his breath. The boy had Maurice's eyes, Maurice's slim brown body, but there the resemblance was at an end. On his lips the desired avowal, once sought, was a parody. Worse, an obscenity. For this he had jeopardised a knighthood, his future, his reputation. All of a sudden, Stafford Briscoe lost control. His hand came up, and for an instant he was aware of the thrill of contact against the satin cheek before the sound of the slap was drowned by a voice he did not recognise.

'You little brown bugger, get out!'

For an instant Ravi stood motionless. Then he stumbled out, blinded by tears.

Briscoe also stood motionless, feeling the unfamiliar jerk on his strings. Circumstance – or fate – pulls all our strings, old Haldingham had said, and now it was his turn to be manipulated, to discover depths to which he had not known he could sink. He was still lost in contemplation of their fathomless immensity when bells and whistles split the night in a jangling and a shrilling such as he had never heard before, though like all passengers he knew what they signalled: Fire! Fire! Fire at sea!

Bobby Vane sat bolt upright in bed and looked about him. He had been deeply asleep and something – he did not know what – had wakened him. As always, he was instantly, fully alert.

It was never quite dark in the cabin. There was always a line of light under the door from the corridor where all-night lamps were burning. The porthole sometimes showed a star, and sometimes at the beginning of the voyage it had shown the phosphorescence of tropical waters, but tonight it was unremittingly dark, and the motion of the ship seemed more noticeable even when you were lying down. Captain Meiklejohn had told him that the Channel could be choppy – 'like a nagging wife who scolds you for leaving her and scolds you yet again for coming home.' 'Does *your* wife nag?' Bobby had asked, and the Captain had answered, 'No, laddie,' before Bobby's scandalised mother could say, 'Hush!' 'I do apologise for my son,' she said, turning great eyes on the Captain. The last thing she wanted was for him to remember he had a wife. But he only smiled, shook his head, and said, 'The lad does well to remind me.' Bobby had felt vindicated.

Now he looked at his mother's bed. It was empty, as he had known it would be, though he switched on the bedside light to make sure. After she came to bed he would lie simulating sleep and watch between lowered lashes as she removed her make-up and brushed out her hair, before disappearing into the bathroom to emerge later in clouds of scented steam and the rose-patterned peignoir whose sash fastened in a great bow not unlike a blossom nestling against her left hip. After that, for the first few nights of the voyage, she had climbed into bed, whispered goodnight – he carefully didn't answer – sighed, and turned out the light. But recently she had been much concerned to discover if he was asleep before switching out the light from the door and slipping into the corridor, leaving Bobby alone. Towards morning she returned, though he never heard her, but when he awoke she was there. 'Where have you been?' he asked once, drowsy, but she didn't answer and if she had she would only have said, 'Little boys mustn't ask questions,' which was what she always said when she did not want to answer them.

Bobby had early learned that answers were best obtained by observation and deduction, though his two and two did not always add up to four; but they made somewhere near it, and to an eight-year-old not good at arithmetic, somewhere near was enough. Besides, from now on he was going to be good at arithmetic; a captain had to be. Captain Meiklejohn had explained that he needed to be able to plot a course, work out times and speeds and distance, and still make allowance for the sea. 'The sea's the incalculable,' he had explained only yesterday. 'She's like a woman. Everything else you can predict, but the sea has her squalls and tantrums, her contrary winds and tides. Sometimes she does all she can to hinder you, and then, just as you resign yourself to a late arrival, she fairly pushes you into port.' – 'Are we on time this voyage?' someone asked him. – 'So far. We should make Tilbury tomorrow night.'

There was general satisfaction. Everyone was growing a little tired of the ship, especially now that it was no longer pleasant on deck, the dining saloon was depleted, and more and more passengers were cabin-bound. Bobby wasn't, and nor was his mother. 'Born sailors, both of us,' she laughed, with a quick look in the Captain's direction to see if he had heard her, which he undoubtedly had. The Captain was important to his mother, Bobby had discovered; she liked to talk of him. Not that she ever said much: 'The Captain thinks . . .' 'Captain Meiklejohn was telling me . . .' but his name was often on her lips, and there was a brightness in her eye as though she were perpetually smiling at something which Bobby couldn't see. She hummed a little tune too, under her breath, as she moved about the cabin; she had been humming it last night. 'What is it?' Bobby had asked. 'Just something from an old musical,' she answered; and went on humming 'Lady, Be Good'.

Did Bobby know? Cynthia sometimes asked herself. He couldn't, could he? Nobody knew where she went. Of course the stewardess was aware of her nocturnal expeditions and lay in wait for her in the mornings with a knowing smile. Doubtless the woman expected a fat tip for her discretion, but what had she got to be discreet about? There were others who also wandered the ship's corridors at night and emerged from the wrong cabins. The difference was that they did not emerge from the cabin of Captain Angus Meiklejohn.

Angus was waiting for her as usual when she opened his unlocked door. In a trice he was beside her, locking it after her, and then she was in his arms. The smell of him; the hard muscles of his arms and shoulders now a-quiver; his face, freshly shaved, hungrily demanding hers. He was husband, father, brother, even father-in-law, rolled into a mighty One. When they moved towards the bed she did not know if she led or followed; the rose-printed peignoir lay tumbled on the floor together with her slippers, and his hands, strong, a little stiffened, were on her body rousing it to unsuspected frenzies of desire. She was aware of the narrowness of the bed, of the ship ploughing steadily beneath them, of the bells for the changing of the watch, but they were all subsumed in Angus, part of Angus, which made this experience unique. Sometimes at the height of ecstasy she thought of Robert. If he could see her now! But there was no disloyalty; the ecstasy would have been his if he had not forsaken her; he was with her still, but in another form.

She never asked Angus if he loved her. The word seemed inappropriate. Love was something at once particular and universal, spreading out from one relationship to embrace the whole of mankind. But from her relationship with Angus there were no waves outwards, only an ever-deepening inward turning until at last she was completely fulfilled. And if I have a child? The thought recurred often. She knew Angus craved a son, another Andrew with all his promise unblighted – but she, what did she crave? Wasn't it the security of having Angus beside her, the child (together with Bobby, of course) bonding them with a hoop of steel strong enough to resist whatever magnetic pull might be exerted by the woman and her son in Aberdeen? If Angus leaves me I cannot bear it. That thought also recurred. But why should he leave her when she could draw forth his very essence as they lay locked together in his bed?

Yet he was the one to remember time and duty, to indicate that she should go. Sometimes, stealing through deserted pre-dawn corridors, she wondered if he thought of her as a whore. Or even as a light woman. He had used the phrase in jest when he had swept her up in his arms on the occasion of her first visit and laid her down on the bed. 'Who'd have thought ye were such a light woman?' And then: 'In the physical sense, of course.' But the other had occurred to him, however briefly. Would it vanish if she were heavy with child? 'Would you like a little brother?' she had once asked Bobby, and been daunted by his uncompromising 'No!'

'But you'd like a father like the Captain, wouldn't you?' she'd persisted.

'I'm going to be a captain when I grow up. So I shall go away to school like you want me to because I have tickets to get. First a mate's, then a master's, and it takes years and years and years.'

'That's wonderful, darling,' Cynthia said thankfully. (When had Angus found time to indoctrinate the boy?) 'We haven't had a sea captain before in the family.' If he couldn't inherit land, he could the sea; Robert's rolling green Lincolnshire acres could become the oceans of the world, and his son – her son – could rule the one from a bridge as surely as they had once intended he should rule the other from the estate office of the Big House. She wondered for a moment what they would say at Robert's old school on learning that his son wished to enter the Merchant, not the Royal, Navy, but there was time to think of that. And Angus would help. He'd have to. Provided Angus was there . . .

Unknown to her, at this instant Bobby was finding the idea of being captain of a liner less than attractive. He was well and truly lost in an unfamiliar part of the ship, and the fact that it was entirely his own fault did not make it any more comforting. He could not have said what had prompted him to follow his mother that evening, except that they would soon be docking at Tilbury and his curiosity had become too great to bear. She was *his* mother and no one else's, and he had a right to know where she went. So almost before the cabin door had closed behind her he was out of bed and opening it again. Yes, there she was just disappearing round the corner. He ran lightly down the corridor. The stewardess did not hear him – she was not expecting a second click of the door – and by the time she next looked out he had vanished in pursuit of that figure who seemed anxious not to be noticed and, on hearing the approach of late retirers, shrank back against the wall.

Bobby too shrank back, but when he allowed himself to move forward, his mother was out of sight. Where had she gone? The companionway before him led up, but also down. Upwards led to the bridge; she wouldn't be going there – it was prohibited to passengers. Bobby decided to go down.

He hurried faster and faster, but there was no sign of her. The corridors with their grey carpeting were identical to those he had already left. Perhaps she had gone back to their cabin; she would be worried if he wasn't there. In panic, he tried the handle of a cabin occupying the same position but on this lower corridor. It was locked, and a voice cried out, 'Who's there?' Any moment the stewardess would come and he would be scolded. Captain Meiklejohn might get to know; he would be reprimanded. He turned blindly to the right. The carpeting ceased at the next corner. He turned right, and right again, but instead of coming back to the central staircase, he found himself confronted by narrow iron steps leading downwards. There was a chain across the top and a notice saying 'No Admittance', but by now he was too frightened to care. He ducked under the chain and began the descent headlong, not considering where he was going, or why.

It was hot down here. His dressing-gown seemed suddenly stifling. Sweat was breaking out on his face. He could feel it gathering in his eyebrows, as it had done in India, and trickling down his nose and chin. People would think he was crying – if he met anyone, that is. The thought of this humiliation provoked the tears he so dreaded, and he was obliged to halt long enough to sniff. If only his mother would come! She couldn't have come this way, she would never have ducked under that chain, but at successive levels there were galleries leading left and right, any one of which might contain her. Despite the heat, Bobby began to run.

He did not know where he was or where he was going. He knew only that he had to run as though the Devil himself were behind him, black and squat against the flames of Hell. He turned a corner, and there was the Devil in front of him, arms held wide to bar his passage and enfold him in a lethal embrace. Bobby had not enough breath left to scream. He halted, panting. The Devil stepped towards him and smiled. His teeth were very white against his dark skin – black with coal dust, Bobby saw, but brown beneath it. He was naked save for canvas shoes and a loincloth. The sweat made patterns in the blackness of his face and chest. His hands were strong on the child's shoulders as he swung him round and began pushing him ahead of him in the direction from which he had sprung. They turned into a doorway, a concealed side turning. The heat had become intense and there was smoke – the light had become much dimmer and Bobby could feel a rasping in the back of his throat. The shoulders of his dressing-gown were filthy where the Devil gripped him. He wanted very much to cry, but his earlier tears had dried and stiffened, as much from fright as from heat.

In front of him the Devil capered in exultation as he pointed to a massive steel door which closed off the side turning ahead of them, forming a cul-de-sac. Bobby did not realise it, but it was the entrance to a bunker where coal for the furnace was stored. It was in fact the reserve bunker, for use in emergency, for near the end of her voyage the *Karachi* had devoured most of the coal taken on at Aden, and this was the only bunker still full. The man capering in front of it, who was no less frightening for having become recognisably human, seemed intent on saying something Bobby only half understood. 'Fire – burn!' He rubbed his hands gleefully. 'Burn ship.' Unexpectedly he spat, the gob sizzling on the hot firedoor. 'All burn.' He spread his arms again.

Suddenly Bobby realised what the man was saying. The *Karachi* was on fire and they would all burn – or drown. Unless someone told Captain Meiklejohn. He must tell the Captain at all costs. He turned and ran, gasping with fright and heat, not knowing where he was going so long as it was away from the fire. He dared not look round in case the Devil-figure was behind him, its hands reaching once again to grab. The corridors and companionways seemed endless. The heat followed him, or else he generated his own. His throat was still rasping, and he had no breath to tell his tidings, even had there been anyone to tell.

With a sob of relief he felt carpet beneath his feet once more and realised he was back in the passengers' quarters, but he did not recognise these doors. Behind them everyone was asleep, and beneath them the ship was burning, a great orange-gold cavern spreading wider and higher, devouring her very heart. And the Captain did not know. He had to tell the Captain, despite the stitch in his side which made him pause at the foot of yet another companionway, whose top was out of sight. He took a deep breath and pressed a hand to his side to still the stabbing – and suddenly pandemonium broke out. Bells ringing, whistles shrilling, doors opening, startled faces . . . 'What is it? What's the matter?' A steward hurried past looking scared. 'Is it a fire drill? At this hour?' – 'No, madam, it's the real thing. I'm afraid. Please get your life-jacket and go to your lifeboat station.' – 'Is the ship going down?' – 'No, sir, but passengers are asked to assemble on deck for safety.' The steward, an unfamiliar one, caught sight of Bobby and turned. 'Get your life-jacket, sonny. You know your boat station, don't you?' Bobby nodded, too scared to admit he did not. He knew the way from his own cabin, but this region was unfamiliar. Nevertheless, he was glad to dart away as the steward addressed other passengers: 'Yes, sir, I should take a coat with you . . . No, madam, not a suitcase . . . Excuse me, sir, the life-jacket goes over the head . . .'

And as the frightened, sleepy people began to mill about, shocked into a semi-awareness of danger, the jangling bells kept up their message: Fire! Fire! Fire at sea!

John Joseph Fitzgerald was off duty. This time tomorrow night the *Karachi* would have docked and his first voyage would be over. He had been to Bombay and back. He did not actually feel any different for having seen places that from Munster Street, Dublin, would have seemed impossibly far, but his head was a kaleidoscope of impressions which he hoped would some day fall into place. Yet the recollection of individual passengers on the outward voyage was already fading. Was this something that always occurred? He must ask Dr Bladon, also making his first voyage, if he too found that a face you thought you would remember for ever was now no more than a blob attached to a name. Would it be the same with passengers on this homeward voyage? Surely not; there were some who would stand out. First and foremost, the stowaway – His Highness, as he must now call the boy who had pleaded for water in the darkness of the boat deck. John Joseph had glimpsed him earlier this evening in all the silken glory of his gold and emerald coat, the dagger that had clattered to the deck when Third Officer Strode leapt upon him now thrust jauntily into his cummerbund. He was a handsome lad; the girls would have looked twice at him in Dublin as surely as they must have done in Maggapore, only he had no eyes for anyone except Mr Stafford Briscoe, who was someone else John Joseph hoped not to forget. The patrician features, the cool assessment of everything around him, the hawklike turn of the head – if anyone could discover who had attacked Miss Nina Martin it must be this man, yet the rapist was still at large. John Joseph's fists clenched. If he could only lay hands on him! And Miss Nina going for a nun. She should have been as sacred as if her vows were already taken, and no one could say they didn't know, what with Miss Con announcing it at the dinner table, shocking these Prods who did not understand that to be chosen by Our Lord was to be highly favoured, as once His Holy Mother had been. And anyone could see why He would have chosen Miss Nina with her gentleness and piety, whereas if it had been Miss Connie . . . Yet they said it was often the unlikely ones He chose. Like Ellen. Who would have believed the deaths of Kieron and Bart Collins would have changed her so utterly, Ellen the most outspoken and irreverent of them all? John Joseph prayed for her every Sunday at Mass, as he knew she prayed for him, but the years had not succeeded in imposing the image of a holy woman on the sister he and Kieron

301

had most loved. But at least Ellen had been able to enter upon her chosen life, whereas Miss Nina now wandered the ship like a ghost, avoiding all company save Miss Connie's, her waxen face seeming drained of life and blood. 'It will take another shock to jerk her back to reality,' Dr Bladon had said when John Joseph confided to him his disquiet, 'and it might just as easily send her over the edge. I suppose you pray for her?' John Joseph nodded. 'Then that's as much as any of us can do.'

One thing John Joseph was sure of: he would not forget Edmund Bladon, to whose continued presence on the ship he had looked forward and who instead was returning to the life of an English titled gentleman. The news had soon spread among the First Class passengers that he had inherited a baronetcy, and they were divided between those – mostly women – who felt that this made up for any deficiencies in his war record and ensured that he could not be Nina Martin's rapist, and those – mostly men – who did not. John Joseph did not care about the war record and he knew better than anyone else on board the *Karachi* that Edmund Bladon had been otherwise occupied at the time of the rape. Miss Connie must know it too, for it was unthinkable that if she didn't her face would light up in his presence, as though someone had lit a candle before a holy statue in church. Perhaps now the doctor would ask her to marry him. Fellow stewards had told John Joseph that there was usually one engagement announced on every voyage, and it would have been pleasant to have something better to remember than that between Captain Archibald Johnson, M C, and Miss Imogen Stiles. Not that he had anything against Miss Stiles except that she was dull and plain and haughty, but against Archie Johnson the tally was already long. John Joseph almost regretted the ending of the civil war in Ireland, for it would be good to think of Captain Johnson caught in an ambush or summarily executed for the crimes he would undoubtedly commit. Kieron would sleep the sounder for knowing there was one less casual life-taker in the world. Perhaps in Palestine, or wherever else fate might take the gallant captain, there would be a bullet awaiting him. The pity of it was that there would be no knowing. Once disembarked, the passengers would go their separate ways, and though some of those who administered and controlled the King's Indian Empire might someday sail with them again, the majority would scatter into so many unfinished stories, in which the voyage was no more than an interlude.

Like the Haldinghams. He would never now know why they hated him, John Joseph realised with regret. He had no hope of cancelling out their hatred, but he ached to know its cause. What could this aged couple who had spent all their lives in a remote region of India have against an Irish steward? They had never set foot in Ireland. They had no sons whom the Troubles might have harmed. Yet he could not forget the horror in the old lady's eyes as she turned away from him, nor the protective arm which the old gentleman interposed as though to shield her from the Irishman who sought only to serve.

Meanwhile the problem of Christmas and where to spend it had to be overcome. He could not afford the fare home to Dublin, which left no alternative but to rent a room or take refuge in a seamen's hostel, and neither prospect appealed. At home they would all crowd into the house in Munster Street, whose walls seemed elastic for that day. His sisters and their husbands, the steadily increasing tribe of nieces and nephews, Mam flustered and happy, Da dispensing drink with a generous hand. Those who couldn't cram into the front room piled into the back room; there was a steady procession to the outside lavatory; and then at some moment in the festivities there would come a silence, unheralded, unrequested, and eyes would turn to the photographs on the wall: Kieron with the sash of the Irish Republican Brotherhood; Ellen – that last photograph, taken in a studio – seated, eyes downcast, gazing at the crucifix in her lap. Look up, Ellen, and smile, for that's how I remember you, John Joseph wanted to say; but his mother's and sisters' tears, the masculine clearing of throats with his father loudest, froze the words on his lips. In her convent in Connaught Sister Mary Bernadette doubtless prayed for them among her sisters, and in Paradise (for surely he was released from Purgatory by this time) Kieron looked down and did the same. Happy Christmas, Ellen. Happy Christmas, Kieron. I shall never see you in this life again.

John Joseph pulled himself up as if he were indeed at home sharing the family Christmas. It was time he went below. He had come up on deck for a breath of air and to escape Preston's offensive presence, but the wind was keen and his overcoat proving thin. Most passengers had already retired. There was an air of packing and suppressed bustle common to the end of a voyage but new to John Joseph, whose own neatly stowed belongings had not been augmented by a single souvenir; whereas Preston seemed to have half the gaudier trappings of the East thrust in among the white shirts, underpants and dark socks, of which he had a generous supply. 'Never know when you might strike it lucky and need to impress a lady,' he confided, implying that on this voyage once again he had. John Joseph listened and said nothing. He would have loved to cast Preston as Nina Martin's attacker, but he did not see how it could be, when they had both been serving in the bar that evening. Which brought him up against the Great Moral Problem of Edmund Bladon and what he ought to do, for by confessing to Captain Meiklejohn his own role in sustaining the stowaway and Edmund's assistance, he could clear the surgeon of any suspicion of rape. Yet Edmund forbade it, saying, 'I've already resigned for personal reasons and am leaving at the end of the voyage, but if you admit breaking the rules by aiding a stowaway they'll have to dismiss you, and neither Ravi nor I will be able to intervene. You need the job. Hang on to it. You'd be a fool to throw it away, especially when it can do you no good. It's all rumour. I haven't been formally accused.'

This was true, but John Joseph knew of the rumours and they disturbed him. It was all very well for Miss Connie to make plain that she discounted them, for Miss Nina to continue to consult the doctor – they were dismissed as naïve. Popular opinion had cast the doctor as villain, and was intent on exploiting it. John Joseph tried not to hear the smothered asides in the bar, the more open remarks when ladies were not present, but could not shut them out. It was in his power to scotch them. Ought he to keep silent, as the surgeon said?

He was brooding on this when he turned a corner and saw Nina Martin gazing out to sea. For an instant he did not recognise her, she looked so different. His second thought was: how did you get here? Nina had strayed far from the First Class quarters and was in a part of the ship reserved for crew. Was she meeting someone? Was that why her hair was swept up in a great coil at the back of her head, accentuating her pure profile? In the dim deck lights she was all pale face and pale hair above some dark garment. Perhaps it was the changed hairstyle, but her face looked strangely at peace. It was as John Joseph first remembered it, when he had been struck by the luminous quality that seemed to emanate from her skin.

He said, 'Good night, now,' and made to hurry past, having decided against offering to escort her back to First Class in case it seemed too much like a rebuke. To his surprise, she turned round.

'Are you in a hurry? I wanted to thank you, Joe, for your kindness and – and sympathy.'

' 'Twas nothing, miss, nothing at all. Every gentleman on board would like to see the madman who attacked you safely behind bars.'

'Please –' she held up her hand – 'I don't want to talk about it; it's behind me. The future matters more than the past.'

'I'm glad you feel that way, miss. We've all grieved for you.' Curiosity overcame John Joseph. 'What'll you be doing, may I ask?'

'I don't know – beyond being bridesmaid to my sister.'

' 'Tis engaged they are, then – she and the doctor?'

'They will be by the end of the voyage.'

'He's a lucky man – and she a lucky woman.'

'No more than she deserves to be. I'm the lucky one, to have such a sister.'

'Miss Con would never let you get away with that.'

'But she isn't here, is she? I'm my own woman now.'

It was true. John Joseph felt it. The girl beside him had in some mysterious way grown up. Her composure was that of womanhood, not innocence. He smiled in acknowledgement of the fact.

The answering smile that lit her face stayed in his mind long after he had turned the corner and made his way to the lower decks. Miss Nina, thank God, was emerging from nightmare, and there was nothing more to fear. She would be all right. She had come to terms with what had happened, Mary Mother of mercy be praised, and whatever the future held John Joseph, never a betting man, would have taken a wager she wouldn't be her own woman for long. Some man would claim her – may he be a good one. May she know the happiness of being a wife –

The alarm bells ringing blasted his thoughts and brought him to a standstill. Now whistles shrieked as well. It was the signal dinned into even the newest member of the ship's company as one of emergency. Fire! Fire! Fire at sea!

It was true Nina Martin was at peace. She recognised it as someone swimming against a current recognises when he is no longer in its grip, when his actions produce expected consequences and he is once again in control. No doubt the sense of destiny not being a blind force had been growing quietly within her, but she could pinpoint the moment when she had first become aware of it.

It had been at sunset this same evening when the sky was ragged and stormy and the sinking sun sent shafts of light over choppy seas. She was on the First Class deck where she should be, not hidden away as now, when she had become aware of Third Officer Strode beside her, pointing.

'Your first sight of England, Miss Nina.'

England! That grey blur on the horizon that she couldn't be sure wasn't cloud.

'Are you certain?'

'Yes, miss. The bridge reported it just as I was coming off watch.'

So it was official, and this was her first sight of the country from which Daddy had come out long ago, with his Irish bride clinging to him and laughing because he loved her so. Nina could not have said why that picture flashed into her mind, but she knew as clearly as if she had been present that that was how it had been. And now Mummy was dead, she had died in sin, refusing confession and absolution, and Daddy was all alone. With that first sight of her own country a number of things became clear in Nina's mind: Connie's half-hints, her father's silences – of course it was Major Orrey to whom they both referred. Mummy had loved him! Nina gave a little shudder compounded of shock and distaste, for she had never cared for the handsome officer with his impudent dark eyes. How Mummy must have grieved when her younger daughter reported seeing him out riding with a girl fresh out from England. No wonder Con and Daddy had shut her up. What a fool that younger daughter had been. But then, she was her mother's daughter, and her mother too had been a fool.

The heresy was so enormous that it took some time to sink in, during which Third Officer Strode explained that what she was seeing was the south-west tip of Cornwall, a little to the east of Land's End. Land's End – or in this case, Land's Beginning, the start of a new life, new in a way she had not expected, for now, like Connie, she would have to find a job – if Connie did not marry Edmund. There would be so much explaining to do. What would Aunt Eileen – Mother Imelda, that is – say when she told her? What would Daddy say?

He'd be pleased, of course – pleased that she was not to enter and that Connie was marrying a good man. My sister, Lady Bladon – Nina tried the

305

words cautiously. She need not tell her father the reason for her own change of plan. He would be only too thankful that she had changed her mind and would assume that common sense had prevailed; either that or that he had been right in insisting that she should first have a good time, know what she was giving up – though he could not have foreseen that she would have such a brutal introduction to the passion for which her mother had died.

Because that had been the most troubling thing about it. Despite the fear and pain and degradation, a spark of pleasure had been struck which not all the remorseful sessions on her knees had been able to smother, any more than confession would extinguish it. The woman within her was aware that the experience to which she had been subjected was a travesty of what it should have been, but it was that woman within her, only now awakening, who was responsible for Nina's calm. She had experienced desire, but in circumstances so shaming that she was only just beginning to admit it, convinced that her mother at least would have understood.

You are your mother's daughter. There was a new meaning to those words, because it was of Con, who looked so like her, that they had always been said in the past. Whereas I was the holy innocent, Nina thought with a tinge of amusement, whom Mrs Major Barrett and Mrs Magistrate Beer could not believe 'the gay Mrs Martin' had bred. And what an innocent – though I wouldn't say I was holy; I just pretended I was. And Reverend Mother saw through that game of make-believe. No wonder she urged me to pray. No wonder I found prayer such a burden. You can fool yourself; you can even fool other people; but you can't – ever – fool God.

O my God, I am heartily sorry . . . The act of contrition came tripping to her tongue, but it was contrition for her own self-deception, now so cruelly exposed. Yet could there have been any painless way of eradicating something so deeply ingrained? Is it possible I ought to be thankful I was raped? Nina wondered. And then: What if I have a child?

She was overdue by more than a week – she who had always been so regular. Already she believed her breasts were tender, which Con said was one of the signs. But such an arch self-deceiver as she was might easily imagine it. There was a new life to which she was going. Was there also a new life conceived within her womb? The thought was too overwhelming to be faced. The holy innocent a fallen woman and her child a bastard? What was she going to do?

But that was what they must have said of Our Lady, when she was found to be with child. No one had believed that Holy Ghost story, until St Joseph had his dream. No one would believe her either. Oh, for a little of Our Lady's faith. Holy Mary, Mother of God – that proudest of titles that could so easily have been refused. But I couldn't refuse, Nina pleaded. I never said, 'Behold the handmaid of the Lord.' Oh, this was blasphemy. She was sinking deeper, deeper into the sin of being what she was.

And all the time Third Officer Strode was chatting brightly about the weather, the voyage, how they were nearly home and he would be going to stay with his widowed mother, and a part of her was responding, offering the expected answers to conceal the turmoil within. When he left she could scarcely hide her sense of deliverance as she thanked him for pointing out the land and hoped his last night on board would be pleasant – a sentiment which he politely returned. Then she was alone, with the grey blur on the horizon illumined by a sudden flash of sunlight into a land of brightness in which she seemed to distinguish the green of fields, and white gulls swooping and squawking about the ship brought with them the assurance that they were indeed approaching land.

Unfortunately she had lingered too long, and it was in the very act of turning to go below that Mr Gurslake caught her.

'All alone, dear?' he enquired.

On the chilly, windswept deck she was patently alone. He came and stood beside her.

'I was just going in,' she murmured.

His ungloved hand came to rest over her gloved one. 'Stay a little longer, dear. With me.'

Never was invitation more reluctantly accepted, but convent training told. 'Always be gracious,' Reverend Mother had instructed. 'A lady never allows it to be seen that she is put out by others' demands upon her. She is selfless at all times – especially when the demands are made by those less fortunate than she is.' Well, poor Mr Gurslake, recently widowed, was certainly unfortunate. Nina wondered if she was expected to call him Uncle Bert to match the deceased Auntie Florrie. No, even Mr Gurslake couldn't expect that.

'Won't you be cold?' she asked, assuming a solicitude she did not feel as a prelude to suggesting they should both go below. Indeed, he did look peaked. He wore a cap pulled low on his forehead and a muffler wound about his throat; his suit was strained over a knitted pullover, but he had no overcoat. The truth was that Bert had no idea in which trunk Florrie had packed it, and couldn't face opening them all, since he had decided his best chance of escaping a possible reception committee from the Consolidated Finance Company was to abandon his luggage in favour of a quick getaway. So it was more than ever necessary that he should catch little Miss Nina alone before the ship docked. He did not want Florrie laughed at, even though she was now beyond laughter and tears. There was one other person he wanted to see alone, and that was Stafford Briscoe, but that meeting could wait till tonight, preferably in Briscoe's own cabin. Bert looked forward to that. Who would have thought the impeccable Mr Briscoe would so far forget himself as to write compromising letters to Prince Ravi? Well, it was going to save Bert Gurslake's bacon. Make his fortune too, perhaps. But this business with Nina was different. It was something Florrie would have wanted him to do.

He had never thought much about Florrie while he had her, but he had soon discovered that her absence caused a hole at the very centre of his being. It was as if he now existed only on the periphery of himself. It was not just that their cabin seemed empty; that he lay wakeful in the night waiting for her to snore. He craved assurance that in some way she still existed, not – as that creep of a padre would put it – in a better world or in a higher life, but here and now in this one, by virtue of some tangible reminder that would say 'Florrie' for evermore.

'I've been wanting to see you,' he assured Nina. 'Get you on your lonesome, like.'

A shiver ran through the girl. What did he want with her – alone? Her terror of the unknown rapist had receded a little, but it lurked like a tide on the turn. Since it happened she had avoided being alone with any man, except Edmund in his capacity as a doctor. Now, as she glanced round fearfully, she was very much alone.

Bert seemed unaware of her alarm.

'Got something for you,' he continued. 'Just from me to you.'

His grip on her wrist had tightened. He was fumbling in his trouser pocket. Her throat had closed up with terror – otherwise she would have screamed.

Bert drew out a long, thin object crudely wrapped in brown paper.

'Something of Florrie's. She'd have liked you to have it. Very fond of you, she was.'

Nina took the package, which needed no unwrapping because its contents were already sliding to the deck. Bumping heads, they both stooped to retrieve the ivory hair ornament which had adorned Florrie's head.

Nina looked at Bert with eyes moist with relief as well as gratitude.

'Oh, Mr Gurslake, she was so fond of it. Are you sure you want to give it to me?'

'Ain't no one else,' Bert said; then, realising that that did not sound generous: 'We never had no little 'uns, but Florrie said you was like a daughter and you got the right sort of hair.'

'Yes.' Nina fingered the intricately carved object. 'I'll put my hair up with it tonight, the last night of the voyage, and I'll treasure it always, Mr Gurslake. Thank you.'

Always be gracious . . . even when the object in your hands brings back the memory of a fat woman sprawled gracelessly on the deck, her colour changing from pale to ashen, her breasts heaving uncontrollably. Could she really bring herself to bind her own hair with what had secured Florrie's walnut tresses? She needed no reminder of Florrie Gurslake, let alone one as personal as this.

Bert was patting her hand. 'I'll look forward to seeing it. Make tonight something special.' As it would be in any case, once he and Stafford Briscoe had had their little talk . . .

Nina steeled herself. She would have to do as promised and put her hair up, but Con would help her and she need never wear the ivory dagger again. Always be gracious . . .

'It's very good of you,' she said sincerely. After all, it was kindly meant. 'I shall always remember Mrs Gurslake – Auntie Florrie.'

Bert said, 'I'm glad you was with her at the end.'

The end. A sudden slumping to the deck. A gasping and a choking sound, like Mummy. No one knew when the end might come. 'Therefore be ready at all times,' Reverend Mother had said. 'Treat each night as if it were your last one. Clear your conscience and lie down as if to die.'

O my God, I am heartily sorry . . . but for what? For being me? For having misheard your call, or hearing only what I wanted of it? For having mocked you in deceiving myself? The thoughts chased each other through Nina's mind on that last night of the voyage, like the shadows crisscrossing the deck. The *Karachi* was ploughing her way up the Channel against a stiffening breeze, and with each movement the pattern of light altered, so that what had been illumined was suddenly dark and shadowed corners in this unfrequented part of the ship were unexpectedly subjected to a searching swathe of light. Nina knew she ought not to be here, but after dinner, which had been overhung by the expectation of arrival, the sadness of farewells, and a pleased surprise at the change in Miss Nina Martin's appearance – 'Quite a little beauty,' was the general verdict – most passengers had retired early to be ready for immediate disembarkation as soon as the *Karachi* docked. Nina too had returned to their cabin, but to her surprise Connie was not there and when she had not returned by the time Nina had finished both her own and her sister's packing, she could not help being alarmed. Since the attack Connie had never been far from her, and if she did leave her for a short time, it was always with details of where she could be found. Nina put on a topcoat and went in search of her, pausing only for a second glance at herself in the long mirror, for the upswept hairstyle made her seem unfamiliarly tall. Her face too looked thinner, its structure beginning to show beneath the smooth pale roundness that had characterised her features till now. She could not resist a half smile at the young woman in the mirror who had left an unformed girl somewhere between Indian and English territorial waters and tomorrow would set foot in a new country to begin a new life. She ran her hands down her body, apprehensive yet again of the possibility that it too might harbour new life, but what she was chiefly conscious of was the smoothness of silk underwear against her skin. How right Connie had been to insist that she have a trousseau, for though no heavenly bridegroom waited, she could at least give herself up without guilt to those small pleasures of the flesh which a short time ago had seemed so sinful because she was soon to renounce them for good. A memory of her mother surfaced. Just so had she seen Bridget Martin stand, smoothing slim flanks before a mirror and, with a similar half-smile, perhaps recalling the touch of other hands. I understand, dear, I don't condemn you – Nina wanted to cry the words aloud; and though I may no longer offer myself unsullied for your soul's salvation, perhaps you are in less danger than we have been taught. God be merciful to me, a sinner. Holy Mary, pray for us. For what use are prayers if there is no mercy? And if there is, what need have we to fear?

These thoughts were still with her as she stepped out on the deck and saw almost at once on the lee side two figures merged as one. Tall and short. Edmund and Connie. So this was where her sister was. Something about their stillness held her back from approaching. She turned, hoping they had not seen her, and went the other way. My sister, Lady Bladon. If Edmund were indeed proposing, that was what she would soon be able to say. God bless Con, she deserves her happiness. If only Mummy were here to see!

She had wandered away from the passengers' quarters and leant against the rail in the dark. Away to her left – no, to port – was England, but she could not see the coastline now. Instead she was conscious of the peace within her which that first sight of land had brought. As that burst of setting sun illumed it, it had seemed a land of brightness, of promise, whatever of good and ill was to come. Behind her she heard footsteps, but she did not turn as they approached her, for the ship was never entirely still; there were always creakings and groanings, soft footfalls, the muted bells of the watch. They were a part of the peace that enveloped her. Even the Irish steward's voice as he paused to bid her goodnight blended into the calm of the moving deck, the slap of water, the steady pulsing of the screws.

Their brief exchange did not disturb her peace; rather, it enhanced it. God bless Connie and Edmund; the Irish steward for his kindness; Captain Meiklejohn who looked so stern and was not; Mr Briscoe, eternally aloof . . . For three weeks the *Karachi* had been their world, and love, violence, death had all been part of it under God's all-seeing eye – that same eye that would follow them to England, or wherever else in the world they might go. That it was a loving eye she was now certain: it belonged to a merciful God, who in this dark corner of the ship sought out a girl who had doubted His existence, and filled her full of hope. The land to port was bright with promise. Her God was with her still.

O land of brightness, fade not.

O God of mercy, fail not.

Gloved hands came suddenly out of the darkness behind her and closed about her throat. Colours swam before her eyes worse than in a migraine, noise sounded in her ears: a harsh jangling interspersed with whistle blasts. She fought desperately for breath against the hands that were strangling her, and all at once everything she had been taught about emergency procedures flashed clearly into her mind.

In the event of fire the alarm will be given by the ringing of bells and blowing of whistles.

It was fire! Fire! Fire at sea!

III

Angus Meiklejohn was not asleep when the alarm bells sounded; he was only pretending to be. Sometimes, if you pretended long enough, sleep itself was deceived and came stealing over you, and make-believe slid into reality. Cynthia was asleep beside him, he could tell by the evenness of her breath; there was a little pause at the end of each inhalation, as though she were not certain whether to die or live. She lay fitted into the curve of his body like a nut inside its shell. Only her right arm lay outflung, demonstrating independence in a touchingly childish way. She was taller than Ailsa, less rounded, for Ailsa had been sturdy even as a girl. Ailsa was built for bearing burdens, but Cynthia was differently designed. The burdens thrust upon her were too heavy: widowhood; an only son. She needed someone to support her, to share with her the problems of Bobby's upbringing. Above all, she needed someone to give her another son.

If there had been a second son, would he have taken Andy's tragedy so hard? Angus wondered. But Ailsa had not conceived again and, proud of their golden boy and mindful too of the Australasian Line's not over-generous pay packets, they had not appealed against this fiat from On High. Yet Jamie Sutherland was raising four on a salary less than a captain's. Surely, then, a captain's salary would stretch to two without excessive hardship for Ailsa and Andy, or for Cynthia and the son that she might bear.

Angus looked down at the woman curled against him, at the thin shoulders, the white nape of neck revealed by the bobbed hair, whereas Ailsa's spread over her back, over the pillow, tickling and delighting his nose. Ailsa. She would not forgive him. He had no more hope of making her understand than he had of making Jamie, and Jamie had made his feelings all too plain. For these last nights there had been no six o'clock tap at his door, no sitting in companionable silence over a pipe and a wee dram. Soon there would be no Jamie, when he transferred to the *Hyderabad*. Without him, voyages would be lonely; but at least at the end of them there would be Cynthia and perhaps a new child to take in his arms.

But would she have him? What could he offer? The stigma of divorce on the grounds of his adultery committed *pour la forme* with some unknown and undesired woman in a 'suitable', that was to say, sleazy hotel; and then a life of long separations and brief reunions, scarcely better than in the old days when a sailor's life was governed by winds and tides. 'The wind commands me away' – that phrase from countless hastily penned letters in captains' cabins said all there was to say.

For the past ten days she had been his mistress, both of them so bemused that they hardly knew how they had made the assignation under watchful eyes on the bridge. The first time her tap had sounded at his door he had not dared to believe it, despite her punctuality. He had drawn her in – she was shivering.

'Are you sure you want to?' he asked.

'Yes, oh yes.'

'And Bobby?'

'He's asleep. So long as I'm back by morning . . .'

'Morning's a long time away.'

He slid the rose-printed robe from her shoulders and gathered her into his arms. 'Who'd have thought you were such a light woman?' he said jestingly. And added: 'In the physical sense, of course.'

She hid her face against him. 'This is the first time since Robert died.'

Then they were lying on his bed, and though he sought to still her trembling it communicated itself to him until they both shook with the violence of desire and it was as though the ship vibrated with them in a plunging rhythm that was succeeded by infinite calm. If this is adultery, Angus thought, I'm surprised it is not more common; and then was horrified at himself, for it was a breaking of the Seventh Commandment, but – had Moses been a married man? 'I ken fine ye have a mistress, Angus,' Ailsa had once whispered, 'but I'm no jealous. At least your wife doesna have ribs of iron.' And he had taken her in his arms and vowed that for him there could be no other woman – and lo and behold, there was. I ought to feel remorse, shame, guilt, Angus told himself, but I feel nothing but fulfilment because this act is right. I should do a greater wrong by denying what is between me and Cynthia than ever yielding to it can do. He was aware that Jamie Sutherland would make mincemeat of this argument, but at the end of every voyage when Jamie returned home there were four lively youngsters to greet him, not a tall, thin young man with a muted 'Hello, Daddy.' What did Jamie know of adultery?

But this last night was different. For the first time Angus could not sleep, although their love-making had been as satisfying as usual and beside him Cynthia slept. 'I ken fine ye have a mistress, Angus' – but her ribs were of iron, not of ivory, like Cynthia's, and it was his old mistress who was crying to him with every creak and shudder of her body, telling him something was wrong. Did Jamie also feel it? Angus would have reached for the telephone and rung the Chief Engineer but for arousing Cynthia, so certain was he that the Chief would also be wakeful, aware of the *Karachi*'s distress. He listened, but he could detect no difference in the weather, in the way his ship clove through the water. They were within hours of port. The voyage had been eventful, but in no way dangerous. Yet he was awake, alert, muscles tensed and nerves straining because his ship needed him – needed him as she had not done since he stood watching the white wake of the torpedo racing towards her, knowing that he and his ship were one.

Almost before the first alarm bells sounded he was on his feet, falling into the clothes left always ready. Behind him, Cynthia sat up.

'Angus! What's the matter?'

'There's a fire,' he said curtly. 'Please go back to your cabin and do exactly as your stewardess says.'

'A fire! Where?'

'I don't know. It may be only a small one. Please, Cynthia, do as I say.'

He left her sitting up in bed, the sheet clutched to her, her eyes great round O's of fright.

In seconds he was on the bridge. The duty officer turned towards him. 'Fire reported in the First Class writing-room, sir.'

The writing-room with its fancy wood panelling which aeons ago he had assured Cynthia was no risk.

'Is it contained?'

'For the moment, sir.' The voice said more than the words.

Angus considered. The writing-room was amidships. If the fire broke through, the danger was to the decks above, to the superstructure, possibly to the lifeboats, and the stiff Channel breeze would not help.

'All crew at fire-fighting stations, sir,' the officer reported. 'Passengers assembling on deck.'

Angus gave his first order. 'Prepare to lower the boats.'

The officer turned to relay it, but not before concern showed in his eyes. The Old Man was evidently taking no chances. He hoped it was caution, but everyone knew that where his beloved ship was concerned the Old Man had a sixth sense. He didn't like the sound of it.

The bridge telephone rang again.

'First Officer Stocks, sir, asking for reinforcements to help contain the fire.'

Angus gave instructions where to find them. For the time being, the lower decks and holds were safe, since the fire would burn upwards before burning downwards. The Chief could spare some men.

Meanwhile the passenger decks bristled with aggrieved agitation as stewards began shepherding their flocks. 'No need to take a suitcase, sir . . . Just a precaution, madam . . . Please take your life-jacket, let me help you . . . Yes, sir, it's fine up on deck, take an overcoat by all means but you won't need that umbrella . . . Yes, up the main staircase, just as in the boat drill. Remember your lifeboat, do you? Number six starboard, that's on the right.'

'First passengers coming up now, sir.'

Angus could see them for himself, some still fully dressed, others obviously roused from slumber, and in every variety of clothing. There were First Class passengers in the forward part of the ship, but astern the scene would be repeated as men and women welled up from Second Class. Except that it would take longer to assemble the First Class passengers

313

because too many routes were blocked: by the fire itself, by fire-fighting equipment, by hurrying reinforcements. He had done well to give the order when he did.

He fancied he could smell smoke, but apart from the crowding humanity below him, the night was so normal that he knew his imagination must be playing tricks. Away to starboard were the lights of other vessels in the busy Channel. To port lay England and safety. Safety? He checked himself. They were not in real danger. Not yet.

Nevertheless: 'Radio our position and alert other shipping that we have fire on board and may need assistance.'

He tried not to see the careful control on his officers' faces. He was being over-cautious, but where passengers' lives were concerned . . . Where Cynthia was concerned . . . She was somewhere below him in the darkness made more intense by the brilliance of the ship's lights. The *Karachi* continued to plough forward. Another whiff of smoke. The Chief would already have rung the bridge for instructions . . .

The bridge telephone again. Its constant burring and the quiet voices of his officers in reply. He was proud of them, proud of his crew, his ship . . .

The duty officer turned towards him. 'First Officer Stocks, sir. They're unable to contain the fire.'

Angus moved forward and took the instrument.

'The Captain speaking, Mr Stocks. Any casualties?'

'No, sir, nothing serious, but the fire's now broken through to A deck, spreading slightly towards the stern.'

'Do you need further assistance?'

'Not yet, sir.' Stocks was stubborn. 'Fire's still contained amidships, but there's a lot of wood above us and –'

Decking, hatch covers, please God not lifeboats . . .

'– and it's possible it may break through.'

'Thank you, Mr Stocks.'

So – cut the engines, lest her way should fan the flames. Angus gave the order, hating the sense of helplessness created by leaving a ship at the mercy of the sea. Fortunately the sea was showing mercy. They could have met a Force Nine gale. Even so, he felt the shudder as, far below him, the engines went hard astern. The ensuing stillness was louder in his ears than all the sounds around him. In some mysterious way the *Karachi* had just died.

'Are all passengers now on deck?' he asked the duty officer.

'All Second Class passengers, sir. They're still coming up from First Class. The main staircase is out of commission, so they're re-routing them.'

Of course. The writing-room was near the top of the main staircase. Angus could picture the scene: smoke making an effectively dark background for the orange glow of flames; passengers guided away from their normal exit, perhaps scenting or seeing the fire . . .

'Any panic?'

'No, sir, but they're edgy.'

314

Meaning it wouldn't take much. The moment perhaps to go down among them, setting an example of monolithic calm. It only needed a woman to start screaming and some of them might stampede out of control.

The smell of smoke had reached the bridge – he was certain.

'I'm going down to the boat deck,' he announced.

The bridge telephone burred again.

'Mr Sutherland, asking to speak to you, sir.'

Angus turned at the head of the companionway leading from the bridge. Only emergency would cause Jamie to ask to speak to him in present circumstances. He knew almost before he reached the instrument what he was going to hear.

'Sutherland here, sir.' Jamie sounded his most Scottish. 'Fire in the reserve bunker. It's taken quite a hold.'

The reserve bunker, for use only in emergency, still held its full load of coal. For an instant Angus pictured it: a gigantic glowing ember from which the heat would be intense, while flames leaped out in all directions in search of further prey.

'I've every available pump playing on it, sir, but we may not be able to contain it. We need assistance, fast.'

Angus turned to the officer beside him. 'Fire reported also in the reserve bunker. Send out a call for immediate assistance' – and then turned back to the instrument in his hand. The two fires couldn't be connected; they were so many decks apart. But . . .

'Is the cause of the fire known?' he asked, and felt his vitals turn to stone at Jamie's answer:

'Aye, sir. We've got a fire-raiser on board.'

'Oh, Ivo, not fire!'

'I'm afraid so, dearest. It may not be much. I believe they're required by law to sound the alarm.'

'What should we do?'

'I think perhaps we should put some clothes on. One always feels better when dressed.'

Clothes make the man. A cliché, but a true one. His own good-quality suit of old-fashioned cut epitomised him: the best of England, but somehow out of touch. In twenty years his figure had not thickened, though recently it had shrunk. The good tweed hung loosely on him; there was room for two fingers between the collar of his shirt and his neck.

His wife's clothes were equally dated, made by a native dressmaker, each garment modelled on the last with allowance for change of figure; by now they were far removed from their originals, which had themselves been out of date. Ivo was aware of the smiles of other passengers, but he knew Kate did not care. They had never intended to leave India, so England must accept them as they were.

A brisk knock on the cabin door interrupted these reflections.

'All passengers on deck, sir, if you please.'

'Ivo –'

'It's all right, dear. A very wise precaution.'

'Ivo, I'm sure I can smell smoke.'

'We should smell smoke if the waste-paper basket in the next cabin were blazing.'

'You know it isn't that.'

He did not deny it. The smoke was pungent. He recognised it as wood. How different it smelt in a forest clearing, or at the edge of a path when the countryside fell in great timber-clad folds below him and the mountains on the opposite side of the valley reared polls as white as his to the sky. Such mornings were the ultimate in stillness; only the sun moved, climbing higher and illuminating fresh snowfields, or the dark cleft of a ravine. Far below a great bird floated, so motionless that its sudden swoop left him as startled as if the earth itself had fallen away. Behind him, his servants busied themselves with the first fire of the morning and the inevitable brew-up of char. By sunset they would have progressed perhaps ten miles further along this forest trail. So each day's span was measured, trees marked for slaughter, and agreements with village headmen made. Months later the great tree-trunks would be hauled along this same pathway and delivered to a collecting point. And at every halt there arose a trail of wood-smoke as his servants lit their fire. But in those immensities fire was no more than a puny claim by man to domination; on board ship fire might have the mastery.

He said nothing of this to Kate, though the smell of fire was undoubtedly stronger when they opened the cabin door. Other passengers were being marshalled by stewards and stewardesses. Sartorial solecisms were rife. For once the Haldinghams were not conspicuous, and Ivo was thankful for that, just as he was thankful not to see the Irish steward. His presence, linked with fire, might have been too much for Kate to bear. Too much for him also, he suspected; his self-control might well have given way, causing him to lash out verbally or even physically at someone so willing and cheerful that there could be no excuse. Except that a willingness to oblige had been characteristic of the Irish tenants on the demesne of Curraghmore ... Their daughter Joyce had written often enough of her happiness among these soft-spoken people of County Cork, where her husband's family had held land since the sixteenth century and administered it with care. Good farmers, good landlords, these Beauchamps, whose Norman ancestors had crossed the Irish Sea with Strongbow nearly eight centuries before, but whose English connections and Protestant religion had counted for more in the end with those soft-spoken Irish tenants than generosity, just dealing, or a common land of birth. Two years ago, one crisp night in October, they had burned Curraghmore to the ground.

'No, sir, not the main staircase. Please follow the route indicated.'

As Ivo shuffled forward, because swift movement was impossible in this press of bodies, he fought down rising unease. Why this unfamiliar route which took them up narrow companionways – servants' stairs, he called them – in a little-known part of the ship? 'Where is the fire?' he asked one of the crewmen who at intervals lined the route like some travesty of guardsmen at a royal procession. The man smiled and shook his head. Ignorant of the answer or of the question? – for despite official regulations, there was little knowledge of English among the native crew, or even of Hindustani, that great *lingua franca* that united the sub-continent.

'It's in the writing-room,' said a voice behind him. 'You can't expect these buggers to understand what you say.'

Ivo winced, both for the language in Kate's presence and for the sentiment, as he turned to see Archie Johnson behind him. The young man smiled – he's enjoying this, Ivo thought on the instant – before adding, 'It's apparently got quite a hold.'

'Then don't say so,' Ivo snapped. 'No need to alarm the ladies.' He could feel Kate trembling against him as he spoke. He laid a hand on hers. 'You mustn't worry, dearest. One more flight and we should be out on deck.'

He would have expected Johnson to be escorting his fiancée and her parents, but in the confusion caused by the closure of the main staircase people had become separated. Somewhere behind them a woman was crying. 'Where is he?' her voice rising in hysteria. But there had been no confusion on Curraghmore's main staircase as Joyce fought her way upwards to where her husband lay. The drawing-room was on the first floor – she had described it to them so often – its great windows facing southwards towards the sea, but on that October night they had spouted flame and their hereditary owner lay somewhere behind them, felled by a falling beam. 'We saw Mr Beauchamp at the window shouting defiance,' the estate steward had written in a black-bordered letter whose lines were branded on Ivo's brain. 'Then all at once he staggered and fell back. Mrs Beauchamp was like someone demented – there was no holding her. She rushed in through the portico and up the main staircase which was burning fiercely, and that was the last we saw.' *And in their death they were not divided*, Ivo thought bitterly. He had caused that to be engraved upon their tomb.

His hand tightened on Kate's. They would not be divided in death either. Sometimes when he had been away up country and had thought of all the ills that might befall one or other of them in absence, such as accidents or sudden fevers with no European aid to hand, he had offered up thanks to his gods for their well-being and a fervent petition that it might endure. Ivo's gods were neither the Hindu pantheon nor the Classical pantheon of his youth, and nothing at all to do with the God of the missionaries as represented by the Reverend and Mrs Stiles. No, his gods had more in common with tree spirits, or the force that drove the sun across the sky. This was a power he understood, neither benign nor malign, but forceful, leaving human beings too occupied with coping with its effects to speculate on its origin. It was a

317

power that fuelled the flames that raged through Curraghmore, and was equally responsible for the jet of flame that now shot across the head of the companionway above them, to the accompaniment of screams.

No one was hurt, but everyone on the narrow staircase turned and began to descend. The crowd, hitherto orderly, showed signs of panic, despite reassurances shouted from below. An officer with a rope appeared briefly above them and cordoned off the stairs, and the closing of one more avenue of escape left everyone with the feeling that what had at first seemed no more than an exercise, like boat drill, was deadly serious. Kate, clinging to the rail with one hand and Ivo's arm with the other, whispered, 'I can't turn round,' and as he braced himself against the tide of bodies, Ivo cursed once more his own diminished strength. Once he would have swept Kate up in his arms, but now both her heavy figure and his own weak muscles were against him. The years when he could shoulder a great log had sunk into the swamp of retirement, where no exertion ever raised its head. Why should it? That wide-verandahed bungalow with its stupendous view was designed as their last resting-place, and they had thought never to leave it. Would never have done so had it not been for Hugh.

Joyce's boy. Hugh Haldingham Beauchamp. The grandson they had never seen. Born late in a hitherto childless marriage and orphaned at the age of fourteen. His father's brother had acted as guardian, coping as best he could with the gutted house, land running to ruin, dwindling income and ever-rising costs, but it had all been too much for him; he had died suddenly six months ago, leaving Hugh dependent on the administration of a solicitor and a steward, in neither of whom Ivo had much trust. He and Kate had never questioned the decision to return home to offer what they could of comfort, guidance, a sense of family to an unknown grandson who might not need them, but who was still blood of their blood.

If the boy had been at home instead of at boarding-school in England, would Joyce have insisted on that act of self-immolation? Ivo had often asked himself that. If Kate were in danger, would he abandon her for the sake of this boy he had never seen? He hoped he need make no such decision, as he helped her turn on the narrow iron stairs; there were few people behind them now, most having pushed past with muttered apologies in the best cases and an impatient shove in the worst. Smoke darkened the artificial lighting and caught in the back of their throats, but at least there was no more flame, though they could hear shouts and the hiss of water above them, the cries more urgent now. Ivo suspected the fire was spreading, shooting upwards as it must have done through Curraghmore, where the watchers ringed it in a mingling of sympathy and hatred, and its owner hurled defiance into the night.

'The IRA men gave Mr and Mrs Beauchamp every opportunity to leave along with the servants,' the steward had reported, 'but Mr Beauchamp wouldn't go. When the fire took a hold we shouted to him to jump from the windows and we'd have caught him, but still he refused to

318

budge. Then something fell on him and he staggered and fell back.' And Mrs Beauchamp – Joyce – had been 'like someone demented' and had rushed up that blazing staircase to her death.

They were making their way up yet another narrow iron companionway when Kate stumbled. Ivo tightened his grip, but her heavy body slewed and fell, dragging him after her. It was only three steps to the bottom, but they ended in a tangled heap.

'You all right, sir?' A steward was standing over them.

'Yes, thanks, but my wife –'

'Easy does it. If you'll take her other arm, sir . . .'

Between them they hauled Kate to her feet.

She bit her lip to keep from crying out. 'My ankle, Ivo. I've sprained it.'

The steward, whose duties demanded his presence elsewhere and who could see the crowd ahead milling about without direction, looked round for assistance. Ahead of him the figure of Archie Johnson loomed.

'Excuse me, sir –' Archie felt a tap on his shoulder – 'but would you mind helping the couple behind? The lady slipped and sprained her ankle, and I'm needed up ahead.'

Archie turned. Of all infuriating requests! Why couldn't the old fools have been more careful?

'Thanks so much, sir.' The importunate steward was gone.

There was nothing for it but to put a good face on things. Too many people had overheard and were watching with relief and approval as Archie offered a strong arm. He tried to look concerned and helpful, but all the time people were pushing past and Kate's slow, painful progress relegated them to the rear of the crowd.

Archie was no fool. He sensed the unease of officers and stewards behind their outward calm and that, more than the swirls of smoke or the sound of fire-fighting above them, told him that matters were getting out of hand. If things were as bad as he suspected they'd be taking to the boats. That's if they ever got as far as the lifeboats, and at this rate they never would. Why the hell hadn't he pushed ahead, got farther away from this old couple, instead of hanging back because it was women and children first? With their slow progress they'd either be overtaken by fire behind them or find their way blocked by it in front. It was the devil of a situation, and he could see no way out of it.

Unless . . . The old boy was obviously tiring, his breath coming in short gasps, and the old woman, a dead weight, could barely struggle along. If he suggested that they rested, he would appear considerate, and once the tail-end of the crowd had passed them, there would be no witnesses . . . Not that he was proposing to do anything very dreadful; reinforcements were becoming essential and he was the obvious person to go in search of them. Nevertheless, it was only too easy for a situation to be misunderstood, as witness Maggapore, and he wanted no further misreading of his actions. Better to play it safe.

They turned a corner and there was a space before the next companion-way reared before them. He could smell fresh air as well as smoke.

'Why don't you wait here, sir,' he suggested, at his most winning, 'and I'll go and find some sturdy crewman to give Mrs Haldingham a hand.'

Ivo spoke with difficulty, he was so breathless. 'That's thoughtful of you, but I think we'd better get on.'

'If Mrs Haldingham can make it, sir.'

'What do you say, Kate? Do you want a rest?'

She shook her head, lips pressed together to keep from crying. Anything rather than fire. She had lived Joyce's fate so often in imagination. She couldn't be asked to share it now. But it wasn't her wishes that were going to prevail – she saw that as Captain Johnson thrust her aside into the space underneath the companionway, already crowded with feet scraping on the metal treads. She found herself pushed down on a coil of rope, unable even to sit upright, as Captain Johnson said:

'You wait here and I'll go for reinforcements. I promise I won't be long.' Then he was gone.

Kate looked at Ivo standing breathless beside her. 'I could have managed,' she said.

He patted her hand. 'You could. He couldn't. Our young friend has lost his nerve.'

'You mean he won't be back?'

'I doubt it.'

The tears came now in good measure. 'Oh, Ivo, what are we going to do?'

'Where is he? Where's Bobby?'

'I don't know, Mrs Vane. Isn't he with you?'

'No, he's not. He's not in our cabin. What have you done with him?'

The stewardess, tense and tired, could have done without Cynthia Vane at this moment. If the woman hadn't gone whoring off – oh yes, she knew what these lady passengers got up to – her child wouldn't have been left alone. And who knew where a boy of eight might end up if he went wandering? Bored or frightened – bored probably, knowing Bobby – he could be in any part of the ship. And the silly bitch was blaming her for the boy's absence. Well, she'd other things to do than to play nursemaid. The boy would turn up all right. Other passengers or crew would take charge of him. Her responsibility now was to get his mother to the boats.

'I expect Bobby's up on deck already,' she said firmly. 'He's probably waiting for you.'

'He'd never have left this cabin of his own accord. Something must have made him.'

'Perhaps he was frightened by the fire alarm and went running to one of your friends.'

Though who they were she wouldn't know. Mrs Vane didn't mix much. Those two Martin girls were her nearest approach to friends, and she hadn't

320

seen either of them in this pandemonium, the stewardess recollected. She hurried along to their door.

To her relief, the cabin was empty, the beds not slept in. They must have been making the most of the last night, along with some of the other First Class passengers who as evidently had not retired. Mrs Vane, it seemed, had; she wore an overcoat over her silk peignoir and her feet were thrust incongruously into mules. If this alarm was anything serious, she'd be frozen up on deck.

'Won't you put some stouter shoes on?' the stewardess suggested. 'And you'll need your life-jacket.'

'Why? Is the ship going to sink?'

'No, of course not. It's just part of lifeboat drill.'

'Bobby's life-jacket is still here. He'll need it.'

'Take it with you and give it to him on deck.'

'What if he isn't there?'

'We carry spare ones. Someone will see to it he's kitted out.'

'I won't go without him.'

'Now, my dear, you're being silly. Come along with you, and up on deck.'

The stewardess took her arm but Cynthia resisted. What was it Robert had said when he went back from leave that last time, while the car waited to take him to the station and she clung to him, trying not to cry? 'Take care of our son for me, darling.' Already he was convinced that the child would be a boy. And she had whispered, 'I will, oh I will,' holding him to her as though to imprint him on her flesh. Perhaps that was why Bobby was so like him. Now, in losing Bobby, she had lost Robert over again. And not just lost him: cancelled out his very existence, of which his son was the outward pledge. And for what? For a moment's ecstasy in the arms of a married man old enough to be her father. How Robert would despise her if he knew!

The tears splashed down, and someone took her other arm in a firm grip as the stewardess signalled for aid. They didn't want this one panicking. Her screams might set others off.

'What's the matter?' the new voice asked.

She moaned, 'I've lost Bobby.' And amplified: 'My little boy.'

'Just separated,' the stewardess insisted. 'He isn't far away.'

'How do you know? You didn't guard him. He could have fallen overboard.'

'Not very likely, ma'am,' said the voice Cynthia now recognised as a steward's. 'Let's get you up to the boats and then I'll go and look for him.'

By now they were in the confusion at the foot of the main staircase, and the man released her arm. 'It's too narrow for three abreast,' he explained; and in an undertone to the stewardess: 'Is the child really lost?'

'He's certainly missing. He may not have gone very far.'

'How old is he?'

'Eight.'

'How long has he been gone?'

'I don't know. An hour? Maybe longer.'

The man drew in his breath in a low whistle. 'Christ! He could be anywhere.'

He could be anywhere. That was Angus Meiklejohn's first response to the words 'fire-raiser'. His second was practical.

'Are you certain?' he asked Jamie Sutherland.

'As certain as I stand here.'

'Do we know who it is?'

'Aye.' The Chief paused for an instant. 'That black bastard Gopal.'

The words 'whom I wanted to put ashore at Aden' were loud between them.

'Is he under restraint?' Angus asked.

'Not yet. He will be when I lay hands on him.'

'Jamie, be careful, even so.'

We don't want you on trial on a murder charge, and black or white, innocent or guilty, Gopal has his rights – something you are apt to forget in your righteous anger, just as you forget your own strength. If the bastard hadn't rights, do you think I'd have kept him on board a moment longer than I had to, endangering my passengers, my ship? But Angus knew better than to voice such thoughts.

Jamie's voice came again, strictly formal. 'I'll be careful, sir. But we have to catch him first.'

And he could be anywhere in the ship, for with the crew at emergency stations and passengers being herded up on deck, there were empty cabins, galleys, lounges, storerooms, all open. The fire-raiser could choose where to strike. Even in normal conditions he'd set two blazes going. He'd never be able to resist a third.

'I thought you had confined Gopal to quarters?' Angus queried.

'He escaped, sir. He's as wily as the monkey he resembles, and the man guarding him was as thick as two planks.'

And confining a determined man to quarters without an armed guard is hardly feasible on a passenger liner, Angus added mentally, and felt himself to blame. If he and Jamie had still been meeting as friends every evening, he might have convinced that stern Scots disciplinarian that mercy was sometimes politic.

The Chief was still speaking. '. . . I've flooded Number One cargo hold.'

Unavoidable, though it meant loss of cargo, trouble with the Owners . . .

'This fire's a nasty one, sir. It's too near those new hull plates for my liking.'

The *Karachi*'s battle scars, replacements from when the torpedo had struck.

'Are they holding?'

'Aye, sir. So far.'

The Chief had never been happy with that repair job. He maintained it

322

was done on the cheap. As perhaps it was. Everyone said there was no money in shipping in post-war England. But there was danger all right.

'Thank you, Mr Sutherland,' Angus said, echoing Jamie's formality. 'Please keep the bridge informed.'

He replaced the handset just as the duty officer approached.

'Two fire-fighting tugs putting out from Plymouth, sir. The French liner *République* altering course to stand by and give assistance with offloading passengers if necessary. She should be here within the hour. Three lifeboats being called out. All fishing-boats in the area alerted. It'll be like Piccadilly Circus by and by.'

'The passengers?'

'All at lifeboat stations, sir.'

'Any danger?'

'Not immediate, sir, but the fire in the writing-room's still not under control.'

And with one fire they knew of and one they didn't, the passengers' danger was greater than they knew. Greater than Cynthia knew . . .

Angus checked himself. He could no longer be a private man. The mistress who needed him had ribs of iron, not ivory.

He turned to the officer beside him and said tonelessly: 'Give the order to lower the boats.'

I can't breathe. I can't breathe.

Nina Martin struggled, but the gloved hands remained round her throat. She kicked backwards and felt her shoe connect with a shinbone, but still the pressure went on. Lights danced before her eyes, her head was bursting. It was last time over again except . . .

Except that this time he wants to kill me.

Her fingers tore at his hands, but the leather gloves protected him. Her hair was coming down. There was a roaring in her ears, a ringing, any moment she would sag like a rag doll . . . And all the time she could hear the alarm bells. Her attacker heard them too.

He released his hold for an instant. She staggered, gasping, and would have gone overboard but for the rail. She clung to it, heaving, retching.

Oh God, he's coming back!

The dark figure moved purposefully towards her, and she saw that, as before, he was masked as well as gloved. She put up weak hands to ward him off, half tangled in the tumble of her hair, and felt something slither through her fingers.

Florrie Gurslake's hair ornament.

She sensed her attacker pause, as though aware she now had a weapon. His awareness communicated itself to her. In the darkness she could see the whites of his eyes quite clearly: they were such a little way away . . .

She grasped the long, dagger-like implement and drove it straight at him.

323

He staggered back, raised his hands, and she heard the thud as he hit the deck and lay there twitching, while she stood petrified.

I have killed him. I must tell Connie.

There was no other thought in Nina's head as she turned and ran blindly.

And still the whistles went on shrilling and still the alarm bells rang.

Stafford Briscoe stood calmly at his lifeboat station and surveyed the confusion all around. The First Class passengers had finished welling up through unfamiliar narrow doorways, though there were still some he could not see. Ravi was there, of course – he had checked that; a habit of mind died hard; though in any case the Prince's costume marked him out in a crowd whose garments ranged from the most ridiculous night attire to evening dress as immaculate as Stafford Briscoe's own. Nevertheless, there were familiar faces he had not spotted, such as the Martin girls. He assumed they were together because they always were, but their boat was on the port side whereas his was starboard; perhaps it was simply that he could not see them, for the artificial lighting dulled even Connie's bright hair. More definitely, the Haldinghams were missing, for they were in his boat. They wouldn't move fast – Kate Haldingham was too heavy – but they ought to be here by now.

He turned to Archie Johnson standing near him.

'Have you seen the Haldinghams?'

'No.' Archie modified the lie – you never knew who might have been watching. 'Not since they left their cabin.'

'I suppose they're all right?'

The implication was obvious: you're a fit young man, go and see.

Archie chose to ignore it. 'There was a stewardess looking after them. She seemed to have them well in hand.'

'They're not here,' Briscoe pointed out.

The silence lengthened.

'Stand back! Stand back, if you please!'

A flurry of crewmen erupted among the starboard passengers, urging them towards the stern of the ship.

'These are our boats,' someone protested.

'Yes, sir, we'll get that sorted out later on.'

There was no mistaking the urgency. Briscoe moved back with the rest, just as there was a sudden roar, a crackle, and a tongue of flame leaped up. It was followed by another and another, and a great belch of orange-tinted smoke. The lighting dimmed, though whether due to smoke or to electrical failure Briscoe was uncertain. A sudden scream, shrill and marrow-freezing, set all heads craning. High on a lifeboat a figure blazed against the darkness, the hair lifting in a crown of fire. For an instant it seemed to be dancing, then cartwheeled over the side and spun downwards towards a black extinction of agony.

'It's Bobby! I know it's Bobby!'

The woman's voice rose in a thin wail.

Turning, Briscoe saw and did not recognise for an instant the haggard face of Cynthia Vane.

'That was no child,' he said calmly. 'Some poor devil of a crewman, I fear.'

His tone had its effect on her. She said, her voice more normal, 'Bobby is missing, you see.'

The old and the young . . .

'He'll turn up,' Briscoe said, not believing it but not knowing what else to say.

Now a cry of dismay went up from those shaken into silence by the fearful death they had just witnessed.

'The boats! The boats are on fire!'

Briscoe looked and saw that it was true. The boat where the man ablaze had capered was already engulfed in flames. A hose jet arced above it and they heard the hiss of steam. Darkness for an instant. Then another flame, and another. Part of the superstructure seemed on fire. And all the time great puffs of black smoke coiled and roiled skywards and made a second night beneath the night of stars.

'They're never going to be able to lower the starboard boats,' a man cried, voicing the general opinion.

In such circumstances one voice could make or break a stampede. Briscoe braced himself.

'Nonsense,' he said in the same loud, clear tone that had before now quelled impending trouble even among tribesmen who did not understand his words. 'Look, the stern boat is already swinging out. Only the boat amidships is affected, and its passengers will simply be redistributed.'

'Are you one of them?' someone called.

Briscoe addressed no one in particular. 'As it happens, I am.'

It wasn't true, but already he judged they had a situation in which it might be women and children first. Only one boat was ablaze and the damage might be limited, but the boats on either side could not be swung from the davits until it was possible for the crew to get near enough to try. And the fire, though still localised, burned fiercely. A spontaneous movement of the crowd became official as crewmen herded them further astern. 'Keep to the sides of the ship, please. Keep to the sides!' Briscoe wondered why, since this increased the confusion between port and starboard passengers, but concentrated on keeping those around him in a tight knot as the starboard stern boat swung level with the deck. The crowd moved as one towards it, but an officer barred the way.

'Ladies first, please, gentlemen. Don't crush their dresses.'

The attempted jocularity fell flat.

Some women were helped into the boat, others clung to loved ones. Briscoe heard Cynthia Vane crying hysterically, 'I won't go! I won't go without my son!' And it wasn't even her boat; she was turning down a chance of safety and endangering other lives with the same lack of discipline

325

he had observed in her on other occasions and which she had doubtless communicated to her child. But Briscoe was in no doubt that someone on board would see to it that the child was rescued: children were first priority. There were others he was more concerned about. He asked loudly, 'Where are the Haldinghams?'

Of those who heard him, no one seemed to know. Briscoe repeated his question, his eyes scanning the crowd. Ivo Haldingham was the only other man as tall as he was. It should be easy enough to pick him out. And Ivo would never leave Kate. Theirs was the kind of long-term marital devotion that Briscoe understood. He began to pick his way towards the officer controlling the loading of the lifeboat.

'Stand back, sir, if you please!'

Affronted, Briscoe drew himself up to his full height. 'The Haldinghams, a very old couple – they ought to be in that boat.'

The officer nodded, raised a loudhailer to his lips. 'Will Mr and Mrs Haldingham please come forward.'

The crowd checked briefly, heads craned, but there was no sign of the tall old man and his dumpy wife, though the officer repeated his call before turning back to Briscoe. 'They're in another boat, perhaps. I can't do anything more.'

Briscoe nodded, glanced towards the port side, where a similar scene was being enacted as passengers were helped into the boats, and began to thread his way towards one of the narrow companionways up which he and the other First Class passengers had made their way on deck.

A steward bobbed up in front of him. 'Sorry, sir, no going below.'

'There's an old couple trapped below decks. I'm going to get them.'

'Sorry, sir. Captain's orders. No passengers to go below.'

'But they're old. They may not be able to manage.'

'Are you sure they're not here, sir? The lighting's very bad.'

Smoke had indeed dimmed the lighting and blotted out the stars. Every now and then a burst of flame lit a few faces ruddy-orange, but many were blackened by smoke and those which were not were death-pale. The Haldinghams were not among any of these.

Briscoe said, 'Stand aside, I'm going down.'

The voice which had quelled a panic had no effect on the steward, who remained immovable. Briscoe considered whether to rush him, while debating if this was a case of stupidity or a concept of duty equal to his own. He decided on an appeal to emotion.

'Look here, he's eighty and she's not far off it. They've been married for nearly sixty years. Someone's got to help them. We can't abandon them and let them burn.'

The appeal worked, but differently from what he had expected as the young steward said, 'I'll go myself, sir, if you'll just take my place and make sure no one else attempts to go down. And keep away from the centre of the deck, sir. With this heat, they're afraid the glass may go.'

So that was the explanation. If the centre of the deck was showered with glass from the public rooms blown violently outwards, it would be like a battlefield. Beneath his impassivity Briscoe shuddered, but all he said was, 'Noted.'

And as the steward turned to descend into the ship's smoke-ridden interior, he added softly, 'Good man.'

.

'I saw him! I saw the Devil!'

'So did I! So did I!'

Bobby Vane, running, panting, gasping with the stitch in his side, collided with someone he did not at first recognise as Nina Martin. They clung to each other, not knowing what else to do.

'He was all black, and when he opened the door there was a great fire behind him.'

'I stabbed him, I think he's dead.'

'We've got to tell the Captain.'

'No!'

'We've *got* to, Miss Nina. Otherwise we'll all burn.'

'Yes, in Hell.'

But she was shivering . . .

'Please, Miss Nina, come on.'

Nina allowed the child to propel her forward through the underworld of the ship. The smoke here was no more than a suggestion; were it not for the ship's stillness and the absent heartbeat of her engines you could almost believe all was well. There was no one about; Nina was convinced they had all gone to look at her victim's body and then they would come for her, they would assemble on deck at dawn next morning as for Mrs Gurslake's funeral and after the Captain had pronounced sentence and read prayers they would proceed to hang her. Unless Connie intervened . . .

She stopped, causing Bobby to bump into her.

'I don't want Captain Meiklejohn, I want Con.' Her throat hurt too much from those bruising hands for her to explain further.

'We'll go and find her after we've told the Captain.'

'No, I want her now.'

Bobby looked at the white-faced girl before him, her hair tumbling about her shoulders; she was like a young horse he had watched his uncle breaking in in Quetta, all nervous starts and wildly rolling eyes. But Miss Nina counted as a grown-up, someone who had to be listened to and obeyed.

Bobby took his first big decision.

'If you won't come I'm going to go alone.'

He set off. It wasn't any worse than it had been before he met her, only there were so many companionways to climb and they seemed to get steeper and steeper. He glanced back and to his relief saw Nina following him, still with that same distracted air. She was muttering to herself, but he did not at first understand what she was saying because her voice was so hoarse.

'I never meant to kill him but he was throttling me, and it's the same man, I'm certain, it was like living through it again, and now they'll ask endless, endless questions and I won't be able to tell them a thing because I never saw him through the mask and the gloves but I never meant to kill him, I'm not a murderess . . .'

Bobby realised she was talking about the man who had attacked her, a subject on which his mother had been irritatingly vague. He took his second big decision.

'It wasn't Dr Bladon,' he said.

Nina looked blankly at him.

He went on. 'It wasn't Dr Bladon I saw. I told the Captain I saw him hiding near your cabin but I just made that up because I didn't like him. I never saw anyone.'

Then, as though frightened by his confession, Bobby turned and scrambled up the companionway ahead, and suddenly they were out on deck in a part of the ship neither of them had ever seen before, with boats being loaded and amidships a column of smoke rising skywards and the orange glow of flame.

Immediately rough hands seized them – 'Let's get you two kids aboard!' – and the ten years that separated them vanished as they were thrust into a boat for Second Class.

In Second Class all was more orderly, for they were away from the seat of the fire, their boats were undamaged, and the wind which fanned the fire towards the First Class quarters carried it away from them. Nevertheless, several boats were overloaded, though not dangerously so, for no one had sent back those First Class passengers who, by accident or design, had penetrated the barriers that separated the classes. Bobby and Nina found themselves among strangers, but kindly strangers for all that. 'This your little brother?' – 'Where's your mum, love?' – 'Don't cry, it'll all get sorted out.' Their boat swung out over the water some sixty feet below and remained poised there. 'Like the funfair at the Wembley Empire Exhibition,' someone observed, and a wag promptly quoted a catch-phrase, 'I Wemble, thou Wemblest, he Wembles,' to laughter and applause.

Bobby and Nina clung together, both lost in their own thoughts. Bobby's were of his mother, of the Captain he had lied to, of the Devil dancing dementedly in the depths of the ship. Nina's were of prison walls and wardens, of a judge putting on the black cap, of a cell very different from the one she had thought to occupy, and the minutes creeping round to eight o'clock.

Of course it was not Edmund who had attacked her; she had never believed it was and nor had Connie who was in love with him, as much as he with her. Edmund and Connie. If she could believe in their happiness some good might yet come of all this pain, but she did not even know if they were safe, Edmund at his post – was it near the fire? – and Connie who might be anywhere.

Crouched in the bottom of the lifeboat, Nina began for the first time to

328

pray, not the ordered, formal prayers of the devout schoolgirl who thought she was going to be a nun, but the racking, tearing, inchoate supplications which Bridget Martin would have understood, Connie . . . Edmund . . . *I confess to Almighty God* . . . but I didn't kill him, Mrs Gurslake, God rest her, never meant me to use her ivory dagger for that . . . *mea culpa, mea maxima culpa* . . . please let Connie and Edmund be safe . . . what do I do about Bobby? Suppose Mrs Vane is drowned . . . his eyes through the mask were so glittering . . . my throat aches . . . why are people cheering, looking upwards? They must be lowering the boat . . . no one will ever believe me, will they hang me, what's it like to know you're going to die? . . . perhaps we are, should I make an act of contrition, will they let me have a priest? . . . Connie will get me one . . . Connie . . . O God, I wish Con were here, look after her, let her be happy . . .

Blessed Mary be with her, pray for her, Blessed Mary pray for me . . .

The boat hit the water and a wave sloshed over the side.

'Sir, we've got him!'

Excitement sounded in the Second Engineer's voice.

'Where is he?'

There was no need for Angus to ask who 'he' was.

'He's penned in near the entrance to the reserve bunker. Mr Sutherland's gone in after him.'

Trust Jamie to take the dangerous mission. The heat must be intense. Big man though he was, the Chief would have difficulty in holding the fire-crazed demon that they knew as Gopal.

'He'll need assistance,' Angus said.

'Sir, he won't have anyone with him, though I've a group of men waiting outside. If he dodges the Chief he'll not get past us.' The Second Engineer's voice rang with confidence.

Angus tried to share it.

'What about the blaze?'

'Under control, sir.'

'And the hull plates?'

'They're holding, sir. Mr Sutherland asked me to tell you, he thinks there's no further danger so far as the engine-room's concerned.'

Thank God for that. Thank Jamie. While the fire above board raged out of control, that below decks devouring the *Karachi*'s vitals was ceasing to be a threat.

'And no more fires?'

'No, sir, though we found a pile of paraffin-soaked rags hidden in an empty locker. He was planning further devilment.'

'Thank you, Mr Martin. You'll please keep me informed.'

'The Chief will report to you himself, sir, as soon as Gopal's under lock and key.'

And what then? Angus wondered. A Board of Enquiry and some

maverick lawyer trying to make out that Gopal had been victimised. Not that it would save him, but it might blacken Jamie and by inference himself. He could imagine the questions: 'Would you describe Mr Sutherland as a hard man, Captain? What was his attitude to native crew? Had he had occasion to discipline this stoker?' – on and on until a fine man and the Australasian Line's best engineering officer was presented as a kind of Simon Legree. And all this in a useless attempt at mitigation of a crime for which there could be no excuse: the putting at risk of innocent men, women and children, of Bobby and Cynthia . . .

No, better not think of them, though he had – briefly – when giving the order to lower the boats. The lights of the *République* were coming up on the starboard quarter, some small craft had already arrived, there were the first reports of casualties. That had decided him. If there was no longer safety on board it must be sought on the sea despite the overcrowded lifeboats, before all discipline broke down. As it threatened to do, for with three starboard lifeboats out of action there had been an attempt to rush the last boat, and it was in the ensuing fracas that casualties, not serious, had occurred. Something else that the Enquiry would doubtless go into, but in this gusty darkness with a choppy sea sounding loud against the silent hull, a man's decisions were not necessarily those he would make in the company's boardroom, and Angus could only pray that his were right. His years of training and experience must count for something, as they had when the torpedo struck, but that had been wartime, his ship was not carrying women and children, and – though he hated to admit it – a proportion of self-seekers and cowards.

Meanwhile from every quarter the messages flooded in: offers of help from other shipping; hospitals alerted on shore; the blaze in the bunker contained without further flooding of cargo; that amidships still raging out of control, the bridge itself lit by the flames though not yet smoke-filled, thanks to that freshening breeze. How long before the fire-fighting tugs arrived? Could they save the *Karachi* or was he going to have to give the order 'Abandon ship'? Except that he never would abandon her; he would go down with her, a kind of suttee in reverse. The British had stamped out in India the practice of wives dying on their husbands' funeral pyres, but here in the English Channel a form of it might live on. Ailsa would understand, and she'd get a pension . . . Andy would neither know nor understand . . . Cynthia . . .

The bridge telephone rang again. The duty officer came towards him.

'Mr Bladon, sir, reporting a fatality.'

Angus forced calmness into his voice, demeanour, as his lips formed the one word: 'Who?'

Ravi stood a little apart, in so far as it was possible to do so amid the crowd of men on deck. Just as his exotic costume distinguished him, so too did his reserve. Briscoe sahib should see that a little brown bugger could die as

330

proudly as an Englishman. He glanced across to where Briscoe sahib was standing, ramrod straight and tall, and against his will a little of the old admiration forced its way to the surface and spread over the tumult of his emotions like oil. Briscoe sahib was indeed a prince among Englishmen, and the tribute due to one prince from another was that he, Ravi, should die with equal calm.

For he never doubted he would die, despite reiterated assurances from officers and crew that there was really no danger so long as they kept to the port side where the lifeboats were loading and away from the open deck. Listening to the tone rather than the words, Ravi was convinced they were lying. He would never see Maggapore again; neither Briscoe sahib nor Dorothy would ever sit in the court of the fountains where the peacocks strutted and screamed; and the Watermans would be sad, Barry perhaps affording him a brief 'Poor old Ravi', and Dorothy the tribute of a tear.

The last boat was being loaded, but Ravi still held back. If the time of your death was written in the stars, as Indian astrologers claimed, what use to try and avoid it? You could not alter fate. True, you might be given the chance to determine whether to burn or drown; or both, like that terrifying figure on the starboard lifeboat whose fiery outline had been extinguished in the sea; but there was no need to push forward, as some of the remaining passengers were doing, although the shower of sparks which suddenly descended might argue otherwise. Ravi slapped angrily at the smouldering hole which appeared in the sleeve of his silk jacket, and then, seeing a similar hole appearing in the coat of the man in front of him, slapped that too. The man turned in protest. It was Bert Gurslake.

'You were on fire,' Ravi explained.

'Sez who?'

'Take your coat off and you'll see for yourself what I mean.'

This suggestion was too practical for Bert. All he knew was that he was having to queue up for the place in the lifeboat which should have been his by right. The buggers who ran the country, ran the ship, had screwed it up once again, with the result that a wog in fancy dress, a nancy-boy, stood an equal chance with him of being saved. It wasn't fair. Bert addressed this silent condemnation to whoever was responsible and turned on Ravi.

'Keep your filthy hands off me.'

'With pleasure, Mr Gurslake.'

Ravi stepped back, bowing. Several passengers turned round, and Bert, feeling as so often that he had been outmanoeuvred, reacted in the only way he knew. They weren't going to keep him out of that boat, not if he knew it, not now he'd got a new life ahead. He patted his jacket which concealed the jewelled dagger. For a moment he'd thought the little wog had been trying to get it back. No, it was safe, and with it Bert Gurslake. The Consolidated Finance Company wouldn't be able to touch him now. He'd got more than enough to pay off that old debt, even with the interest they were charging; enough for a new start. Or at least he would have if these daft buggers would only get moving. Bert used his elbows and shoved.

The action was so unexpected that the crowd parted. The lifeboat, though full, was still accepting passengers from among the older men.

'Hey!' someone shouted in protest as Bert pushed his way to the fore. 'You there! Wait your turn like anyone else, can't you?'

'It's my turn now,' Bert said.

'Sorry, sir.' A crewman barred his way. 'Lifeboat's full. We can't risk overloading.' He gestured to the crowd of men at the rails. 'You're safe enough. Just keep away from the centre. The old *Karachi* isn't going down.'

'You let me on that boat,' Bert said, fists doubled.

'Sorry, sir.'

Bert struck out blindly and felt his fist connect. The crewman staggered back, winded. An instant later someone seized the collar of Bert's coat.

He twisted his head and met the coldest eyes he had ever encountered.

'Don't try that again,' Stafford Briscoe said. 'I've a good mind to pitch you over the side and there's not a man here would be sorry. You're a disgrace to whatever spawned you, and it can't have been much, God knows.'

'Sod you!' Bert wriggled but the grip remained unbroken. 'Sod you, you fucking old queen! Who d'you think you are – Lord Muck and then some, is it? What about His Highness there? Don't you want your nancy-boy saved, or are you keeping him by you to bugger as the ship goes down?'

Briscoe's blow caught him and sent him sprawling into the centre of the deck. The jewelled dagger fell and slithered a few feet from him. Quick as a flash, Ravi swooped.

Bert raised himself on all fours. 'That's mine! You gave it me, you bastard!'

Ravi held the hilt towards him. 'Come and get it, Mr Gurslake – if you dare.' With an effort Bert stood upright. 'You bleeding little sod, I'll crucify you!'

'*Look out!*'

No one ever knew who shouted. The words were lost in an almighty crack as the great windows of the passenger lounge shattered outwards from the heat and glass flew everywhere. The silvery crash and tinkle of its fall was mixed with cries of pain as, despite all precautions, one or two splinters found human mark. Then the cries were engulfed in a pool of silence in which could be heard quite clearly for an instant the roar and crackle of flames.

Bert Gurslake lay on the deck where he had fallen, pinned like a beetle in a collection by a great triangular shard of glass. His blood was already running in streams and rivulets. It was obvious to all that he was dead.

'Dear God, don't save me, save Nina.'

Connie was convinced her prayer would go unheard because for so long

332

she had refused to listen to what God was asking of her that He must be angry, but at least let Him take it out on her. There was no need to be angry with Nini, whose only fault was that she had been too young to understand the relationship between Mummy and Major Orrey, and had reacted mistakenly.

Crouched in an overcrowded lifeboat, cold, wet, surrounded by people who were frightened but doing their best to conceal it from themselves and one another, Connie had no doubt of her own punishment. God intended to let her live to mourn Nina, who had been sacrificed to expiate her sister's sins; to let her hear forever in her ears the blasphemy to which she had reduced Edmund in that final raging cry. *Curse God and die* – it was in the Bible somewhere. But don't let Edmund die, he didn't mean it, accept my lifelong penance instead.

Introibo ad altarem Dei – I will go in unto the altar of God. *Domine, non sum dignus* – I am not worthy . . .

'Move up, dear, if you can.'

The brisk voice broke in upon her, a voice from another world.

'Don't keep fretting about your sister,' the voice added. 'She'll be safe in another boat.'

'I hope so.'

'Of course she is. Didn't you hear the officer saying that all passengers were safely away?'

'How does he know?'

The woman looked annoyed that her attempts at comfort were unavailing.

'Wireless,' she said positively, if incorrectly.

The latest scientific miracle, by which people at a distance, in other countries even, could still communicate. But there was no wireless communication with Nina. If she were alive still, Connie thought, I'd surely know.

When the fire alarm had sounded she had rushed to their cabin, but Nina was not there. The stewardess was coping with an hysterical Cynthia Vane who was crying out for Bobby – it was no use asking her. Moreover, it was impossible to make headway through the press of passengers who moved at a snail's pace, slowed by the elderly and infirm such as the Haldinghams. Connie reproached herself for her lack of charity. But Captain Johnson was at hand; he would be sure to help them; whereas Nini might be anywhere . . . So long as she had enough sense to make her way to her correct lifeboat station . . . When they emerged on deck, Connie saw that she had done no such thing.

It was then that she began to panic. What would Daddy say? She had promised to take care of Nina. How could she face him again? Then she remembered that she would not have to, except through a convent grille. That was if he came over to England, tried to dissuade her . . . No, please. I can't bear more argument. Let him settle down with the Widow Moloney. Let Edmund marry someone else. Let him be happy. Let him forget me.

333

It will be better if we don't meet again – oh, the coldness in his voice as he said it. It would quench a thousand fires. But not the fire that burns within me which I cannot subdue because it is the fire of love, of life . . . O God, you have demanded Nini and Edmund in sacrifice – do you demand that too?

Useless question to which she already knew the answer. Nothing less than all she had and was would do. You didn't make terms with God. He demanded unconditional surrender. Only by becoming nothing did you become a part of Him, His will your will because you no longer had a will with which to resist Him, what Reverend Mother called the Great Peace. But peace was the conclusion of war, of many battles; not all who fought would live to see the peace. I am not worthy . . . Dear God, don't save me, save Nina. Only – isn't death the easier way? Edmund would say so. Am I still hearing my voice, not God's voice . . .

Connie became aware of a stir of excitement all around.

'What is it?' she asked, not caring.

The woman with the brisk voice replied.

'The French liner, dear. They can see her lights away to starboard. She'll be taking us all on board.'

'Thank God,' said a voice like a groan beside her.

Connie recognised the Reverend Septimus Stiles. His wife, equally wretched, clung to him.

'Where's Imogen?' Connie asked.

'We don't know. We were separated. We can only hope and pray.'

'She'll have Archie with her,' Mrs Stiles insisted.

Nina would not even have that . . .

'And your sister?' Mr Stiles remembered.

Connie found she could not answer. She turned her head away.

'*The Lord giveth and the Lord taketh away,*' Mr Stiles said, mis-understanding. '*Blessed be the name of the Lord.*'

When it isn't your sister, Connie thought resentfully. Would such acceptance extend to the loss of Imogen? If she were not with Archie? Or if Archie proved powerless to save her? He had been alone when she saw him near the Haldinghams . . .

Dear God, don't save me, save Nina. No, that was not how it should go. Dear God, not my will but Thine be done, because Thy will is mine, I can have no other as I go in unto the altar of God.

'Oh, Ivo, what are we going to do?'

At the foot of the narrow companionway Kate Haldingham clung to her husband's arm as tightly as she had clung to it when he had led her down the aisle as her bridegroom almost sixty years ago. But now her small face was pinched and puckered, and eyes which had then been bright with happiness glistened with unshed tears.

'We'll make our own way up as best we can,' Ivo said soothingly. 'Take your time, dear heart, and lean on me.'

He was surprised his voice sounded so normal, in view of the black anger which choked him; anger at himself first of all, at his own age and weakness; anger tinged with violence towards Archie Johnson who so obviously did not mean to return; anger at the crew of the *Karachi* for forgetting their oldest passengers; anger at the Irish, whose burning of Curraghmore had robbed him of his son-in-law and daughter and made this present nightmare all the worse.

'Oh, Ivo, not fire,' Kate had said when the alarm bells had sounded. He knew it was her secret dread. In the past two years even the innocent house fires lit on chilly evenings had caused her acute distress. She would not stay in the room to watch sticks and paper kindle; the crackle of dry wood made her weep. The servants were kind if uncomprehending and did their best not to occasion her grief, but Ivo knew that in every cheerful blaze she saw a staircase climbing upwards to a dark wall of smoke, and the comforting embers they had used to sit by were the ruins of Curraghmore.

Ivo found that his own emotions were directed outwards to those who had deliberately destroyed. What price the kind, soft-spoken ways of the Irish when they had stood by and let a few fanatics wreck centuries of loving pride? Because the Beauchamps were good landlords; there had been no trouble on the demesne until that night when half a dozen men on Harley motor-cycles – British government surplus, Ivo noted grimly – had ridden through its gates. 'They were armed,' the steward had written, 'and there was nothing we could do.' Nothing? Ivo was certain he would have done something; the men were outnumbered, after all. 'We carried out what we could from the downstairs rooms,' the steward's letter continued, 'while their leader tried to persuade Mr Beauchamp to come out.' Ivo could picture his son-in-law standing in the doorway of his domain defying them. Had he hoped they might be deterred? 'Many of us were in tears,' the steward's letter had stated, but Ivo dismissed this as superficial distress, for no one had ever come forward to identify these murderers, who had made no attempt to conceal their faces behind masks.

He could understand Kate's hatred of the never-to-be-trusted Irish, Ivo admitted, even though he had attempted throughout this voyage to induce some modification in her attitude to the Irish steward, who was obviously upset by it. Somehow he had never expected to find Irish staff aboard a British vessel, but of course England and Ireland were indissolubly linked. And not only by language: the centuries of commerce and settlement had always been two-way. There were Irish names throughout the length and breadth of England; Irish titles sat in the English House of Lords. But Kate, who had never consciously heard an Irish accent, would not let 'that murderer', as she called him, near her, would accept nothing at his hands, would not answer if he addressed her, and looked at him with undisguised hate. 'My wife doesn't care for the Irish,' Ivo murmured needlessly to other passengers, who nodded as if they understood.

A billow of black smoke appeared at the head of the companionway, hesitated, and rolled down towards them, setting them both coughing. The water in Kate's eyes brimmed over and made tracks down her smoke-grimed cheeks, but whether from inflammation or emotion Ivo could not tell. He produced his handkerchief and handed it to her.

'Put this over your nose and mouth.'

She shook her head and pushed it away from her. 'It makes no difference, Ivo. I can't go on.'

'Of course you can,' he said. 'One more step – there! We'll soon be in the open.' He dared not say fresh air.

To his horror, Kate slumped down on the step above them, almost pulling him with her. 'No, Ivo, I'll go like Joyce did. I've always known I would.'

Mrs Beauchamp was like one demented . . . So too Mrs Haldingham? But Joyce had rushed into the inferno in search of her husband and never found him. At least Kate was not alone.

Ivo sat down beside her, noting how dark it had become. The electric lights had no radiance, pale moons in a swirl of fog. He longed for a lungful of that dawn mountain air which had always surprised him with its sweetness as the mist in the valleys rose like petticoats tossed over the shoulders of the mountains and peak after peak disrobed to meet the day . . .

He put an arm round Kate and tried to raise her. 'One more step, dearest, for my sake.'

Her body resisted, but he was still the stronger. There was such a little way to go. As the smoke cleared he could see the exit above them; then, abruptly, it darkened again.

'Hold on, sir, I'm just coming.'

Kate jerked as though from an electric shock, almost overbalancing both of them. Someone grasped her other arm.

'No! Murderer!' She struggled to free herself.

'I never murdered anyone in my life,' John Joseph Fitzgerald said to Ivo. 'What's the old biddy – what's your wife got against me?'

'Nothing,' Ivo said. 'Against you.' It was a time for truth. 'Our only daughter and her husband were killed in the Troubles, when the Republicans burned down their house.'

John Joseph's spark of anger was quenched. The poor old woman. He knew how she felt: it was how Mam felt about Kieron. How he himself still felt.

'That makes two of us, ma'am,' he assured Kate, 'for my brother was shot by the British in Easter Week 1916. I saw it and I'll never forget it, but he died a martyr to Ireland's cause.'

Imperceptibly they had got Kate on her feet again and moved a step higher; she was unresisting now. Ivo did not know whether she had heard what the young Irish steward was saying, or whether she had given up in despair.

'And your daughter too, ma'am,' John Joseph went on. 'Another martyr when all the names are written down.'

336

And all the tears are shed and all the rancours buried . . .

'There've as many English died as Irish in our poor country . . . Come on, ma'am, lean on me and take another step. Sir, if you're ready . . . That's it, ma'am, not so bad now, was it?'

Encouraging, coaxing, always supporting, John Joseph led the Haldinghams out on deck.

'Put Mr Sutherland on. I want to speak to Mr Sutherland.'

Angus's voice was sharp.

'The Chief'll be along in a moment, sir.'

'You said that last time.'

'Yes, sir.' The young engineer's voice was cracking. 'I'll get Mr Martin, sir.'

The seconds stretched to eternity while Angus drummed his fingers. At last another voice sounded in his ear.

'Martin? For God's sake, man, what's happening? Has the fire broken out again?'

'Fire under control, sir,' the Second Engineer reported.

'And the hull plates?'

'The plates are holding, sir.'

'Then what –'

'Sir, there's been a bit of an accident. The stoker Gopal – he's dead.'

Angus's first thought was: Thank God. Then he remembered the Enquiry. Poor old Jamie would be for it now. 'Mr Sutherland, when you arrested this man, will you tell us exactly what happened?' – 'I had him cornered by the reserve bunker' – 'You were alone?' – 'Yes, sir.' – 'Why?' – 'I judged the situation to be dangerous.' – 'I see. Please go on.' That much Angus could project, but what *had* happened?

He asked the Second Engineer, and Martin's voice came clear over the bridge telegraph. 'He fell into the bunker, sir.'

'Where the fire was?'

'Yes, sir.'

'You actually saw him fall?'

'No, sir. Mr Sutherland told us what happened.'

So there were no witnesses . . .

'Mr Sutherland –' Angus could hear them at the Enquiry – 'you have heard Mr Bladon's evidence that on an earlier occasion when he was injured Gopal claimed to have been pushed. Is it possible, however accidentally, perhaps when you were striving to arrest him, that you could have pushed him in?' – 'No, sir, I never touched him.' Of course Jamie would say that. Then: 'He lost his balance,' or: 'It was deliberate.' – 'You mean he committed suicide?' – 'Yes, sir.' – 'How . . . convenient.' And there the slur would rest, ineradicable because unstated and the truth of the matter be known only to Jamie and his God.

Once it would have been known to me also, Angus reflected. Jamie would have told me the truth. But that was in the days before Cynthia . . . For the first time he wondered if Cynthia was worth what he had given up.

The duty officer approached. 'Message from the *République*, sir. She'll be here within half an hour, ready to take all passengers on board and return to Cherbourg.'

'Very good, Mr Stocks.'

The passengers still on the stern deck would also be transferred to safety – not before it was time. They'd been incredibly lucky when the glass blew to have just one fatality. That and the crewman who had Catherine-wheeled into the sea. And now of course Gopal. Angus prayed there would be no others, but the danger was not over yet. The fire amidships was still blazing, sending a burning cresset into the sky, marking their position better than any chart to those speeding to aid them; marking too their helplessness. His ship, his beloved, was blazing. Apart from damage below the waterline, unspecified as yet but not fatal, some of her public rooms were gutted, three of her lifeboats gone, her superstructure seriously damaged. Would it be the scrapyard rather than a refit? Angus could not bear to dwell on it. He would sooner lose Ailsa, lose Cynthia, lose the promise of another son . . . Only one man would understand his feelings.

He turned to the bridge telephonist. 'Get me Mr Sutherland again.'

'Mr Sutherland's not available, sir,' the man reported. 'Will you speak to Mr Martin?'

Angus snatched the instrument. 'Martin, where's the Chief?'

A hesitation. 'We've taken him to the hospital, sir.'

'Is he injured?' (But why else would they take him?)

'Yes, sir.'

'Badly?'

Again that hesitation. 'I would say so, sir.'

He must go to Jamie the first moment it became possible for him to leave the bridge, but there was no point in ringing the hospital: Bladon would have his hands full. A phrase from the references he had seen for Edmund Bladon came suddenly to mind: 'a dedicated doctor'. Please God let it be true.

The bridge screen ahead of him was misty, and it was nothing to do with swirling smoke. If the *Karachi* sailed again it would be without Jamie; he was transferring to the *Hyderabad*. But I'll make him change his mind, Angus promised; we make too good a pair. Either of us without the other would be diminished. He'll see reason in the end. He'll even accept the situation with Cynthia – if I ever see Cynthia again. For the first time it occurred to him that she might not wish to be reminded of the *Karachi* and her captain . . .

The bridge screen misted again.

Then it was struck by a sudden whoosh of water. Shouts. Men running

338

from all sides. The duty officer approaching with an air almost of jubilation. The fire-fighting tugs had arrived.

In the ship's hospital Edmund Bladon awaited casualties. After the horrifying discovery of the fire-filled writing-room, he had stayed just long enough to ensure that the first fire-fighters had arrived and that an officer had taken charge of them, and then returned to his post. Fire at sea. Even now it seemed impossible to credit that the blaze had taken hold so quickly. In one corner, perhaps, as the result of a careless match or cigarette, but not the whole room. It was almost as though it had been dowsed with paraffin. Could it have been deliberate?

Uneasily the episode with the stoker Gopal came back to him. Almost three weeks ago, between the blue sky and sea of the Indian Ocean, when Miss Constance Mary Martin was no more than a name on a passenger list. He had reported the man's accusations and much good it had done him – he recalled the Chief Engineer's scathing dismissal – but he had never reported the man's threats. 'Burn! All burn!' he had said. Had he meant it? Was this the result of the Chief's repressiveness? Edmund had not warmed to James Sutherland in their brief meetings: he had seen that kind of handsome, blinkered face before, too secure in its own conception of righteousness to be shaken by anything less than the Last Trump. It reminded him of his father: not because there was any physical resemblance, but because the two were of a type.

Well, the Last Trump had sounded for Jeffrey Bladon. He knows it all now, Edmund thought. *I shall know even as I am known.* How disconcerting, when one had no idea what God might think of one. His father would expect to be received as a social formality, but suppose the pearly gates were closed? For an instant Edmund enjoyed the thought of his father's expression, in which outrage, anger and amazement would rapidly combine. Then he remembered there were no pearly gates, no God whose existence postulated judgement if only by comparison with Him. His father, like himself, like most of the population, was the victim of a con trick. And at the word 'con' Edmund blanched.

Was she safe? She must be. The danger wasn't as great as all that. They'd get the fire under control and limp into port a day late with blackened superstructure and journalists and press photographers lined up on the dock. It would be a two-day wonder; then the public interest would die down and they would get on with the business of living. And Connie would see reason: he was sure of that. This wanting to be a nun was a temporary derangement, brought on by guilt, however mistaken, over Nina's fate. Once ashore, with life back to normal, she would see it for what it was. Dammit, he'd *make* her: take her to meet Anne in London, take her to Gloucestershire to see the house and grounds. If after all that she still wanted to go on with this nonsense, he wouldn't stand in her way. But she wouldn't, if only because she'd never leave Nina. He supposed he'd

339

have to accept responsibility for his sister-in-law. So long as she wasn't pregnant . . . Yet even if she wasn't, her future was still in doubt. The convent would have been so neat a solution, though even in Nina's case he'd considered it a waste. Then how much more in Connie's; she wasn't created for that, not with that hair, those eyes, that body less voluptuous than Nina's but supple and springy, inviting mastery by its very resistance, that proud carriage as she walked –

He was interrupted by the first of the casualties, a crewman with a burnt arm.

'How's it going?' Edmund asked as he dressed it.

The man shook his head. 'Not good. Captain say lower the boats, take passengers, but fire –' he spread his hands – 'whoof!'

A small chill seeped outwards from Edmund's stomach and settled itself round his heart. Of course it was no more than a precaution; for Connie's sake he should be glad; yet the thought of those small boats afloat on a choppy sea in darkness was enough to fill anyone with dread.

Thereafter minor casualties came thick and fast. Through them Edmund learned of successive disasters: the man, clothes ablaze, who had thrown himself into the sea (pray God he had no casualties like that to deal with); the starboard boats on fire; the confusion because the main staircase was impassable; the passengers crowded into the port boats; the second fire in the reserve bunker and the fear that there was a fire-raiser on board, at which point Edmund almost said 'Gopal' and then forced himself to silence in case it was no such thing. He heard about the little Irish steward and how he had single-handedly brought the aged Haldinghams up on deck. 'Reckon he saved their lives, Doc,' said the man reporting it. 'They was just in time for the last boat.' He saw some of the casualties caused by the glass splintering outwards from the lounge windows. 'Though there's one you won't be able to do anything for,' a man with his cheek lacerated assured him. 'They just covered him with a tarpaulin and left him there. My God, you should have seen him, Doctor – he was laid open from here to here –' The man's gesture was graphic and he turned, retching, away.

Edmund gathered that a number of male First Class passengers were still on the stern deck, but that all the women and children had been taken off.

'You're sure?' he asked a man.

'Dead sure.' The man laughed shrilly, his hysteria barely under control. 'Sorry, Doc. Funny expression.'

'Forget it,' Edmund said.

'Forget it!' The man's voice rose sharply. 'No chance I ever shall, what with the smoke and the light of the flames and the darkness – it was like something out of Hell. And all those boats being lowered into blackness, the upturned faces like white flowers; then bending forward against the wind and spray, and the outline of the boats becoming fainter as they pulled farther and farther away.'

340

'What about rescue?'

'They say there's a French liner on her way – she can't get here too soon. Otherwise there's just a handful of fishing-boats which are anxiously standing by.'

Edmund thought of Connie – and Nina. He hoped they had warm clothes. He hoped they weren't too frightened. He hoped they would be picked up soon. They would be together in the same boat – that was something. He should have been in it too. He remembered Connie saying that they had never been apart and that both dreaded their impending separation. Surely that alone would justify her in a change of heart?

Awkward footsteps and a bumping sound in the corridor outside alerted him. They were carrying someone down. He went to the door. Two men with a limp tarpaulin-shrouded bundle. Could it be the man laid open from here to here? No, he was pinned to the deck, his informant had told him; they couldn't move him yet. Then who . . .?

'This one's a goner, Doc,' one of the men said, panting, 'but we thought we'd better bring him down.'

Edmund did not recognize the men, presumably crewmen; all red-rimmed eyes in smoke-blackened faces were beginning to look alike. 'Put him there,' he said, pointing to the examination couch. 'You're probably right, but it isn't always easy to tell.'

The men deposited their burden and stood back, seeming expectant.

'It's all right,' Edmund said. 'I'll take over.'

Still they hovered.

He drew back the tarpaulin from the face.

The first thing he saw was Florrie Gurslake's ivory dagger, which earlier that evening he had admired in Nina Martin's hair. Now it protruded from an eyeball; if he drew it out it would be sticky with blood and brain. Despite his training, Edmund felt his own gorge rising. He swallowed and looked away.

'I'm afraid you're right, he's dead,' he said with an effort. 'Where did you find him?'

The senior crewman described the place.

How on earth had he got there? How had Nina . . . Edmund checked himself. This was no time to speculate.

He re-covered the face.

'Since you're still here,' he said to the two men, 'perhaps you'd move him over there. There's nothing I can do for him and I may need the couch for others.'

Like zombies they obeyed, and still like zombies departed. Edmund breathed a sigh of relief. Would they have recognised the dagger? It was unlikely. They did not mix with passengers. Steeling himself, he withdrew the weapon and cleaned it first with cold water and then with surgical spirit. He was destroying evidence, but there were other ways in which the man could have come by such an injury – ways that would not implicate

341

Connie's sister, or even Connie, for who knew what she might do in Nina's defence? Edmund hid the dagger away; time enough to dispose of it later. He wondered what Stafford Briscoe would advise. He had a strong suspicion Briscoe's instincts would be the same as his: prevent a bad situation from becoming a worse one, and limit the suffering involved. Perhaps some day they would have a chance to discuss it in an abstract, theoretical way, naming no names and referring to no particular incident, yet each knowing what was meant. Meanwhile he must do his duty and report the fatality . . .

Scarcely had he replaced the bridge telephone when footsteps, voices cursing, a cry of 'Careful!' warned him another casualty was on the way.

This one arrived on a makeshift stretcher. Two bearers escorted by an officer and followed by an anxious, grim-faced crowd congested the corridor outside the surgery.

Edmund commanded, 'Bring him in,' after a glance at the man's face, the only visible portion, which appeared to have been flayed. Extensive burns. The type of casualty he had prayed he would not be faced with – his resources were too limited. Bad enough in a well-equipped hospital, but in the middle of the English Channel . . .

'Who is it?' he asked briefly.

Half a dozen voices answered and their words fell away from him.

'The Chief . . . the Chief . . . the Chief . . .'

Archie Johnson was exhilarated and ashamed of it. He was also cold and wet, though not more so than he had been many times in the trenches; but now, as then, the sense of danger stimulated him, making him acutely aware of his surroundings and at the same time unaware, except in so far as she was an irritation, of the sodden bundle of misery beside him that was Imogen.

Another wave slopped into the lifeboat. Imogen gasped and shuddered and tried to draw her feet under her, away from the eight or nine inches of water that slurped in the bottom of the boat.

'Are we going to drown?'

'I shouldn't think so.' Archie's tone verged on the hearty. 'That French liner's here. It's her wake that's causing us to bob about like this.'

'I feel sick,' Imogen moaned.

She was not the only one. The bad sailors among the passengers were already suffering, and in the overcrowded boat their suffering was not confined to themselves. The elegant Mrs Vane looked like one of the damned on Resurrection morning. Even so, she called at intervals for her son.

'He'll be safe in one of the other boats, dear, you'll see,' the woman beside her promised.

'But he's so little. I ought never to have left him.'

'Someone will take care of him.'

'It should have been his mother.'

'Of course, dear, but they'll make sure a little boy's all right. Oh –' as Cynthia succumbed to another surge of sickness – 'you are in a bad way, you poor thing.'

The officer in charge of the lifeboat was standing up, giving orders. The boat began to swing in a wide arc, and as she did so the passengers saw for the first time the lights of the *République* towering above them and realised rescue was at hand.

The scene was extraordinary. The *République*'s lights illumined one stretch of sea, while behind them the red glare from the *Karachi* turned another stretch to burnished bronze. Where waves broke, or where the wakes of lifeboats and tugs created them, they were tipped with flamingo pink. And otherwise all was darkness, stretching to the horizon's rim. It reminded Archie of No Man's Land, as he had seen it so many times: a sea of mud, barbed wire, and shattered trees and buildings, watched over by these same indifferent stars, and broken here and there by the lights and fires of man's activity which still failed to dent the darkness all around.

Out of that darkness the ship's lifeboats were converging on the *République*'s welcome lights. They manoeuvred with more or less skill according to the degree to which they were overloaded and the experience of whoever was in charge. Archie was pleased to note that his boat was one of the first to reach the liner, not only because it indicated the efficiency he expected, but because he fretted less at not being in command. No one had ever suggested that Captain Johnson was less than an efficient officer – too efficient, some said – but opening fire on the crowd at Maggapore was not the first time his zeal had outrun discretion. The Colonel in his report of the incident and its outcome had intimated that he was not entirely surprised. The surprise was all on Archie's part, for what else could he have done when British troops were faced by hostile natives who had to be taught their place? Not that one could expect the little princeling to see it that way: it was damn bad luck he had been aboard the *Karachi* and there had been that showdown in the lounge. Some of old man Haldingham's remarks still rankled; of course he was too old to count, but they had reopened the wound of dismissal, which festered enough, God knew. Dismissal for doing his duty, for safeguarding the lives of his men; more correctly, dismissal to placate the Nawab and his simpering faggot of a son. If there was anyone Archie would have been glad to see drown it was Ravi, but he thought it unlikely this wish would be fulfilled. They wouldn't dare let anything happen to him – too much of a diplomatic incident. Men like Briscoe and that old fool Haldingham would go out of their way to make sure he was all right, even at the expense of British lives, their own for preference, though there too Archie suspected he would not have much luck. Someone would have been sure to help the Haldinghams; he hadn't really put them at risk, just made it clear that he wasn't going to be fool enough to help a man who had condemned him before his own kind. Damn it, if the

343

British didn't stick together, what hope was there for the Empire? It was men like Haldingham and Briscoe who were undermining it, for which they would retire full of years and honour, while he, Archie, was turned out into a world he was ill-equipped to deal with and in urgent need of a job.

The injustice of it rankled only slightly less with Archie than the injustice of his physical plight. A dose of clap for spending a brief paid hour in the arms of loveliness, letting her soothe away some of the hurt. And now shame was piled on shame. That prissy doctor and his preaching about celibacy – well, he'd shown him how little his lecturing counted: he'd got engaged to Imogen Stiles, and though their caresses had so far been limited, it wouldn't stay that way for long. Of course he'd go to a clinic, do something about that burning throbbing, but they needn't think he was going to keep away from women when it was a woman who'd started it. And Imogen might yet prove an asset. The daughter of a clergyman, even an Evangelical, was the sort of wife a young officer ought to have. Except that he was no longer a young Army officer, and Imogen was being sick again.

Their boat had been made fast to the side of the *République* and a ladder was being lowered. Archie stood up and grasped it, helping to make it fast. This won him a nod of approval from the officer in charge of the boat. Other boats were approaching, and the red glare from the *Karachi* was subsiding as the fire-fighting tugs did their work, sending great snakes of water into the vessel which hissed and blended smoke with steam. Suddenly a fresh spear of flame lanced skywards. Archie, standing with his back to the rescuing liner, was the first to see. One of the tugs backed and manœuvred swiftly to reach this fresh outbreak, setting the small craft bobbing in her wake. At once Archie realised the danger, but his mighty shout of warning, though delivered at maximum lung-power, was puny on the night air.

In trying to take avoiding action, one of the lifeboats had turned too sharply and heeled over in the surging wake. It hung there for a moment while water poured over the screaming passengers who had rolled to the bottom of the boat. Then, before the horrified eyes of those in the lifeboats, on board the *République*, in the fishing-boats hovering protective and helpless, even on the stricken *Karachi* herself, the boat capsized and floated dark hull uppermost, surrounded by a flotilla of round dark bobbing heads.

'Is there nothing you can do for him?' Angus asked.

'No.'

Edmund had spent the night doing what he could for the Chief Engineer, but it amounted to no more than antisepsis and efforts to alleviate pain. That the efforts were largely unavailing did not deter him. He could not hold Jamie Sutherland back from that abyss towards which he was slipping, but he must give him ease while he could. Some part of himself was also slipping towards it, because in struggles like these patient and

344

doctor fused, and though at the last Edmund knew he must step back and allow the Chief to travel on alone, whatever part of love and labour had been expended on him as an individual would go with him, leaving the doctor exhausted and emotionally drained.

That it was love Edmund recognised. He had not liked the Chief, but the man's massive courage had won his admiration, and as they fought through the small hours, each knowing the fight was hopeless, the bond had been irrefragably forged. For much of the time the Chief was conscious, yet scarcely a groan escaped his blackened, blistered lips. The big body lay inert, apart from the rise and fall of the chest, each involuntary movement ending in a gasp of agony as it was transmitted to the burnt flesh. To die instantly, as Bert Gurslake had done, now seemed to Edmund the apotheosis of good fortune – or like that other who lay covered with a sheet in an annexe, Nina Martin's ivory dagger no longer protruding from his eye.

The hospital in the forward part of the ship had so far escaped both fire and water, though smoke hung heavy in the air and only a short distance away amidships the fire-fighters struggled through inches of hose-water which the *Karachi*'s pumps were now attempting to clear. For the fires were out: that was what Captain Meiklejohn had come to convey in person, and now that there was no further immediate danger, his concern was all for his friend.

To Edmund the Captain appeared to have aged twenty years since he had last seen him, less than six hours ago. His face was grimed with smoke and grey with exhaustion, his hair lank and no longer combed to conceal incipient baldness, his eyes red-rimmed from lack of sleep. The bones of his face stood out like those of the dying. His voice was hoarse when he spoke. Even so, he had still knocked politely on the surgery door, had enquired, 'May I come in, Doctor?' as though his visit were routine and he had not had to avert his eyes from the stained and crumpled uniform lying where Edmund had thrown it, on which were clearly visible the four gold and purple sleeve rings denoting a chief engineer. Edmund had tried in vain to prepare the Captain for what he was going to see, but 'You forget, Mr Bladon, that I was on this ship when the torpedo struck her,' was all the acknowledgement he received. Then the Captain had moved gently but firmly past him to the inner room where Jamie Sutherland lay, and only the briefest check in his stride, an indrawn breath, betrayed his emotion as he caught sight of his friend.

'Is he conscious?' he asked Edmund.

'Unfortunately, yes.'

The Captain nodded and advanced.

'Jamie, it's Angus.'

The blistered lips moved, repeating the name.

When words fail, gesture mediates; but there was no part of the Chief Angus could touch without adding to his pain. He realised it with horror, at the same time as he became conscious of the smell. No dressings or antiseptic could quite conceal it: the unmistakable odour of burnt flesh. Angus breathed deeply, forcing back the desire to retch. This was Jamie; Jamie needed him; nothing about Jamie could disgust. And Jamie was trying to speak to him; once again the tortured lips moved.

He leaned forward, striving to catch the whisper that was all that remained of that once-resonant voice.

'I didna push him, Angus. It was no deliberate, ye ken.'

Jamie absolving himself. Jamie saving his captain trouble. Jamie considerate to the end. There was a force about a death-bed confession, and Angus had no doubt it would be believed. But Jamie would never now face an Enquiry: that would be for his captain to do, and to ensure that the name of Jamie Sutherland emerged spotless.

'I never doubted it, Jamie,' he said.

The Chief appeared to relax, if that were possible. Looking up, Angus met Edmund's eye and the two men withdrew out of earshot.

'Not long now, I'm afraid,' Edmund said.

Angus nodded, and nodded again in acceptance when Edmund informed him that there was nothing more he could do. Jamie had been too late to grasp Gopal before his final plunge into the bunker, but in time to meet head on the mighty blow-back of flame. He had known from the moment he saw him that Jamie was dying, and known that Jamie knew it too. A short while ago he had wanted to touch him, but touch was irrelevant now. Their communion was not of the flesh but of the spirit. They were two souls face to face. To the last Jamie had done his duty as he saw it; no man living could do more. If perhaps his conception of duty had been narrow, distorted, that was part of the condition of being human and he was paying for it now. Whereas he, Angus, despite being given a very clear perception of duty, had listened to the lure of the flesh, which, now that he saw it burnt and agonised before him, revealed its meaninglessness. What mattered was not a handclasp with Jamie, but what transcended flesh; but with Cynthia, however close the embrace, there was nothing except the chimaera of a boy somewhere between Bobby and Andy, who would never now exist. It was for this boy, whose parents were destined never to come together, that Angus bowed his head.

Edmund stood awkwardly by, supposing the Captain was praying. When the Captain spoke he almost jumped.

'I shall stay with him.'

The voice brooked no denial, and Edmund stood aside for him to re-enter the room where Jamie Sutherland lay. It was a small room, no more than a cubicle, white-painted, with barely space for an iron bedstead, locker and upright chair. Edmund saw at once that the figure on the bed had moved slightly; the head was turned towards the door.

Angus saw it too.

'Did ye think I'd deserted you, Jamie?' He settled himself on the chair.

Edmund, sensing this was an intimacy he could not intrude on, withdrew behind the door. How long could this agony last? When the Chief had been brought in and he had first seen the nature and extent of the burns, he had thought him dead already, yet hours later he still lived. His great strength, which had seemed a blessing, was proving at the last a curse. How much longer would the morphia supply hold out? Edmund ran his eye over the phials: he had injected as much as he dared – no, more, knowing that the case was hopeless, and there was not a great deal left. If another serious casualty arrived . . . But there would be no others. Only a skeleton crew remained on board. He himself should have gone long since, except that the Chief could not be moved and a doctor stayed with his patient. The passengers at least were gone, Connie and Nina among them in that lifeboat that should have held him too. Would he ever see either again? Nina he must, if only to learn the truth about that dagger, but Connie . . . Yet even now she might change her mind, see sense, admit the force of his arguments. A thrill ran through him like returning life, only to be checked and held as his body had been held earlier by the steady gaze of those blue eyes. She would not change – he knew that. A part of him would not respect her if she did. Instead she would immolate herself on the altar of the non-existent, and in such a wilderness of nullity he could no longer even damn God.

In the cubicle he heard the Captain speaking. 'I'll break the news to Barbara myself.'

The head on the pillow moved. In acknowledgement?

'And, Jamie, there'll be no word of blame at the Enquiry. I'll make sure of that.'

This time there was an acknowledgement; then, after a while, the lips moved again. Angus leaned forward to catch the whisper.

'Minna?'

Had he heard correctly? Had the dying Chief Engineer of the *Karachi* really murmured the name of the ship's cat?

'I'll look after her,' Angus promised – if she hadn't lost all her nine lives.

The Chief lay silent as though waiting. Angus knew what he was waiting for.

He lowered his voice, never doubting Jamie could still hear him, though Edmund from the doorway could not.

'Jamie, at the end of the voyage I'll be going north again. As usual.' He could not bring himself to utter Cynthia's name, still less Ailsa's and Andy's.

The blistered lips parted in what could have been a smile. 'Good man.'

There was another, longer silence. Then the Chief exhaled a little more slowly than usual and Angus waited in vain for him to draw another breath. From the doorway Edmund stepped forward and drew the sheet over the staring, lidless eyes.

347

'Be thankful,' he said.

'Aye.' The Captain's Scottish accent was more pronounced. 'I'm thankful for Jamie right enough, and grateful to you, Doctor. I know you did what you could.'

'It was so little.'

'He waited for me. I should have come sooner – would have done, if it hadna been for the boat.'

'What boat?'

'The lifeboat that capsized, man. But down here ye would not know about that. She was caught in the wake of one of the tugs and heeled too far over to be able to right herself.'

'The passengers . . .?'

'Most were saved. The fishing-boats and the lifeboats did a grand job, and so did the *République*'s boat. It could have been worse, but even so, there's no knowing how many are missing. The boats are scattered, ye see, and the darkness does not help matters, though night's giving place to day.'

The blackness was indeed giving way to greyness, but in this small, artificially lit room where life and death fought it out, the struggle between day and darkness went unnoticed.

The Captain laid a hand on Edmund's arm.

'A boat from the *République* will fetch you, Mr Bladon. You can do no more here. Go aboard and get some sleep.'

'And you, sir?'

Angus squared his shoulders a little stiffly. 'The Captain stays with his ship. We can maybe get her engines going and she should make port under her own steam. Plymouth is the nearest, though the *République* will return to Cherbourg. We must thank God things are no worse. Apart from the Chief and the four fatalities we know of, we must hope no more lives have been lost.'

It was a vain hope, and he knew it. Screaming passengers in the capsized lifeboat cascading into the sea would be too shocked to act rationally and die as much from drowning due to panic as from any other cause. The fishing-boats were not equipped with radio, and were returning to their home ports. Until some tally could be made it was impossible to tell the extent of the catastrophe, but he saw no need to spell this out.

'Which boat was it?' Edmund asked idly.

The Captain allowed himself a grim smile. 'Yours. Number three on the port side. The Chief maybe did you a service, Mr Bladon, keeping you occupied below.'

348

IV

At Cherbourg the dock was crowded. An alert reporter in Plymouth had phoned a London daily, and phone calls through the night had gone out to every English-speaking newspaperman in Paris, as well as one or two elsewhere. A young man sent to do what he knew would be a dull article on the equally dull subject of Deauville out of season was roused from sleep and commanded to get to Cherbourg by whatever means he could find. This proved to be a local taxi at truly exorbitant cost. Others took the first train from Paris, Americans well to the fore, for by no means all the English papers maintained a Paris office and the scent of freelance pickings added to the over-excited reportorial air.

Photographers had also gathered, but whereas to begin with the reporters concentrated on any available survivor disembarking from the *République*, the photographers selected those distinguished by physical beauty, social prominence, or extreme emotionalism, and since Cynthia Vane possessed the first and last qualities in abundance, pictures of her with her arm round her son were available in Fleet Street in time for the late evening editions.

It was Bobby, however, who supplied the journalists with a scoop. 'I saw fire-raiser, says Bobby, 8' was the first hint given to the world that the fire might not have been accidental. The Owners, in fear of liability, immediately issued a statement to the effect that the cause of the disaster would be revealed only in the course of the official Enquiry, but Bobby's version spread with the speed of the fire itself, and a number of sightings of the fire-raiser were promptly reported, though they varied significantly.

To Bobby the whole thing was a bewildering experience. His failure to reach the Captain rankled, for which he felt Miss Nina was to blame. His mother's survival he had never doubted, and the emotional reunion to which she had subjected him when he was at last landed, wet and shivering, on the deck of the *République* seemed and still seemed to him excessive. He was reluctant to have it reproduced for the benefit of these men crowding around him with notebooks and cameras, particularly in view of his attire. The passengers on the French liner had generously donated clothes for the soaked, bedraggled victims whom they had watched arriving on board, but Bobby's relief at being warm and dry was tempered by awareness that a blouson with a sailor collar was not something a self-respecting English eight-year-old ever wore. His statement about Gopal had been intended to distract rather than to draw attention, and he was mystified by its effect.

'Say that again, sonny,' a reporter called. 'Did you recognise the man?'

Bobby shook his head. He had been by no means certain that the figure was human, though he was beginning to suspect that it was. The Devil and things supernatural had receded from his consciousness; he was almost enjoying himself, especially now that the weight of his lie about Dr Bladon had been lifted. He had not told the Captain, but he had told Miss Nina, and she was the one who had been hurt. If he could only change his clothes and get away from his mother! The anonymity of school uniform seemed suddenly a relief. Already he sensed that having been a passenger aboard the *Karachi* would invest him with interest. He pictured himself holding forth to a group in the dormitory, their excited questions and his own nonchalant replies. Like other, older passengers, he was in the process of adjusting his story so that it told the maximum of what his hearers wanted to know – a process which required that Gopal's diminutive figure be transformed into a towering giant. The reporters scribbled busily.

Those who had cornered Stafford Briscoe found him less forthcoming. Yes, there had been a fire. The alarm had been given towards midnight. He believed it had started in the writing-room. No, he did not know what had caused it – possibly a cigarette. He had seen no fire-raiser, did not know if one existed. Everyone had behaved very well. Even when some of the starboard boats had been destroyed there had been no panic and one or two heroic acts – the Irish steward making his first voyage, for instance, who had braved the heat and smoke to go below and rescue an elderly couple who had somehow fallen behind.

As he had calculated, this had the effect of diverting attention, as reporters made off in search of John Joseph Fitzgerald, whose name he had been delighted to give. Stafford Briscoe respected courage; he admired what the young man had done; at a later date he must acquaint the Captain and the Owners with the steward's action and make sure it was recognised. Meanwhile there was another young man – Ravi – to be considered. How much could be salvaged there? Thank God for the death of Bert Gurslake – who could have foreseen an end like that? And Ravi had been quick to seize the jewelled dagger: he was a brain as well as a body, and that was all to the good. Once they were en route for London it should be easy enough to seek him out: the man to man compliment, the lightest touch on the shoulder, the offer of hospitality . . . And of course a word with the India Office, making sure that Ravi knew . . . It was regrettable to conclude that the fire might have its blessings, but it was also true.

For one thing, it would take the heat out of the investigation – he allowed himself a smile at his unconscious choice of phrase – into the so-called rape of Nina Martin. If it had ever taken place. Stafford Briscoe was honestly doubtful: the trouble with over-sexed girls of that age – and anyone could see the girl was ripe for plucking – was that their imaginations ran away. No doubt there had been an encounter of some kind: no smoke without a fire – again he smiled; there seemed no way of avoiding an incendiary connotation – but it had surely stopped short of rape. And if it hadn't, there was no hope now of identifying the culprit: too much evidence had been destroyed. The man might be dead. His mind ranged over the casualties: Bert Gurslake; the seaman who had cartwheeled into the sea; several passengers and crew unaccounted for in the capsized lifeboat; the Chief Engineer, so they said; and the fire-raiser, because of course there had been one, only it was not politic to tell reporters so. In disaster the first priority was containment; only then did you assess what could be done. And if the Resident in Maggapore knew his business something would be: Ravi's marriage could be postponed . . . In imagination Briscoe saw himself already on that terrace with its fountains and its peacocks, and breathed a more liberated air.

Imogen Stiles too felt the yoke of parental restraint slide from her shoulders. The reunion with her parents had been tearful on all sides, but while her father praised God, Imogen praised Archie and saw to it that her praise was heard. She was not too specific about what he had done (had he really saved her?), but of his presence at her side in the open boat there was no doubt, and she had clung to him, exaggerating her weakness as a means of boosting his strength. By the time the *République* docked at Cherbourg and she had seen the crowd of reporters, she had determined that, newly engaged, they were worth an interview, and a little rearranging of their position as they descended the gangway ensured that they were prominent. Nevertheless, it was a sense of theatre such as had marked her father's Armistice Day service which caused her to command her fiancé as they neared the bottom of the gangway, 'Lift me up.' – 'What's wrong?' Archie asked. 'Don't argue – do it,' said the voice of his future wife. Archie obliged. 'Not like that, stupid.' Imogen rearranged herself and smiled brilliantly – she had good teeth and it was perhaps as well she had lost her glasses – as Archie set foot on shore. Several photographers responded as she had expected; reporters crowded round. 'War hero saves bride-to-be' announced the caption above the photograph, which was another to make the late-night extra in time.

The elderly couple with their arms round a young steward was another picture rushed to Fleet Street. The Haldinghams did not mind. They were so intent on praising John Joseph and his heroism that they would gladly have paid for it to appear. As it was, they vied with each other in heaping praises upon him until John Joseph blushed to such an extent that they desisted out of pity, though Kate Haldingham soon began again. 'You see,' she explained, 'I have hated the Irish since they burnt our daughter and her husband in their home at Curraghmore, but I see now I was wrong to condemn a whole people for the excesses of a few. I never thought I'd live to bless the day I heard an Irish accent, but I'm thankful I've lived that long.' At any other time it would have made a story, but the reporters were spoiled for choice. John Joseph's nationality was of little import; what mattered was his heroism.

John Joseph was surprised they made so much of it. When Mr Briscoe had alerted him that the Haldinghams had not come up on deck, he had naturally gone to see what had become of them – well, he couldn't have let Mr Briscoe go, a passenger and an older gentleman: it was as simple as that. The whole trouble was Mrs Haldingham had sprained her ankle, but with the two of them it hadn't taken long to get her up the companionway. Yes, he told reporters, the smoke had been a nuisance, it had set Mr Haldingham coughing, but they'd managed, as anyone could see. And praise be to all the saints, they'd been in time for the last lifeboat. Yes, of course he'd prayed – to Blessed Mary and to St Patrick, and once – when things looked bad for a little – to St Jude. The reporters were not interested in the details of his devotions, but it gave them another line. 'I prayed, says trapped steward.' Fleet Street loved it, and New York wasn't far behind.

Nina Martin dreaded descending that gangway. Her one instinct was to hide, to pretend that none of this had happened and that it was Connie, not Edmund, by her side. Not that Edmund hadn't been good to her. He had been one of the last to come aboard the *République*, and at sight of his worn face her heart went out to him. He had seen her and come to her at once.

'Any news?' He meant of Connie.

Mutely she shook her head.

'Don't give up hope.'

She had never had any. From the moment she had heard what had happened to the lifeboat – that boat she should have been on – she had known she was alone. God was punishing her. Connie – friend, sister, protector – was gone.

'Connie's dead.' She tried saying the words aloud, but they were still meaningless.

'Not necessarily,' Edmund said. He stopped at sight of the hopeless face turned towards him and contented himself with the promise that they would talk again.

'Connie's dead.' He too said the words aloud and could not believe them. Could so much brightness be extinguished? Drowned? He glanced at the grey waters of the Channel heaving in the November morning. Was he looking at Connie's grave? *We therefore commit her body to the deep* . . . The words of Florrie Gurslake's committal came back to him. How long ago it seemed. Yet it was less than a week since he had watched the black-scarved heads of the sisters bow in unison as Florrie's coffin slid from the protection of its pall and tilted, tilted, before arcing its way to the sea. The splash had been inaudible, there was no ripple, scarcely a trace of foam.

352

But Connie went uncoffined, unhallowed; she would float for a time just beneath the surface of the sea and already small scavengers would gather . . . Edmund shook his head to clear away the thought. It was better to think of Connie living, even behind a convent grille, than rising, falling, sinking, to become one more secret of the sea.

Meanwhile there was Connie's sister to be cared for, at least until Uncle Charles and Aunt Maura arrived. Though Edmund had been beside her as they descended the gangway, it was not until they were temporarily installed in a hotel in Cherbourg that he had a chance to seek her out. The First Class passengers had hotel accommodation, the Second Class were sheltered in schools and local halls, until cross-Channel steamers could arrive to ferry them back to Weymouth and waiting boat trains, and the arms of relatives.

Heavy-hearted, Edmund tapped at Nina's door that morning. Many passengers had congregated in the hotel lounge, glad to talk and exchange stories in the euphoria of safety, but Nina was not there. He had glimpsed Cynthia Vane and Bobby, the old couple – the Haldinghams – and Archie Johnson, which surely meant that the leech-like Imogen could not be far away; but there was no sign of Stafford Briscoe's tall figure, nor of Ravi's handsome one – were they together again? He would have Briscoe as a neighbour in the country until he could sell the estate and buy himself a practice somewhere – perhaps in London, not too far from Aunt Anne. He had already dispatched a telegram announcing his safety. Nina had presumably done the same to her aunt and informed her that Connie was missing, but with the helpless, unworldly Nina you could not even be certain of that. Connie, now – Connie was efficient; Connie would have taken charge; but someone would always have to look after Nina. For the moment it fell to him.

There was no answer to his knock. He knocked again, more loudly. This time there was a scuffling, followed by a frightened 'Who's there?'

'It's me, Edmund.'

The door was opened a crack and a blue eye in a sliver of face peered out at him.

'Oh! – it really is you.'

'Who did you think it might be?' Edmund asked as she admitted him.

'I wasn't sure. It might have been the – the rapist.'

'I think you know very well it couldn't be him.'

He watched her crumple on to the bed as he held out Florrie Gurslake's ivory hair ornament.

'I believe this now belongs to you.'

'Where did you get it?'

'From the body of a patient brought to my surgery.'

She began to cry quietly, hopelessly. 'Will they hang me, do you think?'

He was about to say they didn't hang women, but the Thompson-Bywaters case had put an end to such comforting delusions. For the first time in eighteen years a woman had gone to the scaffold, and for far less than Nina had done. Instead he said, 'Tell me what happened.'

Haltingly, Nina began.

'Are you sure it was the same man?' he interrupted.

'Yes, I would have known him anywhere. He was wearing a mask and gloves, only he didn't have a knife this time: he put his hands around my throat instead.'

'And there was no one else about?'

'No.'

'You're certain?'

'I saw no one.'

'So you stabbed him in self-defence?'

'I suppose so. My hair came loose and the dagger slid downwards. When I found it near my hand I thrust it at his face. He was choking me,' she added. 'I only wanted to make him let me go.'

'Show me your throat.'

She undid the high-necked dress she was wearing. The bruises were dark on her white skin.

'Did I really kill him?'

'I'm afraid so. By a chance in a thousand, the dagger penetrated the brain.'

Nina shuddered.

Edmund reached a decision as he retrieved the dagger. 'I think I'd better dispose of this, don't you?'

'Isn't it evidence?'

'Of what? In hurrying to take up position when the fire alarm sounded Third Officer Strode obviously stumbled and fell on some sharp object which pierced his eyeball. Who is to say what it was?'

It was easier now he had said Strode's name. Nina also seemed to find it easier.

'I can't believe it was him. He was always so polite and helpful. Why should he have done this?'

'I don't know,' Edmund said, thinking of that neat, small figure about whom so little was known and who would never now reveal the motives that lay behind his twisted lusts.

'He tried to kill me,' Nina said in wonder.

'He must have been out of his mind with fear, thinking you'd recall some detail that would betray him. He decided to make sure.'

'I suppose I did recall something in a way,' Nina said slowly. 'I mean, it wouldn't have identified him for certain but I think it would have helped.'

Edmund waited.

'He was wearing a wristwatch,' she went on. 'It came back to me when he put his hands around my throat. Most men still prefer fob watches – you do yourself.' She smiled. 'So do the Captain and Mr Briscoe and almost all the other men on board. Archie Johnson doesn't, but I knew it wasn't him – and there's something else I remember: that first time he wasn't wearing a dinner jacket, which means he must have been crew. But I never suspected Julian Strode. Why, I even danced with him.'

'As you did with me,' Edmund reminded her.

'I never thought it was you. And anyway, that horrible little boy confessed to me that he'd been lying and he never saw you at all.'

A weight slid from Edmund's shoulders. There would be no need now for it to come out that he and John Joseph Fitzgerald had been aiding the stowaway. John Joseph's job was safe.

'What about the men who brought Mr Strode's body to your surgery?' Nina demanded, showing an unexpected practical streak.

'They were native crewmen. It's unlikely they will be questioned.' Or that, if they were, much reliance would be placed on what they said.

'And you don't think I'm a murderess?' Nina persisted.

'I think you acted as any courageous young woman would in self-defence. I doubt if a jury would convict you. Not that they're going to have the chance.'

'And God?'

The God who made Julian Strode and Nina Martin could judge between them.

'I don't know anything about God.'

'You don't think He's punished me by killing Connie?'

'Where would be the justice in that?'

'I don't know. I don't know anything any longer. Oh, Edmund, I'm so tired.'

Had he ever thought her an image of faith and certainty, Edmund wondered, as he asked a few brisk medical questions. In some ways she seemed to him the greatest casualty of all. Others had lost life or loved ones, belongings, but Nina had lost her faith and her sister, the two things which informed her life. The second loss Edmund shared; the first he had lived with since that moment not yet twenty-four hours ago when Connie's faith had confounded his own, but he couldn't tell Nina that. She needed support, someone to take over the practicalities, as Connie would have done. And that meant seeing Stafford Briscoe, who would sooner or later be asked for the report which Captain Meiklejohn had requested. Briscoe at least would have to know the truth. Edmund believed his discretion could be trusted, but there remained a glimmer of doubt. It was with unease that he left Nina, promising to call again later, and made his way to Briscoe's door.

When he knocked the response was an immediate call to come in. Briscoe was alone – Edmund had half-expected he would have Ravi with him – standing by the window looking down on the bustle of the port. The *République*, her unscheduled passengers discharged, was preparing to sail, her captain anxious to make up as much time as possible on the North Atlantic run. Voyagers lined the rails, flags were flying, gulls screaming and swooping under a filmy sun just bright enough to set her superstructure gleaming; she was all grace and luxury. Even in their short time aboard the rescued had been conscious of her spaciousness compared with the often cramped conditions on the *Karachi*. The *République* belonged to the future; the *Karachi* was already of the past.

Briscoe turned from the window to survey the doctor standing in the doorway. His voice was neutral as he said, 'If you've come to give me a medical check-up, there's no need, I assure you. I'm a survivor, as you see.'

'I came to enquire about the progress of your investigation into the attack on Nina Martin.' Edmund's voice was equally cool.

'My dear fellow, I admire your priorities. We have fire at sea, passengers taking to the boats, a dramatic rescue, some loss of life even so, the ship possibly a total write-off, and you concern yourself with a hysteric who claims to have been raped.'

'Is that your conclusion?'

'It's my conviction – as it has been all along.'

'Then allow me to tell you you're mistaken.'

'You have evidence?'

'Yes.'

'Whose?'

'Nina Martin's.'

Briscoe brushed this impatiently aside. 'It's her "evidence" in the first place that started this witch-hunt. You're not taking her seriously?'

'As seriously as I did the first time. I examined her, you recall.'

'But you can't prove sexual penetration.'

'Zealous scrubbing had removed the evidence.'

Briscoe shrugged elegantly.

'What would you regard as proof?' Edmund demanded.

'How about pregnancy?'

'The girl isn't pregnant, I can assure you.'

Thank God at least for that. Possibly she had been, but shock might as easily have delayed her period as further shock had brought it on. To Stafford Briscoe, however, this mercy removed the last possibility of proof, and he was quick to point this out.

'So you can't stand up in court and swear she was raped?'

'No, but I can support her claim.'

'And I can as easily demolish it. There are other explanations for the condition you found her in.'

'Then you may like to know that shortly before the fire was discovered, Nina Martin was attacked again.'

'Did she recognise her attacker?'

'She killed him.'

'You're joking! A girl like that!'

'A girl like that, when desperate and provided with a long sharp weapon, can inflict a mortal wound.'

356

'What weapon?'

Edmund produced the ivory hair ornament.

'You're joking,' Briscoe said again. 'It's another of her stories, a bid for attention.'

'The body is in my surgery aboard the *Karachi*. I myself withdrew the weapon.'

Briscoe was silent. 'Who is it?' he asked at last.

'Julian Strode, the Third Officer. Like me, making his first voyage.'

'Were there witnesses?'

'Not that we know of.'

Briscoe noted the change of pronoun. 'Why are you telling me this?'

'We thought you should know the truth.'

'In order to suppress it?'

'You might otherwise have uncovered it.'

'You're asking me to condone murder.'

'It was an attack in self-defence.'

'You've only the girl's word for it.'

'There are no witnesses. What good will a trial do? Even if she's acquitted, her life will be blighted, and you won't bring Strode back from the dead. Instead, you'll cause distress to his widowed mother. Better to let her think his death an accident.'

'So what are you suggesting?'

'You were going to dismiss Nina as an hysteric.'

Briscoe began to laugh. 'You mean you'd go along with that?'

'Better an hysteric than a murderess. The child has suffered enough. You know she's just lost her sister?'

'No! What happened?'

'The lifeboat that capsized.'

Briscoe gestured in sympathy. 'I'm sorry. You were fond of Connie Martin, I believe.'

'I loved her.' It was the first time he had ever said it.

'Believe me, I know how you feel.'

Edmund bowed his head, aware that the words were no idle convention. This was a man who understood loss. The layers of detachment were no more than a dressing laid over a gaping wound.

'I have had no chance either to condole the death of your father,' Briscoe continued.

'Thank you. That's a different order of loss.'

'Will you return to Gloucestershire?'

'Only to sell the estate and clear the house out.'

'My sister would be delighted if you would call.'

Remembering Jean Briscoe and her quarrel with Anne, Edmund doubted it.

'I mean *I* should be delighted,' Briscoe said.

For the first time Edmund smiled. 'Thank you. I appreciate it.'

357

'I know Jean has missed her friend. Perhaps your aunt may visit you?'

Edmund thought it unlikely, and even more unlikely that if she did, Anne would call on Miss Briscoe, but he chose not to look that far ahead. Nevertheless, for the first time since he emerged from prison, he felt a member of society. Sir Edmund Bladon, even if he never used the title, was still a descendant of an old and honoured race. It was perhaps time to forget the past and turn to the future, even one without Connie by his side. He wished he had that belief in life eternal that Nina Martin possessed. She would pray for her sister, light candles, find comfort in believing herself of some comfort still; whereas he could find comfort only in serving the living, and one man could do little against poverty and disease; he could not even relieve pain. The Chief Engineer's teeth had been clenched so rigidly against any murmur that even in death his jaw had not relaxed.

As though picking up his thought, Stafford Briscoe observed, 'The Chief Engineer's death was a sad affair. Sad for you too, since you couldn't save him.'

'No doctor anywhere could have done that.'

'But it was a hero's death. I understand he died trying to save another.'

'Yes, the stoker who started the fire.'

'Ironic, don't you think? The man had been disciplined by the Chief and his arson was an act of revenge. Mr Sutherland was not one to suffer what he saw as insubordination, and he had no sympathy with native crews and their aspirations; nor had his officers, thanks to him. His death does not entirely absolve him from blame for what has happened, though I doubt if any condemnation will be made at the Enquiry, which in the circumstances will be a whitewash job. Nevertheless, the times are changing. Despite the exhibition at Wembley, the great British Empire is no longer a stable force.'

'Is that a bad thing?'

'Perhaps not in the long run, but instability is always bad.'

A long blast on a ship's siren brought both men to the window. The *République* was under way. Slowly the gap between ship and shore opened. A group of passengers from the *Karachi* cheered. Then, picking up speed, the great white liner headed for the harbour mouth and set course for the New World.

Briscoe sighed, and smiled. 'Even so, I expect the Empire to last my time, but yours . . .? I couldn't say. The Gopals of this world are massing. Some day there will be more of them than us. And then what? A universal conflagration? I hope not, but I fear –'

He was interrupted by the sound of running footsteps, a positive tattoo on the door. Edmund, who was nearer, moved to open it, and Nina Martin, panting and dishevelled, collapsed into his arms.

He had never seen her like this, flushed, breathless, bright-eyed in the grip of emotion. It was a revelation of what might be.

'I knew you were here,' she gasped. 'I came to tell you. Oh, Edmund,

Connie's safe. She was picked up by a fishing-boat which had no wireless, and until it put in to Brixham, no one knew. The hotel manager came himself to tell me – look, there's a telegram. She'll be waiting for us at Weymouth, with Uncle Charles and Aunt Maura. You'll be able to marry her after all.'

His Highness Prince Ravi Rabindranath Banai stepped ashore at Weymouth every inch the Indian prince. He had worn borrowed clothes only for as long as it took for his own to dry, but now, well pressed by the hotel though still stained with sea water and with the colours running here and there, his embroidered silks stood out on the drab quayside as he tried not to shiver in the breeze. He was determined to show these English, and one of them in particular, that he came not as someone seeking refuge, but as a prince in his own right. The little brown bugger who had been humiliated in Briscoe sahib's cabin was still the hereditary prince of a state as large as England, with power over more than a million lives. It was an added humiliation that one of those lives had been unjustly taken by Captain Archibald Johnson, M C, who was now being fêted as a hero without anyone quite knowing why. As he made his way to the warmth of the waiting boat train, Ravi was careful to seek out a compartment well away from the gallant captain and his fiancée who seemed unable to stop clinging to his arm, while her parents beamed in the background and told anyone who would listen that they detected the hand of God in what had happened. They did not say which hand.

'The hand sinister, I presume,' Stafford Briscoe murmured, though not so loudly that the Reverend Septimus could overhear and detain him in conversation. Instead he hurried after Edmund Bladon, who represented more congenial company. What he would really have liked to do was to seek out Ravi, but he judged the time not yet ripe and cursed again that unguarded outburst in his cabin, so uncharacteristic of him. Only now that the danger was past was he beginning to admit the extent to which Bert Gurslake's attempted blackmail had shaken him. He had shrunk from the thought of losing the handle of knighthood, of feeling unable to enter his club, of being out of the running for any public position, and all for befriending – and at the Captain's instance! – a lonely, handsome boy. He chose to forget those episodes with other handsome boys in Arab countries where hospitality included pandering to a guest's tastes; they had no meaning beyond physical release, whereas with Ravi, for the first time since Maurice . . . Perhaps it was not too late.

The boy looked like a bedraggled peacock, he thought, as he watched Ravi reserve a place in the train. Strange how tawdry his colourful silks looked under the grey skies of England, and where on earth was he off to now? His eyes followed the slight figure as it hurried towards the head of the platform and the station buildings. He'd better be quick – the train was due to leave in twenty minutes. What in the world could he want? A bar of chocolate? A daily paper? A belated announcement that he was safe? About the last he need not have worried. From Cherbourg Briscoe himself had notified the India Office of that fact, and already cablegrams were on their way to Maggapore informing the Nawab and the Resident that their hereditary prince was unharmed. Nevertheless, it was with unease that Briscoe stationed himself at the carriage window that commanded a view of the platform's length. At this delicate moment the least thing could determine whether the relationship with Ravi – if relationship were not too strong a word – was re-established or lost for ever, and Briscoe did not intend it to be lost. But whereas before it was part of the game that the approach should come from Ravi, this time it must come from him, and not in any form that could be mistaken for apology but as the hand of friendship once again outheld. The hand sinister? Never! His intentions were wholly good. Ravi would receive nothing he did not end by entreating. But – suppose he was running away?

The thought disturbed Briscoe so greatly that he jumped out on the platform and began pacing up and down. He could not appear to pursue or spy on Ravi by following, yet with every minute his tension rose. Edmund, from the corner seat opposite, hoped his own did not show as much. He had barely glimpsed Connie since they landed, though he knew Nina was with her now. Uncle Charles and Aunt Maura had been waiting on the dock standing one on each side of her as Nina ran down the gangway and into her sister's arms. Fortunately there were no photographers present to record the moment – they were massing again in London – and the little group had hurried away. They had not joined the train, so perhaps they had a motor-car waiting; he realised that beyond knowing that Uncle Charles and Aunt Maura lived near Reading, he had no idea even of their name, and though Connie knew his, she did not have his Gloucestershire address. They were effectively sundered, although he refused to accept that that could be. After what they had been through she must surely see as clearly as he that separation was impossible; she was here, now, beside him, in all but physical form, which seemed suddenly unimportant, so strongly was her presence felt. He saw Cynthia Vane and Bobby hurrying down the platform, and waved to show forgiveness. The boy lowered his eyes; the mother bowed stiffly. At least the little beggar had admitted his lie. There was hope for him yet, especially if removed from his over-loving mother. He and Connie would do better with their sons . . . But it was not Connie but Nina whom he saw hurrying down the platform, looking in every carriage window and carrying a letter in her hand.

Edmund called out to her: 'Nina!'

Anxiety, happiness, relief, despair, darted over her features as she turned at the sound of his voice. 'Oh, Edmund, I'm so glad I've found you. Connie wanted me to come.'

'What's wrong with Connie?' he asked in sudden alarm.

'Nothing. It's like a miracle. It *is* a miracle. She hasn't even caught a cold.'

360

'Then why isn't she here?'

'She thinks it's better. Another parting would be distressing for you both.'

Another parting . . .

'She's not still thinking of going into a convent?'

Nina nodded. 'Isn't it strange, she's been thinking of entering all her life, only she wouldn't admit it. I still can't believe it, not Connie – and yet it seems so right.'

'You too were thinking of entering – until you were forced to reconsider it.'

'And I see now I was wrong. I was in love with the idea of self-sacrifice, but I'd never considered what it meant. To give up all the things you want, even the desire for them, in order to do God's will – it's too hard for me. I could never have done it.'

'Connie too may be making a mistake.'

Nina faced down his accusing gaze. 'No – because she loves you, Edmund. Trust me – I know her. She could never have given you up for anything less than God.'

'She's not going to be allowed to give me up,' Edmund said firmly. 'I'm going to marry her. Where is she?'

'She made me promise not to tell.'

'Nonsense, Nina. This is no time for silly games. Take me to her.'

'I can't, Edmund. I can't!'

He gripped her shoulders. 'You can, Nina. You *will!*'

Her pliant body was unexpectedly resistant. 'No, Edmund, it's better so. She loves you. This is the most difficult thing she's ever had to do. Don't make it harder for her.'

'She'll regret it.'

'She thinks not. After all, she might regret marrying you.'

'Never!'

Out of the corner of his eye Edmund saw Ravi walk past, head held high, a blur of bright silks amid November's greyness. Or was the blurred effect due to tears?

Nina was holding out the letter she carried. 'Connie asked me to give you this.'

A plain white envelope addressed to Sir Edmund Bladon. It was the first time he had seen his title written down. It was unreal, like everything else about this scene. He took it, feeling the texture between his fingers as though he had never touched paper before. This was all he would ever have of Connie, all she would allow him of herself. His anger was such that he would have liked to tear it up unread and see the pieces swept along the gusty platform. He pocketed it instead, and inadvertently put his hand to his face as though the cut from the ring Rosemary had hurled at him had opened up afresh. He could well understand why the bearers of bad news had in the past been executed. He could have struck Nina then and there.

But training again triumphed over instinct, and just as he had pocketed the letter, so now he leaned forward and kissed the girl.

'Edmund, you'll keep in touch, won't you?'

'I don't have your address.'

'Connie's given it in her letter. I'll ask Aunt Maura if you may call – after Con's left, that is. Please, Edmund. I'll be so lonely. I'm going to lose her too.'

For Nina the immediate loss would be greater. She had lived her whole life in Connie's shade, relying on her sister for all those decisions she would now have to make for herself, until a suitable husband took over and she could once more lapse into passivity. Edmund eyed her assessingly; she would make someone a good wife. But not him. Connie's sister was not Connie. There could be no second best.

'All aboard!'

The guard's voice was welcome. Gently he turned Nina round.

'You'd better go.' He gave her a little push in the right direction.

She looked back at him. 'You'll write?'

'Yes, yes.'

Did she expect him to send a message by her to Connie? If so, her expectations would be unfulfilled. She was walking faster now. Doors were slamming. The guard's whistle shrilled again. Don't let her turn her head. She's nearly reached the end of the platform . . .

The train gave a mighty grunt.

. . . Let her keep going. No turning back. No more reminders of Connie. No more a part of my life . . .

A hand reached out and gripped him. He felt himself jerked backwards.

'You're going to miss the train,' Stafford Briscoe's voice informed him.

It was his hand which hauled Edmund aboard.

Very gradually Ravi allowed his spine to relax against the upholstery of a first-class carriage and his head to sink back against the white hemstitched linen antimacassar provided by the Southern Railway Company. He kept his fingers interlocked lest anyone should see that his hands were trembling, but the discipline of an Indian prince and an English public school upbringing combined to keep his features impassive. Haughty would have been Archie Johnson's word.

From the moment he had disembarked, Ravi had felt England reclaiming him. However hard he tried to be a visiting prince in oriental splendour, he had become an Englishman in fancy dress. Although his skin was darker than that of those around him, his accent was no different from theirs; he commanded the same easy nonchalance; and if his hair was blacker, his eyes more liquid, his movements more imbued with feline grace, that merely lent him the exotic air of a Westerner who carried with him an aura of the mysterious East.

The question was how Dorothy Waterman would see him. Or rather, which aspect would more appeal to her. As he made his way to the public

362

telephone outside the station, Ravi was conscious of a wildly beating heart. Was it only a year since he had left England? So little seemed to have changed. Not even an English public telephone could confuse him: he had used one often enough. He enjoyed the assurance with which he asked for a trunk call, gave the Watermans' home number, and jingled the coins in his pocket while waiting to be told how much money to insert.

And then – demoralisation. The maid who answered told him Mrs Waterman was out and Miss Dorothy with her – they were on a shopping trip to London and would not be home till late. Could she say who called? No, Ravi answered, replacing the instrument with a feeling of defeat.

But all was not lost. There remained Barry and his father who could be reached at Watermans Bank, only whereas he had memorised the home number, Dorothy's number, the telephone operator had to find him the number of the Bank, which entailed delay and the insertion of further coins. She recommended a personal call. Ravi waited as the seconds ticked by and he saw that there was less than ten minutes until the train left. Then Barry's voice sounded in his ear.

'Barry? Ravi here. I'm in England.'

'Dear old chap, how marvellous that you are. Dottie will be over the moon, and of course so will the parents. Where are you telephoning from?'

'Weymouth.'

'Don't tell me you were aboard that ship that caught fire, the *Karachi*! Are you absolutely positive you're all right?'

'Unsinged.'

'Trust you! It must have been pretty exciting. I can't wait to hear it all at first hand. We must meet. Lunch tomorrow?'

'All right.'

Was that all he was to be offered? No chance of seeing Dorothy?

'Fine,' Barry went on. 'Shall we say one o'clock at my club? It's Father's club, but now I'm at the Bank I'm a member. Bit of string-pulling, you know, chip off the old block and all that nonsense. Jolly useful, though.'

Surely Barry's voice had a plummy resonance it did not possess before?

'I'll be there,' Ravi promised. And then: 'How is Dorothy?'

'In top form. Getting excited about the wedding. She'll be so thrilled to have you come.'

'What wedding?'

'Oh, I forgot. You won't have seen *The Times*. Our little Dottie's getting married, and after her first Season too. My mother's no end pleased. My father says it's damned expensive, but at least it gets it all over at once. You probably know the bridegroom. Remember Freddie Forde?'

The voice went on sounding in his ears as Ravi leaned against the side of the call-box, and there stole into his mind the memory of a young man, tall, stooping, sandy hair already receding and what seemed more than the usual number of front teeth. Two years ahead of him and Barry. Without a penny to his old and distinguished name.

'You mean the Marquis of Forde?'

'Got it in one. Dorchester's heir. Our Dottie'll be a duchess one day and a marchioness by Christmas. It's at St Margaret's, Westminster, by the way. December 14th. You'll be there, won't you? And afterwards you must come down. I'd ask you before, but my mother's so taken up with the wedding she can't think of anything else.'

'And Dorothy? Is she in love with this Marquis?'

'Better ask her yourself, old chap. No one forced her to accept him, if that's what you're thinking, so I suppose the answer's yes.'

But when would he see her to ask her? Did he stop her as she came down the aisle? 'Excuse me, Miss Waterman, but are you in love with this title?' For surely Dorothy of all girls could not be in love with the man.

As though picking up his thoughts, Barry continued, 'Of course Dottie was always a sucker for a title. We used to say it was what she liked about you. Outside the family she always referred to you as Prince Ravi. Fellows like you and Freddie have an unfair advantage.'

Fellows like you and Freddie. Ravi quivered with the shock, but his voice was controlled as he replied, 'There are disadvantages also. Dynastic responsibilities and all that.'

'Yes, I suppose you'll be expected to marry some dusky beauty.'

Ravi fought down the desire to retch.

'Tell you what: why don't we do a show some evening? I know a place we could go to afterwards where the girls – oh damn!'

'What's up?'

'Just realised I can't make lunch tomorrow. There's a meeting that doesn't finish till one and an important client coming in at two who my father wants me to meet. Where are you staying in London?'

'I'm not sure yet. I –'

Ravi broke off before his voice cracked. He had so counted on going to the Watermans, on being welcomed as part of the family and luxuriating, however briefly, in their warmth. Instead, Barry had become a stranger, and Dorothy, who was marrying a title, had never cared for him except as another title, unacceptable on the marriage market but useful for dazzling her friends.

He was saved by the call-box telephone's three pips signalling the end of his time.

'Are you having another three minutes?' Barry demanded. 'No? Then give me a ring when you get to town. I'm at the blasted Bank every day. We'll fix a –' The phone cut off before he could specify.

Ravi continued to lean against the glass wall of the call-box, the coins for another three minutes in his hand. But what was the point of continuing the conversation, or of calling Barry again? They inhabited different worlds without a bridge between them, worlds which were spinning ever further apart. In his, the dusky beauty waited; in the Watermans', dynastic marriage of another kind.

Someone jerked open the door of the call-box. 'Have you finished?'

Ravi nodded, unable to speak, and came out.

'Bleeding wog,' the man said to no one in particular. 'Looks like he ought to be perched on a barrel-organ, dressed like that.'

Not even this could rouse Ravi. Despair enfolded him like a pall. For this he had stowed away, endured thirst and hunger and the humiliation of working in the galley; for this he had grasped Briscoe sahib's hand held out in friendship, only to see it suddenly withdrawn.

He returned to the train because there was nowhere else to go. On the platform he saw Dr Bladon deep in conversation with the younger Martin girl, the one whom they had briefly suspected him, Ravi, of raping – it seemed an age ago. She was not really like Dorothy except in her fairness, but he would never look longingly again on English flesh. Instead he glanced at Nina with something like loathing, and was proceeding down the train when a hand fell on his shoulder and a voice said, 'Well met, dear boy. Come and join me.'

Briscoe sahib.

Ravi turned. The hawklike features were composed, the gaze sincere and interested, that of a concerned older man eager to help, just as he had helped when Ravi first joined the First Class passengers aboard the *Karachi*. The difference was that Ravi no longer believed. He had seen that immaculate façade crumble and the words 'little brown bugger' form on those thin lips.

'Thank you, sir,' he said stiffly, 'but I have a seat reserved further down.'

And he moved on, never realising that the look which followed him was one of reluctant respect. For the rest of his life, which was to be a long one, Sir Stafford Briscoe would speak highly of the young Nawab of Maggapore.

In the train Archie Johnson sat next to Imogen and opposite her parents. He did not exactly have his arm around the girl, but it certainly rested along her back, while Imogen leaned towards him at an angle that must have made her neck ache. Her hand lay in his, but not passively; it was forever twisting, turning, withdrawing, as though seeking some response. It was his hand which lay passive, reflecting the concentration of his thoughts.

Archie was not used to thinking. It was something he had never been required to do. From school he had gone unthinkingly into the Army, where he had unthinkingly obeyed orders, especially the unformulated overriding one to kill. He had never understood why his shooting that sniper had had such a bad effect upon his men, any more than he had understood his Colonel's decision to ship him out of Maggapore stripped of his commission when all that had happened was that a native had been hit by a stray British bullet and had died as a result.

And now here he was engaged to a padre's daughter. He wasn't quite sure how this had come about, but he hadn't been drunk: of that he was certain. Never again, after that night in Bombay. Almost he could fancy the scents of that room still in his nostrils: musk and sweat, with an overlay of joss-sticks, and those thin, supple hands at work . . . Imogen's hands were white and podgy, like her body. It did not excite him, but it promised welcome relief. But only after marriage. That was the snag with girls like Imogen: they knew how to keep themselves tantalisingly out of reach until after the nuptial knot was tied – and the knot in Archie's view was a slip knot, very like the hangman's noose.

He shifted position, seeking ease from the burning in his groin which for the last twenty-four hours he had been too occupied to notice, but which now seemed to have returned with redoubled force. He'd have to do something about it, but he shied away from the thought. Those backstreet clinics and censorious-eyed doctors, like that conchie on board ship. It wasn't right that cowards like him should live to condemn men decorated for gallantry. The conchies should all have been shot.

This conclusion heartened him sufficiently to respond to the pressure of Imogen's hand, and even to smile at his future in-laws, who were very ready to smile back. A fine young man, decided the Reverend Septimus; decent, upstanding. The slanderous hints of that doctor were a disgrace and ought to be reported, if only he knew to whom. But of course the fellow was leaving the ship, even turned out to have a title. The gentry weren't what they were . . . Except for that chap who'd offered Archie a job; he was clearly an exception. Bit of real talent-spotting there.

The gentleman in question, another First Class passenger, ran a small business manufacturing machine-tool parts. He had offered the hero a job as a salesman as soon as he cared to start. Apart from providing a car, the job was on commission only, but the implications of this were lost on Mr Stiles, who was already thinking of 'my son-in-law the sales manager' and staying at 'my daughter's place'. If only there had been another gentleman who was patron of a vacant living, someone right-thinking who would have responded to the service on Armistice Day . . . Still, at least Imogen would be all right married to Archie. It would mean separation, of course, when at the end of their leave they returned to India, but how different her circumstances would be. A missionary was too often regarded as a kind of clerical poor relation by the Anglican Establishment. Small slights at the hands of garrison chaplains and the incumbents of well-endowed churches in the British communities surfaced in Septimus Stiles's mind. At the time he had convinced himself that he suffered them for the Lord's sake rather than because he had to, but every single one had left its mark. It was good to know that his daughter would escape them, would be able to make a new start.

Daddy was really pleased about her engagement, Imogen thought, responding belatedly to his smile. Just as well, since she was anxious to hurry on the wedding; no long engagement for her! It was a pity Archie was so unexpectedly reticent when she longed for him to demonstrate mastery. Had she held back too much and produced the reverse effect from that intended? Should she show more initiative? Of course she didn't want to shock him by seeming less than a lady – perhaps the fire had affected him? It had certainly affected other people – that old couple, the Haldinghams, seemed to have gone ga-ga at last. She now clung constantly to the arm of that Irish steward she had always refused to be served by, and her husband had cut Archie dead. Or that was what it had looked like, when they all came face to face. Archie swore the old man was short-sighted and hadn't recognised him, but to Imogen there had been nothing vague about that hawk-sharp gaze: it had been directed straight at Archie and held something very like contempt. Could he have mistaken him for someone else – someone from the past, perhaps? That seemed the likeliest explanation, considering his great age. It had been an uncomfortable moment, but Imogen was resolved on charity. The Haldinghams could not be long for this world, and could therefore do little harm.

They must now be somewhere aboard this train bound for London, but so many people seemed to have disappeared. What had become of the redhead and her convent-bound sister who had allegedly been raped? Not that she, Imogen, believed it for a moment; it was a ploy for attention, that was all; but there had certainly been enough fuss about it. Why, every man on board had come under suspicion, including her Archie, who was unfortunately proving a gentleman to the core. And since they were no nearer to discovering the culprit, the suspicion hung over them still. That was what came of entrusting the investigation to a man like Mr Briscoe, who was, Daddy said, a civil servant through and through. If it had been entrusted to a military man like Archie it would have been different. Archie got things done. An army officer had to; it made them valuable in civilian life as well. She could look forward to the future with confidence: his heroism had won him the offer of a job already. She was, as they said, marrying well.

Nearer the front of the train John Joseph Fitzgerald also leaned back in a first-class carriage. It was the first time he had travelled in such luxury, and the starched white antimacassars draped over the backs of the plush armchairs, the curtains at the window, the shaded reading lamps that could be switched on and off at will, all impressed him because this was how the gentry travelled and he had never thought to taste what that was like. And now here he was adopted by the gentry – employed by them, at least – because Mr Haldingham had offered him a job at more than the Australasian Line was paying, and his written notice would be handed in as soon as they reached London, where they were going to stay in one of the grand hotels. And then they were going on to Dublin; John Joseph could hardly believe his luck, except that it was no luck, it was an answer to all those desperate prayers he had put up as he looked down that companionway to the smoke curling up from below. St Patrick and St Jude were powerful protectors, but nothing less than the Blessed Mother of God would do. He had begun a Hail Mary, but the smoke caught in his throat and set him coughing . . . *pray for us now and at the hour of our death.*

It hadn't been the hour of his death but it could well have been the old people's. Mrs Haldingham was sitting on the stairs crying quietly, and the old gentleman was hovering above her like a guardian angel who didn't know quite what to do. But he hadn't left her – though with his long legs he could have been up those stairs in a minute – John Joseph was to remember that as he seized Mrs Haldingham's arm, wondering if she might still reject him, and urged her to her feet.

At Cherbourg Mr Haldingham had sought him out and offered him money, which John Joseph had at first refused because you didn't take money for helping an old lady who could have been your grandmother to escape a cruel death. But Mr Haldingham had insisted so kindly, saying his wife meant far more to him than the sum offered, that in the end John Joseph had accepted. And then had come the offer of a job.

'But Mrs Haldingham can't bear me, sir,' he had burst out. 'She'll never be happy having an Irishman around her. She'll not give me so much as the time of day.'

'I think you'll find things will be different now,' Mr Haldingham assured him. 'It's not just gratitude. You've laid to rest a cruel memory.' And he went on to remind John Joseph of those hurried words on the stairs – how their only daughter's home that had been in her husband's family for centuries had been burned by the Irish, and how she had insisted on dying with her husband in the flames.

John Joseph listened, appalled. Of course he knew of the Troubles – what Irishman didn't? Mam had even mentioned them in her letters, though he had sometimes been hard put to it to make out what she meant by all these references to trouble between Republicans and Free Staters. She usually concluded by saying it was a mercy Kieron was taken else he'd have been in the thick of it, and then went on to tell how some Republican friend of Kieron's had been killed in an ambush and no one even knowing what it was all about. Sure 'twould take all the prayers of Ellen in her convent and the intercession of the Holy Mother of God herself before Ireland was a peaceable land for John Joseph to return to, but they must pray that it would some day be so.

And behold, their prayers seemed answered. The civil war was over, the Treaty signed, and John Joseph was coming home. He could scarcely wait to tell Mam. She'd never believe he was working for the English, not after all he'd said against them after he'd seen Kieron fall. But it was only since meeting the Haldinghams that John Joseph had ever considered the English side: the bitterness that could make a woman who had never set eyes on him shrink at the sound of his voice. And she was a sweet lady, Mrs Haldingham, and she must have been a beauty once. Her eyes were so blue they might have been Irish, and the way she had of laying her hand on your arm . . .'Twas no wonder Mr Haldingham adored her and wanted her to have everything she desired. He wasn't far from feeling the same himself about her, and that after forty-eight hours. He'd do his very best for them in Ireland, where they were going to survey the demesne, see the solicitor, sort out what was left for their grandson away at school in England and alone now that his uncle had died. They'd need an Irishman to make sure they were treated decent, but John Joseph felt he could trust himself to see to that. And the English were good employers – hadn't the Mullens in Munster Street been treated kindly by those they'd worked for? It was going to be all right.

He leaned back, hardly daring to rest his head against the cool white linen, and smiled into Mrs Haldingham's blue eyes. The eyes smiled back, faded but still sparkling, as her husband's hand closed over hers. He hadn't left her. John Joseph wouldn't leave them. They were old, they mightn't live long, but for as long as they did they would have a devoted servant, and after that there would be memories to console. The English and the Irish didn't always understand one another, but the peace that passeth all understanding could still be theirs to keep.

Somewhere on the line between Weymouth and Winchester, the bitter memory of Kieron Fitzgerald was finally laid to sleep.

Somewhat higher up the line, just south of Woking, Edmund Bladon scattered from a lavatory window the fragments of Connie Martin's letter to him. Connie was no letter-writer, never had been. The immature schoolgirl hand, the naïve phrases, the platitudinous pieties, which, despite the best efforts of the good Sisters, were all a convent education had equipped her with to express the deepest feelings of her heart, had failed to carry their message to a more sophisticated mind. Worst of all with Edmund, her failure to come in person still rankled; it was a kind of cowardice which Nina's stumbling explanation had not managed to dispel. Those military ancestors whose gaze would greet him from bad portraits when he returned to the house in Gloucestershire would have understood the sentiment which gripped him: Connie had run away. The future mother of his sons had been unable to face him. What might those sons have been like?

He had not kept the address in Reading Connie had so carefully copied out. He did not mean to keep in touch as Nina had begged. Aunt Anne had said when she left Gloucestershire for London that if a break had to be made it had better be a clean one. She had never again seen her friend Jean Briscoe, never sent a letter or exchanged a Christmas card. She had seldom even spoken of her, Edmund now realised; had Briscoe's sister felt the same? He would have liked to ask Stafford Briscoe, but the question smacked too much of intimacy. They were not friends; what united them in their present situation was not mutual liking, still less former acquaintance, but the realisation that they were two of a kind, their responses filtered through

369

the same background of education and expectation that made an English gentleman. If Briscoe was right and the British Empire was failing, there remained the poor of their own land to serve. If he became a doctor among the English natives, Edmund suspected that Briscoe would understand.

He had caught the other man's eye on him as he first read Connie's letter, though Briscoe had immediately looked away, embarrassed to have been caught out in what he would consider prying. Nevertheless, Edmund had the feeling that Briscoe understood and that the experience of rejection was one more thing that united them. He had to resist the temptation to hand the letter over and say, 'Tell me what you make of that,' well knowing that it would be handed back with a veiled smile and an ironic comment such as 'The Lord's handmaids are less well educated than they might be, don't you think?' Instead he had read it through a second and a third time until its stilted phrases seemed branded on his brain, before making his way to the toilet compartment where he could dispose of it. The white fragments vanished at once in the train's slipstream, as if they had never been. There would never be another Connie, but there might someday be someone else. He was not the one taking vows – he would leave to her that nonsense. With a sudden spurt of joy he accepted that he would not remain celibate.

He returned to the compartment to find Briscoe with one elegant leg crossed over the other and deep in a copy of *Eugénie Grandet*, which he had – typically – procured while in Cherbourg. He looked up as Edmund entered.

'Another twenty minutes to Waterloo.'

The train seemed to be hastening through the Surrey landscape as if anxious to ignore the housing estates burgeoning among woodland, the first intimations of industry. The British Empire might be failing, but its heart was enlarging. A sign of decadence?

'I suppose the newshounds will be out in force,' Edmund said tentatively.

'Yes, all those who couldn't manage to send a man to Cherbourg, or weren't satisfied with what they got. The only bigger reception will be for the Captain when they bring the damn ship in.'

'You think so?'

'I know so. Someone has to be to blame. They're going to crucify him unless passengers like us give evidence at the Enquiry. I assume you'll testify?'

'Of course.'

Briscoe consulted his watch. 'We shan't get down to Gloucestershire this evening. Where are you staying in London? I could put you up at my club.'

'Thank you, but I've my aunt in St John's Wood.'

'I was forgetting. Naturally you must go there. Please give her my regards and say my sister and I hope to see her in Gloucestershire. Jean has missed her friend, I know.'

Edmund inclined his head, afraid to jar the fragile moment with any expression of bitterness on Anne's behalf.

As if understanding, Briscoe changed the subject. 'Since we are perforce unencumbered with luggage, shall we make a quick getaway? I know a short cut to the taxi-rank. We might even share a cab.'

Edmund agreed, and the two tall thin figures were among the first off the train, Briscoe leading the way, brushing aside reporters with a practised, 'No comment. Sorry, nothing to say.' Edmund followed, every inch the dedicated doctor he already sensed himself to be. In both of them emotion was a force, but a controlled force, not permitted to break its bounds, channelled deep into the stuff of being like rivers crossing a tableland. Only where it escaped at those permitted estuaries of marriage, birth of children, death, was it possible to gauge the extent and depth of the torrent and through what chasmal courses it had flowed. In Edmund a girl's red hair would always cause a momentary check, a damming, before the water overflowed, churning for a little among the rocks and potholes of past feeling before resuming its onward course. In Briscoe a boy's slim body, a dark and liquid eye, would have the same effect, though less pronounced, less frequent, before the river continued its slow and stately progress to the sea.

The sea which heaved about Angus Meiklejohn was grey and surly, as if angry at being required to keep afloat the vessels who sailed on it. One such was the *Karachi*, making a slow and troubled progress into port. The tugs escorted her like fussy nurses as she nosed into Plymouth Sound. It was very different from all her other arrivals, and it caused her captain no pride.

Angus had refused to leave the bridge, despite the entreaties of the First Officer who headed the skeleton crew still aboard. Eyes red-rimmed, jaw stubbled, uniform crumpled, Angus remained upright and solitary, with a monolithic grandeur that forbade approach. His ship, the love of his life, was crippled, perhaps dying, and he must watch over her to the end, as he had watched life leave the blackened hulk that was Jamie Sutherland, the finest chief engineer of the Line. When they docked he would go north to see Barbara, the three fine sons and the beloved little daughter – that would keep his promise to Jamie, though he dreaded the reproach he might detect in Barbara's greeting. Had he, as captain, really done all he could?

Reason said yes, but a voice beyond reason reminded him of all those intimate half-hours at the end of the day in his cabin when so much was said and left unsaid. He knew Jamie's views on the native question, had disagreed with him more than once, but had failed to see the danger they represented to the ship they both loved, let alone to Jamie himself. All he could do now was to make sure Jamie's heroism was recognised, and that the Line accorded courage its due. Barbara would get a pension; there were

371

charitable foundations that would help with the education of the boys; as for the beloved little daughter, there was not much he could do for her except ensure she had cause to feel pride in her father, which meant that at the Enquiry Jamie must be fully cleared. 'Was Mr Sutherland a strict disciplinarian?' – 'Yes, sir.' – 'Was his strictness resented by native crew?'—'With respect, sir, a strict disciplinarian is never popular, but Mr Sutherland was always just.' Was it true? 'Never knowingly unjust' might be better, but did that amount to admission of a fault? Thank God Gopal was not alive to give evidence and other native crew would not be asked. But what of the engineer officers? What of Edmund Bladon, who knew that Gopal had originally claimed to have been pushed and that Jamie had declined to take action against the officer allegedly responsible – what might not Bladon reveal? Except that Bladon had watched with him the last agony as Jamie strove to die, and it had been he who had drawn the sheet over those blind lidless eyes that had gone on staring after the mighty heart had ceased to beat.

They had seemed fixed on his friend and captain, and though Angus knew this was coincidence, he knew also that he would never be able to erase the memory of that unblinking gaze which had seemed by turns compassionate, accusing and perhaps at the last forgiving. He hoped so. More than anything in the world he wanted to hear again that whispered accolade – 'Good man' – and to believe that in full health and vigour it would have grown into Jamie's soft Scots voice saying, 'I canna approve your conduct, Angus, but ye ken fine I understand.' More than anything in the world? Ah no, even that was a betrayal. More than anything else he wanted to bring the *Karachi* safe to port.

It should be possible. Thanks to the fire-fighting below decks – Jamie again – her weakened plates had not buckled. Her hull at least was sound, and so were her bridge and engines, and to a seaman those were her vital parts. Decoration, paint, wood, superstructure – these were important to passengers and Owners, but they would not keep a ship afloat. And possibly if the Owners had been less insistent on that wood panelling in the writing-room the fire on the main deck would never have got such a hold; but he could not see them admitting it at the Enquiry when there was so much else at stake. Would they refit the ship? She was basically seaworthy, but she lacked the elegance of design which was creeping into post-war vessels, and her coal-fired engines were slow compared to the latest oil-fired ones. Of course he would fight for her, plead for her, with the hard-headed, hard-faced men of business, but their decision rested on considerations of profit and loss. It might be cheaper to sell her for scrap than to refit her, and to invest in a new ship with the attendant publicity. In any case she would sail under a new captain – Angus was in no doubt of that. If he was lucky they might offer him a shore job or command of some coast-hugging vessel, but his days as captain of an ocean-going liner were past. He minded less for himself than for the *Karachi*. Without Jamie it

372

could never have been the same, and there came a time for all men when it was better to go than to stay, even though it would mean less money, less comfort for Ailsa and Andy, and goodbye to Cynthia.

Cynthia. For the past forty-eight hours he had scarcely thought of her, not since the terrified young mother had stumbled from his cabin and gone in search of her son. Not their son, as Angus had begun to think of him, but hers and another man's. And if by chance she carried also their son, Angus would never know it. She and Bobby were safe – he had checked that their names were not on the mercifully brief list of casualties – but he knew without the need for farewell scenes or letters that she was no longer a part of his life. The whole affair had now the quality of a half-remembered dream where reality blurred into illusion and illusion mocked reality. Between that time when he had sat in the panelled writing-room and poured out his heart to her about Andy, and that moment in his cabin when the fire alarm had resounded in their ears, there was a vacuum, as if emotion so intense had burned itself out of existence and destroyed every-thing else in its train. All the many incidents of the voyage stood out clearly, but they seemed to have taken place in a void, within which he had functioned efficiently and correctly, while no one but Jamie realised that his true being was otherwise.

It still was. He existed in and on and for his ship, but there was no world beyond her, even though that world was beginning to impinge. He must write to the parents of the dead crewman, to the widowed mother of Third Officer Julian Strode. The inevitable phrases . . . 'your great loss . . . a young life tragically cut short . . . a promising officer diligent in the performance of his duties . . .' rang hollower than usual but they were kinder than the truth. Even now he found it difficult to assimilate the information conveyed by Stafford Briscoe in a swift note from the Cherbourg hotel marked *Urgent – Strictly Private* and hand-delivered to the London head office of the Line. From there it had been sent special delivery to Plymouth, and brought out to the ship by launch, together with the letter from Ailsa which would normally have awaited him at Tilbury. He had not opened Ailsa's letter: there would be time enough later to learn that Andy was unchanged; but the unfamiliar black spiky handwriting carried its own urgency. Briefly he had forsaken the bridge for the privacy of his cabin, where the disordered bed and what he fancied was a faint scent on the pillow reminded him of Cynthia. Yet as he sat down he could no longer recall her except as a warm, responsive body and that strangely shorn dark hair. All his life he had been accustomed to twine his fingers in Ailsa's tresses, but with Cynthia there was nothing there except a neck so slender it reminded him of a kitten's . . . Or Minna's. He must remember to enquire about the well-being of Jamie's pet. He shook his head and slit the envelope, only to be shocked into forgetfulness of her and all else by its contents, which described briefly the end of Julian Strode. 'Poor child, poor child,' he heard himself murmuring over Nina Martin and the terror that directed the dagger-like weapon in her hand; but for the spruce, correct Third Officer he felt nothing but a kind of angry disbelief. That they could all have been so deceived! Yet who knew what passions, healthy or unhealthy, lurked beneath the anonymity of uniform? He recalled the entry in Edmund Bladon's log on Archie Johnson. And for himself, what could he say? All men were capable of moments of madness, but what they did in those moments was due to an infinity of factors once self-control had gone. Young Strode's dominating mother, who would be shattered by the truth if she ever learned it, might have more responsibility for it than she knew.

At least it would not be necessary to write to Gopal's illiterate family. Instead, the Line's Bombay representative would call and hand over the pitifully few rupees that represented the compensation to be paid. Later, when the *Karachi*'s native crew returned, stories would circulate, becoming wilder each time round, but all emphasising the iniquity of the British and the need for their overthrow. Along the waterfront the agitators would muster, the union claim new recruits, but despite Stafford Briscoe's forebodings it would take more than that to make the British Empire tremble; it was safe for a few years yet. And while it was, ships like the *Karachi* would ply between its ports. The Owners wouldn't scrap her; there was too much life left in her; even burnt and bruised and wallowing, that life pulsed beneath her captain's feet.

He returned to the bridge strangely comforted. Dawn was breaking, or at least the pre-dawn paling of the sky. The water in Plymouth Sound was calmer, the shore lights brighter; the bulk of other anchored ships loomed dark. One day succeeded another in an unchanging round. There was no change, it was all change, the past blurred into the present and the present reached forward to the future. What had one man to lose or offer against eternal years?

The tugs hooted, heralding their arrival. The sky brightened further in the east. Already it was evident that the clouds overshadowing them since Biscay had broken and it would be a clear, sunny winter's day. Sounds of activity penetrated from the dockside; motor vehicles starting up; gulls' cries mixed with men's cries; the splat of a falling rope. Against this background Angus took out Ailsa's letter and tore open the envelope with his thumbnail. Ailsa's letters were usually short, at least half the first small sheet taken up by the address which she insisted on writing out in full. 'Dear Angus . . .' After more than thirty years of marriage and all the hundreds of letters they had exchanged, still this formal, guarded opening. His letters to her began the same.

'Dear Angus, I have good news. I scarcely dare believe it, but Dr Murchison assures me it is so. Andy shows signs of recovery . . .'

Angus Meiklejohn read no more because of the blurring of Ailsa's handwriting, as firm and rounded as herself, due either to tears or to the trembling of the hand that held the paper, shaken by the thumping of his

374

heart. 'Andy shows signs of recovery . . .' It was what they had lived for, prayed for. Fearful of finding something to spoil it, he forced himself to read on. The letter was dated a week previously, and was as factual as a medical report.

'I have thought for some time his eyes seemed brighter and he was more aware of his surroundings,' Ailsa wrote, 'but supposed it was wishful thinking. I have fancied such things before. Then last week he said to me, "Mother, when are we going to Glengowan?" – you mind how he loved going there. So I took him. He was quite calm on the bus, and when a van backfired he took no notice, though loud noises have always upset him, as you know. When we reached the glen he went at once to his favourite spot, just like he used to, and then began following the burn. When I called to him to wait for me, he turned and said, "What's the matter, Mother? Aren't I old enough to go by myself?"

'Next day he was quiet and I was worried, so I asked Dr Murchison to call. Andy greeted him like an old friend. I thought the good doctor would have dropped dead of shock. Since then there has been a steady improvement, which Dr Murchison confirms. Yesterday Andy said, as if the past eight years had never existed, "When is Dad's ship due home?" I dare to hope our prayers have been answered, and our boy will get completely well . . .'

Completely well. A young man instead of a shadow figure. *We know so little about the mind* – the words of the specialist in London came back to Angus. Who knew what clouds of fear had rolled away from Andy, dismantling the barrier they had formed between him and a world he could not face? For the first time since that July day in the Somme's watermeadows the sun shone on him again. The sun. His son. Andy might even resume his studies. He might marry. There might be grandchildren some day . . . A kaleidoscope of possibilities shifted before Angus's eyes. His own future no longer mattered. The parent receded before the child, which was what Nature – or did he mean God? – intended. Uncertainly Angus bowed his head.

'Sir –' the First Officer was speaking – 'we're docking in a few minutes.' Then, seeing the Captain's face, 'Not bad news, sir, I hope?'

Angus smiled – a smile such as the First Officer had never believed could overspread those craggy features.

'No, Mr Stocks, good news. The best.'

He did not elaborate, and the First Officer was left wondering briefly if it had all been too much for the Old Man. He need not have worried. The figure before him was Captain Meiklejohn still.

Replacing his cap at a firmer angle and squaring his shoulders, Angus stared full ahead from his bridge as the tugs nosed his ship into the berth made ready for her and activity heightened on the dock. The great cables snaked round the bollards. Port officials and representatives of the Australasian Line waited to come aboard. Beyond the dock gates reporters were massing. A gangway stood waiting to be brought alongside, and a new life waited to be born.

The voyage was over, but it was a homecoming like no other homecoming. For Angus it was the most triumphant one of all, as silently, still expertly under the eye of her captain, the SS *Karachi* docked at dawn.